FORGOTTEN MASTERS IV

AWAKENING CONNECTIONS

SCOTT M. SWAINE

Primix Publishing
East Brunswick Office Evolution
1 Tower Center Boulevard, Ste 1510
East Brunswick, NJ 08816
www.primixpublishing.com
Phone: 1-800-538-5788

This is a work of fiction. Names, characters, places, and incidents either are the product of the author's imagination or are used fictitiously, and any resemblance to any persons, living or dead, is entirely coincidental.

Published by Primix Publishing: 11/06/2024

ISBN: 979-8-89194-145-8(sc)
ISBN: 979-8-89194-255-4(hc)
ISBN: 979-8-89194-146-5(e)

Library of Congress Control Number: 2024907433

CONTENTS

"In this space, you have will, and your will can alter this space."
Tyanna Nazég to her young daughter, Kali.

Chapter 1

REVIVAL

Morning was rising on the city of Bya'an Tamoranth on Tae'Eladar. Life was stirring for a new day of business among the shops and inns in the busy urban center. And within the city's main temple complex, known as the Temple of the Planes, a pair of familiar faces was visiting an unlikely new friend.

The couple were Tristeen Macaid and Haran Carronel, two former students once belonging to the mage academy in the city of Rolsklinde, on the world of Therinë. That world had been the subject of a four-century long siege and occupation by a villain known as Marshal Darumon, along with his military strong-arm, leaving it generally devastated. And on the final day of the siege, Rolsklinde had come under attack by a band of dwarves under the potent influence of a mind-altering drug, and equipped with Suuden-Aryku weapons, no thanks to the Marshal.

As a result, the city was destroyed, although the people managed to evacuate with only a minimal loss of life. However, there was one serious casualty, and he was the reason these two were now visiting the temple's Healer's Ward, the medical annex that served the needs of the local community.

Tristeen sat on one side of the bed while Haran sat on the other.

They were in a recovery room and waiting expectantly for the patient to awaken. On the bed was the Dean of their former academy. During the evacuation, he got caught in an explosion where he took serious injury. But curiously, up until those last moments, he was often regarded as the enemy. It wasn't until the intrigues laid down by the old Governor, who was actually Darumon in disguise, were uncovered, when the Dean realized his own mistakes along the way and tried to repent for his errors. This earned him a special reprieve.

The Dean had been kept in a special sleep trance, a kind of forced slumber, similar to a form of anesthesia, but using a divine chant, rather than drugs. This was to prevent any further trauma due to his injury, which by now had been attended. Now it was simply a matter of recovery.

He slowly began to stir on the bed. He was sluggish at first, taking a deep breath as he lazily opened his eyes. He squinted as his vision adjusted. The surroundings were unfamiliar in his blurred eyesight, but as he began to focus, he noticed two people nearby. He turned first to one that appeared female, trying to make out her face.

"Tristeen…?" he murmurs softly.

"Hello, Dean," she replies with a gentle smile. "Welcome back."

"Back…" he whispers uncertainly.

He then turns to examine the other visitor.

"Haran…" he mumbles.

The Dean now begins studying the room, rolling his eyes around at the architecture, and the various medical tables and equipment, most of which were unfamiliar to him.

"Where am I?"

"You're in a Healer's Ward," Tristeen responds soothingly. "In Bya'an Tamoranth…"

"Huh? Where is that?"

"On Tae'Eladar, actually. This place is amazing compared to our old city."

"Our old city… Great gods, I remember now, but still so much is fuzzy. What actually happened, and why am I here. I remember dwarves, and such horrible noises, and smoke and fire…"

"The dwarves from the mining enclave attacked the city using Suuden-Aryku energy weapons, and basically destroyed everything. Our people had to run to evacuate the city, but unfortunately you got hit by some debris."

"Oh, I did? How bad was it?"

"It was pretty bad. You were killed," she smirks tenderly.

The Dean gazed at her, and then passed his glance at Haran, who was smiling playfully.

"Tristeen, I think I'm not really in the right sorts for jokes at this time. What do you actually mean to say?"

"You were dead, Dean. But apparently, death isn't a complete end for these people. Lady Aerlie told me that if they can catch it quick enough, and under the right conditions, they can actually bring a person back to life."

"You can't be serious! They actually hold such knowledge?"

"They do, but she also told me yours was bad, so they had to call in a little divine aid in your case."

"Divine aid?" he winces.

"One of the Estelar," she affirms. "Do you recall anything of those last moments? We were pulling back along the main avenue, but you were apparently late in returning to us. It seems you had gone off to find more stragglers, but by the time you came back, we had already pulled away down the road. And so, you had to make a mad dash for it. We tried holding back the dwarven line to give you a chance, but it didn't work. One of them got a shot off and hit a building. You took a big chunk of wood in the side, and even though we managed to pull you away, you didn't last more than a few brief moments in our arms."

"Good gracious! I'm trying to recall the moment, but I'm uncertain if it's clear to me yet. What happened after that?"

"Priest Garrain of the temple...you remember him, right? His Lordship's people which he used to replace our own..."

"Um, wait...I do recall he managed to infiltrate some of his men. Yes, spies of one kind or another, and very effective too," he pauses to recall the moment. "He had them everywhere, it seems. Oh dear..."

"Yes, he did," she chuckles. "Well, he called on one of their gods, one named Ilmater, known here as the Crying God. He apparently specializes in such things as perseverance, suffering, and endurance. He's known among these people to offer forgiveness and relief from their pain so they can carry on with more productive lives. And he gave you a special gift. He brought you back to us."

"Oh good gracious," he leans back on his pillow and sighs.

The Dean lays there trying to recall the recent history and sequence of events in the city before the attack. He recalls making a visit to the temple, where he inquired of these new priests about the Estelar, hoping to understand these strange new gods in relation to his recent encounter with their former Governor.

"The Estelar," he mutters distantly. "He told me about them when I made a visit. It was right after my visit to the Governor, and not long after His Lordship came to my office. Pleasures...yes, this is the word that creature made to me. And these Estelar apparently interrupted these so-called pleasures."

He tilts his head forward to glance at his body, which was wrapped in a blanket. He gingerly tries lifting up a corner to examine himself.

"An injury, you say? Where was it? I don't actually feel anything..."

He reaches under the blanket to feel around for any tender areas, finally to open a portion of a gown which had been placed on him during this time.

"What injury, Tristeen? I don't see anything."

Haran leans over to give direction.

"It was a stick of wood that impaled your left flank. They said it pierced almost completely through and punctured your kidney."

"But Haran..." the Dean sits up in bed to make a better inspection. "Here, you say?" he points to his left lateral. "But I don't see anything."

"Their healing technique barely leaves any scars behind. It's another divine gift. They can close an injury with the touch of a hand, and leave the area appearing perfect."

"Good gods, and apparently in a literal form."

"Furthermore, they gave you a new kidney, so it seems."

"Huh? Wait a moment. How is that possible?"

"They have a treatment salve that when applied to an injured area, one where a body part is lost, like say an arm or a leg, or in your case an internal organ, they can regenerate the missing part back to normal."

The Dean was dumbfounded by the statement. He simply gaped at Haran as he tried to envision the process, then returning his gaze to his body.

"Does anyone ever actually die on this world?"

"Well, yes, I suppose they live and die much the same as any other, but they apparently live much healthier lives along the way."

"My goodness, this is unbelievable. But why would they do this for me, after all I've done?

"Dean," Tristeen declares. "Thaelyn says your contribution to our cause in those last moments granted you a special merit. You earned what he describes as a ticket to redemption."

The Dean instantly felt a wave of emotion wash over him as he began to put it together. This was a second chance for him, one where he could repay for all his prior sins. His eyes became moist as he reflected on his life in the old academy, where he once held such ambitions as to make the city a better place, but soon lost those dreams when the Governor, or rather to say Marshal Darumon, twisted his ideals into the nightmare that would become the future course of his position.

He gazed longingly at his two callers, then again at his body, which showed no outward signs of injury. He glanced around the room once more, taking notice of several priests who were in attendance with other duties.

"It would seem I owe a tremendous debt to someone. Not simply to His Lordship for granting this to me, but also to this god for actually delivering it. How can it be possible for anyone to hold such authority as this, and yet walk amongst such meager creatures as we?"

"It's true that Thaelyn is an exception to the usual rules," Haran affirms. "Normally, a Celestial would not be found in a place like this, certainly not in such form as he is, but my studies here so far have told me he's something special."

"Your studies? Are you now taking studies here, Haran?"

"Well, yes," he chuckles. "After our little, um, dispute in your office that day, I decided to come over here to continue my mage studies. Sorry, Dean, but they really do have some fine lessons available here."

"Oh, I can't blame you for running off, Haran. Not after my tirade, and certainly not for the poor treatment our students so often received. In fact, I wouldn't be at all surprised if the remainder of them would join at your side after this."

"Some of them already have."

"Indeed! Well, I should wish them better luck. What's the final condition of our home, by the way?"

"Dust, rubble, and ash… The clean-up will probably take months, but Thaelyn is promising to help us rebuild."

"He would even offer this…" he muses deeply. "That man, or whatever word is appropriate to describe him as, must be a saint. Very well, I should probably find a new occupation for myself. It would seem my old job is no more."

"Well, at the moment…" Tristeen relents. "But I'm sure they'll build a new one."

"Tristeen, dear, I think I've had my fill of trying to be a dean. My last effort turned so sour on me that I think I cannot look at another one."

"Then if not this, what else would you do?"

"I can't be sure right now. But I think I should first see what manner of payment I should offer for all these services they gave me. How much longer do I need to stay here?"

Haran turns to one of the priests in attendance to refer the question, which had to be spoken in the local language. He returns to the Dean with his reply.

"He says they would like to keep you until later today for observation. After that, you may go."

"And what about payment? Surely, they must take some form of payment for their services."

"While I'm sure that's the case in most situations, first of all we're in a state of war, and some part of it is falling under a war fund. And second, you and everyone else from the city are now regarded as refugees, so it's also falling under a disaster relief declaration. The kingdom apparently has a rather robust emergency fund to accommodate such things."

The Dean simply gawks at Haran for the outrageously surreal statement.

"But..." he wheezes. "What do you mean...I just simply stand up and walk away? We're not even members of his kingdom, and he is offering to pay for people not his own? For all that is holy... good gods, listen to me," he slaps his forehead. "And look at who it is we're speaking of here."

Both Tristeen and Haran laugh at the Dean's unfortunate bewilderment while he tries to recompose himself.

"No..." he shakes his head. "I cannot simply do that. I want to pay back something. If I am to prove my...redemption...in any form, I need to offer myself into some service."

"Well, Dean..." Tristeen begins. "Um..."

"Please, Tristeen," he interjects. "Don't call me Dean anymore. I think I want to distance myself from that title. It carries too many ill feelings by now. Just call me Alin."

"All right, Alin..." she smiles. "My best suggestion, at this point, might be to speak with either His Lordship, or maybe Lady Aerlie, who usually works out there in the main part of the temple. Although today I think she's out by Firstfall giving aid to the others. But maybe one of them can suggest something."

✦✦✦◆✦✦✦

The daily activity was just beginning in the village of Firstfall. This small settlement was located in a region that was historically known as the Badlands. The terrain, which once was an arid wasteland, had been radically altered into lush, wooded pastures, due to the extraordinary forces brought into play by Lord Thaelyn, King of Tae'Eladar. This transformation was the result of his arrival, and a corollary demand to the destruction of a large orcish occupation he found here after pursuing them off Tae'Eladar.

However, unknown to him at the time, those orcs were but a smaller part of the larger machinations enacted by Darumon, and from a much earlier moment in history as Darumon had designs for a revenge attack against his old rivals, the Estelar.

The local races were all heavily oppressed as part of the siege of the world, and their ability to comprehend the truth of it was so badly muddled, few of them could even recall their own history of how it got started. Fortunately, Thaelyn was not as limited in his scope, and much to Darumon's chagrin, he unraveled these plans and chased Darumon away. But the world was a wreck by this time.

Outside the gates, on the north side of the village, was a huddled mass of refugees from the city of Rolsklinde. The city was one of the last surviving cities in this world, but now a smoldering heap of rubble. These people were the homeless survivors waking up after the nightmarish event that took place the day before. And had it not been for Thaelyn's spies investigating so many bad deeds, they may have been lost completely.

The masses had been gathered around a series of campfires. Many tents were erected around the area to offer shelter, and blankets delivered the night before to afford them some comfort. Care workers walked amongst the people representing members of the citizens of Tae'Eladar, along with some of the local races, including the Night Elves and High Elves. Another local faction, known as the Daanen-Aryku, set up a medical field station to provide for the needs of those who suffered injury during the attack.

As the morning progressed, wagons were arriving with food supplies, and a series of makeshift kitchens were preparing the morning meal. Several key figures were gathering, some waking up within the barracks of the local garrison, and others who had found occupancy in a few inns on Tae'Eladar.

Tristeen was one of those arriving through the gateway from Tae'Eladar. She was soon joined by two friends, Willit Sarens and Jared Galwen, and a young female accomplice, Leesa Gobbard, the latter of whom were taking up temporary residence in one of the barracks. After finishing breakfast, they were joined by Tristeen's father, Josef, and their personal friends, Abraim Whitcord and Seth Farlind, and now they hoped to use their combined skills to bring some order into the chaos out in the fields.

"How do you suppose we are going to manage all that?" Abraim mumbles as he scans the morass of bodies in the northern fields.

"Badly," Josef relents. "But manage it, we must."

"I can already tell you one thing," Tristeen considers. "We need to bring the families together into groups. And I'm starting to get an idea. In fact..." she smiles mischievously. "Yeah, this might work to solve a few things at once."

Both Jared and Willit studied her, and then glanced at each other at the obvious implications.

"She's got that look in her eye," Jared mentions.

"Aye, I see it," Willit agrees. "If we hop to it now, we can get a head start before she catches us."

"Aye, but to where?"

"Now just a minute, you two," Tristeen chides. "We're in this together, remember?"

"All right," Willit affirms. "But what do you have in mind?"

"You remember how I used to organize group activities in the old academy, right? Well, if we apply a little of that, I think we can make some progress. But I'm going to need help, and a number of assistants. Willit, Jared, Leesa...that means you."

"I didn't go to the academy," Leesa admits. "So, what can I do?"

"Just follow my lead. But now, we need help from His Lordship's people."

Tristeen scanned the activity of the village looking for any familiar faces.

"We need to find Master Dastien. He can probably help. Who else do we have handy? Oh, look there..."

She points toward the tactical office where Thaelyn and his officers would often meet. Outside in front was a military officer who stood watch.

"Him… Captain, um, Hagmaert, right?"

"Aye," Willit offers.

"He holds some authority, doesn't he? Can we get him to help a little?"

"We could surely go up and ask."

"Good. Now listen carefully…"

Tristeen pauses to consider her plan of action.

"First, I need a platform to stand on so I can speak to the people."

"Tristeen, my dear," Josef muses curiously. "Just what do you have in mind on this occasion, hmm?"

"I think your daughter is bucking to be a new political aspirant," Abraim admits.

"But is she simply looking for a Council position?" Seth considers. "Or create a new Governor's seat?"

"I'm not saying I want to be the next Governor…" Tristeen pauses to consider the idea. "Although it does sound like fun," she giggles. "But we do need to draw their attention to some manner of presentation. Next, I need a way to direct them into groups to sort out the madness of that jumble out there. For this…yeah, maybe if we hold up a number of signposts with letters of the alphabet on them and organize them by the spelling of their surnames."

"Indeed," Josef nods. "This sounds fair enough. A bit crude, but under the circumstances, given what we have to work with, it would provide a workable solution."

"Crude or not, it's the end result that matters."

Tristeen starts giving out orders for each of her cohorts to bring the various pieces together while she goes out into the fields to survey the situation.

✦ ✦ ✦ ✦ ✦

Thaelyn had arrived for his morning report in the tactical office. At this time, only the General and a few other officers were in attendance.

"General," Thaelyn begins. "If our greater enemies in this world are no longer to be considered an issue, I should wish to see about the remaining orcs as quickly as possible. According to our scouts, the last of Darumon's people departed last eve, correct?"

"Yes, my Lord. That last team of scouts you sent out there came back with a report of sighting a large mushroom cloud rising up over the region, and they were able to confirm the base was completely destroyed as the result."

"And so we see the last of that, but it is a bittersweet solution, as now we have to rely on luck to find our way to Sargeras, if such a thing is actually possible."

"Indeed, I must agree. And I think we still have many steps to go before we might happen across that luck."

"Very well, until then, let us finish up with what we have so we can free ourselves in preparation of that lucky event."

"Yes, my Lord. So far, the orcs are running scared, which leaves them vulnerable. But my Lord, this does leave me with an important question on my mind which I feel I must ask at this exact time."

"And what is that, General?"

"When we first declared our war on them, it was on Tae'Eladar, and as the result of the atrocities they played on our people. I still recall your words that we shall leave no orc standing on our home soil, and we did exactly that. They are gone from our world. But now we find ourselves on another world, and while I fully realize the threat they pose with their use of portals, which could allow them to launch an attack on us without warning, I must ask what our ultimate intentions are here. Are we to continue this war until no orc stands on this world either?"

"I understand your concern, General, and I must also sympathize. I do not take lightly the prospect of wiping a species out of existence, but at the same time, I cannot abide by their treatment of others. Our issue here is largely centered on their use of portal magic, which they should not have in the first place, and neither should they have access to direct it at Tae'Eladar. Both of these are clearly the work of Darumon teaching them something they were not ready to learn, and further to use it as a means to assault our world."

"Of course."

"If it could be as simple as taking away some item or device to prevent them from holding this power, I would do so, but we also have the prospect of them apparently using portals from Ruuki uy'Daan to this world. This leaves the source of this power out of our reach. And if any of them still holds knowledge of Tae'Eladar, the threat is not entirely resolved."

"I understand."

"Until we can resolve this, I feel there is no other way but to continue our campaign as it is. Maybe a solution will present itself at a later moment. But ultimately, unless we can find a way to remove this knowledge from them, the only real solution..." he sighs and pauses to consider his prospects. "Well, the only sure way might be to simply remove their capacity to perform magic at all. But this presents its own complications, as we would need to relocate them to a world outside the flows."

"An interesting solution, but yes, I think this is also outside our current capacity."

"And let us not forget their manners. If you will recall for a moment, our war on Tae'Eladar began with the uprising of their aberrant manners. During this time, we considered how and why they were suddenly taking this new direction, as we once had control of their numbers."

"Yes, I recall this, and our conclusion, now that we find ourselves here, was largely a combination of new leadership, meaning to say Darumon leading them as part of his crusade, and also a new religion in the form of worshipping Sargeras."

"And we cannot necessarily find a solution to that unless we can somehow convince them not to follow him any longer."

"But orcs aren't ones to negotiate, so this leaves the idea virtually unresolvable, especially if he is still driving them in some manner, like he was doing with the Flame Elves."

"It does. And with or without Sargeras's so-called songs, I think I will not choose to trust those who are currently running from us, as they have never impressed upon any of us to learn from their mistakes. Give them the opportunity, and they might try fooling us again."

"Very well, my Lord, then we shall continue pressing forward."

◆ ◆ ◆ ◆ ◆

Morning was progressing to midday as an elder Night Elf arrived from her home city of Solinaia. Lady Amariyn was making a brief visit to the Daanen-Aryku medical station for a review of their services. She was currently speaking to the chief medical technician in charge of their operations.

"One of my most important concerns right now," the Med-tech infers, "would be those who still have the implants in their bodies. For as long as those remain, they are at risk of infection, and this needs to be addressed as soon as possible."

"I agree," Amariyn reflects. "But for this, we will need to take a careful account of who is here and their age groupings. We need to take a census of some kind, which would ultimately allow us to monitor who has been processed and who has not."

"Absolutely!" she nods. "And we need to find a way to do this quickly. I took notice of some people over there near the gate putting together something like a stage. I was thinking of going over there to see what they're doing, and if we can work together somehow."

"I can certainly go investigate for you."

Amariyn and the Med-tech both orient themselves to examine the activity in front of the north gate, which had brought many laborers into action by now to assemble Tristeen's stage platform. Amariyn saunters over to find someone to speak to about the Med-tech's concerns, which centered on the implants carried by the human population of Rolsklinde, potentially threatening a deadly illness. This was one of Darumon's little games he was playing to keep them under control.

"Eh, excuse me," she asks of a laborer. "But who is in charge here?"

The man turns to her address, but didn't understand her immediately as she was using the local dialect.

"Sorry, madam," he responds in Elvish. "I didn't understand you. What was it you needed?"

"Ah, my pardons, you must be from Tae'Eladar. Once again, we have this issue of language. I am looking for the one in charge of this here."

"But of course! Then you need to see that ambitious young lass over yon," he points at Tristeen, who was directing a flow of workers. "She's the boss in this case, along with that man standing nearby."

"I see, and thank you."

Amariyn now ventures over to meet with Tristeen as she supervises the work effort. Master Dastien had been coordinating with her to help with the translations.

"Excuse me, do you speak Elvish?"

Tristeen turned and gazed blankly at the elder Night Elf, not understanding the native language. All she could do was interpret how to respond.

"I'm sorry, I don't understand you. But you look like a Night Elf, am I right?"

"Good gracious, my apologies…" she smiles. "So many people, and so many languages. I thought you might be one of His Lordship's people. Are you instead from the city up there?"

"Oh, yes, we have a lot of mismatched people here. This man is one of his people," she directs at Master Dastien. "As for me, my name is Tristeen Macaid. My family is one of the noble houses of Rolsklinde, or whatever is left of it."

"A noble? How interesting. I came to ask what it is you are building here. The Daanen-Aryku Med-tech over there has a few of her own needs to address, and we were wondering if perhaps we might find a way to coordinate ourselves."

"Oh? What does she need?"

"Our concern is with these implants your people have that could set off this dreadful illness. We need to remove them as a priority, and do so as quickly as possible."

"Ah, right! I nearly forgot about those, for all the other troubles we've had. Yes, I'm hoping to apply myself to bring some kind of order into all this, reuniting families and sorting out this mess. Along the way, I'm sure we can find time to address that as well."

"Are you hoping to take some sort of census of the surviving population? I think it might prove useful."

"A census…" she muses as she glances over the large gathering of people. "I don't think I have the resources for that, at least not personally. Perhaps you could help?"

"Oh, but of course! By the way, I should introduce myself. I am Lady Amariyn Moonshimmer of the Elven Council of Solinaia, or at least until we more fully assimilate into His Lordship's kingdom. We are still passing through a number of transitions as our city integrates with his cultural and economic methods."

"So, your whole city is joining his kingdom…wow," she sighs and looks again at the confused array of refugees. "I can't help but to wonder where we might end up."

"It might serve you to know that he has offered this to the High Elves of Kynesoth as well, and I am sure he would offer it to you too."

"You think so? Well, I don't think I could make that decision by myself, naturally. But maybe, once we gain control of the situation out here, we can talk about it."

✦✦✦✦✦

"I do not wish any to escape, only to resurface at some future moment," Thaelyn asserts to the new meeting. "If they do, they could pose a surprise danger, especially if to use these portals. But I am also growing concerned over the sense of loss they might be feeling at this time."

"My Lord!" Relissa yips. "Don't tell me you're starting to feel sorry for those buggers."

Relissa, Marelle, and Lieutenant Padriyl Lapäli had joined the meeting by now, having returned from their language classes on Tae'Eladar.

"Perhaps, but Relissa, we must remember that we do not wantonly destroy all that stands in our way, as the Suuden-Aryku have so blatantly demonstrated. We only apply ourselves if it threatens our own or other innocent lives. The orcs do still pose a threat due to their use of portal magic, but their support in the Suuden-Aryku is at an end. And yet, if they willingly give their worship to Sargeras, we must consider them a danger to whomever they encounter for as long as that persists, unless we can find an alternative solution."

"An alternative solution?" Marelle wonders. "If they worship him as a god, the only alternative I can see would be if Sargeras was dead, if such a thing can actually be accomplished."

"Not simply that, I would say," Relissa adds. "But even the simple image of him as a god, whether or not he's physically present to demonstrate it."

"Yes, that too."

"This is correct, in a very simplistic manner," Thaelyn nods. "But short of this, we must consider what else we can do. While we may have no other choice but to continue our campaign of genocide against them, if they can be contained somehow, perhaps we could remove their threat potential, and at the same time, avoid destroying their race completely."

"And how do you suppose we do that? Are we talking about the threat of them worshiping Sargeras as a god, or their use of portal magic...or both?"

"Technically, both would be preferable, but until we can find ourselves in a position to do away with Sargeras, we should perhaps focus on their use of portal magic. If they cannot use it, they cannot travel to places beyond their physical reach. Currently, they can apparently reach from Ruuki uy'Daan to this world, and if any of them still remember the way, they can reach from here to Tae'Eladar. Remove this ability, and we may have containment."

"How do you know if it's removed? If their shamans are the ones conjuring these portals, then I guess we need to remove all of them, right?"

"Normally, I would say yes, but the knowledge might not be fully contained if they maintain records of it, or perhaps an artifact to point the way. As primitive as they may seem compared to us, they do still understand such a concept as writing, and future shamans may arise to learn from it."

"Then we look for all of their books, or whatever they use for this."

"Possibly, but this could then become problematic, especially if they get wise and attempt to hide these items from us. There is one other idea that comes to mind, however, and it could also allow us to preserve even their shamans if we are able to accomplish it properly."

"This should be good," she smirks. "So, what is it?"

"The General and I were discussing this earlier. If the orcs could be relocated to another world, one outside of an arcanic cloud, they could continue to survive using whatever means they are accustomed to, but without the use of magic."

"All right, that's an idea. Do we know of any worlds like this?"

"I cannot answer that at the present time, but we would need to choose one that is supportive of life, yet currently uninhabited by anything of a highly evolved nature, such as other sentient forms. Naturally, the orcs would need the means to hunt and gather food, as well as to harvest other resources, such as wood and stone. If this becomes their primary home, the only thing we should concern ourselves with would be the long-term implications."

"My Lord, sometimes I wonder how you come up with all this. What sort of long-term implications are you referring to now?"

"Over the course of time, all things, even orcs, can grow and learn. In their case, we could be speaking of thousands of years of advancement. But someday they might grow to understand such forms of science that they could learn to build ships to travel amongst the stars as the Suuden-Aryku do. I wonder what sort of society they might have at that moment, and how they would differ from what we see today."

"An interesting thought... Scary, if they keep their current manners. But in thousands of years, who knows? Still, they could be quite dangerous if they develop science like what the Suuden-Aryku have."

"Yes, but in such time, we will also evolve, Marelle, and probably much more efficiently. But we cannot find a reasonable answer to this until perhaps we arrive on Ruuki uy'Daan. We need to cut them off at the source. Therefore, those present in this world must still be considered a threat."

"All right, so the war goes on a little longer. What about Darumon and the Suuden-Aryku. You said something about speaking to High Commander Geilv, right?"

"Yes, and as expected, he did seem to be under a control effect. His voice betrayed a suppressing force governing him. He was kind enough to inform me that there are indeed implants that control their manners. One is described as a medical device, but it also apparently suppresses their emotions, and another holds a military purpose to impose a governing effect on their compliance."

"Jiggers!" Relissa snaps. "That doesn't sound at all nice."

"One is a medical device?" Padriyl wonders. "And THIS is what causes them to show no apparent emotion? Fascinating... I wonder what sort of medical condition they're speaking of here that requires an implant as a curative procedure."

"It sounds as though it might date back some distance," Thaelyn recalls. "And it became a kind of universal demand as a preventative effort."

"That sounds as weird as it does bad for those people. As for the other, I have to agree with Relissa. A military control chip simply isn't nice."

"Indeed, but it certainly follows with how Darumon tends to treat those around him. And yet, the Commander gave an interesting impression, along with what I might suggest was a local officer, maybe on the communications station. They shared a few words here and there as they carried some local conversation relating to our subject matter."

"What sort?"

"Firstly, the officer seemed much more cognitive, so I am wondering if he was under the same influence, or if it was limited only to the Commander."

"That would represent a curious twist."

"Curious like using the Dean, and then the rest of us?" Marelle offers. "Or maybe Sehnisavain and the Flame Elves? You have a top man under his control, and the rest are simply cronies following orders."

"Yeah, Marelle, you have a point."

"Generally speaking," Thaelyn continues. "They were questioning the integrity of their orders. Initially, they apparently felt justified in their actions, at least within reason, as they were told the local societies were to be contained due to their association with some alleged opponents. But then I began questioning just how much they paid attention to who and what they were trying to contain. If we say the Estelar are the opponents, how do you justify wiping out a society that is not space-capable, and therefore incapable of holding relations to anything found on another world, or another universe? They apparently did not make this connection, and this reminds me of Darumon's deception and control of information."

"Cu'Nar help us! So, the Suuden-Aryku are being told to do things without even a proper explanation? That doesn't help matters at all."

"No, it does not, and he also seemed to hint at this not being the first time. We have him pursuing you all the way to another universe, presumably by way of a tracking probe following you through your wild jump. In my mind, this sounds like an excuse to justify finding a way into a new universe by means that should otherwise be outside their capacity, much like those orcs and their probe aiding them to find this next destination."

"Wonderful, an excuse to find us out here. And maybe like all the others."

"And laying waste to worlds with populations that should not hold the potential to travel outwards to be a threat to anyone. And yet, Darumon instructed them NOT to find a conveniently empty world, and instead devastate this one for his staging operation."

"That's sickening. And worse to think our people would actually follow these instructions...chip or no chip."

"Indeed. He said the Marshal apparently keeps his secrets, and HE, as the High Commander, although he believes he SHOULD be in the know, very often is not."

"I swear, that's even worse than our revelation of Darumon controlling things, rather than the HC. My Commander isn't going to like this one at all."

"And then, once I began to chastise them over this, they almost sounded as though they regretted it. Some words were mentioned agreeing with me about the errors made, and he even apologized for himself."

"Great cu'Nar!" he yelps. "I would never have expected that one!"

"I also heard a number of sounds relating to a pain reaction."

"A pain reaction?"

"Yes, apparently coming out of the High Commander. When I tried interrogating this, his officer, I must again assume at the comms station, informed me this medical chip contains some sort of feedback feature to enforce itself. This apparently relates to that emotional control."

"I don't believe this!" he shouts. "So, even if they DO try to have an emotional reaction, they get zapped for it?! In all the nether-space, Commander Nazég is seriously going to lose his horns over this."

"No doubt! But even with this control effect, their minds must still be capable of some level of rationalization. If this is the case, I might wish to play on this more, if we should find the opportunity."

"Incredible! This is simply shocking, and a little difficult to accept, when you consider all of our suffering at their hands. But it does offer something new to think about."

"And finally, during my conversation with Darumon, I was able to manipulate the direction ever so slightly as to involve a few tender details, such as the first invasion of his orcs, and him seeding this world at a point in time that should well predate anything the High Commander might otherwise know about to a presence in the local space. I cannot know what he might think of this, but if he and his people were paying attention to the wording, it might leave an impression of foul play and premeditation on the part of this world and its population, and maybe Darumon's overall attitude towards lesser lifeforms."

"To refute anything Darumon might have told them earlier? Yes, but if he likes to play with things, THEY should be careful now."

"Yes, I also left a small note to be aware and not fall into the spotlight should things turn the other way. And I also made a recording of the conversation. You can review it if you like, and share it with your Commander."

"Oh, absolutely! I would certainly like to listen to that. But now, where does this actually leave us?"

"It leaves us with a rebuilding effort, and we must do so on no less a scale as this calamity to restore what was taken. We must first bring help to clean up the remains of Rolsklinde so we can begin our efforts there. I would also wish to investigate the mining enclave up north. General, perhaps you could arrange a scouting expedition to investigate that for us. Have them make a cautious approach by air, and report what they see from afar. We will move in at ground level only if it appears safe."

"Yes, my Lord."

"Next, Lieutenant, would be your people. We will call in additional aid to assist you and yours to build some manner of proper settlement, the beginnings of a new home for you."

"Us?" Padriyl responds. "You want to help us rebuild?"

"But of course, Lieutenant. Why not? Your society makes use of certain industries in order to provide for your needs. We can assist in furnishing you with labor and materials to give you a jump start. You can then reciprocate by providing some product or another as part of a mutual trade agreement. When was the last time you engaged in any manner of trade with an outside body?"

"Not in my lifetime, other than the orcs of Ruuki uy'Daan, but I wouldn't exactly call that a very productive form of trade. And I don't recall mention of any kind of trade with anything else on any of the other worlds we crossed."

"Then it is about time for you to regard yourselves to be part of a proper societal network again. We must work together to find our way to a combined purpose. And for this, it occurs to me that we need to form an official diplomatic treaty for trade and other forms of political interaction. After all, we are neighbors," he smiles.

"Criminy," Relissa wheezes. "New neighbors, and not just for fighting some bleedin' war! Now we have peace and a chance to build something. I never thought I'd see the day."

"Indeed, Relissa, I must admit, for all the trouble you had here, I would agree. But Lieutenant, we must arrange for a proper form of alliance. Your people and mine will need to work together if we are to take this war back to Sargeras. And we MUST take it back to him, or else other worlds like this may fall."

◆◆◆

"Tristeen, our signposts are arriving."

"They are? Good, bring them over here."

Leesa was overseeing the arrival of a wagon with new supplies coming in from Tae'Eladar. It carried a collection of long wooden poles, and several stacks of wooden plaques.

"We have these long poles," Leesa announces as they examine the supply cart. "But they look heavy, so we may need a few extra hands to manage them. Then all these signboards, and several pens to mark on them."

"Good," Tristeen affirms. "Let's gather up some people and place them around the area. The platform isn't quite ready yet, so I'm using a stack of boxes so far. If anyone ever said to stand on a soapbox to make their presentation, well, I'm living up to that by now."

They called up Willit and Jared, and together they marked the signs with individual letters of their alphabet. Then they gathered a few additional laborers to stand them up at intervals around the field.

Amariyn had called in a group of auditors and a table to take down a proper census with names, ages, and relations of the people as the assembly found some organization. Josef and the other noble fathers assisted in coordinating the data, while Tristeen stood on her soapbox pedestal giving her announcements.

"Keep in mind," she shouts to the audience. "It is very important for us to conduct our initial census so we can see exactly who is present here. Our people are in great disarray, and need to be brought together so family members can find each other, and we can better organize ourselves into groups. We can further use this to understand who is in the greatest need to undergo the removal of that horrid little device those priests once gave us with their Festival. Those in the higher age ranges are at the greatest risk, therefore they must go first. The rest can surely wait until they finish, and we will work our way through the population with all due haste. For this reason, when you find your assigned group, you should remain there until we can attend to you. Thank you."

Thaelyn and the others were taking a recess from their meeting and stepping outside for some fresh air when they overheard the announcement.

"'Ere now," Relissa perks up. "What's that ruckus all about?"

She directs the group around the corner of the office building and towards the gate, where they observed the crowds being herded under a series of tall signposts, and Tristeen up on her makeshift platform giving out instructions.

"How interesting," Thaelyn muses. "Is that the same young lady we met in the city?"

"Aye, that's Tristeen again. Jiggers, that girl doesn't know when to quit."

They pass through the gate to see the auditors and a small army of attendants making relays to and from the groupings under the signposts. Thaelyn notices Josef and the others participating in the affair, so he ambles over to check on things.

"Sire Macaid, it would seem you found yourself some curious occupation."

"Yes, Your Lordship, but I think the true credit goes to my daughter up there. This was mostly her idea. I'm just giving her a hand."

"You mean to tell me your daughter brought all this together?"

Thaelyn turns to survey the full scene, which involved the

continuing labor to build the stage platform, Tristeen and her soapboxes, the signposts, and the army of attendants.

"Yes, Your Lordship," Josef continues. "Before I could even get a word in edgewise, she already had her friends rounding up support in cooperation with this fine woman here," he points at Amariyn, "along with a Daanen-Aryku medical officer, further with some of your people, and apparently some supply stores to deliver the materials."

Thaelyn gawked at the man as he directed the attention to all the elements Tristeen had conjured up ad hoc to serve her needs.

"Now she's up there helping us take a census," Josef continues. "And furthermore, to prioritize the removal of those implant devices."

"Dear Powers, I think I may need to pay close attention to this one. Was it not stated that your family, along with the others, once held some form of political authority in your city?"

"We did, once upon a time, and to some extent we still tried to maintain some of those old teachings, although mostly in private amongst our own. But dear Tristeen up there, she is a true gem. She seems to hold some practical experience from her time spent in the academy with the other students."

"Indeed. And she certainly did not waste any time in coordinating all this. Very well, carry on, and if you have any additional needs, do not hesitate to ask."

"Thank you most graciously, Your Lordship."

Padriyl studied the scene as Tristeen gave her announcements, shouting nearly at the top of her lungs as she tried to reach out to the vast assembly of people, which numbered in the tens of thousands. An idea immediately came to mind, so he stepped up to gain her attention.

"Um, excuse me up there."

Tristeen halts her presentation to respond to the Daanen'kai officer.

"Wow, even from up here, you people are tall. I remember seeing you yesterday. You went inside the Governor's Manor for something, right?"

"Yes, we had to shut down a reactor he had in his basement, in order to prevent it from overloading."

"Whatever that actually means, but I'll take your word for it," she giggles. "Is there something I can do for you?"

"Actually, there's something I think I can do for you. My people could probably make life a lot easier if we provided you with a few pieces of equipment and set it up over here. We can bring out some loudspeakers for you to make your announcements without the need to blow your lungs out at the same time. How does that sound?"

"I actually have no idea what that is, but if it can help me reach out to these people, I'm all for it. My throat is already going hoarse."

"I can certainly understand that," he grins as he pulls out his trans-com to make a call.

✦✦✦✦✦

In the city of Bya'an Tamoranth, in the temple Healer's Ward, the former Dean of the old Rolsklinde academy is being released from his stay. He makes his way through the ornate temple complex into the main audience hall where he finds the priests attending to their worship, with some of them teaching students and others coordinating choirs. Among these was Aerlie, who was offering some of her own lessons.

The Dean knew right away he would have trouble speaking to the locals, as the people of Tae'Eladar used their own unique language as compared to those on Therinë. But he recognized Aerlie from his previous interactions, and hoped she could offer some direction.

"Eh, my pardons," he calls gently as he approaches the dais.

Aerlie broke from her lessons and turned to the address.

"Ah, Dean," she replies politely. "How do you feel today?"

"Actually, considering I was apparently dead for a time, I feel remarkably fine. I don't know who to thank first for this uncanny gift, but perhaps I could ask for some direction on where to begin."

"We do not place demands on our guests, Dean..."

"Please, as I was saying to Tristeen earlier, I do not wish to use that title anymore. My name is simply Alin Malorn. I think I have had my fill of trying to be a dean."

"I see. Well, all things considered, I suppose I cannot blame you. From what I understand of it, the experience would likely have left a bad taste behind."

"That it did. It's my understanding that not only do I have your priests to thank, but I apparently owe a significant debt to His Lordship, and this god of yours named, eh…Ilmater, is it?"

"Yes, he is the one we called upon to provide for us on this occasion."

"I was never a religious man before this, but then the priests we had in our temple back home weren't exactly the sort you would give proper homage to. And yet, as I reflect on the conversations I had with yours, I began to realize there may actually be some kind of Power watching over us after all. And now, I vaguely recall a voice, but I can't be sure where it came from."

"A voice? Do you mean from one of us?"

"No, I don't think so. It almost seems like a dream. I've been trying to place the image, and all that comes to mind is a gentle face of a man who appeared battered and bruised, but he seemed undaunted to hold his composure."

Aerlie listened to the depiction and smiled. She impulsively turned to glance along the rows of religious icons lining the walls around platform. These represented the various gods the people of Tae'Eladar worshipped, specifically the local pantheons of the Estelar.

"But anyway," Alin continues. "His voice seemed so soothing, but also firm."

"What did he say, can you recall?"

"The voice did not speak in such way as to use plain words, rather a feeling of some kind. And there was meaning behind it, as if to convey a message by means other than simple words. Does this actually make sense to you?"

"It does. You must be referring to Ilmater himself, as the image you describe is often what he uses to depict himself to us. The battering you mention represents the suffering and torment he draws away unto himself from those who ask for his aid. And the Estelar usually do not use a spoken language as we do, unless they wish to converse in a more primitive form with a younger society like ours. Our priests most often interact with them using a form similar to your experience, and we teach lessons here on how to interpret these sensations. We then use this to convey their teachings to our people."

"How interesting. To communicate with a being of such high capacity that they don't even use words anymore. But still, I would wish to offer my thanks to him. I cannot believe I would be regarded as worthy of such a thing as what he gave to me. And still, there was what he said…"

Alin paused in deep thought as he tried to recollect the interaction he had, which occurred during the time when he was regarded as clinically dead, and when Ilmater brought him back into his body.

"My service is not complete. I must represent my own message."

"This is curious," Aerlie admits. "He must hold a purpose for you."

"But how do I fulfill that purpose? I'm not a priest…" he halts his statement as he silently asks himself about the implications. "Do you actually think…? Yes, that must be it. I must repay for all my past sins, and I do hold a great many. A ticket to redemption, and there can be only one way for it. Your Grace, can you perhaps give me a few of these lessons?"

"We certainly can. Let's first pay a visit to Ilmater's icon and introduce you to him personally. Maybe he can offer some additional guidance."

She leads him across the dais to a row of statues lining the rear of the platform. Among them was one with a symbol on a golden plaque representing a set of bound hands. They kneel and Aerlie directs him to place his hand on the plaque while she summons the mind of the associated deity, and together they begin his lessons.

+ + ◆ ◆ + +

In the mountains north of Rolsklinde, a pair of scouts rides a gryphon in the skies looking down at a mining enclave where a band of dwarves once served as slave labor for Darumon and his follies. A sturdy door sealed off the mining entrance, but the door wasn't the primary focus of their inspection tour.

"There it is," points one scout. "That's the door, and the large hollow the Suuden-Aryku used to set down their flying craft."

"That's all well and good," the other one replies. "But most important is the mountaintop is still in one piece."

"Aye, so that bomb they left behind must still be sitting down inside there."

"That doesn't make me feel any better, but if it's not going off, then maybe we can move ahead and take the mine."

"That'd be a fine one, another adamantium mine. But before you can get me to set foot inside there, I think it would be a good thing to have someone go in and make sure it's all neat and tidy."

"Aye, so call this in and let them know."

The scout pulls out a trans-com and dials in a number. Soon, a voice answers.

"This is Thaelyn."

"My Lord, we're up here by the mine. It looks fine enough, the place is still in one piece, so we're thinking we should send in a ground crew to check on things inside."

"Very good, then I will have you return to camp, and we will contact the Daanen-Aryku to participate in a closer examination of the area."

"Aye!"

They end the link and Thaelyn turns to the General and Lieutenant Lapäli.

"Lieutenant, contact your people. I suspect you must have some manner of environmental or radiation hazard equipment on hand, correct?"

"Yes, we do."

"Good, prepare a team to infiltrate that mine and inspect that bomb. If all appears well, we will use a portal rune on it to remove it to a safe location on Tae'Eladar, probably within reasonable proximity to the new research base, but I do not want it to be positioned too close, just in case."

"Will do," he nods. "I can call in a few of our engineers to see about any activation triggers, and what is necessary to disable them. But an atomic is a dangerous weapon, no matter how you look at it."

"Indeed it is. We do not at present have a reasonable method to dispose of it, so for now perhaps we can simply bury it in an underground bunker for storage until later."

Padriyl pulls out his trans-com to forward the instructions while Thaelyn continues with his own plans.

"General, once it is safe, we are going to take that mine and move some of our own people into it. I want a careful inspection of the forge, and any other equipment to be found down there. Also, be sure to give instructions to clean out that kitchen of theirs and to quarantine that farming area. Although I cannot see what we might use that farm for, at the very least we do not want anyone tampering with it. Lieutenant, perhaps your people might find this an interesting biological study."

Padriyl shrugs as he continues his call.

"Knowing Ankhia, she might want to save a few specimens."

"This is reasonable, but beyond that, we may simply wish to remove those mushrooms entirely. Unless...hmm...a biological study. Maybe we can simply close it off as a laboratory project. Who knows, perhaps we could find this useful one day."

"That's an interesting prospect," the General accedes. "Our first example of life from another world to study. This could open a new field of science for us."

"It could! And this one is particularly alien to us. And then we have the mine itself. This brings to mind another interesting matter, while we are here."

"And what might that be, my Lord?"

"Are there any other deposits of adamantium in this world?"

"Gods above..." Marelle mutters. "Yeah, that's a very good question. If we have one, there should be more, right?"

"And quite often mithril can also be found on worlds such as this if adamantium can be found. You just need to know where to look. I must now wonder if there is indeed such a resource."

"None of us apparently found any, but if we don't even know what to look for, I suppose that answers it."

"In addition, my Lord," the General suggests. "Since we seem to be of the opportunity, I would recommend sending scouts, cartographers, and other such people into the field to make a careful study of this world. Even if not to survey for such resources as these, but simply to give us a better idea of the lay of the land around us."

"Very good, and surely there are other resources that could be of use, especially in our rebuilding effort. Local supplies would be preferable over importing our own."

"And this would give the local societies their own industry, and a boon to their local economy."

"Speaking of which," Thaelyn reflects. "Even though we have the favor of the Night Elves, we have yet to work an arrangement with the human and High Elf populations, and this world belongs in part to them as well. And then there are the Daanen-Aryku."

"Your Lordship," Padriyl relents. "Technically, this isn't our world at all. If you recall, our ship crashed here, so even though we're stuck here, we can't make any official claims to anything."

"Lieutenant, foreign or otherwise, the fact that you are here now, and generally accepted as neighbors with the rest, to say nothing of the, ahem, unfortunate fact of this world having been devastated by Darumon and his antics, I feel we have more than enough space for you and yours. You must fit in with the rest, and find a comfortable place amongst us, as I suspect we have far to go together."

"All right," he chuckles ironically. "Great cu'Nar, you're more demanding than my Commander."

"Perhaps, Lieutenant," Thaelyn grins. "But we need you as much as I suspect you need us. You have lived a nomadic lifestyle for a long time, and this may have jaded your social capacity somewhat."

"Especially if you consider that last world we were on."

"Indeed! Now I think a little rehabilitation is in order as we prepare ourselves for what lies ahead. I still regard us to be in a state of war, even though that war is in recess for a time."

"Yeah, for as long as Sargeras is out there. All right, then I'll pass this on to my Commander for our Elder Council to consider."

A late afternoon recess was in session for Thaelyn and his officers. They were retiring to an officer's lounge tent that was assembled just off to the side of the village square in the settlement. Josef and his team, along with Captain Kholgard, formerly of the Allegiance Guard from Rolsklinde, as well as Tristeen who was taking a break from her soapbox lectures, had all been summoned into a casual meeting. Lady Amariyn was also attending, as was the High Elf delegation, which involved the High Priestess Sehnisavain and her two daughters from the city of Kynesoth.

"We are gathered here at this time to see about a few issues that need resolving," Thaelyn begins. "The Night Elves of Solinaia joined our kingdom just over a month ago. With their involvement, our kingdom can declare itself an official member state in this world, and therefore neighbors with all the rest. As such, we must establish for ourselves some manner of official treaty to declare our relationships. This world is currently at peace, within reason, and we must make full use of this opportunity to rebuild what we have."

"Your Lordship," Captain Kholgard submits. "Marelle was suggesting to me not long ago that since you will be basically rebuilding our city for us, that we might owe you virtually everything we own. I was speaking with Sire Macaid and his people earlier, and we're all asking ourselves how we might go forward with this."

"He's right," Tristeen adds. "Lady Amariyn told me you once made a similar offer to the High Elves, and you might make the same to us. But when I look at the plans you have for our city, I'm actually asking myself if we are expected to offer ourselves to you, or if we will become citizens by the simple merit that we will be occupying space you built on our behalf."

"I would never make such a demand as that," Thaelyn affirms. "While on one hand we can say you are abducted members of our society on Tae'Eladar, on the other hand, you built new lives for yourselves in this world independent of ours. I was sent to Tae'Eladar with a purpose, to unite those people into one nation. This technically occurred after your abduction, but I would surely welcome you back home again if you desired it."

"From what I've seen of your world, it sure does look inviting."

"Still, that city is your home, even though it is currently in ruins. But the land belongs to you. I could suggest we do here as I did on Tae'Eladar, and unite everyone together, those who are not already aligned. Unity bestows strength, and right now you need this... you, the High Elves, and even the Daanen-Aryku. If, however, you should desire to join with us, I can offer a number of benefits for your inclusion into our kingdom, not the least of which would be the more advanced wisdom and cultural amenities we have. With respect to you, your society, even without this chaos, did not represent such a refined condition of advancement as what we have accomplished on Tae'Eladar."

"I understand. I've visited your home city briefly with Haran, and I can see with my own eyes that you have a lot to offer. Then, is this to say you would create the same for us here? And would this be only on the condition that we offer ourselves into your service?"

"This is actually a good question, and I must answer that I hold a belief, which is handed down to me as part of our cultural background with the Estelar, that it is considered inappropriate for a more advanced society to bestow upon a lesser one their higher wisdom, as this can create an imbalance within the local environment in relation to others they might interact with. It tends to follow as part of the Measure of Balance, the philosophical teachings of the Estelar. If you were to choose to remain independent, I could only provide that which you are already familiar with."

"Interesting. So, this is to say, the gods may be all-knowing, but they don't actually share this in order not to corrupt people like us."

"Correct, as they believe in the growth experience. But if you were to join us, you would share in everything we have for ourselves. We would likely need to engage in a careful assimilation period to bring you up to our level, but once done, it should flow naturally from there."

"Your Lordship," Padriyl wonders. "Just for the sake of continuing this thought from a different perspective. There are a number of quiet rumors circling around the Naarg uy'Sodrad stemming all the way back to that famous visitation you made with Velen's holo-disk. You apparently made quite an impression with some of our people."

"I would certainly hope so. Your people, with all due respect, appeared grossly demoralized. A good solid dose of inspiration would work wonders for you."

"Yes, I suppose it would," he smiles. "So, we have your statements about a conjoined effort to take our fight back to Sargeras, then we have the Night Elves joining your kingdom, and we have these other suggestions for the humans and High Elves. You have offered us aid, both military and industrial, and you are now offering more elaborate political and trade agreements. Furthermore, my general impression, from what I hear of people on Tae'Eladar, is that you make it your life's goal to unite people from different backgrounds. So, I can't help but to wonder about us, especially when you're practically twisting my horns about behaving as part of a larger society in this world," he chuckles.

A round of laughter ushers up from the group.

"Lieutenant," Thaelyn considers. "My purpose to unite people is at least in part to find their greatest strengths and bring these together into harmony where we can all benefit. And I hold a policy where any that can follow our creed may join with our people. And my impression of your people certainly fits this mold."

"All right, but now, about your statements concerning the differing levels of technology… We would represent a higher form than yours, at least in your present day, and if you hold such a policy of keeping things separate…"

"Ah, but of course, this is a fine topic. If such a junction should ever occur between us, we would need to consider this same principle, only in reverse, of yours holding back until ours reaches a compatible level. This also follows with our combined research, as much of it would have to be kept secret until our people are ready."

"That's what I thought, but it sounds like it might become complicated after a while."

"Indeed, it would be a delicate balance, but in time, we will eventually find equilibrium."

"So, what we have here," Tristeen reflects, "is coming down to us making a decision of some kind…us, and maybe also the High Elves. But if they join together with you and yours, that kind of leaves us out in the cold if we stay independent. And if you make it your goal to unite people into one big nation, and we're just one little city with hardly anything to call our own, good gracious, that doesn't sound like a good place to be."

"You can also look at it this way," Sehnisavain offers. "In a manner of speaking, we are all returning to our roots. Our ancestors once migrated here from Tae'Eladar, even though this was thousands of years ago. Therefore, our ancestral kin are still found there, which means we will not be alone any longer, as we were here."

"We should also consider," Thaelyn asserts. "That portal device your people used along the way must surely have been created by Darumon to bring you here intentionally."

"Right," Tristeen affirms. "And this is disturbing in itself. It's enough to make you WANT to run home, especially after all he did to us after we arrived and built this lovely civilization. But, like you said, in this same time, the differences have grown rather wide between us."

"Clearly," Josef interjects. "If we did join, we would need to undergo some manner of adjustment. And for this, if we are in such a position to rebuild nearly from scratch, I should think this adjustment might actually go a little smoother than if to convert all that we had before to a new standard."

"Which, by the way," Amariyn adds, "is what we're doing in Solinaia right now, and it's causing a little disruption, as we have to study these new methods. We also need to install some of these new amenities, and for this we may have to redesign a number of buildings to find room for it."

"And at the same time," Sehnisavain admits. "As much as I hate to say this, we are all down to the last of our kind, at least in this world, and this represents a terrible loss. Although we are not dead yet, and we can still rebuild, I think rather than rebuilding as isolated societies struggling in a world so far from home, we have this remarkable opportunity to come together for our mutual benefit. I would further suggest we are blessed to have His Lordship and his people making this offer to us with such a prestigious welcome."

"Then, what we need to do next," Josef concludes, "is we need to bring our people together and make a survey. Then we need to take a vote."

Chapter 2

RECKONING

It has been two days since the final departure of Marshal Darumon and his Suuden-Aryku military. The masses of refugees outside of Firstfall had found better organization, with family units now clustered together, and friends helping neighbors.

A temporary gateway node had been established just outside the south gate of Rolsklinde to enable the easy transit of laborers to and from the settlement, and a constant flow of workers was moving around the area as part of a massive clean-up effort. The city was in total ruin, where the outer walls are mostly mounds of rubble, and the homes, taverns, inns, and other buildings inside the city had been blasted to splinters by the invading army of dwarves and their borrowed weapons.

Broken wooden beams and frames, along with fractured portions of stonemasonry, were being carted off outside the city to a dump site. Gravel, splintered woodwork, and smaller debris were being taken to another dump site for sorting to recover any personal belongings that might still hold value. Mercantile items from destroyed marketplaces were being collected into boxes and bags for storage in the hopes they could still be of value to the refugees. Many items of food were being carried off and disposed of as damaged goods from the attack.

And despite the evacuation effort, there were still a few bodies found amongst the debris of those who could not make their escape.

"My Lord," the General announces. "With all the volunteers arriving to give aid in the clearing of debris from the city up there, we would do well to begin establishing some manner of local shelters for them. The flow of workers through the portal gates is becoming rather burdensome."

"Indeed, General," Thaelyn responds. "It also appears we are starting to experience a shortage of tents to use as temporary shelter for all these refugees. What are the most recent reports from our scouts in the vicinity of Kynesoth?"

"So far, we have seen no activity of any kind, other than the passage of a few wild animals through the area. So, if Darumon and his ambitions are truly departed from this world, I might suggest we make use of that city again."

"Good, then share this with Priestess Sehnisavain, and send some of her people down there to make an inspection. We will begin relocating them back into their native housing again, and perhaps, if we have any spare room available, we can try moving some of these refugees into inns or temporary homes, or at least to place them within the city walls for better protection."

"Absolutely, my Lord."

"Perhaps we could provide a small convenience if we set up another temporary portal gate, at least until we can arrange for something more permanent."

"That would be a fine suggestion."

"I am also asking myself about some form of temporary housing… something simple. Do you recall the old stories of the nomadic tribes of the north and their longhouses? That might work for us. The construction materials were simple and quick to assemble. Can we put something like that together up near Rolsklinde to bring the people closer to home so they can assist in the clearing and rebuilding process?"

"That would be a grand idea, and quite functional. I can pass the word to some of the contractor associations back home and have them organize things for us. If we give this to the commercial sector, they can carry some of the workload for us."

"Excellent. We have a seasonal change coming up soon, so we need a solution to it. Now, what is the latest word on the orcs?"

"The orcs have been pushed well to the south by now. Our front line has advanced several hundred miles and continues to make steady progress. Their front line, on the other hand, is becoming sparse by compare. I am asking myself recently if most of their warriors had been accumulating more to the north where they might find more action, or if there could be another reason."

"Possibly. But then, we must ask ourselves, if they were accumulating to the north, where are they coming from to make that journey? Thus far, we only know of one portal, and it was already to the north. There must be one or more additional portals out there to supply this many."

"I agree, and we are still searching for those. But if their numbers are thinning out as much as they are, I must wonder where the lower line is to be found."

"This is an interesting question. We may in fact discover it soon, but I would still wish to make a careful search, at least by air, just in case we have any stray pockets lying in wait."

"Absolutely. But overall, at the rate we are moving on that front, I would think we should have solved that problem before too long. That is to say, other than for the continued outpour from their portals arriving from Ruuki uy'Daan. Clearly, there is still a driving force motivating them on that side."

"Indeed, and I might think them to be too stubborn to simply give up. It could be they continue to make their incursions for little more than the thrill of the fight, and they cannot know what waits for them until after they arrive, only to be cut down on their first step into our garrison outposts blocking this side of the portal."

"And, of course, we cannot close those portals until we can find a way to reach Ruuki uy'Daan and shut them down at the source."

"We will have our day with that. For now, we must push ahead and secure ourselves, and then plan for the future. This now brings me to another matter of the local politics."

"And what is that, my Lord?"

"I will need to speak with Lady Amariyn briefly concerning the further assimilation of her people into our kingdom. This also brings to mind the other two populations and what direction they might take. I see young Miss Macaid out there still running her political campaign, and this brings yet another note to mind."

"Good gracious, your mind must be spinning in circles by now."

"Yes," he rolls his eyes. "And it would do all of us a good turn to unload a few of these thoughts. Therefore, depending on the outcome of her efforts, I might wish to see her play a special role for us."

"And what role might that be?" he smiles expectantly.

"Before I can answer that, I would like to make a review of the events from these last few weeks. I will have you call in our field officers, including Master Dastien and the priests we had up there in the temple, then Master Cydulean and Priest Sumisal from their efforts in Kynesoth. Take reports from each for their impressions of the events leading us up to where we are, and most importantly the participation of those native elements that offered themselves into our service. I would like to give out a few commendations where appropriate to reward these people for their efforts."

"Very good, my Lord," the General nods. "I'm sure they would appreciate the thought."

✦✦✦✦✦

"With respect, Miss Macaid," calls a male voice from the crowd of refugees. "Some of us out here are still not sure how we're supposed to interpret this situation. Sure, some of us went to the temple and listened to these new priests, but a good many stopped going to the temple years ago. So, for those of us who are not quite up on things, it's a little hard to trust anyone when your home is a burning heap under a mountain of rubble."

The man gave his statement through a wireless microphone

being carried by Leesa as she made her way through the assembly, offering the people an opportunity to speak publicly. The strange equipment, which was donated by the Daanen-Aryku and set up on Tristeen's stage platform, was a curious but very useful addition to assist in arranging a public forum for debate.

"I understand your feelings," Tristeen announces through her loudspeaker system. "Then for those who didn't catch the explanations given by His Lordship's priests, after they essentially took over our temple from our old priests, then I'll give it to you again."

She pauses as she paces across the stage to collect her thoughts.

"We'll begin with what is most apparent before us. Four centuries ago, the noble families recorded the sequence of events that began at the start of this war. This also included the beginning of this plague. A man came to our city with the claim that he could help us, but he demanded to be made Governor, with full authority over the mage academy and the temple."

"Bloody hell," shouts one man in the audience. "And now you're telling us this plague isn't actually by the Flame Elves, but something put inside our bodies by the old priests?"

"Yeah, I know. It's shocking, perhaps even horrifying, but we were simply used as toys to play with until either we found special purpose for him, or no further value at all, which is where we are now."

"Grand."

"The device is called an implant, which the Daanen-Aryku explain is most often used for medical reasons among their kind. But this one was made by the Suuden-Aryku, and certainly not for anything medical. It contains a substance which is the true cause of the plague. We suspect the man was actually the same as our current Governor, and not human, but rather some kind of being that serves this godlike creature they call Sargeras. Therefore, four centuries for him is not too much to ask, as he's probably an immortal being, so time simply doesn't affect him."

"And then what? Why do this at all?"

"Here, we need to step back even further in time. We're not native to this world. We were brought here from Tae'Eladar, where these people in this village came from. We, the Night Elves, and the High Elves, which we've been describing as Flame Elves until now, are all immigrants brought here many thousands of years ago by some mysterious person using an equally mysterious portal device."

"Why don't any of us recall this in our schools?" calls one woman.

"Why don't we recall anything? Just look at the expression, 'for as long as I can remember,' and you have your answer. Our schools were wiped of any actual history and this rubbish given to us instead."

"Well, that's just bloody dandy!"

"The Governor, who was actually this Marshal Darumon, controlled our education system through his control of the mage academy. He erased everything he didn't want us to know about, and then filled our heads with his rubbish about our neighbors so we wouldn't go out asking THEM these questions, either. He was using all sorts of tactics to keep us bottled up inside our walls."

She continues pacing across the stage as she speaks.

"But anyway, according to Lord Thaelyn over here, the descriptions we have of this portal device, given to us by some old journals held by the Night Elves, describe something that shouldn't otherwise exist on Tae'Eladar. It requires a unique form of knowledge to build, and this can't be native to those people. Therefore, it had to be Marshal Darumon again. At the same time, Tae'Eladar also saw an invasion of orcs, and this didn't make sense, as orcs should NOT have the ability to move between worlds. This also had to be the Marshal, as he would be the only one who could grant access. This represents an intentional effort to pollute Tae'Eladar with his minions while stealing us away for later. And it all culminated here on this world, where we have him and his Suuden-Aryku military sieging our homes, confining us to our last remaining cities, and destroying everything he didn't otherwise want or need as too much fluff to be bothered with. We are tools for him, to do as he wants and no more."

This announcement caused many of the people to raise their voices in protest and anguish, not simply for their homes being destroyed, but for their entire world, to say nothing of being used.

"He invented these stories about the war to distract us," Tristeen continues. "And then, his agents inside the academy and temple further confounded our ability to ask questions with such nonsense, including the gods themselves denying us to speak out. We were given to repeat such fashionable expressions as, 'for as long as I can remember, such-and-such,' to stifle our ability to recall anything. And then, 'if you can't trust our authority, who can you trust,' as a means to give ourselves to the one and only thing intended for us to bow down to. And unfortunately, as this was committed against us by a superior being against a lesser society using unfamiliar methods, our people bought every word for four centuries, until Thaelyn came along and broke the cycle."

The crowd ushers up a cheer, although it was strained for the burden of their misery.

"Didn't I hear once something about a conspiracy over the elven war?" asks one man.

"Yes, they suffered a series of crimes, also due to the Marshal. They have an ancient religion that offers a special devotion to a sacred tree they call a Tree of Life. This isn't a normal tree, and certainly not something you cut down for firewood. If you look inside this settlement, you'll see a young sapling. It's surrounded in a circle of fencing, and it carries a very special kind of spirit inside that the elves can talk to."

"Talking to a tree?" he winces.

"Yes," she smiles. "We humans might think this is strange, but I was speaking to a few people about this, and this tree comes from the ancient elven home, where things tend to work differently. It represents a binding link to the natural world, and the elves thrive by this principle. We humans usually like to think of ourselves as detached from everything else out there, even though this is generally wrong. Anyway, this conspiracy killed all the trees on both sides, and the elves found evidence of the other side doing the deed when neither would do anything of the sort."

"And so they went to war for it?"

"This is generally what we are made to believe due largely to the Marshal's control methods. We believe it was just one of many lies he fed us to give him an excuse to turn our attention the wrong way. The High Elves fell into despair at the loss of their tree, and also a set of holy items stolen from them at the same time. This allowed Sargeras to essentially abduct them through a form of mind control. From that moment, they called themselves Flame Elves, and due to his control methods, he drove them to burn everything around them. They had no knowledge of this plague either, but we were made to think they were responsible."

"And so, where does that leave us now?"

"Lord Thaelyn managed to reclaim them and brought them back to our side. In the meantime, he also found the Marshal was involved in a number of other devious plots, not the least of which involved the dwarves, who by the way are ALSO not native to our world."

"Wait a minute!" shouts another onlooker. "What do you mean, not native? Where did THEY come from?"

"This is a good question, and it also involves knowledge found with the High Elves. At some moment in the early years of the war, the Marshal ordered them to spend…or maybe I should say to squander…some part of their population on an attack against a world filled with dwarves, so he and his Suuden-Aryku military could possibly capture it. Those dwarves are no doubt the result…a slave mining crew with no other purpose than to serve his needs."

"And the iron they were supposed to be giving us?"

"The term, supposed to be, is very subjective here. They were not supposed to be giving anything to us. It was mostly a play in our eyes to make us think they're doing something useful. Most of the iron they were producing was going to the elves and orcs out there. Therefore, the shortages, as we were not intended to have it. It was barely enough to keep us in operation, and one more control effort to restrict us. But this was secondary to their REAL purpose, which was to mine up a metal called adamantium. The Marshal apparently has a special use for it, and it doesn't have anything to do with us, as we didn't even know what it was until recently."

"Wonderful, but this means we must know something now, if you're using the word?"

"Yes, Thaelyn's people know what it is. It's a super metal that's much better than steel, but you need special skills to use it. The Marshal is likely hoping to use it as part of his revenge on these other gods."

"Revenge! Is that what this blighter is out for? Bloody hell, lass..."

"The dwarves were also found to be under an effect, believed to be a drug of some kind that placed them completely under his control. They may have looked like they were acting independently, but they weren't. His Lordship told me earlier that once they finished their job, they just stood around like they were waiting for someone to come along and give them another task to perform."

"How can someone do something like this to a person?" shouts a woman.

"That largely depends on who that someone is, I suppose. If we are speaking of the Marshal, the way he was behaving with our people, he apparently takes pleasure out of it. He seems to spend people like a drunkard bellying up to a tawdry bar. I saw him with my own eyes as he called on the Suuden-Aryku to make that bombardment of the Upper Ward. He was watching the show from his window."

The crowd murmured in vigorous debate amongst themselves as they discussed these alarming revelations. Tristeen listened for a moment longer before continuing, realizing she needed to bring this into order to finish her presentation.

"Good people, listen carefully. I understand this is all very disturbing. I'm no better for my part in it, and I lived through a portion of this trying to sort out these activities to help our people. But here we are, all of us...you, me..." she sighs. "Right now, we have the opportunity of understanding what has been driving our lives throughout this entire period when we were told this world was at war. The Marshal set us down here, then left and returned later to finally take us once his other plans were no doubt ready to move forward. I have also learned he and his Suuden-Aryku loyalists have been chasing the Daanen-Aryku from one world to another, playing with them as if they were toys."

She pauses to pace across to the other side of the stage.

"This is apparently typical of his kind, and His Lordship knows this. We learned that Darumon and Sargeras are apparently the last of their kinds as part of an ancient godlike society called the Primordials. They absolutely hate these others we call the Estelar, and I'm sure at this point the feeling is mutual. Therefore, once we understood this, Lord Thaelyn used his relationship to these new gods in those last moments to force that creature off our world. But as we all saw, the Marshal did not go quietly."

"Aye, you got that one right," shouts a man. "But now, where does this leave us sitting out here in the open?"

"We are currently clearing the debris, and have plans on rebuilding. But at this time we also have a question standing before us that I believe is very important to ask. As I said, we are all immigrants from Tae'Eladar to this world, and technically, I might also say, we don't belong here, if only due to Darumon luring our ancestors away. Now, we can call this world ours by the merit that we are here, and we made our homes, such as they are. So be it. Regardless of the city up north, the elves still have theirs, and we will rebuild ours again. But this is not the question. We find ourselves reunited with our ancestral brothers and sisters, who are giving us aid without asking for anything in return. Their society has progressed far in this time, so they can apparently afford this to us."

She continues pacing across the platform as she collects her thoughts.

"Herein lays our question: How do we repay them? The Night Elves have joined with Thaelyn's kingdom. The High Elves are also considering this. Now ask yourselves, where does this leave us standing out here in the open?"

Now the crowd ushers up even louder murmuring and debate as they discuss this new suggestion.

"Consider this," Tristeen continues assertively. "His kingdom is a very robust and prestigious society filled with wisdom, culture, and prosperity for all of its citizens. Amazingly, they have solved virtually every problem they ever faced, all because of His Lordship and the teachings he has delivered to his people during his tenure. And this is clearly demonstrated right here. So far, he has given us food and blankets, and he is offering to rebuild our homes, but he could do much more. As citizens, we would benefit from everything else he has to offer. He would teach our children and provide us with good work with good pay. We have hundreds of volunteers arriving to help with our troubles, as well as donating food and other things. And while he does not make any demands on us, the offer of joining his kingdom carries its own merits."

The assembly continued to whisper their opinions until another man spoke out.

"Miss Macaid, while I'm sure you have a point, I think at least a few of us might see this as a little too good to be true, don't you think?"

"Too good to be true, perhaps. But then, this is the whole reason he was SENT to Tae'Eladar to begin with. They were not doing this themselves. And I might further say, neither did we."

"Uh oh… That rings with something."

"There are many things in life that can easily be regarded as too good to be true. But then, so is his presence on Tae'Eladar, which was apparently a divine mandate for him. He didn't just wake up one day with the idea to conquer a world. He was sent there explicitly by these gods to do so. I think that carries a message that goes beyond being too good to be true. It was arranged this way intentionally. Tae'Eladar is someone's garden world, and he was sent there to cultivate it. And now, here he is with us."

This statement caused the gushing of voices to rise with oohs and ahs, and further mumbling over the implications.

"I should also point out," Tristeen continues, "that I have personally visited Tae'Eladar, and have friends living there right now who have informed me of what they have to offer. Therefore, if you feel this is too good to be true, just inside these gates is a device they call a Gateway. The simple fact that they hold this kind of knowledge already places them above us for their wisdom, as it creates a portal leading from here to Tae'Eladar. If you desire, just step through and see for yourself. His Lordship would welcome your objective opinion. Just be advised that they don't speak the same language as we do, so this is one thing we would need to correct."

"And just for the sake of argument," offers another man. "What if we should decide to go it alone?"

"This is a reasonable statement, but to answer this, we need to realize where we stand as an independent body. I can already predict a few issues of concern. We suffered shortages of almost everything in our city, and I think most of us know this. Trying to find and establish new resources for such things as wood, stone, iron, and other things, will take time, labor, and the creation of an infrastructure to collect and transport this to where we need it. When you have nothing to start with, trying to build something that allows you to build other things represents a paradox with no easy answer, unless you think you can cut down a tree or a block of stone with your bare hands and haul it on your back."

"Aye, that's a good one!" he chuckles.

"He has merchant societies that will help us establish new marketplaces, industry to provide new tools and building materials, and a lot of skilled labor, plus schools and universities to teach our children, and even our adults. We barely even had schools for our children, and those were the shoddy result of the Marshal corrupting our education system. But on Tae'Eladar, the people are all very highly educated, and often encouraged to seek more as they go along."

"Grace of the Gods, girl, just how do you expect a bunch of flaming fools like us to be able to fit in with all that?"

Tristeen giggles at the suggestion as she composes her response.

"Well, good sir, you'll just have to work at it, the same as the rest of us. I don't expect this to go over quickly. Surely, we'll need time for it, and we can easily say we did solve our local problems as they presented themselves. I'm sure each of us will have plenty of opportunity to find a place for our skills simply to rebuild what we have. And once done, we can push ahead as time permits. Our children, on the other hand, will be the ones most likely to carry us into a new era. We may have some difficulty in the beginning, but surely, it'll smooth out over time. We'll just take it slowly and adjust to it. So, what do you think? Do we go it alone, or hand-in-hand with his people?"

As Tristeen finishes her statement, the murmuring of the crowd resumes. People moved around the camp speaking of the potential merits, and comparing to what they had before. Among the human refugees were many High Elves who had been attending the service and participating in the census Tristeen was conducting. As they listened in, they felt a similar motivation in her words.

It was passing into early afternoon when Tristeen, Amariyn, and Sehnisavain were visiting the tactical office during a break in the activities outside. They were holding a meeting concerning a few rising issues.

"Your Lordship," Tristeen wonders. "Assuming we were to join up, just what sort of government would you suggest for us here?"

"What we have back home is a modified form of monarchy," he admits. "What this means is it uses an elected civilian parliament. I divest some portion of my rule into that body to manage many of the domestic affairs of law and policy, although I still hold on to an overriding authority in case of any critical events or dire emergencies. The only stipulation is I need to justify myself for the occasion, and this usually goes through the High Council. In a non-wartime scenario, they act as a system of checks and balances, working parallel to my authority to aid me in the higher-level administration and advisory protocols. They might oversee such as the legal process of our kingdom, also to attend to such things as emergencies or disaster relief. And if we should ever see the occasion, to make decisions on our policies with foreign cultures."

"Wow! That sounds complex. But how would this apply to any of us here?"

"Solinaia is already undergoing the transition, so we can use this as our example. For instance, Lady Amariyn..." he directs. "In order to give your people proper representation within our government, we would need to admit a number of you into my High Council. But at the same time, we have a peculiar circumstance here that we are located on a completely different world. Although we can extend our existing parliament to involve this, I think it would serve us better to create a local body instead, then to have it manage those issues specific to this world. We could then extend the High Council as a supervisory layer to manage the individual parliaments across these bounds, bringing everything into harmony with a common form of rule overall."

"That sounds like a curious blend," Amariyn admits. "And what sort of representation are we looking at within the High Council? That is, if we involve the others."

"Firstly, the High Council is populated by members of each of the races in bodies we call quorums. Some races, like the elves, divide their society into clans, but they still tend to speak collectively. Traditionally, we used a quorum of three for each. This allows representation for each clan and their native needs. The human population does not follow this same practice, so we compensate by offering them five. However, the inclusion of this world and its local societies might force us to reconsider this aspect, as we now have additional populations that should carry their own representation. But at the same time, these populations are not evenly distributed. For instance, we have a Mori'Quessir society here, but not on Tae'Eladar."

"Unless you consider those you call Drow, but they are not a part of your kingdom."

"Correct. Perhaps at some moment, we can resolve this, but for now we must still refer to our usual traditions for your people. You only occupy one city, but we need a quorum, therefore we must give you three positions. And then, as time progresses, you can grow to fill in with more population for better saturation."

"I suppose," she nods.

"The humans and High Elves, on the other hand, are robust societies back home, and therefore already have quorums. But if the local groups join up, I feel it is appropriate to give them a voice, therefore we should offer additional positions for this world. I might further suggest this could change as the populations grow and thus have a need for greater representation, to say nothing of them migrating to-and-fro. The needs of any one world may hold special interest as the conditions may vary."

"This could become very complex over time," Sehnisavain cautions. "If our population grows and builds new cities, and if you have any others come here and build anything, this could become rather burdensome after a while."

"It could, so we will no doubt need to examine the structure to find a happy medium as our combined population matures. If we can create a more homogenous blend, perhaps we might find a fair equilibrium together. In the meantime, Lady Amariyn..." he pulls back from the table to conclude his thoughts. "Your efforts in our relations, and the aid you have provided outside, leads me to desire you to represent your people within our High Council. We can decide on the other two as we review some of the other members of your existing Council, and choose appropriately."

"I would be most honored, Your Grace," Amariyn affirms with a nod.

"One concern I hold at this time, when mentioning the Drow, is that I ask you and yours to demonstrate patience with our people. We have a long and very jaded history with them, and these feelings run deep. I have made a number of concerted efforts to relay word of your discovery to our people, so they will know the difference. Therefore, time is the only real enemy here."

"I understand. I will share this with our people and inform them to be on their best behavior."

Thaelyn glances at an assortment of papers on the table as he continues.

"Our next order of business is the resettlement of Kynesoth..."

◆

Relissa and her group, along with Haran on this occasion, were just arriving back from their final language class in the guildhall. As it was their usual practice during the course of the war, they made their way to the tactical office to report in. On their arrival, Relissa instantly spies her mother.

"Mum!" she calls and moves in for a hug.

"Are you just returning from your class today?" Amariyn wonders.

"Aye!" she replies with a broad smile on her face. "We finally bloody did it. I never thought I'd be so happy to finish up with a language class, and then get ready to start something new."

"Speaking of those language lessons," Tristeen relents. "I need to take a few. Trying to work with all these people of yours out there is becoming troublesome for the language issue."

"Indeed," Thaelyn admits. "Amariyn, Sehnisavain, I would strongly recommend you as well, plus as many of your people as you can muster. We will have a great many people in need to educate for the language alone, so we should make our best use of time for it."

"Of course," Amariyn affirms. "I will call on some of our people to participate for the next available session. As for me, while I would be happy to be involved, I am not as young as I once was," she smiles.

"I as well," Sehnisavain offers. "Along with my sister, though my two daughters are surely anxious for it," she chuckles. "How much space do you have in these classrooms?"

"We will no doubt need to assign additional facilities to accommodate everyone," he considers. "But I feel this should be a priority, especially for those in the more prominent positions of authority."

"Naturally."

"And Marelle? Haran? How do you feel this day?"

"My Lord," Marelle responds. "I'm ready and eager to get started. Maybe it's just my imagination, but it seems the sun is shining brighter, and the air is a bit sweeter today."

"And as for me, my Lord," Haran adds. "This is a day I've been looking forward to for a good long while. I think I would even say since my early days of study in our own academy, to which I never really found proper satisfaction."

"You'd better be careful with your words, Mister Mage Academy Transfer Student," Tristeen teases. "Some of that time you spent over there should count as a little more important than others."

"Well, yes, of course," he grins. "But I was speaking of the study time we spent under the old instructors, not those moments when we were sneaking away from it."

"I think I should not be listening to this…" Thaelyn groans and rolls his eyes. "But anyway, this is good to hear. Now, from this day forward, and until your graduation, I think you should place the greater part of your focus on your studies. The war, as far as this world is concerned, is essentially over, so there is no further need for you to attend our meetings. Instead, I will have you collect all your instructional materials and organize yourselves for your introductory classes, which will bring you up to par with our educational standards. We will see about rushing you through some of it, to compensate for your existing education, and in order to get you into the next season's class schedule."

"All right," Marelle agrees. "In the meantime, is there anything we can do around here?"

"The war is proceeding along nicely against the orcs, and we think it may not be much longer on that front. This leaves us with only a forward direction, but it also brings up a curious reminder."

"What's that?"

"Priestess Sehnisavain, we need to understand that portal your people were sent to find, and then where it leads. We must discover what was so important about it that Darumon would take such a risk entering our space. Can you recall anything, for instance was there any mention of its purpose and who you sent there?"

"As for who was sent, I can't recall personally," she admits. "It was my husband who led the expedition, but…" she lowers her head as she continues, "…he didn't return from it."

"I am very sorry. Was there an explanation for his loss?"

"I recall there was one survivor who returned to us, a young mage, I believe. She said they came under attack by something big…

monstrous, I believe, is the word she used. The others were killed. But they did succeed in deploying that device through the portal."

"I see, so we have a near total loss of the party, but a success to the mission. This is bad on all sides, actually."

"Aye!" Relissa agrees. "And how long ago was this?"

"I believe it was several decades ago by now," Sehnisavain recalls.

"Very well, Priestess," Thaelyn advises. "You must make it a priority to find that survivor, assuming she is still with us today. With any luck, she might still recall something of their journey, enough perhaps for us to follow. Then we need to know where it leads. Do you have any information on that?"

"Not precisely. The Suuden-Aryku did not generally reveal anything specific to us unless they needed us to know about it. But I recall a conversation they once shared, which is probably as meaningless as anything else. They mentioned something about the orcs, who were sent ahead of us, if you recall, having discovered a wheel of some kind."

"Bloody hell..." Relissa giggles. "Who would've thought, the orcs have discovered the wheel!"

"Indeed, Relissa," Thaelyn grins softly. "But on this occasion, I think it is not the sort you will find on a wagon. This actually tends to fit well with that book the Dean had in his possession," he glances at the item on a table behind him. "If we are to suggest the contents of that book to be the result of research by Darumon on the 'Who, What, and Where' of the Outer Planes, and it apparently contains some outdated subject matter by now, then the mention of a wheel becomes evident, at least in my mind."

"And how does a wheel help where the Outer Planes are concerned?" Marelle wonders.

"This takes us back to the time of the Spellplague again. It was a terrible disaster that occurred a few centuries ago."

"That's the same one you told us about on that first day, ay?" Relissa recalls.

"It is. Our world suffered terribly from the effects of it, but we were not the only ones. The rest of the Outer Planes also took immeasurable damage."

"What sort of event was this?" Padriyl asks.

"It was a moment when there was a conspiracy amongst the Estelar where one of them, named Shar, coveted a possession owned by another named Mystra, and so she devised a plot with one known as Cyric to kill her. Unfortunately for everyone, this possession, which was a fabric layer of the flows we call the Weave, was pulled so tightly that when Mystra died, it backlashed across the planes, tearing many of them apart. On Tae'Eladar, we suffered from waves of blue fire coursing through our skies, and the shaking of the land so fierce, it devastated many of our cities, and opened up several gaping chasms."

"Great cu'Nar! That sounds cataclysmic."

"It was, and as a result, I decided two can play at this game. I broke from my traditions of progressing our people in a timely manner, and gave them a few things to allow for a rapid return. We had come far during the years and centuries before this, and much of that was lost, all due to the foolhardiness of a Power who overstepped her bounds and brought a great amount of harm to the rest, to say nothing of how she violated the Measure of Balance."

"What did you give them?" Tristeen asks.

"The same, actually, as what I will use on your city," he smiles. "Yours is not the first city we had to rebuild from scratch. Among the gifts I gave to my people was an organized city planning committee. The cities of our world had grown in a rather organic fashion, simply adding on as more people needed space, which ultimately left the result rather disorderly. We would change this to permit better structure, allowing people to find their way from home to work to shopping, and back again, with minimal effort. We also began developing our Gateway network at this time."

"Incredible," Padriyl gasps. "And all this before you even understood the principles from the scientific side, as we had to do."

"Indeed, we had portal magic for a few centuries before this. It was not my original invention on Tae'Eladar, as others had found this by themselves, namely a potent group of mages we once had, called the Guild of Red Mages. They were a rather unpleasant sort who lauded themselves for their prolific mage craft. I simply brought my own and shared it with those who served me to spread it further. We later developed the devices you see now based on these principles."

"You know, Elder Vankkar was once a history teacher. I'm sure he would love to read up on this, as this is truly fascinating."

"He is welcome to visit our libraries, but like all the rest, he will need to study our language first."

"Of course."

"As for the cities, I also gave them the knowledge of how to make concrete, as we did not have this before. Our architectural designs were much the same as what you had up in Rolsklinde, using wood timbers and quarried stone. Concrete, however, comes as a mixture of ingredients that can be poured into a mold to create any custom design you need. It carries the strength of stone, perhaps more if you reinforce it with iron or steel, and it allows for new architectural designs that might not otherwise be possible with the more contemporary methods."

"Really!" Tristeen perks up. "Is this what I'm seeing over there on Tae'Eladar now?"

"Much of it, yes, although we might still apply some decorative layers for a more traditional appeal from the street...we do so adore our native charm," he grins. "But Tae'Eladar was not the only one to take damage from the Spellplague. The rest of the planes also took hits. Some were destroyed completely, and others tossed as marbles on the ground."

"Dear cu'Nar," Padriyl relents. "I can't even begin to imagine the forces that need to go into play for something like that."

"Trust me...you do not want to, either. But in the end, the alignment of the planes shifted. And this is where we come to Sehnisavain's mention of a wheel."

"Oh grand..." Relissa moans. "So, this portal leads up to the Outer Planes, which we sort of figured by now if he has plans for revenge against the Estelar, but what is this about?"

"The Great Wheel, as it was once called, was the peculiar alignment of the major planes of Positive and Negative polarity, along with the cross-alignment of Order and Chaos, all with neutral buffer zones in-between. This formed a type of matrix with the plane we call Cynosure as a hub in the center."

"Ay, wait… That one…is that the one where we went to interrogate those…eh, with apologies to those present…" she glances at Sehnisavain, "…the Flame Elf scouts we caught once?"

"The same."

"You took them all the way out there?" Sehnisavain wonders. "Why so far just for a simple interrogation?"

"To remove them as far as I possibly could from Sargeras's influence, since I suspected he had his thoughts inside your heads. I have a private location hidden away there where I had hoped he would not hold the power to reach inside. But the Wheel, in this case, would be the former arrangement of these planes. And if Darumon is going on outdated knowledge, as might be evidenced by this book, he will not find whatever he is looking for, at least not in its expected location. This might buy us a bit of time, but I do not wish to tarry, nonetheless."

"Aye," Relissa affirms eagerly. "That much I can agree on."

"Very well, Your Grace," Sehnisavain offers. "I will make every effort to find that survivor, and pray to our gods she is still among us. But I do not know precisely who it was, and with so many to question, this may not be easy."

"Speaking of which, do we have any final tallies of the surviving population out there?"

"Yes, we do!" Tristeen affirms. "We got a census for our people, and it came out at around thirty-nine thousand."

"That sounds like a fair bit," Relissa muses.

"It does," Thaelyn offers. "But I would also suggest it to be a little shy of my expectations. For the size of the city, I might instead expect the upper forties. I think we can blame Darumon's population control, which likely stifled the growth factor and kept them to within a certain margin."

"Maybe so," Tristeen concedes. "And then the High Elves are coming up at around fifty-two thousand."

"That seems fair enough to me," Sehnisavain admits. "And I think this is likely because of our people gathering up so many refugees during this time from the other cities we abandoned."

"Do we have anything new on the dwarves?" Marelle asks.

"At last word," Thaelyn responds. "They were still in a catatonic state, same as when we first captured them and placed them inside the detention yard. Our people have been trying to feed and shelter them, but they are largely unresponsive. We have managed to invoke their dining ritual by providing tables and benches similar to what they used before, along with dishware resembling their original set. But our concern is how they might respond to us if and when they should ever recover."

"You're using that camouflage décor, right?"

"Yes, to make it appear as a smallish dwarven camp with dwarven attendants. We were debating whether we should make this appear as a simple work camp, or a military one, as we would ultimately need to reveal to them that they are in a type of detention facility during a time of war. We cannot know the situation over there, and dwarves tend to be a bit temperamental," he chuckles softly. "Therefore, we chose to go military."

"That sounds like fun," Relissa smirks. "What do you think they'll say to it?"

"We know at one time Darumon sent orcs into their world, then later the High Elves. This would suggest a condition of war occurring over there on at least two occasions. Now, I am going to make a very delicate assumption here and say the Suuden-Aryku must have taken that world, likely by force, and also perhaps subversively, as they did here. These dwarves were under a drug influence during their slave labors, which goes beyond being forced into it consciously. Therefore, I must suggest something is occurring over there behind their backs. If, however, we can also suggest a quiet action of some sort, like an underground movement..." he holds his statement and chuckles impulsively.

The rest of the room puzzles a moment at the strange reaction, and then erupts into laughter as they realize the pun.

"Aye!" Relissa blurts. "Underground would be a fine one for dwarves!"

"Yes," he smiles. "It is on those rare occasions that such things emerge so conveniently. But anyway, we need to feel around for what information they have to offer. At the very least, we will aim for a suggestion of one such movement in light of where and how we found them. We will suggest they were…captured…away from their previous captors. I suspect they will be disoriented, and likely feeling a number of ill aftereffects from this drug, so we should try to use this as best we can."

"I wonder how they'll respond to being captured away from anything," Marelle muses. "Much less, other captors…"

"Indeed, I wish I could answer this. For now, our people have instructions to go slowly with the details, and gently dig for our answers."

"Sounds fair enough, but how long has it been? Almost three full days since we brought them out of the city. How long do you suppose this drug will hold out?"

"It must have been very deeply saturated within their bodies for it to keep them this long. This makes me fear for their health. For this, Med-tech Tad'vaal has supplied us with a quantity of medicines, some of which are chelating agents. These are used to remove heavy metals from the body."

✦✦✦✦✦

In an open field just outside the city of Bya'an Tamoranth, stood a formation of pylons emitting a shield-like projection which effectively represented a virtual barrier. It was a similar arrangement to what had once been used around the settlement of Firstfall during the course of the war, only inverted to create something better resembling a holding pen, rather than an outward defense. It formed a rough circle with a twisting corridor leading off to one side into a garrison post.

By using theatrical props, they carefully disguised the entire assembly to resemble natural stone walls, making the pen look more like a rocky cove. The corridor was closed off by a neatly crafted entryway, a sturdy wooden door sealing the corridor as a means of privacy and protection.

Inside the cove, there were a number of buildings resembling domiciles, a dining area, a small shrine, and personal relief and wash facilities. It represented a military appeal, but of a diminutive stature, as if to say a small frontier outpost. They fashioned most of the buildings as lean-to structures, with a basic open-air construction that included three walls and a roof, leaving the front exposed to the common area.

Row upon row of makeshift bedding was laid out within the structures. Each of these served as a bed for a single dwarf, a full three hundred of them. The dwarves being housed here were captured after they had finished their rampage through Rolsklinde a few days earlier. Although they could not be accurately described as prisoners, they were being carefully watched as if they were, with guards, caretakers, and priests seeing to their needs until they recovered.

They had been silently resting on their beds, occasionally to take food according to some preprogrammed ambition to follow a scheduled feeding ritual in the dining area. Beyond that, they made no other movements, until now.

A soft groaning issues forth from one of the dwarves as he begins to shift about, clutching at his head and grumbling something unintelligible. One of the caretakers who was sitting at a table overlooking the gathering, signals to the guards at the gate to call in some of the priests and the warden in charge of the facility. Moments later, the others arrived to join the watchman and prepare to assist the captive as he tries to pull himself upright. The dwarf takes notice of the people gathering around him and attempts to speak in a rough voice...and using a curious dialect of Old Dwarvish.

"Oi! Me head... It feels as though a great stone be a-crushin' down upon it."

The warden passes a glance around at the other caretakers in wonder at the strange accent. It resembled something unheard of for as long as any could recall. He then motions to an elder member sitting at a side table with a pen and journal book to begin scribing the dialog as the warden moves forward to interact with the prisoner.

"Take ease there, lad," he soothes as he offers a hand to the prisoner. "Ye don' look right to me, like ye've been hit by the small side of a mountain."

"Aye, it feels that way, too. Ye speak in a strange way, brother. Where d' ye come from?"

"I might ask the same of ye, brother," he chortles to ease the tension. "I'll bet ye come from a far place, as ye're far from anythin' in this range."

The prisoner dwarf tries looking around at his surroundings, taking notice of what appears to be a mountain cove with a smallish military outpost making camp here. He sees the attendant dwarves, all dressed in some manner of uniform, with several females tending to the kitchen area, an elder dwarf at the table with a pen and book, and more lying about on the beds, seemingly resting.

"What be all this about here? Where be we?"

"Again, take ease, brother. Let's take it slowly. I don' think ye're in the right sorts for jumpin' about."

"Aye, 'tis true, that. But can ye tell me who ye are an' where we be?"

"Me name is Jorn Ironbeard, and I'm a military captain."

"A captain? Be ye fightin' the point-ears then?" he glances once again around the camp, now more eagerly trying to gauge their numbers and composition.

The Captain studied him carefully, watching his reactions and trying to assess his meaning. He suspected there was something occurring where this man came from originally, and this already suggested an ongoing war.

"A war, ye say? Aye, we're fightin' a war, of a sort, but the one ye mention is different. Point-ears? The word might hold meanin' to me, but we know of them by a different name. We call them elves."

"Elves, be it? So, that be their proper name?" he huffs indignantly. "Grand, but what war be it ye're fightin' if nay the elves?"

"Take kindly, dear brother. I think ye're lackin' a wee bit of knowin' of the nature of the true war."

"Ay?" he responds curiously. "True war? Wait now, what be this ye say? The Thane back home tells tale of a great war a-ragin' across the land. He tells of the point…erm, these elves, ravagin' everythin' they see, an' all the cities up top be a-burnin'…" he once more glances at what he interprets to be a rocky cove setting. "Be this here hidey-hole yer war camp? Are ye here mayhap because yer city be burned already, an' this be all what's left for ye?"

The Captain was getting a good impression of the details by now, at least as far as this dwarf understood the conditions back home, but it didn't help matters for the implications.

"Lad, we need to take this slow. Look here at yer brethren. Do ye see them lyin' in these beds, barely knowin' if they're alive or not?"

The dwarf looked around carefully, taking special note of the condition of those who had yet to recover from their drug-induced vacancy. A few were starting to wake up, and thus becoming aware of the conversation, trying to focus on it, but no more certain of the content as the first one.

"Great All-Father, what happened t' us," he emits woefully. "Did we lose any, d' ye think?"

"I don' know how many ye had to start, but I know ye were all found together like this, so it seems fair enough ye're all here."

"But what happened t' us, brother? What be wrong with me lads here?"

"Do ye feel yerself strong enough for it? Lad, ye and yer friends were found in such a state that ye didn' know up from down, nor right from wrong. Ye were walkin' about, but in a daze like ye didn' see where ye were goin'."

"What? But how can we nay be a-knowin' where we be?"

"Do ye see yer friends, and the same if ye look at yerself. Ye say ye have a bustin' headache? Ye were all under a powerful drug that put ye in a type of sleep where ye didn' know what ye were doin'. And we found ye in a mine pullin' up adamantium."

"Adamant!" he surges. "But what were we a-makin' with it? Ye say ye don'na know of the war with these elves, but we were sent out to make up fair for it."

"Makin' up fair for a war, is it? Aye, that's fine enough. Are ye a smith, mayhap? And by the way, ye never told me yer name, friend."

"Oi!" he slaps his head. "All-Father forgive me, where be me manners. Me name be Tol Bronzeheart, Chief Forge Smith of the grand city of Glimmerheim. Mayhap ye know of it?"

"To be true, I nay know of the name, but if it puts such a sparkle in yer eye, I'll wager a month's pay it be a fine one."

"Aye, that it be! But if ye don'na know of Glimmerheim, where be we now? I thought Glimmerheim was such a grand one that all the land would know of it. We must be far t' distant lands by now…"

"Aye, that's one way to put it…far and farther, to be sure. As for the fair ye were makin', it was simple ingots."

"What?!" he blasts. "Bricks? We were a-makin' bricks, nay any fair for the war? But…that nay be any different from what we be a-makin' back home!"

"Aye…" announces another dwarf as he was taking notice of the elevated tensions. He lumbers over and sits next to Tol on the bed. "Me name be Whurgan Ringforger, an' I be a forge keeper in Glimmerheim. The Thane keeps askin' us for bricks, bricks, an' more bricks. It be said he rages at the poor Chancellor for more an' faster t' send off t' the war, an' then he calls on us t' attend this feast of his t' send out smiths t' make up fair for the warriors who be a-fightin' it."

"Really now…" the Captain muses thoughtfully. "Instead, ye were simply makin' up more bricks. And worse is that ye were under this drug where ye didn' even know what ye were doin'. Lads, we have a few small notes here that don' add up nicely. As a military Captain, I need to pay mind to this, because it may give me some clue as to where and how we found ye, and why ye were makin' up bricks in the first place."

"Aye, it does," Tol admits. "But Captain, where be we now that ye don'na know of Glimmerheim?"

"I'm tryin' to go slow with ye, lad, as ye're not in good sorts for any big surprises."

"This here be a big surprise already," he mumbles.

"Aye, so let's take it one piece at a time. What's the last thing ye recall before ye found yerself here?"

"That would be…ehm…the feast, I think."

"The feast…by yer Thane… This is already bad, because if he was the last one to see ye up and about, he becomes suspect in me mind as the reason ye're here now, especially if he was callin' ye up for a special duty."

"But…he be the Thane of Glimmerheim! Ye don'na go 'round callin' him a liar!"

"Lad, at this moment, I think he's the most likely one we can say is responsible for this. Listen to me. We found ye in a mine. Ye were pullin' up adamantium and makin' ingots. Ye were stockpilin' them for later pickup. But it nay be for any war against elves. There was another group comin' for it, and they nay be dwarves. This be the war we're fightin' here."

The two dwarves reeled back from this suggestion, and more attention was coming around from others who were waking up and taking notice of the conversation. Now a third dwarf stumbles over to join the group. Like the others, he sits down still clutching his head.

"Friend," the Captain begins as the new participant joins up. "I'll bet ye feel as bad as ye look. What's yer name?"

"Me name be Balur Gravelfist, I be a minin' foreman. The Thane has us diggin' holes everywhere we can under the city. May the All-Father protect us if the caves ever fall in."

"Aye! We saw ye doin' much the same in the mountain where we found ye."

"Sounds familiar," he sighs. "But the last thing I recall was the feast, an' it tasted bad."

"Aye," Whurgan agrees. "Like the 'shrooms were wrong somehow."

"Is that so?" the Captain responds. "How did they taste to ye?"

"Foul, a wee bit bitter, and with a taste like metal."

"That sounds like a nasty 'shroom, if ye ask me. And this was in the feast?"

"Aye, but he be the Thane, ye know, an' ye don'na go 'round complainin' about his food. He gave us a stew with some meat, which was fair enough, an' these 'shrooms. It made me feel a bit queasy at first, an' I recall I was a-feelin' a mite wobbly after a while, an' then nothin'."

"Right, this sounds good enough, but if ye thought that was the end of it, I didn' tell ye yet what we found ye eatin' in that minin' camp of yers. It sounds much the same, and the 'shrooms were a gnarly bunch that we think hold heavy metals in them."

"Wait now!" Tol exclaims. "What be this ye say, the Thane was a-feedin' us 'shrooms t' poison us?"

"We think it's nay to poison ye, although they're doin' that nicely enough. And we have some medicine for ye to help purge this and make ye right again. But these 'shrooms carry this toxin that puts ye under this spell I mentioned. After that, he put ye to work in a mine makin' up more of these ingots for his friends."

"Friends! What sort of friends would the Thane have that nay be dwarves?"

"The ones that started the true war, Tol… Those point-ears, as ye call them, were a diversion, I think. What do ye recall of this war as it's described to ye?"

"A diversion?" Balur argues. "That would be a grand beastly diversion, Captain. It be a-ragin' for a great long while now."

"Ye're TOLD it was ragin' for this long, but word on my side is these elves were sent at ye for only a hand or two of years, and then stopped when they used up their numbers. Everythin' else is likely yer Thane ragin' at your Chancellor with stories of a war so he can justify pullin' up more adamantium for his friends."

"Huh?"

"Wait," Whurgan interjects. "Just wait, I be a-thinkin' of the old tales now. Me father an' his father passed down the tales of the war an' how it first came t' us."

"Aye!" Balur offers. "We have these old tales, though I nay be a-hearin' them much by now. But they started with the point-ears a-comin' through portals at us. This was in the old days."

"Portals?" the Captain wonders.

"Aye! This be the tale. An' they just kept on comin' without end, throwin' such like magic at us, I think."

"But wait," Whurgan reflects. "That nay be the end of it. I recall hearin' of the magic, but they nay be good at anythin' else, an' even the magic nay be as good t' hold up a fair fight with a proper warrior. They were weak as babes floppin' on the ground, an' I think I also heard how they could'na even breathe proper. The tale, as I heard it, was it be as much like a mercy killin', nay a bold fight for any warrior."

"Aye, an' this may be why we nay hear any new tales by now. Who wants t' tell a tale of a weak fight against babes who can'na even stand up for it?"

"This sounds a bit strange to me, lads," the Captain considers. "Elves are nay as strong as yer average dwarf in full armor, but they're nay so weak as to simply fall over with trouble breathin'. This makes me wonder if they were sick in some way. But regardless of this, our tales are different. We hear of a time when these elves were sent at ye about four hundred years ago. All we have of it is they were called into this for a hand or two of years, enough to use up a great many of them, but no word came back to this side, whether win or lose. Then, one day, they're told to stop."

"Told to stop by whom?" Whurgan asks. "Do they have a Thane or some such?"

"Wait!" Tol snaps. "What d' ye mean, came back t' THIS side? Just where in all the blazes are we?"

"On the other side of yer alleged war, me friends," the Captain responds. "The elves weren't yer true foes. They were pawns sent to draw ye away from the real beasties that likely came down behind ye, an' yer Thane must be in league with them, especially if ye blame the elves for yer troubles an' don' even know about the rest. This stew is his way of stealin' ye away to work in yet another mine."

The three dwarves glanced around at each other, and then the remainder of their crew, some of whom were still trying to shake off their hangovers.

"Just how does this stew play in t' it, Captain?" Tol asks. "If it puts us t' sleep, how d' we go about minin' up Adamant an' makin' bricks?"

"It doesn' truly put ye to sleep, but a blank-faced stare where ye take orders easily and don' talk back. Our soldiers saw ye in that mine, and ye didn' speak or do anythin' else a normal person would. Then, ye went an' did somethin' horrible, all because yer masters gave ye instructions, and ye simply followed yer commands like a doll with only half a mind."

The three of them turned to gaze at each other again, much more cautiously. The room was becoming more alive by this time, and others were trying to listen in.

"What did we d', Captain?" Balur asks tenuously.

"Ye flattened a full city using powerful weapons that blast away buildin's with nay more than a single shot."

"What?" he shouts. "How could we d' that? An' what sort of weapon was it? I nay know of anythin' this powerful."

"It belongs to the ones who came down behind ye, the ones takin' up all the adamantium. They're a highly advanced sort, with knowledge and dealin's way beyond the likes of us. They set ye up with adamantium armor, to make ye virtually invincible to the locals, and then gave ye a type of shoulder-held cannon to do the work. Then ye blindly went in and blasted the entire city to rubble. When ye were done, ye just stood there, like mindless lummoxes, waitin' for yer next command."

"Great All-Father, could we actually d' all that?"

"That's when we took ye down and brought ye here. This place is a kind of prison, but we nay can rightly say ye're prisoners for this drug effect ye were under. So, I'm tryin' to get the story of how it got started from yer side."

"An' that be the way of it?" Tol concedes. "Ye're a Captain in this military, fightin' a war that we were on the wrong side of. All-Father forgive us…how many did we kill?"

"Thankfully, we were watchin' ye before ye got started. We evacuated the city and let ye have yer fun. Ye were too dangerous to approach with those weapons in yer hands. The city folk are safe, as best they can be, but the city is a total loss. Now we need to rebuild."

"Captain," Whurgan relents. "I swear t' the Soul Forger himself, I nay can remember any of this, an' this be a right disturbin' tale ye're tellin'. What will ye d' with us now?"

"For now, we need to take care of yer sickness. We have medicine for ye over here. This is to help with yer aches and the heavy metals in yer blood. But the man who leads us will want a few words with ye…and he's no thane. He's the King of the world we're on right now. I don' know where they carried ye from, but this isn' it. Neither was the world where we found ye."

"Nay even the same world?" Tol wheezes. "All-Father help us, what did that beastly Thane d' t' us? He feeds us this gnarly stew with poisonous 'shrooms that taste like metal, puts us t' slave labor for his friends, who are the real fiends behind the war, tells us lies about the rest, an' then we wake up only t' find we're on a new world after blastin' a city t' ashes. Home? Ye're a dwarf, friend, be this much true?"

"Aye, but I'm a native citizen to the world we're standin' on, which we call Tae'Eladar. My clan, and a few others, arrived here many thousands of years ago during a pilgrimage from our ancient home, but then we became a bit lost and had to make do. Since then, we and others who live here, includin' a bunch of elves that make their home here, all came together under the rule of a very powerful man, and he now leads us in this new war. And also, this is likely the reason we speak such a different dialect by now."

"Elves again," Balur muses. "Be these the same ones ye said came at us before?"

"Nay, brother, those are on a different world, one we call Therinë, and the war they had there spilled over here, which brought us into it."

"Who be it that started this war, then? Ye say these elves are nay more than pawns?"

"There is one at the top, and he's the one to worry about. The rest, we think, are all servants, probably no better than the elves during their time under him, or you with the drug. We liberated the elves, once we found them, but this other crew, the ones we think are on your world now, are out of reach for us to help so far."

"So, ye're in this war at least as much t' rescue these others as t' fight the one that drives them?"

"Generally so..." he nods. "The one at the top shouldn' even be alive by now. He belongs to an ancient race that some call titans."

"Titans!" Tol shouts. "I know this name. This be an' old tale, some say ancient legend, but mostly we tell it t' the babes at bedtime. Are ye sayin' they be real?"

"Real, yes, but ye're right that it's ancient history, well beyond our time. Folks like us shouldn' even know of it, except mayhap if ye listen to something older than we. They should be long gone now, but this one is still out there, and he's makin' a grand bit of trouble."

"Grand it is..." he mumbles woefully. "Oh, me dear Eiki... T' think she still be inside there behind those doors."

"Excuse me, friend?" the Captain wonders. "What doors do ye mean? And who is this Eiki?"

"Me beloved wife... When the war with the point-ears first came out, the Thane told us t' dig deep under the mountain an' close the doors so nay anythin' could bother us. Then he told us we need t' make up fair for the warriors up top...Adamant bricks, that be the whole of it. An' it be the same t' this day, we nay can go outside t' see the world, an' the Thane tells us the land be a-burnin' from it. So, if there nay be a war at all, what does the land actually look like, an' why has nay a soul come t' check on us?"

"That's a good question, brother. The world we just took away from him didn' have much left on it, so it makes me fear for yers now. What world do ye come from, anyway?"

"Ye say yer clan came here on a pilgrimage?" Whurgan wonders. "I be a-tryin' now t' think of any tales of a pilgrimage, but if it be so long ago, mayhap they were lost by now. Well, Captain, our world goes by the right proud name of Morndindor. D' ye know this name?"

The Captain's face suddenly went blank. The other native dwarves in the area also went pale, and all activity stopped and turned in Whurgan's direction. Whurgan and the others could tell something peculiar had just happened.

"Aye," he mutters softly. "Methinks ye d' know this name."

"Morndindor..." the Captain whispers faintly. "That name is nearly a legend to us here. It's the land of our ancient home. We thought it was lost to us forever when we couldn' find our way back. So, we made our home here, until one day, after so long a time of wanderin', and leavin' behind one ruin after another as we had to fight our way through all our local troubles, we lost most of what we had of our ancient home. It wasn' until recently, when our Lord and King helped us learn new ways, and go in search of our old history, that we even have this name at all."

"Then ye're a lost clan t' us," Balur muses. "Our lost brothers an' sisters from a pilgrimage we can'na remember. I wish I could offer ye fair greetin's, but it seems a bit dim after all the other tellin' ye made. An' now that we're here, where d' we go after? We had families back home, an' now I worry for them with that cruddy Thane runnin' about."

"Ye say these elves came at ye through portals? Aye, and we think we know who sent them, but they're also a world away. Ye'll have to be patient, friend Balur, ye and all yer kin here. We're workin' up a volley of ideas, but time is bumpin' against us. Mayhap ye and yer kin could offer a kind hand or two to help?"

"Captain," Tol offers. "I think it yay be the least we can d' for all the harm we did here. Ye say we blasted a full city? That still sounds like a hard one t' swallow, but mayhap if we can offer up a few wares t' rebuild it, it would make the All-Father happy again."

The Captain smiles and nods. He pats Tol on the shoulder, then gets up to stroll over to the elder dwarf who had been so diligently scribing his notes. There, he picks up a completed set and passes them through to a guard by the door. The guard leaves the area, travelling along the corridor to the outpost, where he finds a mage who will carry them back to Firstfall.

✦

The meeting in the tactical office was just about to adjourn for the day. Tristeen, Amariyn, and Sehnisavain had returned outside to see about the refugees again, leaving the rest to finish up their war details. Then a runner arrived in the camp through a custom mage portal directly from the dwarven prison. He quickly proceeds into the office to deliver the notes made thus far.

"My Lord, the dwarves have awakened. I have here some of the initial details our people have gathered. It's a fair bit, to be sure, and already troubling for what it tells us."

"What is their condition?"

"They're apparently suffering from severe headaches and disorientation. Other than that, they seemed able enough to speak and tell their story."

"This is promising. See to their medications, and go out there to inform Aerlie and Med-tech Tad'vaal on the matter."

"Aye!" he salutes and rushes out the door.

"What do they have to say for themselves?" Marelle asks.

Thaelyn takes a moment to read through the pages for a quick overview.

"Hmm, this is interesting as well as disturbing. And this tends to follow with some of our previous interpretations. Their behavior is friendly and polite, but also disturbed by their situation, which I cannot argue with. They appear to be civilians, with such occupations as smiths and mining foremen."

"So, they were working mines for a living, I suppose. I guess this makes them perfect for the job, but it sure is a nasty way to spend your skilled labor."

"Indeed, and especially if you consider adamantium is a particularly difficult material to work with. It takes many long years, a good portion of a lifetime, to understand all of its secrets. To spend this sort of talent so frivolously, and on such folly as this with a poisonous drug eventually taking it away from you…" he shakes his head.

"Do they say where they actually come from?"

"Their home is a city they call Glimmerheim, and by the mention, they regard it rather highly, so it must be a prominent city over there. However, they also mention they are barred from going outside due to a constant situation of war. They claim they are under siege by what they call point-ears…" he chuckles briefly.

"Ay!" Relissa gripes. "Don't you go making fun of my ears now!"

"But of course, Relissa," he smiles. "It is simply a curious way of stating the obvious, especially for a society that apparently never encountered elves before. But anyway, they claim their Thane, which is the traditional ruler of a dwarven clan, feeds them stories of a perpetual war outside their otherwise closed doors that is…" he coughs for emphasis, "…raging, is the word they use here, all across their native lands."

"Gods above," Marelle relents. "That sounds so much like the Governor back home."

"No doubt he is using a similar tactic on this occasion, with the exception here being this city is buried under a mountain. Unlike Rolsklinde, where there was a wall looking out onto the land, they remained locked behind a set of doors, which is likely the only way in or out."

"So, even without passing through the doors, or gates in our case, we could at least see what was out there from the walls. But they're completely boxed in."

"And like you, they are forbidden to go outside and check on things."

"So, their Thane tells them whatever he pleases about the outside world, and they have to accept it, just like the Governor did to us. I wonder if it's the same guy. He can change shape, right? Could he be running two jobs here?"

"I suppose it is possible, and if we are right in suggesting he can fold space, he could jump from place to place at will, even across worlds."

"That sounds bad. All right, if and when we can find a way over there, we need to be careful of that. The trouble now is how do we find it to help them? Do we know the name of their world? Not that it actually helps much."

He continues reading through the papers until he comes to a later section that catches his eye. His brow furrows, and he leans back in his chair, as if in deep consideration.

"Incredible," he whispers. "We found it. Or at least in concept, we found it."

"What do you mean?"

"Marelle," he sighs. "In our long history, we know the dwarves of Tae'Eladar arrived there as part of some ancient pilgrimage, as they tend to call it, from their ancestral home world. But for all the troubles they encountered since that time, much of their original history was lost to them, at least until I came along and began teaching the science of archeology. This allowed them to go in search of those ancient relics and reassemble them to piece together their forgotten past, including the name of their ancestral home, Morndindor."

"Good gods!" the General wheezes. "Morndindor? Is that where they came from?"

"Indeed, General, we have found their home at last, at least in concept. It is still outside our reach, but we do have one potential opportunity."

"An opportunity? What sort?"

"He says these, ahem, point-ears..." he flashes a broad grin at Relissa just to tease her.

"Buggers to you," she returns playfully.

He continues, "...Are said to be arriving through portals."

"Portals!" Marelle considers. "All right, we were talking about the orcs using portals to reach us, and the Suuden-Aryku making another covert operation to infiltrate the dwarven world. So, if we say the Suuden-Aryku transported the elves from here to Ruuki uy'Daan, allowing the orcs to use their newfound portal magic, which our dear Marshal blessed upon them, and if the orcs were once used in an earlier attack on that world, they might still know the way, so they could do it again. Am I right?"

"Very good, Marelle, but this becomes our next bane. We must find our way to Ruuki uy'Daan to deal with the orcs, but at the same time try to discover how they are able to use this portal magic in the first place, and then to use it for ourselves to find Morndindor."

"And do you think they'll just come up and offer it free of charge?" she smirks.

"Indeed, this is the one question we must answer rather delicately."

"The next thing to ask is this," Relissa offers. "How do they find themselves all drugged-up and working in a mine?"

"Yes, this report tells us their Thane is responsible for that as well, it would seem. He apparently puts on a feast during a selection process to call up laborers for the purpose of providing wares to the ongoing warfare outside. This feast, by their description, matches that same stew we found up in their enclave, including the mushrooms. They claim it tasted foul, and with a tinge of metal. This is apparently the last they can recall until now. And further, they do appear to be suffering some aftereffects."

"Anything serious?" Marelle asks.

"I cannot be sure from this report. It mentions headaches and other symptoms that might be typical of awakening from a drug-induced stupor. They also mention a general pallor which may indicate the poisoning from the heavy metals. We will have Aerlie, and perhaps Med-tech Tad'vaal go in, once the situation stabilizes, to thoroughly check on things."

Thaelyn once again reviews the report, now taking note of the stories the dwarves gave of their war, and again he pauses in deep contemplation over some of the wording.

"Weak, falling to the ground, and with difficulty breathing…?"

"My Lord?" the General utters softly.

"Yes, right here, they mention these elves again. They have old stories of the early battles, but these apparently stopped after a while because they were not very appealing."

"Not appealing?" Marelle wonders.

"Well, yes… Dwarves have a tradition of pride during warfare, and they tend to celebrate strong leaders and other war heroes as the finer examples of bravery and valor. But in this case, their opponents did not bring such gallantry, therefore the stories they might normally tell of such occasions stopped."

"Oh, all right, I suppose I can see that part. So, why did they stop? What was wrong with their opponents, in this case?"

"The elves were described as weak and unable to stand up, nor even to catch their breath. I must ask myself, what could be the cause here? Is it something in the air, perhaps a strange mix of elements, or maybe something relating to the local flora that taints it in some fashion that the elves were unaccustomed to?"

"Could it be the elves were injured after their arrival through the portal, or maybe they were sick?"

"At this moment, it could be any number of concerns. Elves may not be as sturdy as dwarves, but they are very nimble. To say they could not dance around their opponents, and even that they had trouble breathing, suggests to me there is indeed something wrong here. Unfortunately, there is nothing we can do about it from this side. Whatever it is, it may have to wait until we actually arrive there. But we will keep this in mind just in case it holds special relevance."

+‧+◆+‧+

A new day was dawning over the Badlands valley. The refugees from Rolsklinde were just waking up to the smells of fresh-cooked food drifting out of the kitchens. Once again, the medical staff returned to continue the process of removing the implant devices from the populace. Aerlie had several of her priests with her taking one group, while Med-tech Tad'vaal and her people took another. The process would take time, if only for the sheer volume of patients on the waiting list.

Tristeen had been assembling her team again, which included Amariyn and Sehnisavain, along with her father and the other nobles.

On this day, she needed to begin a serious campaign to bring the people to an agreement for their future.

"I think we should create some manner of memorial," she muses, "to symbolize what happened here...for all the lives lost, and the hardships we suffered, all of us. Maybe we can create a day of remembrance, as well as a tribute to our victory, if you could call it that. This could also serve to teach future generations. We should never again allow ourselves to be so ignorant."

"Josef," Abraim notes. "I think your daughter is looking to become a new folk hero now."

"Or at the very least, an inspirational social leader," Seth offers.

"Will the two of you stop encouraging her?" he jests. "She has enough ambition as it is."

The group all smiled at the thought.

"Miss Macaid," Amariyn affirms. "I think this is a most noble suggestion. Sehnisavain, what do you think?"

"I have to agree," she nods. "I think it would do us all a good turn to make the day of departure of that horrid Marshal and his people into a tribute of victory, but we should also build some manner of monument, perhaps for each of us. The humans certainly need one to remember their suffering and the loss of their loved ones to this illness, as well as their homes, and I would also wish one for ourselves for all that we endured."

"You mean for the terrible madness afflicted upon you by that... creature?"

"Yes. Surely, you also suffered, Amariyn, and for this, you deserve your own. But I think our people held the worst of it for what he did to us."

"Oh, I do not pretend our suffering to be anything as great as yours. Four centuries of his domination is more than enough for you to desire your peace. Perhaps we could present these ideas to His Lordship for consideration."

"It seems so unreal by now," Tristeen reflects. "I'm trying to recall all the recent events, like those up in the city, where we were fighting a hidden war to reveal all these truths to the people, while at the same time trying not to get ourselves killed by his military."

"Indeed, Tristeen," Josef admits. "And you did a fair amount of that if I recall. You singlehandedly saved the full student body of the academy from poisoning. Then you saved all our lives in the Upper Ward..." he ponders.

"I had a little help in the academy, Dad."

"Yes, but as I understand from the reports they gave, you orchestrated the whole affair."

"The part about the Upper Ward was simple intuition," Seth considers. "You don't learn that in a school, it just comes to you."

"Well, now, just a moment," Tristeen protests. "I did actually have advice from His Lordship that the Governor may hold a pet peeve over me, at the very least. And the Dean...uh, well, Alin... Mister Malorn, as he likes to be called now. He also warned me that the Governor knows about my involvement. So, the answer was obvious."

"Yes, but it was an answer that brought us completely out of that demon's line of sight. Even if we were to simply hide in the basement, it wouldn't have saved us from that blasting. I heard that the whole of the Upper Ward was reduced to giant holes in the ground. Not even a basement shelter would survive that."

"Well, yeah, I have to admit, that was a bit dramatic. And I had been told about this, so...well, all right, I just put it together and came up with an answer to solve the problem. We were expecting to be evacuated anyway, and I suppose the noble families were Number One on the hit list."

"And let us not forget your efforts out here," Josef adds. "We had in mind to combine our skills, such as they are, to give aid to these people. But you, my dear, got up on the soapbox and started preaching to them. If that is not the mark of a proper political aspirant, I don't know what is."

"Fine, Dad, but let's not get carried away with it. I'm just doing what I feel is necessary to help these people. I'm mostly making it up as I go along, since we really never had anything like this before, but that's all. Anyway, I just feel like so much of it happened so fast. At one moment, I'm just a student at the academy, and the next, I'm a rebel leader working undercover to overthrow an oppressive ruler from who-knows-where with nearly godlike power. You don't see that every day."

"Indeed, I must agree," he chuckles. "We were essentially in the middle of a type of warzone, with you on the front lines against some rather outlandish odds."

"You know, Josef," Abraim considers. "Didn't she actually tell us once that we should NOT go out starting any rebellions?"

"Actually, she did! Hmph!" he teases. "I'll bet she simply wanted to take all the fame to herself."

"Well," Seth grins. "She certainly accomplished that much."

"You people are going to drive me mad one day," she smiles and shakes her head.

"And yet," Josef muses. "You do bring up a good point. When speaking of godlike powers," he pauses to survey the landscape. "I still can't get over what happened out here. Just look at this place! Just what manner of beings are we dealing with here?"

"I agree, Josef," Seth admits. "I was noticing this when we first arrived. It was dark, but even in the moonlight I could see it wasn't anything like the stories told. It was supposed to be a dry desolate wasteland."

"And even with an army of men, you couldn't plant this much greenery during the full time he was out here. And yet, I'm told this was done in a matter of moments. You want to talk about godlike..."

"Well, Dad," Tristeen relents. "He is descendent from these Estelar, so that might suggest something."

"Yes, the child of a god...with the power to turn a desert into thickets and meadows, then to unite the people of our world together, and turn around a four-century long war of intrigue played by another godlike creature."

"And now he's going in pursuit of that other one," Abraim adds. "This isn't over."

"As for the valley," Amariyn advises. "His association with the dryads and the druidic powers of his priests astounds even me. He must've empowered them somehow, though don't ask me how. I can understand how they can enrich life, but this goes well beyond that. I had never actually visited this place before his arrival, but from what Relissa told me of her scouting expeditions, it was devoid of anything living…the remnants of a forgotten battle from centuries past."

"Well, forgotten battleground or otherwise," Abraim mentions. "I think if we are to have any play in this, I'd like to contribute a suggestion to this idea of a memorial."

"And what is that, Abraim?" Josef asks.

"This valley… We've always called it the Badlands, but I don't see anything bad about it now, do you?"

"I agree," Seth adds. "He came in here as the result of the war intruding into his home, but as I understand it, he asked permission before building this village over here, so we can't say he simply took something away from us."

"Not that it actually belonged to us in the first place."

"Despite what the Governor tried telling him on that first day," Tristeen recalls.

"Right," Abraim affirms. "And so I think we should make a special tribute to him. He won this war for us, and shooed away a creature that likely would've eaten us for breakfast, if he held such an interest."

"No…" Tristeen conjectures humorously. "This one definitely liked to play with his food."

They all shared a laugh at the idea.

"We should give this place a new name," Abraim asserts. "The old one simply doesn't hold any relevance by now. And with this village over here, with such a name as Firstfall, which gives its own tribute to the orcs he blasted to their maker, we should name the entire valley to his honor."

"What a most noteworthy idea," Amariyn admits. "It should describe the occasion of how it came to be this way, and perhaps even how it brought us to where we are now."

"All right," Tristeen issues. "You people put this one together and we'll present it with the rest. Meanwhile, I need to get back on my soapbox…" she sneers playfully at her father, "…to preach some more. I've been trying to conduct a little research on the people of Tae'Eladar, along with their social customs and culture. Haran has been really helpful for this point since he's been living there these past few months. I want to present this as part of my campaign to convince these people that joining up would be the best course of action for us, in both the short and the long term."

She moves away to collect Leesa, who had been assisting her previously with the microphone, and prepares to take up her stand on the stage again. As they exit through the gate into the field, she makes a slight detour behind the stage to an area further along that was partitioned with portable walls to offer some privacy. This was the medical station, which was positioned away from the crowds in order not to disturb them, or the patients, with a lot of traffic passing by.

"I need to do this sometime," she mutters quietly while peeking around the corner.

"I did mine a long time ago on Tae'Eladar," Leesa admits. "Lady Aerlie did it for me."

"Did it hurt?"

"Not at all…although it's probably moot, as it still needs to be done."

"Yeah, true, I'm just a bit squeamish."

"Anyway, she and her people used some trick to make my body feel numb, so I didn't feel a thing."

"But that was Lady Aerlie. We also have these Daanen-Aryku out here. I wonder if they do it the same."

As she continues peeking around the corner at the operating tables, she happens to take notice that Captain Kholgard was coming out. He was just finishing up, and now leaving the facility.

"Captain?" she calls to him. "You look a little pale."

"Girl, I just had a hole cut into me and something ugly pulled out. You expect me to be all plums and roses after that?" he chuckles.

"Probably not, but count yourself lucky you got it out at all. If it weren't for His Lordship discovering all these nasty little secrets, we'd all still be dying from it."

"Granted. And I have to admit, it's actually a relief to know that I won't be dying from this accursed plague in another few years. That's been on my mind for a while now, and sending chills along my back every time I think about it."

"I'm sure you're not the only one, Captain. My mom and dad are the same way, though I doubt they'd actually admit to it like that."

"Everybody deals with it in their own way, I guess."

"Who did it for you, Lady Aerlie or the Daanen-Aryku team?"

"In my case, it was that Med-tech lady over there, but they all seem to be doing a fine enough job at it, so if you're worried about who does it, I don't think it matters much."

"Well, all right, but in the case of the Daanen-Aryku… Leesa here said Lady Aerlie did hers and she didn't feel anything from it, but I get shudders when thinking of someone taking a knife to me for any kind of surgery. Did the Daanen-Aryku use anything where you don't feel it?"

"Yeah, actually… She used something she called a hypo-spray device that put some kind of medicine into my shoulder to make it numb. In fact, it still feels that way. They say it'll recover on its own soon enough."

Tristeen's curiosity causes her to try peeking at his shoulder. The Captain notices this, so he leans in and pulls his collar down.

"Here, you want to see it? There's not much to see at this point."

Tristeen feels a little shy about looking at someone's surgery scar, but as she leans in to take a closer look, she finds she can't discern anything noteworthy.

"Um, are you sure they actually did something? I mean, at the very least, there ought to be a bandage or something, and then what about the stitches?"

"They're using a combined effort over there, even with the Daanen-Aryku team, using Lady Aerlie's priests to heal up the leftovers. They use a divine touch, so they say, which instantly heals the injury, so there's nothing left to look at, not even a scar."

"Gods be blessed," she wheezes. "Then why am I so worried about it, sign me up!"

The Captain chuckles vigorously, followed by Leesa.

"The experience isn't even enough to tell your grandkids about," he explains. "But I'll admit one thing; the stress of thinking about it is enough to give you the shivers."

"All right, I'll see about my turn soon."

Thaelyn and his officers were in their morning meeting in the tactical office. On this occasion, Lieutenant Lapäli was attending, having finished his language classes along with Relissa and the others, and now able to spend his full day at his post.

A soldier comes in with a delivery, which arrived at the receiving area for inbound portal rune transport. He carries a note and a rune just received from the front line of the assault on the orcish hordes.

"My Lord, this just came in from our western front."

"What do we have here?" Thaelyn asks as he receives the delivery. He reads the note and begins to form a modest smile.

"My Lord?" the General grins. "Do we have good news today?"

"It will do. Our forward line on the far western front has found another orcish camp with a portal. This makes two."

"Ah, grand. Then we should do with this as we did the first one...to take the camp and settle a garrison until we can find a way to shut it down."

"Correct, but this was on the far western front, and it makes me wonder. For the quantity of orcs closer to this side, I feel there should be one more. But this will certainly put a crimp on their reinforcements entering this world."

"Do you wish to make another personal visit on this occasion?"

"No, this time I will leave it to our local commanders to decide. The orcs are running scared, so taking this outpost may not be as much a task as before. We can send word to soften it up with gryphon-mounted archers and mages, and then move in with ground troops later."

"Before too long," Padriyl suggests. "You'll have this war completely under control."

"We must give our credit to all those who have played their roles," he nods. "But then, we need to look forward to the next one. With Darumon out of the way, we have some freedom to ourselves, and I wish to make good use of it. He thinks we cannot follow, and we will take advantage of this perception to sneak up behind him."

"But with respect, you don't have any space travel capability, nor do we hold any navigation logs to help us find Azgarén again. How do you suggest we find our way back there?"

"We may need to depend on luck, which in itself is problematic, but if Kaliya could find her way to Ruuki uy'Daan once, we will see if we can train this to help the rest of us. Then we have the orcs to deal with, and at the same time, they might also hold the key to Morndindor. If this is true, we have another step to look forward to, and on Morndindor, I hope to find a well-suited Suuden-Aryku outpost managing their mining operations."

"And if that outpost has a conveyor unit, that gives you access to Azgarén. All right, I follow you, but these are lot of ifs we speak of. It's also a very strange way of travelling between worlds," he chuckles.

"Indeed," he grins. "And certainly not what I was expecting to see when our proper moment came to us. But Lieutenant, I will need to begin coordinating our efforts directly with your Commander Nazég, if you do not mind. I will need his level of clout and authority to see our next steps through efficiently."

"I understand. I've been keeping him informed of our efforts and I can tell you he is quite impressed by your success factor so far, as well as the timing of your movements. But at the same time, he also confided in me his trepidation over pursuing Darumon back to Azgarén."

"I can appreciate his concern, but this is not a choice we can ignore. You need only to see what he has done to this world to know he is a great danger to all life, not simply the trouble he caused you and yours. I must also ask myself about Morndindor, and the stories we are receiving from those dwarves we captured. If he holds a presence there, what has he done to it, and for that matter, even your former home of Azgarén?"

"I was born on Ruuki uy'Daan, one of the first new generations, and like so many others, I can't actually call Azgarén my home anymore. We consider ourselves in exile, which is actually how our name is defined. The term Daanen-Aryku, in our language, means the Exiled Ones. Except for Master Velen, who is the only surviving member of the original crew, the rest of us were born somewhere along the way, and none of us ever expected to return home again."

"You have lived a rather nomadic life since then, which some might say is not especially healthy, although there are those who actually enjoy it. Still, no matter where it was you might call your place of birth, as a species, Azgarén is still your home."

"Yes, I suppose you're right, but it feels so…alien…by now, especially when you think of who controls it and what happened to the rest of our people."

· ✦ ✦ ✦ ·

Tristeen was once again up on the platform, this time preaching her campaign to inform the people of the benefits of joining the kingdom. Her audience had gathered around in a mass of bodies that filled a broad area outside the north gate, and her voice bellowed out of the loudspeaker system, echoing across the land for everyone to hear.

"Just imagine, my friends," she announces. "Good work for good pay and equality for everyone. Our children will go to their schools and likely learn many times what we had in ours, if only for the sheer volume of what they have to teach. And apparently, they use a very peculiar system of education, where it is highly compressed and accelerated to teach what could easily amount to a lifetime of lessons to one of us, but in only a fraction of that time."

"How do they do that, Miss Macaid?" ask one man. "I mean,

good gracious, how can a person study so much even in a single day and be able to recall anything from it?"

"I have several of my friends over there right now taking language lessons. This would make a good example for us. Normally, if you can recall from any of your old studies in school, you read from books and listen to the instructor at the head of the class giving a lecture, right? Over the course of time, pounding this into your head, plus testing, and then more pounding, you eventually learn something. Well, from what I'm hearing on Tae'Eladar, you can forget the books; it's just not fast enough. They give you a textbook that is laid out a certain way, mostly the raw details of the lecture for your eyes to follow, while they blast your ears with multiple instructors speaking at the same time!"

The crowd suddenly gushes up a series of moans and boisterous murmuring.

"Yeah, I know the feeling," she giggles. "But I have one special friend who has been attending an academy over there these last few months, and he tells me he was able to learn their full language during only this short period of time, and he hopes to take more lessons, which would place him in a rather prominent position of academic esteem, and he's estimating it to take only seven or eight years, depending on some of the prerequisite courses he needs in order to prepare for it. And we're talking about the complete mastery of magic, plus history, science, mathematics, political science, culture, several additional languages, and more, depending on his choices during that time."

The crowd again ushers up a series of groans for the sheer volume of content involved.

"And in order to do this," she concludes. "They combine this accelerated form of delivery with a unique alchemical elixir that similarly accelerates a person's memory recall. Therefore, you can learn what could be ten times or more the volume you might get in a very prestigious academic course, but in only a fraction of that time."

The crowd gasps and emits a resounding set of oohs and ahs.

"And they are able to give this to their children also, although in a milder form to compensate for their growth rate. So, by the time they grow up into adults, they already have a top-level education, as compared to your traditional childhood courses. Then they can take additional courses in the higher institutions to further expand on it."

"Bloody hell, ma'am!" shouts another man. "How do you expect any of us to keep up with that? Most of us are already adults. If their children are already above us...uh..."

"Fear not, for there is always a place for every man and woman out there. Lord Thaelyn doesn't leave people in the gutters. He encourages everyone to find their best purpose, and go from there to improve on things whenever possible. No one is left behind. We will probably have more than enough work for us trying to rebuild our homes and reestablish our basic needs here, and I think you'll all find good work for yourselves, no matter how much education you have in you right now. We can work on the rest later."

"Aye, that's for sure. But what can he do for us on that side of it?"

"Indeed, his world carries other blessings besides this. They're more advanced than we are, due largely as the result of his enlightened teachings, which he brought to his people from his former home in Mount Celestia."

"Where is that?" asks another onlooker. "I'm guessing it isn't Tae'Eladar, like the rest."

"That's right. Most of you probably do not know this, but I learned of this on the day when that creep in the Governor's Manor ordered that demon to be sent against him."

Another round of groans echoes across the field as many recall the occasion in the upper district plaza.

"Yes, I was there, and I saw the whole thing, and I'll tell you, it was as frightening as anything to see that monster storming through the streets. But his men took it down with barely a scratch. That's how tough they are, and how dedicated they are to their faith. And although I understand he could've done this himself, he was instead trying to make a statement in Darumon's eyes that he and his people are not to be trifled with, and I think it worked, at least within reason."

"Within reason?" shouts another man. "How do you describe that with our city being wrecked?"

"Well, yes, I understand. Darumon doesn't apparently take no for an answer. When I say, within reason, it is to say to stifle HIS opinion of superiority against everything else out there. And this has to extend beyond our one city. It caused him to refrain from attacking anyone else around here, which he likely would've done to punish, as some might say, all those who were otherwise opposing him. Instead, he tried playing a trick using those dwarves, rather than a direct launch of the Suuden-Aryku forces. The bombardment of the Upper Ward was a quick hit-and-run tactic, apparently because he hated the noble families so much. So, the message was to keep him from destroying what's left of our world. But as we saw, he did dare to hit our city, and likely because he felt he could get away with it before anyone could catch him."

"Bloody wicked, that..."

"His Lordship's warning was to suggest the Estelar would be watching everything else, and if those Suuden-Aryku were to try anything...well..." she shrugs and gives a prominent thumbs-down gesture. "But that Darumon!" she huffs. "He used a non-military target to hit another non-military target."

"And that's even more wicked! Doesn't he hold anything sacred?"

"I guess not! This is why we decided it was more worthwhile to sacrifice our city if only to get him to leave the rest alone. We can rebuild after that."

"That's a mighty sacrifice, but I guess I can see your point. But how is it you can say he would be afraid of these new gods? We barely even know of them here. Does this mean he knows them from this other place?"

"In a way, yes... I'm told they're ancient enemies from a forgotten war that occurred long ago. Lord Thaelyn and others of his kind recall this, which is just another aspect of knowledge he brought with him. And in this case, I think it is very convenient that we have access to this knowledge to understand who he was in reality, if not our Governor."

"Uh, excuse me," calls a woman. "But did I just hear you correctly? Did you say he and others of his kind know something that's also said to be on the level of these new gods?"

"Yes. When Lord Thaelyn visited inside the academy to speak with the Dean, he was delivering a message that the Dean would be expected to relay to the Governor. His Lordship was apparently trying to keep himself personally at distance, and work this indirectly through the Dean."

"Why is that?"

"The reason is generally because Marshal Darumon belongs to an ancient and largely forgotten race of beings also on the scale of gods. The Estelar found them once and the two got into a dispute, which resulted in a battle with these others losing. This one, however, along with his master, who we know of as Sargeras, escaped and went into hiding. His Lordship figured this out, after some investigation, but these two are thought to be very evasive, and Lord Thaelyn has in mind to pursue them to finish what was started long ago. Therefore, if Darumon were to see Thaelyn coming, or any of these Estelar, he might run again. And for now, we want him to stay where he is, which we think is the Suuden-Aryku home world."

"And this might also include him popping into his office there in the plaza?"

"Rather than Thaelyn going in personally, we would use the Dean to reveal that Thaelyn is a being called a Celestial, which carries a special definition. As I understand it, there are two flavors: One is natural, meaning to say a society of beings who have advanced so far up the ladder, they are partway to godhood by now."

The crowds draw back with oohs and whispers about the potential meaning.

"The other side is a form of hybrid. These are special cases, as I understand it. Thaelyn is one of these, along with his wife, Lady Aerlie. These are beings that are mixed with mortal blood, like ours, and half Estelar. So, they are literally the Children of these Estelar."

Now the crowd reels back with howls and yelps.

"Easy now..." Tristeen coaxes. "All his people revere him as a father figure, and I've even heard how they regard him as a kind of messiah for the nature of who he is and where he comes from. His Father is one they call Lord Tyr, the predecessor to Torm. And while this particular member of the Estelar is no longer among us, as apparently even gods can die on occasion, he was once known as the Just God, because he presided over the domain of Justice and Law, and Lord Thaelyn follows that same path. These references would be enough to send chills into Darumon, and we believe they did. He made a hasty retreat once he figured it out. But as we saw, he didn't go quietly."

"Aye, but at the same time, I'm sorry I asked now," she chuckles weakly. "So, he brought his wisdom, which I guess is borrowed from these gods, to his people on Tae'Eladar?"

"He did, but he needs to follow a delicate process here. The Estelar hold a number of philosophies, which they call the Measure of Balance. I believe we heard this mentioned during some of the sessions in our temple with his new priests trying to teach us about their gods. He cannot reveal his teachings directly. Instead, he must allow the people time to grow and simply encourage them to learn things by offering what he calls knowledge quests, which direct them into a new study to learn something important. This encourages their growth beyond what might come naturally, but not too fast. In this way, his people have progressed quite vigorously during the many centuries he's lived on Tae'Eladar."

"Centuries?!" the woman shrieks.

"Yes, as I understand it, he's immortal, just like his Father and the other Estelar, so he's not going anywhere anytime soon. And he'll do for us the same as he did for them. But we need to work hard to meet him halfway. He doesn't just give things away, he expects us to do our part, as well. Haran, my friend in the academy over there, tells me he likes to test people on occasion, just to keep them active and using their heads. This is how they built their world, with everyone doing their own part."

Tristeen now takes a break to allow the people to discuss these new details amongst themselves. She steps back from her podium on the stage and calls Leesa away from her runs through the crowds with the portable microphone.

Aerlie was again helping the medical teams process the patients for the removal of the implants. But during this time, she was taking a break to listen in, and as she overheard the speech, she relayed the details telepathically to Thaelyn inside the tactical office.

Thaelyn had been sitting quietly in his chair, trying to focus on a few reports he had in front of him, but distracted by Aerlie's polite intrusions. The General watched him, casually glancing over to check on his reactions and realizing he was in communion with his wife outside. He could hear, at least partially, the echoing sounds of Tristeen's lecture through the fields, but when the voice stopped, he began to wonder what Thaelyn's final result might be.

"My Lord?" he ushers gently. "Do we have anything?"

"General, that young lady out there will have those people eating out of her hand before long."

"Do you think so?" he laughs. "Well, I have been taking these reports from our field officers. You've seen those, correct?"

"I have, and I am forming a determined opinion on this matter. If these people should join us, we will require some form of representation in our government. And dear young Tristeen is demonstrating herself to be more than capable as a leader."

"Are you thinking of perhaps appointing her to some position up there in the city?"

"That is one thought, but mine is a bit higher, actually," he smiles cautiously.

"Good gracious," he grins. "Well, I can't wait to see this one played out."

"In the meantime, I need to make a visit to our dwarven associates and introduce myself. We need to find a place for them, as well."

"Yes, according to Captain Ironbeard, they've been mostly relaxing as our people are treating their ailments, although they also seem a bit anxious to get back on their feet again."

"I cannot blame them, and we will certainly have work for them, if they should so desire it. Good smiths, ironworkers, toolmakers, and the like, will be in great demand in the coming months and years as we rebuild Rolsklinde."

As they wrap up their meeting, Thaelyn makes himself ready to return to Tae'Eladar. The business of the war might be coming to a close in this world, but the preparation for the next step will be a difficult one.

✦✦✦

Today was orientation day for Relissa and the gang. They had collected their instructional materials and cadet uniforms, and now they were on tour around the guildhall academy. Haran joined in as they reviewed their scheduling, and he assisted in locating some of the classrooms. The first assignment they noticed on their list was Arcane Studies: Circle One.

"Jiggers," Relissa smirks. "Looks like we'll all be sharing a class together. Who would've thought I'd be sitting next to this spark-thrower studying the same books?" she giggles while thumbing at Haran.

"That'll certainly be fun!" Haran laughs. "But I suspect my previous experience in mage craft will allow me to push ahead in there rather quickly, so don't get used to it."

"Aye, you might need to study their books, but you already have the practice, so half of your class time will go on to something new. This first year is going to be a bit of touch-and-go for us till we can find our niche."

"Relissa," Marelle inquires as she peruses her schedule list. "What do you have after that?"

"Looks like I need to hop over to a history course, and then we have lunch. After that, they have me doing a math class, then going into creature lore, whatever that is, and finally combat practice."

"Creature lore, I've heard of that one," Haran notes. "It's a study of various types of creatures they have around here, most of which you don't want to meet in a dark alley, or a well-lit one."

"Nice. Do we need to worry about any?"

"I think it's mostly for information. It's a way of knowing their strengths and weaknesses. Apparently, they still have a lot of dangerous elements hidden away in dark places, like caves and underground catacombs."

"Wonderful."

"Hmm," Marelle muses. "It looks like they're putting us through the same classes as a way to fill in these prerequisites, and I suppose we all need this since we're new in this world. I can't wait for that combat practice session, though. Maybe I can finally get to learn some of those fancy moves Thaelyn was showing us that one time."

"Aye, but I wonder how hard it is to learn. He made it look easy, but I'll bet there's a lot of work to it."

"I had a few opportunities to watch them out there on the training field," Haran recalls. "Even we mages need to learn a little bit, but rather than use swords, they teach us a few tricks with staffs."

"Well, easy or not," Marelle relents. "We still need to do it, so let's stick together. And who knows, maybe we'll see Kaliya out there and we can all gang up on her!" she giggles. "We could use each other as training dummies."

Relissa eyes Marelle suspiciously as she finishes her statement.

"Right, but just remember, my bones break easier than you humans. Still, I'm quick on my feet, so if you're thinking of laying one on me, you'll need to look sharp to catch me."

"Sounds like a challenge. All right, you're on."

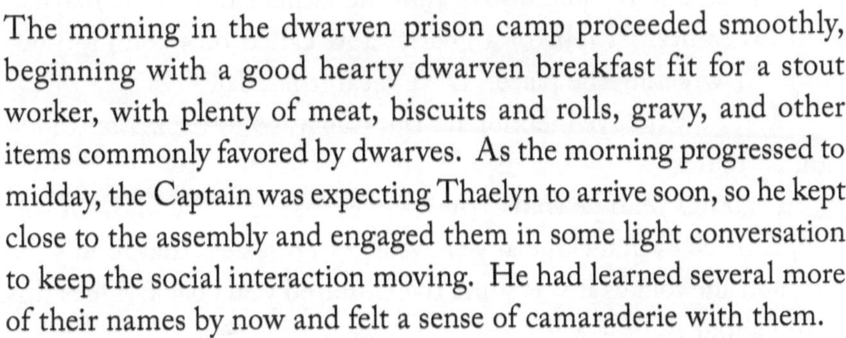

The morning in the dwarven prison camp proceeded smoothly, beginning with a good hearty dwarven breakfast fit for a stout worker, with plenty of meat, biscuits and rolls, gravy, and other items commonly favored by dwarves. As the morning progressed to midday, the Captain was expecting Thaelyn to arrive soon, so he kept close to the assembly and engaged them in some light conversation to keep the social interaction moving. He had learned several more of their names by now and felt a sense of camaraderie with them.

"How are ye feelin', Tol?" he asks. "Has yer head stopped poundin' by now?"

"Aye, for the better part, though me eyes be a bit hazy an' me head feels thick, even without the poundin'."

"Aye, we think ye'll feel this way for a fair bit until we can get those heavy metals out of ye. The good thing is ye're in our care and we have some fine people pullin' for ye."

"Ye know, Captain, ye say ye have all these people, but I be a-wonderin' where they be. All I see yay be the few of ye here inside this wee nook with us. Where be the rest of them?"

"That's a good one. This wee nook, as ye call it, is just somethin' of a wee illusion. Ye see…these rocky walls around us aren' actually rocks. They're just panels coverin' up another type of wall to make it look like rock."

"Why d' ye have this? D' the other walls look so gnarly that ye have t' cover them up?"

Tol and the other prisoners let out a bold round of laughter at the thought.

"Well, actually, Tol," the Captain grins. "While that's good for a laugh, the other walls are nay true walls at all, at least nay in the normal way of it. Now ye need to know what sort of knowledge we have here in our world, and it be a right fine one if I must say. Many years ago, like I said, war came to us from that other world. It came in the form of orcs invadin' our land and makin' trouble for our people."

"Orcs!" shouts Whurgan. "I know that word. It comes from another old tale handed down from me father's father, an' mayhap even his father. It tells of a gnarly crew called orcs comin' t' our home an' wreckin' the place. D' ye recall that, Tol?"

"Aye, now that ye mention it. But this was way back…how long ago, I wonder…"

"I can tell ye, if ye want," the Captain offers. "We know of this also. The elves that came at ye have a high priestess that recalls the tale, and she told us it was some five hundred years back. Does this sound about right to ye?"

"Five hundred...mayhap...an' methinks they also came at us through portals, or so it was said."

"Aye, we think the same. These orcs used portals to come at us also, but we turned it around on them. We fought them back and used their own portals to chase them instead."

"Har har!" Balur roars. "Now there be a right fine one. An' this here be when ye found yerself on this new world?"

"Aye! And also when we found so many others in trouble, includin' ye and yer kinfolk."

"How long ago was this?" Whurgan wonders.

"When we arrived on Therinë? Just over three months ago. But we couldn' be sure who some of our friends were. We made friends well enough with a few, but there was that one city...the one ye blasted, by the way...run by a Governor who was behavin' strangely for a man blamin' all of his ills on a war he also claimed to be ragin' across the land."

"That one sounds a wee bit like our Thane," Balur reflects.

"He's the one who runs the bloody bastards, as it turns out, hiding in disguise and pretendin' to be their Governor."

Tol and the others paused a moment to gaze at the Captain as he continued his dialog.

"His true name, as we learned later, is one Marshal Darumon, leader of this military that goes around blastin' whatever he pleases to have his way with it. He makes slaves of those he wants to work for him, and seems to blast away the rest. We saw this on Therinë. It was down to only three cities, one of them under his control, the other two heavily oppressed in case he needed them for later."

"Great All-Father," Whurgan moans. "How can such a beastie like that go 'round in such way? Be there nothin' t' stop it?"

"Aye, there is... Us!" he thumbs at himself. "We just didn' know of it until now. It seems this Marshal Darumon has a pet peeve against some old foes, the gods we all know and love. His kin were once ancient enemies in a great battle, but they lost. Now he wants revenge. But he needs minions to do his work for him, and this is where people like ye, these elves, and others come in."

Tol and his friends all shake their heads at the scene.

"All-Father protect us. But what now? What can we d' about it?"

"First, we need to prepare ourselves. In our fight, we had to invent a few new things…these walls, for instance. Behind these panels are a series of spires, and these spires create a wall of energy that forms up a solid barrier. We used this to create a defensive wall around our outpost."

"A wall of energy made solid?"

"Aye, we have some fine workin's of magic here. But we found this was useful for a few things beyond our walls, like the types of weapons these other folks use, the Suuden-Aryku. Those weapons they gave ye to blast the city were a large cannon that shoots great blasts of energy to rip things apart, but these walls can actually stop it."

"It sounds t' me like ye have a fine few tricks t' play, once ye meet up again."

"Aye, but first we have to find our way over to it. He's a world away, and we don' quite know how to get there yet."

✦✦✦

Thaelyn was just arriving at the prison to make his appointed visit and see about establishing a formal relationship with the dwarven captives. He first checked in at the garrison outpost in front of the prison housing for a brief update on the situation.

"Milord," calls a resident lieutenant. "We've been expecting ye. The Captain is inside with the prisoners."

"Very good. How do they appear? Does that medicine seem to be offering any relief?"

"I nay can be sure yet. They tell how they feel a wee bit better, but methinks it'll take some time before we see any real progress. 'Tis only the first day for it, ye know."

"Of course, but now our affairs must press forward, and I wish to see where we will go together with them. Let us go make our visit. I would wish to speak to the Captain briefly about his impressions."

"Aye, this way then…"

The Lieutenant leads the two of them along the corridor of the oddly aligned shield walls up to the door. He unlocks the door and brings them inside. Their entrance is keenly noticed by the majority of the occupants, many of whom rise to their feet as the door opens, only to discover how high they need to angle their heads to see Thaelyn's face, as he towered over the group.

"Grace be t' the All-Father," mutters one of the prisoners. "An' this must be their king."

"Aye," responds another, panning his view across Thaelyn's full form. "An' take a gander at what he be a-wearin'. That be some of the finest smithin' me eyes have beheld in a good many years."

"That there yay be some fine Adamant, t' be sure," suggests another one. "A right proud set for a king."

Thaelyn rolls his eyes around the scene, gauging the reactions of the internees. He then sets his sights on the Captain.

"Captain Ironbeard," he announces calmly. "How are our prisoners this morn?"

"Milord, good to see ye," the Captain replies as he steps forward. "These good folks are turnin' out to be a fine crew of hardy citizens, but as ye can probably guess, they're nay at all pleased about the situation they find themselves in."

"Are we speaking of the situation of being held here, or the overall situation of the Suuden-Aryku occupation?"

"Aye, that one… They don' mind being here after what they did outside, and they're willin' to help us, but the thought of their Thane and what he's doin' back home is grindin' on them harshly."

"I can certainly understand that, and I hope we can find our way there in a timely manner to give aid, but our hands are tied at the moment. Very well, let us see what we have to work with and where we can take it."

"Aye, good enough. Here ye go. But be mindful! They carry a swanky accent," he chortles boldly.

"This should be rather interesting," Thaelyn muses privately.

He steps forward and clears his throat, now in need to use the Dwarvish language for the remainder of this discussion.

"My name is Lord Thaelyn. I am the noble sovereign of this world. To my own people, I am addressed as a King, though I understand within dwarven society, your people tend to address such a man with the title of Thane. The world you find yourselves on now is called Tae'Eladar. Once, long ago, people from your world came here during a moment of migration, the same as it was for a few other races we know of who also travelled in this fashion. But history can sometimes become blurred, and some of these people lost their old knowledge, only to find themselves driven to survive in places not as commonly known to them. Recently, we found one such world, known to the local societies as Therinë. They can easily be said to be worse for the wear after a four-century-long war devastated their home. And as it turns out, the cause for this is the same as what brought you here amongst us."

"Aye, so we've been a-hearin'," sounds a voice from the crowd.

"May I know your name, good friend?"

The prisoner steps forward to make his address. He carried a serious demeanor, but he checked himself in the presence of the royal mention.

"Me name be Tol Bronzeheart, Chief Forge Smith in the Thane's service in the grand city of Glimmerheim, though I nay be too happy t' say much about the Thane at this time."

Thaelyn glances over at the Captain briefly for recognition. The Captain returns a subtle nod that this was one of those he had been speaking to at length before.

"I would offer you a pleasant greeting," Thaelyn resumes. "Assuming it might serve us in this situation. And further, I fully sympathize with your feelings. We have had a few of our own falsehoods thrown at us during this time, and many have suffered for it."

"Aye, so I've been a-hearin'. I also hear where these other beasties made us go an' d' a mighty deed of harm t' a full city. Be this the way of it? It sounds a grand bit hard t' swallow, as I was tellin' yer Captain here."

"Indeed, but the weapons they gave you were a very extraordinary sort. We are not as familiar with this design, but you can be sure we are studying it now, as we might find more of this pointed our direction in the future."

"Aye! I nay would want t' be a-standin' in yer boots, if that be the way of it!"

"Absolutely," he grins. "But unfortunately, no one else can fit my boots, so I may not have a choice in it."

The full assembly now erupts in a bold laugh.

"Yer Kingship," Tol continues. "I can accept that we were made saps by our own Thane, as I could see with me own eyes the lads here when we first woke up. An' me head still feels a wee bit thick on the inside, so I can'na doubt these words. I recall tales of how the Thane rages at the poor Chancellor every time he goes in, always callin' for more bricks, more an' faster it be. The man can ne'er get enough. Then t' hear we were found in another mine haulin' up more of the same..." he shakes his head.

"An' that nay be all," another voice ushers up.

The attention is drawn to Whurgan, who steps forward to join Tol.

"Yer Kingship; greets t' ye," he bows modestly. "Me name be Forge Keeper Whurgan Ringforger, an' I've been a-standin' here tryin' t' recall the old tales. There be two feasts put on by the Thane. They go every year, mayhap half a year apart. We were called t' one of those, an' this be where we find ourselves. I nay be a-knowin' what becomes of the other one, 'cept t' say it goes t' another place also said t' be a-makin' up fair for the war."

"Wait now, Whurgan," Balur calls. "I know that one. D' ye recall the old tales from the start of the war? I remember as a wee lad me father tellin' me these tales. It started as a great need t' go out minin' up Adamant for the war, an' there was said t' be another mine t' the south, mayhap t' the east a ways of Glimmerheim."

"So, you are saying there are two of these external mines?" Thaelyn asks. "What is your name, good man?"

"Oi, me pardons," he bows briskly. "Balur Gravelfist, a minin' foreman in Glimmerheim. Aye, two of them outside, an' the one we have 'neath the city proper."

"Does he feed this odd stew to you while you work within the city?"

"Nay t' that, but life nay be so grand down there. With the doors closed, we need t' be careful with all our wares. We see almost no trade with the outside, 'cept for a few small bits the Thane calls for... coal for his braziers an' straw for the herdin' beasts."

"Animals? You keep animals down there?"

"Aye! 'Tis a common thing for us, ye know. Many a city can be found 'neath the mountains, an' we need food, so we bring herdin' beasts, an' also set up farmin' in special gardens. But we also make trade with the families up top. I recall a tale of farmin' folk, herders, weavers, an' many a fine ware could be found up there. Glimmerheim be a right proud city, or at least it used t' be. We had the outer city that did much of the trade, an' the inner city minin' an' smithin' our own wares."

"It sounds like a fine arrangement. Are we speaking perhaps of a capital city?"

"Aye, mayhap this be the right word for it. Our Thane lives there, an' it be the main home of his rule for all our native lands."

"And unfortunately, Darumon chose this particular example to play his tricks. I worry for what condition the rest of it may be in if he has his hands in any of it."

"Oh grand... All-Father protect us if he did anythin' foul t' it."

"Yer Kingship," Tol continues. "About this Darumon, where be all these bricks a-goin', an' why...an' for how long? It pains me t' think of it... D' ye know just how much we admire our Adamant? It be a precious thing t' us, an' this beastie ye tell tale of runnin' about, he be a-tossin' it away like it was no more than slag t' him."

"Good sir Bronzeheart, I think you may be closer than you think with that statement. My understanding is he holds a personal grudge with a collection of ancient enemies, and he hopes to use this to make a very unique type of weapon. But the adamantium, as we call it here, is not his direct interest. It is the magical energies contained within that he wants. And these comprise a relatively small amount of the material, which means most of it is indeed very likely going to waste."

The dwarves all hang their heads and sigh.

"As for how long," Thaelyn continues. "If he took your world as much as four centuries ago, we might have an answer to that, as we are suggesting he might also need skilled labor to extract it, and we all know how good dwarves are at this skill," he smiles gently.

"Aye, ye've got a good point there. We know our Adamant well enough."

"But at the same time, Tol," Whurgan admits. "Mayhap this nay be such a good thing."

"Aye, he came t' us because he saw how good we were with it. May the All-Father curse him for this."

"As for the rest," Thaelyn resumes. "We are working our way to meet with him again, but we must first prepare ourselves. For this, I would wish to make you a kind offer."

"Oh?" Tol perks up. "What sort of offer?"

"I believe my Captain mentioned this before. We can always use a few additional skilled hands, and right now we have a city to rebuild. I can take you there and show you, if you find it so difficult to believe, and then we can make some plans on how we can assist those unfortunate people who are made homeless. Then, when the time comes that we are able to move forward, therefore to find your home, I would return the favor to help you and yours, if we should discover your own city to be suffering any damage, or those on the outside."

"That yay be a right grand offer. No wonder ye're a King in this world, offerin' up such fine deeds as this. Aye, I would like t' see this city ye speak of, just so I can wrap me head 'round what we did t' it. An' we'll set ourselves down t' work up a few ideas on what we can d' t' help."

"Very good. Then we will attend to this on the morrow. This will give you a little more time to rest and recover from your illness. I will return for you then."

Thaelyn smiles graciously and turns to leave, allowing Tol and the others to return to their beds and another dose of their medicine.

Chapter 3

REESTABLISHMENT

A young woman makes her way out of a local wooded glen and down a hill. Before her is a pleasant river cascading through the foothills into the valley below. The river descends from a local region of mountains and over a waterfall into a broad pool. From there, it continues to flow across a plain in a northerly direction, eventually to empty into a local sea. But from her perspective, that was simply too far to be of concern. Her immediate focus was a makeshift bridge crossing the river just after the pool.

She works her way along a type of path, one gently patted into the ground, in part by her own hoof steps, as well as others who have passed through the area. The path led into the wooded hills on this side of the river. It was a place often visited for hunting and gathering ventures by others in her group, though she had her own interests out there. She was returning from gathering the latest crop of herbal ingredients from a collection of small gardens she had been painstakingly tending to over the years. These gardens were carefully hidden away within the woods.

The young Daanen'kai female cautiously makes her way over the rickety bridge. It was intentionally fashioned this way as a means to dissuade the curious from suspecting any form of current habitation in the area. She, along with the others in her group, could not afford to be discovered by those they were hiding from.

They were refugees, and generally living off the land in a very primitive setting. Even their clothes suggested as much, being mostly ragged pieces of old cloth, those that hadn't disintegrated altogether, intermixed with scraps of crude leather and bits of furry hides stitched together to make up Stone-Age style garments that just barely covered their bodies. In her case, where she held a bit more modesty than some, she tried to assemble enough to cover her shoulders and upper chest, and a wrap around the middle.

As she crosses the bridge, she enters a work camp, formerly belonging to an old mining operation once used by her people to harvest ore out of the mountainside. There was a large yard hosting a scattering of structures, including storage sheds, workshops, and refining facilities, most of which now stood dilapidated and rusting. It was just another attempt at keeping the appearance of abandonment. Only one building amongst the set held any real value to her people at this moment. As she approached it, she saw another young woman struggling with one of the machines, grumbling and cursing at the large apparatus for its constant breakdowns.

"Suli!" the girl calls out. "Are you still at it? Have you made any progress getting that beast working again?"

The other girl pulls out from a large machine housing, her bushy black mane of hair only roughly groomed, and her face smudged with dirt. She leaned back on her knees to see her friend arriving, and tried straightening out her fur bikini top and sarong waist wrap.

"Túfu, I hate this thing!" she replies in frustration. "It breaks down almost as soon as I get it fixed and fire it up again. That first century we had it working, it was a blessing to us, but ever since, it's been just as much a curse."

"Miss Sulíma Tad'vaal!" she retorts mockingly as she sets her hands on her hips. "How many times…oh, forget it," she relaxes back. "Maybe you should just give up on it. It's been what… How long have you been fighting with this thing? Ever since you were old enough to open it up and look inside."

"Yeah, at least a century and a half, maybe two by now. I can't even keep track of time anymore. One day just blends into another around here."

"To be honest, I was amazed to see you get it working at all, especially after the reactor went down."

"Yeah, well, engineering wasn't one of my original study topics, not that we had time for it. But it was nice to have, once I figured out how to configure and charge a few super-capacitors..." she chuckles.

"Right, I remember that. You had half of us out here turning old-fashioned cranks around an iron core rotary generator. Thank goodness we were able to scavenge those parts from our old engineering class in the city."

"Yeah, but then we had to fashion that step-up gear system to amplify the magnitude in order to generate any appreciable amount of current. We can't burn anything for fear the orcs will see the smoke, so steam power is out."

"We had that one idea to use the waterfall and try a waterwheel arrangement."

"Yes, and while it's not a bad idea, the problem is it stands out too much. If anyone should happen to walk by..."

"Yeah, I know, they'll see it and get curious."

"So, all we have left is manual labor..." she glares at the machine again and smacks it with her wrench, "...and this thing! It was the only machine we had left that was worth anything to us. We could recycle our old scrap and at least have a few materials to make something on occasion."

"Well, Suli, I can't blame you for being angry, but it was inevitable. Still, we've done well enough, haven't we? I mean, we're alive, we're able to hunt for food, do a little bit of farming..."

"So long as you keep it hidden up there in those hills."

"Well, yes, but the woods do a good job of that for me. And then, I learned how to use some of these herbs to make medicine. It's not great, I know, but...well..."

"Little Miss Túfula, the optimist," Sulíma retorts. "But that's just about ALL we can do, Túfu. One day is just the same as the next.

There's no place for us to go, nothing to do, and, um, you know me. My tail just can't stop twitching."

"Yeah, but your tail has never stopped twitching, as far as I ever knew."

"Well, yes, but I'm actually speaking of ambition here."

"Ambition, sure, but I know boys are involved somewhere along the way," she grins.

"Well, naturally! But they must be useful for something else. You know, during the downtime," she giggles. "Túfu!" she urges more seriously. "Look at me..." she stands up and glances at her particularly scant attire. "And look at you. Look at Tana, for cu'Nar's sake. She's the worst of all. I may swing my tail a lot, but I wouldn't actually mind a nice dress and some jewelry to go along with it. One wrong move in this, and something falls apart."

"Yeah, I know, and hunting for pelts is problematic for all the competition with the local orcish camps, which we need to keep clear of to begin with."

"Right. I had hopes one day to be like my sister and maybe work in a medical lab, or find something else really useful for myself. Even I need a break from chasing boys once in a while to be a part of something important. But look at us. All we can do is hide inside the mine."

"All right, I concede, and I know what you mean. We don't dare go outside except to hunt for food. We can't even be sure to go searching for a better place to live. All we ever seem to do is hide. After all, the orcs are everywhere in this world. It is theirs, after all. We would stand out no matter where we were. And if they should ever catch us, well..."

"Right...I know the speech. I realize it's enough just to be alive at all. But what kind of life is it, when it all comes down to this," she finishes, slapping her palm against the side of the machine.

"Let's take a break for a moment and go inside. I need to bring these herbs down to my lab anyway. You can sit down, cool off, and maybe take in a little conversation to distract yourself from your worries."

"Can I swing my tail a little this time, or will you get on me again for taking up all the possibilities?" she smiles cautiously.

Túfula grins and shakes her head disbelievingly.

"Are you sure you're still a virgin?"

"Yeah, and that's the problem!" she gripes.

The two share a laugh before Sulíma continues.

"You know, Túfu," she sighs wearily. "I'm glad we're friends. Being stuck in this place has been a real burr in the tail. If it wasn't for people like you, I think I would've gone mad a century ago."

The two young women turn and make their way around to the mine entrance, trudging up a ramp and into the tunnel.

The entrance to the mine was carefully concealed behind a row of shrubs planted just in front and tended to regularly to keep them bushy and full. It was yet another attempt to hide their home from prying eyes. They had been fortunate in making their way to this location, and even more fortunate that their enemies did not show any interest in reaching out this far.

The two girls strolled through the tunnel system, past a watch post being attended by another of their group, and further along to find their way into a large gathering chamber. The room was filled with tables and chairs, and often used for dining and casual relaxation. To the right, a tunnel exited the room to find its way to a kitchen area. On the opposite side was another passage leading off to a series of sleeping chambers, and to the rear of the room was one more leading further into the mines where the group had managed to create some simple workshops and storage for whatever scavenged goods they were able to collect outside.

In one corner, off to the side, was an arrangement of desks they were able to relocate from an old office building in the city. It was a remnant of their former home, part of the Sentinels service that once acted as a law enforcement and security agency for the city. Sitting at these were a few surviving Sentinels officers, including the ranking Captain in charge of this detachment.

Sulíma glanced over at him as she and Túfula entered the room. He was sitting quietly and staring at an old portrait he kept on his desk. His manners were such that he often felt depressed, and it was at times like these when Sulíma noticed he was feeling even more disturbed and lonely. The portrait was that of his wife and son.

Sulíma stepped over to see if she could once again try to cheer him up. This was becoming as much a chore for her as it was for Túfula to act as her support.

"Captain," she calls gently. "Don't tell me you're doing this again."

He turns away from the picture frame to gaze longingly at the young girl. Even though he didn't look like it on the outside, she knew he was weeping for their loss.

"Please, Captain," Sulíma begs. "Túfu and I just went through this outside with my own misery."

"I'm sorry, Suli, but there are times when I wonder what they're doing...or if they're even alive."

"You think they got away on the ship, right? If that's the case, then we can hope everything is alright with them."

"Yes, but for how long. You know how it goes with those tail-crazy Suuden'kai forces chasing us."

"Well, I can't say what will happen. You and the others have told me stories of how we keep jumping from one world to the next, but they always find us. This last one was the worst, and the most puzzling, since we did that wild jump thing. So, by all rights, they should NOT know where we were."

"I still say they were tracking us somehow, but no one could find anything like a tracking device or a beacon emitter."

"Who knows," she shrugs. "But I might also suggest, for what it's worth to us now, that they shouldn't have any reason to come back here."

"Not unless they have further dealings with the orcs. I just know they were involved somehow in the attack on the city. There's no way those orcs could've done all that damage by themselves."

"Yeah, this much I may have to admit to. The orcs used this magic stuff to burn everything, but according to your stories, we lost power and communications somewhere along the way, and I can't imagine orcs knowing how to turn that off."

"And I still can't understand how you kids got trapped here. We had the order from the Elder Council to evacuate once we realized the orcs were invading the outer districts and doing so much damage to our power grid and comms network."

"We've already been through this…many times. Blame the administrators for that. I can't be sure which one, because none of those who survived knows anything about it, but someone got the order wrong."

"Suli, listen to these statements carefully and tell me how you can get it wrong: 'Evacuate the city', as compared to 'hide in the shelters'… Can you tell me if there is any way to misinterpret those two?"

She giggles at the obvious flaw in the suggestion.

"No, Captain, I can't, but I was in my classroom at the time, as were the rest of the kids."

"And I think this is the biggest tragedy of all, you were taken down into those shelters while the rest of the city was loading up on the Naarg uy'Sodrad."

"One thing I think I can be sure of," Túfula offers. "My father was probably screaming at someone, to say nothing of whatever else he was doing."

"I'm thinking of my big sister now," Sulíma reflects. "We loved each other so much. I know I lost my parents, both of them, but you didn't find her in the medical lab, so she must've made it to the ship."

"I remember when the Captain and his team were able to find their way back into the city and saw all those bodies, many of them burned, stabbed, broken bones, and such."

"That was a gruesome sight, kids," he relents. "And one of the things that twists my horns more than anything else about the attack. They came in, burned everything they could, killed many of our people, and just left their bodies there to rot. It took months to drag them out into the fields and bury them. I swear, if I had enough of an army, I'd do the same to them."

"Captain," Túfula cautions. "That's not our way, and I think you know it. Even my father would object to that, and we all know he can have a bit of a temper at times."

"Túfu, I think it's precisely because your father is Elder Vankkar, with a temper over so many injustices we've had to suffer, that he would have a few words to say about this. This goes beyond retribution over the brutal treatment of others. Even the orcs hold certain customs, and burial is one of them…that, or cremation on a funeral pyre. One or the other would at least show a little respect, and they did neither."

"All right, I withdraw my argument. You are right in at least this much."

"And Túfu," Sulíma suggests. "I think a number of us, beginning with Tana, at the very least, would disagree with the part of this being…our way. It's our way that got us into this in the first place, by not fighting back…ever!"

"Furthermore," the Captain continues. "I regret being trapped here as well. Even though I had instructions…and those instructions were…well, controversial, to say the least."

"Controversial or not," Túfula admits. "It's good you were available to help the rest of us."

"Yes, this much I'll agree with, but it still hurts, and on multiple levels. Those orcs behaved as crazed animals out there. They were throwing everything they had at the ship, trying to burn it like they did the rest of the city. But in the end…well, I think maybe I should keep my mouth shut for the rest."

"It's alright, Captain, I think we all understand. None of us wants to be here, and yet here we are."

"Well, all right, I'll put it away for now," he sets the picture back down on his desk. "Do we have anything special happening outside today?"

"We've got some nice weather outside," Sulíma bids. "And with some cool breezes for a change. I think the wind turned, and now it's coming in off the ocean, so this tropical heat is a little lighter today."

"That's nice to hear. Of all the places we chose to settle down, it had to be in the middle of a jungle."

"Yeah, well, I guess we didn't have too many options at the time. As I understand it, we were trying to keep to a small corner so as not to take up too much space. This isn't our world, after all, and for all the times we've been evicted by the Suuden-Aryku, we can't feel comfortable anywhere."

"But Suli, we really hoped we had escaped from them this time. What can you possibly expect after a wild jump into a completely new universe? The simple fact that it IS a new universe breaks many of our scientific theories. And then to have them show up stepping on our tails again."

"You're right, but again, like I said, I can't see why they would come back here with the Naarg uy'Sodrad gone. As unfortunate as it may sound, they'll be chasing it to some new world, leaving us stranded here on Ruuki uy'Daan, the place of outcasts, lost societies, and refugees of exile!" she huffs. "But at least, if we're to be forgotten, it's better to be forgotten by THEM rather than anything else."

"Right. But then, I think of all of you kids. You barely even got started in life, and it was taken away from you."

"Captain," Túfula interjects. "Life wasn't taken away from us. I was just trying to convince Suli outside a moment ago that we are, in fact, alive and surviving. It might not be a very luxurious way to survive, but I'll take this over what the orcs might have to offer any day. We have enough food to keep us going..."

"So long as we ration it and try to pace ourselves with the hunting season. You need to remember that, Túfu."

"Well, yes, I remember, as well as the planting season for my gardens out there. But it's working."

"But Túfu, there's something you're missing here, and that is, what happens if any of you want to pair up and try starting families. We need to provide for that, and we're barely providing for what we have now."

Túfula sighs, as she knew this was likely to come up in conversation sometime. She and the others were all adults, still young, but adults that would eventually feel the call of nature pressing on them. And hiding in an old mining complex was no place to start a family.

"Right, Captain, and with nowhere else to go, we're stuck here."

"Yeah," he sighs. "So, what else is happening out there today?

Túfu, did you see anything interesting? You went up the hillside again. That should give you a good vantage."

"Actually, yes," Túfula responds a little more enthusiastically. "I saw some colorful birds in the trees today. They seemed to be enjoying the springtime weather, but not much else up in the hills this time."

"You always did like watching those birds," he smiles. "Suli, how goes your work on that processor out there? Were you able to make it work again?"

"It's the same story as always," she relents. "I fix one thing, and another one breaks. I don't have the right tools to do the job, and even if I did, I'm not even sure if I know how to do the job right. I've fought with it long enough to learn a few things, but it just keeps fighting back trying to show me I don't know enough."

The Captain lets out a gentle laugh at the girl's predicament.

"It was only a matter of time, Suli," he offers solemnly. "Without the proper industry to provide us with the right replacement parts, it was just a matter of time. It's rusting away, like everything else around here. Like we will one day, I'm sure."

"Captain!" she snaps painfully.

"Yes, Suli… We just finished with this. You don't need to yell at me. But I'm something of a pragmatist, and our situation doesn't leave much flexibility. That machine provided us with some good work while we had it up. But the components needed to fix it were becoming more intricate as the wear built up. I'm not at all surprised it's finally given up on us. Other than the fact that it requires such a large input of energy, like that of a fusion reactor, to power it in the first place, I think the only way to fix that pile of junk would be a complete overhaul of the nano-disassembler array."

"Yeah, and the tools for fixing it don't exist around here, and I really don't know how to fashion alternatives. We're talking about micro-engineering and nanotech assembly. You can't do that with a hammer, a pair of tongs, and a handful of cooking grease."

"Then give it a break for now. We'll just have to think of some other way to recycle some of that scrap out there."

"But how, Captain? None of us knows anything about turning old scrap into new materials. That's what we had the machines for."

"Perhaps, Suli, but there was a time when people used to work this problem by hand. It's just that we haven't seen times like those for so long, none of us remembers how to do it. It may finally be time for us to learn. But this brings to mind our other little problem," he finishes with a glance back out the tunnel.

"The orcs…"

"Right, if we should attempt any kind of serious work outside that raises smoke or dust, it could draw attention. And in our condition, we really don't have the proper means to stage a fight with them. Our pulse weapons died centuries ago when the power cells drained, and the recharging units also failed after a while from the continued wear, like everything else around here. We've been stepping lower and lower back along our technological tree for virtually this entire three and a half centuries since the attack. I wouldn't be too surprised to find myself one day wearing the same animal skins and wielding the same pointed sticks those orcs use out there."

"Um…" Sulíma coughs emphatically as she waves at her own apparel, then to glance at Túfula standing next to her. "And should I also mention Tana, who not only wears just barely enough to cover the important parts, but she actually does carry a wooden spear."

"At least she learned how to weave a grass skirt," Túfula notes.

"Yeah, but we were children when this all happened, and now look at us. All our original clothes wore out centuries ago."

"That's right," the Captain nods. "And we can't simply send you on a shopping spree since the orcs essentially burned all the clothing stores, along with the rest of it."

"I have to admit, however…" Túfula considers. "A few of us…" she glares at Sulíma, "…actually seem to like running around half naked."

"Hey, I resemble…er, resent…no, resemble that remark," she jokes.

The three of them find a small moment of inspiration to share a laugh together.

"All right," he suggests. "Let's talk about something else for a while. I should think the hunters will be returning soon. I hope they found something decent today. It's been a while since we had any good meat, and the dried stuff we've been keeping down below is showing its age."

"Captain," Túfula mentions. "While I was out, I noticed some of the berry plants were starting to bloom. I think we'll be able to enjoy some fresh fruit soon. That'll be nice. I don't mind the occasional small cup of preserves, but the fresh harvests always seem to perk me up."

"My favorites are the hazel-berries," Sulíma recalls. "They won't be out until summertime, but you can bet I'll be the first one out there to pick a few!"

"Yeah, I remember that one time, Suli," echoes a voice from behind the girl.

A young man walks out from the tunnel leading to the sleep chambers. He had just woken up from a brief nap and overheard part of the conversation.

"Petrith, are you awake finally?" she calls to him.

"Just taking a short rest after my patrol. Not much to speak of in the city today. I didn't see any orcs moving through the streets, and as far as I could tell, the mutants are quiet."

"Again? Petrith, is it just my imagination, or is there something happening here?"

"What do you mean? Not seeing anything is better described as something NOT happening," he chuckles.

"Yes, well…" she shrugs. "But aside from the mutants, which may not be quite as much of a problem as the orcs…"

"Suli," the Captain interjects. "You do recall the stories I told you of how they attacked our people alongside the orcs, right?"

"Yes, Captain, but it doesn't help to think they may be someone's mother or father when you see them. I know we keep away because of what they did during the attack, and we don't want them to know about us any more than we want the orcs to find us. But let's be practical for a moment. They never go outside except to forage for food, and never travel beyond the city limits. So, I think the orcs represent a more pressing issue than the mutants, so long as we keep out of the city, or at least away from wherever they hide themselves."

"Granted."

"But anyway, Petrith has often come home with one or another report of seeing orcs wandering through the streets, at least once in a while, if not every day. Why they come into the city, I don't know. But why are they NOT coming through anymore? How long has it been, Petrith, since the last time you saw one?"

"Um…" he pauses to think. "Well, actually, I have to admit, I wasn't really counting the days, but it seemed to be slowing down during these last couple of months, and now nothing."

"Captain, maybe I'm just looking for an excuse to get some excitement around here, but I think we should look into this, if only to understand this change in behavior."

"You know," he nods. "You may be right. At least when we saw them in the city, we knew where they were. But if they're not going into the city anymore, we need to know where they ARE going, if not around our backs and up the other side."

"Cu'Nar's grace, Captain…" Túfula moans. "Do you think they may have figured something out about us finally?"

"I think if they did, we would know about it, as they would be on top of us by now. But it would do us well to find out. We should send out a few scouting parties to see where they're going, if not into the city. There's that river canyon on the other end of these hills down there. If they're going through there, they could circle around these mountains and up the valley to the west. And that's our blind spot. It also represents open space for new occupation in case they want to spread out."

"Maybe it's nothing serious," she suggests. "For instance, maybe they simply got tired of rummaging through all those ruins. There's not really anything left for them there, it's been pillaged and ransacked so many times, and not just by them. I know many of us have gone in there searching for any odd relics we can scavenge. And over the years and centuries, the overgrowth and decay has wrecked whatever didn't collapse during the initial attack."

"All those burned-out buildings," Sulíma reminisces. "Everything collapsed into a series of heaps. I know I can just barely find anything whenever I go hunting for new tools and such. And at least I know what I'm looking for."

"The fun part was watching that skyscraper fall over," Túfula chuckles. "It fell right on top of the Social Relations building, which is where most of our interaction with the orcs took place within our civic structure."

"All right," Sulíma concludes. "So, we go see where the orcs are moving off to. If they're simply ignoring the city because it's no longer interesting, that's fine, I guess. But if they're going around these mountains, maybe in the direction of this valley over here…"

"But why around the mountains…the long way? Going through the city would be much simpler."

"Yes, it would. And we never actually saw them come this far out. Nevertheless, this space out here is vacant land, so why aren't they setting up a new camp?"

"If they did," Petrith admits. "That would be bad. That puts us in the middle, and that side is also our hunting ground, so it would effectively cut off our food supply. We may find ourselves in a fight before long."

"Dear cu'Nar, and that's really bad. All right, so it's not just me trying to find a little excitement, we need to know what they're doing. They never came out here before, and now they're not even going through the city like they were. Something is up."

◆◆◆◆◆

"So, this is where these peeps eat their lunch, ay?" Relissa smirks as she picks up a tray in the guildhall cafeteria.

It was lunchtime, and Relissa, along with Marelle and Haran, had finished their morning classes. This was their first time inside the cafeteria, now being full students. Before this, they were taking their language classes, and then travelling off to Firstfall for their review of the war. Haran, for his part, instead took his meal elsewhere before serving his apprenticeship with one of the master scholars.

They received their plates of food for the midday meal and set out to find a suitable table where they could sit together. They spied an opening near a strangely familiar student wearing an appropriately large training uniform to suit her tall, blue-skinned form. They step over and sit down next to her.

"Hey there!" Kaliya rings out as she sees her long-time friends slide in on the benched seating. "Nice outfits. Are you now officially enrolled?"

"You bet we are," Relissa replies cheerfully. "Our first day in school, and I never thought I'd feel this good about sitting in a stuffy old classroom listening to a bunch of old crones jabbering like there's no tomorrow."

"Some of them aren't crones," Marelle grins.

"And many of them aren't really that old," Haran adds.

"Nitpickers…" Relissa retorts. "Fine. And I suppose you'll next say the classrooms aren't that stuffy, right?" she snickers.

"I remember our old school on Ruuki uy'Daan," Kaliya recalls. "It wasn't really all that bad, but I have to admit, this place is a lot different, on many levels. What sort of lessons are they giving you?"

"We got our first taste of arcane studies and some history this morning," Relissa reflects.

"I would actually say the mage studies were interesting," Haran states. "But since I've already learned so much from my old academy, it's mostly just rehashing a lot of terms in a different language for me so far. I actually can't wait to get into the higher-level courses to match my previous studies so I can start making some new progress."

"Yeah, yeah, Haran," Marelle concedes. "We all know you, but let's try to stay the course. We all have some previous experience and need to catch up to our level, but there's a ready-made program to follow, too."

"I'm perfectly willing to follow the course. I'm just excited."

"What about you, Kaliya," Relissa asks. "How are your lessons going?"

"I was able to pass several of them already, due to my old education. They created some special testing for me to fill in some of my prerequisites. Now, it's mostly to fill in things necessary as a new citizen of this world. Things like history and culture, whatever might be specific to this world, that they include as a requirement for future lessons. I've been trying to put in some overtime on occasion to hurry it through, since Thaelyn wants me in the full swing of actual training as soon as possible."

"Sounds like he has you working harder than most," Marelle suggests.

"Yeah, and I'm trying my best. It's hard work, and I get tired quickly, but I found some help with the priests over at the temple. Apparently, one of the things they can do for me, and I'm guessing because I'm a special case here, is to provide me with occasional revitalizing treatments to keep me going during the day. This has really helped a lot to give me the extra push I need to get everything done."

"They don't do this for anyone else?"

"I don't think anyone else has the schedule I have, or the workload. Plus, most of them are probably accustomed to this sort of scheduling to begin with."

"Ouch, then I feel for you, Kaliya. I really do."

"I suppose it's not as bad as it sounds…vigorous, yes. We need to take it in context. From what I see and hear, for people like you, this might be normal. But for me and mine, it's like crunching a century of study into a year, especially if you factor in that elixir. Yikes! My horns were spinning so fast, I thought I might take off into orbit!" she chuckles. "You need to remember, our schools stretch things out, if only due to us taking so long to grow up. So it's like, learn a lesson, wait, learn a lesson, wait…"

"Oh dear. That sounds bad…for you, at least," she giggles.

"In those first weeks, I was sore from horn to hoof, simply because I wasn't used to this level of activity. But then I got into the rhythm of it. It reminded me of my old athletic training back home. Of course, I was much younger then, but still…"

"Oh? What did you do there?"

"Well…" Kaliya pauses as she recalls her old school accolades. She starts to blush slightly.

"All right, girl," Relissa teases. "I see that color in your cheeks. I know you well enough to know it's no fever. What are you hiding?"

"I was a star athlete in our school track and gymnastics competitions. I even won several awards."

"'Ere now, what's this? You never told me that before!"

"It never came up, to be honest. I hid so much of my youth, even from myself. But yeah, I won some high honors for my floor dance routine, as well as I set a couple of speed records on the track."

"I don't know about the other Daanen'kai kids," Marelle comments. "But looking at those legs of yours, I wouldn't be surprised at that."

"Actually, when we're young, we're all fast runners, especially the girls."

"No doubt to keep away from the boys," Haran smirks.

Marelle nudges him in the ribs as Kaliya continues.

"The young boys tend to be rather quick, but it seems to be short-lived as they get older and more mature. They develop bulkier bodies which aren't as nimble as they once were. They're strong and sturdy, but not nearly as fast, while the women are much more agile."

"That's actually rather interesting," Haran muses. "To see how a race endures such diverse physical development between the genders as they mature. Humans tend to be a little more homogenous in this regard, I think. Relissa, how do the elves compare?"

"We're all quick and nimble, and none of us ever really gets bulky like she says. I've seen her brother…you know, Kailen. Have you ever seen him? Or Lieutenant Lapäli, there's a good one. Compare that with her."

"Yes, indeed."

"It's called dimorphism," Kaliya offers. "And in our case, between the genders, it really stands out."

"So, how do you feel these days?" Marelle asks. "Do you think you could ever set any of those records again?"

"I doubt it. I'm seriously out-of-practice. I spent a lot of time out on the field in our old school training myself. I could probably set a few outstanding records here in this world in comparison to the local people, as I'm sure I could outrun any of you, but I think that's not really the point. I'm just happy to find myself rediscovering my old talents."

"Speaking of old talents," Relissa remarks. "Anything new on this bleedin' head-hopping you were doing before?"

"We haven't tried any formal training yet, but Thaelyn says he knows of an old friend up in Sigil who might be able to help."

"Ay! That place? Criminy, girl, you better watch yourself. I hear those people don't mess around neatly. Half of them are half of something mixed with half of something twice the size."

"Yeah, I've heard a few stories from the other students, upper classmen mostly, and some of the scholars who were helping me to understand what I might be getting into. But it actually makes sense to have someone from up there teach me, as Thaelyn says this gift shouldn't ever occur in mortal beings. Certainly not to the extent of what I have. So, where else do you think you'll find someone who knows anything about it?"

"Jiggers... And that tells you something."

"A small part of me is curious about that city," Marelle considers. "Relissa, do you remember when Thaelyn brought us to that place of his? You know; when he was interrogating those Flame Elves."

"Aye! A bit hard to forget, that one."

"Thinking of this city called Sigil has me wondering what it's all about. Of course, I remember my reaction just to find myself in the Outer Planes when he was taking us to that place. I'm not so sure about going to a city where you might meet who-knows-what kinds of people, and I use the term loosely."

"Right, but Thaelyn grew up in that place, at least partly. It's where he met that girlfriend of his...if you remember the tale he told."

"A girlfriend?" Kaliya muses.

"Aye, when we were waiting for that one Flame Elf to wake up after being touched by the dryad, he told us a little story about his time up there. It seems our dear and noble Lord spent time in a brothel," she giggles.

"You're kidding me!" she shouts.

"Nope, but it wasn't your normal type of brothel, so he says. It's some kind of place where students of a local guild go to work for the public. He says Sigil has several types of guilds, and each one has a different philosophy of life, and I guess death, and how you're supposed to play it out to meet your maker. His girlfriend used to work in this place, at least till she got too old for it and finally passed on."

"So, she was a mortal? That doesn't sound like a very happy story, especially considering Thaelyn is immortal. I have to wonder how many people he's outlived in his years so far. And this actually reflects back on me and my people too, where all of you come in."

"That's right," Marelle admits. "You'll probably outlive all of us, our children, grandchildren, and many more generations after that, all things permitting. I surely can't envy you for that, especially for all the friends you'll make, and then lose along the way."

"This thought has crossed my mind many times, and I've already outlived many of your kind, which really doesn't help. My understanding is that the elves also have this to some extent, with lifespans lasting several times longer than you humans, so we each have our problems, it seems."

"Aye, so we do," Relissa relents.

"Whatever happened to this girlfriend?" Kaliya asks. "Did they actually do anything? Or is this something better left behind closed doors?" she grins.

"According to his story, they couldn't. He was on this contract of his, and obligated to remain chaste."

"Ouch," Haran moans. "That sounds painful, especially if you're a young person in love."

"Aye, but then she did something wacky. He didn't tell us what, and this reminds me… One of these days we need to check the library for the answer."

"What do you mean?" Kaliya inquires.

"You know how he is… He leads you on, and then makes you figure out the rest with your own bit of research. Ours apparently needs to go through the library over here."

"Oh, he did that to you?" she chuckles. "Well, good luck with it. I doubt I'll have time to help, but if you learn anything, let me know."

✦✦✦

"I can'na believe what happened here!" Tol exclaims as he and the other dwarves finish up their tour of the ruins of Rolsklinde. "This place looks like a wreckin' crew stormed through with many a barrel of powder blastin' everything away. An' ye say it was all from some sort of weapon we were a-carryin'?"

"Indeed it was," Thaelyn affirms. "Our own people, as well as many of the local citizens, saw you use this on their homes. We chose not to engage you here, as we considered it might be too dangerous. Instead, we waited to see what you would do after your current task was finished. As it turns out, it would seem Darumon only gave you this much, as he set his own trap with a device under his house capable of a very powerful explosion, enough to finish you and anything else that might still be standing. He was essentially throwing you away, along with everything else, as he was leaving this world."

"Now THAT burns me boiler!" he hollers. "He steals us away from our families, poisons us with his foul 'shrooms, gives us these blastin' cannons, an' tells us t' wipe away a city, then tosses us away like so much rubbish. Argh! All this wickedness for a demon that uses us for our Adamant," he growls. "The All-Father will surely show his ire for this one, t' see His children used for somethin' so vile. 'Tis an outrage! I don'na want this on me hands! But someone has gone an' put it there just the same…an' worse, without me knowin' about it!"

Tol's voice roars in the street as his obvious rage intensifies. His breathing quickens and his blood boils as he stomps in circles around the mounds of debris left behind from several nearby buildings. His characteristically short dwarven temper was settling in after their tour of the mines and now the city, and the realization of his part of it.

"When I find me way back home again, I'll rip that man apart, I will!" he roars. "I'll drag his wretched backside out on t' the barrens an'…an'…"

Suddenly, Tol begins gasping for breath. His face turns pale, and he seems unable to catch himself. The attention of the other dwarves turns to his inexplicable drop in temperament, and they rush to his side.

"Tol!" Balur screeches. "What be the matter with ye?"

Thaelyn quickly steps over and kneels next to the stricken dwarf, who is now dropping to his knees. His breath seems ragged, and he appears faint.

"Tol, you need to calm yourself," he commands. "Can you speak? How do you feel?"

"Me breath…can'na…catch up," he wheezes. "Feelin'…like…"

Tol collapses into Thaelyn's arms as the nobleman helps lay him on the ground.

"We need to return to the settlement immediately," Thaelyn urges. "Balur, Whurgan, you go first. I will send Tol through as he is. Wait for him on the other side and pull him away from the portal exit to allow room for me to pass. We have priests and others there who can see to his condition."

Thaelyn pulls out a rune and casts an enchantment on it. Balur and Whurgan both touch the rune, as they have learned to do earlier in the day while on their tour, and each vanishes in a ball of light. Thaelyn then turns the rune over and touches it to Tol, sending him away to be collected in the settlement. He then dismisses the energies for the secondary transport and re-casts for a first-person exit.

They arrive in Firstfall, with Balur and Whurgan hovering over their unfortunate friend. Thaelyn arrives a moment later and immediately sends a telepathic command to the druids near the tree, as they were the closest. He sends another one to Aerlie, who was once again stationing herself near the Daanen-Aryku medical professionals, and she brought Med-tech Tad'vaal with her.

"Hold on, brother," Balur pleads. "Help be a-comin'."

"Priestess Rumoren," Thaelyn calls out to the druidic high priestess. "This man is showing signs of hypertension, or perhaps hyperventilation. He appears faint, and is complaining of being unable to catch his breath. It began as an emotional reaction to the carnage in the city. Check his heart and lungs. Also, see if you can calm his nerves."

"Right away, my Lord."

Others join the group as the scene draws the attention of the camp. Along the way, Whurgan takes notice of the curious appearance of the druids.

"Ehm, Yer Kingship, I can'na help but t' see this young lass t' be a-wearin' her clothes a wee bit thin. Is this normal?"

"She is a wood elf, and also a druid, and they have their own style of dress code, so you will just have to excuse her for it."

"Oh, I nay be a-complainin'. She be a fine young lass, pert and healthy, if ye know me meanin'."

"I believe she also speaks Dwarvish," he grins subtly. "So she can understand every word you are saying."

"Oh grand…" he relents sheepishly. "Ehm, I be sorry, lass, I did'na mean anythin' improper."

"It is quite alright," she responds with a smile. "I will actually take that as a compliment, especially from a dwarf, as you tend to favor certain qualities, and we elves don't usually fit that style."

Another moment passes and Aerlie rushes in with the Med-tech.

"Oi!" Whurgan groans. "Look at that one now."

"Which one, brother," Balur offers. "There be two of them rightly odd."

"This one with the wings is another clan of elf," Thaelyn informs. "In her case, they are rather special due to their wings. She is also my wife," he smiles gently. "Her name is Lady Aerlie."

"Oh dear," Whurgan cowers. "I nay be a-makin' right with me manners. Sorry Yer Queenship…ehm, be that the right way of it?"

"Not to worry," she responds politely. "Lots of people react to me that way. Mine is a rather unusual breed, as Thaelyn said."

"Whurgan," Balur whispers. "I think ye should keep yer mouth shut for this next one. She has horns like a briar sheep, an' a good four times as tall."

"Aye."

"Actually," Aerlie grins. "I doubt she knows your language, so you can talk about her all you want."

"Oh, so ye're givin' me permission for it, are ye?" Whurgan smiles softly and shakes his head.

"Thaelyn," she asks. "What happened here?"

Thaelyn flashes a telepathic record of the events up in the city since it was far more efficient for him to use this method than to speak it aloud. Both Whurgan and Balur watched, expecting him to actually speak, but when no words came out, and Aerlie seemed to nod in affirmation of the message, they couldn't help but to wonder what just happened.

"Ehm, a question, if I may," Whurgan begs. "She asked ye what happened, an' all ye did was look her in the eye. How does that help?"

"Aerlie and I are two rather special examples in this world. We both share a series of talents which are rather uncommon to find amongst such people as you will see here. One of these is the ability to communicate telepathically. Do you know what telepathy is in your world?"

"Nay t' that, Yer Kingship…"

"It is the ability to share our thoughts, and this is actually a very efficient method for us."

"Whoa now, that be a fine one."

"Your Lordship," Med-tech Tad'vaal announces. "What actually happened here? I'm not seeing any serious injury or other critical medical conditions in this man."

"We were in the city on our little tour when he had a classic dwarven rage reaction to what he saw. He began gasping for air and appeared faint. I am concerned whether this could be part of his illness from those mushrooms, or perhaps his heart and lungs may simply be weak."

Med-tech Tad'vaal runs a medical scanner over the man's head and chest to check for physical defects. She examines the results on the display.

"His heart rate is elevated, this much is sure, though your priests here seem to be bringing it back under control by now. I sure wish I understood how you could do this without drugs," she chuckles. "But anyway, the rhythm is strong. His respiration seems strained, however. One moment…"

She recalibrates and runs another scan over him. At the same time, she instructs one of her interns to prepare a mild sedative. She looks at her results once more on the display.

"This is strange. I'm showing a mild form of hypoxia."

"Hypoxia!" Aerlie retorts as she makes an exam of his lungs.

"Yeah, it seems his oxygen intake isn't meeting up to demand. His heightened nervous state is using it up faster than he can take it in."

"This is unexpected," Thaelyn wonders. "Can this be a condition possibly relating to the toxic effects of those mushrooms?"

"No, this is between his lungs and his other tissues. We need to settle his heart rate some more. It's too fast, and his body isn't picking up enough oxygen from it."

"Interesting. What could be the cause, then?"

"I'm not showing anything physically wrong with him. The symptoms seem more like what you'd find of a person suffering from oxygen deprivation at high altitude."

"Indeed! How curious…" Thaelyn muses, turning to the other dwarves. "Balur, Whurgan, how do the two of you feel at this moment? This is to say your ability to breathe effectively."

"What?" Balur retorts. "What d' ye mean, t' breathe proper?"

"The medical technician here believes Tol is simply suffering from a condition of being unable to breathe easily due to the air here being too thin for him, though I am at a loss to understand the meaning as none of us have this difficulty. What about you?"

"Well, now that ye mention it, me breathin' seems a wee bit thin.

I don'na know if it be from me worry over me kin brother, or if it be some other cause."

"I think it be the same with me," Whurgan offers. "More so now than before. When ye first brought us here, it was fine, but now a-seein' poor Tol like this, makes me feel almost as weak as he looks lyin' here."

"Then you should both try to calm your nerves. It may help your breathing. Tol, can you hear me?"

"Aye, good King, an' I hear ye talkin'. This blue-skinned lass did somethin' on me neck an' I be a-feelin' a wee bit more relaxed by now. I be a-catchin' me breath better, too."

"But what can it mean?" Balur asks. "I did'na feel this way in the morn, nor while walkin' through the mine, only just now when Tol fell before us."

"Gentlemen," Aerlie explains. "This would represent a condition most often seen if you were standing on top of an especially tall mountain, where the air is rather thin. The air around us has certain critical components we need, including one we call oxygen. If your body is using it too quickly for your lungs to draw it in, you may feel faint. This can occur if your heart is pumping too quickly, or if there simply isn't enough to satisfy you to begin with."

"Really now! That be a fine one."

"The curious part of this is we are standing on low ground here… well, within reason…so trying to understand why it is occurring at all is a strange one. But to compensate, I would suggest you try to maintain calm and keep your heart and body in a relaxed state as best you can, at least until we can find the cause, or maybe until you can adjust."

"Aye t' that!"

They wait several minutes longer until the medicines take their full effect to return Tol's heart to normal. Color returns to his face, and after a while he is able to sit up.

Balur relaxes back, feeling calmer that the crisis is over. He takes note of all the people who came to their side offering help, as well as so many others rushing across the settlement as they move materials from one location to another.

"Well now, if ever we had a question of where all yer people be, I think we know the answer t' that by now. Good King, what be this place?" he asks.

"This is the village of Firstfall. It was in this place where I established our first garrison camp after we arrived in this world fighting our war with the orcs who invaded our home. We pursued them back to this place and continued pressing forward from here."

"This be what ye call a garrison camp?"

"Admittedly, it has grown somewhat since then, as our interactions with the local races grew. We have expanded it into something better resembling a village by now."

"Aye, it would seem that. An' a busy little place it be."

"It is currently so busy because of all those people you might notice sitting about in the fields just over there."

Thaelyn directs their view to the mass of refugees huddled together outside the northern gate of the settlement. There were rows of tents arranged around campfires, a makeshift kitchen center, and a small army of caregivers moving throughout the area.

"Are those the poor souls left behind after the rendin' of that city?" Whurgan asks.

"They are. When Tol feels himself sturdy enough to walk again, I will bring you over for a closer look."

"I think I can manage that by now," Tol groans as he pulls himself upright.

They begin walking slowly towards the north gate, keeping a gentle pace for Tol's benefit until he felt sturdier. As they proceeded forward, Whurgan couldn't help but to speak up again about the strange sights.

"Ehm, ye know, Yer Queenship, since ye went an' gave me such privilege t' ask…who, an' for that matter, what be that tall lass with the horns?"

"Her name is Med-tech Ankhia Tad'vaal," Aerlie advises. "And she is a medical expert. Her people call themselves Daanen-Aryku, and we found them here along with the rest. They are also refugees, of a sort, from a world called Azgarén. You have been told of Marshal Darumon; I suppose. It was their world he invaded, and these people tried to escape, but he has pursued them all the way to this world, hunting and murdering them across many worlds along the way."

"Great All-Father, be that the way of it? Oi! But then, the rest of their kinfolk be the ones ye say came down behind us?"

"Yes, unfortunately, he now uses them to serve his needs. And this is just one more obstacle for us to overcome."

The group arrives just before the gate. The dwarves roll their eyes around the field at the large number of refugees, awestruck at the sheer volume of homeless people.

Up on the platform, they noticed a young lady giving an announcement. As she began to speak, the unnatural amplitude of her voice shook them.

"By the Almighty, that lass has a set of lungs on her!" Whurgan exclaims.

"Those are not actually her lungs you hear," Aerlie grins. "The Daanen-Aryku are a very advanced society with many scientific and technological achievements to their credit. They donated some equipment that allows her to speak to the masses out here without the need to stress her lungs by shouting."

"It seems ye have a great many valued followers," Balur suggests. "I see here those of different sizes an' colors, an' each of them comes with barely a whisper from yer lips."

"Some might say this is the mark of a good leader," Thaelyn admits. "Though, I will leave that for others to judge. I live by the teachings of my Father, and I share this with all who would follow me, as if they were my own children."

"That be a grand way t' live, Yer Kingship," Tol affirms. "We dwarves admire our fathers greatly. T' see it the same in yer people warms me heart."

"But now, as you can see, we have much work ahead of us. The city needs to be rebuilt. I already have several plans in the making for that, and we wish to bring these people back into their homes before the seasonal change causes too much hardship for them."

"Aye t' that. Just show us where ye need our help, an' I'll whip up the lads t' make a good service for ye."

Chapter 4

INTREPID EXPANSION

A week has passed, and a new week was beginning. Many refugees were still huddled in their clusters outside the north gate of Firstfall, but the situation had become more routine as their basic needs were mostly satisfied. The city of Kynesoth had been resettled by the High Elves, and with the aid of a temporary gateway node, there was a slow migration of humans moving their temporary occupation to within the city walls for better protection and support. And yet, today there was a large gathering outside the north gate of the settlement as Tristeen was wrapping up her political campaign.

Thaelyn was just arriving from Tae'Eladar for his morning review in the tactical office. He couldn't help but notice a larger-than-usual level of activity moving around the settlement, as people made liberal use of the local amenities in the village square.

"General, in all my years of developing Tae'Eladar, it would seem we have created, in only a small fraction of time, a considerable volume of trade and commerce occurring just outside here in this one small area."

"Indeed, my Lord! I noticed that as well. Not only do we have the locals making good use of the shops and cafés, but we also have a fair number of visitors from back home passing through the area."

"We may need to expand the boundaries somewhat to accommodate the flow. But I hesitate to make this move without first becoming more aware of how our political interaction will proceed."

"Well, I think I could possibly answer that, at least in concept. Young Miss Macaid out there is preparing something for a later presentation, and she feels rather confident of her progress. She bade me not to reveal the details of it, as she still needed to make the final review of her work, but she feels she should have something ready later today."

"It would be a fine achievement, if she is hoping to bring together what I suspect she has in mind. I see both humans and High Elves out there. Managing one by itself is a task, but both..." he rolls his eyes as he takes his seat. "In the meantime, do we have anything of notable import on the war today?"

"Largely, it is business as usual. The garrison outpost has settled nicely around that second orcish portal, and they are keeping it secure for us. So far, they report the flow to be sporadic, however. I was comparing this to what I am describing as Portal One for now, and that one has been producing supplies and occasional reinforcements at regular intervals."

"Interesting. Perhaps they have a larger camp on their side in that case. And the other one, Portal Two, I suppose, may be a smaller camp with fewer resources on that side."

"These are my thoughts as well. I was collecting some details on what we can see through the portal aperture. Portal One gives the appearance of a jungle environment, and we can see a fair amount of activity through the window. Portal Two, however, gives the appearance of the camp backing up to a hillside in a grassy valley bordered by other hills."

"How interesting, a small peek into Ruuki uy'Daan, if only through a window made by a portal. What about the population?"

"They can see what appears to be a relatively small camp, one that is not as heavily populated as compared to the first. So, I think the idea of a lower population would explain the infrequent manner of incursions."

"We should keep this in mind for when we arrive, so we know what to look for. This still makes me wonder if there are any other portals lurking about. Two would account for a fair portion of what we see out there, but three would fit my expectations better, especially as we continue to move further south."

"Only time will tell, but I think that time will not be long. As our troops move further along, pushing deeper into their territory, we continue to see a diminishing number of camps with smaller populations."

"Then are we to assume our previous suggestion to be correct? Let us consider the possibilities. When we made our push across Sein'amar, we saw these same diminishing numbers after a while, and we had originally thought this to be due to them spending their best up front. But we later began to realize, with the inclusion of this portal magic, that they were instead escaping from us. Are we seeing more of the same here, or simply that they did, in fact, send their best to the front, and these are the support crews on the rearward lines?"

"I suppose we could easily find our answer by sending some long-range gryphon scouts into the region to investigate just how far south they extend."

"Good, do so. Let us at least discover how much more we have to face. And have them pay attention to any form of migration of troops to-and-fro; in case they are attempting to escape from us. And if any of those other camps contain portals leading away, it would be prudent for us to capture them to prevent any surprises."

"Very good, my Lord, I'll see to it immediately. And if they do not, in fact, extend so far to the south, might I also suggest a new tactic for us?"

"And that is?"

"Perhaps we could force a rapid advance of the line on the eastern side of our bowl formation, cutting them off on this side. We could then sweep around under them, across the south, thus allowing us to close in around them on all sides with nowhere else but the western shoreline open to them. And we both know they are not good swimmers. This could possibly cut our war effort nearly in half if we move in from two directions."

"And allow our people to find rest sooner than expected," he nods. "A fine idea, General. Let us see about this as a way to solve this front quickly."

As the conversation neared its close, Lieutenant Lapäli arrived in the room after making a visit to the joint military research base being operated by Thaelyn's gnomish scientists and a selection of Daanen'kai engineers and technicians. With Darumon out of the way, his role in this campaign was starting to evolve, from an intermediary with the Daanen-Aryku High Commander, to coordinating their combined research projects at the Bahlaie Research Center on Tae'Eladar. All their efforts had to take on a new forward momentum.

"Lieutenant, good to see you," Thaelyn offers as the tall Daanen'kai officer makes his entrance. "Have we made any progress on that disk?"

"Yes, Your Lordship. My mother is leading the project now, along with your Professor Cogswoggle. They pulled out a number of interesting elements from that holo-disk Kaliya brought back, and we're currently assembling several research teams to begin redeveloping some of these old technologies. We're also introducing a series of industrial plans that we often use when settling in a new world to establish our local industry quickly. We're hoping to adapt some of these to this new cause."

"Excellent. And this will give us a nice little jump start into production."

"The only stumbling point we can see at this time would be to procure the necessary resources to begin the early stages of production once we have the facilities up and running."

"We already have some industries that can provide for you, although I must admit, some of the materials you may require are likely still outside our current capacity. Therefore, we shall build whatever is necessary, and work on this solution as a cooperative effort. Since this is a form of technology you are better suited for, perhaps we could build some of this close to your home, giving your people some proper occupation again."

"That certainly sounds reasonable, but as we proceed forward on this, some of us are beginning to wonder if we will be able to fully manage all these new projects."

"Why is that, Lieutenant?"

"Population. At last count, our people numbered just under nine thousand. Between the research projects, this new industry, and everything else we need to do in order to keep our society running, we may find ourselves with a deficit of workers."

"Then let us approach it this way. How many of your people have the academic qualifications to serve in these industries?"

"I don't actually have those numbers, but I'm sure we can take surveys to find out."

"Good, then relay this to your Commander and the Elder Council. We should identify the capacity of your workforce to know how many we can employ in these new industries. We should try to make the best use of what we have, at least in the initial stages until we can train more. As to the more fundamental needs, we can provide many things to you, such as food, drink, recreation, basic resources, and supplies. If your people would care to integrate themselves with ours on a more familiar basis, perhaps we could solve this issue in a fair and equitable manner; therefore, allowing you to direct yourselves to the more imperative needs."

"That sounds like a fine idea. I'll send the word along. I know there has been a lot of talk recently among many of our people since the close of this war. Some of them have expressed a significant interest in your society and the offers you've presented in the past. And they're also becoming motivated to learn more about these arcane studies, as this has been a mystery to us since we arrived on Ruuki uy'Daan and observed the orcs using this thing they called magic. The orcs were never able to teach us anything, not that they really tried that much, and our science could never understand ways to identify it. But since that time you showed Kaliya how to use it, more of us are opening our eyes to the possibility that we might finally learn how it works."

"This is a marvelous suggestion, Lieutenant, especially as our combined technological developments will include certain aspects of this. We should entice your people to become familiar with this as we proceed forward to finish this war."

"I wouldn't mind taking a course or two, myself, if my schedule should ever permit me enough time."

"At present, it would seem we may have enough to play with, so let us make good use of it. Considering the numbers involved, and the fact of having so many other projects, there may be some logistical issues to resolve. And so, we may need to take this in steps."

"All right then, I think this would make a lot of people back home very happy, even if only to solve a lot of long-standing questions in our minds."

"Simply remember that magic is a powerful force, and must be treated with great respect. As people of great scientific achievement, I am sure you can appreciate the responsibilities of such a gift. This is no different."

"I understand."

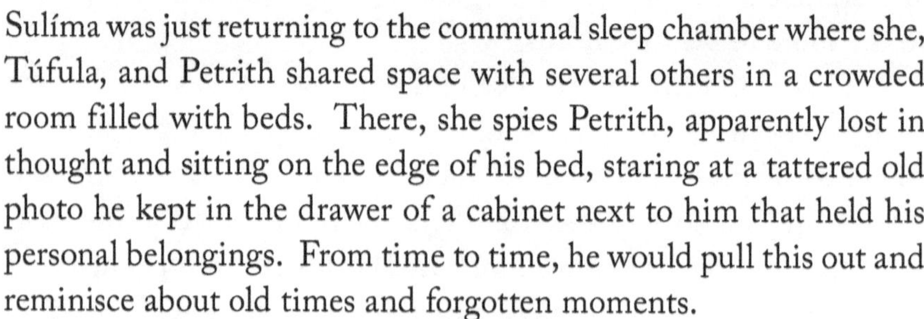

Sulíma was just returning to the communal sleep chamber where she, Túfula, and Petrith shared space with several others in a crowded room filled with beds. There, she spies Petrith, apparently lost in thought and sitting on the edge of his bed, staring at a tattered old photo he kept in the drawer of a cabinet next to him that held his personal belongings. From time to time, he would pull this out and reminisce about old times and forgotten moments.

"Petrith, are you getting ready for your patrol?" she asks.

She moves closer and sits down gently on the bed, then peers over his shoulder at the photo. It was a class photo from their old school, a graduating year that came not long before the attack. Once, Petrith had managed to rummage through the remains of his old home to find it, then bring it back here as a keepsake. It was not uncommon, as many of the refugees made such a search, hoping to find mementos of their former lives and families. It was all they had left of their memories. As Sulíma sat next to him, he looked up to meet her eyes, before returning to the photo.

"Do you remember those times, Suli?" he asks solemnly.

"Yes, Petrith, I do, quite a few of them. But then I have to wake myself up and remember where I am today. It's hard, but there's nothing else for me now."

"Me too. There are times when something brings back those old memories, and then I need to pull this out just to remind myself of what we had back then."

"What things? For all the troubles we have just trying to survive, do you really spend that much time daydreaming about this?"

"It's not just daydreaming, Suli. Sometimes, when I'm asleep, I have dreams, and then I wake up and still have some of those images inside my head. It's not really something I can actually control."

"I think a lot of us have that, to be honest."

Petrith examined the photo and the faces of the students depicted in the image. He picks out several of interest, recalling the occasion of the photo shoot and what may have been going through their minds as the image was captured.

"Look at me here," he points to his image in the photo. "Can you believe that? I wait all year, and this is what I come up with."

"That's kind of a silly look on your face," she giggles. "What were you doing, trying to make yourself look goofy?"

"No, I had an itch, but rather than bring my hand up to rub it, which would probably result in a picture with my hand covering my face, I just let my cheek twitch, hoping I could hold out long enough for the photographer to finish so I could scratch it. Well, it didn't work."

Sulíma lets out a soft laugh and continues to examine the photo.

"Well, if you think that's bad, look at mine over here," she directs their attention to another section of the photo. "I look like I have a pole running up my back, and my head is angled towards the ceiling."

"Is there a reason for that?" he grins.

"I don't know what was going through my head that I was standing so straight, but I think my attention got distracted waiting so long for the photographer to get organized that I was looking at one of the light fixtures."

"Well, then I guess I don't feel so bad about mine now," he chuckles.

They moved their gaze from one face to another on the photo, recalling various friends and classmen, each of whom survived the attack and were currently housed in the same mine shafts where the two of them took refuge. They eventually settled on one face in the front row, belonging to a very attractive young female displaying a flirtatious cock of the head, a bright smile, and resting her hands on the two students adjacent to her.

"And then there's her," he recalls. "She always knew how to make a good photo. Just look at that."

Sulíma studies the image and briefly glances up to look into Petrith's eyes. She could see a distant longing in his gaze as he stared at the girl's face.

"You still think about her, don't you," she states tenderly.

"It's pointless, I know. She's gone, and I'll never see her again."

"Petrith, I sometimes think about her too. She was my best friend, after all. All three of us were, for that matter. We were like a team once. And you always had that special eye for her, I know. It actually made me a little jealous on occasion."

"Well," he sighs, letting out a single muted chuckle. "It's over now. I just wish I knew what happened to her."

"My bet is she made it to the ship. She was Velen's daughter, after all. If anyone would be first onboard, it would be them. Last I heard, Tyanna came running through the school yelling something about orcs attacking, and screaming for Kali to follow. And that's the last anyone saw of them."

"Well, let's hope she made it, but it doesn't help ease our sense of loss for her. She was terrific. She was a good friend, witty, spirited… she had a lot going for her."

"Don't forget, she was also very popular around school. An honor student, star athlete, gymnast… I have no doubt she would've gone far when she grew up."

"If she grew up," he laments. "We can't even be sure of that. We're only guessing she made it to the ship. But for all the carnage in the city…"

"Petrith, stop!" she orders. "Let's just say she did and put it to rest. It's easier on the nerves that way. Surely, they got out early enough to beat the orcs stampeding through the streets, so they should've made it."

"All right, fine," he concedes reluctantly. "It's more comforting to think of this, anyway. And then I can enjoy my dreams and not wonder if I'm just fantasizing over what could've been, or if I'm going crazy with a sense of loss I can't fulfill."

"These dreams… So, you dream of her?"

"Yeah, I'm embarrassed to admit to it, especially to you, but I sometimes have these dreams where I see her doing various things. It started a long time ago, but I'm having a few new ones recently, and it almost seems to be getting worse."

"How do you mean worse? What kinds of dreams are they?"

"Suli," he sighs. "I'm not really sure if I feel right about sharing this with you. First, it's kind of personal, and second, well, you might think I'm going crazy."

"Petrith, we're about as good friends as friends can be, and we need to stick together. Go ahead and tell me. I'll try to understand, even if I really do think you're going crazy. A lot of us are doing that around here…even me. My dreams often involve me fighting that stupid machine outside in a game of tug-o-war, and mostly it's winning," she giggles.

"Really!" he laughs. "Well, maybe next time, you can call me into it, and I'll help. Two against one is usually better in that game."

"All right, I will! But now, about your dreams…got anything really juicy going on?" she smirks.

"Are you suggesting my dreams to be pornographic?" he jests.

"How would I know? The way you had the look for her back

then, and for all the times I've tried swinging my tail at you, but with no results…"

Petrith lets out a spontaneous burst of laughter at the thought, joined by Suli as they share the humorous moment.

"Suli, don't think for a moment that I didn't notice that tail of yours. But to be really honest with you, it's not about you or Kali, or any of the other girls around here. I just can't feel myself really comfortable trying to start a relationship when our life here is so unpredictable."

"I know what you mean. I feel the same way, and so do a lot of others. I've spoken with Túfu on this several times. Regardless of what Captain Lapäli said about pairing up, we've both had thoughts on this, but like with so many others, well…" she sighs deeply. "You know, Petrith; a girl like me probably wouldn't think about a serious relationship for maybe another two or three centuries, and I wouldn't consider trying to make a family for another one after that, at the very least."

"Suli, considering your behavior, I have to wonder about that. Are these your personal interpretations, or what you learned from your parents for a proper young lady?" he grins.

"Well, naturally, my parents both tried to give me a few lessons, and my sister also put in a few words. As for my behavior, this is just a release for me, and it's basically all I have to give me a break from my own tensions. Besides, it's fun."

"Fun for whom? You with all of these plays, or the rest of us following that wild tail of yours?"

"You like it, and you know it," she smirks. "Besides, I figure it's good for morale. But anyway, considering where we are and what's around us, Túfu and I have come to the conclusion, along with a lot of others, that we might not even want to make the attempt. What's the point of bringing a new life into a world that's trying to kill us? We hide in these mines with nowhere to go and nothing to do. Would you really want to bring a child into that kind of environment?"

"You're probably right, Suli, but then I'm reminded of what the

Captain is so fond of saying. We're just rusting away in here, and one day we might fade out completely."

"Yes, it's a depressing thought, but I can't find any reasonable argument for it."

"Suli, I think the only reasonable argument is NOT to rust away. At some point, we may have to learn to fight for our survival. This might then push us to make a stand, find space for ourselves, develop a civilization again, and to the nether-realms with those orcs."

"And do you think you can fight a full world of them?"

"Not all at once, but remember, they don't organize themselves as a nation. Best case, it's an isolated village here, and an isolated village there. If one or more of them should disappear, who would pay attention to it?"

"Um…right. Well, before you go out declaring a war, tell me about these dreams. At least give me something new to think about."

"All right. First, they don't come very often. I've had strange dreams for most of my life, that I can recall, but they started getting weird after a while. They seem to come only on rare occasions, and mostly where I think I see Kali in various places and situations. But in the last few decades, I'm having them closer together. Still, not very often…it might be months, or even as much as a year between. The strange thing is they're not dreams of us as children, like old memories of us in school or walking around town. I see her as an adult, and in fact, there was even a progression of her growing up, just like the rest of us."

"Well, the mind can play a lot of tricks on us, and I suppose it shouldn't be too unusual for you to envision what she might look like as an adult. You're an adult, so you want to see her as one, too."

"Maybe so, but how do you dream of an interpretation of someone you knew as a child, but now as an adult? Or even the progression of growing up?"

"No idea. So, what is it you see her doing? You said you felt almost like you were going crazy with something."

"Yeah, this is where it gets weird. I remember some of those early dreams, where I saw her in what I have to assume to be a room, maybe like a classroom in study."

"This makes perfect sense to me. Was this back when we were kids?"

"Yes, but this is AFTER the attack, and we're all hiding inside here. But she was in an actual room of some sort, and I think with someone teaching her something."

"Well, I think we can still easily explain this, if we were kids and you were probably thinking of our old school."

"Maybe, but after our first centennial? We would normally transition to the senior school by then, not stay in the junior one."

"Um..." she hesitates and bites her lip gently as she ponders the idea.

"Yeah, and here we move into the later dreams, where now she's an adult, like the rest of us. Now I see her in what looks like a Sentinel's uniform."

"Sentinels? Kali? That's not what I would've expected of her, based on our old school experiences. Her brother was in the Sentinels, this much I remember. He was in the security service, I think."

"Yeah, but this new sequence now shows her in the same militia uniform. Sometimes she was wandering through what I think was a grassy field, although I'm mostly guessing, as the scenery is very blurry for me. Another time, I think it was a mountainous region, and there was also a time in a dry barren waste."

"Interesting, at least you have some good imagination for the landscapes. But militia?" she chuckles. "Were there any other people in there with her?"

"Actually, yes, and this is one of those things you might think I'm crazy about. Just like with the landscape, the other things were blurry. Only Kali was in clear focus. It's like my view was only on her, and I couldn't see anything else around her, at least not clearly."

"All right, so in your dreams, you need glasses," she giggles. "Who did you see? Anyone we know?"

Petrith pauses to gaze at her uncertainly.

"Are you sure you won't laugh hilariously at me?"

"Well, I'll try to hold it down to a minor side-bursting," she grins.

"Yeah, sure… Well, I think I could see, and also hear, a few others, and some of them were like us, but there were occasionally a few who were not."

"Huh? You're seeing aliens in that mix now?"

"I have no idea who they could be or how I could create such a weird image, but there was one who showed up quite often in the more recent dreams. I think it was female, only about chest height to us, and I think with medium gray skin and white hair."

"Yeah, I think you probably do have a point about going crazy. All right, so she's walking around in a Sentinels uniform with little, gray-skinned aliens. What else?"

"This is what bothers me. We have this, and I can also hear them talking, and it's not our language."

"Oh dear. And now you have them speaking in strange tongues."

"Yeah," he chuckles softly. "I've had other dreams…normal ones, you might say. Why do these come out so different?"

"Well, you always did have an eye for her. As for the rest, I don't know."

"Yeah, it's kind of funny when you think about it. But then there's the dream I had last night, which is actually why I'm sitting here now. You'll get an even bigger laugh off this one."

"All right, hit me with it."

"I saw her again, but this time in different clothing. Don't ask me what kind. I didn't recognize it, but it looked like another type of uniform, cloth this time, not the synthetic plate armor they use in the militia."

"Ah, so you have her working somewhere else now?"

"The impression I'm getting here isn't work…more like training, like in some kind of academy…maybe a military academy. She looked like she was practicing some form of combat art…"

✦✦✦✦✦

"Yer Kingship, we've got a wee bit of a problem, if ye don'na mind t' listen."

Tol Bronzeheart was making his way through the settlement into the tactical office with one of his recent upsets. He had been making a series of these visits as he and the other dwarves were experiencing a string of anomalies during the course of their newfound employment. They had taken up work in a new smithing shop established in Rolsklinde to help make supplies and equipment for the other workers still struggling to clean up and clear some space in the city in order to prepare for several new building projects.

Since that first day when Tol experienced his unusual anxiety event, Thaelyn had been keeping a close eye on the dwarven workers for any other signs of illness. They had all undergone examination by Daanen-Aryku medical workers for signs of respiratory ailments and cardiac distress, only to turn up with healthy results other than for minor symptoms of appearing to be breathing in a low-pressure environment.

"Yes, Tol, what do we have this time?" Thaelyn responds.

"I hate t' be a-pesterin' ye so much, Yer Kingship, but this be a-comin' 'round t' a bit of a bother by now. Look at this here..."

Tol sets down a large sledgehammer with a heavy wooden handle, which was splintered in the middle.

"Just what is it you people are doing up there to cause so much stress on these tools? This level of damage does not come about easily."

"I can'na say, Yer Kingship. I nay be a-doin' anythin' here that would'na be the practice back home. For some reason, though, things just seem t' be a-breakin' easier here. This wood here be a soft one, if ye ask me. D' ye have anythin' sturdier?"

"This is already one of the hardest woods we use for tools of this sort. How did it break like this?"

"The lads were a-hammerin' a brick of iron down t' a sheet when some of them broke the handles. This here be one of them."

"More than one broke at the same time?"

"Aye! It be a-gettin' t' be mighty hard on us t' make our work with broken tools. We're thinkin' t' make somethin' new with iron handles."

"Iron would make it rather heavy…"

"Nay, we use that often back home for much of the harder work."

"On a sledge like this?"

"Aye, 'tis no great matter t' us. Wood nay be somethin' ye'll find underground, ye know."

"Indeed, this is true. And no doubt, you would build up some fine upper body strength along the way."

"Aye!" he chuckles. "An' in fact, this hammer feels light as a feather, so the swingin' feels softer than a wee one's rattle poundin' a block of stone."

"An interesting description…" Thaelyn muses as he picks up the broken pieces of the hefty work tool. "I would think, by that account, you may be using more strength than is necessary when shaping your iron bars. You say this sledge feels excessively light to you? I know many of our own smiths use these, and none has ever mentioned this before. And I believe many use similar methods of shaping iron as what you describe."

"I can'na say how yer other smiths may d' this sort of work. I see some of them nay be dwarven, so I have me doubts they could hold the strength of a good dwarven smith in their arms. The dwarves ye have in yer employ are another thing. Which of these d' ye most often put in the smithin' shops?"

"Humans can make good smiths for many occasions, although we are also beginning to use more machines in our industry these days, so we do not have quite as many of the original hand-forging workshops. And yet, we do also employ a good many dwarves for this. But even at that, our dwarves, for all their fine skills, have not gone through sledges and other tools as quickly as your men. I wonder… Your men were working with a singular purpose in the mine up there, so perhaps you built up a high degree of strength in your arms from this. Then again, our own dwarves also work long and hard in such mines, and they still do not exhibit quite the level of physical prowess enough to break tools as often as you. Can it be a coincidence that we were given a set of tools with flaws, or could there be another reason?"

"My Lord," offers the General, also speaking in Dwarvish for Tol's benefit. "Could there be a strange side effect in this regard relating to their use of these mushrooms? Or perhaps another odd detail we are missing. This does seem rather peculiar to me that they are breaking these tools so often, and in such close timing as compared to all our other smiths for much longer periods."

"Very well, let us examine this in greater detail, but we should bring in someone with some technical expertise to assist. Have a page outside fetch Med-tech Tad'vaal for us."

The General steps over to the door and summons a page from the line-up near the building. He gives the order, and the young man runs off to find the Daanen'kai medical technician. Moments later, she arrives in the room.

"You called, Your Lordship?" she answers.

"Med-tech, we have an interesting quandary. Our smith here, along with his friends, has been breaking many of our tools up in their shop in the city."

"I'm very sorry to hear that, but I'm not a toolmaker. What do you need from me in this case?"

"Examine this here," he explains, pushing the broken hammer in her direction. "This is one of the most recent examples. The handle is clearly broken, and from his description, it sounds to me as though he and the others are in possession of some rather profound physical strength to break this as it is. A question has been put forth as to whether these mushrooms could offer a peculiar side effect to produce this quality."

"Given what I've learned in my medical studies, and the results we have so far on those mushrooms, I don't actually see it. For a person to develop so high a level of strength as what you're suggesting could possibly be made using steroids, or some other muscle-enhancing drug, but those mushrooms didn't show any such substance in our earlier analysis."

"Could you have missed it? We were looking for mind-altering drugs and toxins before, not steroids."

"That's true. I could order up another analysis to test for it. In the meantime, let me ask this," she mentions as she prepares to pull out her medical scanner. "How long do tools like these usually last for your people?"

"Much longer than what these men have been demonstrating, and that includes our own dwarven smiths."

"So, your own dwarves use the same tools, but not with so much wear on them? Interesting. Your Lordship, I'd like to make a quick scan of this man, could you relay the message to him?"

"Of course," Thaelyn consents, and then translates the request to the dwarven smith.

"And for reference," she adds. "I'd also like to examine one of your own dwarves. I'm hoping to see if there are any clear physiological differences between them. But I should remind you my knowledge of dwarven biology isn't very complete."

"I understand. I will see what we have available."

Thaelyn turns to the General to relay the most recent request, as the conversation with the Med-tech was in the common tongue for Therinë, and she had not yet learned to speak Tae'Eladaran.

The General steps outside again to find a page. He gave an instruction to send him off through the portal gate to Tae'Eladar to find a dwarven smith at the guildhall smithy. He chose this as the best comparison, rather than a dwarven soldier stationed within the camp, as many of those were magically augmented for strength and other enhancements which could skew the results of the study. They waited many long moments for the return of the page with his charge.

Med-tech Tad'vaal began her scan of the newly arrived dwarf from Tae'Eladar. She studied the results on her scanner and called up the results of the previous scan for comparison.

"This is strange..." she mumbles.

"Have you found something?" Thaelyn wonders.

"Just a moment, Your Lordship, let me be sure of what I'm looking at."

She makes another detailed scan of one arm on Tol, and an arm on the guildhall smith, calibrating the display for a more accurate analysis.

"Your Lordship, I've never seen anything like this before. The cellular structure between these two men is significantly different."

"In what way?"

"Is your dwarf here typical of all dwarves on your world? Or perhaps I'm asking something that might be hard to tell if you've never conducted an analysis like this…with all due respect, of course."

"To the best of my understanding, the dwarves of Tae'Eladar should all fall into a category very much like this one."

"May I run a scan on a human specimen?"

"General," Thaelyn instructs. "We need a human subject in here. One of those pages outside should suffice. They are not part of our military, so should make a good example of a common citizen."

"Very well, my Lord. Do we have something of unusual interest occurring here?" he responds as he moves towards the door.

"The Med-tech is detecting some manner of anomaly, or at least an unusual variation between these two dwarves. I believe she is looking for more data to compare."

"I see. I do hope we are able to discover the cause."

He summons the same page into the room that was called in earlier. The Med-tech once again conducts a scan and compares the results with the others. She pauses in deep thought for a moment.

"Your Lordship, is it my understanding the dwarves of your world once came from the same world as this one here?"

"Morndindor, yes, but our dwarves came from there many thousands of years ago during a form of migration."

"How long, do you know?"

"Hmm," Thaelyn considers. "I think some of these migrations, between the elven population and the dwarves, began somewhere between twelve and fifteen millennia ago."

"Really! That's interesting. How long are their lifespans?"

"For dwarves, most often around two centuries, though some go more than that."

"Two centuries per, over let's say fifteen millennia on the inside…" she ponders. "Your Lordship, would you indulge me for a little experiment?"

"Certainly, Med-tech," he responds with a broad grin. "What is it you have in mind?"

"I would like to test what these scan results are trying to tell me. I want to see exactly how strong your dwarf is compared to this other one. Perhaps if you have some manner of weights or something you can use to demonstrate strength in a form we can measure."

"How curious…and rather appropriate…"

Thaelyn begins relaying instructions to the General again, and together they send out the page on yet another errand to Tae'Eladar. In time, he returns with a group of several others from the guildhall, wheeling in a hand-wagon full of gymnastic weights and bars. They begin setting up the apparatus outside the building.

"Yer Kingship," Tol asks. "Just what be ye an' this fine blue lass a-makin' with this here?"

"She has a most curious interest in conducting a little test of strength between our native dwarf and yourself. Would you care to indulge her?"

"Well now, if ye don'na mind me takin' time away from me service t' ye, I'd yay be happy t' give a moment t' show up t' this lass what a true dwarf be good for!" he chortles.

Thaelyn directs each dwarf to step over to the wagon and begin selecting an assortment of weighted disks to apply onto a long rod. The first up was the guildhall smith, who chose several large disks and a few smaller ones. With a heavy grunt, he lifts the prominent mass off the wagon and over his head, then brings it back down again.

"Not bad, if I'm judging those weights appropriately," the Med-tech muses.

Next up was Tol. He steps over and examines the weights in the wagon. He first tests the assembly used by the previous dwarf, but guffaws at the puny arrangement. He then reassembles the weights to just more than twice the original amount before attempting to lift it. With a similar grunt, he hoists the bar over his head, and then lowers it back into the wagon.

"Amazing!" Med-tech Tad'vaal mutters.

"I must agree with you on this, Med-tech," Thaelyn admits in a low voice. "I have not seen this level of proficiency amongst our common dwarves before. Many of our troops are magically augmented, so this would be a much more common sight with them, but this… Unless we are speaking of time spent in a structured form of exercise, this would suggest something outside my expectations."

"I have one more test I'd like to see, now that we have this much."

"And what would that be?"

"This may sound weird, but I would like to test their leg muscles. Can you have them jump for me, to see how high they can go?"

"Indeed, you are a fascinating piece of work, Med-tech. Very well…"

Thaelyn now asks the dwarves to move away from the wagon and give a demonstration of jumping exercises. Once again, first up is the native dwarf from the guildhall. He performs a series of jumps, squatting low and making a powerful effort to propel himself upward. His best attempt takes him to nearly two-thirds his own height.

Thaelyn then directs Tol to make his turn. Tol steps forward with a confident grin, squats low and similarly makes ready to jump. He leaps off the ground with an unexpectedly strong upward thrust, carrying him well over the head of his opponent, twice as high as the best effort of the guildhall dwarf. But he begins to panic slightly as he sees himself continuing to rocket skyward, realizing he is much further above the ground than he has ever gone before. He lets out a yip and twists in mid-air, somehow hoping to stop his motion before the winds carry him away. Finally, his upward momentum comes to a halt, and he is pulled back to the ground again. He lands awkwardly, using his hands to catch himself.

"Great All-Father, what was that?" he exclaims as he regains his balance.

"Powers pay witness," Thaelyn mumbles.

"Did you see that?" the Med-tech bounces with excitement. "Did you see it?! Do you have any idea what that means?" she giggles with joy.

"I am forming some rather unique opinions on the topic, to be sure."

"I think I have an answer for you, Your Lordship! And I'll bet all the other dwarves from the mine are the same, just as yours once were a long time ago when they first came to your world."

"Very well, Med-tech," Thaelyn charges jovially. "Let us hear this extraordinary judgment of yours."

"My scans of the two dwarves show similarities to each other, and a notable difference to your human here. But between the two dwarves, there is also a difference, which is more pronounced in the one native to their home world. If using humans as a base constant, it would seem the dwarven bone and muscle tissue has a denser structure than human tissue."

"Yes, this much I believe I can vouch for from our own experience using them in our world. They are strong and quite durable as compared to humans."

"Right, but between these two dwarves, the one from Morndindor has a much denser structure than the other. Meaning, he should be stronger and more durable than what you are familiar with of your own dwarven population."

"Interesting. So, this might offer an explanation to his enhanced strength, in his arms as well as his legs, I suppose."

"But now, consider this. Around fifteen to twenty thousand years ago, whatever the number may be, dwarves from their world came to yours. This man from your world is an example of what they have become since that time."

"Just a moment, Med-tech. If I am interpreting this correctly, you are speaking of an adaptation of some sort."

"Yes, the one from their home world is what you might call a true original. Compare him to yours by physical features. Short, stout, and physically robust. Compared to a human, yours may be stronger and tougher, but compared to the original, he might fall significantly short of a match. The adaptation essentially degenerated these higher features as it degenerated the tissue density to meet the native environmental demands."

"Very interesting," Thaelyn intones intriguingly. "Please continue."

"Our race is perhaps more knowledgeable of the studies of different species from different worlds, the study of exobiology. Maybe you don't have as much experience in this, if you haven't travelled as much, and therefore collected as much data as we have over the years…and centuries, and millennia…" she sighs.

"I fully understand, Med-tech, and I would suspect your people have discovered many a world during your long trek in front of Darumon's follies."

"Yeah, and I suppose it's useful for us, in a way, but I wish it wasn't as the result of being chased by cold-blooded killers. Of course, it can also involve so much of our old history, too."

"Indeed, so take ease, Med-tech, and please continue with your analysis."

"Right. With what my scans tell me, and correspondingly by studying their physical forms along with this obvious difference in strength, I think I have a very good idea of the type of world the original dwarf came from, and therefore why he has these features we're seeing. Your Lordship, I think Morndindor is a heavy gravity world."

"An excellent conclusion, Med-tech. Their physical stature, strength ratios, and perhaps other features, might surely give clues to this. Perhaps this could explain a few other anomalies we have observed, as well."

"I'm sure it can, and one that comes right off the tip of my horns is why this man had that episode several days ago, and why the others have complained about their breathing difficulties. A heavy gravity world is also likely to have a heavier atmospheric pressure. Move someone from that into ours, and it's like trying to breathe at high altitude."

"How interesting, and therefore, conversely, if to have one of us travelling there…"

"Their atmosphere would be heavy to us, so we might have some difficulty with it."

Thaelyn pauses a moment to make the association, and then a revelation comes to mind.

"Dear Powers, that must be it!" he surges.

"My Lord," the General asks, unaware of the nature of the conversation due to the language difficulties. "What is it? Is there a problem?"

"A problem? Follow along with me..." he replies, then turns to Tol. "Chief Bronzeheart, you once told me of the story your people held when the elves first attacked you. Do you recall that?"

"Aye, Yer Kingship. A sorry bunch they be, at that!"

"But specifically, you said they seemed to fall out of their portals and then appeared to have trouble breathing, correct?"

"Aye, 'tis true that. D' ye think ye know what the cause was?"

"I may indeed. The Med-tech believes you come from a world with a heavier form of gravity, and this would explain your higher strength as compared to anything here. It might also explain your breathing issues. However, if to turn this around... Anyone travelling there might find it difficult to hold themselves upright effectively, as well as your world would likely hold a higher atmospheric pressure weighing down on their lungs, causing breathing difficulties in reverse of yours. Elves would be a poor selection to send to a world like that. They would likely find it very difficult to move around, or to breathe efficiently."

✦ ✦ ✦ ◆ ✦ ✦ ✦

"Can everyone out there hear me?" Tristeen shouts through the microphone. "We need to bring ourselves into order so we can take a final vote. I think it is important to make our vote unanimous, so if anyone here has any objections, let them speak now so we can address it and try to resolve it."

Tristeen had been hard at work all day since sunrise, assembling the huge mass of people in the fields north of Firstfall. The assemblage of bodies stretched far across the grassy plain in all directions. In the days preceding this, she had ordered the repositioning of her stage to a more centralized location where she could cover a greater area at once in a broad semicircle. The speaker system provided by the Daanen-Aryku had been reconfigured for better coverage to accommodate the wider scope and broader expanse.

Leesa had been playing the role of a sidekick to the political hopeful. As Tristeen made her speech, the girl stood next to her with the portable microphone ready to dash out into the audience to interview anyone with opposing opinions, last minute questions, and final comments. But the large mass had mostly settled these issues in the many days that came before. The only thing to do now was to take one last poll of opinions to ensure the full coverage of the population.

Amariyn assisted by sending a group of Night Elves among the people to check for anyone wishing to speak to the assembly. Very few had anything to offer beyond what had already been said. In the end, they took a final tally, not so much to count how many assenting votes were made, as it was already presumed the people were in full agreement, but rather to catch any dissenting votes.

When Tristeen was satisfied with the results, she conferred with the noble fathers, Lady Amariyn, Priestess Sehnisavain, and Captain Kholgard, all of whom had been very instrumental in putting this together. They then moved off as a group through the gate and into the village.

+ + ◆ + +

"My Lord," the General argues. "This is at least as despicable as anything else we have seen come out of that beast."

Thaelyn and the others had returned inside the tactical office. Tol had been dismissed back to his work with instructions to take greater care of the local tool supply, at least until a sturdier set could be made for his workers. Med-tech Tad'vaal had been briefed on

Thaelyn's epiphany about the Elven invasion, and now this same topic was being discussed by his officers.

"Yes, General, I agree, but it also fills in a few details of the dwarven home world. On Tae'Eladar, at least, the dwarven population had long been sworn enemies of orcs. The two simply do not get along."

"Not that those orcs got along with anyone to begin with," the General relents.

"True, but dwarves hold a particular grudge against them. I would imagine the same would hold true on Morndindor. Therefore, it does not surprise me that when Darumon attempted to use them during that first attack, it would fail so miserably."

"Are we speaking of with or without the issue of heavy gravity?" Padriyl asks.

"Well, yes, this would certainly play a role, and let us not forget the adamantium armor and weapons the dwarves would likely bring with them, not to mention the fact that Darumon was trying to fight what we must consider to be a well-populated world. So, clearly, this had to be a test of dwarven resolve. I cannot see how Darumon, or anyone skilled in any form of military exercise, would make such a profound mistake as this."

"I would agree."

"Furthermore, if his tendency is to use deception, and if also to consider the dwarven lust for tall tales, he would want to leave a bitter taste in their mouths for this occasion."

"And so," the General concludes. "He uses what can only be described as an inferior invasion force to distract them, as well as to leave no real interest in these stories of great battles by proud warriors, as dwarves tend to desire. Therefore, the Thane simply calls for his ingots, and tells them the war is raging across the land, but without the actual stories of how or why."

"The elves would never be a good match for dwarves under these conditions," Thaelyn asserts. "They do possess magic, so they could throw off a few fireballs and such. But if these stories begin with such statements as them falling to the ground with breathing difficulties, and describing the fury of battle as a mercy killing, no one will want to hear of it. And here, we might have the Thane use the excuse of digging deeper into the mountain to distance himself from the unpleasantness of the scene."

"And closing off the doors so no one can actually go out there to see for themselves what is truly happening."

"But this now raises a rather dire question in my mind. I recall mention in those reports where neither they could go outside, and no one else came in with any news. Either the Thane is restricting access to the outside world entering the city, or something has happened to that outside world that no one CAN enter the city with an update."

"Cu'Nar's grace, Your Lordship…" Padriyl moans. "That leaves a bad taste in my mouth now, especially when I reflect on our own experiences."

"Indeed, my Lord," the General admits. "At the risk of losing my professional composure as a soldier in your Order, I find this war becoming impossibly revolting."

"You are not alone, General," Thaelyn concedes.

"Knock, knock?" ushers a gentle voice from the door. "Are we interrupting anything critical?"

Tristeen and her troupe had arrived in the village as they came in from the field outside. They stood just at the door, hoping to gain someone's attention.

"Tristeen, please come in," Thaelyn calls, attempting to cover his distressed voice. "Whatever you have for us, I am sure it would be far more pleasant to discuss than our own topics."

"It sounds like the war is weighing heavily on you today."

"Actually, the war is fairly light. It is a recent development that just came to us, which brings most of our current woes. But it is a matter that can wait, as there is nothing to be done about it now."

"Do you need to discuss anything with us?"

"I can brief you later if you like. It will mostly affect Priestess Sehnisavain, as it involves her people more than any other…something old by now, the dwarven home world, and I would not wish to reopen those wounds unnecessarily."

"Oh, all right. Anyway, we have something we would like to say, and I was hoping you might be able to offer a few moments of your time to assist us with something."

"Very well then… I see you have assembled a rather impressive quantity of people out front, and now here you are with an equally impressive delegation of officials. Should I presume we have something of great interest to discuss?"

"Indeed, Your Lordship! It has been decided by the unanimous vote of the people that we, the citizens of Rolsklinde, wish to join with you into your kingdom on Tae'Eladar, though we might still wish to return to our homes here…once they are restored."

Tristeen turns to look at Sehnisavain to offer her part.

"And, Your Grace," the elder High Elf declares. "I am similarly charged by the voices of our people, the citizens of Kynesoth, that we too desire to rejoin our ancestral kin on Tae'Eladar and serve in your honor."

The pleasurable announcement brings a broad smile to Thaelyn's face as he feels the burden of the previous discussion melt away. His pleasure of the favor was so great that he even felt himself blushing.

"Your Lordship," Tristeen resumes. "We have assembled the people outside. There are more than ninety thousand aspiring petitioners, all waiting to see your face and offer their vows. I'm not sure how we're going to manage this, but it should be fun to watch!"

"Indeed, ninety thousand would account for the largest mass swearing-in I have ever conducted."

"Might you have a moment to give us for the ceremony? Then, perhaps, we could all share in a bit of revelry before going back to our normal lives."

Thaelyn glances around at the General and Lieutenant Lapäli before turning back to Tristeen.

"Revelry, is it? I certainly hope you brought enough drink for the occasion!" he chuckles. "Well, I believe we might be able to offer a few moments."

Tristeen and the others share a round of laughter, then turn to leave the building with Thaelyn and the other officers following close behind. He diverts briefly to call up a squire stationed within the village to assist him in straightening his attire, while the General picks up Thaelyn's sword to carry along.

Once his appearance had been tidied up, he proceeded out onto the fields, there to find Aerlie standing near the gate along with a few other familiar faces nearby. Relissa, Marelle, Haran, and Kaliya had all been assembled, called in from the guildhall, as well as Willit and Jared who had been so instrumental with their efforts up in the city during the final days.

"And just what are you people doing out of class at this hour?" Thaelyn asks, raising an eyebrow at them.

"Aye!" Relissa yips. "We got a little reprieve from the chains and shackles for the occasion."

"Really! And I wonder who it was to authorize this…" he finishes by casting a suspicious glare at Tristeen.

"Don't look at me," she retorts. "I don't hold that level of authority. But I did get a little help," she concludes looking over at Aerlie.

Thaelyn passes his gaze around at his wife, and then back to the others.

"Dear Powers, there are conspiracies all around me…"

"Look at it this way, my Lord," Relissa suggests. "If you didn't have all us mortals climbing your back, what sort of life would you have?"

"A peaceful one," he smirks. "But not nearly as enjoyable."

They continued out onto the field and over to the platform used for the earlier presentations. Thaelyn and Aerlie step up on the platform, with Tristeen and Sehnisavain standing on the stairs just below. The General took to Thaelyn's side and slightly behind, while Amariyn and the other officers stayed on the ground.

Leesa took up a position on the platform to assist with the microphone, holding it up to him as he prepared to speak in a bold voice. Padriyl watches her and suddenly gets his own idea to make a video recording, so he pulls out his trans-com and holds it up to observe the event.

"Good people," Thaelyn begins. "It has been brought to my

attention that, after a long and no doubt difficult debate, you have come to a final decision regarding our offer of a union, to share in the many joys and accolades of our society, the prosperity and the freedoms of our people, the wisdom of our ancestors, and the esteem of our gods. I know this time has been hard for you, and you have suffered much for it. But that time has passed, and now we find ourselves with an open future, one where we are in control of our own lives and the direction of our society."

He pauses briefly to glance around at Tristeen and her political party standing off to the side.

"On this occasion," he continues. "We have found ourselves reuniting with our lost Brothers and Sisters, who took upon themselves an intrepid journey to unknown lands in the bargain to spread the seeds of life and the gifts of society. And even though we might have the tales of your journey, and the cause behind it, we can and should hold pride that this new world you conquered holds its own value. But then, you found yourselves cut off from the rest, and yet, even with the misfortunes you experienced along the way, we have in our hands the potential for a future filled with many possibilities. And these possibilities can and will carry us to far distant lands beyond even this one."

He holds a moment to survey the masses all around the area.

"We will not let those who brought so much harm to us demean our spirits or break our resolve. Our future is our own, and we will build on it with all our might. And for they who once thought to use what we have to their own benefit, we shall instead turn this to ours, and demonstrate to the remainder of Creation what WE will bring, not them!"

The crowds rise up in a vigorous cheer. Whoops and hollers echo around the area, along with generous applause.

Padriyl listened and felt his own sense of passion building inside. His people needed this probably more than any, and Thaelyn was a shining example of a leader who could deliver it. He leaned over to whisper privately at Kaliya.

"It's no wonder you joined up so quickly. Kaliya, I need to apologize to you."

"Why is that?"

"Well, regrettably, knowing your history as I do, I considered you just ran away from us. But I think I understand now. You followed a beacon that led you to salvation. We could all use this. I'd do it myself if I didn't have so many other responsibilities hanging on my horns."

She lays a hand on his shoulder and pats him gently.

"Maybe one day you will. Maybe we all will, I don't know. But we certainly couldn't go wrong with it."

Thaelyn was preparing to wrap up his speech. He waited for the cheers to settle down before continuing.

"On this day, we find ourselves travelling on a long and curious road. Our battle against that creature who calls himself Marshal Darumon is not over. It goes without saying that what he did here, he could do again elsewhere, and as enlightened people, we must recognize our responsibility to a great purpose…a purpose that transcends beyond our own miseries. The people of Tae'Eladar understand this, and we offer ourselves to it freely. We strive to find our greatest strength, and we apply this to the noblest of deeds, not only for ourselves and what we believe in, but for all others we may one day touch. We follow the teachings of the Estelar, as their wisdom is eternal. And we will teach you and your children the same."

The crowd once again rises up in cheers and applause.

"Ours is a symbol to guide others. It represents our beliefs, our principles, our determination, and we offer this to lead those who seek this same enlightenment, that they will follow us, joining their strength with ours, increasing the whole, and expanding our greater capacity, such that no obstacle shall stand in our way. We shall aim for that which is beyond our reach, achieve that which is beyond our desire, and stand above all that would tear us down. This is a road we will travel together, and to seal this agreement, we should enact this ceremony to bring you into our society proper. Within this ceremony is an oath of allegiance, as was once committed for the fine citizens of Solinaia. And herein we shall bring this unto you."

Thaelyn straightens himself to stand at attention. The General presents the sword in a ceremonial prose, where Thaelyn draws it out and holds it in a salute, raising it up for all to see.

"Gracious," Tristeen mumbles. "Look at that thing. Up close, it looks even bigger than before with that demon."

He then inverts the sword and brings it down to stand on the platform at his feet. Next, he holds up his right palm to the assembly.

Padriyl was agape as he studied the motions and reflecting on the pageantry of the display. He exchanged a quick glance with Kaliya for her impression.

"I've never seen protocol like this before," he whispers to her.

"He's a King," she replies softly. "When was the last time we saw one of those?"

"Well, there was Saakerav once, but that was forever ago."

"But did he ever give out oaths, or simply conquer the place?"

"Good point."

Thaelyn now prepared himself for the oath. It carried a standard recital as a preamble, followed by the declarations.

"We who are the people of Tae'Eladar, do decree that we hold stewardship of our own. We who are the people of Tae'Eladar, do decree that we hold fast to the principles of the Societies of the Estelar and their teachings, that the doctrines of the Measure of Balance will guide us and our actions for all those we may encounter in our travels. And to this end, we do offer this oath to those who would join with us on the journey of life and the path of enlightenment."

He holds a moment to offer a brief delineation. He takes a deep breath and begins again.

"Be you here, who are assembled, admitting to my call?"

"Aye!"

The great mass of people let out the collective cry, filling the air and echoing off walls and buildings. It even seemed to be rebounding from the surrounding hillsides and canyon.

"Be you here, who are assembled, admitting to my grace?"

"Aye!"

"Be you here, who are assembled, admitting to my service?"

"Aye!"

"Be it known, as by the will of the people, the citizens of the city of Rolsklinde, the citizens of the city of Kynesoth, where they and thee shall come to the side of mine own. Is this, in truth, your plea?"

"Aye!"

"Be it known, for with this mandate, you who are assembled would become citizens of my domain, to serve as my subjects, to bequeath unto me your duty and your promise to the fulfillment of our combined destiny, to the glory of the kingdom. Is this, in truth, your plea?"

"Aye!"

"Be there a man or woman present who would not declare this so, let them speak now!"

Thaelyn surveys the wide swath of people to check for anyone standing out. But, as it was in Solinaia, the crowd goes silent at this statement. None wish to express any discord, and possibly be left out of the most important day of their life.

"So be it! As the Gods above shall pay witness, let these words be borne across the realms! From this day forward, it shall be known that the people of Rolsklinde, and the people of Kynesoth, as will their children and heirs, are welcomed into my arms as they are welcomed into my kingdom."

A boisterous cheer rises up from the crowd as the people raise their hands and begin singing songs of praise. Somewhere out in the mass of people, music begins playing where Tristeen and the others infiltrated musicians amongst the horde of refugees.

Thaelyn beams a wide smile as he replaces his sword in its sheath. He looks around at the celebrating mass of new citizens, and wonders silently how he may ever be able to introduce so many new people into the folds of his existing society. Not only will these people need to learn the language, but they will almost certainly need supplemental education to bring them up to Tae'Eladaran standards, just to make them competent by the higher level of sophistication his people enjoyed, as compared to what they had previously.

Tristeen steps up on the platform and calls Leesa over with the microphone.

"May I be the first to call you…MY Lord!" she announces into the unit.

Thaelyn turns to meet her gaze. She has a grin from ear to ear playing across her face.

The crowd and the music went quiet for a moment to give her a chance to speak.

"My Lord," she continues. "We, the people, have but one or two small requests to make of you, if you would give us this honor. As time passes, and our city of Rolsklinde is restored, we would wish to offer a type of memorial to recall our sorrows and the many tragedies of this war. At the same time, the people of Kynesoth would also make this request to give solace for their own suffering. If you could provide us with this service, we would be most grateful to you."

Thaelyn steps in to make use of the microphone as Leesa moves it up to him. She had been developing quite a talent for handling the curious device by this time.

"Miss Macaid, this is indeed a most appropriate request, and I would wish no less for it. We can call to our service a collection of artisans to help us design something representative of the occasion. We have a good many of those on Tae'Eladar, and perhaps we also have a few amongst us here who would wish to offer their opinions. Then, as we move forward, we will allocate space for it, and provide the proper services to teach our people and their children of this moment in our history."

"Thank you, my Lord. Another small item we would like to ask about. This war has tormented us for four centuries in this world. With the surprising development of the Marshal and his people leaving us, we find ourselves blessed by the joy of victory, even though that victory came at great cost. Still, we will accept it as a victory, and an end to so long a time of suffering. We would wish to ask for a day of remembrance of this occasion, so as each year passes, we may all share a moment of recollection of the deeds that brought us out of that misery. Our thoughts are to consider the day the Marshal left this world, and use this as our day."

"I see you have been hard at work devising these considerations, Miss Macaid. This is yet another mark of a savvy leader."

"Well, I have to admit, I was in consultation with Lady Amariyn and Priestess Sehnisavain for much of this. And of course, the noble Fathers also had to have their say," she grins.

"Indeed, and it would seem we have a fair amount of mischief occurring out here. Hmm..." he glances around the gathering. "But again, yes, this is also a very fair suggestion. We have our own special days on Tae'Eladar for one thing or another, and I see no reason why you should not have yours. You have certainly earned it."

"Again, I thank you, my Lord. And finally, we have one last item to share on this special occasion."

Tristeen calls up Amariyn and Sehnisavain to share her space while she prepares her next statement. She also calls Padriyl to join them. He hands off his trans-com to Kaliya to continue recording the event in his place.

Thaelyn senses an air of charged emotion gathering on the platform with him. He motions for Leesa to pull the microphone away momentarily so he can share a few private words.

"Tristeen, what is you have on your mind right now, Child?" he asks softly.

She passes a curious smile at him as the other two women and the Daanen'kai officer take their positions.

"I think you have been spending too much time with Relissa and Marelle," he continues. "Their mischievous nature is rubbing off on you."

"Oh, I had this long before I ever met them," she smirks.

Tristeen pulls up the microphone so she can begin speaking again, with the other representatives now backing her up.

"My Lord," she speaks boldly. "Your arrival here changed many things for us. Each of the races here owes something to you for your service during this time, and we wish to give a special tribute to you. The people of Rolsklinde owe you their lives for the discovery of these nasty devices that have been taking our family members for centuries, as well as much more. The Night Elves owe you for replacing their sacred Tree of Life, defending their people from their enemies, and allowing them to rediscover their roots within your world. The High Elves owe you in similar ways, but more so by rescuing them from the dastardly clutches of that horrible fiend, Sargeras. And even the Daanen-Aryku owe you a great deal, not only for your defense of their people, but your aid to help them redevelop their science and giving them so much support to rebuild themselves after so much loss. Between the four of us, we represent the surviving societies of this world."

She pauses briefly to look at the other members standing next to her.

"A proposal was made some time ago within our leadership delegation to give tribute in the form of honoring what you have accomplished here in this valley. For as long as any of us can actively remember...and I actually hate using that term after what the old mage academy up there did to our education system...but it still stands that this valley has been described as the Badlands, primarily due to its barren nature after centuries of war. But no longer! From this day forward, the people have decreed it should be given a new name, The Lord's March, in honor of your arrival and your pursuit of our combined enemies. From this place, you sent out your armies to conquer the land away from a power that dominated us for centuries. And you brought our people together and aided us in our greatest time of need. As a representative of the people of Rolsklinde, I support this proposal."

Amariyn takes a turn to step forward. Leesa turns to give her the microphone.

"Your Grace, as a member of the people of Solinaia, we support this as well. Your service has given us new hope for our future. Our people have begun to enjoy so many new benefits, and I am sure more will follow in the years to come."

Sehnisavain steps forward next.

"Your Grace, we of the High Elves would probably not even be here today if it were not for your compassion to help us away from our dominion. We owe you our lives and our freedom, and we can think of no less than to offer this to you as our return for reuniting us with our native heritage."

She steps back and allows room for Padriyl to step in. Leesa stretches herself to reach the microphone up to him.

Thaelyn gazes curiously into the Lieutenant's eyes, quietly wondering how he fits into this, as his people often did not consider themselves official citizens of this world.

"Your Lordship," he begins. "Although we, the Daanen-Aryku, consider ourselves exiles from our home on Azgarén, and cannot feel ourselves a part of any other world, we must bring ourselves to accept that we are here and cannot leave. The other people of this world have welcomed and accepted us, and for this we feel a tender sense of belonging. As they have offered to have us stand among them, I have been granted the authority by Master Velen and the Elder Council to confirm this proposal. We would consider it a great honor to support the decision of the others to give this valley a more appropriate designation to your service."

As Thaelyn listens to the testimonies, he feels a welling up of emotion inside him, the likes of which he hasn't felt for many years. Aerlie senses his feelings and moves to his side, taking his arm and leaning into him. He feels his eyes becoming moist, and tries desperately to hold his composure.

Leesa brings the microphone back around to allow him an opportunity to respond.

"Miss Macaid," he begins with a slight tremor in his voice. He attempts to clear it before continuing. "Lady Amariyn, Priestess Sehnisavain, and Lieutenant Lapäli...along with all the rest who participated in this affair..." he takes a deep sigh. "As representatives of your societies, you do me a great honor this day. The people of Tae'Eladar have honored me on many occasions over the years, but this would certainly count as the highest form of it. The dedication of a monument of this size and magnitude is a most noteworthy one.

And to preserve this occasion, I think it might be prudent to make this valley into a type of national parkland, to keep it pristine. The village here may grow somewhat over the years, but perhaps we should keep it modest, so as not to fill this space with an overabundance of structures, and thus detract from the natural beauty of the land. We could also erect some manner of memorial here to further mention the deeds that took place for future generations to learn from."

A rousing cheer comes up from the audience in support of the suggestion.

Marelle had stepped closer to Captain Kholgard by this time as she listened to the service on the platform. Relissa impulsively followed behind her friend, and they stood together as a group near the front of the crowd for a better view. Also standing nearby was Alin Malorn. Marelle took notice of him as she approached.

"Dean? How do you feel lately?"

"Please, don't call me Dean," he corrects politely. "But yes, I feel much better now, and today is a special one."

Marelle studied his attire, which seemed very unusual for his typical profession.

"Um, if not Dean, then what? Because it looks like you're taking up a religion now."

"Yes, Lieutenant, I feel this is my newest direction in life. I very literally owe my existence to the god Ilmater, so I'm going to follow his wisdom and see if I can pay back for my gift by helping others with theirs."

"All right," she smiles. "It's good to see you found something that suits you. Good luck with it."

The cheering was settling again, and Thaelyn was preparing for his next statement.

"And furthermore," he announces, having regained better control by now. "Over the course of this time since the Marshal departed, I had my officers file their reports for a summary review, and I took special notice of your involvement in so many matters of helping others, coordinating our efforts in the city, even saving the lives of so many innocents. For such a young lady, still so early in her years, you have demonstrated some rather exemplary talent and wisdom, and I do not waste such qualities. Although we have spoken briefly in the past about what manner of government we may bring to this world, for those societies who would join us, I think I would desire something special in your case."

Tristeen suddenly felt a chill run down her back as she started having visions of where this might be going.

"Therefore," Thaelyn continues. "For all the honors given to me this day, it becomes necessary for me to give a few back. I will require a form of representation within my government to accommodate these people out here, both the human population of Rolsklinde and the High Elves of Kynesoth. I also need a proper form of representation for those of Solinaia, as we are still trying to assimilate them as well. Naturally, a city demands leadership, and in the case of a royal sanction, we might use a viceroy rather than a Governor, although the position is essentially the same. We will also establish a local parliament body to define the rule of law for these lands. But you, young lady…I want you on my High Council."

Tristeen screeched at the suggestion, falling back a step, and covering her mouth. She turns to search for her father in the crowd. Josef and his friends all stood nearby. Abraim and Seth both nodded with wide grins, while Josef smiled brightly and gave a double thumbs-up.

Willit and Jared both gaped at the scene on the stage before turning to examine each other.

"Bloody hell, man," Jared moans. "Do you think she'll even still talk to us after this?"

"I certainly hope so!" Willit muses wittily. "If she can come off that golden perch of hers long enough."

Thaelyn surveys the audience as he continues his speech.

"We already have representation for the human population of Tae'Eladar, so we will involve a new position for this world. The same goes for the High Elves, and Priestess…" he turns to Sehnisavain. "I am hereby elevating you to the position of a noblewoman. You may still serve as a priestess if you desire, but you will also serve on my High Council to represent your people. And Lady Amariyn, we have spoken of this before, where you will be appointed to a position, along with two others, to fill that need."

Sehnisavain's jaw dropped as she listened. She was in shock and couldn't speak at first. Her sister, Ilothonna, was in the crowd, as were her two daughters, Tyshalis and Rhyvanith. They all rushed forward to comfort her and exchange hugs.

"Your Grace," she wheezes. "I don't know what to say. I didn't expect this."

"And why not?" he smiles. "You are already a leader in their eyes. Therefore, you are the best choice for this position. And the nature of this position carries its own weight, therefore you must rise to meet it...Lady Sehnisavain," he bows his head politely.

"By the light of the Seldarine, my deepest thanks, Your Grace," she bows deeply.

"And since we are on the topic of appointing honors," Thaelyn considers. "I have one more I would wish to bestow at this time. This has been on my mind for some time now, and especially after the attack on the city, but it was generally outside my jurisdiction to take this action, other than perhaps an honorary mention. However, now that we are here, and you have all accepted our offer of allegiance into the kingdom, it would make sense for me to attend to this on an official level."

"And what would that be, my Lord?" Tristeen wonders.

Thaelyn now turns to the crowd and calls out boldly.

"I wish to call forward Captain Kholgard of the Allegiance Guard. Present yourself and be recognized."

The Captain had been contentedly standing in the crowd watching the display, and the sudden mention of his name surprised him. He yelps unexpectedly and quickly checks his appearance.

Marelle jerks around to see him suddenly fussing with himself. She lends a hand to assist by smoothing out the wrinkles of his shirt and straightening his attire. He runs his fingers through his hair in a vain attempt to groom himself and then looks to her for approval.

"How do I look?" he asks nervously.

"A wreck, but we're all like that, actually. Just go with it. You can't keep him waiting."

He attempts to compose himself and tries to remember how to stand at attention, then to walk with a formal military posture.

"Kneel here before me please," Thaelyn asserts while pointing at the platform.

The Captain makes his way up the stairs and moves in front of his new King, then to kneel on the platform…a position he's never had to take before with anyone.

Tristeen and the others move aside to give the two of them room, unsure what Thaelyn has in mind. Leesa finds herself trying to figure out what she should do with the microphone, so Thaelyn motions privately to bring it up closer to him so he can speak. He straightens his posture and turns again to the General with the sword. He draws it out once again and holds it in a salute as he prepares to speak.

"Captain…hmm… It occurs to me that I do not know your full name. Marelle calls you Roddy, but what is the formal pronunciation?"

"Um, right, Your Lord…er, I mean, my Lord."

"It is quite alright; everyone has that occasion around here."

"Yeah, I guess they do, at that. My given name is Roderic, or do you prefer all of it, Roderic Sabastian."

"Most excellent, and that is a very fine name. But now…" he clears his throat. "In your service, you have demonstrated extraordinary valor, courage, and selflessness in the face of remarkable dangers. You held true to your virtues, and you risked life and limb, in a very real sense of the word, to the aid of others around you, to preserve lives, and to protect the innocent. Such men of your integrity are a rare breed, and when one is found, we must permit ourselves to bestow upon him a most dignified service of gratitude, that he may stand as a symbol of excellence and a demonstration of righteousness. It is to this end that I offer this to you."

"Gracious, he's doing it," Marelle mumbles silently. "I've only heard about this in bedtime stories."

Thaelyn begins moving his sword to dub each shoulder of the Captain as he continues.

"By the authority vested in me as Lord and King of Tae'Eladar, and to the service of Torm, who presides over the domain of Justice and Law. In the memory of my Father, Tyr, and Helm the Guardian, and in the eyes of the Gods we adore who cast their gaze upon us this day, I do hereby dub thee Sir Roderic Sabastian Kholgard, Honored Knight and Patron Saint of the Realms. You may rise."

The Captain can barely catch his breath due to his surprise at the bestowment. He tugs at himself to stand up again, his face twitching with emotion. He forces himself upright and gradually brings his eyes to meet with Thaelyn's.

"Thank you…my Lord," he offers softly, barely able to push the words past his lips. "I just wish my father could be here to see this. I think he would be proud."

Thaelyn smiles as he returns his sword again, and the crowd lets out another riotous cheer.

Marelle lurches forward. She jumps up on the stage and throws herself around the Captain in a generous embrace. Thaelyn and Aerlie exchange glances and smile warmly.

"Did I not hear some music out there?" he calls to the assembly.

"Aye, you did," returns an answer from somewhere in the mass of bodies.

"Then let us hear it again. I recall someone once promising some revelry on this occasion," he finishes with a teasing glare at Tristeen.

Chapter 5

A STEP BEYOND

"Túfu, how do you feel about Petrith, or any of the other guys here?"

"Are you thinking of the Captain again, and his statement of pairing up?" she sighs. "I don't know, Suli. We've had this discussion before. There are a few I'm attracted to, including Petrith. He's cute, and I like him, although I'm half-expecting you to beat me to him," she grins softly.

"To be honest, Túfu, despite my behavior, I don't actually want to get in the way of anyone else. I suppose, eventually, it will come down to some kind of competition, if we're all looking to pair up. But we don't have an even count of boys and girls."

"Oh, so you're actually paying attention to that?" she grins mildly. "Yeah, I noticed that, as well. But you and I both know this isn't a life for us. What would we do together?"

"Túfu, if you need me to answer that one, I think you missed a very important part about growing up," she giggles.

"All right, fine," Túfula returns with a subtle laugh. "But besides that part. It's the part that comes after. Where do we go with it? We're trapped on this world and hiding in a hole in the ground. That's not exactly the kind of future I envisioned for myself."

"Neither did I, but here we are," Sulíma relents. "Petrith and I were talking about this not long ago. He seems to feel that sometime, somehow, we need to make a stand, that it can't stay this way forever. I don't like the idea, but in the end, I can't argue with it either. I want better, but fighting a world full of orcs doesn't sound very promising."

"I've heard Tana speak of this a few times, too. She wants to take back a little for all we had to take from them. And apparently, it's not limited to the orcs."

"Oh wonderful. But this simply isn't our way..."

"Suli, our 'way' is to run and hide from anything that looks even remotely scary. Therefore, we hide in a hole. At least, this is how Tana would describe it. And although I'm not much different from you in this perspective, a piece of me also wants better, and fighting might be the only way. Our lives will carry us FAR longer than any single generation of orc...or ten, or a hundred! And all we do is hide in a hole? For how many centuries, or even millennia? This hole might not even survive that long!"

"I suppose you have a point," Sulíma sighs.

"Even our ancient ancestors, the Eracyodines, did better than we are, and all they had were stone tools. They didn't even have the knowledge we possess to make anything better, and yet they still took over the place! So what are we sitting on our tails for?"

"Fine! But you know, Túfu, as for knowledge, when I was in school, I was hoping to study exobiology, so I could one day follow in my sister's hoof steps, maybe to join her working in the research labs. Then the attack came and tore all those dreams apart. Now, I'm struggling to fix that machine out there. I never expected myself to be working as an engineer. I don't have the background for it. So, knowledge or no, even those stone tools are beyond us. We became so used to our technology; we forgot the rest."

"I may have to agree with you on that, so we may need to use our advanced knowledge to reinvent a few things, stone or otherwise. And yet, it's strange how so many of us have taken up occupations very different from what we had in mind during our school years. My interest was in history and cultural science, to follow after my father. I don't really want to replace him on the Council, but if to find a nice place in some office working to study something intellectual, that would be fine."

"Yeah, you come from a privileged family. He was a history teacher before this, wasn't he?"

"That's right, and he did so love to tell stories."

"Mine was much more scientific, med-techs and researchers. You remember my sister, Ankhia, right? She was an intern at the medical lab before all this. She would come home and play junior med-tech with me, trying to teach me a few things about medicine and health care."

"That must've been fun."

"And I think Petrith was hoping to go into the technology field. He was always so good with computing systems, networks, and, um…" she pauses momentarily to clear her throat, "…well, let's just say…decoding encryption algorithms."

"Decoding? How about breaking into…" Túfula retorts playfully. "That one time he cracked the Security Council mainframe was famous."

"Yeah, and so was the reprimand he received."

"Still, you're right, he was good. But this was all a long time ago, and since then, I think a lot of us have slouched on all our old lessons. We only made it partway through our junior school. We still had the senior school, and then the university. That's a lot of study time robbed away from us."

"And so I, who wanted to be a biotech researcher, have been trying to teach myself how to repair a re-articulating nano-molecular fabrication array. Petrith has gone from computer science to serving Captain Lapäli, trying to learn the role of a militia trooper, and you…" she chuckles. "Let's see, from a history buff to…what was it the Captain called it?"

"He used an archaic term I barely even recognize. It's almost humiliating, but I suppose it's true. An alchemist… Someone who studies herbs and mineral compounds trying to figure out how to make primitive remedies."

"Well, I have to admit, you've come up with some interesting formulas over the years."

"Yeah, I suppose I shouldn't complain. I had some early help from a few of the teachers. That got me started. And Tana also helped from all her studies of the orcs. She pointed out a few things they often use in theirs. One good thing about being sent into the shelters is we all survived together, though it doesn't help much simply to be here."

"We should be thankful for this much, though. We didn't finish our junior school, but they did at least manage to fill in some of our lessons, even without the official classroom study."

"My best discovery was that simple antibiotic made from mold secretions. I think that's probably the most useful item of all. Some of the herbal remedies I've made seem to help with things like stomach upset and nervous tension. I just wish one thing…"

"What's that?" Sulíma inquires.

"I wish I knew how to make soap. Today is bath day for me, and I wouldn't mind a nice soothing bubble bath scented with some type of flower essence to help me relax. The trouble is all our soaps were manufactured in a chemical lab. No one remembers the original invention."

"More of that lost knowledge. And speaking of baths, I need one as well. I wonder what the water is like today."

"Well, no time like the present to find out. The sun is shining, so they say. Maybe it won't be too cold this time."

The two girls rise from their table in the dining hall where they were enjoying their conversation after finishing breakfast. They make their way through the tunnel leading to the sleep chambers, passing several doors leading off to individual rooms until they come to the one where they shared their quarters. They enter the room to find Petrith getting ready for his daily patrol.

"Hey there girls!" he chirps. "Just coming in from breakfast?"

"Yeah, and now we need to go get washed up," Túfula replies.

"Need anyone to come supervise? I'm available. As an official unofficial member of the Sentinels, you might need me to watch over the place to make sure it's secure!"

"Right, Petrith," Sulíma giggles. "And would you also help us wash our backs?"

"If duty calls, I must answer. It's a difficult job, but someone has to do it," he chuckles.

"You know, Suli," Túfula conjectures as she pulls out a change of clothes. "I wonder how many times our duty-bound officer of the Sentinels has been secretly surveying the so-called security situation around the pool while the girls are out bathing."

"That's right!" she muses. "I've actually noticed what I think to be some well-entrenched hoof prints just behind the shrubbery screen overlooking the pond. I can't imagine how they got there, though!" she teases.

"Oh dear!" Túfula feigns her surprise. "Then, I suppose we really do need someone from the militia to protect us in case there are ruffians out there that might wish to defile our virgin purity!"

The trio breaks out in a rowdy burst of laughter as the two girls collect their things and get ready to leave. Petrith also finishes assembling his gear, and they make their way together back to the dining hall and through the tunnel into daylight.

The sun was shining brightly today, and the air felt pleasantly warm. The work camp below the mining tunnel entrance was deserted, as usual, and the grasses in the open fields surrounding them danced gently in the calm breezes. To the north, the plains extended into the distance, terminating on the horizon at a seaside shoreline. The fields continued around to the east, hugging the base of the mountain foothills where their mine tunnel had been carved. In the distance, they could see the remains of the once-proud city they used to call home, now broken and decayed and overgrown with centuries of recovering vegetation.

The jungle environment further to the east of the city was taking back the land, but the city posed a difficult obstacle to overcome before it could move back across the plains where their hideout was found. The region had been largely clear-cut when they first arrived in this world almost eighteen centuries ago. The city paved over a large section of the land, and the region west of it was cleared to make room for the immense ship that settled to the ground. The resources uprooted were used in the initial construction efforts, and then more space was cleared to provide for farming.

The mining operation was established in the mountainside just to the south of the fields and near the river. The river itself was used as a source of water, both for the city as well as irrigation for the farms. But now, the farms were gone, overgrown by native grasses, and everything else was in an advanced state of decay.

Sulíma and Túfula walked down the ramp from the mine entrance, followed by Petrith. When they reached the bottom, the two girls strolled off towards the river and the pool at the base of the waterfall. Petrith watches them as they depart.

The girls continued across the camp until they came to a row of shrubs lining the river shoreline. They circled around the shrubs, casting one final glance back in the direction of Petrith, who was still standing near the ramp. He makes a gentle nod and turns to head off in his own direction. The girls turn to each other with a subdued sense of disappointment, and then continue to the pond for their bath.

Petrith takes off toward the city. He breaks into a sprint, dashing across the fields along the base of the foothills. Over the years, he had developed a sturdy muscle tone and a lot of stamina making runs like this. It was a routine he had conditioned himself to perform on a regular basis. He crosses the open plain and approaches the outer boundary of the city.

A short masonry wall marked the edge of a section of housing. It showed as much deterioration as everything else around here, but it was still standing. He hops over it and drops down into the backyard of a local residence. The house was scorched and collapsed in a heap. Petrith keeps low to the ground, a practice he had learned as part of his training by Captain Lapäli, as well as from his field runs through the city streets and alleys, trying to avoid any hostile elements and keep out of sight. He creeps across the yard to the other side and along the far wall towards the front of the property. Peering around the corner of the wall, he sees the coast is clear, so he dashes out along the edge of the street that passes through the neighborhood.

This area of the city was well known to him. He passed through here often, and nothing ever came up. The orcish patrols he usually saw were mostly on the other side of the city, and sometimes in the downtown section, but never this far out. He made his way through streets and alleys toward his old school. He used that as a perch overlooking the rest of the city, as it was located on a hill and afforded him the best view.

✦

"My Lord, we have some rather interesting news for you this morn."

Thaelyn was just arriving in the tactical office when the General called his attention to a new scouting report received during the early morning hours. It has been three months since they began their new deployment strategy circling the front line against the orcs to the far south on the eastern side and around under their forces.

"Yes, General, what do you have for me?" Thaelyn responds as he takes his position at the table.

"First of all, a brief review. As you recall, a few months ago, we began making surveys using our gryphon scouts to see just how far south the orcs actually extend, and as it turns out, it is not fully to the southern shoreline, as previously thought. This doesn't actually surprise me, knowing how the orcs prefer warmer climates."

"This is true, and that shoreline extends into a subarctic region."

"We can also probably say, with some reasonable assurance, that since most of the action would be found to the north, they would tend to migrate up there anyway. So, our new campaign to circle our troops around on this side and close in behind them is yielding some fine results. We now surround them on three sides against the western shoreline. I think it is safe to say this war will be over very soon."

"This is good to hear, at least insofar as this world is concerned."

"Right, and then we need to consider what comes next. Meanwhile, we just got this in," he flashes a new report. "This would make Number Three, I believe, and personally, I cannot see how there might be any more, considering the remaining landmass and orcish troops seen moving around out there."

Thaelyn picks up the report. It details the discovery of a third orcish portal aperture in a southern campsite which seemed particularly small in comparison to the others.

"Do our scouts report any activity in the area? I am a little concerned by this description of so few orcs in the region."

"Since it is found at such low latitude, one explanation I thought of was that they might wish to migrate to the north at their earliest convenience to escape from the cold. Other than that, the scouts sent to observe it see very little activity in the region at all. We have also been keeping a close watch on their troop movements. I think they are becoming wise to our presence in the south already, and are now clustering in the middle."

"I am almost sorry to think of the panic they may be experiencing at this moment, but war is war, and we have surely seen enough bloodshed on our side of it. Nevertheless, they can still pose a problem if they use their portals to escape, and their escape could be to places unknown, only to rebuild and come at us again. It is a solemn choice, but we must press forward."

"I would tend to agree with you, my Lord. Therefore, considering the placement of our troops at this time, I would imagine no more than just a few months remain in this engagement. After that, and other than for these three portals we need to monitor, I might say our war is complete…on this world, that is."

"This would be a welcome sight. Soon, we can let our people return home to rest, then to find a more pleasant occupation in their reserve status."

"I know I have come to miss sitting in my favorite chair on the rear porch overlooking my wife's garden. She is always so attentive to it, and I often found it relaxing to watch her as she tends to her work."

"I would certainly wish to see you find some relaxation time for yourself, General. You have earned it no less than anyone else. Also, it would seem we are nearing an end to our needs here in this village. I would wish to begin making plans to relocate our command operations to a new home within Rolsklinde. We have made some progress in rebuilding some of the homes and marketplaces by now, and there is work underway in the upper plaza district on new civic and parliamentary buildings. I have been in contact recently with our gnomish engineers to replace the portal gate here in the village with a more permanent structure, rather than the one we have now, which is left over from our original occupation of this site. This will tie into the other local gates, forming a regional network. We will then build a hub in the city linking back to Tae'Eladar."

"Very good, my Lord, and the city up there would most certainly offer us room to build a more elaborate structure from which to conduct the remainder of this war. I would imagine our activities, even after we finish with the orcs, will be more suitably conducted in this world rather than on our own. This world bears a closer link in the progression we are following to achieve our final goal."

"This is my belief as well, and Rolsklinde is as good a place as any to build our base since it has so much open space available. Further, if we build our gateway hub there, and a regional gate linking to the other cities, it could serve as a crossroads for commerce and industry in the region. However, this does prompt me to consider one alteration to our existing practice."

"Oh? And what might that be?"

"Our network on Tae'Eladar is mostly for foot traffic, other than the cargo routes, which may often use vehicles to carry merchandise. Then, within the cities, you may have coaches for hire to transport you around the local sights. However, one thing that disturbs me in our travels here is the excessively long tunnel stretching from one world to another. Going through the network back home, you have a flash, then instantly another flash as you arrive on the other side. Here, you are flying through the ethers freeform, and for the uninitiated, and even the casual traveler, this is inappropriate.

Therefore, I am thinking of a custom transit center using a passenger vehicle for this application."

"Oh dear cu'Nar!" Padriyl moans. "If that doesn't twist my horns. Interplanetary travel using what? Wheeled vehicles pulled by animals?"

"Actually," Thaelyn smiles. "While the thought would surely be amusing to see, I am thinking of using our more recent motorized vehicles for the occasion."

"Uh huh, which is nearly as bad."

"These are fairly new, as part of our mechanized industry back home. But if to design a facility with a parking garage, and an appropriately large portal aperture, much like we use for the existing cargo network, then to use that same carriage service, or perhaps to schedule timed departures, depending on how the flow develops, we could provide a fine service for the people."

"I'm simply trying to envision this. You're barely in an Industrial Age, and now using wheeled vehicles and portals to move across worlds. Yeah, there go my mother's horns again. She'll love this one."

"But just imagine, Lieutenant... She could purchase one of her own to commute to and from work. How convenient would that be."

"Oh, cu'Nar help us. But you do carry a valid point, as we would probably do the same, if only we ever colonized anything and made regular transit between them. But I'm sure we'd be using space-based travel, not ground transport jumping through a hole in space."

"One day, Lieutenant... One day..." he waves a finger. "Which actually brings to mind another issue. Our interactions together seem to be increasing nicely, and I am pleased your Elder Council has accepted my suggestion of providing more of a workforce to the construction of this new industry around you. But we should recall the need to supply basic goods to your people, and for this, it would greatly improve matters to install a more permanent link between us. You are developing a nice little village of a sort, so let us include our gateways there as well, both for personal travel as well as cargo."

"That would indeed help, I'm sure. The one we were using before, that temporary one you hid inside our vehicle hanger, served us well and proved to be very convenient. I'll relay this to the Council so we can make the appropriate plans for it."

The morning proceeded as usual. The clutter of refugees outside the north gate had thinned out considerably as they were relocated to Kynesoth or resettled in Rolsklinde, leaving the level of activity within Firstfall to settle back to a more natural flow for the local business trade.

At around midmorning, an anxious address shouts through the door of the tactical office as an elder High Elf emerges into view.

"Your Grace! I have something for you, finally!"

Sehnisavain appeared with a younger woman, having just arrived from Kynesoth through a mage portal, as the new city portal gate did not yet connect directly to the village. She seemed very excited, and the other elf followed closely behind.

"What is it, Lady Sehnisavain? You seem rather agitated."

"I found her, Your Grace. After all this time, I finally found her."

"Her, meaning…" he raises his eyebrow inquisitively.

"Oh, my apologies, it has been a while since we last discussed this…that one surviving member of the expedition to your world to deliver that probe for the Suuden-Aryku."

"Ah! Yes! Thank the Powers. Although I am truly sorry to hear she is the last of them. But if we have at least this much, it gives us the link we need to discover what Darumon was doing out there. Do we have any interesting details to report?"

"She is able to recall several details, and I was hoping you could assist in piecing together the rest, given your greater knowledge of the landforms on Tae'Eladar."

"Very good. What do we have then?"

The young woman steps forward to give her address.

"My Lord," she begins. "Although it was quite some time ago, I can still recall a few moments of our journey. And when the Priestess here called me forward, I have been trying to remember even more. Firstly, we were sent into your world and led by a group of orcs across many lands, finally into a range of high mountains. There was a group of us led by the High Priestess's husband, may the Seldarine help him find peace. Most of us did not return. I was lucky, I think. I was able to cast an invisibility cloak on myself and sneak away. I felt bad for it, but the others were falling too quickly, and someone needed to return to report our success."

"I understand. What was it that attacked you?"

"I can't be sure what name you might have for them, but they were gigantic. They looked like people, but primitive, and stood taller than some of our homes."

"Then you must be referring to a clan of giants, possibly stone giants. Yes, we do have a number of those in the mountainous regions. They tend to roam as nomadic tribes, and largely keep to themselves. They choose not to be a part of our kingdom, as they once arrived from somewhere outside our world, but they also know their place, and we hold a tentative peace with them, so long as we allow them their space."

"Well, it would seem we must've violated that space rather seriously. The orcs led us up to it, but it was a surprise to see them. If they move as a nomadic clan, they must not have been at home the last time the orcs made their visit."

"This is reasonable, as well as unfortunate. But now, as to the location..."

"Right. I recall it was cool, as if the entire region were that way, though I wonder if it could be a seasonal effect."

"Perhaps seasonal, or maybe you were in a northern region. Did you see any significant features of the land?"

"We began in a barren place and walked for many days in the direction of the setting sun."

"To the west..."

"I recall we had to circle around a great maw opening in the ground. It was quite deep. I have to admit, I was a bit frightened to step too close to it."

"Unfortunately, we have a number of those left behind by the Spellplague, where the eruption of the magical energies after the goddess Mystra's death ripped open the land."

"Gracious, I'm terribly sorry to hear that."

"Can you describe the configuration of this hole…its general shape? Each one is a bit different."

"Well, I recall we were walking near a long stretch of it, still to the west, and then it seemed to turn, branching off to the south. Then, a short distance further, another branch turned northward, forcing us to divert around it."

"Something of a T shape, by the sound of it. Very well, this narrows it down for us. What came next?"

"Once we passed that, we continued west and crossed through some smaller mountains and forests, then spent a while passing through a large forest until we came upon a swamp. The orcs told us we needed to go around the swamp because of something bad that lived in it."

"Did they give it a name or a description?"

"They were not good with our language, and we did not spend much time to study theirs, so there was some difficulty in that, but they called them things that do not die."

"Such a lovely name, even for orcs…" he smirks. "Let me think a moment. There are many creatures in our world that may be especially difficult for an orc to fight, but for them to call it a thing that does not die would suggest they lay into it, perhaps causing great damage to it, but it does not go down…or else it quickly comes back up again. Yes, perhaps that could be it. Swamp trolls. They have the ability to regenerate their injuries quickly, and the only true way to kill them is most often with fire, though these orcs might not be aware of this, especially if they are imports to our world."

Thaelyn pulls out a sheet of paper from a nearby box and picks up a pen to start taking down notes on these details while the girl continues her description.

"After we circled around the swamp, I believe we were moving north now. There were grasslands, I think we crossed a road once, and finally came into more trees."

"We do have a lot of those. What next?"

"We moved into the forest, and by now I think there were mountains to our right, and later, more in front of us, big ones. But then we turned again to run along the base of those until the orcs began to take us up a trail."

"This is becoming complicated, but do continue. Which direction did you turn?"

"Left, to the west again…"

"All right, and then up a trail," he continues with his notes. "Is this the final destination, these mountains?"

"Yes. Now it is getting cold and snowy. We were facing some difficulty here as we were not really dressed for the occasion. The orcs were able to hunt some local animals to provide us with skins, but they were rather smelly."

"I suppose they might be, but at least it was cover."

"At the top of this trail, we came to a cave. The orcs led us inside, but this is where it goes badly for us with those giants. As they saw us come in, I recall they tried talking to us, but none of us understood their words. The orcs, however, they simply charged to the attack…the brutes."

"Yes, I must agree on this point. Like I said, we hold a delicate peace with the stone giant clans, and those orcs may have jeopardized it. Now I will need to go up there and explain our situation here in this world and our new war. But anyway, they attacked you, but you were able to complete your mission, correct?"

"Yes, we knew our priority was to open the portal and send the artifact through. The orcs told us it was deeper inside and against one wall. They occupied the giants, along with some of our men, and the rest of us hurried through to find the portal. We just barely managed to open it and send the thing through before we came under attack again. This is when I knew I needed to escape. It was every man, or woman in my case, for himself at that point."

"I understand. Now, as to this portal… Often, one needs a key to open a portal of this sort. Did you require something in your possession, or to speak a word or make any sort of gesture to this effect?"

"The orcs had an item in their possession which they gave to us during the journey. Unfortunately, it was lost when the giants attacked. Like I said, the orcs charged to the attack first, giving us a small amount of time to see to our task. It was the High Priestess's husband who carried this artifact, and he was soon to fall after we finished. I got away and met with one of the orcs, who also ran out of the cave when he saw us finish with the portal. From there, we worked our way back to the shamans who opened a return portal for us."

"I wonder if they could have been the same shamans we found once," he muses privately.

Thaelyn examines his notes to ensure everything has been covered. He then calls for a page outside to fetch a regional map of Sein'amar from the guildhall in Bya'an Tamoranth. He discusses some of the details with the General while they wait. When the page returns, they begin to compare his notes with the images on the map.

"We start in a barren space," Thaelyn considers, "and move west to one of the Spellplague chasms. But by the description, it did not take long for them to circumvent that, so it must be a small one."

"This would leave out the hole in the southeast," the General suggests. "Depending on where they arrived at that one, it could take weeks to work around it, perhaps more."

"And the one in the central west is more of a round hole, rather than one that branches to the east in a T configuration running north-south, which leaves us with this in the northwest."

They continue to study the map, pointing out the various features and cross-referencing with the notes.

"Very well, if it's the one up here..." the General points at the map, "...then we have trees and mountains... Good, there are some of those along the way here, and then a large, forested region after that, and a swamp. My Lord, this must be the one, and we also know there to be swamp trolls living there."

"Next, we head north, so the grasses and forested region she is speaking of should be this region of plains and the forest beyond that."

"And further, my Lord, here may be the road she was referring to, stretching across just north of the swamp."

"Based on where we seem to be heading, General, we are moving into these mountains here..." he points at the map. "And I know of a band of stone giants in the region. This will most certainly complicate things from the diplomatic perspective."

"I don't envy you this, my Lord, but if anyone can smooth it over, it is you."

"We have not had dealings with the giant populations for a while, and if they suffered an attack involving elves..." he shakes his head. "Orcs would not be a bother if it were only them, but they know we control the elven population, so this might appear as a strange new alliance in their eyes. We will need to proceed gently and perhaps make an offering. Furthermore, if they killed the one carrying this portal key, we must find a way to take it back. But more than likely, the one who killed that member of their party is using it as a trophy."

"Complications, my Lord, but this cannot deter us."

"Absolutely. Order up a few gryphon scouts to survey the region. Maybe we can spy on the cave from the air and monitor any activity in the area. If these giants are nomadic in nature, we need to find them. Hopefully, they still carry that key."

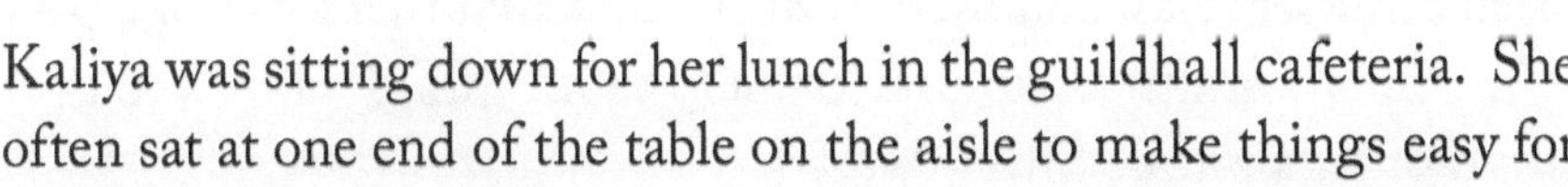

Kaliya was sitting down for her lunch in the guildhall cafeteria. She often sat at one end of the table on the aisle to make things easy for her to slide in and out of the benched seating, due to her size and the awkwardness of the design for smaller bodies.

The cafeteria was busy, as usual, with students coming and going through the room. But one individual was seen browsing the assembly, and she wasn't carrying a plate of food. Instead, she was an elder High Elf clutching a set of thick notebooks and journals. She scanned the room, as if looking for something, and finally set her eyes on Kaliya, so she struts over to join her.

"Hello," she begins politely. "I'm sorry to interrupt your meal, but I was hoping to take a moment to ask you a few questions. Do you mind?"

Kaliya looked up at the woman. She was well-dressed as a

professional businesswoman, and presented an image of someone important.

"Oh, not at all, have a seat." Kaliya motions to the other side of the table.

The woman sits down and begins to introduce herself.

"My name is Vonafel Windsong. I'm the Senior Archivist over at the Royal Historical Archives down the road. My specialty is studying the many ancient tomes, scriptures, and other fascinating literary works we have seen occur during our history."

"Really! That sounds interesting. You might want to talk to Elder Vankkar, in that case. He was once a history teacher before he was appointed to our Elder Council."

"Indeed. Well, if he's anything like me, he would probably get lost in it," she giggles. "Anyway, I'm currently trying to conduct a little research on a few things, and I needed to ask you a few questions, if you don't mind."

"A history researcher asking ME questions? That's a new one. Am I listed in your history somewhere?" she chuckles.

"Actually, that's what I'm trying to find out. You see, we have a few noteworthy individuals in our history who left behind some fascinating legacies, and there's one in particular that I've made part of my life's work to try to understand the meaning. Have you ever heard of Adalon the Silver?"

"I think the name may have passed by me a couple of times in the hallways, why?"

"She's a founding member of our Order, and an exceptionally wise individual, but also extremely aloof and very cryptic at times. She's best known for her prophetic verses."

"A prophetess? Oh wonderful. My father sometimes has visions he receives from a race we call the cu'Nar, and these tend to represent prophecies for us, but they're also extremely difficult to figure out."

"Who are these cu'Nar? Is this a race you encountered somewhere during your journey?"

"They're a race that came to us back on Azgarén, our old home world, to warn my father about Sargeras. But they're a strange one.

Thaelyn says they're likely a race of positive elementals. Does that mean anything to you?"

"Indeed, it does, but to see such as that anywhere outside their natural realm is highly unusual, to say nothing of warning a society like yours about such a creature as he."

"Yeah, I think Thaelyn mentioned something like this once. Wow, so does this mean we're really privileged or something?"

"I can't say for sure, but let me write this down..."

She sets her books down and separates her journal from the stack. She also brings out a pen to scribble her notes.

"Do you always carry so many books wherever you go?" Kaliya asks.

"It's an old habit I developed when I was once attending the academy."

"You were in the academy?"

"Yes, but that was a few centuries ago by now. I was attending at the same time as Aerlie. We're good friends together."

"Wow, that must be fun, to have your best friend also as your Queen."

"She and I hold a special relationship. We're the only ones remaining of a social group we had in the old days. The others passed on many years ago."

"Were they elves like you?"

"No, one was a half-elf named Amaree, and the other two were humans, one named Annah, the other Deena. But, as with all things, nothing lasts forever. I miss them, but I still need to carry on."

"That's rough, but I know the feeling. I'll probably go through the same, in time."

"All right, now let me see. You and your people came from this place you call Azgarén. It's my understanding you were running from this Sargeras and essentially being hunted by your former military, correct?"

"Yeah, we would jump from one world to another, settle a bit, just long enough to build new homes and try to relax, but then they came again and pushed us to the next world. Thaelyn thinks it was all just a game Marshal Darumon was playing with us. His kind apparently likes to toy with little things like us."

"This is what I've been coming to understand about these Primordials. I've been asking around, trying to piece together a number of curious little clues to help me understand a new set of passages in these prophecies, and so far, I'm coming to the conclusion we have entered into the final chapter of her second book…a period I have come to describe as the end times."

"Yikes! I'm not so sure I like the sound of that. What does it mean?"

"Well," she smiles gently. "It's not actually as bad as it might sound, simply the end of this book with an open future, as far as I can tell. She hasn't written anything new since then."

"What sort of book is this, prophecies about what?"

"About the Lord and Lady mostly, except for this last chapter. The subject matter changes radically in this one, like suddenly her focus is on someone else, and it can't be local."

"Huh?" Kaliya blurts and leans forward. "Not local, meaning to say what?"

"Meaning to say those elements we are discovering right now… including, I think, you and your people."

"What?" she wheezes. "You mean I really am in that book?"

"She seems to break with many of her previous traditions in this chapter. Everything else reads like a story of the lives of the Lord and Lady. I'm sure Adalon knows what is happening, more than she would ever let on. She's hiding something. These books read like a story yet to unfold, and we see these passages like hints as to what's coming next…somewhere and sometime. But she makes it so impossibly cryptic to understand. They apparently hold private, perhaps also privileged knowledge that only a handful of people would actually know about, with her being one of those. But the real puzzle in my mind is WHY she does it like this. Something is happening, and she's making a chronical of it ahead of time."

"Great cu'Nar, that sounds worse than, well, the cu'Nar!" she chuckles ironically. "Can you give me an example of where it talks about us?"

"There is a mention of a war, which has to be this orcish invasion. It's described as a vulgar tide…here, let me read this to you."

She pulls open another of her notebooks with many handwritten notes, scribbles, scrawls, and doodles. Every corner and margin was covered with something. Kaliya winced at the horrid mess.

"And you work in a historical society? In all the nether-space, I hope you're not a teacher in the academy as well."

Vonafel giggles at the mention and prepares to read several excerpts.

"She uses a lot of metaphors, which is the worst part of this, because like I said, it often demands someone's private knowledge to interpret their meaning. The chapter begins with someone called the Forgotten One. I'm going to make a guess here and say Sargeras, since he's likely forgotten by now among the Estelar, and anyone else who might have once known the Primordials. But this also brings a paradox, as Adalon uses this reference, so where did she get it, unless she's simply using a metaphor based on her interpretations of these visions."

"What does this Forgotten One do…other than make life miserable for my people?"

"The chapter starts like this. Alone in the dark, they lie in wait, Forgotten and Ignored; two Ancient Ones, from times unmeasured, and a life they once adored."

"Yeah, that sounds a little like these cu'Nar, except they don't make poetry out of it."

"The reference to this Forgotten One is used multiple times, so it seems he is becoming active with something. And if we are referencing two of them, the other has to be the Ignored entity."

"I wonder which is which, to be honest. One is Forgotten, the other Ignored, which might suggest he wasn't worth thinking about to begin with. Let me think a moment, based on what I've been hearing from my friends during that war. We have Darumon and Sargeras, both of whom could qualify as Forgotten, I suppose, but

Ignored? Darumon seemed to like to stay hidden…and, oh! No one even knew his name until we asked my father, who just barely recalled it. It was always 'Sargeras this, Sargeras that,' therefore pointing the finger away from him. But is this to say HE is the Forgotten One? You say he becomes active, right?"

"Yes, I see this term used multiple times here."

"So HE must be Forgotten, as if to say he wasn't important enough to qualify, or he's trying to defer attention. After all, he's only a servant creature. What good is that in comparison to the Estelar?"

"Yes, you have a point. But then, how would we describe Sargeras, if Darumon is only a servant creature. Sargeras would be the Primordial, right?"

"Yes, so he would surely be one to remember. But Ignored? Um, let me think…" she pauses in deep thought. "Hey, what about this? Yes, this might be a possibility. He was controlling the High Elves over there, but not solidly enough that a bit of careful wording could turn them around. And my father also recalled him arriving in poor health on Azgarén, which means…OH!" she snaps her fingers. "Yes! The dynamistic flows! He needs them, apparently. Without them, he would be in poor health, and according to something I heard, would likely be very weak, probably to the point of being too insignificant to worry about. He's in a barren fold, so who cares, he's a non-issue."

"Ah ha! Yes, very good! See what I mean about personal knowledge?"

"Wow, and to think I actually contributed something to that. And I'm not even native to this world."

"But now, a later verse has this to say. The Forgotten One, long in slumber, seeks to take his prize; a race of Children, slowly grown, shall lead to his demise. I have no clue who or what these Children are, how or why she describes them as slowly grown, and then leading to his demise. It almost sounds as if he made something, but it turns on him at some moment."

"Interesting, and a little ironic," she chuckles softly. "Anything else?"

"Later, she talks about someone described as an imposter who seems to hold a lot of hatred for someone else, and he looks down at them very coldly. The trouble with this one is I have no idea who 'he' is or who 'they' are, as they're both referenced indirectly. But if we move to the part that I can be reasonably sure of, it's this one here," she points at one section of her scribblings. "We are talking about a war here. War, as far as we're concerned in this world, shouldn't be possible any more with all our society united under one rule. So, it has to come from outside, and it's described like this…"

She clears her throat again for the next one.

"A tide of vulgar manners flows, from a place of unknown shores; the Son and Daughter travel fast, when the song of battle roars."

"I think my horns are about to fall off now," Kaliya sighs and shakes her head. "And I just grew a new set recently. I guess this is why you had to make it your life's work, because it'll probably take you that long to figure it out!"

"Yes! And I'll tell you, I have been pulling my hair out over these things ever since my academy days. All right, the song of battle must be our invasion of orcs, and their manners were indeed very vulgar when you consider how they were treating our people. The references to the Son and Daughter are common metaphors she uses for the Lord and Lady. He's often described as the Son of the Mountain, and she's the Daughter of Sky."

"That's truly…weird, actually. All right, next?"

"From unknown shores makes sense to me at this moment, if you consider your world would be unknown to us here, and your war essentially spilled over onto us."

"Makes sense… So, she predicted the coming of this war, these orcs invading, and where they came from."

"Correct, but now, this next one. This is where I think you come in, or rather your people. I've been racking my brains over this until recently, when I spoke to Aerlie to get a few ideas. She tells me you essentially told us about Sargeras when you first met with Thaelyn. And naturally, as a Celestial, he would recall those old stories handed down by the Estelar. But now, listen to this…"

Once again, she collects herself to recite the passage.

"A battered home of forlorn souls, in desperation fight; from foreign shores, a haggard chase, is a message borne in flight. Now, Kaliya, tell me you aren't in our history books. You brought this to us!"

Kaliya's expression sagged as she made the connection. She was agape at the very idea of having a role in this at all, and simply stared blankly at Vonafel.

"Just a moment here," she gasps. "Are you saying we were intended to bring this message? But…but wait a moment, then what about the cu'Nar? You said they don't normally come outside like this."

"And Sargeras would be forgotten to just about everyone else. Let me ask you this, what words did they use when they gave you this message?"

"Oh please, let's not go into that one again. When I told Thaelyn, he reacted so furiously, his voice nearly blasted my horns off."

"Oh? He used his Celestial voice? Wow…that must've been a surprise for you."

"A surprise?!" she balks. "I was lucky to still have my skin attached. Anyway, the cu'Nar used a word like 'Titan', or at least this is how we are interpreting it. Thaelyn says that's an ancient word that only a handful of beings might use for such as the Primordials, and elementals are one of those."

"Then this is a personal issue we're talking about here. Someone is following him, and these cu'Nar are messengers, or maybe spies. As elementals, they might hold this ancient knowledge, but they can't be the ones in charge if they're only passing messages. So, the question is who they're serving, because I doubt they would do this on their own."

"This reminds me of our ship. It's massive, and according to Thaelyn and Aerlie, it would be very expensive to build, and NOT likely by the cu'Nar, as they're the ones who delivered it. And it was simply given to us."

"Then it was planned as a way to bring you out of there, along with this message. So, whoever it is, YOU are also messengers."

"But for whom? Would Adalon know the answer? You said she seems to be holding back."

"Yeah, I'll bet she does. Her kind are notorious for their mysterious behavior. But I doubt she would say anything until AFTER it actually happens. This is her way, so we're left scratching our heads and trying to associate things as we go along. But at least we're starting to get a few ideas on the direction now."

"A few ideas?"

"Partially... They delivered this to you, and you brought it to us so that we could take action. This suggests we have a direction to follow, a path of Fate. I've seen this many times in the earlier sections of these books. And the passages that follow seem to describe this direction, at least within reason for how she talks. Eventually, I think I will need to bring this to His Lordship and see what he has to say about it, but there are still a few pieces I'm missing."

✦✦✦✦✦

Several days have passed and Thaelyn is making his way through the guildhall courtyard. He has taken time out from his duties in the war room to visit the guild and refresh his mind on the more productive activities to be found there. Students were coursing their way through the courtyard and along the halls and corridors between classes. Several scholars were making their way between the academy and administration buildings, and a number of attendants and secretaries were dashing around the compound.

Aerlie descends from out of the sky above into the courtyard to meet with him, having sensed his presence visiting the local planar realm and deciding to have a spousal reunion. She was arriving after flying up to the guildhall from the temple in the city.

"Thaelyn!" she calls to him as she settles on the ground. "Are you taking time away from work today?"

"Yes, the burden of this war has played its role, but things are settling into a modest routine now, so I hope to find more time around here as we proceed forward."

She approaches and they share a tender embrace.

"We have made some good progress with our efforts in Rolsklinde," he continues. "And I am also pleased to say we have managed to stabilize much of our concern with Kynesoth, as well. The only true shortfall at this time would be education."

"Yes, I know this already, and we've asked for an increase in production of the Elixir of Visions to assist with it. Also, we're arranging additional classes in many of the cities to make space for the language courses. This must be our first step, of course. Then we must consider what is required to bring the people up to our standards to meld with our original society more evenly."

"This may be the most difficult, not so much for the actual needs to be met, but for the volume of people to process."

"Indeed, ninety thousand is no small matter. That's the size of a large city already, and then we must consider what we are already engaged upon with the Night Elves."

"This represents a lot of work, and no doubt it will keep us both busy for a fair amount of time."

"Just so long as you don't forget who you are married to, my love," she smiles.

"How could I ever forget something as desirable as that," he replies, then plants a gentle kiss across her lips.

"Thaelyn, there is one other thing that came to mind recently, and I wanted to speak to you about it."

"Oh? And what is that?"

"I've been leading our priests in the temple to study those charts and diagrams provided to us by the Daanen-Aryku on their physical anatomy, so that we can learn how to treat their injuries, if the need should ever arise. But one can only learn just so much from a book. You know, as well as I, that our people need the occasional hands-on approach to train our younger members. For the moment, though, I would wish to finish our study with the group I've already assembled."

"Very well, and how would you wish to go about this?"

"Many times, in cases like this, we might use a training doll, but we don't have any for the Daanen'kai model. We could make some, of course, but it would help us a lot if we had something to get us started. A volunteer perhaps, to serve as a model and to give us the initial jump.”

“Male or female…or would you wish to have one of each?”

“One of each would be preferred, of course, to give us examples of both. The diagrams show some rather interesting variations between them, and naturally we would want to fill in our knowledge to its fullest.”

“Then we should see if Commander Nazég can provide us with a few examples to begin this study. I should think this would be a workable solution, as I would imagine their medical professionals must follow a similar practice.”

“Good, but in the meantime, I had a thought. We have one female already among us that we could possibly convince to offer herself as our first victim…I mean, our first study subject,” she giggles.

“Why do I get the impression you, along with so many others around me of late, are working to make the affairs of my life seem so conspiratorial?”

“My dear, you are a millennium and three-quarters. A person can become rather dull after that much. We’re just trying to keep you on your toes!”

Thaelyn forms a pleasant grin as he peers into her crystalline blue eyes. He quickly glances around the courtyard at the various people moving through before responding.

“Aerlie, with people like you at my side, I think we have nothing to worry about. As for this, I will ask Kaliya if she would assist us, the next time I see her.”

◆◆◆◆◆

“Suli, you’ve been gone almost all day. I was starting to worry a bit.”

“Sorry, Captain. It took longer than expected. That place is a wreck, and every time I visit, it seems like more of a wreck.”

“Is that from the orcs rummaging through it, or you?” the Captain chuckles.

"Maybe a little of both, actually," Sulíma replies with a smirk.

"I really can't see the purpose of you going back to the city and that hardware shop. By this time, it should be thoroughly pilfered of anything useful."

"Yeah, I'm sure it is. I just keep hoping there's something still there, maybe hidden in a corner or under a collapsed rack of shelving… anything. I can't fix that stupid machine outside with what I have. And I really don't have much else to do around here, so this is where it takes me."

"You're going stir-crazy, Suli. I can understand this, but I should also remind you to be very careful whenever you go into the city. Even though Petrith hasn't reported any orcish patrols coming in, we shouldn't become over-confident. And let us not forget those mutants. We don't see them often, but we know they're there."

"I know, and I'm being careful. I move quietly and low to the ground, just like you taught me, and I try to keep to the shadows to hide myself from view. I remember the lessons."

"Good. So, did you find anything this time?"

"Yeah, I found that I'm apparently allergic to dust," she chuckles. "Other than that, it's mostly a lot of little scraps. I did notice a set of long-nose pliers lost under a cabinet, so I grabbed those."

"Great! It might not be much, but every little bit helps."

Sulíma steps over to one of the tables and sits down. The dining hall was mostly empty at this time as the people were either resting, or attending to their chores elsewhere. She rests her elbows on the table and lays her head in her hands to think. Her posture betrayed a clear and sudden change in her demeanor.

"Suli? Are you alright?" the Captain asks.

"Yeah, I'm fine," she murmurs through her hands as they covered her face. "I made another little detour to my old house. That's all. Old memories, lost times…you know the feeling, you do the same often enough with that old photo of yours. The place looks a lot older than the last time."

"It's probably not very healthy for you to keep going back there.

It just brings you into more depression, as if we didn't have enough of that going around anyway, like me and mine."

"Yeah, but I had to, just to see what it looks like this time. Call it feminine curiosity."

"That feminine curiosity may one day get you in trouble. And being alone as you are..."

"Yes, Captain, I know, but also remember I'm a girl, which means I can run a lot faster than those orcs, and a lot of other things out there."

"That you are," he grins.

As the day moves to late afternoon, Petrith returns from his patrol. He had spent most of the day at his usual perch located on the field just outside their old school, overlooking a large portion of the city from atop a hillside. As he enters the dining hall, he makes his usual announcement and a brief report to the Captain.

"Captain? I'm back."

"Yes, Cadet Girhani, what do you have for us? Do we have anything to report?"

"Nothing to report on the orcs today and the mutants seem quiet. I saw no unusual activity in the streets...no activity at all, for that matter."

"Another day, and all is calm. It's pleasing to hear, but I would actually feel better if we saw at least something occurring out there. Those orcs are up to something, I can almost feel it."

"Captain," Sulíma suggests. "Maybe you're just going stir-crazy like the rest of us."

"Maybe, and I wouldn't mind if that's all it was. But some of the other scouts have been telling us of movement within the orcish camps."

"Yeah, ever since that day we were talking about the apparent decrease in their activity inside the city. Any word on what's going on?"

"As you may recall," he leans forward. "A few months ago, we started sending out long range scouting patrols to spy on the orcs. This is something we've never done before, so we had to take it slow to learn our way around the local terrain, and to find safe vantage points. What we saw was the movement of orcs from one settlement to another."

"I remember this, but do we know of the reason for it yet?"

"None, so far. We're still studying the situation, but one suggestion was it could be some form of migration. Of course, I'd really like to be able to extend our patrols to the farther regions, just to get a broader scope of the situation. The trouble with that is the running distance and teaching our people how to survive in the wilds for extended periods until they return."

"We have a hard-enough time just trying to survive here."

"I know. I've been trying to recall some of my survival training from the early days as a cadet in the militia. Things like using natural camouflage to cover the body with materials so you can blend in better with the surroundings. Remember, we're not a militaristic society. We don't go to war with just anyone we meet. Such tactics as these are mostly unused by us, so a lot of this will need to be reinvented."

"Just talk to Tana, she's halfway there."

"Yes, you're right, so maybe she can provide us with a few pointers. She already uses natural materials for her clothing, as well as body paint to cover herself in the field. In fact, she's our best scout out there, when spying on the orcs. But the next issue is, since the attack, we've been keeping ourselves hidden in this mine, mostly because of all you kids. You were just children when we found our way in here, and it's taken this long for you to grow up."

"We were grown up two centuries ago, Captain. We were just too scared to go outside because we have orcs everywhere."

"Well, all right, and we do tend to stand out, being as tall as we are in comparison. But now that you're old enough, I guess we should start thinking of what to do with you."

"Well, it's about time!" Túfula shouts from across the room.

The young lady was coming out of her lab deeper in the mine when she overheard part of the conversation. She strolled up to join in.

"Captain," she announces. "Some of us have been talking about this, and we generally agree, at least in concept, that we can't spend all of eternity in this mine. Petrith, Tana, and even Suli and I have to admit we need to make some sort of movement for our future. We don't want to simply rust away, as you like to say it."

"Yes, Túfu, and I suppose I must also agree. But my habit is to take things cautiously, especially with all you kids. But since you're not kids any longer…"

"Right. And as a result of so many of us feeling our horns sagging, I've spent the better part of these last two centuries trying to maintain what little morale we still have left. Still, like so many others, my tail's been twitching for a long time to get out there and do something. If we could actually go out and start behaving like people who want to live, it would do us a world of good."

"Or is it an orcish world of good," Sulíma muses cautiously. "Just what is it you're hoping to do out there, go to war with them?"

"Well, like I've heard Tana say, and I think you mentioned the same with Petrith, we need to make a stand of some kind. I don't think we should go to war with the whole world, but to claim some small piece of it for ourselves…"

"But Túfu," the Captain interjects. "This isn't actually our world to lay claim to."

"Captain, I won't argue with that, but unless you know how to build a star cruiser and carry us away from here, it's either we TAKE a piece of it, or they take all of us. Which will it be?"

"Yes, of course…" he sighs.

"I might wish to add something," Petrith notes. "The orcs DID allow us this land to settle on, right? Therefore, by merit of that old negotiation, this land IS ours."

"I suppose you can say that, but…"

"But?" he interrupts. "Captain, the only 'but' here is they reneged on the deal. Furthermore, they attacked us unprovoked. WE certainly didn't do anything to warrant it, regardless of our opinions of the Suuden-Aryku getting involved or not."

"Also," Túfula continues. "My father would probably say, the old Eracyodines TOOK their world from whatever else was out there in competition with them. We may not originate in this world, but this is where we are, and survival must come into it somewhere."

"All right, Túfu," the Captain relents. "I see your point."

"Therefore, there's got to be somewhere on this planet where we can set up a better home for ourselves and start building again. If it's empty of orcs, great. If not…um, well…" she shrugs.

"Clean it out? I suppose this might be our only choice. But let's not get ahead of ourselves. As far as we know, this place is crawling with orcs, the worst of it in that settlement just on the other side of the city…the one where they launched that big attack. And according to our scouts over there on the edge of the city, it's actually grown in size recently, which is just another curious question on my mind. The camp is growing, but we're not seeing anything entering the city, not even as it used to be, to say nothing of what that increase in population would offer."

"They must be interested in something else," Sulíma suggests. "And it's attracting a big mass of them."

"The last time we saw this, it was just before the attack. Something about a religious tribute to their god."

"Great, another of those?"

"So, until we know more about this, as well as where the rest of them are and what they're doing, we should continue to stay low."

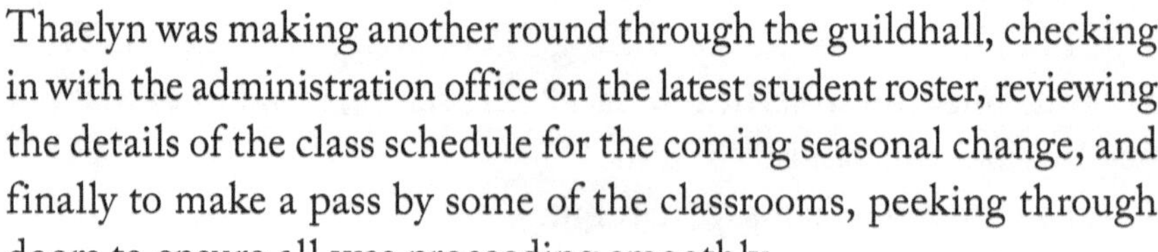

Thaelyn was making another round through the guildhall, checking in with the administration office on the latest student roster, reviewing the details of the class schedule for the coming seasonal change, and finally to make a pass by some of the classrooms, peeking through doors to ensure all was proceeding smoothly.

His last stop was the combat training hall. This was actually one of his favorite places to visit, aside from the mage academy, as it reflected on some of his own personal skills. He would sometimes attend the classrooms to supervise and offer a few of his own lessons to the students in attendance. On this occasion, however, he was only interested in reviewing the training session. He was also looking for Kaliya, as it was at this time of day when she would be taking her training course in this room.

As he enters the room, the training instructors bring the class to attention to give a proper form of salute.

"As you were, everyone," Thaelyn calls into the room.

"My Lord," announces one of the instructors as he approaches. "To what honor do we afford this visit of yours?"

"I am simply making a casual review of affairs and seeking a little relaxation."

"Most excellent, my Lord! The burdens weighing upon you of late have surely brought a fair amount of grief, but it is good to see you back in here."

"And it feels good, Sergeant. Is Cadet Nazég available for speaking momentarily?"

"But of course, my Lord. Allow me to fetch her for you."

The Sergeant moves to the head of the room to make his announcement.

"Cadet Nazég, present yourself forward..."

From near the rear of the hall, a tall, blue-skinned female takes a break from her exercises working a punching bag hanging from the ceiling. She turns and sprints forward, arriving at the front of the hall and taking up a position in front of the Sergeant, standing perfectly at attention.

"My Lord, Cadet Nazég is ready for your inspection," the Sergeant advises.

Thaelyn casually strolls over, making a cursory inspection of the tall cadet. Her poise was well practiced by now. She stood fully erect, her feet spaced proportionate to her hips, her arms close by her side, and her head and face proudly positioned forward. Even her tail was held at attention, straight and centered down behind her, with a slight outward curve at the tip.

Thaelyn circled around the recruit and nodded his approval.

"Nice form," he observes to himself openly. "Good posture, a most interesting presentation of the tail, especially as most of us around here do not have one… Is this how you do it in your old service?"

"Yes, it is, my Lord," she announces proudly.

"Indeed! Sergeant, we should see about adopting a few of these traits, in the event we should ever see more of them join up, to give honor to their native charm."

"Absolutely, my Lord!" he asserts.

"Aside from that, thank you, Sergeant, I will take it from here."

The Sergeant makes a salute and returns to his supervision of the training exercises.

"Cadet Nazég, rest at ease," Thaelyn orders. "How are you faring today?"

"Quite well, my Lord," she responds boldly as she takes a more relaxed posture. "Is there something you require of me?"

"In a way, more of a request for a volunteer effort. Aerlie is making a study of Daanen'kai physiology, and could use some assistance. You may be aware that she and some of her colleagues have been busy studying a series of Daanen'kai anatomical charts, as provided to us by your people. This is to assist in our native understanding in case we should be called upon to provide medical aid. But now she is looking for a few volunteers for a hands-on study. We will be contacting your brother about this, but she also wanted to ask if you might be willing to offer yourself to this cause."

"I'd be happy to serve. Um, my Lord, may I have permission to speak freely?"

"Absolutely."

"Will this require me to get naked and flaunt myself in front of a room full of people?"

"Most likely, yes, but I imagine it will be a closed room to offer some privacy, and the people are all priests and healers. I am sure Aerlie will try to make the experience as inoffensive as possible for you."

"Of course, and I've had some experience with this already; for instance, attending the baths. At first, it felt like every pair of eyes in the room was on me."

"Under the circumstances, they probably were, with you being such a foreign sight for many of us. But I would imagine it was more out of curiosity about your race, rather than anything lewd or impolite. Ours is a society with a different perspective on nudity than some. If yours instead regards this as a practice to be kept behind closed doors, you may find yourself ill at ease in ours, at least in the beginning. Here, we tend to use public baths nearly as often as private ones, and over time this has affected our public opinion on the matter."

"Right, this is what I've heard, and since that time, I've gotten used to the idea, if kept in the appropriate environment. It actually feels a little bit liberating after a while," she grins softly. "Also, a lot of people have come to admire me for that thing I did during my ritual, and I've made some new friends too, which helps. So, I feel a better sense of fellowship now than in those early days, and this makes me feel a little more at ease with it."

"I am very pleased to hear it, especially as you are the only one of your kind here. I would imagine you may feel isolated and alone, in this regard, but from the sound of it, you may be earning a kind of celebrity status with many of the other students. Simply remember your ultimate goal."

"I understand. This study you're talking about sounds like it'll be a lot more personal, but I understand the need…for science, that is. So, I'll try to keep a straight tail and bear through it."

"This is the sort of spirit I like to see. If you can attend to this at your earliest convenience, I am sure we can see it through, and then you can move on to other interests."

"Yes, my Lord."

"That is all, Cadet. You may return to your practice."

Kaliya returns to attention and makes a proper salute, then turns and walks back to her former training exercise.

Thaelyn leaves the room and makes his way out into the courtyard again, working his way out the gate and finally through the portal back to Firstfall. When he arrives, a page greets him with instructions to divert to the officer's lounge where the General had been taking his afternoon break.

"General," he calls as he enters the lounge. "You left word for me?"

"Ah, my Lord, I trust your little excursion was refreshing?"

"Walking amongst the halls of the guild is often a relaxing treat for me. It is a pleasure I have been missing for a while."

"I am pleased you were able to indulge yourself, my Lord. But now I fear I must disturb you with the articles of war again."

"As always, General, what do we have?"

"First, I would like to relay to you our success in taking that camp with the third orcish portal gate inside, not that it was actually any great effort. They tell me the camp was empty when they arrived."

"Empty? Meaning to say it might be abandoned?"

"It would certainly seem that way. I was asking myself if we happened to catch it when the last of the current inhabitants had already migrated away northward."

"What about the portal itself? How does it appear?"

"I am still waiting for an update on that, but so far, they tell me they do not see anything of special import on the other side. They see a smallish camp with no one moving around, at least not in front of the window. But we will continue to study it to see if anything shows up."

"How about the terrain? What do we have on this one?"

"By the descriptions, it seems to be a prairie-like setting, perhaps near a river of some sort on the other side."

"Interesting, but with no orcs in view... This is strange, as the setting might suggest a favorable site for a camp, especially with a river nearby."

"We will be establishing a garrison around it soon, so we will have plenty of time to study it. We are also pushing our line up from the south and experiencing fairly light resistance, which I suppose is to be expected for the lower population count in that region."

"Very good, and what of the other portals, are we still receiving reinforcements?"

"At last word, Portal Number Two was still producing orcs in small groups and at odd intervals. They report it does not appear to have a great many moving around in front of the window on that one. Portal Number One seems to be the most productive, as it seems to be sending not only warriors, but occasional supplies, and the flow there has increased slightly since the time we first took it."

"I see, and this is rather curious. How might we interpret this if to look at it from the source?"

"That might be a very difficult perspective, my Lord. We have encountered many them in this world, and we have been cutting through them quite efficiently. One must wonder now..."

"Yes, General?"

"I am forced to think about how Darumon and the Suuden-Aryku treated the elves. They used a large number of them in their efforts against the dwarves, and it seemed mostly as a sacrifice, simply to make trouble. We also know he has declared the orcs to be no more than fodder. They were abandoned to us as we made our earliest attacks, and I recall how Darumon noted in your last communication that he had no desire to support them further."

"Correct, but how would this affect the orcs, I wonder."

"There may be more than one way to explain this, but it would all be very speculative. First, the orcs may be making stronger incursions through Portal One hoping to regain favor with Sargeras if they realize he has gone silent on them. But this does not explain the other two portals. One appears empty and the other close to it. Now I must recall the aspect of the elves, and how many were used in their engagement. This brings me to wonder how many orcs might still be on Ruuki uy'Daan at this time."

"Indeed, for instance, how many did they start with, how many were relocated here previously, and how many remain currently. And if they continue to flow through, might they use the last of their race in this wasted effort?"

"Although I would not necessarily wish to be the destroyer of a full race, we may find ourselves in this position by default, if this is the case."

"You will recall this was the issue when we first began this war on

Tae'Eladar. Of course, we did not know they were making incursions into our world from another one at that time."

"Yes, of course. But I suppose we can also say, if they were migrants, they had to migrate FROM somewhere, and this would represent their source."

"With more of them on that source," Thaelyn nods. "So, despite my edict, a full genocide of their race would only be limited to that of Tae'Eladar."

"Indeed."

"But if looking now at Ruuki uy'Daan, this complicates matters if they hold any information that could lead us to the next step."

"Absolutely!" the General affirms. "If they spend the last of their kind on this folly, we may yet be trapped with no way to continue forward towards Azgarén."

"And so, as for these portals..." Thaelyn considers. "One is fully active, perhaps increasing the flow, while another is decreasing and the third has run out. General, this bears the appearance of a consolidation effort, with Portal One being the focus. It was our first conquest, and the nearest to us. Maybe the orcs received an instruction to focus their greater efforts on that one to oppose us."

"And they are pulling in from the other locations to support this. Then the region where Portal Three is located may be largely abandoned at the source. We should watch for this, as well as any obvious signs of activity through the windows of the other ones. Perhaps we can gain some impression of what they are doing over there."

"This is a fine suggestion, General."

"All right then, my next topic is the cave with the giants. I just received word that our scouts found one such cave on the eastern end of that mountain range, and it seems to be the current home to a group of stone giants. There is a trail leading up to it from the valley below which might take the better part of a day to navigate."

"Good. I want to make a trip out there as soon as possible. Tomorrow, perhaps. We shall organize a small guard contingent. I want mages, at least one of which is an Elder. We should also prepare several spell scrolls with rune marking and activation enchantments on them in case we find ourselves travelling to a place that is low or absent of the flows. The scrolls carry this within them, so a mage can still cast the spell even without a natural source."

"Very good. Is there anything else, my Lord?"

"Pray that we do not have any significant trouble with the giants. If they do possess this portal key, I may try negotiating with them. Perhaps some form of barter. Also, I want that young elf with us who was there once before. She can point out the actual portal to us when we arrive."

A new day dawns, and with it an expedition is forming within the guildhall courtyard. Thaelyn has assembled a guard detail, along with a few scouts and high-ranking mages. Also present is the young female elf brought forward by Sehnisavain, with the knowledge of the route she once took, and the location of the portal within the cave. Another mage stands holding a rune to the region, ready to send them off.

"Is everyone ready?" Thaelyn inquires. "Then we should be on our way. We will have a long walk up the mountain trail. The portal rune only takes us to the base of it, for reasons of safety, so as not to provoke the native giant clan in the area. Mage, open the portal for us."

The lone mage standing on the side casts the enchantment, and orients the rune for the third-person transit, which opens a portal aperture for them to jump through. One by one, Thaelyn leads the group away.

They arrive at the base of a broad range of tall mountains, well to the northwest corner of Sein'amar. Ahead of them lies the trail leading up into the mountains. Now they set off on their long hike.

The day wears on as they continue through the mountain pass. The weather was clear, but the air was cold, still in the clutches of a late winter chill. They had dressed themselves with heavy coats and scarves overlaying their armor. They wore wool hats and gloves, and heavy boots with course treading to find better traction in the snow.

It was approaching midafternoon, and up ahead they spotted a pair of giants sitting near a large cave entrance. Thaelyn motions for the group to pause momentarily.

"All right, listen carefully," he states. "We do not wish to provoke them, but more than likely, they may express a cold attitude after the event with the orcs and Flame Elves. I will need to be careful with my statements in order to ensure we find satisfactory results. Nevertheless, we should keep alert. They know the strength of the kingdom, so it is not likely they will attack on sight, but they will certainly move to intercept. We once granted them this easement to use this territory as their own, so we are essentially treading on their land at the moment."

The group begins moving forward again, working along the trail towards the giants and their cave.

The two giants had been sitting outside the cave entrance essentially on guard duty, though nothing ever dared come this close to them. They take notice of a line of men hiking their way along the trail and immediately jump to their feet, moving forward to meet them. Their actions were more to stop the men rather than to attack, realizing they held a truce with the men of the southern kingdom and did not wish to provoke a war.

"You there, stop," commands one of the giants in a sluggishly low rumbling voice. "Why do you come here?"

Thaelyn signals his troupe to halt as he prepares to reply.

"We come because of a great evil threatening our world," he begins, speaking loudly for the giants to hear him, and using a simple dialect to meet their linguistic needs. "We think this evil is looking for something, and that he sent his followers to this place."

"Evil…what evil? Followers…what followers, we do not see men come this way."

"I am told they came this way many years ago. We found ourselves at war with foreign people from a foreign land. We found elves, like this woman here," he directs to the elf. "They were following a false leader, and this false leader also had orcs following him. Maybe you remember this time, a time when elves and orcs came here."

"Yes," the other one admits. "I remember that day. Orcs and elves of pale skin come here and attack us. Our Chief is not happy. He wants to know why the Kingdom of Thaelyn sends elves to attack, and why they make friends with orcs."

"We did not make friends with the orcs. We are at war with them. Their false leader sent them here to look for something, but my understanding is they did not know you were here. I am told the orcs started the fight, and then the elves joined because they saw danger."

"Yes, there is much danger in attacking us. But why do they come here? What do they look for?"

"I am told they found a portal here, and this portal leads somewhere their false leader desired to travel. I must understand why and what is on the other side."

"A portal? There is no portal here."

"This woman tells me there is, but it is hidden. You need a special item to open it. The story goes that it is an ancient portal from ancient times, and probably created by an ancient being. This being stole some of our people away to this foreign land and made slaves out of them. Our war has found this land and freed them, but we are now told of this arrival and this portal. I cannot allow this false leader to find his way to some new land, so I must pursue him."

"You chase him now?"

"Yes. The other elves in that group were carrying this item, and they used it to open this portal, but then they were killed, and the item was left behind. I need to find this item, and I need to know what is on the other side of this portal. I believe our world is in danger for this false leader and his evil desires."

"A false leader who can make danger for all the world?"

"He is an old god, one who should not exist by now, and yet he does. We believe he hopes to attack the current gods. If he does, our world is in danger as well."

The two giants glare at each other, and then the first one speaks up again.

"You say this portal is hidden. You need an item to open it. What item? How does it look?"

"The woman tells us it was a carving of silver, in the shape of an open eye. Have you seen this?"

The two giants turn to each other and grumble something in their native language, then turn back to Thaelyn.

"Yes, we know of this item. Are you here to take it from us?" the giant asks, his tone becoming charged.

"You are a strong warrior, and I would not wish to challenge you. Your people took an attack, but I did not know of this until recently. I am King Thaelyn of the kingdom to the south. We hold peace with you, and I wish to keep that peace. I apologize for the attack, even though it was not mine, and I would make efforts to assure we hold to our word of peace. The item is bad. If it can open this door, bad things may happen."

"Our Chief keeps this item; no bad things happen to him."

"As I said, it can open this portal. I do not know where this portal goes, or what is on the other side. This is what I consider bad, and I need to learn more of this. I must do this to protect my own people, as well as yours. Perhaps we can make a trade. I carry some treasures with me. He may choose from this and trade for the item."

The giants turn for another brief discussion in private before offering a reply.

"We will bring you to the Chief, but only you. The others stay here."

"I will agree with this, but the woman must come with me. She saw this item once before. I need her to tell me if this is the item we seek."

The giant grumbles once more.

"You and the woman, come."

Thaelyn follows behind the giant with the elf in tow. The other giant stays behind to keep watch over the other men.

They climb up the remainder of the trail to the entrance of the cave. Thaelyn takes note of the carved entrance, with a framework of stone columns and an archway. The stone had been etched with runic engravings in an ancient language, and not one native to the giants. As they pass through, Thaelyn whispers to the elf.

"Where was this portal you mentioned? Do you recall?"

"I believe it was further inside. I remember it was set inside a frame of some kind. I can't see it yet."

"Let us hope it is not too far ahead. The Chief should know me well enough to give me time to speak. We will see where this takes us."

As they move deeper into the cave, they come to a large open space. There is a gathering of giants here, one of which is decorated with many trinkets and bones on a leather strap hanging around his neck. The giant who was leading them announces their arrival and relays the story from outside.

"You are King Thaelyn," he grunts. "Yes, I know your face. You say orcs and elves come here who follow a false leader. I remember this. I try to talk to them, but they do not listen. Instead, they attack."

"I am told it was the orcs who started the attack. You know orcs as much as I. They love to fight."

"Yes, so it is with orcs. But why do elves fight with orcs?"

"This false leader lied to them, gave them stories of great victory, but then he sends them to war, and many die from it. Then he comes here looking for an ancient portal. We think he wants to make war with the gods. He and they are old enemies, and he holds much hate for them."

"He wants to make war with the gods? He is crazy. The gods are all-powerful."

"Yes," Thaelyn chuckles to release the tension a bit. "I think you are right. But he is making a powerful weapon. This is extremely dangerous. And then we have this portal. We think it may take him closer to the gods, but I need to know for sure. Then, I need to stop him. Therefore, I must find this portal and go through it. I need to find where he is going, and bring my own people there to continue my war."

"King Thaelyn, you have always been true to us. I will take your word that you did not break our pact. But you want an item to open this portal? What item is it? And what do you have for trade?"

"I have a bag here with many things. I will show you, but I also ask to see the item to be sure it is the one I seek."

The chief rocks to one side on his stone seating to consider the suggestion, then pulls his necklace off over his head and brings it low to the ground for Thaelyn to see.

"What item is it?" he asks as he shows off his trophy band.

Thaelyn looks over at the elf as she examines the necklace. She points out a silvery symbol resembling an open eye.

"This one, my Lord," she declares. "I recognize it. This is the one the orcs gave us."

"Chief," Thaelyn calls up to him. "The woman knows the item we seek, and she has chosen."

"This was taken from orcs and small ones like the woman. Weak ones... It is small. This is what you say opens the portal? Hmm..."

"Portals are strange things, and many strange items can be used to open them. I know this from my lessons back home where I come from."

"And you make war now. You fight this evil god?"

"We do, but we must move quickly before he attacks the other gods."

"Then you want this, and I will trade, but only for something precious."

"I understand. I will show you what I have."

Thaelyn sets down the bag he had been carrying and opens it up. Inside he had collected an assortment of baubles, mostly of silver and gold, and each of them magically enchanted to enhance their value. He suspected the giants would not let this item go without a substantial offer.

"This item here..." he offers while holding up one of the selections, "...can protect you from poisons. This other one can make your skin hard against blades and claws. This next one can increase your strength…though I would imagine you have much of that already," he chuckles.

Thaelyn rattled off the list as he displayed the collection of trinkets. The choice of what to bring was based mostly on the known preferences of giants, due to previous experience, as well as the presumed desires for the type of lifestyle they lived and the demands of the environment they lived in. Thaelyn's earlier experience with giants also told him they tended to be greedy and selfish. He assumed they would not let this artifact go cheaply if it would call the king of another land out this far to find it.

The chief examined the array of choices and reflected back on his smallish offering. Realizing his adversary in this arrangement was showing a strong interest in the trade item, he felt confident in his position to make a hard deal.

"I take all," he declares.

Thaelyn was not actually surprised to hear this, but he knew he couldn't so quickly accept the offer without a few words of debate, or else it might weaken his own image.

"You would take all for this one small item?"

"King Thaelyn, you are King of all the south lands. You have much. You come here for this small thing? It must be worth much to you. You say you go fight an old god, and this old god can bring danger to all the lands…to you, to us. I understand. I will take all, you take this. We make a new pact of peace, forget orcs and bad elves."

The offer was as much blackmail as it was a demand to correct for the past offence, and Thaelyn suspected this might be necessary. So, in the interest of keeping the peace, he would need to accept. After all, the wealth of his kingdom could surely afford it.

"Very well, Chief, we will make this new pact. We shall enjoy the peace between our people. We are good friends. We understand each other. But now I must ask you to allow my people inside so we can follow this portal. We think it is inside this cave somewhere. This woman tells us she knows where it is. When we are done, we will leave you with your home again."

The chief looks around the cave, wondering where and what this portal is about. He recalls what was said about the artifact being able to open the portal, but that the portal may hold bad things inside.

"When you open the portal, will bad things come out?"

"I have warriors outside. We will watch and be aware. You do not need to worry."

"And when you go, will the portal open again?"

"The portal will only open if the item is brought close. I will take it with me and keep it away. You will be safe."

"Then I will agree. You go fight the evil god. Keep your people safe. Keep our people safe."

"Very good..." he nods.

The chief unties the necklace string and removes the artifact. Thaelyn returns all his offerings back into the bag to keep them together, and they make the trade. The Chief gives instructions to allow Thaelyn's men through, and the group reassembles in the large gathering space.

"My Lord," calls one of the guards. "We were beginning to wonder what was occurring in here. Should we assume, since there are no bodies lying about, that you were successful?"

"Indeed. The Chief is a fair and reasonable leader, though he also drove a hard bargain, as I expected, but we made a trade. I have the artifact here. Let us now go find the portal and be on with ourselves."

The group proceeds deeper into the cave, with Thaelyn and the young elf in the lead. She brings them over to an alcove on the side where she finds a strangely carved stone framework, not unlike the one outside the cave, but smaller in scale.

"My Lord," observes the Elder Mage. "I was studying the runic carvings on the frame outside, and these here look largely of the same work. This is not the language of the giants, however, and appears much older."

"Yes, I was noticing that as well, and it disturbs me, as I think I have seen such as these before."

"Where might that be, my Lord?"

"In the ruins of the Sarrukh..."

"The Sarrukh?" he winces. "But, just a moment, this is very curious. Was it not said that we believe Darumon built this in order to steal away those immigrants some ten thousand years ago?"

"Yes, this is the assumption. And to see this writing again can only associate two elements that should not normally associate. Now I wonder how he relates to them."

"Or they to him, perhaps. For instance, if Tae'Eladar was refurbished by them, did he play a role in it? Then later, he would return to steal away some of our people."

"I actually believe Maker Kuroku to be involved with Tae'Eladar, so unless there is a common language being shared along the way… Ugh…" he shakes his head. "I cannot be sure of anything at this time, and I am already getting a headache from it. Let us simply proceed forward and see what lies ahead of us."

"Very well, my Lord, and perhaps one day we can come back to it. If it were not for these giants, I would love to study it further."

Thaelyn holds a moment to think. He glances again at the framework, and then pulls out his trans-com to invoke the photographing function. He steps back and takes a snapshot of the frame.

"Scout, take this and run back outside to photograph that front entrance. This can serve as a substitute for us."

"Aye," he nods.

The scout takes the device and rushes back through the cave.

Thaelyn turns again to face the framework. He steps closer and brings the artifact up to the portal archway. The runic carvings begin to glow softly, and the interior of the framework starts to swirl with an ethereal vortex.

"And here we have it," he remarks. "Young lady, I believe this is where we should part ways. I would not wish to endanger you further, and the places we must travel will most surely hold some mystery."

"I'm not afraid, my Lord," the elf replies. "And I would surely like to know where this leads for all the suffering we went through to find it, and how many were lost along the way."

"I understand, but if this leads to the Outer Planes… Such places as those are not commonly for mortals from the Prime worlds, at least not without a considerable amount of preparation."

"Well then, I am so glad to have my Lord and King at my side to protect me," she smirks.

"She's got you, my Lord," the Elder mage chuckles. "This young lady knows her way around words."

Thaelyn gazed bemusedly at the audacious young lady for her brazen remark, and then glanced around at the rest of them.

"Remind me, when we get back to camp, to have the General take down her name for my special list."

"Aye!"

"Very well then, so here is the plan," he begins. "We cannot know what is on the other side, so we must make several assumptions. First, although we all know that portals can take us into realms that can be very dangerous, we will assume this one, by reason of its maker, as well as the fact that Darumon might be hoping to send some of his own people through to further investigate, must therefore hold a hospitable environment for us, at least within reason. Still, we will take our precautions."

He turns to one of the mages while he continues.

"We are equipped with a number of spell scrolls to provide us with the capacity to cast our rune enchantments even if the other side is short of the flows. We will first mark a rune at our present location for an emergency exit if the other side is harmful. Mage, you should perform this now, please, over in this open area, if you will," he directs to a clear area away from the group.

Thaelyn observes as the mage steps over to the clear space and begins enchanting a fresh rune.

"We shall first send the Elder Mage through," he asserts. "I have provided him with a special high-level spell that can produce a shield bubble around him, offering him protection from outside harm, as well as a safe internal environment in case there are any serious issues of concern, such as the local air supply or some other. The bubble will not require the typical chanting, like the Infinity

Shield does, but it also only lasts for a limited time. Once it is cast, I will telekinetically lift him and send him through."

The mage had finished marking his rune and was now passing it over to the Elder Mage as he made his preparations for his shield bubble spell. He checked his pockets for his spell scrolls and confirmed all was well before beginning.

"Our initial purpose here," Thaelyn continues, "is to make a quick assessment of the situation on the other side, then return to report. If all is well, the environment is safe, and there are no hostile forces waiting for us, then we shall all pass through. However, if any of the aforementioned is present, we may need to reconsider our methods."

"My Lord, one thing quickly," asks one of the guards. "Since this is such an old portal, could the Spellplague have caused any harm to it? If it passes into the Outer Planes, and they shifted about so, could this portal now point to a new location?"

"This is a good question. It could be this portal now opens to an empty space, which is yet another reason for the shield bubble. We can only try it and see, and hope for the best."

The Elder Mage draws up his energy and makes ready to cast his bubble spell. Thaelyn moves slightly off to the side, but not so far that the portal key leaves the close proximity of the frame, thereby keeping the window open.

The Elder begins his casting. Swirling energies start rotating around him, forming into an elongated shell surrounding his body. The casting takes several moments to process, as it was a high-level spell and therefore more complex, but also more powerful as compared to lesser spells. As he nears completion, the bubble solidifies around him with a subtle clap, and he is suspended inside while it rests on the ground.

Thaelyn quickly brings his attention onto the man inside the bubble. He levitates him away from the ground, giving space between the bubble and the cave floor. The bubble follows the motion of the man inside, as it is anchored to his form. He then orients the man to pass through the portal, and away to the other side.

Now they wait. The expected amount of time for a result is not presumed to be long, as the time limit on the bubble is a predictable quantity. Thaelyn pulls out a timepiece from his pocket and studies the passage of the seconds. He forces his tension to remain under control, but he can also feel it coming from the other members of the group. He checks the location used for the return rune, but as yet, it is still empty.

The scout returns with the trans-com, handing it back to Thaelyn as they continue to wait. He checks his timepiece once more and passes a glance around the group. Then a crackling sound engages in the return portal space. A ball of light forms, and within it is an elder man in a flowing mage robe.

"Thank the Powers," Thaelyn sighs. "I have not had to wait such a painful few moments for a long while. What do you have to report?"

"My Lord, the other side is safe and seems devoid of any hostile bodies, and in fact of many things. I believe it does open up into the Outer Planes. You will see when you arrive. We should be well enough to pass through here, as I believe it should land us safely on the ground."

"Excellent. Then we should proceed."

Thaelyn glances back into the passageway, where he notices the giant chief standing and waiting for his final evaluation.

"Chief, I think we have what we need now. I thank you, and now we shall be on our way."

"Good. Fight well, King Thaelyn."

Thaelyn instructs the group to pass through the portal while he waits, still holding the key to keep it open. He follows up the rear after the last man.

They arrive in a flat open expanse, representing a wide, barren, and featureless land. The air is dry and at a moderate temperature.

"Aye, my Lord," calls a guard. "I would indeed say we're in the Outer Planes, and I think I know which one already. There, look yonder."

The guard points off to the distance. Across the expanse is a solitary feature of rock, an impossibly tall column of it standing above the land.

"Indeed," Thaelyn mutters. "Cynosure… A nice neutral location for an arrival zone."

"My Lord," announces a scout. "I see no signs of the Suuden-Aryku probe in our local vicinity. Might they have been here already and collected it?"

"It has been a good few or several decades since the elves delivered it. Almost anything is possible in that time. But I am hoping that it would take time for the Suuden-Aryku to discover its voyage. Largely because it was small enough to be carried by a man and light enough for an elf, as they were the ones transporting it, apparently. These two conditions would suggest it to be rather weak for the signal it may produce. Such a thing might take even more time to detect."

"If we're lucky…"

"Luck has been with us on a few occasions, so far. Let us hope we can hold on to it for just a bit longer."

They survey the area for a moment, trying to gain their bearings. Some of the scouts search the local grounds for any signs of tracks or other recent activity, but nothing noteworthy comes up.

"All right men," Thaelyn declares. "We should consider the possibilities. From time to time, there may be nomadic bands that roam this region. In all the years this probe may have been laying here, one of those bands may have discovered it. Thinking perhaps it to be of value, they might have taken it to one of the nearby border towns for trade. We will begin our search with this."

"Right then, but which border town?"

"Considering where we find ourselves, let us take the path of greatest temptation. The border towns tend to ring the outer regions of the plane. We are far from the Spire already, which marks its center, so let us continue away from it and see where it leads. We may not be long before the next one."

"But walking? That's a far distance if you ask me. And worse if it's not the one we want."

"I agree. Let us mark a rune at our present location and send a mage back to fetch us a flight of gryphons. That will make our work much easier."

***

Kaliya was passing through the guildhall courtyard after some morning exercises in the mage training field, followed by a brief visit to the baths and a quick sprucing up of her appearance. Today was part of a weekend break, but she still spent some of her time in practice, hoping to make the best use of herself for all the demands placed on her. As she progressed through the yard towards the front gate, she noticed Relissa, Marelle, and Haran assembled along some benched seating to one side of the memorial statue depicting Aerlie and Thaelyn in their thoughtful repose. Tristeen was also present, and they were deeply engaged in conversation together. Kaliya diverts herself to investigate.

"Hey there kids!" she calls as she approaches the group. "Are we conspiring on anything important today?"

"You know, girl," Relissa retorts. "You're not much more of a kid than the rest of us, in your own way."

"I know, Relissa. I might be four centuries old, but by Daanen'kai standards, that's still rather young."

"It's hard to believe," Tristeen reflects. "To describe oneself to still be rather young at four centuries…"

"It goes with the territory, I guess. So, what are you all doing here?"

"We're going over some of our mage studies together," Haran replies. "Tristeen and I have been reviewing some of our past experience with Relissa and Marelle to help them understand a few of the finer points."

"Sounds like fun. I just came from a practice session, myself."

"Putting in more overtime, ay?" Relissa jokes. "You'll be so far ahead of the rest of us, we won't have a chance against you."

"The burdens of the violet, Relissa…" she shrugs. "They don't mess around with you if you get one of those."

"Violet?" Tristeen asks.

"It's one of the color grades you get in the testing for application," Haran answers. "They conduct a special test for the purity of your spirit, which is a marker for how dedicated you are to the virtues and the philosophies the Order worships. Blue is the minimum to get in, and what most people get, but this misfit got a violet, of all things."

"Why? Is it so unusual?"

"Yes. According to the specs, mortals shouldn't normally qualify for that due to how we're made. I heard it said that only one other person ever got a violet score, and that was Lady Aerlie, probably because she's a Celestial."

"Wow, so what does that mean for you, Kaliya?"

"I don't know, and it scares me a little for the implications. And when you combine this with the Prodigy Child gift that allows me to project myself out-of-body, which is another thing mortals aren't supposed to have, it paints a scary picture for who and what I may be."

"Scary, perhaps, but it might also mean you hold a special power you don't know about. Don't be afraid of it, Kaliya. Embrace this as your special gift. Learn from it and use it wisely."

"That's a very kind, and also a wise suggestion. Thank you, I will, but first I need to meet up with whoever it is Thaelyn has in mind to train me for it."

"How are your other classes going?" Marelle inquires.

"Things are progressing smoothly, I suppose. Among other things, I've been trying to spend extra time in the training hall for my combat practice. I can feel my body toning up again, after all these years. It feels good."

"What do you mean…again?" Tristeen wonders.

"I was once a star athlete in my old school, so this was a common routine for me back then. Since that time, after the orcs attacked and we had to evacuate, everything sort of fell apart. I lost a lot of my ambition, I was angry, hurt, frustrated, and just gave up on a lot of my old hopes and dreams. When I was old enough, I joined the Sentinels. Actually, I joined it before I was technically of age, but we were kind of desperate for militia people, and I was itching for a fight. The trouble is all my negative feelings got the better of me on a lot of occasions."

"And that's why your bleedin' Elders ranted on you so much," Relissa finishes.

"Yes, but after meeting Thaelyn, listening to his advice and accepting his help to overcome all of this, I feel almost like my old self again, though wiser for the wear."

"Just like old times…" Marelle reminisces. "I remember my old school, though it was nothing like this place. I didn't really care much for it, though. The teachers would tell us what they wanted us to know, but I always felt there was something missing, and they didn't like me asking so many questions. Now, after all that is said and done, it's hard to believe…here I am, almost the middle of my life, and going back to school."

"It's not so bad, Sis," Haran remarks. "I know most of the students from the old academy are signing up here now. Granted, many of them are not as old, but it's basically like starting over for them. And then we have a lot of people from the city who need to take up supplementary classes just to become proficient enough to compare with the average Tae'Eladaran citizen."

"That's going to be hard for a lot of people," Tristeen reflects. "You still need to put food on the table, and if you're spending all your time in a classroom, when do you find time to make any money to pay for yourself."

"It'll be hard in the beginning, but they'll get through it. They can take courses that don't occupy all their time, maybe half a day and during certain days of the week. This will afford them time for the rest."

"How are Sara and Jon, by the way? I hardly ever see them now that they came over here."

"Sara is ranting over all the courses she wants to take, and poor Jon is simply trying to find time to balance between that and a part-time job to pay for things."

"Isn't Sara helping?"

"They're both taking up apprenticeships, like I did in the

beginning, to give them a little money, but you know Sara. When she first saw the academy study hall, she went wild with all her cravings to learn. I'm sure she'll settle down in time, but she needs to find her niche."

"I don't remember any of the kids from my old school anymore," Marelle admits. "Too much water under the bridge since then. Kaliya, do you remember any of yours?"

"A few..." she reflects. "I had a lot of friends, really, but a couple of them stood out as my all-time favorites."

"That sounds nice. So, do you talk much to them lately, or are they...um..." Marelle's voice trails off.

"Marelle, none of them made it."

"Oh dear gods! Just what happened over there?"

"The orcs, of course! When they first attacked, they made quick work of many of our critical power and communication networks, cutting off a lot of people from knowing what was really happening. Kailen says he was sure the alert went out for people to evacuate before the lines went down completely, but the end result leaves a bitter taste in our mouths."

"For all the people lost?" Haran muses.

"Yeah, especially in our old school. I remember when my mother came running into the classroom and dragged me away by the horns, screaming something about orcs. But I had no idea what she was talking about until we were well outside the school and running for our lives."

"Ouch!" Tristeen yips. "How does that feel to be dragged by your horns? I can't even imagine it."

"It's not actually that," Kaliya laughs. "It's an expression we use. To be dragged by the horns is to say to be forcefully made to follow."

"Oh, so she didn't actually take you by the horns and, um...well, that's not really coming out right either," she giggles.

"Yeah, something like that," Kaliya grins. "In reality, I didn't actually have horns at that time. I was still too young. But anyway, none of the other school kids followed. We have no idea why. Most of us think they just didn't get the evac order when they were supposed to, probably due to the comm lines being cut. My mother got the word early because she was at the university at the time, and my father contacted her personally."

"That's terrible. How old were you at the time?"

"Around half a century..."

"Half a century," Tristeen muses. "Almost a lifetime for one of us, and you're still a child in school."

"Kaliya, if this bothers you too much," Marelle winces. "Then maybe we should change the subject."

"No, it's alright. I had to come to terms with this a long time ago. A lot of kids were lost in that. I think our school was host to over nine hundred."

"Wow, that's a lot. I don't think our little schoolhouse could even hold that many."

"I'm sure ours was much larger. We tend to design them that way to accommodate for multiple classroom grades and different age categories. Also, we had a series of baby booms after we landed and got settled. It was to compensate for our losses from the previous world."

"A baby boom? Do your babies go boom when they come out?"

The group shares a round of laughter at the idea.

"Not quite, Marelle," Kaliya smiles. "But if you were to ask my mother, she might have something to say about it in my case. No, a baby boom is where you have a sudden cascade of many births at once. We lost a lot of people on the world we had just escaped from, which is nothing new, as it was often this way when we were attacked and pushed to a new world. So, it became something of a habit for us to try to repopulate as quickly as we could before it happened again."

"You make a bunch, you lose a bunch, you make a bunch, and you lose them again..." Tristeen ponders. "That could get tiring after a while, and very dispiriting. How do you manage?"

"Dispiriting, yes... It wore very heavily on my father, more than anything. But it was a matter of survival, I think. We became accustomed to it over the many millennia as we were running from the

Suuden-Aryku, and trying to survive on worlds that weren't always friendly to us. We didn't really have much choice on the matter."

"Kaliya, may I ask you something?" Marelle solicits. "Did you have any boyfriends, or at least any hopefuls?"

"At one time, yeah... We were good friends. Like I said, I had a lot of friends, but there was this one guy, his name was Petrith. He and one other, a girl who was probably my best friend ever...the three of us were inseparable."

"Who was the girl," Haran asks.

"Her name was Sulíma. She was Ankhia's little sister; quite a playful little tart too, on occasion."

"Ankhia? Who's that?"

"Oh, sorry, you don't know her given name. That's Med-tech Tad'vaal to the rest of you."

"Sounds like you had a rather closely-knit group there."

"Yeah, she was Kailen's new wife at the time. So many people lost children and other loved ones. Petrith was Elder Girhani's son..."

"'Ere now," Relissa teases. "Kissing up to the elites, are we?"

"Actually, Relissa," she chuckles. "She wasn't an Elder on the Council at the time. She was an undersecretary to another one, Elder Drescuul, but he was killed in the crash, so she was bumped to take his place. Then there was Elder Vankkar, he lost both his wife and his daughter, I think her name was Túfula. I remember he was in a deep depression for a long time after that. He hardly talked to anyone."

"Wow, that's bad," Tristeen relents.

"I didn't know her personally. We didn't share any classes together. And even Lieutenant Lapäli lost someone close, his father. He stayed behind, and I know a lot of people argued this. According to my father, the cu'Nar apparently passed a message of some kind saying he held a purpose. But it was VERY controversial, and most people disagreed with it."

"Did they give a reason for it?"

"None that I know of. Then, last I heard; he was presumably fighting on the lines trying to hold off the orcs to give the ship time to escape. It seemed so pointless! Later, the Council honored his memory with a commendation for his sacrifice. If only he could've known what was waiting for us on the other side."

"That's a lot of tragedy, girl," Relissa admits. "Those bleedin' orcs and the Suuden-Aryku have been laying into you for a long time. Let's hope from this day forward you can get a proper breather."

"Speaking of breathers, I think I should try making use of this one. I have some time off, so I'm going over to the temple to see Lady Aerlie."

"Taking up a new religion now?"

"Well, no, but I'll tell you a little secret. From all the things I've been learning in this world, I wouldn't actually mind offering some worship to these gods here. It couldn't hurt, and it might even help to know there's someone big out there watching over me. But as far as Aerlie goes, I need to speak to her about an examination she wants to perform on me."

"What kind of examination?" Haran asks.

"She and some of the other priests have been conducting a study on our physical anatomy to expand their medical services. So far, it's all been charts and diagrams, but now she's asking for a few volunteers for a physical study. And I'm one of them."

"Can I watch?" Haran offers with a broad grin spreading across his face.

"Hey, you..." Tristeen objects and slaps his shoulder. "You've already got some of that."

"But Tristeen, it's for science!" he croons.

"I'll 'science' you if you go anywhere near that place."

They share another round of laughter at poor Haran's misfortune, and Kaliya bids them goodbye as she gets up and continues out the front gate.

She strolls through the gate and down the avenue to the cross street that runs along at the base of the hill from the guildhall. She turns left and follows the road for a block before crossing another street, then continues partway along the next block until she arrives at the grand Temple of the Planes. It was an ornate and well-appointed temple structure, neatly apportioned to the service of the capital city of the kingdom. She enters the front door and strides along the isle of a seating area lined with many rows of pews, most of which were currently empty, as it was not the typical time of day for the people to gather for worship. As she approaches the dais, one of the attendant priests steps over to greet her.

"Welcome, Child! Are you here for a service, or is there another need on your mind?"

"I was sent here to speak with Lady Aerlie about an examination of Daanen-Aryku physique. She was asking for volunteers, and I'm offering myself."

"Ah, yes! I recall this. So, you are here as our first study applicant? I will inform her at once. I believe she may be expecting you. One moment, please."

The priest hurries to an office near the rear of the temple and disappears through the door. A moment later, he and Aerlie both emerge. The priest returns to his former activities while Aerlie walks over to greet Kaliya.

"Kaliya, I am very pleased to see you are doing so well. You are here for our little study? How do you feel about this?"

"A little nervous, but I'll get through it. All I ask is that you don't try dissecting me. I think Thaelyn might still have plans for me later," she chuckles weakly.

"Aw, and I was so hoping to take a peek inside," Aerlie jokes. "Very well, we have a room over here waiting for us in the Healer's Ward. Follow me, please."

They proceed through a side exit and down a corridor into another section of the temple where they conducted most of their healing services for the general public. The Ward was composed of a number of individual examination rooms, a trauma center and emergency receiving area, alchemy labs, and recovery rooms for those who were resting from the more serious treatments.

Aerlie continues through the corridors to a specially prepared examination room where several other priests were assembling to make the review. When they entered the room, they saw a bed being prepared for Kaliya to lie on. A collection of papers had been laid out on a table nearby with medical diagrams and charts detailing the internal and external anatomical features of a typical Daanen'kai body, with this particular selection representing the female form.

"Now, Kaliya," Aerlie declares. "We will try to make this as pleasant a procedure as possible for you. I will have you disrobe for us and lay your clothes over on that table," she directs to another item in the room. "Are you wearing any jewelry?"

"No, not today," she replies as she begins removing her tunic. "I don't actually own any. Most of it was lost on Ruuki uy'Daan, and we haven't had anything new since."

"I'm sorry for that. Maybe, as our two societies learn to interact more commonly, you'll be able to find something new in one of our own jewelry stores once they begin supplying something."

"Now there's an idea. To buy my horn chains and tail ring at a store on a world populated by people without horns or tails."

They share a laugh together while Kaliya continues removing her clothes.

"When you are ready," Aerlie continues. "We will have you lie down here on the bed."

Kaliya sets her tunic on the table, and then unfastens the waistline of her pants, pulling them off and piling them up with the other item. She follows this with her undergarments and leaves them with all the rest. She was dressed very casually today, to make the process easier, knowing it would all come off during the examination. When she was done, she stepped over to lie down on the bed.

The priests picked up some of the charts and began to pour over them while referencing the corresponding aspects of Kaliya's body. Aerlie tried to engage the uneasy participant with some polite conversation and questions to help her relax into the study process.

"Kaliya, I hope you'll understand that this is a very important part of learning for us. Do your people ever perform such a ritual while training their own medical students?"

"Yes, I think they do. I don't really ever hear of it, but I've noticed on a few occasions, while visiting our own medical labs, that they might have a few interns in there with the more experienced members going over some form of instruction while examining someone on a table."

"And no doubt this was to teach those interns how to perform some aspect or another of medical aid. It really isn't any different here. We all need to go through it, and while you may feel a little bit exposed, you should also understand from our perspective that we are placing our hands in areas not normally suggested for such casual contact," she giggles.

"You know, it might feel different if you were all Daanen'kai interns, but for some reason this doesn't feel quite the same with you being of a different race."

"In what way?"

"Well, I think if you were all Daanen-Aryku, it might feel more personal having a lot of people studying me like this. The other way, it feels a little more like a science project to me, even though I'm the one under the microscope."

"A most interesting perspective… Then you wouldn't object to me asking you some rather personal questions?"

"I guess there's only one way to find out. Go ahead and try, and we'll see where it leads," Kaliya responds with a gentle smile.

✦✦✦

"I'm glad we were able to shed those heavy coats. This place is a fair bit warmer than those mountains."

"Aye, and the saddlebags came in good and handy to store them, too."

Thaelyn had been leading his expedition across the barren expanse of the Outer Planar region known as Cynosure. A flight of gryphons had been delivered by one of his mages, and now they were continuing their survey of the land for the Suuden'kai probe that was presumably delivered some number of decades ago by the Flame Elves.

"There!" Thaelyn shouts. "That must be the border town, or at least what is left of it."

"Not a pretty sight, that," replies one of the guards. "What do you suppose happened?"

"Let us go down and take a closer look."

They drop down out of the sky, bringing the gryphons to a calm landing on the ground. They have arrived at their nearest destination along the path they took to find a border town, hoping to discover what had happened to the probe. But this border town was in ruins. There were no mounds of rubble or burned buildings. Instead, it appeared as though the entire town had been ripped off its moorings and carried away.

"My Lord, got any ideas on this place? It looks worse than the wreck left behind by the dwarves after they finished with Rolsklinde."

"It does. But at least they left behind something to study. This one is missing entirely, and I think I can give you the reason. It slid into the adjacent plane."

"I don't think that was on the study list in our classes, my Lord. What does it mean?"

"From time to time, a border town can become too heavily influenced by the nature of the plane it borders. The realm we are in now is one of neutrality, but the border towns back up to portals leading into the other planes, such as those of Positivity or Negativity. This influences the nature of the town and its people. If they should ever lose themselves too deeply to this, the effect might be what you see here. The entire town shifts from this plane into the next."

"That doesn't sound like a very pleasant outcome, my Lord. So, if the Suuden-Aryku artifact was found in this town, would that mean we'd now have to pass into the next plane to find it?"

"It could, but rather than that, let us consider if this occurred before or after the artifact was found. These ruins look rather old to me. It may be possible this occurred quite some time ago. If this is the case, the nomads may have taken the artifact to the next town, instead."

"Right then, let's hope that, but which one? Where should we go from here?"

"To answer that, it would help to know where we are. This is actually fairly easy for me. The portal is still intact, the only thing remaining after the shift. It has carvings on it to identify the link it shares to the bordering plane. Let me examine this briefly."

Thaelyn walks over to an ancient archway standing upright alone in the ruined town. It sits on top of a platform, and appears to be made of an unknown type of stone, inscribed with runes and glyphs all across its surface. He stands in front of it and studies one set of glyphs running along the base, reading the name of the connecting planar realm.

"Carceri... How typical. This town has a history of sliding. It is likely this occurred some time ago, maybe a long time ago and has not been rebuilt since. I would suggest we move on to the next town."

"My Lord," remarks the Elder Mage. "Carceri, if I am not mistaken, is the realm of Negativity with a character between Chaotic and Neutral. A sort of transitional realm, is this correct?"

"It is indeed, and not one I would show any great desire of visiting at this time."

"Very well then, but which way would you suggest at this point? To our right should be the realm of The Abyss, and to the left, if memory serves, would be the Gray Wastes."

"Very good. If I were a nomad trader with an artifact I wished to sell, I might find a better deal in the town bordering the Gray Wastes. The one adjacent to the Abyss would be too chaotic for my taste, and more likely a person might be robbed rather than find a decent trade opportunity."

"You know this place far better than the rest of us, my Lord. Lead us onward."

Thaelyn orients himself to face the Spire rock formation still visible in the center of the plane. Using it as a reference point, he turns to his left to indicate the direction they should travel next. The troupe then returns to their gryphon mounts and sets off.

✦✦✦

"Such a curious story, Kaliya... So your people, as a species, once evolved from a type of creature that roamed your home world, bipedal with hoofed feet and hands with gripping digital appendages. Many of our local animal species equipped with hoofed feet are quadrupeds, and those that use hands also have feet with digital appendages. The fact that yours made use of both is very interesting. Do you know if they were carnivores or herbivores, or maybe both?"

Aerlie and Kaliya were enjoying a productive interchange while the priests made their intimate inspection of her body. They had been discussing the Daanen'kai physiology and their evolutionary history, which would similarly relate to the Suuden-Aryku, as they were all the same species, and trying to understand the process that created them.

"Keeping in mind," Kaliya responds. "This isn't actually my specialty. From what I recall of the lessons I got, partly in my old school and partly from a few people on the ship after we arrived, the Eracyodines, as they're called, were thought to be herbivores, at least up until this evolutionary transition. Kailen had a much more detailed study in this than I did from his old university classes. He tried sharing some of this with me on Therinë as I was growing up. Our ancestors apparently underwent a radical transition from this into a newer form that learned to use tools and became more predatory."

"But Kaliya, this already speaks to me as a strange paradox. Granted, I'm mostly studied in the medical arts, but I also spent some time with biology studies, and your example seems to defy a few of those lessons."

"Oh, how is that?"

"Let me first ask you this. How long was it for this transition to take place?"

"Um, well let's see. Kailen was teaching me about this, and I think he said it was largely thought to be the result of some extraordinary environmental event that forced us to make a do-or-die evolutionary advance. It was quick, like only half a million years or so until we formed the first civilized society."

"Half a million is indeed fast, especially for a species with such long lives. Do all the species of your world share this quality?"

"I don't actually know. I didn't get any of those lessons."

"So, we are suggesting a species with this extended longevity… Perhaps it was not as much then as it is now, but evolving from what is essentially an animal species to a sentient form on the edge of civilization, in only half a million years. But this still presents a paradox, Kaliya. Would you like to know why?"

"Um, well I suppose I need to ask, now that you mention it."

"Because you still possess so much of your original herbivorous physiology. How did you make this advance above and beyond any other predatory species if you do not have any natural weapons?"

"Wow, that's a little beyond my study. For this, you would probably need to talk to someone who spent more time in an actual school. Unfortunately, mine was interrupted by the attack."

"I'm very sorry to hear this, but perhaps one day we can discover the answer together. And yet, you still represent such a fascinating case study. In so many of the examples I have studied, one thing tends to stand out in the higher forms. Certain anatomical features become vestigial and eventually fade away. Yet here you are defying that rule."

"Which rule is that now, other than looking like I should be an herbivorous herd animal."

"Well, for one thing," she smiles. "You have a tail. After a while of bipedal development, particularly if you are standing perfectly erect, you should no longer have a need for it, as it would largely tend to serve as a counterbalance if you are hunched and pivoting on your pelvic quarters. Therefore, your people shouldn't have this anymore. So, why is it still present, especially one that extends below your knees on this side."

"Ah, that…" Kaliya giggles. "I suppose I CAN give an answer to this, at least partially, as I've seen diagrams of the early species, and they did apparently have thicker tails at one time."

"Ah! There we go. So, maybe it is still in the process of fading. This might also involve your extended longevity and a slow evolutionary process."

"Aside from that, I think it could be that we like it so much."

"Now hold on!" Aerlie grins. "That's not a very scientific answer."

"It is when you're having an intimate encounter…"

The two women let out a sudden course of laughter together.

"Really! I see. So, is it a sensitive region? Would this be some kind of erogenous zone for you?"

"Yeah, so be careful when you handle it, or we might have an accident," Kaliya smirks.

"Very well, I'll be gentle. But tell me, in this case, where do you feel the greatest sensation and what role does it play for you?"

"Ankhia and I talk on occasion…she's Kailen's wife, you know. She and I share a little girl talk sometimes, and she's tried to explain a few of the facts of life to me…in the absence of my mother," she sighs wistfully.

"You miss her, don't you."

"Yeah, I do, and it was really hard on me during this time. But that visit I made to Ruuki uy'Daan has filled me with new hope, so I have something to look forward to now."

"Good. So, what does Ankhia say about this?"

"We sometimes use the term 'tail pit', although this can also be used as a naughty word. That, along with a few expressions we use, like raising the tail as a suggestive act, or flipping the tail as an obscene gesture."

"Oh dear, so you have a dark side to your culture?" she smirks.

"Yeah, I guess we all do. But anyway, the locus point is near the top and underneath, even though much of the length can be sensitive to some degree. It's often used to stimulate the sexual desire and raise the expectancy of the intimate act. Although I've never had an opportunity to experience this."

"Gracious, and you said once you were four centuries old? Are you a virgin?"

"Yeah, which wouldn't be too unusual for someone my age, as we tend to have a slow progression for our development, and then our cultural tendencies to wait for it. But moreover, there aren't any available men for me. Most are much older and already paired up. We have too many females and not enough males, and I'm still a little too young to get involved in any of that yet. I don't think I'll ever get my chance."

"Gods above!" Aerlie winces. "Too young? Just how old do you need to be in order to find a mate?"

"We typically don't get serious until at least six or seven, just to find that special someone. And it might not be for another couple of centuries to settle into marriage and children. And this is with our predicament of being hunted, where we had to break with a few of our old traditions just to repopulate. Normally, we might go a full millennium for the family scene."

"Incredible! That's a long time to wait. Why so long? I thought you went through puberty at close to a century. By this time, you should already be married."

"We do, but it seems like we take our leisurely time with the rest of it. I think the attitude is if your lifespan runs twenty millennia, you just don't rush anything."

"Indeed! But even at that, it's still a long wait. And I thought we elves had it bad."

"Why? How long do you go for it?"

"For us, our turning point is our first century. That's when we consider we come of age and are ready for the true rigors of life, including marriage and family," she sighs as she recalls her moment. "I was actually a little more than that by the time it came for me, and it was such a remarkable moment in my life."

"This is when you met with Thaelyn?"

"Yes, but the meeting wasn't anything you might call normal. There were actually two events that brought us together. The first was when I was still a child, although an older child," she begins to grin playfully. "I was in a circus."

"Huh?" Kaliya blurts impulsively and rolls over to face her. "Just a moment, did you say you were in a circus? Are we saying you were visiting, or a part of it?"

"It wasn't actually by choice. My life had a bad turn in those days. My people had long been suffering a series of attacks by this group of dragons that had been chasing us for many centuries. It all started in a famous moment in our history where they attacked a sacred temple belonging to the elven nations. The temple held a special artifact, and the dragons were hoping to take this and maybe use it as a weapon."

"Uh oh, that sounds bad. What for?"

"Once, there was a time we call the Age of Dragons, where we believed they were trying to destroy us. This was after we arrived here, and they apparently didn't like it. We later came to realize they were actually guarding this world, and we accidentally intruded into it. They were simply responding to us, though we didn't know this at the time."

"Ouch!"

"But this one group apparently held a pet peeve. It was some time after the rest of them were in retreat, realizing we were here to stay, and their Maker, one of the Estelar, had called them off. Again, we had no way to know this in those days. But this bunch didn't get the message, or else they just weren't listening by now, holding such a grudge that they were now going against orders. So, they launched their own independent attack on this temple in the hopes of taking this artifact and following what they believed to be the original orders."

"Oh wonderful!"

"But the temple was located in a very craggy line of mountains, and nearly impossible to reach, at least efficiently, by ground. Thus it was considered safe from any conventional form of attack. Unfortunately, dragons can fly."

"Yeah, I can see the problem with that already. So, they came down on you, probably took it fairly easily, and you lost the temple?"

"Initially, yes. Then, our people rallied together and attacked by air, but the battle was very bloody, and many of us were killed. We routed the dragons, and reclaimed the temple, but those dragons held a serious grudge against us for our ability to fly."

"Oh no, and yeah, I think I can see what came next. So, they harass you in much the same way the Marshal was harassing us?"

"Yes, actually, very similar. Slowly, over the following centuries, our people were diminished down to our last village. It was just after one such attack when I was angry and argued with our village

Patriarch about the situation, but to no avail. Then, in my frustration, I decided to go for a little flight in order to relax. The next thing I know, I'm getting curious about what's on the other side of the mountains, which was actually forbidden for us. Our Patriarch held his own grudges against many of the surrounding kingdoms over their poor treatment of us in past times."

"I'm sorry to hear that. Why did they treat you this way?"

"Probably due to our unique differences, perhaps also from their own arrogance and conceitedness. Also, we had isolated ourselves away from the world, and much of it had nearly forgotten us by that time."

"Is this to say you turned a little xenophobic?"

"We did, actually. I'm told the persecution we received due to these dragons chasing us turned us into a hunted race, and the few times we actually did reach out to anyone, asking for help, they turned us away. No one wanted to fight dragons."

"I've learned a few things about dragons in my classes. They're said to be huge and extremely powerful creatures."

"They are. But anyway, after this one attack, I was angry, so I went flying, until I decided to take a peek over the mountains to see if there was anything else out there to lift my spirits. I found myself passing over a green meadow, and before long, I noticed what appeared to be a young girl down there running from some men."

"Oops, that doesn't sound at all good. What happened? Or should I guess?"

"I had a thought that maybe I could do a good deed by helping her. If I could swoop down, maybe I could pick her up and lift her away to safety. Well, it didn't work. She was frightened of me and fought back. I couldn't speak the local language to explain anything to her, and before you know it, those two men had tossed a net over our heads."

"Oh no! Who were these people?"

"Slavers… It was apparently a trap, although I didn't know this until much later. I was locked in a small cage and sold to a circus."

"You're kidding me!" Kaliya exclaims, now propping herself up on her elbows. "But you didn't know until later? How?"

"Well, this wouldn't come out until my next official meeting with Thaelyn. I learned that during his continued campaign across the land, he absorbed the town they came out of, eventually to find those men, even though they apparently tried to escape from him…" she smirks, "…and also that girl, who was herself a slave and forced to run around out there as a target to draw my attention."

"Oh great! Is that how they do things around here?"

"In those early days, yes," she shrugs. "This town was one of those governed by a lot of corrupt people."

"Unbelievable. So, you were captured and put in a cage. For how long?"

"I was in that cage for a long while, I think it was some number of months, easily. It was too small for me. I couldn't stand up, my wings were abrading on the bars, wearing off my feathers and inflaming the skin, and I developed lesions, some of which became infected. I was malnourished and unkempt because the horrible men in charge of the circus didn't take care of me. I was feverish and weak, and thought I was sure to die. I prayed to our goddess, Aerdrie Faenya, to just let me go, but there was no answer. I thought she had forgotten me, maybe turned away from me for my foolishness."

"That's awful. How did you get out of there?"

"I didn't know this at the time, but my goddess did hear me, and who do you think she called to my aid? Thaelyn… The story that follows is a strange one. Apparently, one day he was summoned to the temple. In those days, it was much smaller than what we have now. Lord Helm, one of our gods at the time, had received a call for aid. He was to pass this along to Thaelyn. When Thaelyn arrived, the goddess Aerdrie Faenya had physically manifested herself within the temple to speak with him."

"Great cu'Nar!" Kaliya wheezes. "She's one of the Estelar, I guess, right? And she came down here personally?"

"Yes, much to the surprise of everyone in the room. Our people didn't hold such a close association with them in those days, so to actually see what an Estelar looks like was a shocking experience for them. She told Thaelyn to go look for me, giving off clues as to where he might find me. Apparently, even though she came here with a request for aid, she wasn't just going to give away the answers. He had to work a little for it."

"I don't believe this," she shakes her head. "Go help my lost child, but I'm not telling you precisely where she is."

"Exactly!" Aerlie giggles. "The Measure of Balance, right up to the top. She told him that one of her Children was in pain and needed aid, and this Child was in a prison that moved through a dusty land of sin and corruption."

"Did that actually mean anything? To me, I wouldn't think that was enough information."

"The clues she gave were enough for him, as he knew this land well enough to put together a few ideas. To the south was once a nation called Menenbahd. It's a dry, arid land, and it was truly filled with corruption at that time. The clues suggested I was on exhibition for their greed."

"All right, that's a little better, therefore something like a circus."

"Right, in this case a display of what they called exotic creatures. But the first issue of concern is the bad political relations they had with our nation here in the north. This is obvious for our code of law and their absolute lack of it."

"Oh, I'm sure of that!"

"Thaelyn had to move carefully if he were to avoid an all-out war, which he eventually did anyway, but that was later. At this time, he tried a covert operation to lure the circus owner out of his safe spot."

"Oh, this should be good. How did he do that?"

"A little bit of intrigue. He enticed the circus owner out with some, shall we say, bait."

"You know, whenever you people say, 'shall we say', I'm getting flashbacks of Thaelyn and some of the tricks I've been hearing him play on the people over in Rolsklinde. What did he do on this occasion?"

"He sent one of his agents, a young female mage with some very voluptuous assets, to make a play for the circus owner."

"Oh really! He's into that, is he?" she chuckles.

"Hey! It worked! She made the announcement that he could make a lot of money, which he was apparently lacking, if he were to bring his circus up to the city of Amberdain, which is over on the coastline from here. It holds the reputation of the City of Wealth, which is enough to entice anyone for a lucrative business opportunity. But it's up here in OUR land, and this is the first stumbling block. He would never want to come up here and risk being caught with all his contraband."

"All right, I'm with you so far. So, how did you overcome this?"

"Thaelyn held a considerable amount of power in those days, having merged most of this side of the continent into his nation by then. He simply arranged a special holiday event which he called Open Gate Day. It was originally an experiment, but ultimately it started a kind of revolution in commerce within the kingdom to open up the trade lanes. It would encourage free trade, and attract merchants from across the kingdom, even at distance, to come to the city and ply their wares. Normally, the city guards who watch the gate would make routine inspections of the merchandise coming and going, to ensure the legal aspect of things, but this would be waved on this occasion to expedite the free trade allowance."

"That's clever, and on the outside, very innocent. So the circus owner might feel confident he could sneak in without anyone noticing, right?"

"That's right. Thaelyn had his scouts following us, and sneaking into the wagon where I was being held to provide food and medicine for me along the way. When we arrived, the circus settled in a district we call the Promenade, which is a large bowl-shaped market plaza, often used for travelling caravans. The circus set itself up during the evening to be ready for all the wonderful money they were hoping to make the next day."

"Uh huh, wow, but something tells me this isn't what happened," she grins expectantly.

"Thaelyn had to play this very carefully, in order for it to follow within our code of laws. He and his Captain knew the details of it, but they gathered up a contingent of city guardsmen who knew nothing, and made what they called a routine spot inspection of the arriving caravans…you know, to provide assurance of the quality of the merchandise to the local citizenry…" she smiles.

"Oh, so THAT'S how things are done around here! I need to remember that the next time I'm carrying illegal goods."

"They made a circle around each of the arriving caravans, in order to follow a pattern of legitimacy that they are spreading themselves equally."

"I'm not specifically trained as a law enforcer, but so far this sounds good to me."

"When they came around to the circus, they made a few cursory passes to examine the merchant stands and some of the boxes of novelty goods they hoped to sell. They did apparently have a few legal items, like toys for the kids."

"Oh, so they actually do sell something legal…how boring," she smirks.

"However, one of the baskets of…legal…goods smelled strange to one of the guardsmen. It would seem someone misplaced some of their illegal narcotics into a basket and then…accidentally…placed it out in the open with all the other stuff. How unfortunate!"

"Oh, yes! I'm sure it was very unfortunate. Um, who was it that accidentally misplaced something that shouldn't have been out there in the first place?"

"Well, the jury is still out on that one, but according to the official report, a young lady was passing by the guardsmen while they were still arranging themselves on a side street and informed them of something she smelled. Of course, she couldn't be precisely sure where it came from, other than one of those caravans, so the guardsmen had to go in search of it."

"Uh huh…Measure of Balance again. A young lady? Does this have anything to do with that agent he sent?"

"Well, actually, from what I heard, she was last seen leaving the Promenade on a shopping spree. She only returned afterwards when the arrests were made."

"I swear," she grins and shakes her head. "You people are amazing. So, if I'm interpreting this right, the guardsmen, who didn't actually know what to look for, made this 'accidental' discovery of the drugs, and this ultimately led to the arrests. But then, what about you?"

"At first, the circus owner tried weaseling his way out of it. He made the mistake of attempting to bribe Thaelyn to turn his back on it if he split the proceeds."

"Oh dear... Yeah, I'm sure that would go over fantastically with someone like him."

"Naturally, Thaelyn had to play the role of the city guards, as well as the local council, requiring reports and such to explain the local happenings, and this could stand out."

"Uh huh... Naturally."

"Now, we COULD say, if the man held any decency, or even a sense of tact, he would simply let it go and try to excuse himself for the unfortunate error, maybe to sacrifice this small quantity to dissuade the interest. Therefore, he could get out of any further questioning for the rest of it. But he didn't."

"Oops!"

"Instead, he made an attempt to include all the other witnesses, meaning the guards and such, into this deal, by suggesting a private arrangement for a larger-scale operation to import and distribute this illegal trade within the city."

"Oh fabulous!" Kaliya shouts. "And I can already hear the screaming."

"Yes!" Aerlie giggles. "This invoked an immediate arrest for bribery and possession of illegal goods, followed by a thorough search for anything else in there. And this led to discovering me, which only compounded matters. But then Thaelyn needed to release me from the cage, which at this point was rusted shut."

"Rusted shut?"

"The lock... The circus handlers were nasty brutes. They abused the cage while I was inside, therefore the lock was corroded."

"Corroded... I'm not sure if I want to know this, but abused how?"

"They urinated on it...repeatedly."

Kaliya grimaced at the suggestion.

"You actually had people like that in this world at one time?"

"Apparently so, and that place down there was especially notorious for it. As a result, the key wouldn't work."

"Wonderful. So, how did he open it?"

"With his sword. Do you recall that tree in the Badlands? Well now, imagine an iron bar cage, and cutting off the top."

Kaliya gaped at the suggestion, trying to envision him swiping his sword through a series of iron bars to lop off the top of a cage.

"And you're still in one piece?"

"He's very good, but I'll admit, when I saw it coming, I felt sure someone was going to lose something. Anyway, he brought me back here for my treatment. But my wings were so badly infected, they were irrecoverable at that point, and they had to be amputated."

Kaliya pauses uncertainly, raising her brow at the statement, and then blinking to reexamine the woman for her current condition.

"Um, you know, where I come from, the word amputate means to surgically remove some part of the body. You said it was your wings?" she wonders while glancing at the clearly apparent and fully formed appendages.

Aerlie giggles pleasantly as she continues.

"It would seem that between Thaelyn and Adalon, they had our people invent some miraculous medical treatments over the years. My involvement since then has brought it even further, but at this moment in time, they had a treatment they called the Unguent of Regeneration, which restored my wings back to their full form."

"Huh?" she wheezes. "Cu'Nar's Grace, you have something you can use to regenerate lost body parts?"

"Yes, we do, although nowadays we call it a regeneration salve. We also had antibiotics, which came well before we had a proper form of microbiology study."

"I don't believe what I'm hearing, and there go my horns yet again! You people simply aren't following the evolution of science like you should," she chuckles ironically. "All right, so you're still a young girl at this time, I think. What happened after this?"

"Once I recovered from the treatment, he brought me back home.

But then, our delightful Patriarch laid into him, believing him to be some enterprising human looking for a reward or some such. Our village, what was left of it, was extremely impoverished from the attacks and the other interactions we had before, which essentially robbed us of anything we once held. So, he didn't trust anyone after that."

"That's bad."

"This is also when I learned my mother was my real mother."

"Um, wait, I think you just lost me. Why didn't you think your mother was your real mother?"

"Because I was raised to believe I was an orphan found in the woods."

Kaliya closed her eyes and shook her head again.

"I feel like my horns are sagging now. Why did she tell you this?"

"I was originally a divine gift from Tyr. You see, our goddess, Aerdrie Faenya, called her to serve a role. She was to receive a child who would one day be our savior from those dragons. I was her Chosen One, and I would be delivered to her in those woods, away from prying eyes as it had to be private. No one was to know the truth, at least not yet. Tyr was the one to deliver my spirit into my mother's body to produce a child, and she told me a seraph aided in the immediate delivery of that child."

"Blessings of the cu'Nar, you were instantaneously conceived and then born? Ouch!"

"I'm basically a clone of my mother, but ascended to Celestial status."

"Incredible! And there go my lessons on where babies come from," she giggles. "But how does that make you feel?"

"It's a curious sensation, especially when you consider where I came from originally. But I try not to think about it as anything bad. I'm just me, and I think I'm unique enough to make a good example."

"Well, that's good to know, but she didn't tell you this from the start?"

"The story was she found a child in the woods at the request of our goddess. This is how our people had to interpret things as she was not pregnant at the time to produce her own."

"All right, I suppose you still need an alibi, even if you are having a secret tryst with a god," she chuckles.

Aerlie shares a laugh with her.

"Also, my features, like my hair, eye, and wing colors, are unique to anyone in our village. Therefore, I can't be a native offspring."

"Interesting."

"But later, I learned I was this special gift, and I also apparently had a path of Fate to follow. This was explained in Adalon's prophecies."

"Wait! Adalon, um…the Silver, I think, right? I had a woman from the Royal Archives come to me not long ago with some of this. It seems you have a few lines in there about me and my people, as well, and she describes it as another path of Fate we're following."

"Vonafel came to you?" Aerlie raises her brow. "I know she came in here asking a lot of questions, some of them concerning you and this war we're into. What did she say?"

"She said Adalon apparently saw us arriving and carrying this message about Sargeras to you here."

Now Aerlie dropped her jaw and stared.

"Gods above, I need to share this with Thaelyn. Does he know about this yet?"

"She said she would need to meet with him sometime, but she still needed to put a few things together."

"This is incredible. I wonder what she has to say about this. I've known her since we shared time in the academy, and she's basically dedicated her life to deciphering these riddles. Adalon doesn't make it easy on us. I recall my own days. I was at my first century, so I was of age and could make my own decisions in life, and once again I was angry at the Patriarch following another of these attacks. I went in search of Thaelyn's kingdom, not truly knowing how to find it, other than a vague memory of our return home. I didn't expect to see him again, thinking, just like the Patriarch, that he was human and therefore mortal, and this was something like seven decades later, so he shouldn't be around any longer. But sure enough, there he was."

"That must've been a little surprising."

"Yes, it was, and then he started to explain who, and therefore what he truly was…which surprised me even more. I came to him to beg for his help with those dragons, and this is where I learned a few lessons on the Age of Dragons and why they were actually bothering us in the first place. We weren't supposed to be in this world."

"Uh oh! Is there a reason for this? Other than you aren't native, I suppose. You mentioned you intruded on something…"

"Yes, this world is apparently a kind of special project, maybe like a garden being cultivated by one of the Estelar called Maker Kuroku. She revitalized an otherwise dead world and seeded it with everything you see here, up to the original human population."

"In all the nether-space," she gasps. "Now THERE is a story! To refurbish a full planet with new life…"

"And the dragons were guarding it against any outside interference. Well, here we come, and boom!"

"Yeah, now I get it. Wow!"

"Anyway, I tell him about our troubles, and before I know it, he's asking how many and what kind. The NEXT thing you know, there are bells ringing, people shouting, guards rushing all over the place, and I'm being dragged around to the gryphon stables."

"Oops! You splashed your hooves in the wrong puddle with that one!" she grins.

"My goodness! And he is not one to waste time on something like this. I had never seen a gryphon before, so I had no idea what they were, or that these people could actually fly at all. Our kind once had this unfortunate bias for our ability to fly naturally, describing the rest as land-walkers. This is actually a derogatory term, and we have since banished it. But then he did something else surprising. He invoked those transport spheres, and we shot through the sky like lightning! I had never seen, or even imagined, one could travel so fast."

"That would shake your opinions about flying, I'll bet."

"To say the least!" she grins. "And not simply that, it put us to shame for our sudden LACK of ability. And to make matters worse, Adalon joined us, which nearly frightened my feathers away."

"Um, would you like to elaborate on that? Why would she frighten your feathers away?"

"Oh, you haven't actually met with her yet, have you? Well, perhaps later for that. Anyway, um..."

"Yes, I see you circling around that one," Kaliya chuckles. "You should pair up with Relissa. All right, next?"

"We arrived home very quickly, and Thaelyn set me down in our village. He shared a few more happy words with our Patriarch, and then joined with his men out on the field."

"More happy words, I wonder what those were."

"Then Adalon made a call to attract those three dragons that were bothering us."

"Excuse me? I seem to recall you used the term in plural, but three? I've heard a little bit about dragons, my Lady. One is bad enough, but three?"

"Yes, two whites and a blue. When they arrived, Adalon apparently tried sharing some conversation with them to understand what they were doing, but it didn't result in anything favorable."

"Oh dear..."

"So, it came down to a fight. Thaelyn flew his gryphon over the head of the Blue, and jumping off onto its back. His men took one of the whites, and Adalon took the other."

"All right, let's see if I have this. Thaelyn is insane, Adalon is also insane, and your soldiers are suicidal. Right, got it..." she smirks.

"Oh, come now, they're still alive, in case you haven't noticed."

"Yeah, and I'm wondering what miracle of miracles permitted this."

"Thaelyn was wearing some special gear designed for fighting dragons. His boots were equipped with gripping teeth to anchor onto the dragon's scales, affording him a sure footing, and he had a long whiplike lasso he could swing around the dragon's neck to hold onto it. He then pulled out his sword, and started cutting through the wing tendons to cripple it."

"Doesn't anything in this world scare him?" she grimaces. "He jumps right onto the back of something said to hold legendary power, rides it around like a horseman in a competition show, and starts fileting it!"

"Yeah, that was actually a very surprising spectacle, I'll admit. I was watching, along with the Patriarch, and it changed a few perspectives," she chuckles. "So, he brought it down, jumped off, and started cutting tendons in the leg joints next. He danced around it like a bug on a hot foil, finally climbing up on its back again, ready for the final blow. I was standing near a cave entrance we used for shelter. I watched the whole thing. At the last moment, he and the dragon seemed to be sharing some words, but I didn't understand the language. I've since come to understand it was their native tongue. Apparently, the Blue realized his errors in the end, maybe as the result of what Adalon said in the beginning, as I'm sure she must've been chastising them, and he took full responsibility for himself and the others, and regretted his actions."

"Wow!"

"But what was done, was done, and they shamed themselves along the way. And the Measure of Balance holds some strict doctrines for these sorts of actions, especially by such beings so high in the rankings. Thaelyn had to portray his adjudicator side to decree law and justice. The Blue requested forgiveness, which he gave, but the rules demand the purification of the polarities, and for this, Thaelyn granted him an honorable death as befitting a warrior. Here is where he finished it by leaping off the shoulder and bringing his sword down across its neck, beheading the creature."

"Ouch, that sounds a little gruesome. But I guess, from what I've been hearing, such a thing becomes necessary to keep things aligned. Wow, the things you learn around here. What about the other dragons?"

"The soldiers made good work of the one white, although I saw several of them tossed around like toys in the process."

"Oh no, were they hurt? I've heard a few things about these enchantments you use around here, and Relissa told me about that demon in Rolsklinde."

"Yeah, the same here, and it was yet another thing to surprise us.

They just stood up and charged back into it. And given our history with dragons in the past, none of us, including the dragon itself, was expecting that level of proficiency or durability in Thaelyn's men… it went down so fast. As for Adalon, she played a clever role with hers, apparently feigning a ploy to lead it into a trap, where she was able to expose a weak spot and thereby finish it."

"Sounds like she knows a thing or two."

"Clearly! But she was also sad afterwards. I watched her as she moved away and hid her face."

"What? How come?"

"I asked the same question. So I flew out there to see what was wrong, thinking she may be hurt. But when I arrived, I thought I could hear crying, if only barely. I asked her why, and she said these dragons violated some kind of rule. And even though she had to bring justice, she wasn't happy about it in this case."

"I'm still not sure if I understand the meaning here."

"Her kind holds certain cultural values, it seems. And this sort of conduct is offensive. Still, it had to be done."

"Interesting. She must hold some very deep feelings. Maybe, if I should ever meet her, I can ask about this."

"Perhaps, but just so you know, she can be very elusive."

"Uh huh… So, I guess they finished, and now I have no idea where we are. I forgot what we were talking about that got us into all this."

"Me and Thaelyn, silly!" she giggles. "After the battle, he came back into our village, and our people were very grateful, of course, but we all expected him to make some extraordinary demands on us now, based mostly on our older experiences with the other kingdoms. He and our Patriarch shared a few more words, calmer ones, this time, and then he did something curious. He called me for a little play, just the two of us. That was fun."

"Fun…in what way?"

"We got into this debate. It was all a play, like we were arguing, just like he and the Patriarch were doing earlier, but this time on a few things I had learned by now. So, I played into it as if he were making these outrageous demands of rebuilding our city and supplying us with fresh…everything. I acted as if this was some form of oppressive servitude, forcing us to live in houses that actually stood upright, working in actual workshops, producing actual goods to sell at an actual marketplace to earn actual coin, and therefore we could buy actual merchandise for ourselves, like new clothes and such…none of which we had before since the dragons wrecked our village every time they came around."

"And you complain about Relissa playing tricks?!" Kaliya balks. "I don't think even SHE was that bad!"

"Yes, well," she chuckles. "This was completely new to me. But then I learned more about this Fate…that I was intended to bring him to help us, and I had some kind of future with him, although I didn't know exactly what it was, other than maybe to study in the academy. Then, one day, as I was sitting out there in the courtyard, trying to decide what courses I wanted to take, Adalon sits next to me and throws one of her famous knowledge quests in my direction. Lo and Behold, it would seem my family was in possession of a very old and mysterious book of unknown origin, with a bizarre alchemical formula in it called the Elixir of Visions."

"Wait a minute! A mysterious book of unknown origin. And this is where that elixir came from…due to HER again?"

"Yes, she is the one to hint at me to go look for it in my grandfather's library. We had no idea where it came from or why it even exists. And then the ingredients, which themselves are strange."

"Yeah, I recall an alien plant growing in an otherwise inhospitable tundra region. My guess on that one is someone genetically engineered something and planted it in your backyard."

"You're probably right, but who it was…that's what we're still asking about."

"Great," Kaliya sighs. "Do your people have anything like insurance policies for losing horns?"

"Um, I don't think so, but I'm sure we could probably put something together."

"Good, because I'm going to need it before too long. What about this book, how far back are we going here?"

"Nearly to the time when those dragons started chasing us. So, our best guess is Maker Kuroku again, as she seems to be the one directing this Fate for us. We think SHE got involved, making a number of backroom deals with Aerdrie Faenya and Tyr to see all of this through."

"I swear, if I thought my horns were feeling weak before, I think they just fell off and ran away. And people say these gods work in strange ways. So, are we done here? Given all these nether-wild stories of yours, I think I need to find a rock and crawl under it."

"Oh, Kaliya," Aerlie jests. "One day, your time will come, and you'll be the one jumping onto the backs of dragons. Everyone here in the Order holds that same high esteem. When Thaelyn offered his aid to us, I knew where I wanted to be, and that's when I decided to join up. I may not be very physically strong, but I won't back down from even the greatest of threats, and neither will you. You've been a good listener, Kaliya. Yes, I think we are done here."

◆◆◆◆◆

"Over there, my Lord. Looks like we found it..."

"Let us hope our suspicions are correct in this case. I do not look forward to spending an extended amount of time in this area. The stench of it offends my nostrils."

Thaelyn and his group have arrived at the border town adjacent to the portal leading to the region known as the Gray Wastes, the realm sometimes described with the alignment of Neutral or Unbiased Negativity, as was often used by those in the Outer Planes. Although it held the negative polarity, its neutral character could possibly afford a more predictable interaction than the other one connecting to the Abyss, which was purely chaotic. Yet, Thaelyn was still aware of one detail that would stand in his way. He was of Positive alignment, and would not be openly welcomed here.

The team lands at a distance from the town, within easy view of the buildings and their occupants. The town was encompassed by a low rock wall acting as an outer delimiter to the barren wastes around it. On one side was an open gate guarded by two men. They stood firm to their ground, with their posture quickly stiffened by the arrival of the flight of gryphons a short distance away. Most of the citizens inside the town had not taken notice of the arrival, and simply continued with their local business.

Thaelyn and his men dismounted and walked the remainder of the way in, leading the gryphons on foot. As they came near the guard post, the guards moved in to bar the way.

"You there, halt!" one guard shouts. "State your business or begone."

"My name is Thaelyn," he replies. "I have come seeking knowledge in an effort to locate an artifact that may have passed this way. The item in question is the product of a race I have recently found myself at war with, where they passed by us in this direction with unsound interests for the realms beyond. My journey to locate this item has now brought me here."

"You come here seeking knowledge? Followed by soldiers and whatever those beasts are? I find that unlikely."

"And how would you define what is likely? Do you make these definitions that others must follow? This event took place in MY home, not yours. What YOU find likely or not is outside of reason."

"Fine, but you travel with soldiers seeking some simple bit of knowledge?"

"Very well, I will grant you this much. But surely if you know anything of the Realms, travelling alone is not always advisable, especially if those travels might take you to places unknown, and with dangers unknown."

"And these beasts with you?"

"You do understand the concept of a mount, do you not? Ours are imported from our home and hold the capacity of flight, to make the journey quicker. And this place is rather broad in scope. Walking is not sufficient."

"Very well, I suppose this argument is sound enough. But why should any of this be of concern to us, outsider? Why should we care what you want? I can smell your stench from here."

"Really now," he smirks. "And I so hoped the bath I took this morn would have covered that."

The soldiers all let out a muted chuckle at the obvious play.

The guards glared at Thaelyn and his soldiers, then finally at each other.

"Are you making a joke?" he retorts brashly.

"Guard, I am as much a soldier on this crusade as these men behind me, and our crusade in this war supersedes your personal concerns or your comfort level. These people I am fighting are led by a powerful being with specific designs on some ancient enemies. This item we seek is simply a device to lead him here. I hope to find it, perhaps to deny him this, or at least to discover where he might travel afterwards, as I suspect this might not be the final destination."

"All right, let's speak of this. Who is this being you speak of, and what ancient enemies does he seek that it might bring him here?"

"The enemies are no less than the Great Powers, as his kind was once an opponent to them in an ancient Age. He is a survivor of the old Celestial Wars, a Primordial."

"A Primordial?!" he screeches. "Impossible! There shouldn't be any more of those."

"I would agree. My own teachings tell me their kind should have been fully destroyed an epoch ago. But I have recently discovered a lone survivor and his servant out there in one of the Prime domains. He has gathered minions who now serve his cause, and seems to hold designs to move in this direction, back to where I think he had his final stand with the Powers. But along the way, I found information leading me to suspect he hopes to find an ancient prison portal where he might find more of them, perhaps to release them as he destroys the Estelar."

"Ridiculous!" the guard refutes. "How could he hope to accomplish this? If he is alone, surely, he would not pose any sort of threat to them."

"This is true, under any conventional circumstance. Unfortunately, this one is not conventional. I also hold information granted to me by a close friend who serves one of the Estelar that his methods might involve a weapon of the sort once used during the final Celestial War that erupted the flows in a cataclysmic wave of destruction. The result of that episode destroyed an entire Prime fold. If he were to use this here, I dread to see the result."

The guards both reeled back at this mention, again glancing at each other for the audacity of the statement.

"And you are here to discover his methods? This sounds like a rather outlandish story. Do you think YOU can stop such a plan as this? This sounds like something better suited to the Powers themselves."

"It may yet fall to that, but I must lead the charge in case he is watching for them. I suspect he has been in hiding during this time, and likely would not hold still for THEM to find him."

"Uh huh, and just who are YOU to lead a charge against one like THAT?"

"Look closely at me, mortal. Do you know what I am?"

The guard steps in slightly to take a closer look at Thaelyn. He examines his features, including the flowing silvery-white hair and golden eyes.

"You look like a Positive, although I don't recognize your race. You call me a mortal? That might suggest something. Are you perhaps a hybrid?"

"I am, and my Father is, or rather was, the one known as Tyr. My actions are also sanctioned by the Power Torm, and this should also speak for me."

"Figures, and that just makes you even more undesirable around here. Torm isn't a favored Power in this place, and you should know this," the man sighs faintly and retracts his posture somewhat. "But nevertheless, he is a Power."

"Indeed. And so, despite your preferences, does this at least answer your question of my capacity to pursue a Primordial, if only to discover his ways for others to take action?"

"I suppose it does, but it still seems a bit outlandish."

"Perhaps, but I have the support of those who believe ours is a viable course to take."

"And this device you speak of? What is it?"

"The device is described to have been sent through a most unusual Door we discovered on the Prime world of Tae'Eladar. It was likely built there, sight-unseen by any of us, by his servant, and we found it leads to this plane, some distance coreward of the Carceri gate. But in the absence of the border town proper, I am hoping to find evidence of it here, instead."

"Yes, that town has been vacant for a long while," he chuckles softly. "They never could hold their own."

"So I have often heard," he smirks. "The device is a beacon to attract them on this side of the planes. Therefore, if they should learn of its passage into this place, it gives them access to the Powers, and perhaps also the prison plane used for the remainder of the Primordials."

"And what do you hope to do with this thing, take it away?"

"That would certainly be a desirable choice, to disable and remove it. Surely, those others will no doubt desire to find it as well, and they do not carry such manners as to simply talk about it."

"Others?" he hesitates and turns to the other guard. "What others are these?"

Thaelyn took quick notice of the change in the guard's demeanor. The thought comes to him that they might hold valuable information regarding this item, but further is the thought that the others, in this case, have already been here.

"They are tall, bipedal, with curved horns, hoofed feet, slender tails, and appear disfigured with blue skin mottled with red patches. They would probably wear a form of advanced battle armor, and as I said, they would not likely speak as much, but simply march forward and take what they want by force, using powerful energy-based weapons. Does this sound familiar to you in your altered manner of conduct?" he grins impishly.

The guard displayed signs of recognition, but he also realized

Thaelyn noticed his change of attitude. The pretense of bravado would no longer hold up.

"You're an astute observer, Celestial. All right, yes, we have seen such as these. They came barging in here several years ago. They blasted their way through the gate, killed anyone who stood against them, and then paid a happy little visit to the local inn. One witness said they stood there apparently studying an object we have hanging on the wall in there. They stayed a short while, fiddling with some device they were carrying, and then left. Does this answer your need to know?"

"It does, but it also tells us we are too late to prevent it."

"Yes, you got that much right. But now what?"

"I would still desire to examine the artifact, maybe bring it away with me for further analysis back home. But unlike those previous visitors, we are asking for admittance. Will you grant it?"

"Are you going to make trouble in here?"

"I am the Child of Lord Tyr. I do not make trouble, but I will most certainly finish it. I hold no hostile interests in you and yours. So, for as long as you do not start anything against me and mine, I will attend to my business, and then depart."

The guards looked at each other and spoke privately for a moment. One of them turns to look inside the town, and then returns to Thaelyn.

"You may enter, Celestial. Just keep it under control. And leave those things of yours out here. You can hitch them up to these posts on the side."

Thaelyn waves for his men to bring the gryphons to the hitching posts to tie them up. He then leads his troupe inside the town.

"Gracious, my Lord," the young elf mutters. "Is it always this hard to deal with such people around here?"

"Only on this side of the realms," he responds privately. "If we were on the opposite side, it would go much easier, at least for me. Of course, if one of THEM were to show his face, it might go similarly from our side of the argument."

They proceed into the town square. People are milling about in the course of their daily affairs. The square is a center of activity in this town, with marketplaces and trading stalls hosted by travelling merchants. Further along were several large buildings, including a tavern, a town hall, a small barracks with a training yard, a stable with several examples of some form of bipedal reptilian mount, and finally an inn. As Thaelyn and his group move through the streets, a young woman approaches from the side.

"Well, look at the sweet thing that just rolled in off the plains, will ya?" she announces in a sultry tone. "What say I give ya a bit o' local flavor over here at the inn? It'll put a fresh look on that puss o' yours, and not cost you more than a few simple coppers."

"Back away from me, woman, I am a Celestial," Thaelyn retorts boldly.

The woman suddenly jumps back and hisses fiercely at him.

"I knew ya had a bad smell when I first saw ya come in!"

"Then why did you approach? Did you not pay close enough attention to your senses to know the difference?"

She hisses at him again and dashes away from the square.

"My Lord," remarks one of the scouts. "Is this the sort of place you used to frequent during your service?"

"I have indeed visited this place before, and many others. Those were memorable days, and nothing has changed about it. Let us move to that inn and see about this artifact before any more of this occurs."

They strode across the square and through the door of the inn. The building was crowded with many patrons, and stank of beer and cheap perfume. They stood inside the doorway, studying the activity. Thaelyn recalled the guard mentioning an item hanging on a wall. He looks around the room and notices an odd item resembling an artifact of advanced technological design hanging on the wall behind the bar.

He directs his men to move forward and attempt to mingle, while he steps up to the bar and draws the attention of the barkeeper.

"What is it you want, stranger?" the barkeeper asks. "You don't look like the sort we usually get around here. You just stopping by, or do you have some other business?"

"I have a special interest. I am looking for something of unusual origin. This item would also be of interest to others, however, and I believe they have visited here once already, several years ago, disrupting the affairs of this town and its inhabitants. Might you recall this occasion?"

The barkeeper draws back hesitantly, and clearly nervous about the statement.

"And what is it you want with this…item…stranger? Are you here to make trouble for us, like the last ones?"

"I already engaged in this debate outside with the guards. So, rather than repeat myself, allow me to simply summarize. There is a war occurring in other realms. I am fighting against these others, but I have recently discovered they sent this device through a portal on my world to this place so they could follow its passage and arrive here themselves. I had hoped to locate this item in order to prevent this. Although, according to the guards outside, it would seem we are too late for that."

"Yes, we did experience such an occasion of outsiders who came in and blasted the place without reason for it."

"They were following this device, as it represents a form of beacon transmitter to lead them here explicitly. They serve a being thought to be long extinct, and he has designs for himself here. Therefore, my war, as it first crossed my space and drew me into it."

"A war, is it? What space are we talking about? Your use of the word suggests it's not within this region of the Planes."

"It is not. It is the Prime world of Tae'Eladar. But that point is actually irrelevant, as these beings possess the ability to jump between folds. This makes them especially dangerous, as they can arrive and make trouble for you and others without warning."

"You're right about that much. And what is this thing you seek?"

"The item is a probe of technological design, small enough to be carried by a man, but surely not the sort of thing you might find locally. This race I am pursuing is a Prime society, and not native to this region."

"I see, and they're serving this being? What sort of being is it that a bunch of Primes would follow to a place like this?"

"A survivor of the old Celestial Wars, a Primordial."

The room suddenly went quiet. The barmaids stop in their tracks, and the other customers, who were previously enjoying their drinks, set down their mugs to listen. The wenches standing around the upper balconies halt their beckoning, and lean over the railings to observe the discussion.

"Oops…" the young elf mutters quietly as she watches the scene.

"Aye," a scout affirms. "That sure got their attention."

Thaelyn passes a casual glance around the room. The other patrons have all turned to look at him. The bartender also casts his eyes briskly around the room before continuing.

"I thought there weren't supposed to be any more of those," he mentions solemnly.

"So did I until my war spilled over onto another world, where I discovered the truth of it. We believe this one escaped and went into hiding. We encountered his servant as he was laying siege to that world with the apparent purpose to launch a large-scale assault. We found troop movements, but the numbers suggested it could not simply relate to that one world, as he had already obliterated most of the population there. Then, as our battle came to a close, and he began to realize who I was, he ran from me, but not before leaving a few hints as to his greater purpose."

"What was that? And why would he run from you if he's serving a Primordial?"

"I am a Celestial; therefore, I serve his sworn enemies, and he is generally in hiding from them. This is his goal, to take revenge."

"A Celestial…that figures. It also explains why I'm feeling so uncomfortable with you in here."

"If you help me to understand this device, I will be on with my business and take my leave, and then you and these others can return to your normal comfort level."

"Fine by me, but just what does this device look like?"

"Sir, if you are aware of those others that came in here several years ago, I think the issue is moot. It is likely to be that thing hanging on the wall just behind you, as the guards at the gate mentioned it to me on my way in. Let us not play with words here. Time is precious enough for us as it is."

The bartender glances over his shoulder at the object on the wall.

"Yes, I suppose you have a point. Old habits…you develop those around here."

"Of course," Thaelyn nods. "Where did you receive this item, perhaps from a travelling merchant or a nomad?"

"I wasn't working here at the time; the previous attendant took up new work for himself after that incident. But as I recall, it was a group of wanderers who came in off the plains. They were looking to make a trade, and claimed to have found it out on the wastes not far from the Carceri gate."

"Yes, this is where we first arrived when we entered the portal I mentioned. It makes sense if this is what we are looking for. Would you permit me a closer inspection?"

The barkeeper studies Thaelyn a moment, and then glances around the room, taking note of the many eyes on them, including Thaelyn's men near the front. He turns around to face the artifact, reaching up and unhooking it from the wall mount, then bringing it down to the counter.

"This thing has already caused us a lot of trouble. You want it? You can take it. Get it out of here and don't bring it back. I don't want any more of those creatures blasting their way through here. I don't know what you have in mind to do with this Primordial of yours, but keep it in your realm, not ours."

"I would desire to do just that, and then to corner him where we can finish him. But these are plans that need great care to devise. As for this…"

Thaelyn makes a careful examination of the probe. It has a central spherical hub with long narrow panels reaching out to either side. The panels appear to have striations coursing their way in a zigzag pattern underneath the metal sheeting. The hub is smooth except for a panel door set on one side with a key lock. Thaelyn studies the lock closely.

The barkeeper watches him as Thaelyn focuses intently on the lock. Then, the lock begins to turn as with a life of its own, and the panel pops open.

"A Celestial," he mutters. "Yeah, that much is for sure. But now what?"

Thaelyn peers inside the compartment. He sees circuit boards and other electronic components, along with a sturdy metal box. The box had numerous wires and tubes attached between it and other components, including a small storage reservoir filled with liquid. The apparatus appeared to be circulating the liquid through the tubes into the box and recycling it back to the reservoir. One set of wires connected to an assembly with grounding attachments.

"I think our first order of business is to deactivate the device so it will no longer send any outward signals. If I am to take this with me, I do not wish them to discover its travel away from here. We are trying to keep our movements secret thus far."

He pulls the plug from the circuit assembly and a small indicator light goes off. The device goes dead.

"If instead to have it appear to fail," Thaelyn asserts. "This would be a better solution. They may have no further interest in it, but I am not taking chances."

"All right, that seems smart enough. But if they already know where it is, what does that mean for us here?"

"I suspect you are not their target. I believe they have interests elsewhere, and this is simply to grant them access to this domain. Unfortunately, now that they have this, I must pursue a number of other leads to see if I can cut them off before they can progress any further."

"Blast! And then what? What do they actually hope to accomplish once they arrive? You said this servant is looking for revenge, but against the Powers?"

"Yes, we have observed him amassing a large quantity of materials which we believe he hopes to produce a unique form of weapon. This is extremely dangerous, and if he succeeds, it will wreak havoc on everything we are familiar with."

"What kind of weapon can do all that?"

"The knowledge would be largely limited to those like the Powers, and also the Primordials. It is not something we would normally be granted to know. But the advice I received comes from a valued source, and it would reflect upon the old Celestial War...this last one...and the final outcome brought about by it."

The room suddenly ushered up a collective moan as the people recalled the historic event and the resulting damage to the realms.

Thaelyn continues, "But we also believe he has in mind to attempt a release of the others who were once imprisoned during that time. Combine these and you have good enough cause for a Celestial like me to offend you and yours in such a place as this on my quest to resolve the issue."

"Right, I get it. Look, I don't want to sound as though I'm supporting you...you know, because we're on opposite sides...but this Primordial would be even worse than having you around, so I hope you can stop it."

"I understand, and I am sure you are not the only one. The Measure of Balance may carry its obligations, but this one extends beyond those bounds. I thank you for your patience."

Thaelyn takes the probe and steps away from the counter. He moves to join his men and together they leave the establishment. They continue outside the gate to retrieve their mounts, and then make ready to open portals for a return back home.

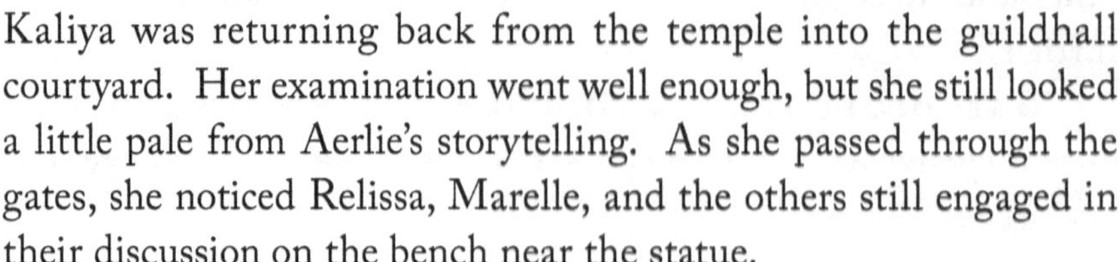

Kaliya was returning back from the temple into the guildhall courtyard. Her examination went well enough, but she still looked a little pale from Aerlie's storytelling. As she passed through the gates, she noticed Relissa, Marelle, and the others still engaged in their discussion on the bench near the statue.

The group looks up to see their tall blue friend arriving and call her over for a talk.

"Kaliya," Relissa asks. "How did your exam go?"

"It went, along with my wits."

"Why is that? Did they stick you in all your unmentionable places?" she snickers.

"Yeah, but at least they were polite about it, so it wasn't too bad."

"Then why do you look so peaked?"

"Don't ever ask that woman about her personal history. She enjoys telling stories nearly as much as my father, and with such clever undertones as to compete with you," she chuckles.

"Ay, you mean I have competition now? Jiggers..."

"What kinds of stories?" Tristeen wonders.

"Oh, I'm sure you'll hear about it eventually. It sounds like a well-known bit of history around here. Her people had a lot of troubles once upon a time with a group of dragons."

"Wow! That sounds like some serious trouble. How did it end?"

"Thaelyn and his people came to the rescue. But I don't think I can take any more today, so I'm going to my room to lie down a bit."

Kaliya offers a feeble wave and turns to find the dormitory building where she had her room.

The day pressed on into early evening, and the sky above the guildhall erupted in several flashes of light. Thaelyn and his team were returning home.

They made a gliding descent arcing around the guild fortress towards the stables located behind and to one side along a mesa in the hills. There was a landing strip located in front of the stables for the gryphons to use when coming to a rest. They circled around and made their approach one by one, then strolled up to the receiving area where the handlers would take over by unloading their gear, and removing the armor and harnessing equipment.

Thaelyn and his men dismounted and turned over the gryphons to their handlers while he and the others proceeded around a walkway to a rear access of the guild. He was carrying the Suuden-Aryku probe with him as he entered the compound, and maneuvered his way through the halls to a tactical war room found onsite where he made his delivery. He would store it here for now until arrangements could be made to deliver it to the Daanen-Aryku.

After a few moments to relax in the familiar setting, he set off to visit the temple. He made his way out of the guildhall, down the avenue, along the cross street and into the temple building. Aerlie was on the dais directing a service at the time with some other priests. When she saw him come in, she excused herself from the group to join with him.

"Thaelyn, I sense you were successful?" she asks as he approaches the dais.

"We found the probe, yes, but not without complications. It travelled to Cynosure, but was apparently discovered by wanderers some time before, then taken to the border town at the Gray Wastes and used as a trophy for display at a local inn."

"Sounds pleasant enough, but I presume you were able to bring it back?"

"Yes, but it seems we are too late. We heard a story of the Suuden-Aryku apparently making a visit some years earlier. They know where the next step is. Now it is only a matter of the prison gate, and whatever else Darumon has in mind."

"Oh dear. So, where do we go next?"

"Unfortunately, I am not privy to the location of the prison gate. This is a tightly held secret, and as far as I know, there is only one who knows what it is. Lord Ao."

"Gracious! And he's not one to approach on matters like this, or any other."

"Indeed, but we must bring word to him so that we can take the appropriate precautions, assuming we are not already too late for it."

"He does not listen to worship, Thaelyn. He sits above all the others and lets them manage his affairs."

"Then we must send word through someone else and see if we can receive something back. For this, I should review these details with Torm. I have been keeping him informed of the affair of this war, so he is aware of Sargeras and his ambitions. I will speak to him about this latest result and have him carry our message."

Thaelyn breaks from the conversation and steps over to the set of deific icons where the symbol of Torm was found. He kneels before the altar, calms himself and enters a meditative state to summon the mind of Torm. In a moment, the statue overlooking the icon on its pedestal begins glowing softly, indicating to all that Torm was present.

Aerlie stood by quietly. She had brought the attention of the other priests in the room to be still while Thaelyn was in communion. The temple had gone silent during this time.

Thaelyn communes his message with the details of the probe and the need to secure the prison gate. He asks if it is possible to learn where the prison gate is located, and if the Powers themselves can do it, or if an alternative method is required. When the message is delivered, the glow around the statue fades and Thaelyn comes out of his meditation.

"Thaelyn?" Aerlie calls softly as he makes his way back across the dais.

"We must wait. He will speak to Lord Ao and give his response at a later time."

Chapter 6

CLOSE INSPECTION

"Captain Lapäli, I have a strange report here. It could possibly offer some answers, if only we could get a better look, but under the circumstances, that may be, well, difficult to say the least."

"All right, what is it, Cadet?"

A young male enters the gathering hall inside the mine to report to the Captain. He had just returned from a scouting patrol with his latest observations. Over the past couple of weeks, the Captain had given orders for better surveillance of the orcish camp east of the city, located opposite to where their hideout was found. It represented the nearest and greatest threat to their local security, and in recent months, it appeared to have been receiving new forces from outside.

"We've been able to gain a better perspective of the flow arriving in the camp, but strangely, our estimates of their numbers haven't changed by much."

"Are you sure you're able to count them all? It's very literally a jungle out there."

"Yes Sir, we're able to see them reasonably well in the main part of the camp, and it seems they've been clearing some of the local trees to supply more wood for the campfires. The problem is, from what we can tell, we see a steady flow coming in from the outlying areas…not a strong flow, but certainly a flow, and yet it seems the camp isn't growing by the same numbers."

"Do we have an answer for this yet?"

"I still say they're cannibalizing each other," Sulíma snickers.

"While I wouldn't put it past them these days, I'm not ready to accept that just yet. Continue Cadet."

"Sir, so far, we don't have a full explanation for this. We tried circling around the camp for a different perspective, thinking we may not be seeing everything from our position close to the city. The camp does seem to extend further to the east, but then we saw something on the far side."

"Oh? What did you see?"

"Structures of some kind, but not orcish," the Cadet replies. "They were nestled amongst some of the native buildings."

"But these others were not orcish? Are you sure? Maybe they stole something from the city and used it as construction material."

"We thought about that, but it looks too clean, and it's not big enough for housing or anything else. And that's not all."

"All right, what else is there?"

"So far, the trees are obscuring much of our view. We're trying to keep at a distance, not to get too close. But one structure is a large box-like shape, and another looks cylindrical standing upright. This doesn't make sense if the orcs are stealing from the city. Why would they want this?"

"A cylinder and a box…hmm," the Captain muses. "How large are they, can you tell?"

"They both appear to stand over the heads of the orcs that walk through the area, but not by much."

"And those orcs are shorter than we are, only up to about chest height. Were there any markings or other details?"

"Like I said, the trees block our view, but they do stand out amongst the terrain. They appear to be in good condition, at least as compared to any salvage you might find in the city, and white in color."

"White…and geometric… This does stand out, as the orcs

are more organic than that. That cylinder, are we talking about something like a storage tank? What, in all the nether-space, is an orc doing with a storage tank in his backyard?"

"A better question might be what the other thing is," Sulíma wonders. "If we have a storage tank, is it linked to that box?"

"Cadet, try to check on this. See if there's anything like pipes or tubing. And try to see what else is out there. You say the trees block your way? Circle around some more to another vantage point, but be careful and don't let them see you."

"Yes Sir!"

"In the meantime, I'd like to know more about these orcs coming in. I want better counts and a point of origin."

✦ ✦ ◆ ✦ ✦

"General, what do we have today?" Thaelyn asks as he arrives for the morning review.

"Nothing exciting beyond the usual reports, my Lord. Here, see for yourself."

The General shuffles through a collection of papers stacked on the table. He pulls out the most recent updates on the war front, and some reports by the garrisons keeping watch over the three orcish portal exits.

"My Lord," the General adds. "We still have not seen any activity at Portal Three, so I am coming to the conclusion that we may be right about it. Nevertheless, I would not dare suggest abandoning that post, just in case the situation changes."

"Agreed, we will keep it through to the end, when we find the portal and shut it down."

"Other than that, Portal Two is largely unchanged, as is Portal One."

"And what about our observations?"

"Our observations at Portal Three are nil. In the beginning, we thought we saw something, but it turned out to be a wild animal of some sort passing through the area. There are still no orcs."

"That would certainly indicate an abandoned camp, to have wild animals running free. Otherwise, hunting groups would clear them out. But this also raises a curious question. If there are indeed no orcs in the area, then who, or what, is powering that portal?"

"Indeed, my Lord, this would follow naturally. Even in the case of an abandoned camp, you would still need their shamans to open the portal. But if we see wild game moving through the region, then where are the shamans, at the very least, to say nothing of any others who would normally be a part of a local occupation...such as hunters."

"Then we might need to consider a few additional possibilities. First would be this magic of theirs if it maintains a level of persistence even without the shamans to support it. Some spells, when cast, will persist in the world for at least a brief period of time afterwards. However, this portal has been persisting for a fair amount of time. So I might be apt to suggest it is not a conjuration at all. Perhaps it is a device of some kind."

"My Lord, this is a frightening suggestion. Are we to say the orcs have invented such a thing as to compare with our own Gateway nodes?"

"This would indeed be a problem, but it might also answer the question of these portals maintaining themselves day and night. It would demand a small army of shamans on a rotating schedule to keep this up. Even our own mages will only engage a portal on demand if we need it. We do not simply open one and keep it that way for any casual passerby to make use of it."

"This is true, of course. Then if we are to suggest it is a device, we must also consider who invented it, if we are saying Darumon may be responsible for teaching them this technique in the first place."

"We saw orcs using portal magic on Tae'Eladar once, and we can be fairly certain he was responsible for that much. It might then follow he would do this. The only thing to ask now is if he taught them how to do it, or if he simply delivered something into their hands."

"If he taught them how to do it, this makes them at least as dangerous as previously with the simpler form of portal magic, and perhaps more so now as it would not even require as much work on their side to generate. But if it was a device delivered into their hands, they may only know enough to step through it, leaving the internal workings as a mystery to them."

"Then we must examine this carefully once we arrive. What about the other portals?"

"As before, Portal Two shows signs of activity, but not a great amount. It bears the resemblance of a smaller outpost, based on how many orcs pass in front of the portal on that side, but very few are coming through by now. Portal One, however, is another thing."

"What do we have there?"

"There is constant movement around the camp on that side. We can see occasional transport of materials, such as food and wood, which suggests a heavy population and a lot of activity."

"If we have such an influx of orcs consolidating in that camp, this leaves me to wonder about the security of the garrison. If they are massing so heavily, they could surge and overrun our position. General, we should assign more troops to that garrison and think of ways to protect ourselves from anything unexpected."

"Yes, my Lord."

"In the meantime, if there is nothing else of great interest on the war front, how are our activities in Rolsklinde?"

"Construction has begun on both a regional portal gate, as well as a hub gate. We have restored enough of the upper district plaza to make it usable to us, so the hub is being built in the area formerly used by the old city temple. We will build a new temple around the corner. Construction of the parliament building is proceeding nicely in the space left behind by the former Governor's Manor, since that held such a nice location to begin with, though our building will be much larger. The housing and marketplaces in the southwest quarter are almost done, and the workers are transitioning their progress in that area towards the eastern side. We should see the completion of this in a cascading fashion within the coming months. This will surely make our new citizens happy to see the last of the dust settle in that area."

"And the schools?"

"We are still in the early stages of the primary school, and have yet to make the foundation for the junior academy. Since so many people still need to learn our language, and many of these are currently occupied with this in our world, we will focus on the primary school first, giving the younger children the chance to resume their education ahead of the others. We will work on the rest later. We can only do so much at one time, my Lord."

"Yes, the logistics involved are complex, but keep it up, General."

✦✦✦✦✦

"This is fascinating."

"It certainly is, my Lady. The variations between male and female seem to diverge during the course of puberty, developing in some rather profound manners."

"They mostly start out the same, though. As children, they both seem to have light skeletal structures...that is, in comparison to their overall size and physique. And if I'm judging these charts correctly, I would think they should share many of the same physical qualities and abilities."

"Yes, but look at these examples as they reach adulthood. The females maintain much of that slender design, while the males build up a considerable bone and muscle framework."

Aerlie and her team of priests had been pouring over the Daanen-Aryku medical charts, as well as their own notes gained during the examinations of the Daanen'kai volunteers. They were now comparing them to analyze the development of a typical member of that society during their life stages.

The team had already come to a careful understanding of Daanen-Aryku medical needs, so they were well underway to developing training dolls for future study sessions. At this moment, however, she was taking an interest in the particulars of Daanen'kai physique as a favor to Thaelyn to determine if any improvements could be made to Kaliya's training sessions to make them more productive for her. In the process, she was noticing that not all Daanen-Aryku are made the same.

"They must develop a rather healthy appetite during this time," she giggles. "With this much body mass, the males should slow down considerably on the field. But at the same time, they ought to pack quite a punch, I would think. That is, assuming they ever tried fighting with hand weapons."

"Do they even use such weapons?"

"I know only of the ranged pulse weapons they used during the battles outside the Naarg uy'Sodrad, and occasionally small blades if they came into close combat. I wonder…if you put some heavy armor on one of these, and a large two-handed blade in their hands, or perhaps a polearm… No, this much strength should use a blunt item, like a maul or a dire mace," she muses.

"Such a weapon like that would send their opponents sailing, my Lady," the priest chuckles.

"I think Kaliya once had a two-handed item of some sort, but I think it was still a ranged weapon…something technological, one of their own designs. But in the case of a female, a longsword might work, and yet…"

Aerlie pondered the situation, using her experience at helping Thaelyn in the past to derive solutions at making the best use of the physical qualities of their members.

"She should be capable of high agility, certainly as compared to a male. If this is the case, a two-handed rod weapon of some kind might suit her, or perhaps chakrams as a thrown weapon."

"Chakrams would be a dangerous one, to be sure…a set of spinning circular blades thrown at the enemy. If he were still intact by the time they returned to her hands, the second round would likely finish him. As for a rod weapon, are we speaking of a bo staff here?"

"No, I think it should still involve a blade attachment, perhaps more like a crescent-shaped or twin-bladed staff of some kind."

"A sword-staff…yes! That would certainly make her deadly to anything that came too close. And it would suit her general body proportions nicely."

"And her level of dexterity would make very efficient use of it, too."

"One thing's for sure, I wouldn't want to be on the receiving end of it."

"She would not be as physically robust, but her agility could be useful in martial arts training for both offensive and defensive tactics, which brings me to another thing…"

"What's that, my Lady?"

"Those legs of hers…"

"Are we speaking of the general female, or Kaliya? I noticed hers were quite well-toned."

"Yes, I should ask her about that sometime. I know she was sent out on a lot of scouting runs, and often without a vehicle, so this might apply. But I wonder if she ever practiced anything to develop that level of fitness. I didn't see that on the other female we received for study."

"That other one was a medical intern, if memory serves, so maybe she didn't get out as often. But as for Kaliya, since she is so readily available, maybe she can help us confirm some of these other details."

"From what I've heard," Aerlie considers. "She's been progressing very nicely in her combat training. Her martial arts skills are developing, and she's showing improvements in speed and accuracy. Now I wonder about her movement speed."

"If you think she is capable of more than what she is training right now, perhaps we could conduct a few tests and see what her limits are."

"It would also be nice to compare to a male, just to confirm some things from that side."

"But consider this, my Lady, testing and comparing is only as good as their current physical training. If they are not prone to train as highly in their physical prowess, it might not show their true potential."

"Yes, so what we could do is perhaps bring in a few more volunteers for occasional training sessions to see how far they can go. Kaliya is already in training, so let's start with her."

Aerlie gets up from her desk and checks a clock on a table across the way. It was midafternoon. She reflected on Kaliya's training schedule and surmised she ought to be in a practice session at this time.

"I wonder if the Sergeant would mind me stealing one of his students for a little while."

"Oh, I doubt he would complain, my Lady. Do you think you will do this now?"

"No time like the present, and she should already be in session. I can bring her down to the practice field for a few laps and check her running speed, and have her perform some maneuvers for me to check her responses."

"All right, my Lady, and perhaps in the end you might find ways to improve her training ritual. Good luck to you."

Aerlie leaves her office and walks outside the temple. She then spreads her wings and takes off from the ground to fly up to the guildhall. She flies around to the side where the training hall is located, setting down directly into the outdoor training yard often used for practice sessions during fair weather.

The Sergeant takes notice of her arrival as she uses her wings to glide in, then flapping gently to slow her landing. He orders the assembly to come to attention, just as he did when Thaelyn stopped by, and give their salute.

"My Lady!" he calls as he rushes outside to meet her. "So nice of you to drop in, and quite literally so... With all these visits of late, between His Lordship and yourself, you might cost me my beauty sleep while watching these greenhorns practice."

"Sergeant, I find it hard to believe you could ever do that," she grins. "But I do need to borrow one from you for a while."

"And which of these mud-wumps would you wish to take out for a trot?"

"The tall blue one, if you please."

"Very good, my Lady, one moment while I call her up..."

Once again, the Sergeant calls into the room for Kaliya to present herself. She rushes up and stands at attention waiting for Aerlie to respond to her.

"Here you go, my Lady," the Sergeant continues. "Will there be anything else?"

"For the moment, no, but I may return later."

The Sergeant salutes and returns to his supervision.

"Kaliya, how are you after our little visit the other day?"

"Quite well. Thank you, my Lady," she replies, still at attention.

"Rest at ease, this is not a formal engagement. I would ask for you to help me with a little testing to see just what you're capable of. I hope to make an analysis of your physique, based on our studies, to discover if there can be ways to improve your training."

Kaliya relaxes her posture and contemplates the suggestion.

"Is there anything in particular you're thinking about? A lot of this is already working out well for me."

"We always look for ways to improve our methods, and yours is a special case since we are so new together. There may be ways to apply your natural talents above and beyond what you are already practicing."

"All right, I'm all yours. What would you like me to do?"

"First, let's go out to the lower practice field and test you in the open space. There is a sports track there, and I'm very curious about your running speed."

They begin making their way through a rear gate and down some stairs towards a large field. The track was often used for developing muscle tone in the legs, and to train running speed and stamina.

"My Lady," Kaliya mentions. "If you're thinking of testing my running, you should know, I'm already a lot faster than most of the others, just for my gait."

"I might suspect that regardless, but our examination of you, and then another female volunteer that showed up, informed us that your legs seem exceptionally fit. Did you ever do any sort of practice before?"

"Well, actually, yes. When I was a girl, I made a lot of practice on the field back home. I was training as an athlete, and one of my talents was running the track.”

“Really! Then you should still have some of that in you.”

“I suppose, but that was a long time ago.”

“What about more recently, after you came to Therinë? Did you do any sort of practice there?”

“Not really. After the attack, a lot of my ambitions were spoiled. Though I will admit, there were plenty of occasions when I’d go out on patrols, and I just wanted to run for the feel of it again.”

“Wonderful! And that probably kept you in fair shape, even if it wasn’t on a regular training schedule. Is there anything else you did?”

“Gymnastics… I used to perform a floor dance routine. A lot of jumping, flipping, cartwheels, that sort of thing.”

“Interesting. Just how nimble are you on your feet, Kaliya?”

“My high jump was always very good. I used to do vaulting exercises, like on training benches and walls. And I practiced a lot of different step patterns for my dance performance.”

“But let me ask you this, and I hope you take it the right way. For someone with hoofed feet, how does this work for you? Your example would be different from ours.”

“I’ve never had any problems with it. For instance, during my gymnastics routines, I’ve done jumps, flips, spins, twirls, and never fell down. Well, at least not once I got trained. I won several awards for my routine, also. But once again, I was a young girl at the time. Now I’m an adult, and seriously out of practice.”

“Awards? How wonderful. Perhaps we can give you back some of that practice so you can win a few more. What about your classmates…other girls, and were there any boys involved?”

“There were a lot of girls in my class, and some boys, although they didn’t often carry it through, once they grew up. They might go into strength training though.”

They arrived at the base of the stairs and moved out onto the track. The track was currently empty, so they had the whole field to themselves.

"All right, Kaliya, even though you are out of practice, I'll have you make a lap for me, and I will check your speed."

"Sure. Just give me a moment to limber up."

Kaliya begins a series of leg stretching exercises she recalled from her youth. It had been a long time since she was last tested on the track, so she wanted to make it good. She stretches each leg out, and walks around checking herself, then makes another set of stretches just to make sure.

"All right, I'm ready. You want just one lap? Are you going to time me?"

Aerlie considers the prospect and checks her pocket for her timepiece.

"Certainly, why not."

She pulls out her timepiece and makes ready to signal for Kaliya to go. As the hands on the clock reach their topmost position, she waves her hand at the girl.

Kaliya takes off in a dash, picking up speed quickly. The pounding of her hooves thunders against the ground. She feels the wind whistling in her ears as she nears the first turn. Reflecting back on her old training practice, she hugs the curve as she comes around into the stretch on the other side, then pushing herself for a hard sprint until the next curve. Her long legs allow her to cover a lot of ground in a single stride, and her fast gait keeps a quickened pace. As she approaches the next curve, she once again hugs close to the inside, now coming around to the home stretch. She makes one more hard push, leaning into her advance as she crosses the line.

Aerlie looks down at the clock to check the time. Her eyes grow wide as she reads the numbers.

"Gods above, Kaliya, I'm trying to recall the running times for our own people, those who practice out here. We don't use speed enchantments on the field, and you clearly beat their time by nearly twice."

"I told you I was fast, and I'm not even in the right condition for it anymore."

"What about other Daanen'kai women. How would they compare?"

"Well, we all start out fast when we're young, and we all take at least a little bit of physical education in school. Some do more, others less. I was heavy into it, of course. I suppose many of us keep that even until we're adults, some just might not practice as often, and especially not after we crashed, since there's no place for us to go out and simply enjoy life."

"Of course. And what about the men," Aerlie wonders. "I was noticing they develop differently from the women. I suspect they might lose a lot of speed as they get older, is this correct?"

"Yes, a lot. As boys, they make good runners, but after they grow up, they just plod along."

"For all the thick bones and muscles, how strong are they usually?"

"For that, I can actually refer to my brother, Kailen. He did some strength training early on, and got really big. This was during his early days going into service. Of course, just like me, he got out of practice after the attack. But I'll tell you this much, if properly trained and conditioned, they might not be fast, but they could probably bulldoze right through a squad of your people if you should ever stand in the wrong place."

"Really!" she grins. "I'm thinking of calling up more volunteers to see about helping them practice, and then observing how far they can go. Would you like to help?"

"Sure, if I can find time in my schedule. Thaelyn already has me working overtime on just about everything."

"I'll see if we can make some adjustments. But if the end result is to improve your style, I'm sure we can make the sacrifice. But now, there are one or two other things."

"What's that?"

"I should think, by the charts I was reviewing, as well as our little chat, that you should hold a considerable amount of agility. You said you did some manner of gymnastics?"

"Yeah, that was one of my specialties."

"I don't suppose you remember any of it?"

"My Lady," Kaliya chuckles softly. "If you're hoping to get me to remember my old routine…"

"Oh no, I don't think I would have you go into all that. My interests are a little more in line with our needs here. For instance, have you ever used anything like a baton or a staff?"

"A baton? Hmm…" she considers. "Not in the way you might use a stick or a club if that's what you're thinking. There was a time when I was practicing twirling and tossing a baton. As for a staff, well, my father has a staff he uses for walking, but we don't really use those for much of anything else."

"Twirling a baton…one-handed or two-handed?"

"A little of both…"

"Come with me, please. Let's go back up to the training hall and try you out."

Aerlie leads Kaliya back up the stairs, through the gate, and into the training hall again. She steps over to a weapons closet where they kept a selection of practice weapons. Inside she finds wooden swords, daggers and maces, axes and hammers, and several long and short versions of staffs. She pulls out one of each type of staff, giving Kaliya the short one first.

"Now, try to recall your lessons and show me how you used to twirl your old baton."

"The size and general mass of this one is different from mine. Ours were often synthetic or a lightweight wood."

"Yes, this might be an issue, as this here is denser. But do your best."

Kaliya holds the short quarterstaff in one hand and tries twirling it in her fingers, though her bad practice causes her to drop it. She picks it up and tries again, carefully spinning it between her fingers. She drops it again, but remembering the old rule to pick up and go again, she keeps on trying.

"I'm going to interpret your fumbling is mostly because of it being so long, right?" Aerlie suggests.

"Yeah, three and a half centuries is long enough to forget a lot of things, and this is something you need to do a lot if you want to keep it in good form."

"Try using two hands instead."

Kaliya changes to spinning the baton between her two hands, faring much better this time as she was better able to control it.

"I could get used to this easily enough. I just need the time to practice."

"Good!"

Kaliya continues her practice, now recalling more of her old lessons and switching from one hand to another as she started feeling better in control. She was able to toss it up gently and catch it in her other hand, then swapping for another round. Then taking it near one end for a slow swing, flipping it over her shoulder, catching it as she spins, and repeating on the other side. After a few more twirls, Aerlie feels it's time to move up.

"All right, that's enough, and that was a very nice performance. All those early lessons seem to be coming back a little," Aerlie smiles. "Now let's try this one."

Aerlie swaps the quarterstaff with the longer bo staff.

"Do you want me to do this with one hand? I don't think I'd be able to twirl it in my fingers like the smaller one."

"No. When using a long staff like this, you most often use two hands, or sometimes one changing to the other."

"Can you give me a little demonstration to get started?"

"Certainly…"

Aerlie sets down the smaller staff and picks up another bo staff from the closet.

"Now watch and pay attention. It takes some coordination, but I think you can pick up on it, especially with your other experience."

Aerlie holds it in one hand and begins flipping it over, grabbing it with the other hand as it comes around and reorienting herself to grab it for another flip. She demonstrates this slowly at first so Kaliya can mimic the motion.

"Keep your hands in the center, Kaliya. It can easily go off-balance if you lose the center point."

Kaliya follows Aerlie's example until she picks up on the motion and is able to increase the rate of spin. They practice this for a while before trying another motion.

"Now, a bo staff can be a dangerous weapon in the right hands, as any weapon can be. Just because it is often no more than a long stick of wood, doesn't detract from the harm you can inflict with a solid hit. Here is an example of a strike..."

Aerlie takes the staff in both hands, one palm up, the other palm down, and twists in a semi-circular rotation at the elbow to cross the upward hand over her other one, bringing the staff horizontal again, followed by turning it outward with the back end laying against her body. The front end was now in a striking position. She reverses and changes her hands the other way, now performing a similar maneuver in the opposite direction.

Once again, Kaliya tries to mimic the motion. They continue the cycle several times until she is able to follow it naturally.

"There are many ways you can use a staff; twisting, flipping, turning, and so on. It is not used like a club, where you simply bash your opponent over the head with it. It is a graceful weapon, and very often used in martial arts combat, as what you are currently practicing."

"So, does this mean you think I should focus on using this?"

"I think you should practice with many weapons. Each of our members learns to become proficient with several different types, but to specialize in just one or two. This is because you should understand how to use whatever might be in your environment in case your preferred weapon is unavailable to you for some reason."

"All right, but why do you think a staff would be best for me?"

"If you are a graceful and dexterous sort, a weapon like this can take better advantage of that. But I'm not just thinking of a staff like this. There are other weapons that may be wielded in a similar fashion, but include other features like blades, flails, or mace heads. That might be your final choice, but you need to start here."

"Just what are you turning me into?" she chuckles.

"A living weapon, Kaliya..." Aerlie grins.

"But you know, that actually sounds like a contradiction. Aren't you a priestess who's supposed to heal people?"

"Yes, and I do, often. But I must also fight evil, and do so vigorously. Priests may carry the appeal of the kind and gentle caregiver, and it is true that we are. But there are still those moments when we must rise to the occasion no different from a warrior. The only true difference here is what role we actually play, which is very often a supportive one, rather than the front line."

"And as for me, are you placing me on the front line?"

"Your skills would give you this advantage, but not simply as an armored body plowing through a sea of enemies. We'll leave that to your male counterparts," she grins. "Yours would be more of a dance of death, enough to teach your opponents it is much healthier to keep at a distance from you."

"Yikes…" she winces. "All right, so I guess that's where we are, and I'll do what I can."

"Sergeant," Aerlie calls across the room.

"Yes, my Lady?" he replies as he trots forward.

"Have you been listening to any of this?"

"I may have overheard a word or two of it," he smiles.

"Good, teach her the basics of what we talked about. I have some special instructions for her to focus on. We will have her learn proficiency in the standard forms, but I want her to become intimately familiar with a staff-like weapon, much like a kensai with his sword. Further, I want her to master the martial arts."

"An interesting choice of weapon for a kensai, but if it's only for training, what kind of weapon were you thinking of for her final choice, if I may ask?"

"Either a twin-bladed staff or a sword-staff; those would be my best choices. But we must first test her to develop her skills better. We can refine her talents once we see if she can demonstrate the high degree of dexterity that I think she's capable of. However, I will ask for a few variations from the standard kensai model."

"You know, a kensai will need a specialist trainer in time."

"I'm sure it will, but for now, we will work on the basics. Further, we cannot be sure of what manner of foes she may face as time goes by, so she will need adequate protection, meaning to say plate along the critical areas. We will suggest a lighter form of plate in her case, but still sturdy enough to take a few hits, and designed with wider joints for greater flexibility. She will need the performance like that of a kensai, but the protection more like that of a paladin, and we need her trained up to handle it. Can you do this?"

"Oi, my Lady..." he responds sarcastically. "Give me something a little harder, and then ask. Right, then, I'll give her a good working, and have her build up as best I can."

"Which brings me to wonder what one of their males can do," Aerlie muses. "Hmm, a walking bulldozer..."

❖

"Captain," Petrith announces. "One of our long-range scouts has returned."

"Good. What do you have to report?"

A young female recruit has just returned from her extended patrol, ordered up a week before. She was chosen for this due to the fact that she had sports training in school, and therefore the practice and conditioning to run farther and faster than those from other study subjects. She steps up to Captain Lapäli to give her report.

"Captain, I've managed to follow several individual orcish migration lines, keeping myself out of view and hidden amongst the local shrubbery. What I found was an odd chain of travel between camps."

"A chain of travel? How do you mean?"

"For instance, I followed one line from the camp by the city outward to the south, through the river canyon. It was coming out of another camp in the valley on the other side. The orcs seemed to be travelling in small groups. But then I saw more orcs coming from further away into that camp. So, I followed that one, and it came out of yet another camp to the west along the backside of the mountains."

"One spills into another, which spills into another. That doesn't make any sense at all, even if it is some kind of migration, and especially if the one out here isn't getting that much bigger for all of them coming in. There must be a reason, but we can't get close enough without the risk of revealing ourselves, for all those we see wandering around."

"Captain," Petrith considers. "If one is spilling into another, then where is the first one spilling into the second? And how many are left in that first one if this is a kind of migration? Then, what about the second, and so on?"

"You mean to say they might be emptying out some areas and consolidating into this one? It's an interesting theory, but on the other side of it, I also want to know what's swallowing them up. But you're right; if they're all moving to one point, then somewhere out there might be some empty space. Let's start sending out scouts to further regions. We'll follow these lines back to the start if we have to. It might be a lot of running, but you kids have enough energy in you, so let's use it. We'll go over some new tactics together, and I'll have Túfu make up some more of that paper of hers for you to take down notes."

"This will have our people crawling all over the place, Captain," Sulíma cautions. "And we don't have any way of knowing if they get into trouble except, maybe, if they don't show up for a month or two. We don't have any trans-coms or relays. If something bad happens out there, they're on their own."

"I know, Suli, but it's all we've got. We just have to make sure we're smarter than your average orc. They don't know we're here, and seem focused on other things right now. The hardest part is being patient enough to see it through."

"I just wish there was some way we could communicate with them out in the field."

"We could use reflectors, but the distances are often too big, unless we have a long line of them. This also opens us up to detection by the orcs if one of them sees it. Without trans-coms, relays, or even a simple short-wave radio broadcast network, things will be tough for us."

"A long line…of relays," Petrith considers. "Like a network routing system."

"Leave it to a hacker to come up with that one," Sulíma smirks.

"Well, at least it offers a solution," he shrugs. "What about a relay of people? We set up camps in hidden locations, send out scouts to the local areas, run messengers between those camps to deliver new intel, and chain deliver it back here."

"Now there's an idea!" the Captain extols. "Maybe that bit with the Security Office mainframe did something good after all. But then, we need to teach a lot of people how to survive in the wilds."

"And poor Túfu will need to start mass-producing her paper," Sulíma adds. "We'll be using it up quick at that rate."

"She can always get help. And also that ink of hers…or maybe our people can use charcoal from their campfires."

"I'll try to give her some help sometime. That machine outside is a hopeless cause anyway. If we're going to reinvent the wheel, we might as well get started. I just wish we had a good power source to help invent it with."

"That's been my thought also. We had the example you created once using so much manual labor to turn a crank, but I think we'll need something more efficient than that if we're going to make any real work. The only problem here is a supply of materials, such as magnets, wire coils, and something to automate it with, like an old-fashioned steam furnace."

"And that'll make smoke, which could give us away."

"We'll think on this for now. So far, this is a low priority until we can learn more."

"We could use better weapons, too," Petrith offers. "Using clubs and pointed sticks is demeaning, to say the least. And trying to cut and bend sheet metal into a sharp point is nearly as dangerous to us as it might be to the bad guy, for all the cuts and scrapes we get along the way."

"I know, but once again, if we light a fire outside and try to forge it somehow…"

"Yeah, the orcs again… And trying to do it in here will asphyxiate us from the poor ventilation."

"One alternative is gunpowder, if we can figure out how to make it again. But that stuff can be dangerous."

"We have bows," Sulíma offers. "That's better than simple spears."

"This is true, Suli," the Captain nods. "So, for now, we'll make do, just like in the good old days…"

"…That none of us remembers," she finishes.

✦✦✦✦✦✦✦

A page arrives in the village of Firstfall and rushes into the tactical office with an urgent message. Thaelyn had been in conversation with his officers during the morning meeting about the usual news of the war, and speculation over the intentions of the orcs in the first portal camp.

"My Lord, your presence is required in the temple in B.T. The Lady is calling you."

"What is it, page? Is there some sort of trouble?"

"Lord Torm has summoned you."

"My Lord," the General notes. "This is a call you should answer most promptly."

"Indeed," Thaelyn affirms. "And I hope it gives us an answer to our worries over the prison portal."

Thaelyn hurries out of the building and up to the portal gate. He passes through and rushes along the avenue towards the temple. As he enters the temple main hall, Aerlie calls to him.

"Thaelyn, he made his appearance just a moment ago and bade me to call you. He is waiting."

Thaelyn rushes over to the altar and kneels down. He struggles to contain his anxiety and calm himself to enter into meditation so he can commune with the deity.

Aerlie hushes the assembly of priests and the other visitors currently in the temple so Thaelyn could have his moment of silence. She stands at a distance to give him solitude, attempting to clear her own mind so as not to confuse him with her thoughts and emotions intruding into his.

The idol glows softly once more, as it did before when Thaelyn first passed word to Torm about the Suuden-Aryku probe and the potential threat to the portal. Several images are imposed upon Thaelyn's mind in rapid succession, and then the glow fades. The entirety of the communion seemed exceptionally short, but the skill of Thaelyn's telepathic interpretation allowed Torm to communicate in a more advanced form than what the gods tend to use with the common priests.

Thaelyn pulls his attention back into the real world. He stands up and slowly turns around, then begins walking slowly back towards the others. From the look in his face, it seemed clear his mind was in deep consideration of the message and his future objectives.

"Thaelyn?" Aerlie whispers gently.

He takes several steps away from the altar, still in contemplative thought, but the severity of the message weighed in his expression. As he approached his wife, he gazed deeply into her eyes, but it was an image she had never seen before. It was a countenance of muted disquiet.

"I need to go to Sigil," he declares.

"But Thaelyn, why do you show such distress? You've been there so many times before…"

"But never with this purpose. I must gain an audience with the Lady."

"The Lady?!" she shrieks. "Thaelyn, why do you need to talk to her?"

"Lord Torm has revealed to me, though with much reluctance by Lord Ao, that the portal is inside the city. As you know, the Lady has forbidden the Powers from entering the city proper, which is most unusual for any being to demand of the Estelar. There has always been some question about this, but now I think I have the answer, or at least a good cause for one. The prison portal is in the city, and she guards it by keeping all others away, including those who made it."

"Very well, but considering how powerful she is, I would hardly think the Suuden-Aryku, or even Sargeras, would pose a threat."

"Perhaps, but if she is not made aware of this, they could possibly sneak in under her view and access it."

"How would they do that? It would need a key, right? Do we know if they possess one?"

"In answer to that, consider this... What sort of key do you suppose one would need to open a portal to a place holding such creatures you never wanted to see released from there again?"

"Ooh! Are you testing ME now?" she grins.

"My dear, for all the mischief you have been playing on me lately, I think this is a fair return," he smiles.

"Uh huh..."

Aerlie ponders the question for a moment.

"It would have to be personal," she muses. "Something you would not commonly find outside the portal gate. Thaelyn, would it relate to the Primordials themselves?"

"It would. A fragment of their essence... Something that should not exist outside the portal, but it does, with Sargeras."

"Dear gods above, Thaelyn! So, all he needs to do is come close to it personally, or have someone with a piece of him come close to it...like the Suuden-Aryku."

"And if he, or perhaps even Darumon, in this case, uses the Suuden-Aryku to transport components of a conveyor into it, they could construct an escape inside the prison plane without anyone knowing the better. Then, it is just a matter of time for them to accumulate enough Arcanicium to make their weapon, and there go the realms."

"This is deeply troubling and getting worse. And then YOU... you need to speak to that...woman."

"She is not necessarily an evil person, just very strict of mind and directed of purpose."

"Oh! Strict of mind... She frightens the wits out of everyone who lives there. They don't dare think about her, speak her name, or offer her tribute. And any action that threatens the city is punished harshly and without compassion. Simply to see her passing by causes the streets to clear out and the people to take shelter."

"I am not without my own hesitation to perform this duty, but the Powers are forbidden to enter, therefore a messenger must be sent in their stead."

"Eh, my Lord?" ushers the lead priest, who had been cautiously eavesdropping. "A simple question if I may. These are the Estelar we speak of. And as much as we might revere them as gods, they are also recognized as a society of exceptionally high scientific and technological esteem. Would they not have some manner of internal communications network where they could simply pass a message from one to another, rather than to require a runner make the effort?"

"Yes, Priest, you are right, and they do," he chuckles ironically. "But the Lady of Sigil is very isolationist. My impression of her is that of someone who does not pay much mind to missives simply arriving at the foot of her door. You very literally have to knock to gain her attention."

"I see. Oh dear..."

"Thaelyn," Aerlie asserts firmly. "You be careful! You know what she's capable of, better than anyone else. Let's just hope she's willing to listen, and you return with your skin still attached!"

"I think, under the circumstances, this ought to proceed in a predictable manner. Naturally, we have a serious threat, and even she should recognize the importance of it, therefore my reason to disturb her. Her reaction to it is another matter, as she does not get out much...or at all, for that matter. And she does not socialize with anyone other than her servants...who, by the way, are forbidden to speak verbally. Hmm..."

"Right, and she is also known to hold a rather volatile temper and vivid response tactic to those who upset her...and I'm quite sure this will upset her."

"Very well, Aerlie," he sighs. "I will take this with all due caution. This does also bring to mind another reason to make my visit, and I should attend to this before attempting my meeting, if only to begin the process so, um…" his voice trails off abruptly.

"Don't you even dare speak like that!" she chides. "Which one is it?"

"Kaliya… I should speak with Aelwyn, and see about gaining her assistance to give the girl instruction on this gift of hers."

Aerlie sighs heavily.

"When will you do this?" she asks wearily.

"I will plan this trip over the next few days. Perhaps I could go out this next weekend so as not to interrupt Kaliya's tight training schedule."

"Just be sure, before you go, that you spend a moment with me. And I'll pray for you, my love," Aerlie pleads as she leans in and wraps a tender embrace around him.

✦✦✦✦✦✦✦

"General, we need to establish a few contingencies, um, just in case…"

"My Lord," he relents. "When you begin with such words as these…"

It was the morning of the first day of the following weekend. Thaelyn was in the tactical office in Firstfall and had assembled the full attendance of his officers and assigns. He was giving each of them their duties as a precautionary measure in case something should go wrong during his visit to Sigil.

"I know," Thaelyn nods. "I have been listening to this from Aerlie ever since that day in the temple. Nevertheless, here we are."

"Indeed, my Lord, please continue."

"Although I hope this will proceed as expected, and so far, I do not sense anything exceptionally foreboding, I do know the Lady has something of a temper. Therefore, I feel it is prudent to give a few instructions to carry out during my absence, and also in case something unforeseen should occur."

"I understand."

"First, you will continue as planned with the orcs in this world. I will request Aelwyn's assistance to train Kaliya, and you will use her to mark a rune on Ruuki uy'Daan, once she is appropriately skilled. This will grant access to that world and enable you to finish the war there. We once discussed the relocation of the orcs to a world outside the flows. While I would surely desire this over the complete destruction of their race, if I am unable to return, and therefore to find the means using my own connections, and if you cannot find a satisfactory alternative, we may find ourselves with no other option. Use whatever resources you have, and your best judgement in this matter to find your way."

"Absolutely, but I will most surely EXPECT your return, my Lord, or I might go up there and share a few of my own words with that Lady," he chuckles softly.

"Well, all I ask is that you take care of the language," he smiles. "We must also secure our way to Morndindor somehow, and if this involves knowledge or capacity held by the orcs, you must do what you can to secure it and lead us forward. After that, I am at something of a loss to advise, other than again to use your best judgement and whatever resources are available to seek a final result. This may also include involving one or another of the Estelar themselves, if need be."

"This will surely require some careful planning, but we have some fine talent available to us, and so we will see to it."

Thaelyn makes a quick pass around the room before continuing.

"Now, Amariyn, Sehnisavain, and Tristeen," he gazes at the worried attendants. "The three of you must focus yourselves on your appointed tasks, restoring this world and rebuilding the local societies. Rolsklinde is coming along nicely. Keep pushing forward. Educate your people and treat them well, and pray for the safety of the realms."

"My Lord," Tristeen pleads. "Is this really necessary?"

"It may not be as bad as it seems. The Lady, as I said, has something of a history behind her for her reactionary behavior. But this is an important task to attend, and surely even she should realize the need to maintain some level of composure. I am simply laying down a few words as a precaution."

"Uh huh. All right, a precaution. I think I will probably join at the side of the General here if that 'precaution' doesn't play out nice for us."

Thaelyn smiles gently at the girl as he turns to the tall Daanen'kai officer.

"Lieutenant Lapäli, you are a fine young officer, and I wish you to follow your best wisdom. Encourage your people to stay close to mine, and you will not be disappointed."

"I will ask our people to call on the cu'Nar to watch over you."

"I appreciate the mention. Just make sure the cu'Nar are not standing too closely."

Thaelyn makes a final pass around the room, laying a hand on their shoulders and offering a parting smile before leaving the room.

He goes outside into the village and strolls over to the portal. He stops briefly to look around at the bustle of activity before stepping through. He arrives outside the guildhall and moves away from the portal gate, pausing again, as he did before, to turn and look at the grand city he worked so hard to build over the course of so many centuries.

The guards standing in front of the gates study him, not knowing about his upcoming mission, and wondering why he has taken this moment to pause in his steps. When Thaelyn finished his deep reflection, he turns and continues up to the gates.

"My Lord," calls one of the guards. "Is everything all right?"

"Yes, guard, I am simply reflecting on so many of our combined achievements. Every so often, I feel such a moment of nostalgia," he smiles disarmingly.

"Absolutely, my Lord, it's a fine view from up here."

He saunters contemplatively into the courtyard area, studying the large statue in the center which shows him kneeling in a knight's repose with Aerlie standing over his shoulder pointing off in the distance, representing to look towards the future while remaining vigilant over the present.

The students were taking the day off today. Some were simply ambling about, enjoying moments of conversation, while others were using their off-hours for some extra study. None of them were told of Thaelyn's travel plans, as this was a mission of high security and closed details.

Kaliya and her friends were in the courtyard talking about their classwork as Thaelyn approached. Kaliya was informed to meet him here for her trip to Sigil to speak with Aelwyn. Even though Thaelyn had not yet gained Aelwyn's official support, he felt confident enough that she would agree to perform this service.

"Kaliya, are you ready?"

"Yes, my Lord, although I'm a little nervous about going up there. I'm hearing from people it's a strange place, and someone like me might draw a lot of attention."

"Perhaps, but you are not the same as any of the fiendish races, even though your appearance might give some minor allusion to one. I will simply suggest staying close to me and all will be well."

"Is that before or after your visit with the Lady up there?" she grins.

Thaelyn simply smiles at the thought.

"So, it's time then?" Marelle asks. "Oh, I wish I could come along. I've heard so much about that place from various people here, and I also remember your story once. It must be a strange and fascinating place to visit."

"Yes, Marelle, it is," he nods. "But this is not a simple bit of tourism I make. I must go speak with the lady governess of the city to warn her of Sargeras and the Suuden-Aryku, and to pass instructions to safeguard the prison portal gate which is apparently hidden somewhere within the city itself."

"Really. Well then, maybe you'd like us to come along and stand by you? After all, everybody needs someone to back them up on occasion," she smirks.

"Yes, but my dear Marelle, this lady is not your typical sort that one would casually walk up to for any manner of speaking."

"Um, what do you mean by that?" she asks tentatively, now feeling a cold chill running down her back.

"She has something of a reputation for a firm-handed rule over the city and its population. Most people keep clear of her. She has expressly forbidden any of the Powers from entering the city, and keeps a close watch for any who might cause harm to it. She is a form of deity, some have suggested she is a member of the Estelar, but she tends to be very secretive, perhaps also isolationist, and she does not take kindly to people offering piety to her. It is said that if you should come under her shadow, meaning to draw her attention by some manner of wrongdoing, she would flay you alive from the blades that surround the mask she wears."

"Flay? Like…to remove the skin…?"

Marelle now felt the cold snap turning into a strong shiver.

"Also, if you offend her by offering worship, or even to speak her name too boldly, she can imprison you within a custom demi-planar maze, forever struggling to find your way back out again."

"Gee…" she shudders. "How nice."

Marelle's face was now flinching with fear and hesitation. She gulps and unconsciously takes a step back.

"Now," Thaelyn grins impishly. "Do you still wish to back me up while I attempt to face her with this most disturbing news?"

Marelle stammers as she tries to formulate a reply.

"Well, um…my Lord. That is to say, I…uh, you, and her, and then me… Aw hell! Bully to all this, you're going to need me up there!"

"Oh buggers! Marelle!" Relissa groans.

The young dark elf had been growing paler with each word mentioned by Thaelyn during his brief interlude. She was fidgeting and growing visibly nervous, but at Marelle's announcement, she was now clearly agitated. She dropped her gaze to the ground and placed a hand on her hip as she realized where this was fated to go, then cautiously raised her free hand to gain the attention of the group.

"Right, so if the bleedin' round-ear is going up there, this means I need to tag along to keep her out of trouble."

"Relissa," Thaelyn asserts. "The last time this round-ear got into trouble, you were her accomplice!"

"Well, I didn't say I was good at it."

"My Lord," Kaliya states nervously. "Are you sure we really need to do this? I mean, I could always find a cliff and jump off. It'd be much simpler."

"Simple or not, I think there is no other way. Now, are you ready?"

Kaliya takes a deep breath and exhales slowly.

"All right, so let's do it."

"Not yet, you're not!" cries a shout from above.

Aerlie drops into the courtyard, just arriving from the temple after sensing Thaelyn's return to the city.

"Not without a solid kiss goodbye," she continues.

She runs over and wraps her arms around Thaelyn, as the two exchange a deep kiss.

"Ahem," Relissa coughs. "Maybe the two of you would like a room?"

"Um..." Marelle mutters softly. "You're not trying to delay the inevitable now, are you?"

"Maybe..."

"Actually, no..." Aerlie chirps. "That won't be necessary, we already did that part."

A round of laughter spreads between each of them until Aerlie speaks up again.

"Dear, if you get the time, I was wondering if you could do me a little treat."

"And what might that be, my little cherub?"

"You know," Marelle observes. "I don't think they need a room. I think they need a full boarding house."

"Oh you...hush," Aerlie teases. "This is serious..." she redirects at Thaelyn. "It's been a long time since you last went up there. And you know how much I love those little chocolate quasits."

"Serious?" Marelle retorts. "He's going to meet with that Lady up there, perhaps to be eaten alive by her, and you're asking him to bring back sweets?"

The group let out another round of laughter, which at this point was actually helping calm their nerves greatly.

"Ah, yes," Thaelyn nods reassuringly. "Very well, I shall see about it. And I am sure Vrischika would take a special delight in my visitation after so long an absence."

"Oh, indeed!" Aerlie intones enthusiastically. "I still recall that first time meeting with her. Such a delightful personality! And so entertaining! You simply cannot leave without saying a friendly hello."

"Vrischika?" Marelle asks.

"She is a shop owner in the Clerk's Ward," Thaelyn explains. "And she runs a rather lucrative little trade in curiosity items. There was even a time when I brought her a truly fascinating proposal for trade with one of our researchers."

"Really! Sounds like you hold something of a history together."

"Aye, that sounds cute enough," Relissa quips.

"But we should go now," Thaelyn resumes. "I wish to get on with this quickly, if only to see it to the end."

"I really wish you wouldn't put it in quite those terms, my Lord," Marelle moans.

"Well, yes, perhaps that was an unfortunate term to apply here. I should also note, I would not normally bring students on a mission like this, but I suspect you will not be satisfied to remain here, is this correct?"

"Damn right it is...with all due respect," Marelle states.

"Then we will proceed as we have done in the past. Stay close and do as I say."

"Not a problem here."

As the briefing came to a close within the group, outside the guildhall and running hurriedly along the street below, was a frantic elder High Elf clutching her favorite stack of books. She turned and proceeded up the hill to the front gates, trotting feebly the last few steps into the courtyard, and pausing only long enough to gain her bearings. She then lumbered over to the group. Her obvious condition and ragged panting portrayed her clear intention to arrive before Thaelyn had a chance to depart. The group all took notice as she came into view.

"Archivist Windsong?" Thaelyn muses.

"Vonafel!" Aerlie interjects. "What happened? Did you run all this way?"

"Well, yes…actually," she replies breathlessly. "I mean… Well, that is, I heard of his journey up there… You know, to that place… And I, um…"

Thaelyn and Aerlie both exchanged glances.

"Archivist," he begins. "Just how is it you knew about that? We have been keeping it largely a secret."

"Oh! Um, I…uh… Well, I heard about it…you know…through someone I know…who is, um, actually…well, I have a spy watching things for me…several spies in fact," she titters. "But I have a good reason for it!"

Thaelyn eyes her suspiciously, and then turns to look at Aerlie again.

"My dear, I think you need to make a careful review of your staff members. I as well, for that matter."

"Yes!" Aerlie affirms with a grin. "But more importantly, I'm still wondering why she's here at all."

"Well, it's because…um…" Vonafel hesitates, and then glances at her books.

Thaelyn and Aerlie both studied her, and intuitively surmised what she must have on her mind.

"Vonafel…" Thaelyn pauses tenuously to glance again at Aerlie. "What is it? I am going to assume you have been swimming in these notes of yours again, correct?"

"Swimming?" Aerlie retorts. "More like drowning if you ask me. And she's been especially active of late."

"Did you find something new in there?" Kaliya mentions. "I remember you from the last time…you know, when we met in the cafeteria."

"She came to you in the cafeteria?" Thaelyn wonders. "Here in the guildhall?"

"Yeah, she says there's a prophecy in these books of hers that mentions my people."

"Indeed!" he croons. "And most curious…"

Relissa and Marelle both gazed at each other, so far unaware of the subject matter.

"Um, what are we talking about here?" Relissa offers.

"She works at the Royal Historical Archives down the road," Kaliya responds. "She apparently specializes in some books written by someone called Adalon the Silver."

"Ay, I know that name, I think. Isn't that the same one you told us to go look at in the library about that friend of yours?"

"It is," Thaelyn replies. "And if you have not yet done so, I think it might prove educational. But what is the special occasion here? And why are you in such turmoil?"

"Turmoil? Me?" Vonafel returns shyly. "Well, it's just that..." she hesitates. "My Lord, we're in the end times, and I'm watching things unfold right before my eyes."

"When you use such a term as end times..."

"Oh, don't worry about that, it's just the end of her book coming up, so I call it the end times. Although this also seems to be leading up to something, and I can only see one direction ahead of us for what it could be."

"Indeed, and the sensations I am drawing from you at present suggest this is enough to cause you to run all this distance in a panic to see us off."

"Oh, that...no, I was just anxious to see you before you go...oh, wait, that's the same thing as what you just said," she titters again. "What I mean to say is, well, the book tells of this moment, but in Adalon's usual manner of speaking. I only just now put it together, and so I had to rush out here to see it."

"This day is mentioned in her book?" he frowns uncertainly.

"Yes," she affirms. "If you recall, I've stated in the past this reads much more like a story, with a lot of pieces that often require private knowledge to interpret, ever since that day the two of you got married. Do you remember that?"

"Indeed, I do!"

"But the more I see unfolding, the more I'm finally able to put together. My Lord, this isn't a book of prophecies, it's more like a chronicle. I can't even be sure if I would describe it as simple prophecies anymore. More like a series of statements to explain certain prominent moments fated to occur, as if someone, or something, is directing us into it."

"Oh great," Aerlie rolls her eyes. "And here we go again with the Maker, I suppose."

"How would this apply to my journey to Sigil?" Thaelyn wonders. "I cannot precisely see how someone, or something, could have previously directed us towards this."

"Maybe not on this occasion," Vonafel suggests. "It could simply be a process of Fate leading us into it. But she knew about it."

"One moment, Adalon actually knew about this? Are we speaking of the prison portal?"

Vonafel peers down at her books and pulls at a corner marked by a ribbon. She opens the page to reveal her latest finding, and begins to read.

"A city of circular marvel spins, a cage as much as a zoo; a secret kept behind a door, shall raise old fears anew."

"Dear Powers, Vonafel," he wheezes. "If this suggests what I think it does..."

"Right. You've told us about Sigil many times in the past. It's a city enclosed in a curious geometric shape called a torus...circular, and sometimes described as the Cage due to the fact that it has no physical doors or windows looking out, so it's a fully enclosed space. It's filled with beings from all across the realms, so I guess it really is a zoo up there," she giggles softly. "But you also told us that those people tend to refer to portals as Doors, and the city has tons of them inside. And this one we're speaking of would surely count as the realm's best kept secret, even to the Estelar, and we all know how we feel about Sargeras and the threat he poses."

"Wow," Kaliya moans. "This is getting a little scary now."

"Aye," Relissa agrees. "So, what does this mean for all of us going up there? Does it say something?"

"Actually, no," Vonafel admits. "It doesn't say anything bad will happen, and given how Adalon has a history of telling this story from their perspective," she nods at Thaelyn and Aerlie. "I think if something bad were to happen, she would say something. My Lord, we need to talk. When you return, I would request an urgent conference with you, Aerlie, this young lady," she points at Kaliya, "and maybe some of your officers. There's more here I need to go over, and I think it's time to review some of it."

"Very well," he admits. "We will see to this as soon after as we can; given that I may need a few moments to myself to ease my own tensions."

"Oh, of course, and I hope it's not too bad for you this time."

"May I ask for my brother to be involved?" Kaliya offers. "If this concerns our people, he needs to know."

"Yes, this is reasonable," Thaelyn affirms. "I will pass this through Lieutenant Lapäli and see if we can arrange something. I need to begin working more directly with him anyway for our future engagements."

Vonafel nods and backs away as Thaelyn and his group continue their preparations.

"Now," he continues. "In order to reach Sigil from here, we must take an indirect route."

"Why is that?" Marelle asks. "No runes to it?"

"The Lady does not like the opening of random portals within the confines of her city, so we must use one of the existing portals that are a part of it. In this case, we will use an old method I am very accustomed to from my days in the service of my Father."

"Sounds good to me, so where do we go first?"

"Mount Celestia…"

Marelle suddenly goes pale at the mention of that name.

"Isn't that where you were born?" she asks with a tremor in her voice.

"It is."

"And isn't that where the gods live?"

"Some of them, Torm for one…"

Vonafel giggles as she watches the scene develop.

"You have to get used to this sort of thing," she mentions. "I've never had the occasion, but this becomes a familiar sight to us."

"Easy for you to say," Marelle retorts. "All right, so…how do we get there? Do you use a rune for that?"

"Not quite…" Thaelyn smiles. "Kaliya, you stand opposite me, Relissa and Marelle to my sides, and everyone hold hands in a circle."

"Marelle," Relissa groans. "I hate you."

Aerlie moves away while Thaelyn forms a circle with the others, and they all hold hands.

"Like many Celestials, along with others who make their homes in the Outer Planes, I am blessed by my Father with a special ability that allows me to return home from anywhere in the realms. Behold…"

He closes his eyes and draws a breath. When he opens again, his eyes are glowing brightly. He angles his head upward, and a column of light forms around the group reaching skyward. It intensifies into a brilliant beam reaching into the heavens.

The other students in the courtyard all stop what they're doing to observe the abnormal sight. The guards at the gate notice the radiant glow and turn to see it. Out in the city, people who are walking along all take notice of the anomaly reaching upward from the guildhall, many of them realizing what it is from previous experience.

The column sparkles with wispy streaks of light, enveloping the group and lifting them off the ground. They accelerate through the air and into the sky above, finally vanishing into a planar vortex.

The light blinds their vision, but it's not painful. They feel a sensation of flying, though it doesn't truly feel as if they're physically moving. The rush of energies around them makes a gushing sound, with luminescent streams racing alongside through a kind of tunnel composed of light and energy. Strange sights zip along outside, until finally they feel a subsidence of the flow as new scenery comes into focus.

They arrive in an open setting resembling a field of bold green grasses in front of an ornate temple structure of marble columns. The sky is a vivid blue with occasional puffy white clouds passing by. Small orbs floated by like tufts of disconnected starlight drifting on a gentle breeze. And in the background stood a majestic mountain reaching high into the clouds and beyond.

"My Lord," Marelle squeaks as she takes his arm and holds on tightly. "Is this...?"

"Welcome to Mount Celestia, Children, my first home."

"Aye, and just look at the place," Relissa shudders. "So, that over there..." she points. "You have an actual mountain in this place?"

"Some of the mortal races describe this as the Seven Heavens. There are seven layers as you ascend the mountain. Various members of the gods make their homes at different levels. That is, those who reside in this plane."

"I feel strange," Marelle comments as she examines her body. "Like I feel something tingling, or maybe a warm fuzzy feeling, I'm not sure how to explain it."

"The Outer Planes are charged with potent energies, as you have a much closer association with what we generally describe as the dynamistic flows. On Tae'Eladar, we would simply describe this as the arcanic energies, or maybe an arcanic or dynamistic cloud, but here we are much closer to the source, so we might feel it more prominently. In addition, as these are also the homes of those gods who release their own vitalities into the local environment, you may feel their essence weaving its way into you."

"Absolutely amazing," Kaliya mumbles. "To think of my people, who for so long thought we understood a few things, but now to see all this, it simply tells me we actually know so very little. For instance, we use the term nether-space, which is largely a fantasy term for us to depict a void space of undefined dimensions. But this here, are we actually inside something like that?"

"Technically speaking, I think we could say yes, if you are referring to a space of dimensional proportions above your more common three-dimensional universe."

"Well, there goes another set of horns," she shrugs.

"And depending on which realm you visit, you may feel a different sort of sensation in the space around you...positive versus negative, ordered versus chaotic. This realm is the one we call Ordered

Positivity. We might also use such terms to describe things that normally reside here as being Positive Ordered. So, the sensation you feel may also be the nature of the plane imposing itself upon your personal nature. If a mortal being, like yourself, were to spend any significant amount of time in this space, you might even feel the essence of your spirit turn somewhat to come into alignment with the realm itself."

"Fascinating..." Marelle muses.

"What are these little light things floating through here," Relissa asks.

"To a Prime like yourself," he responds. "I would explain these as the resident spirits of those who ascended here in the afterlife."

"Bloody...I can't even say it," she winces. "These are people?"

"It is what becomes of them after they have merged with the plane to become a part of it. They must first go through a process we call Petitioning, which is a sort of acclimation process as they align themselves more fully to the nature of the realm before merging with it."

"Well..." Kaliya sighs deeply. "There goes whatever belief I ever had in what happens when you die, not that I had much of a belief to begin with."

"All right," Marelle utters meekly. "So, now what do we do?"

"Now we must travel locally to the portal gate that crosses into the city," Thaelyn responds. "It is over that way," he points off in the distance, "in the structure near that small outcropping of rock near the mountain."

"That's kind of a long walk from here, but..."

"Walk? We are in Celestia, Child. We do not walk here."

"Um, right," Relissa counters. "What do we do then; float around like these little twittery things?"

"Remember my demi-plane. The mind has power here, enough to fold space and reshape matter. If it is properly disciplined, it can do many things. I chose not to specialize in this very deeply, but I do have a modest ability. Hold hands again, and take mine."

Thaelyn takes Kaliya's hand on one side, chaining to Marelle and then to Relissa. He then holds up a hand to frame his destination with his fingers and focuses his attention on the endpoint across the field at the structure in the distance.

The local space seems to blur and distort, with the center point of their focus enlarging as if under a microscope, while everything else twists and stretches behind them. The sensation was quick, and before they realized it, they were zipping across the local space, only to arrive in front of the structure.

Kaliya tries to cough up a word to express her reaction, but it gets stuck in her throat midway.

"Is there something about this place that you can't speak certain words?" she asks.

Thaelyn laughs as he leads them into the structure. Inside, they see a neatly carved archway with runic engravings.

"Aye then," Relissa asserts. "So, what kind of key do we use here, I wonder?"

"This is the realm of Law, and Law must be blind to the interests of the contestants. Therefore, we must apply a hand shielding our eyes."

"Isn't it a wee bit hard to see where you're going that way?"

"It is best to line yourself up in front of the portal before you do so."

"And what if it doesn't work the first time? You hit the wall behind it?" she grins.

Thaelyn defers to the women, and Relissa finds herself taking the first step. She holds up a hand in front of her eyes and pauses a moment to give the portal time to react, then takes a blind step forward, fully expecting to hit something hard. She takes another step, and one more after that, finally to feel a sensation of passing through something and arriving in a new place. She moves out of the way to allow the next person to pass. Marelle follows next, then Kaliya, and finally Thaelyn.

They look around at the extraordinary sight, a city built inside a closed tubular structure circling around like a donut. They study the sides as they curve up over their heads and down the other way, coming back under their feet.

"Criminy," Relissa whispers.

"Are we on the bottom, or the top?" Marelle wonders. "Or is there a difference?"

"And what holds us here on the ground, or is it the ceiling?" Kaliya adds.

"Gravity, as you commonly know it," Thaelyn responds, "works a little bit differently in this place. Wherever you are, you are technically considered to be on the ground. There is no true ceiling, unless you are inside a building, of course. So, from where we are, if you had the power to jump that high, you might feel the effect of gravity beneath you fade into that which would come down from above."

"Oh!" Kaliya erupts energetically. "I get it. And someplace out there, right about dead center in the middle, you might find a point of null gravity where it balances in all directions."

"Correct, and very good. But that point would be rather small, so any part of your body that may extend outside of it could pull you in that general direction. It is not likely you could very easily become trapped in that place."

"Just be careful of the landing," Marelle considers. "That's a long way up, even though."

"Now," Thaelyn asserts. "What I would first wish to do is seek out someone to pass a message to the Lady, to inform her of my desire to speak with her. It might take time for her to respond, so we should begin this process now."

"That's the scariest part of this trip," Marelle mumbles.

"I think our first effort should be to find a dabus."

"A dabus?" she asks.

"They are servants to the Lady. They monitor and maintain the city on her behalf. They are likely to be the best way to make our inquiry and gain her attention."

Thaelyn leads the group through the streets linking the various sections of the city. They pass by the local citizenry, many of whom turn to examine the strange visitors, especially Kaliya, but mostly go along with their own business. Among the populace, they notice figures of many sizes, colors, and physical features, including tails, horns, hoofed feet, and fur-covered goat-like legs. Some even have leathery or scaly wings.

In a section of recent construction and remodeling, Thaelyn finds what he's looking for. There are several beings hovering above the ground hammering away at the buildings with mallets. They were tall and wore flowing robes, with a shock of white hair and thin corkscrew horns coming out of their foreheads.

"There, that is what we want," Thaelyn declares.

"Those are dabus…dabuses…dabi…" Kaliya puzzles. "How do you pronounce that word?"

Thaelyn pats her on the arm as he approaches one of the creatures.

"May I have a brief word, please," he announces to one of them.

The dabus initially seems to ignore Thaelyn, instead continuing its work without pause.

"Not very polite, are they?" Relissa mutters quietly.

Thaelyn tries again.

"I have a need to speak with one of you about gaining an audience with the Lady."

As he finishes his statement, they each stop their work and turn to him, looking down into Thaelyn's face as if to gauge his sanity. The nearest one begins fashioning a series of floating three-dimensional symbols over its head.

"What's that?" Marelle inquires softly. "Some kind of writing? Don't they speak?"

"This is how they communicate," he replies, before returning to the dabus in front. "I carry word that needs to be delivered to the Lady. It is most urgent."

The creature produces more symbols over its head while forming a curious expression.

"It concerns the safety of the city," Thaelyn replies. "And indeed all the realms around us. There is a great danger approaching, and she needs to be made aware of it so that she can take action, if need be."

More symbols come into view above the dabus's head.

"She will need to be made aware of this article, regardless of her concerns for anything outside the city, as it could destroy all the Outer Planes and the city with it."

Again more symbols. The dabus appeared to be growing impatient with the pointless raving. The others in Thaelyn's group were fascinated by the varied display and how it could simply form out of thin air above the being's head. But the one-sided conversation proved difficult to follow.

"The danger involves a survivor of the old Celestial Wars...a Primordial."

A sudden explosion of symbols spurs across the collective space above the group of dabuses. The flurry of exclamatory remarks and anxious proclamations overlapped and combined, creating a jumbled mix of meaningless forms.

"That got their attention," Marelle remarks.

"Aye," Relissa adds. "But I don't think I want to know what it all means."

The dabuses turn to each other and begin speaking amongst themselves. Rows of symbols appear over their heads as they rant about Thaelyn's last statement, until finally the forward member returns to communicate with him again.

"I have reason to believe he has in mind to return here to find the old prison portal," Thaelyn responds. "I carry Lord Ao's authority to deliver this message to the Lady as a warning for her to secure it from tampering. Beyond that, I am limited in what I can say directly to you."

The dabus turns and speaks with his fellows once again for several moments, until finally he turns to give his response.

"Very well," Thaelyn submits. "I will be travelling next to the Clerk's Ward to visit a friend near the Guild of Sensations. If the Lady will see me, you may find me there."

Thaelyn offers a polite bow, turns, and leads the group away.

"My Lord," Marelle relents. "By the time I finish studying with you, I don't think I'll have any wits left in me."

"This is just the beginning. Wait until the Lady arrives."

"I don't think I want to, thanks. So, what's next?"

"Now we go for a little sight-seeing and look for Aelwyn."

They travel through the city, making their way around the curved architecture until they arrive in a plaza in front of a large building. The plaza held many smaller buildings, including residences, a number of shops, and a couple of cafés. The large building in the background bore an appearance almost to that of a temple, with people occasionally entering and exiting through the double doors.

"Now then," Relissa jests. "What was this I heard once about a brothel?"

"Ah, would you like to take a closer look?"

He leads them up to the doors of a moderately-sized building in the upper part of the plaza. He opens the door for them to go inside.

They entered a lobby lined with sofas and leisure chairs situated around several small casual tables. It was a very pleasant environment, well becoming of a place of social relaxation. The room was occupied by a number of visitors in conversation, but the noise level was kept low to offer a polite setting. As they moved further into the room, a voice rang out from a member of a group at the far end.

"Thaelyn, how pleasant it is to see you again."

A woman breaks from the group and strolls over to meet them. She had pleasing features, at least from the knees up, but her feet appeared as claws. She also had wings…scaled demonic wings.

"Jiggers…" Relissa moans. "Suddenly, I'm sorry I asked."

"Grace," Thaelyn responds pleasantly. "It has been a long time. How have you been faring?"

"Business has been steady," she replies cordially. "And the girls keep themselves occupied. What brings you here…old memories, perhaps?"

"Surely, it brings back a few, but I also have serious business to attend on this occasion. Still, along the way, I just had to spend some time refreshing myself on a few old acquaintances."

"I am pleased you remembered. And who are these friends of yours?"

"Indeed, here we have some of my more recent students, though we have also created something of a special rapport along the way. This is Relissa, Marelle, and the tall one is Kaliya."

Grace offered a polite bow to the trio and examined Kaliya's unusual form for a brief instant. She also took notice of Relissa's dark coloring and pale hair.

"Are these people from Tae'Eladar? I recognize the human. This dark one appears as an elf. She reminds me a bit of Nemelle's mother. A Morier, is it?"

"Aye," Relissa nods gently. "You have one of us up here?"

"Nemelle is an Eladrin, but her mother was a Drow. Although, this was quite some time ago. But this is curious, I thought your kind did not openly associate with the rest."

"My people are a migrant group that left Tae'Eladar some while back. Thaelyn and his people found us recently and brought us back home."

"Really! How interesting. And then this tall one, she is new to me."

"Kaliya is a member of a party called Daanen-Aryku," Thaelyn offers, "which is foreign to our realms. We met her people on a new world we discovered recently."

"Gracious, Thaelyn! Are your people travelling to new worlds already? Other than for Shadowfell, that is."

"Yes, although rather unexpectedly, but in a small context, we are. A war came to us, and this opened a new avenue for us to explore."

"I see. So we have a new face from a far place. Such things are always worthy to share a few good experiences."

"Excuse me," Marelle inquires tenderly. "But may I ask what you are?"

"In the Primes, you would describe me as a succubus, which is a lesser form of tanar'ri."

Marelle gasped and fell back a step on hearing the word, though not knowing fully which word she was falling back from out of the two. She recognized the common word succubus from some of her studies, and further reflected on the tanar'ri that stormed through the streets of Rolsklinde months before.

"Do not fear, human," the woman comforts. "I am not the same as the others of my kind. Allow me to introduce myself. My proper name is Fall-From-Grace, though many simply call me Grace."

"Why are you called Fall-From-Grace?" Kaliya asks timidly.

"There is a history to it, but to make it short, I betrayed the practice of my kind, and therefore fell out of grace to my nature. To this end, I took my name."

"Well, that sounds simple enough, although it's also a bit strange to hear such a term used from that perspective."

"Yes, if we consider that you may have learned this from your perspective. This is the true difference within the realms, what we might describe as the Polarities of the Planes. If you are Positive, you might see me as your enemy, and all that I stand for and perceive as my purpose in life would offend you. But I might hold this same perspective from the Negative side. I would perceive my purpose to be just as valid as yours is to you, and yours would offend me in the same manner. We each take our perspectives and carry them as our direction in life, meeting our ends in such a way as to ensure the Measure of Balance. Are you familiar with the principles of the Measure of Balance?"

"I'm currently taking formal lessons in his academy on Tae'Eladar, and I learned a few basic pointers from some of his priests once."

"Very well, but this is a way of life for us here, on both sides. Normally, Thaelyn and I might not otherwise hold such friendly relations. But in our case, we can, due largely to the fact that I have fallen from my original grace, therefore I am no longer considered a part of that alignment. This is why I take up my occupation here, to find a new purpose for myself."

"What about others like you," Marelle wonders. "Or any others of the Negative side, and especially where he might be concerned," she thumbs at Thaelyn.

"While I may not be of this same sort now, under normal conditions, if we were to meet virtually anywhere outside the city, I think the result would be conflict, without question or hesitation. But this city is special in that it represents neutral ground, allowing us that rare occasion and privilege to meet without ripping each other's throats out," she grins.

"Oh… How convenient…" she smirks.

"But it still seems a wee bit wacky to me," Relissa offers. "When we think of the Negative side, we can't help but to think of it in terms of such like theft and murder."

"I understand," Grace affirms. "But here you are making an incorrect perception. Mortal societies often associate such principles as criminal behavior with the concept of evil. At the same time, Negativity is also associated with the notion of evil, in contrast to Positivity for goodness. But the terms of good versus evil do not play out in the same context here. Crime, such as what you describe, would still be a crime no matter what side you are on."

"So, evil," Marelle wonders, "if we use that word in this context, might actually hold something against murder?"

"Let us exclude the words good and evil for the moment, as these might be confusing us within this context. Naturally, theft and murder would be considered unacceptable to the Positive side, but we are speaking of that which is within its own. However, Positive would not hesitate to destroy Negative, so where did your concept of murder travel off to where the opposite side is concerned? And yet, the same holds true within Negativity, as we would still regard murder to be undesirable…within our own."

"But not where Positivity is concerned, as you might consider yourselves to be at war with each other, right?"

"This is generally the case, along with any who might otherwise side with them. Our purpose would be to promote the perception of Negativity, and how we conduct ourselves, which is to say how we approach our side of the Measure of Balance, while Positivity would conduct itself in a similar manner from its side."

"Then how do these two actually relate to each other?"

"They relate in many subtle, but opposing ways. For instance, our approach to the Measure of Balance is to weed out the weak, whereas Positivity is to support the young. Negativity would test their resolve through temptation and adversity, whereas Positivity would choose to strengthen it through careful discipline and moral virtues. Each side would desire to enlist new members to extend their reach, and therefore to further their objectives, but we must also keep each other in check as our roles within the Measure of Balance. One side cannot grow too powerful to imbalance the other."

"That's a truly fascinating depiction," Kaliya muses. "So, in essence, you're each trying to pick away at the other's work, but to what ultimate end? It seems like a never-ending battle."

"It is, but the ultimate goal here is to ensure the continued nature of existence, the integrity of life, and the fabric of Reality. If the Seas of Creation were to fall too far to one side, the harmony of Balance would slide into oblivion, and carry with it everything else, including all of us. Are you familiar with the principles of electromagnetism, perhaps?"

"Yes, actually. My people are a very scientifically advanced society."

"All right, consider this simple principle. What would happen to a body if it held a uniformly consistent charge?"

"A uniformly consistent charge, as if to say all positive, or maybe all negative. Right, I understand. Charges with the same polarity tend to repel each other. So, if you have a body that is uniformly consistent, it will fly apart."

"Now imagine all Creation like this."

"Wow, yeah, I think I get it, but it's a concept that's a bit new to me. Even though we're a scientific society, we don't usually ask this question because we see the universe around us holding its own nicely enough."

"True, but matter and energy still need to balance themselves. The forces you might see at play with your science afford methods to allow these to cling to each other. This is also a part of the Measure of Balance, but it is not limited to these primal elements. Life is also an element in the Seas of Creation, and the essences of living creatures can influence the ebb and flow of the forces at play in other areas. The mind is a potent influence in such places as these, or anywhere you might find the dynamistic flows. It can possibly hold some potential in those areas that are in absence of the flows, but the flows act as a conduit. Therefore, thoughts and desires can alter the fabric of Reality, perhaps to remake some element of Creation into a new form, or to cause it to unravel altogether."

Kaliya listened to the statement, and once again a distant memory began to surface unexpectedly. She found herself mumbling to herself unconsciously.

"In this space I have will, and my will can alter this space."

"How curious!" Grace intones avidly. "Is this some sort of expression amongst your people?"

"It's something my mother once said when I was little, but I doubt even she fully realized the true depth of it, given what you're teaching us now. My father and his faction once studied metaphysics, although many of the other sciences back home never regarded it very highly. But we once posed a curious riddle, or at least that's how some of us think of it."

"Oh? And what sort of riddle was this?"

"It comes in two parts; we might say a theorem and an axiom. First is where perception enables recognition, existence demands definition, and from this, substance becomes our reality."

"That's a very curious one. It almost seems counterintuitive, coming from a mortal society."

"Right, and then we have the next part, which stumped most of us, even though we invented it," she giggles. "In a metaphysical reality, nothing unknown exists. It only exists after it is known."

"Powers behold, Child!" she grins brightly. "And do you have any way to answer this riddle?"

"I believe I solved it, at least within the context of what I had within my reach so far. It can be demonstrated by this magic you people are so famous for, but back home, our people don't have the flows. So to us, it doesn't exist, therefore the riddle is just that, a riddle. But on Tae'Eladar, I finally learned how to use it. Later, I began to realize something even bigger, and this is where I believe the true definition comes into play. But we're speaking of abilities that would transcend beyond where my people are so far. To Know of a thing, meaning to define it within your perceptions as a form of recognition for what you believe it to be, and then to apply this onto the reality of space around you, causing it to form substance."

"And here I suppose we come full circle with that statement from your mother. She must have been on the edge of a realization, as this is very near to my own explanation. And if you can learn the deeper implications, maybe you too can rework some small part of Creation."

"These flows..." Marelle begins, and casts a quick glance at Thaelyn. "This is the same energy we use when we study magic, as I understand it."

"Yes. For you mortals, you might know this as the energies that power your magic. But for those of us of a higher accord, we carry a much deeper intimacy with them. There may come a time when your kind will grow and develop a stronger influence with the natural elements around you, such that your magic becomes more like our affinity to reshape reality. You are just barely scratching the surface so far."

"I swear," she moans. "For all I could learn around here, I don't think I'll live long enough to use it."

"Such is the misfortune with mortals," Grace smiles. "But if you strive fervently enough, you may discover you can evolve, and these shortcomings will then fall behind you."

Thaelyn watched and smiled at their interaction together, examining each of his students and the expressions on their faces as they absorbed these extraordinary teachings.

"You are all very fortunate to hold such a conference as this. Most mortals do not have such an opportunity."

"Yeah," Marelle accedes. "But now, what do we do with it? Are we actually allowed to share this with anyone?"

"I will permit you as you desire. We will consider this as a free excursion to seek wisdom. It is a high privilege to speak with such as what you will find in this place. Most mortals, that is those from the Prime worlds, do not generally travel here. Although, what we have on Tae'Eladar tends to be more knowledgeable than some, and largely due to my teachings. And since you will ultimately benefit from that, you should take these lessons no differently."

"Spoken like a true Positive," Grace smiles cutely.

"Indeed! But I must also admit…neutral grounds or otherwise, one can still find occasional pleasure to hold such a discussion, if only to share our beliefs for the interest of understanding."

"Yes, of this I think I would agree. The sensation alone is worthy."

"But now, as for our visit, I am showing these three around the Ward briefly before I hope to make a meeting with Aelwyn."

"Ah, I see. And would they like to explore our little venture here, perhaps indulge in some interactions with the girls?"

Relissa and Marelle exchanged brief glances, wondering if they should answer that question.

"I think maybe a quick pass around should do," Thaelyn responds.

"Very well, you know where everything is. If you need anything, I am here."

"My Lord," Relissa mutters. "Are you sure we need to take a look around? Just stepping in the door was fine enough for me."

"Come now, Relissa. Just think of the stories you can bring home after we are done here."

"Aye, and they'll lock me away for a fair part of it!"

They peruse the halls and observe the girls interacting with some of the other customers. Some were engaged in debate, portions of it being quite vigorous, while others were playing some manner of game involving strategy and logic. One was sharing stories of love, romance, intrigue, and misery. As they worked their way around the circular hall, they arrived at the last door before returning to the lobby again. Thaelyn paused in front to read the nameplate.

"Ah, how nice, she is still here. I would have thought she might be retired by now."

"Who is it?" Marelle asks.

"She is an old relation who once taught me some valuable lessons. Her name is Kimasxi."

"What kinds of lessons, or is this something I should keep quiet on?" she smirks.

"Let us go inside and see," he winks.

"Oh dear…"

As Thaelyn knocks on the door, the group is greeted with a harsh voice bellowing out a volley of abuse.

"What smelly sewer rat is it that's trying to crawl under my tail at this time of day?! Isn't it enough that I have to listen to the ravings of so many tin-headed berks stumbling through the streets out of that hole gushing up the stenches of the Nine Hells day and night?!"

"And she was your teacher?" Marelle shudders.

"Oh, you should have seen her in her youth!" he retorts playfully.

Thaelyn opens the door, and they step inside. They were presented with a creature that resembled something half human and half goat, and all mean.

"Thaelyn of Celestia," she scorns. "And just when I thought I scraped the last of that goody stink off my hooves. Now you come and smear more of it under my furry bum. Worse than that, you bring a pack of pug-nosed dog-eared scrap-pickers to further tangle my tail and spoil my mood."

The three women in the group are dumbfounded by the laundry list of slurs. They looked at each other, and then to Thaelyn, who simply gazed calmly at Kimasxi.

"And it is a long overdue pleasure to see you, as well, Kimasxi. How have you been faring?"

"I was faring just fine until that smug face of yours rolled through my door. Now I have to redecorate to take the shine off of things. How have you been doing?"

"Life keeps me quite busy back home."

"You call that dung-filled scum-covered slime-pot full of clueless berks a home? You really have lost the last half of your dimwitted thin-skulled head. So, who are these three?"

"These are some of my students, and I had hoped you might give them a lesson. Although, I think by now, they have already had a good one."

"Really! A band of empty-headed snot-nosed prissy-foots with dreams of becoming smug-gutted stuffy-chested rock-brains. Do any of you want to try me out?"

Marelle looks up at Kaliya. Kaliya gazes back in hesitation, and then over at Relissa. Marelle follows this, causing Relissa to feel their stares on the back of her neck.

"'Ere now!" she protests. "What are you both looking at me for?!"

"Looks like you've been chosen, sweet cheeks," Kimasxi observes. "Hit me!"

Relissa felt herself placed on the spot here. She tries to recall every insult she ever heard, and a few she invented, but somehow feels insufficient in the face of this master of curses. Still, she needs to make the attempt. She pulls herself straight and takes a step forward.

"Nice clothes," she begins. "Did you rip them off some dolt in the sewers yourself? Or did you recruit your army of lice to do it for you?"

"You should wash your face sometime," Kimasxi returns. "I can almost see the slag from your smoke-hole on it."

"At least I didn't climb out of some steam pit smelling like a musty skank."

"No, you just wallowed in a scum pool filled with primordial smut."

"But it's a sweeter smell than the foul vapors spewing out of your pudgy mug."

"Aye, but it's a mug that'll untie your mother's innards after she made her first blink at your slimy snout."

"At least my mother walked on two feet, not some pansy's harnessed shag."

"Maybe, but it's one that squeezed out a tastier lump than you'll ever meet. Maybe you'd like to have a lick?" Kimasxi blasts as she turns her hind-side at Relissa.

"I'd sooner stick my lips under this oversized door-knocker's tail than press my tongue against your rancid backside. I doubt you could spread that smelly bum of yours wide enough to toot through, much less make any music."

As Kaliya listens, she modestly tucks her tail downward at the blatant mention of her delicate parts.

Kimasxi withdraws from Relissa's last attack. She pauses a moment to consider the session.

"Not bad…you show promise," she offers. "Thaelyn, you may have something here. Keep working on it."

"Most excellent."

"Are you always like this?" Marelle asks timidly.

"This is my specialty," Kimasxi responds. "The sensation of abuse. It's what I once studied in the Sensorium over there. And being who and what I am, it fits nicely with my temperament."

"I see. Well, for what it's worth, you've got talent."

"Believe it or not, it comes from a lot of years of practice, not simply a bad attitude," she smirks cutely.

"And now I think we should take our leave," Thaelyn muses. "There is still much for us to do. Good day to you, Kimasxi."

"Ah, stuff it in your craw, you midget-mouthed lout."

They leave the room and work their way back through the lobby and into the plaza, saying goodbye to Grace along the way.

"Charming, as well as innovative," Marelle mumbles. "But now, I think I need a bath."

"Just one?" Kaliya adds. "We have a few expressions in our native language, but nothing on the scale of what she put out."

They wandered into another building that resembled a museum. Inside, they examined several artworks that seemed to come alive when viewed, along with a sculpture of spiraling shards of ice that swirled and danced in midair above the pedestal. And in the rear of the museum, they came upon a stone statue of a man.

"Who's this?" Relissa asks. "Someone famous?"

"Better to say someone infamous," Thaelyn offers. "He was once a citizen of the city well-renowned for his skill in applying curses."

"Curses?" Marelle inquires. "Anything like what we just went through?"

"Oh no, this was much more. Recall what was said about the mind having some rather profound abilities in this place. This can also apply to speech if the words are arranged appropriately. A proper curse can inflict harm, debilitate, scald, scorch, and do much more to a person. This man was what you might call an artist, but not in a good way."

"What did he do?"

"He perfected the craft to such a degree that he could quite literally kill with words. His curses became legendary for the damage they could invoke. But then he apparently made the most fantastic of all. He cursed himself to stone."

"Wait a minute," Relissa objects. "Are you saying this bugger actually turned himself to stone? Is this statue him, then?"

"In the flesh, so to speak… But it does not stop there. He is not actually dead in this state. His curse is such that he could be called out briefly, but his temper is so vile that he would spit a curse at the first person he sees for doing so."

"How is he called out?"

"You must speak his name, and the curse will release him for just a moment."

"Aye then," Relissa smirks. "So, what's his name, my Lord?"

"It is written right there on the pedestal. Perhaps you would like to read it for us?" he grins.

"Nah, I'll pass on that today. Let the old guy sleep a bit more."

They exit the museum and continue further into the plaza.

"Let us take this opportunity to visit Vrischika's shop before we go look for Aelwyn."

"Oh yeah," Kaliya recalls. "And then you can buy Aerlie that… thing she was asking for. Personally, I'm not so sure I want to ask what it is."

They step up to a smallish building in the lower end of the plaza. Thaelyn moves off to the side and opens the door for the ladies, allowing them to pass before he enters.

As the women enter the little shop, they are greeted by a female with deep blue skin and yellow eyes. She also seemed to have a small set of bat-like wings on her back.

"Great, another one…" Marelle whispers.

"Ah, customers, come in," the woman calls. "Vrischika can always help her guests. Mayhap I could interest you in a bottle of stygian bladder oil? Or would you instead favor a satchel of balor horn dust?"

Thaelyn was holding back with a mischievous smirk on his face, which wouldn't be the first time for this location. He continued to wait just to the side of the door while the initial introduction was taking place. As he listened to her preliminary offer come to a close, he stepped inside and into view.

"Ah, another cust… NYAAHHH!! YOU!" she hisses violently at him as he enters the shop.

Relissa and her friends jump at the sudden display, instinctively hopping out of the way as the two make eye contact.

"Ah, Vrischika," he declares jovially. "So nice to see you again. How is business for you…any special sales today?"

"You! Again! Thaelyn!" she hisses again. "Why do you keep coming here? Do you take so much delight in my torment?"

"But Vrischika, it has been so long, and we have such a wonderful relationship, ever since that extraordinary deal you once made. Do you recall that?"

She shrieks and dashes around behind the counter, then over to a doorway leading into a back room, and starts bashing her head against the frame.

Marelle and Relissa exchanged glares, and passed briskly up to Kaliya, who could only return the glance as she tried to croak out a few words.

"Did someone mention something about ripping throats out earlier?"

"I recall words like 'entertaining' back home," Marelle winces. "Is this what it means?"

When the woman finished denting the framework, she turned back to speak again.

"What is it you want this time? Are you here to ruin me again?"

"Ruin?" Thaelyn muses distantly. "But of course not, my dear keeper of exotic trades," he responds warmly. "Certainly, I have no immediate desire for such things as a demon's tongue on this day.

Unless, that is, you should coincidentally be carrying a small vial of deva's tears to go along with it…perhaps?"

She screams again and returns to bashing the door frame, further splintering the wood.

Relissa and the others watched the curious display, completely at a loss as to how this relates to Thaelyn and Aerlie's brief mention back in the guildhall courtyard. She turns to her friends to comment softly.

"This must be what happens when you put these peeps in the same room together up here in neutral ground."

"Yeah," Marelle nods. "They can't go at each other's throats, so this is the next best thing."

"Good Vrischika," Thaelyn continues. "I am simply here for a small purchase…for Aerlie. You remember her, of course, do you not? Like an echo of a past memory."

Another scream rattles the jars on the shelves, and the banging on the wall vibrates the building. She continues smashing her head against the framework while at the same time calling out a series of words in odd tongues.

"Ah, wonderful, I see you do recall. She will be so pleased. Naturally, you remember how she adores those little chocolate quasits, right?"

Vrischika finally pulls herself away and staggers over to the counter. She grunts in acknowledgement.

"Excellent. And where might they be hiding, hmm?" he appears to glance around the shop aimlessly.

She glares at him, then looks down at the counter directly in front of her, jabbing a finger at a prominent display.

"Ah, of course, right where they always are. How silly of me. I will take one, please," he offers as he pulls out a coin purse.

The flustered shopkeeper pulls out the item from the shelf and places it in a bag. She takes his payment and shoves the bag across the counter at him, sneering at him as he picks it up.

"Thank you most kindly, Vrischika. By the way, how is your business faring with Zharaden these days?"

"Doing much better than with you, I'm happy to say!" she retorts brashly, then relaxes her posture. "He's making a regular trade for a lot of reagents, and sometimes even a few rare goods. I don't know what he's doing down there, but it must be a vigorous study."

"From our side of it, he has been experimenting with a lot of new ideas in his Art. It has actually improved our other research considerably."

"I suppose that's a good thing. Not from my side of the Measure of Balance, but knowledge is still knowledge."

"It most certainly is."

"Who are these three?" she points at Relissa and the others.

"These are some of my recent students. I am showing them the sights as I make a special visit up here."

"Uh huh…the sights. And am I one of those?"

"I think we would be remiss if we did not include a complete coverage of the locals."

"Naturally."

"But anyway, thank you again, and I will look forward to our next meeting."

"Yes, I am sure you will be," she huffs.

Thaelyn turns to leave the store. Relissa, Marelle, and Kaliya all jump in front and fight to grab the door, nearly stumbling out together as he follows up the rear.

They move back into the plaza, each of them struggling to find their voice again. Kaliya is the first to bring herself to speak.

"My Lord!" she asks with a tremor. "In all the nether-space, what was that about?"

"I thought I was about to get my soul ripped out of my chest," Marelle exclaims.

"Ay, speak for yourself," Relissa declares. "I was out in front there."

"Vrischika and I go back a long way," Thaelyn responds.

"And you're still alive?" Kaliya yelps. "Right, Measure of Balance my crinkled tail. You looked like you enjoyed that little display."

"Yes, Relissa was right in her statement of putting two people in the same room together. But here in Sigil, we can work it out without any bloodshed. Although the furniture and local architecture may not fare as well," he chuckles.

"What was that mention of someone named Zharaden?" Marelle asks.

"And also that history of yours," Kaliya adds. "I heard you speak of Aerlie in that."

"All right," Thaelyn replies. "Firstly, let us reference Zharaden. He is a necromancer in my otherwise unlikely service. As a Celestial, I would not normally permit the study of necromancy, and indeed it is outlawed in our world. However, once upon a time, I came across this fellow during a campaign to rid our world of a powerful group of mages, to which he was taking up studies in his craft. But unlike the rest, he was involved purely for the academic value, as compared to the others who were ruthless oppressors. But he knew my purpose was to essentially take over the world, and his form of craft would not be permitted. Do you recall Grace mentioning the name Shadowfell? This is technically the first new world we ventured to outside of Tae'Eladar, and thanks to him demonstrating why the art of necromancy is indeed important to investigate, even though it might be distasteful for someone like me."

"Uh huh..." Marelle winces. "I'm now asking myself how he 'demonstrated it' to you."

"Yes, as you might suspect, he launched a series of his 'demonstrations' on our native soil, beginning with small bands of what we call simple undead, meaning to say zombies and animated skeletons. Previously, the only time we might encounter such as these was in ancient times, and in similarly ancient graveyards and catacombs, where restless spirits might become entangled with untamed arcanic energies to invoke an occasional uprising. It became something of a habit for local guardsmen to venture into those places to clean them out every so often."

"Interesting...if also a bit creepy."

"But this was the extent of it, so our defensive measures only needed to be enough to counter this fairly minor annoyance."

"Ah! I think I see a direction here. A fairly minor annoyance.

So you were able to put them down with little more than town guards and such. But necromancy, if it works anything like the other magical studies, probably goes much higher, am I right?"

"Indeed, especially if you fancy anything particularly elaborate, as he did. He started small, just to make a little noise, but escalated it with larger bands, bordering on the scale of armies, and now with much more advanced forms involved, including golems of various kinds, spectral apparitions, and a few other things. Our countermeasures fell short very quickly in all this, and the battles to regain control of our lands were very difficult to win. But win, we did, as we thought someone had started a war with us."

"Where was he at the time? This other world? But then, how did he launch them at you?"

"He had escaped from us during that one battle with those mages using a portal, and apparently to this world we now call Shadowfell, where he set himself up in a rather nice fortress keep, along with a neighboring hamlet of his personal undead servants. From there, he continued to develop his skills, then used portals to send them forward. We only learned of this after a massive assault on B.T., then to see his portals out on the field just as they closed up on us. But just after they closed, he remotely opened a new one, a source-end portal, which would be a very tricky application, in this case."

"By remote?" Kaliya wonders. "How would he do that? I thought you needed to be physically present to do that."

"Yes, typically, you do. His method was very advanced, and involved a Seer's Pool to focus his spell through. He was a devious individual, watching us as we fought his…demonstration. But it all held a purpose to prove a point. He was not actually hostile to us, simply trying to demonstrate a principle. And it worked. We followed his portal, which was clearly a calling card to find him, and found ourselves on that new world, which was a fascinating discovery."

"Where is it? Is it in the same universe? But then, if everything out there got blasted…"

"Yes, it is in our local fold, one of two additional Shells created by the Estelar to provide a little diversity. Recall what I once said about our old ice age, and Selûne and Shar's dispute. Well, this was a compromise solution, to create custom playpens, one for each. This one belongs to Shar."

"Oops! And knowing your history together…"

"Yes, this is true, but she has not mentioned anything unfavorable for our presence there, so long as we keep it modest. Allow me to continue. Zharaden left our arrival space vacant, granting us the luxury to set down a rather solid foothold. His army kept at distance until we marched on it, rather than them coming for us."

"Oh, how nice of him."

"Clearly, this was an indication that he was not outwardly hostile, and it did stand out. We realized fairly quickly that these creations were very advanced, and our methods showed their age by now. But when we arrived at his keep, which was also vacant of anything like guards, or even servants, we found him inside waiting for us with a rather pleasant greeting, a congratulations for our victory, as well as his sales pitch to offer his services to us, in the absence of me not doing it myself back home," he chuckles.

"Uh huh…a sales pitch…figures."

"He explained what he did and why he did it, then to offer everything he had to the greater benefit of our world knowledge base, furthermore that he would continue his work there on Shadowfell, rather than coming home, as he believed we would not feel comfortable with him in his, ahem, current condition…"

"Current condition?" Marelle frowns. "What do you mean?"

"He was once a human, but not anymore. It had been a good century and more by this time, and he had since converted himself into a lich, which is an undead form of magic user."

"Jiggers!" Relissa yips. "Aye! Keep him on that side, not ours, thank you very much."

"These were his feelings as well, and also that Shadowfell did not have anything else on it of great significance, therefore it would make a good research base. So, we made a deal to lay a tender claim to his space as a territorial holding, not to colonize, but to use for research and testing, and also a penal colony for those early days when we had the last few rogue nations making trouble, and we needed to offload the burden. We even established some training fields out there. And in fact, you might find one or another of your lessons taking a field trip for a bit of practice."

"Fascinating…" Kaliya accedes. "So I get to kill something that's already dead. Yeah, wait till I try to explain that one to Kailen."

"These are the trials of living in an environment with the flows, as it can sometimes happen. But hopefully not very often. Nevertheless, as he was now involved with some very advanced studies, his demands for reagents and such were similarly exotic. Here is where I had the idea of Vrischika, as she does have access to some very rare goods. So I connected the two together, which keeps her happy, keeps him in his studies, and further enhances our own countermeasure research, in case we ever do find ourselves in a war with someone who is serious about weaponizing the art of necromancy."

"That's simply amazing. You know, this reminds me of some other forms of unconventional warfare, like chemical or biological, maybe even nuclear. And here you are adding one more dimension to it, necromancy."

"Yes, this is also true. But now, on to the next question relating to Vrischika and Aerlie. Relissa and Marelle, do you remember that story I once told you about Ecco? It was in my demi-plane."

"Aye, I do," Relissa admits. "That girl of yours from the brothel, I still can't get over that part," she snickers.

"Kaliya, you were not present, but the others can tell you the story. Briefly, however, Ecco was an old friend of mine in the early days, and she once had a bad association with a powerful mage here in the city who confided in her something quite burdensome. She found it too difficult to bear alone, so she shared it with another to aid her in her discomfort. The problem is, the mage found out, and magically removed her tongue, so she could no longer speak."

"Yikes," she yips. "That's a bit harsh, isn't it?"

"This is how life goes in the city at times. Responses such as these are most often doled out at the interpretation of the individual, whatever interpretation that might be relative to how the planes turn. I searched for ways to help her, but I was unable to come to a viable solution at first. Then a man came through here on his own quest, and needed to speak with her for some clue she held, but in her condition, she could not provide it."

"She couldn't just write it down for him?"

"On this occasion, no. Once again, we must reflect on the nature of the realms out here. To put something into writing carries a form of identity of the one who wrote it. This could then be used by someone with ill intentions towards that person to cast a spell or place a curse of some kind, which would then reflect back on the originator of the note."

"Ouch! This place is simply nasty for that effect."

"Indeed, and given she had already suffered from one indiscretion, she did not wish another one. Therefore, the need to speak it openly, as the words would simply pass without any serious aftereffect. But at this moment, she was mute, and as it turns out, this fellow discovered a curious item in this shop over here…a demon's tongue."

"Ew! I'm not so sure I would like that as a solution. How does it help?"

"The item in question holds the power to restore speech to one who has lost it in this fashion. The tongue cannot be said to be completely dead, and if placed into the mouth of one without speech, it will attach itself and reestablish the quality. Unfortunately, demons, being such as they are, do not hold much of a reputation for polite speech."

"Oh, great. I think I can see where this is going now."

"Yes, it becomes clear once you know the background. I knew this from my teachings within my Father's court, and I had taken notice of this same item in the shop as I was browsing it earlier. Naturally, I reflected on Ecco and her condition, but this by itself was not a solution I could accept. This man, however, was not as enlightened, and Vrischika's sales pitch only carried him so far as to know this would provide speech."

"Uh huh, and she's another tanar'ri, right? She looked like one, I think. But then, I'm new here, so…"

"Yes, she is. Tanar'ri can come in many shapes and colors, but you are right, she is another variation of succubae like Grace up there in the brothel. But this one is much more enterprising. I presumed she knew about Ecco's condition, as it was no great secret in the Ward, and would wish to benefit from this, perhaps even to take some amount of pleasure out of her suffering at the same time."

"But this man didn't know about this, so he went ahead and bought the thing, I guess. What about you? Did you know about it so you could try and stop him?"

"I was present, and I watched and waited to see if he would actually buy it, and he did. But then I had another curious thought come to me, that Vrischika might find it more profitable to offer a solution to this dilemma, but only after we had an emergency."

"Oh grand!" Marelle blurts. "Yes, now you're talking my language. I've seen people like this back home a few times. They sell you only part of something, and get you all excited for a big result. But then… oops, I'm really sorry, but we forgot this critical piece. However, I can sell this to you for the special today-only price of three times what I might have offered it for before we got started."

They all shared a round of laughter at the idea.

"Precisely, Marelle…" he smiles. "And I am sure this is what she had in mind, so I played her game against her. I asked the man and his group to wait while I investigated. Then, I returned back inside and posed as a collector of oddities. And this bottle was indeed odd in its appearance, at least as compared to those around it. She had it tucked away on the opposite side of the shop, and attempting to hide it from casual view."

"What was it?"

"To begin with, there was no labeling or other identification. When I asked about it, Vrischika gave me this fascinating story of how a dying man traded it for a simple bottle of water, but the story he gave of its contents was…questionable. It was claimed to hold the tears of a deva, but devas are not well-known to shed tears very often, if at all."

"That's weird…and strange…and I have no idea what you're talking about," she giggles.

"Of course, this is where a Celestial education comes into play. Devas are another form of servant being often used by the Estelar. They are the male counterpart to the female seraphim."

"Oh, so we use different names for them?"

"We do, and as creatures of the Upper Realms, who are also said to be sturdy agents of Positivity, they are indeed not known to shed tears commonly. In fact, it is extremely rare to see such. But if one could ever capture such a thing as their tears, it is said they hold the power to soothe evil flesh."

"Uh oh… So, she had this tongue to offer the promise of speech, and these tears to correct for the impoliteness issue, but conveniently she didn't mention this right away."

"Correct, and I used her own story as a tool to bargain this item for a reduced cost."

"Oh no, you played your inquisitor bit on her, twisting her words around. No wonder she screeches whenever you come to visit."

"Atta-boy, my Lord," Relissa applauds. "But I also noticed the two of you calmed down a wee bit for that casual talk. So, here we are again, neutral territory, where you can actually behave yourselves, even if you do play these games to torment each other."

Thaelyn smiled as they slowly continued through the plaza.

"Anyway, he applied the tongue," he recalls. "And of course it performed as advertised on both accounts, as she was able to speak, but only blasphemies and curses. Then I applied a drop of these deva tears, and this neutralized the effect, granting her better control."

"So, let me see if I can interpret this with my new education," Kaliya muses. "Ecco was likely on the Positive side if she was a close friend of yours. Vrischika is obviously Negative…"

"I'll bet that'll make her an enemy to Grace up there, too," Marelle supposes.

"Yeah…wow. But anyway, she saw a weakness and was trying to corrupt it to her favor. However, you played your role to support and strengthen Ecco's resolve, and essentially repairing this weakness, thereby maintaining some form of balance between the two sides."

"Very good…" Thaelyn nods.

"But wait," Marelle interjects. "If we say she was hoping to corrupt the situation to her favor, how do we explain these tears… as a mistake to make some extra money, or could this be another part of the test, to see if this resolve was strong enough to find the answer before Ecco fell completely."

"That is a very cleverly put question, Marelle," he admits. "The Measure of Balance is a complex stratagem. It motivates us to seek our greatest strength, as well as those around us, to ensure we maintain the integrity of our own. Vrischika likely did hold an interest in profit, but even Negativity can occasionally drive a person to overcome their weakness, if only by dangling the solution in front of them, but in such a way that you actually need to look for it before you can see it."

"So…" Kaliya considers. "The lesson here is, never take anything for granted."

"Essentially yes, and by following this rule, you maintain your awareness of the viability of your surrounding space."

"Jiggers," Relissa winces and shakes her head. "These are lessons that go a good bit farther than your average schooling."

"Well, this sounds like a good story," Kaliya admits. "But what happened after?"

"The man went on his way," Thaelyn reflects, "while Ecco and I shared many long years together. Relissa and Marelle can tell you the rest, though there is not really that much more to tell."

"Actually, they did tell me something about this once. She did something later that played a trick of some kind, right?"

"She did, but now, if you desire to know more beyond that, I will bid you to follow Relissa and her quest to find the answer."

"Yeah, she already told me about that. But with everything else going on for me, I think I'll just have to wait for it to come out in print after she gets it. I have enough of my own mysteries to solve."

They had been making a casual stroll in the direction of the guild. When they arrived at the door, Thaelyn bid the doorman to allow them to enter. He opened the door, and they passed inside.

They entered a large hall. There were many people in the room, mostly in groups. Thaelyn studied the faces of those in view, but did not see Aelwyn amongst them. There were doorways leading off to the side, but rather than go in search for her in the hallways and offices, he instead brought a hand to his temple and expanded his awareness to search for her mind. He sensed a presence in another part of the guild and sent a telepathic suggestion to it. The others watched and realized this was just another example of his Celestial manners at work, so they waited.

Not long after, a graceful figure emerged from a door on the side of the room. She was dressed in a long robe, resembling a priestly design, dark blue with delicate golden embroidery around the collar and cuffs. There was a golden emblem centered below the neckline depicting a man's face appearing in a euphoric meditative trance. Just below and in front of the face was an open hand turned to the side, facing an ear.

The woman was youthful in appearance. A hood covered her head, but underneath, one could see locks of bright cinnabar red hair. She also had golden eyes, the same as Thaelyn. She walked placidly across the floor of the hall as she approached the group, and began speaking with a strangely disconnected mode of speech as she arrived in front of them.

" 'What is this?' she asks herself. 'Is this her long lost spirit-brother who ventured to the Primes? Has he returned to pay a visit to his dear sister?' "

"Oh wonderful," Relissa groans. "Now we bloody well have to read a walking book to understand what she's saying."

"Aelwyn," Thaelyn begins. "My dear spirit-sister, how have you been? Aerlie and I have thought about you often during this time."

"She is pleased for the mention, and she recalls for him her long moments spent in study, and of several new sensations delivered into the libraries for her to experience. But she pauses politely to take notice that he has brought guests, and inquires as to their names."

"Aelwyn," Thaelyn intones deeply. "I thought you had overcome this handicap of yours centuries ago. But nevertheless, if this is how you wish to play it, these are a few of my recent students, Relissa, Marelle, and Kaliya."

"Yes, Thaelyn," she sighs. "I did overcome that difficulty, at least within reason. But from time to time I still find it appealing, as we have many who pass through the Ward, and even the guild on occasion, that I wish not to apply myself upon, even if by accident."

"But Aelwyn, I believe I have mentioned on at least one or two occasions, perhaps now on the order of dozens, or a few or several score, that if you do not work to overcome this fear of yours, you may never find enough confidence to function within such a society as this, or any other for that matter, without resorting to this shell you place around yourself."

"It is not a shell…" she retorts, but then retracts herself and sighs again. "Perhaps it is. And it is an old habit now."

"I recall those early days. It was quite difficult for you."

"I was young then, the same as Nemelle, for that matter. And so were you. But aside from that, are you here as a pleasant excursion from your other duties?"

"In a small way, yes, but my primary reason for visiting is one of much more serious intent. And then I have a secondary need, also quite serious, for which I must speak to you."

"Serious and more serious, but within this, you desire my involvement? This is curious. And yet, I sense a great burden within you. What is it that weighs on your mind so greatly, spirit-brother? I could feel your tension when you first arrived in the Ward."

"Are you telepathic also?" Marelle asks.

"Look at those eyes, Marelle," Relissa suggests. "What does that tell you?" she angles up to look into Thaelyn's face.

"Well, yes, I can see that part, and I recall the various occasions back home. But I suppose what I'm asking is why she doesn't quite fit the same picture as his example. Sorry," she redirects at Aelwyn. "This is probably my city guard training talking now. They train us back home to watch people for certain behaviors, and yours is different from his, especially for a Celestial."

"You are very observant," Aelwyn admits. "A city guardsman… What manner of service do you perform?"

"Well, better to say I did perform, as I'm now in training in his academy for a new service. But mine was the Civil Watch office, mostly to maintain the peace on our streets."

"Is that before or after picking up all the drunks?" Relissa teases.

Marelle nudges her friend on the arm as she redirects to Aelwyn for her response.

"Ah," she croons. "So it could be said you were a form of law enforcement? This would certainly make sense. Indeed, it is true that I possess the gift of telepathy, although I do not indulge in it quite as often as Thaelyn. Rather, I tend to specialize in my empathic competence."

"Empathic…" Marelle muddles briefly. "Wait, I've been learning a lot of new tricks lately, both in his academy as well as simply watching him playing his games on us. This is the ability to feel one's emotions."

"Correct, to sense at a distance, as well as to apply at a distance."

"To apply…meaning to say you can actually cause someone to feel something?"

"Yes, and as Thaelyn is so fond of criticizing, I tend to fall into a defensive shell very often due to my intense passions that can sometimes escape from me. It is an old fear that I have never been able to fully overcome."

"That sounds like a hard life for you. But if it means anything, don't worry about us. Just think of us as friends you can share a good laugh with, if it helps you relax any."

"Very well, and I thank you deeply," she smiles.

As Aelwyn displays her warm reaction, the group can feel a subtle sensation of gratitude washing over them. It caused each of them to take immediate notice that it was not native to their own minds, but rather an external influence.

"Aye," Relissa notes. "She's got her ways, maybe a wee bit different from his, but no less for it."

"And just one more example of how things work up here," Marelle admits. "And so, you could feel him when he first arrived in this area?"

"I did!" Aelwyn replies energetically. "We are longtime friends and companions, and our minds are very familiar with each other. And his feelings are particularly intense at the moment. I have not felt him to possess such trepidation for a long while."

"Just wait until he explains it to you," Marelle chuckles cautiously.

"If it's anything like his reaction on that first day…" Kaliya grins.

"Aye!" Relissa agrees. "And buggers to that if she lets loose on us even half as much."

Aelwyn listened to their remarks, and could feel their curious manners, taking note of their obvious camaraderie, but also noticing a demeanor which seemed unusual for her expectations, and this only compounded the mystery for their visit.

"I sense the three of you are rather close friends, and apparently you each share a special bond with Thaelyn. How interesting it is that mortal-children can experience such a sensation with one who is a Celestial."

"You don't have this here?" Kaliya wonders.

"I…well…" she pauses as she glances around the room. "I… suppose I must apologize. This once again reflects upon my introverted manner. Thaelyn is right; I tend to shy away from such interactions. We have many mortal residents amongst us here, but my nature tends to lift me into a different category for my skills, and I hold a deep aversion towards applying them, largely because I feel it is unfair that I hold this power, but no one else does, nor do they hold the capacity to effectively resist it."

"Unfair? Wait a moment, where are we again?" she balks. "We have that girl, Kimasxi. She seems like a fairly extreme personality. Do you know her? I'll bet you probably do."

"Yes, we are well-acquainted."

"And she is anything but normal."

"But this is also her profession."

"Profession or not, she's got a mouth on her that doesn't stop. Then we have Grace, a creature that could easily outrank any of us simple mortals, and I didn't see anyone ducking under a table when she was walking around. Then, this lady down there at that shop," she turns and thumbs over her shoulder. "Vrischika, she is an extreme example, at least where he is concerned," she glances at Thaelyn briskly. "But I guess people still come and go without being eaten alive by it. We have a guy in this museum who turned himself to stone, but no one thinks THAT is weird?" she chuckles. "Speak his name and BAM, there you go. And this is apparently normal for you people. And you worry about a little emotional outburst? Cu'Nar help us, if you could've seen a few of the things I did in my life."

"Well, yes, but…"

"Aelwyn, you're a Celestial. Do you think yourself so abnormal around here that you would stand out as an oddity? The stories I've heard tell me this place would be perfectly natural to find someone like you. You can't berate yourself for what you are. No one on Tae'Eladar runs and hides from Thaelyn whenever he goes outside. And he does go outside often, which means he doesn't hide from himself, either. And I know he has some very powerful skills…I've seen them in action. And yet, I would still choose to stand next to him rather than hide behind him, even though I realize I might find a horn or two missing if he should sneeze the wrong way," she giggles satirically.

Aelwyn gaped at Kaliya for her lengthy reprimand, realizing there was a clear wisdom to these words, but also feeling a compulsive rush of amusement flowing into her, in part from Relissa and the others sharing Kaliya's witty rebuke, as well as her own response. She tried holding it back, but it was already seeping out, causing the others to begin giggling uncontrollably.

"You may as well let it out, girl," Relissa notes through her snickering. "We'll all explode if you don't."

Aelwyn couldn't help it any longer, and allowed herself a moment of hearty laughter, followed by more from the rest as her emotions spread across the group.

"Powers behold!" she exalts. "I have never had anyone come up to me like that before. I thank you, Children. That was indeed a pleasurable experience, and one I do not often find in any social circles around here. Thaelyn, are these the recent products of your teachings? It is a rather curious blend."

"I can only take credit for so much," he admits. "These three are just beginning their studies, but they do carry their own special appeal. And I am quite sure this one example is a special case," he glances up at Kaliya.

"I recognize the human...and the elf...a Morier, is it?"

"Aye, in the flesh," Relissa smiles.

"I was unaware your people had reintegrated with the rest of his world."

"You sound a wee bit like Grace over there. I'm not originally from Tae'Eladar. My people are migrants to another world he stumbled into as part of a recent war. The Drow are still the Drow."

"Ah, that might explain it, but this simply begs one to ask how and why yours migrated elsewhere. Hmm...I wonder if Nemelle would find interest in speaking with you sometime."

"Grace mentioned her before. Who is she?"

"She is a good friend of mine, and another Celestial, but in her case an Eladrin, part Morier. In fact, I know of these terms only due to some lessons she shared with me once," she smiles gently. "Her mother was found being held prisoner in a pocket domain with a den of illithids. This was after a conjuring her house Matron Mother was performing, using her own daughter as a sacrifice."

"Jiggers! They do that down there?"

"They are a despicable society, twisted and deranged. Anyway, she tells us how the baatezu who claimed her sold her off as a slave to the illithids, but she was later discovered by a group of githzerai, who are natural enemies of the illithids. She was then rescued, and due to the nature of being a mortal, and in her case elven, they chose to deliver her to the Seldarine, where Corellon Larethian took a special interest in her rehabilitation. Later, he blessed upon her a child, and this became Nemelle."

"That's a pretty wacky story, but then, I guess this is how it goes up here."

"Yes, ours may follow in some ways like yours, but the players are surely different."

Aelwyn continues her examination of Thaelyn's guests, now coming to Kaliya.

"And just where did you find this one?" she asks. "I do not recall her from any of my previous studies."

"She is part of my reason for coming here," Thaelyn asserts. "I have need of your assistance, if you think you can pull yourself away from your duties here. It is very important, and I should procure this before anything else occurs."

Aelwyn flashed back to her empathic sensation of Thaelyn's emotional state, which seemed refreshed with those words. Her reflex reaction caused her to return to her strange dialect.

"She wonders, 'Why does he desire her so?' On this occasion, his words carry a deeper inflection than she has ever recalled of him in the past."

Relissa slaps a hand over her eyes and leans on Marelle's shoulder. Marelle responds by patting the poor girl's head.

"Well, we tried..." she relents feebly.

"No, wait," Aelwyn smiles softly. "You did succeed in enticing me out a little, so let us not despair. Like I said, there are times when I use this because it simply appeals to me. And after a lifetime of this, it becomes as second nature."

"A lifetime..." Marelle wonders. "This makes me wonder how long that actually is...you know, if you're a Celestial."

"Yes, I am just under a full century beyond him. We regard ourselves nearly as brother and sister, for this point. But Thaelyn, what is this you require of me?"

"Aelwyn, let us go outside and speak," he offers. "I do not wish to be overheard in this place. Perhaps we can sit in a local café if it is not too busy."

They turn to leave the building, passing through the doors and proceeding across the plaza to one of the local cafés. At this time of day, the cafés were mostly empty, though the concept of day and night in the city is artificially regulated since there is no actual rising and setting of a sun. So, they found a secluded table and sat down.

A waiter takes notice of their arrival and marches over from the refreshment bar to attend to his latest customers.

"Welcome, Cutter! Yeh look like a fine sort, with a fancy gaggle of friskies hanging about. What can I fetch fer yeh?"

"A round of drinks for each of us, if you please…"

"Right yeh are, Cutter…" he replies and chases off to the bar to fill the order.

"What's a cutter?" Kaliya asks.

"It is a colloquial term here, in polite form, whereas the word 'berk' is impolite."

"Oh, all right, I'll try to remember that."

"This city, like so many others, has its culture, and this culture is rather unique and varied, depending on where you travel."

The waiter returns momentarily with their drinks and receives his payment, then moves away to give them their privacy.

"Thaelyn," Aelwyn inquires. "Tell me, what is it that bothers you so?"

"There are two major concerns, at present. The first involves my need for your participation, while the other is a matter of security."

"Security…of your home, perhaps?"

"Tae'Eladar would be included, but it is not the center. All the surrounding realms are involved, on this occasion."

"Thaelyn, I am at a loss to perceive how any force could affect such an expanse as the full breadth of the realms around us. That is, well, other than the disruption once brought by Shar and her conspiracy."

"You mean the Spellplague?" Relissa mentions softly. "Aye, we heard of that. But this one's big, so you should buckle up those emotions a wee bit for it."

"Very well, so then which of these would you wish to embark upon first…as I sense your desire to reveal both to me."

"Let us first take this young lady here," Thaelyn motions at Kaliya. "We discovered her people on a new world during a campaign of war I was forced into on Tae'Eladar. The war had essentially spilled over from their space into ours, with an incursion made to seek out a Door to be found on Tae'Eladar."

"A Door? Thaelyn, are we speaking in such terms as we use here?"

"Yes, and this is a most unusual one that cannot be native to Tae'Eladar. We believe we were visited once by someone who built it behind our backs, and it brought us out to the plane of Concordant Opposition."

"Why there?"

"This incursion was to deliver an alien beacon probe into it to locate a destination endpoint for a jump index their ships could use later."

"Uh oh…and who would want this, and why?"

"Let us come to that in a moment, as this relates to that issue of security. These invaders used arcanic portals to arrive and exit, so we followed them back to where we discovered even greater perils. Among other things, that world held a population of humans, plus members of the Cala and Mori clans of elves, and all from an ancient migration from Tae'Eladar…and this too is a strange one."

"Strange…" she muses. "I suspect it could be, but for reference, how precisely?"

"This world is in a completely different fold, and they should have no way to find it on their own."

"Indeed! Surely, even I can see this much. So, how did they do it?"

"We suspect this same Door was used. Adalon suggested once it could hold two indexes, one being that other world, the second being the Outer Planes."

"That would require some special configuration."

"Yes, it is no small matter, to be sure. Further, this migration occurred perhaps as much as ten millennia ago, and at roughly the same time as that first orcish incursion. You do recall that from our previous meetings, right?"

"First one?"

"Yes, this new one was more of the same."

"I see. And yes, this was some of that world history you shared with me once. But are we speaking of a coincidence, or something else? You once mentioned those orcs should not hold the capacity to find their own way, and now we have others finding a way out due to a similar paradox, if only for this Door."

"Yes, but I suspect the same individual who built that Door is responsible on both accounts. The elves carry a history of someone… inspiring them…to follow him into new lands, with part of the reason being those orcs arriving."

"Oh, splendid! So, we have someone delivering your orcs, then taking away some of your native citizens, and building a hidden Door to the Outer Planes for later application."

"And here we are seeing the end result. These people are examples of those populations," he points at Relissa and Marelle. "And, as it turns out, they also recently joined my academy."

"Really, so you are bringing together people on a new world now?" she smiles gently.

"But of course!" he grins. "Is it not my purpose to do so these days?"

"I suppose that depends on who you talk to. I recall once a young man who said he did not wish to go to the Prime domains to take control, simply to offer a few pieces of his wisdom. The next thing I hear, you are crowned King of Tae'Eladar," she beams warmly.

At this time, she allowed her feelings to seep out, and everyone at the table could feel her ironic satire. They all shared a reflexive smile at the notion.

"Aye," Relissa offers. "That's a good one."

"And what about her people," Aelwyn directs at Kaliya.

"Kaliya and her people are refugees," Thaelyn states. "They originate on a world we believe to be in a barren fold."

"A barren fold!" she gasps. "And yet they hold the power to fold space?"

"In a technological form, yes. Their ships are capable of travelling across folds."

"Fascinating, then they must come from a rather highly adept society, especially if they originate in a barren fold, and are still able to develop this quality."

"Um," Kaliya interjects tenderly. "Although I can probably answer this one myself, just for the sake of discussion, how do you mean?"

"Certainly. If to use the dynamistic flows, one can perform this fairly easily. I hold certain powers that can alter Reality, though this is largely here in the Outer Planar realms, but if I were to apply myself firmly enough, I can also do this in the Prime domains. And yet, if you originate in a barren fold, this is to say you do not have access to these same flows. Therefore, your society would need to climb a rather difficult technological ladder to achieve the same, and it would be a much longer one, and likely fraught with some rather large hurdles, such as dimensional warping and power consumption. For instance, are you familiar with the principles of…well, some people call them black holes, but around here we use the word gravastar."

"Yes, and we also use that word. And yes, those are some rather extreme anomalies. And therefore, the demands to create something artificial using only the laws of physical science. I think I can probably vouch for that, to the best of my recollection from my childhood studies."

"But here we are with a rather curious dilemma," Thaelyn resumes. "Perhaps more than one, at this time. I cannot be sure of the cause, but during my initial testing stage of this young lady, she demonstrated a most unusual skill to which I would not expect to find in a mortal body."

"A most unusual skill not found in a mortal," Aelwyn muses. "What sort of power is it, and how did she demonstrate it to you?"

"Do you recall the testing procedure I use to define the purity of mortal spirits?"

"Yes, you have told me of this in the past."

"Good. She initially tested as a conditional fail, the quality I allow to permit a possible redemption. But during her redemption, she entered the chamber and passed into a type of sleep, though I wonder if it was more of a transitive form of torpor. While in this state, she projected her conscious awareness back to her original place of birth, which in her case is a different world entirely from where her physical body was found."

"Metaphysical manifestation?" she muses enthusiastically. "And further with directed spatial translocation."

"Spatial? Try trans-dimensional, as she was on Tae'Eladar at the time, and this other world was in another fold entirely."

"Powers help us, that would be a potent gift!"

"And, not only that, but she also visited with her mother, who was still found there, and further, she returned carrying an object from that place."

"In all Creation!" she yips excitedly. "Trans-ethereal manipulation of primal matter while operating as an incorporeal manifestation!"

"Jiggers," Relissa whines. "I didn't even know words could stretch that long."

Aelwyn gazes across the table at Kaliya, with her view spreading out to the other women. The three visitors could feel a wash of exhilaration strike them like a strong wave on a seashore.

"Mortal-child," Aelwyn infers. "Do you know what this represents in you?"

"I'm only vaguely aware of it," Kaliya admits. "My father tells me something about a study project my mother was trying to make on this phenomenon, but it's so rare amongst our people to discover it, we really don't know much about it."

"Then it has occurred before with your people?"

"Very few and far between, from what I hear."

"How old is your race?"

"This is where one of our paradoxes comes in," Thaelyn interjects. "Aerlie and I have already pondered this."

"Oh? Why?"

Thaelyn directs at Kaliya to answer the question. She perks up with a timid but mischievous grin on her face.

"According to my history education, our civilization is said to be about two million years old from the earliest recorded moments."

"Two million?" Aelwyn considers. "Hmm, this is a fair number, to be sure, but a little under my expectations."

"Now ask her the next question," Thaelyn grins impishly.

Aelwyn glared at him, and could feel a sensation of something misplaced. She then looked at Kaliya again, along with Relissa, and could see similar expressions in them.

"Oh, Powers helps me on this one. Very well, what am I supposed to ask here?"

"How old she is," Relissa quips.

"Uh huh… Then, Kaliya, would you be kind enough to give me your age?"

"Of course," she smiles cutely. "I'm four."

"Powers help us, and look at you at only four years?"

"No, not years…centuries!" she flutters her fingers.

Aelwyn recoiled sharply in her seat, and her shock rang out across the table like a bell strike, causing everyone else to reel back from the impact.

"Aye!" Relissa snaps. "And that was an even better one!" she giggles.

Aelwyn quickly realized her error with her emotions, but Relissa's comeback softened it such that she actually felt at ease on this occasion. She gazed at the dark elf in amazement at the comforting support.

"Thank you…again, Relissa. You know, never have I felt like I could open up as much as with you here. Very well then, so we are speaking in terms of centuries. This is surprising, but it would make better sense. I am simply surprised to see what I would normally interpret as a mortal-child using such a term."

"Yeah, we do this," Kaliya remarks. "Especially if you were to ask the next obvious question, which is what's pulling his horns out… at least figuratively."

"The next one…and I think I can guess at this point, because if your society is so accustomed to these terms, you must have some rather profound longevity, correct? So, what is it?"

"Our full lifespans measure about two hundred centuries."

Now Aelwyn's jaw dropped, and if the bell strike of shock wasn't enough the last time, this was more like a screaming fire alarm. Her words stuck in her throat and the other people at the table took a heavy hit of astonishment.

Relissa was expecting as much, as were the others by now, and as soon as she could regain some amount of her composure, she tried piping up again.

"Jiggers, girl, that's got to be the best one yet. Now I know why you try to hide it so much."

Aelwyn turned to her and covered her mouth, then her eyes as she tried to regain control of herself.

"Yes, I am sorry," she whispers. "That one was surely too much."

"Don't worry about it. I think it's expected. You should've seen him at one time."

Aelwyn peeks through her fingers at the girl, and then redirects her eyes at Thaelyn, who simply smiles and nods. She pulls her hands away and tries to find her focus again.

"Indeed, but yes, Thaelyn, I think I can see your paradox now, and with a civilized state of ONLY two million years. Do we know how and why they could carry such profoundly long lifespans with such a young, civilized age?"

"Not as yet, but Aerlie was conducting some recent medical studies on their physiology, and listening to her story of their evolution, and she told me there is something strange about it."

"Something strange, such as…" she raises her brow.

"Perhaps if you ask her, as she is the one with the conversational details."

"Very well, Kaliya?"

"Aerlie thinks I show too much of our early ancestor's physiology to be who and what I am today," she responds. "We call them Eracyodines, an early animal species with very similar physical features as in our modern bodies, except maybe a bit more primitive in their case. They were herbivorous and probably herd animals, but we record a strange evolutionary anomaly where we believe there was something environmental occurring to force our ancestors to make this terrific change from primitive animals to something that learned to use tools and develop into the beginnings of our first societies."

"All right, while in theory, this holds merit, but I think we need to consider the timing, as well as any transitional stages that would be necessary. Further, it comes to mind that any truly sudden and catastrophic environmental changes would more likely cause an extinction event, rather than a struggle to rapidly evolve. This is not necessarily my specialty, mind you, but I think I am educated in this enough to know how the process works. How long a period is this we are speaking of here?"

"I think my school lessons described it as only half a million years from those animals to our first signs of civilization."

"Wow, that is a very short time indeed...and then to compound it with such prodigious lifespans... I think I would have a very hard time accepting this, unless your civilization is the one responsible for the longevity, rather than any sort of evolution."

"What do you mean?"

"For instance, if you are augmented in some way to extend your lifespans artificially. Do you know if anyone in your history ever embarked on such a project?"

"I don't think I ever heard of anything, but then my education was interrupted by an attack on the world where I was born...part of this war we're fighting."

"I am sorry, but this is the only way I could accept such lifespans as yours in such a short period of time as your two million years in civilized form. What about other species in your world?"

"I don't actually know about that, as this isn't my specialty either. But my impression is this lifespan, or at least something close to it, is probably just us and for a long time."

"Then, this is an anomaly in itself...how and why you have it at all..."

She pauses to think a moment, trying to assemble these odd pieces into a conjoined image.

"And then, we have this metaphysical manifestation. This too would be an anomaly. Kaliya, I must agree with Thaelyn, this is not something to be expected in someone like you, with or without your abnormal longevity. Let me see... You mentioned something about others who displayed it, correct?"

"Right," Kaliya affirms. "Our history tells us of a few others, but only very rarely, who showed this same skill. This is back on our home world of Azgarén."

"Do your people hold any knowledge of what this is or how it came about?"

"At this point, we really don't know what it is, where it comes from, or why we have it. My father once told me he thought it could be a sign of a form of transcendence, where we might be evolving into something new, but I hesitate to say anything. I don't want to be the vanguard of a new species."

"Well, Child," she chuckles softly. "It is true we should approach this cautiously. To suggest you are evolving into anything at all, just for this one cause, is to leap forward a bit far without proper study. And if you do not know the cause, we must begin there. How long ago are we speaking of when these first examples were found?"

"This was before we had to leave home..." she considers. "I'm not as familiar with the history, but I think it was not too long before that. My father says he was once part of the early research trying to understand it, so we're talking about...oh, let me see...eight along the way, and then fourteen there..."

Kaliya begins a mental calculation, trying to add up the numbers for their long journey to Ruuki uy'Daan, then forward to the present time on Therinë.

"...And then another three and a half. Yeah, I think this would probably come to almost ten millennia ago, give or take a few centuries."

Aelwyn winced at the figure as it came out. Thaelyn simply frowned at it.

"And here we have that number again," he muses. "I think I am beginning to dislike the repeating occurrence of it."

"Aye!" Relissa nods. "I think I see your point. Something got started over there."

"Why are we speaking in such terms for this occasion?" Aelwyn wonders. "Other than for the simple mention of a number?"

"This again regards that issue of security," Thaelyn offers. "Someone arrived on that world, and this is where things start happening to bring about a series of events that ultimately leads us to where we are now with all of them."

"Are we speaking of that same someone who built that odd Door?"

"The same, and he belongs to an ancient society we thought to be long dead. But again, later for that, let us continue here first."

"All right, do we hold any details of these others with this ability?"

"All I have is from my father," Kaliya submits. "He's getting really old now, at one eighty-two. But he told me it was thought to be a really rare thing. They would find some young child doing this, so they would go in and try to study it, but something apparently interrupted the study. He didn't actually specify what it was, and now I'm asking myself why, as this is unusual for him."

"Unusual?"

"Yeah, because he likes telling stories, and this is one he seems to be holding back on."

"Jiggers, girl..." Relissa moans. "That's sets off a few wiggles in me."

"Um, I'm tempted to agree, but I hesitate to say anything."

"But you say children, not adults?" Aelwyn asks.

"Yeah, after a while, he was developing a few ideas, and started calling them Prodigy Children for this gift, and it was apparently thought only to occur in children, for some reason."

"Curious. What ages are we speaking of?"

"I don't know about any of them, but I was about half a century for mine."

"Ugh..." she grimaces. "Half a century, and you are still rated as a child. At what stage are we speaking, to give me a reference?"

"From my understanding," Thaelyn offers, "based on Aerlie's studies and things I have learned along the way, this would represent early childhood and before puberty. If measured by human standards, we might be speaking of single digits here, so simply take off the zero."

"So, from fifty to five... Great Powers!" Aelwyn shakes her head. "How long until they reach full maturity?"

"Two centuries," Kaliya smiles pertly.

"And again, curious," Aelwyn raises her brow. "And I see you are taking some pleasure out of this. Very well, this is an interesting sensation. So, you mature at roughly one tenth that of a human example, and with lifespans more than two hundred times the overall length. This is simply bizarre. From the biological side, I might find this rather fascinating to study."

"Oh no, not another one," Kaliya shakes her head. "Between you and Aerlie, I'm sure to end up on a dissection table one day."

"Well," she grins shyly. "If we should conduct this up here, we could probably reassemble you afterwards."

"My goodness, Aelwyn," Thaelyn muses sarcastically. "Was that an actual attempt at humor? Astonishing!"

She turns to face him, casting a deep scowl and projecting a teasing sensation of displeasure at him. Thaelyn winces and reflexively recoils from the impact, offering up a subtle laugh at her playful assault.

"Is this what we might call Celestial satire?" Marelle wonders.

"Aye, that's a new one," Relissa agrees. "But she definitely needs to get out more…too many stuffy classrooms where she works."

Aelwyn felt yet another moment of refreshing strength flow into her for the supportive comments. She smiled and shared her comforting warmth with the group.

"You are right, Relissa, it is very liberating to feel so at ease amongst anyone at all. Living in this place can be difficult, for this point. Kaliya, I am tempted to test these theories with commonplace parameters of evolution, but your case would defy most of them."

"All right," she suggests. "Let's hear your opinion on this, just for comparison. We already have all these crazy coincidences back home that seem much too convenient. We might as well finish off what's left of my horns so I can finally grow a new set."

"Finish off your horns...?" she wonders distantly.

"It is one of their many quaint expressions," Thaelyn smiles. "Their language seems to carry a number of them."

"Indeed! All right, first, what evidence do you have of your evolution to give you these numbers?"

"I doubt we have anything with us," Kaliya admits. "Not after being chased so far from home. It's mostly academic study for us, at this point. But I would imagine it was all conducted as archeological studies of fossil remains and such, the same as any study of ancient life would be."

"I see, but I would like to review some of those reports, simply to see how these numbers were calculated. Nevertheless, a civilized form at two million years, and if we say your lifespans started out shorter at some moment, then to grow, but still, if you feel your current longevity is an established figure for long enough that you do not easily recall an earlier moment of anything else, this is a problem."

"How so, for example?"

"You need a rather large volume of generations to impose any significant evolutionary change. A species does not evolve, at least not in a physical sense, with larger brain capacity and other physical attributes, within a single lifetime. You need the adaptation of many generations slowly transitioning to a new design. Even if we say you held a fraction of your current lifespans in those days, you are still moving exceptionally fast. Then, if we say, you slowed down so much that you do not recall a moment in your modern history, and with lifespans of two hundred centuries, this must count as a considerable period of time, where you show virtually no significant signs of this same rate of evolution, those early days must have been very different for you."

"All right, I think I can accept this, within reason. So, the question is what happened in those early days. It's said we had something happen in our environment."

"Fine, but this still represents a problem. For this, I would wish to reflect on any other species in your environment, to see if there is anything similar occurring."

"Yes, but I don't have that sort of information here...sorry."

"All right, so be it. But at the same time, this also limits us to assume yours as being unique in some way. And this imposes an even worse paradox. If you were to say this environmental change caused multiple species to transition, we could suggest yours is not the only one. There should be others, and you should know what they are, even if only academically. I think lifespans on the order of millennia would stand out, would they not?"

"I suppose they would. But I'll also admit, until I met these people, or I think any of us met any other form of life out there, the only real example was our own. So, this would seem normal for us."

"Interesting...in all your two million years, or whatever portion you were spaceborne, you did not interact with any other lifeforms?"

"I don't think I could answer that personally, but my impression is we interacted with more xeno-lifeforms during our chase than we ever did for any other reason."

"Fascinating, and also a bit disturbing. Is this simply to say you were not fortunate enough to meet any before this, or that you did not go out there TO meet any?"

Kaliya could only shrug at the suggestion.

"Very well..." Aelwyn continues. "Alternatively, this event should at least leave behind something noteworthy to suggest a large-scale alteration of conditions that yours somehow survived, rather than to simply say...something happened. Under those circumstances, I must say you were very lucky."

"Lucky...all right," she muses.

"Evolution does not grant sudden changes, not unless there is an external factor interfering with your growth. If we say you suffered a cataclysm that would affect large regions of your environment, such as your climate and other factors, it will more likely cause you to go extinct for the failure of your ecosystem and the associated food chain. Many species of animals become dependent after a while on their native environments and the support elements to be found there. Disrupt this, and you have a cascading sequence of failures, not a desperate struggle to adapt to that which is likely outside your scope of capacity."

"Uh oh..."

"Take a typical example. An animal eats a specific type of food; we will say a plant for this point. But this climate change causes the conditions to alter, bringing an end to the favorable conditions this plant requires to thrive, and so it dies out. That animal now has no more food to eat, so it too dies out. Then, you might have a larger predator animal also losing its food supply, meaning to say this smaller one, so it might also die out."

"Yeah, you have a point, and ours was supposed to be herbivorous."

"Right, and it is far more likely they would search for their favorite food rather than immediately turn to experiment with food found elsewhere that they are not as familiar with. As for meat, the digestive system of an herbivore might not be able to process meat without a considerable amount of conditioning. So, the question becomes, what was this effect and how was it applied? What did it do to your environment that forced you to look elsewhere for that which made you undergo this radical alteration? Also, how widespread was it? Was it localized to a small region, allowing you to migrate elsewhere? Was it continent-wide, was it worldwide...how far did you have to go before finding your next meal, and could you actually travel that far? If the numbers are not kind, you should not have survived. So, a suggestion of something dramatic is unreasonable."

"Did you ever take lessons from Thaelyn in his ability to debate?" Marelle wonders. "You sound just like him."

"Him?" she smiles and thumbs at Thaelyn. "Oh, I know of his talents. He told me a few stories about his exploits. I do not have that same background, but I think many of us hold at least a few skills. But next, Kaliya, I would like to speak of your ancestors learning to develop tools, and in only half a million years becoming civilized. A species with even modest lifespans, and we are speaking in terms of decades here, may see enough generations pass where they might begin to see the viability of using tools. We could be starting out with the understanding that a heavy rock, if smashed on top of something's head, will likely kill it. Boom..." she snaps her fingers, "...here you have meat. A club might also serve, but you may also need a social setting, where multiple individuals work together to grapple the animal in order to get close enough that you do not become the meal instead."

"Ouch," Kaliya mumbles.

"Indeed. But if you are suggesting a tool with a cutting edge, this would not likely emerge until much later when the brain capacity is large enough to realize you can chip away at that same rock, using another stone as a hammer, to create a sharpened edge. This, as opposed to using your teeth to simply tug away at your meal. But this still defies the logic. Why does an herbivore need tools to begin with? This might be to take a hide from the animal, not necessarily to eat the meat. And if your habit is not to hunt other animals at all, with your only prey being the grass under your feet, why would you think of applying a new fur coat? The weather is likely the least of your concerns, outside of those predators that are hunting you."

"Well..." she chuckles. "There goes my education, along with my horns."

"Aye," Relissa nods. "Yours and mine...if I had any..."

"I am sorry for this, Kaliya," Aelwyn continues. "But tools are for thinking creatures that need to overcome something a bit more complex than chewing grass. And if that grass ceases to exist, your biggest problem is not to create a tool to solve the need, it is to find an alternative to the original grass."

"You mentioned something about transitional stages," Marelle asks. "Adapting to use meat... What do you need for that? And what about the timing, at least from your side?"

"All right, let us touch on this," Aelwyn considers. "My best suggestion for a transition would need to involve first the adaptation from an herbivore to something higher on the food chain. But herbivores do not develop a taste for meat immediately, as it is more likely the predators to conquer the world, not the herd animals. They have the drive and the motivation to take action, not run from danger like the rest. So, unless it starts out as an omnivore, able to eat both foods, an animal might transition to a scavenger as one possibility, if it can find some other creature's kill and borrow from this…assuming the one that killed it is gone by now, as it is unlikely to simply let go of it."

"Right."

"This can give one a taste for meat, but you still need the ability to actually kill something. And Kaliya…"

Aelwyn pauses to study the tall Daanen'kai's body a moment, peeking under the table to look at her hoofed feet, and then her hands.

"…I think I need to agree with Aerlie, you are still too much like your herbivore ancestors to represent a threat of any sort. Sorry, no offence…"

"I understand," she accedes. "And we don't actually behave this way, either. The motivation to chase things, not run away from them. This is where the idea of using tools comes in. But you blew that one out the window already."

"Right, you need natural weapons to be a predator, along with a predator instinct, simply to gain the meat you need to develop your brain capacity better before you can learn to create something like a tool to further expand yourselves. And this could easily take millions of years under normal conditions of a species with lifespans well inside a century."

"Yikes…all right…"

"And when you combine this with your lifespans, and especially this skill of yours, there is something seriously wrong with the numbers if you are claiming to be naturally evolved this way. However, let us take an alternative. This would require something external. Say you have this natural event…maybe a body, like a meteor, that comes down and essentially contaminates or alters your environment in some way. This could impose something to radically mutate your species, either with a substance, maybe organic, like an alien organism to intermix with yours, or maybe a radiation effect."

"Hmm, that might be something."

"But I would also suggest yours would not be the only species affected. I would think anything in the area might be affected in some fashion. But your statement of not knowing if there is anything else significant enough to remember in your history, is leading me to think YOU are the only thing worthy of mention for this alteration."

"Um, I see what you mean, and right now I wish I had something to offer."

"If we suggest the other examples were not viable enough to persist long, or maybe they were preyed out of existence, but yours survived, then you are again very lucky. If there is anything else, we have that same problem. And this STILL does not answer the one about this skill of yours unless it is a side effect of this abnormal evolutionary step."

"All right, an abnormal evolutionary step," Kaliya surmises. "Let's look at this from the perspective of what you might suggest as a normal step. How might someone come into this by whatever is normal?"

"Excellent. This is a good direction to take. But Kaliya, my interpretation of this skill, much like with Thaelyn, and I would assume anyone else you might speak to around here, would be that you should not have this, given your lifespans measured in millennia, and with such a meager civilized term to allow you the freedom to evolve in ways beyond the primal needs of survival."

"Uh huh…and I'm starting to feel next month's horns going soft already. Oh well…"

"Yours is a curious culture," she smiles. "To be honest, this is a skill I would not normally expect to see outside of a Celestial."

"Whoa! I know what my father said once, but a Celestial? Thaelyn said something about mortals, but just how far do you need to go for this?"

"Most societies must travel many tens of thousands of millennia before they can claim such extravagant gifts as projecting their thoughts to distant locations, perceiving of intangible bodies and energies, and even reshaping Reality by the power of their will. There can be exceptions to this rule in younger societies, usually the result of an anomaly or an odd mutation, but the rule must follow a much longer path to become commonplace. And yours would be rather profound even for an average Celestial. If I understand correctly, you projected this image of yours to another planet in another star system, and further across a dimensional bound, am I right?"

"Yeah, much to everyone's surprise."

"Naturally. I would imagine, had you evolved as anything I would call normal, say for instance like this human here, you might need at least several tens of millions of years for this, maybe reaching into the hundreds, depending on what sort of longevity they might develop in that time, and therefore the generation count passing by."

"And now, there goes my father's theory."

"Worse! For you, with your lifespans already being so high, if we say you simply evolve so slowly, this skill should not develop even in several orders of magnitude above that. And this is to suggest you are...normal...for where you are right now. So, all I can say is, you were given a significant jump start into this position."

"A jump start, maybe with something alien arriving and contaminating our original species to mutate us into something new. All right, I guess that simply cuts it. I'm out my next TWO sets of horns. And if I share this with Ankhia, or anyone else, they'll follow suit."

"Let me ask about your life cycles a moment. Maybe there is something else to be considered here. You are a child at fifty, and you mature into adulthood at two centuries. When do you go through puberty?"

"For me, that was just before my first century, around nine decades."

"Good, and you appear as a mammalian species, correct?"

"Yes."

"Although these numbers are severely stretched in my mind, if we apply a few common rules we know of for other species, I might say your overall lifespan should only be a fraction of what it is, maybe by a tenth at best, given how young you are as a species at this time. But here you are...you take a full two centuries to mature into adulthood, and then spend the remainder of your lifetimes doing what? What about your breeding cycles? At what time do you start producing children as a habit?"

"As a habit…physical or cultural? Our usual cultural habit is to pass our first millennium before we get serious about marriage and family."

"Great Powers…" she wheezes and closes her eyes.

"Yeah, that's what I say," Marelle winces. "And she's still a virgin at her age, can you believe it? I lost mine…um, well…we'll just say a while ago."

They all share a brief laugh at the statement.

"I am truly enjoying this conversation," Aelwyn notes. "I do not even get this much excitement when I share private moments with Nemelle."

"I am not surprised," Thaelyn offers. "She is even more introverted than you are."

"Yes. Perhaps I should bring her out more often. This is inspiring me now. But on to the other side of it… How many children do you usually produce?"

"I think one or two is the norm," Kaliya ponders. "At least, I think it is from a historical perspective. Our case is different, being on the run as we were for so long."

"Why so?"

"The Suuden-Aryku were chasing us after we left home, pounding on us with each world we tried settling on, and killing large populations. On the next world, we go through one or more baby booms to reproduce in large numbers, trying to rebuild our population, then to see it cut down again. And we often did this at younger ages because we just didn't have the luxury of time to follow our normal habits."

"Luxury of time…a millennium or swore," she rolls her eyes. "But only a small number is normal, like with many of the higher forms of mammaloid species. As disturbing as it is, and on multiple levels, this leaves me to wonder for how many years you are able to do this. At what age are you no longer able to reproduce?"

"I, uh, let's see… I would need to reflect on my mother for this point. She had me well into her late years, which is regarded as medically unsound for an elder member, but still possible."

"Just one moment…" Aelwyn urges. "An elder member? Considering your numbers, just how old are we speaking of here?"

"We use a couple of terms here. When we refer to someone as an elder, this means one hundred fifty and up. As for me, my father is one hundred eighty-two, and my mother should be one hundred seventy-nine by now."

"In all Creation…" she winces. "All right, one seventy-nine, and you are…four, by now? So, one seventy-five at the time… Powers behold, such an example as this. No, this is not natural by any proper example I am aware of. Not for a classic mortal society. We most certainly need to extend ourselves into the realms of a Celestial before we see numbers like these, both for the longevity as well as the reproductive limits."

"Cu'Nar help us now. Can you explain why, just so I can prepare for my next year's horn supply?"

Aelwyn raised her brow at the bewildered girl, and then rolled her eyes at Thaelyn. He simply smiled back at her.

"Right," she asserts. "And how many of these do you usually go through at any given moment?"

"Before meeting him," Kaliya responds. "I was nicely outfitted with one set for a good century or two. Since then, about one a week…"

"Really! Well, if one day I should learn how this is applied, I might wish to take samples," she grins gently.

"How intriguing," Thaelyn ushers jovially. "I cannot recall at any moment to see you so unreserved."

"These students of yours are affecting me in strange ways, Thaelyn. Is this the culture you have been developing down there lately?"

"Recall that these examples are from that other world, but I have noticed they do possess some rather wild ambition."

"Indeed! Maybe I should investigate more closely. Now, returning to our topic, an average Celestial society would have evolved away some of the traditional limitations of their mammalian reproductive deficiencies which might curtail their cycles to a narrower time period. Humans, for instance, and many other…young…mammaloid societies, cut out somewhere at midlife, if for no other reason than due to their reproductive centers running out of their native supply of materials, or progressing into maturity beyond their viability stage. A species may also modify itself, after a while, if their longevity grows to such a degree that it becomes inconvenient for the narrow focus of time to permit them the flexibility they desire for their longer lifetimes to use it."

"Um," Marelle raises a hand tenderly. "Can you explain that a little, for those of us who don't know too much about people with lifespans running into the millennia?"

"All right…" Aelwyn smiles. "Let us take yours for a moment. You might have a lifespan that runs the better part of a century. Your habits would be to have children in your younger years, meaning the first few decades, and from there you dedicate yourselves to raising them for the remainder of your lives. After a while, your bodies are no longer able to reproduce, not that it would even be advisable by then, as the remainder of your lifespans would find it more difficult to raise them."

"All right, got it."

"Now, let us assume, as a species, you evolve to a much longer lifespan, greater than a century, maybe two or more. If your bodies do not modify this limitation of your reproductive timing, you are still being driven to do this in the first few decades, leaving you with the remainder of your lives doing…something else. However…" she raises a finger for emphasis. "If you do not WANT children so young, instead to first occupy yourselves with something else, and then LATER to think of children, like maybe after a century or two of occupation elsewhere, but your body ran out many decades ago…"

"Right, I get it now…you're out of luck for it."

"Therefore, if your society can make a modification of some sort to give you an extension, you can delay yourselves. This might come in the form of simply preserving your reproductive components until later when you are ready, or altering your organs NOT to run out at all. Such as this could be the case in a higher developed society, if their evolution is not meeting up to their cultural demands."

"This is an interesting perspective," Kaliya muses. "I don't really know if my people did anything like this to give us this ability. So, I might need to ask my father or someone else, maybe in the medical lab, like Ankhia, to see if she knows anything."

"Even so, if you did not do this at any moment in your history, and again, if you do not recall any easy memories of your lifespans holding different valuations, this suggests you were given something from much earlier, maybe even before you had the technology to do anything at all. And if THIS is the case, either your species is naturally born with an extended or infinite supply...like the elves, as I know they can do this...or this mutation did something."

"All right, one more count against our evolution. So, by the sound of it, I'm half-god even though I shouldn't be half-god. Wonderful. I suppose this also applies to learning telepathy. My father did that, and it's apparently inside of us, even though no one actually does it."

"Oh? Why not?"

"From what I hear of it," Thaelyn offers. "She tells us the rest are too afraid to use it. They have a fear factor over some of this. Also, her father's science faction, which relates to metaphysics, was never highly regarded, as she and her people, being from a barren fold, know nothing of magic. They are not a religious society, and describe virtually everything outside their highly empirical studies as...mysticism," he smirks.

Aelwyn gazed at him and felt a sudden explosion of laughter erupt inside of her. On this occasion, she simply let it out, and the effect spread like a disease across the table, and even spilled onto a few other tables and several people walking nearby.

"Mysticism indeed!" she resumes through her outburst. "That one is worthy of a sensory stone."

"A sensory stone?" Marelle asks.

"Yes. It is a device we use in the guild to record memories of sensations donated to us by those who experience something extraordinary. We keep these in a library for later study as part of our teachings."

"Right, I just had to ask that one..." she relents ironically.

"Very well, Thaelyn, then let us get down to the reason you are here and what you want from me. This living paradox does not seem to hold any rational explanation, so what are we to do with it?"

"Here is where we come into our issue of security, and the other reason I am here."

"And here is where she blasts us with the rest of her feelings," Relissa quips.

Aelwyn glances briefly at the dark elf.

"Is it really that bad?"

"It's bad, you can be sure of that much, so here's a wee bit of a heads-up for you."

"All right, thank you for the warning."

"For this," Thaelyn resumes. "We will return to her home world and her people. They were visited by these two beings, and as I mentioned previously, these were thought to be part of a dead society."

"When you say this, I get the impression we would know of this society previously."

"We would, as they are remnants of the old Celestial Wars."

Aelwyn jerks back and gasps. She was staring into his eyes, but her emotions seeped out in all directions. Relissa and the others felt a shock of minor panic hit them, but fortunately, since it wasn't aimed in their direction, it was only a glancing blow.

"Aye, that's what we're talking about," Relissa soothes. "Easy does it, girl."

Aelwyn suddenly turns to the address and instantly realizes her error. She covers her mouth and closes her eyes to refocus herself.

"My apologies... This is why I am so sensitive on the matter. It is one thing to laugh, but this is another entirely."

"It's alright, we've all been there. Don't worry about us, we're all friends here."

"I thank you again, Relissa, you are so very supportive."

"And besides, this wasn't really the bad part," she rolls her eyes mischievously.

"It gets worse?"

"Aelwyn," Thaelyn continues. "Here is what we know at this time. Her people, in their present form, being refugees, call themselves Daanen-Aryku, which in their language translates as the Exiled Ones. Their native society is called Suuden-Aryku, the Lifted Ones, which I suppose relates to being lifted into a higher form from their primal origins."

"Interesting, but is this a name they chose for themselves due to their evolution, or some other cause?"

"Um, Kaliya?"

"Ours is a society of scientists and scholars," she admits. "So, as far as I understand it, this relates to being lifted from our primeval origins as thinking creatures."

"But this almost sounds suspect in my mind," Aelwyn muses. "The name implies something almost spiritual. If you are ONLY stating yourselves to be lifted as intellectuals, I might suggest you would apply perhaps a technical name, or simply a name depicting a species. But this almost speaks of a religious origin. A type of reverence for being lifted, maybe relating to that strange evolution you speak of. Did your kind ever hold a religion that maybe an early ancestor derived this name?"

"Wow, I wouldn't know that. Religion is not part of our modern society, and I don't hear anyone talk about having anything in our past. I could maybe ask around. We have some people back home, Elder Vankkar for instance, who is a historian. Maybe he would know something."

Aelwyn nods as Thaelyn continues his explanation.

"So, we have this arrival, which is occurring at this most conspicuous moment in time, ten millennia or thereabouts, with two individuals, one named Sargeras, whom we believe to be a Primordial, and his servant, a somewhat lesser being called Darumon."

"A servant creature," she muses. "Maybe on the scale of the seraphim to the Estelar?"

"Perhaps. They arrived with a story, from what I gather after a few odd conversations, where they claim something to be stolen, and they beseeched the Suuden-Aryku to give military aid to take it back. This, in exchange for a gift of great wisdom as a form of payment."

"Oh, how nice of them to once again defile the Measure of Balance."

"Indeed, and this is only the beginning. Now we have Kaliya and her father, who was a member of their governing council in those days. We have a neutral race, as far as I can tell thus far, called the cu'Nar, which strangely enough is described to resemble a race of Positive Primes, coming out of nowhere, delivering a rather magnificent colony ark into their hands, and telling them to run away."

"Oh, well, that was generous of them. And how and why would Positive Primes be involved…first to come out of their native homes, second to interact with mortals like these, and third to deliver a ship they simply happened to have on hand?"

"Yes, these are good questions to ask. But so far, I do not have the answers, other than to say they were following him, perhaps on behalf of another who built the ship."

"This sounds orchestrated. Someone knows this Primordial, was watching him, anticipating his arrival, and preparing ahead of time for this moment."

"It would, and this ship was conveniently calibrated and configured in their native language."

"Oh! Really! Thaelyn, if I said she was a paradox before, this entire situation is paradoxical. I would say all or most of it should be regarded as suspect."

"Perhaps so, but I do not have any more details to help explain the relations. This could be a completely unassociated body we have here who simply crossed paths once."

"Maybe…"

"What about Vonafel?" Kaliya offers.

"Yes," Thaelyn muses. "Then we have her."

"Vonafel?" Aelwyn wonders. "Wait, I think I recall that name from somewhere."

"She and Aerlie go back to their academy days. She was present at our wedding."

"Oh! Yes, and with Adalon and her prophecy. Oh Powers help us, what role does she have this time?"

"At the present time, she works in our Historical Archives back home, and she recently came forward with some new information relating to Adalon's prophecies, and we are suspecting these cu'Nar are messengers of some kind."

"Interesting, but if this is now involving Adalon...and we all know how SHE is..." she rolls her eyes and chuckles.

"Indeed!" he smiles. "Now, these cu'Nar apparently shared some part of their positive energy with her people as a form of protection or warding from Sargeras's influence, or some such. See her eyes, this is an indication."

"Yes, I took notice of this when you first arrived. I did not wish to say anything initially, but I can actually feel the energy from here."

"Good. These cu'Nar apparently gave a warning to be shared with the others, but this governing body must have ignored it for this promise of wisdom. Therefore, her father packed up a large number of people and they left home. Since then, we believe Darumon, who is likely the one most active here, gave chase, at least as much out of spite for their disobedience at not submitting like the others, and perhaps also for the entertainment value of chasing them halfway across Creation to our doorstep, where I met them on this new world we discovered, called Therinë."

"Entertainment value...of course...such is a Primordial," she sighs.

"Here we have a number of...coincidences...that are simply too convenient to be accidental. This is the world these people were brought to by that individual who inspired them to follow this migration. This is also the timing of that first orcish invasion from places unknown, and by means impossible for orcs to achieve alone. This also relates to that mysterious Door that cannot be native to Tae'Eladar..."

"If a Primordial is present, or his servant, either of them should hold this capacity."

"Indeed. My war also involved a new incursion of orcs, essentially invoking an uprising in the existing population, and I found them returning back to this same new world, now to learn who owns them."

"And therefore associating a few of these pieces by now..."

"And further the orcs have a home world, where she and her people were deposited after what they call a wild jump, which is essentially a shot in the dark using a random jump coordinate from their native fold to this new one, then to find a convenient place to inhabit."

"Oh, Powers behold!" she feigns. "And so pleasant a discovery that must have been! I may not be a traveler by such means, but even I can see this is not a rational outcome. And if we are speaking of this Primordial previously associating with those orcs, he must be the one responsible."

"He is a shapeshifter, so it seems. Therefore, this is very likely. Then, he seems to order another attack, pushing them to Therinë, where we saw him collecting many of his toys, including a large assembly of troops, possibly for a push to his final destination. And we believe this to be a revenge attack on the Powers themselves."

"Um, Thaelyn, an attack on the Powers using a mortal society? Regardless of this half-god gift of theirs, I think they would not hold such profound potential to pose a serious threat to the Powers."

"By themselves, probably not, but he has been amassing a huge quantity of adamantium, and for a purpose we believe is to create a weapon to do the work."

"A weapon...what weapon? We are still speaking of mortals, are we not?"

"And from a barren fold, so they ought not to know how to use this material directly."

"Ah, but of course. So, what is he doing with it if THEY are not using it?"

"I suspect he is probably using some proprietary knowledge here, but according to Adalon..."

"Here we go folks," Relissa teases. "Kaliya, grab your horns. The rest of you, get ready for a hit."

Aelwyn glares at the girl and her mischievous grin.

"Does she do this often?" she asks.

"She and this one," he points at Marelle. "Be aware. These two are developing something of a reputation together," he smiles.

"I see. Very well, I think I will try to deny her on this occasion, simply out of spite," she grins softly.

"We'll see about that," Relissa jests.

"Anyway," Thaelyn resumes. "According to Adalon, this weapon would likely need to reflect on that same war, and the final outcome they brought."

"The war… Powers help us, the Rending? He would do that again?"

"Likely so, especially if he is alone and needs to clear the way. But we are still not finished."

"Thaelyn, what else could that creature possibly do beyond this?"

"We have a statement where I managed to invoke him to reveal what may be a hidden intention. I was trying to push him off Therinë, to preserve the lives of what remained of their local populace, so I could pursue him on my terms, not his. He mentioned becoming a Power again, but he used the term, WE shall be a Power again."

"We, meaning him and who else? Thaelyn, if we are only speaking of the two of them, with him being a servant creature of some sort, they surely cannot represent a Power in the shadow of the existing Powers, especially if they are found in a barren fold."

"This is true, although I suppose they may not necessarily stay there. But I suspect he is referring to those from the old prison plane, where he intends to release them and join together."

"Thaelyn, this is becoming frightening. What about the Great Powers? I cannot believe they would simply permit this."

"I doubt they would, but no doubt this is where that weapon comes in. Once he solves the issue of their potential for dissent, it is a clear and open road ahead of him."

"Oh no…" she whispers and lowers her head. "You said Adalon

informed you of this? She would hold this secret? But this knowledge would be forbidden outside the Powers themselves, would it not?"

"I feel it likely would, so do not ask me how she holds it. I suspect there are a few roles of intrigue at play here," he smiles.

"Only a few? With or without her paradoxes," she points at Kaliya. "This sounds like a history with some amount of background. But Powers pay witness, we cannot allow this. And speaking of which, do they know about this yet?"

"I have kept them informed through my connection with Torm, but so far, we are keeping a very low profile. We believe Sargeras and Darumon may try to escape again if they should see anything coming their way. So, the Estelar are under advisement to keep at distance for now, therefore allowing us to conduct our work in relative obscurity, as the Marshal believes us to be trapped on this world with no way forward. But I intend to foil that plan."

Aelwyn cocks her head at the curiously incongruent suggestion. "The Marshal…"

"Ah, yes. He calls himself Marshal Darumon."

"Oh, so quaint… Does he hold credentials?"

"Actually, I did not have the occasion to ask. Although I will admit, we do have a surveillance recording where he actually admits titles are not commonplace for his kind."

Aelwyn rolls her eyes and let go a small portrayal of humor, causing everyone to share a generous smile.

"Uh huh. But now, I suppose I simply must inquire as to your meaning here. Why would he think you are trapped there?"

"Oh, well, quite simply, and this was also his interpretation, is that our society is not yet space capable."

"Ah, but of course. But hers is, correct?"

"Technically yes, but in practice, no, not by now. Their ship was sabotaged to crash on Therinë, and their navigation logs are gone, with no course plans to find their original home world by now."

"Uh huh. So, with no potential to travel thusly, and no direction in which to aim your trans-dimensional drives, you are…trapped… on that world," she chuckles.

"And this is where you come in, my dearest spirit-sister," he grins boldly.

"Me?!" she balks.

A jolt of surprise blasts across the table, slamming into their guests.

"Ba-boom," Marelle murmurs with a grin.

Aelwyn instantly realized her outburst, and Marelle's cute response made her feel almost at home with it by now. She raised her brow and gestured a pause with a finger as she continued.

"Thaelyn, I am not an engineer, trans-dimensional or otherwise, and neither am I a navigator across planar folds. How am I to help you being trapped on that world?"

"Well, not specifically that," he reflects. "I need someone to assist me in training her gift. She once demonstrated, if only by accident, the ability to travel to that world with those orcs, which we call Ruuki uy'Daan. They are still assaulting us, and likely using portal devices left behind by Darumon as a harassment technique. We need to put a stop to that."

"Using her in a projected form?"

"Well, it is a curious beginning. We also believe he once assaulted a world filled with dwarves. We found some of them being used as slave labor to harvest this metal, so there must be a presence in their world of a mining base. We have a story of orcs invading at one time, so if there is anything of value on Ruuki uy'Daan to carry us to that next step, we need to find it and capture it. From there, we should find access to her point of origin, that world called Azgarén."

"Thaelyn, I think you have been spending too much time around these mortals. It must be those gnomes you told me about several times, I cannot be sure," she chuckles. "This is certainly very inventive. Travel by means of Doors linking your destinations, rather than the more conventional stellar conveyance."

"It certainly carries an element of surprise that he would not otherwise expect. But we need that first step, and it begins with her," he points at Kaliya.

"I see. Very well, if your desire is to enlist my aid to teach this

Child how to use this gift, I will do my best. I would find it most curious to see how you intend to employ it. So, where do we begin? Should I bring her into my care here?"

"Unfortunately, I must keep her at home, as she has a very full schedule already. Therefore, I must ask you to come to Tae'Eladar and engage her teachings there."

Aelwyn gazes into his eyes and forms a modest grin.

"You have been trying to convince me to join with you on that world for at least a few centuries, Thaelyn. Is this some new attempt to attract me with the excuse of this great need of yours?"

"I wish the need was not as great, but I should also remind you that there can be many fine experiences to be had on Tae'Eladar, and your studies here have become somewhat limited simply by your tenure within the guild."

"Aye," Relissa adds. "And just think of all the fun you could have chit-chatting with peeps like us."

Aelwyn studies the perky young elf a moment for her suggestion.

"And you said she is also in your academy, correct?" she wonders cautiously.

"Yes, and I think life for the rest of us will never be the same," he grins and winks at Relissa and the others. "But we still need you."

"Indeed, and I should say this brief time in conference here has been rather inspirational," she sighs. "Well, I will admit life here in the city has become rather mundane. One can only examine and reexamine the same sensory stones so many times before one can tell the story in one's sleep. Very well, I will ask you to allow me a few days to prepare, and I shall meet you on Tae'Eladar. Is there anything else? I believe you said there was another issue on your mind."

"Yes, my other main concern for visiting the city."

She studies him briefly for his statement, once again taking note of his anxiety levels.

"What concern is this?"

"As I said, Darumon seems to hold such intentions as to free the other Primordials from their prison plane. We need to prevent that."

"Naturally. So, why does this bring you here?"

"Because the Door leading into it is here in the city, and I carry instructions from Lord Ao to deliver a warning to the Lady."

Now she loses control.

"You want to speak to the Lady?!" she shrieks.

Her sudden panic unleashes a tidal wave of emotion at the others around the table, causing each of them to yelp, and driving them nearly out of their chairs. The shockwave radiated out like a bomb blast, impacting groups sitting at other tables, causing starts and screams, and further travelling to make contact with those passing by, invoking screeches and moans.

Thaelyn took the heaviest brunt of the wave, as her attention had been mostly focused on him. But as he was at least partially expecting this from her, he knew to brace himself for the effect. Still, the force of it caused him to recoil abruptly.

Aelwyn's attention drifted to the disturbances occurring around her, noticing people screaming and moaning in a wide area throughout the plaza. She finally realized her involvement in this and retracted herself forcefully, slapping her hands over her face, turning in her chair, and doubling over. The sounds of distress gently subsided with people pulling themselves back into their right minds and looking around trying to figure out what just happened. Most simply went on with their travels, treating this event as another typical day in a city filled with people capable of strange acts.

Relissa peeks over the edge of the table, having ducked underneath hoping to find protection. Marelle was slouching in her chair, appearing cross-eyed and checking her heart to make sure it was still beating. Kaliya was leaning to one side, panting as she supported herself between a knee and the corner of the table.

"Great cu'Nar," she wheezes. "It'll take me a year to find my horns after that one."

Aelwyn buried her face in her hands and hid herself in her lap. She struggled to empty her mind of all thoughts, wishing simply to find peace. She was mortified at her actions.

"Aelwyn," Thaelyn calls softly.

"She cannot bear to present herself," she announces in her

defensive third-person perspective, with her voice muffled by her hands.

"We need you to extract yourself from there. This is not a time for hiding."

"She is ashamed for her failure. She has applied herself to so many who cannot resist her nature. This conduct is so very embarrassing and undesirable."

"Be it or not, it is expected, though unfortunate. But under the circumstances, a greater need must be observed here."

Marelle tries to pull herself forward to offer her support.

"Aelwyn, listen to me," she begins. "I can't speak for anyone else here, but we've all been through a lot of rough times. I'm sure whatever trouble you just made is minor in comparison."

"Minor? She would describe this as minor?"

"Well, yeah, I suppose I might. It was a temporary release that didn't cause any actual harm to anyone. I remember His Lordship telling us a story a little while ago about his girlfriend, Ecco. Do you know her?"

Aelwyn brought her face up over the edge of the table, slowly lowering her hands to reveal her face.

"Yes, we knew each other very well in those early days."

"And that perp who took her voice away? That seems a little more violent and permanent than simply blasting an area with emotions. People recover from this, but that would leave a scar, to say nothing of the trauma of him being allowed to simply come in and do something, and no one puts him behind bars for it."

"But you do not understand…"

"What don't I understand? A city where the term 'law and justice' is subjective to what side of the Measure of Balance you come from? Or that you simply don't like losing control. When I think of how many times I've seen people scream and shout, and even get into fights… I've had to break up barroom brawls and haul people off the streets into a prison cell for such things. As for this, sure it's not nice, but you didn't do it intentionally. This is simply who and what you are, much like what Kaliya said earlier."

"Aye," Relissa offers. "Looking out on the street here, I see all sorts of wacky peeps walking about, and I use the term loosely. How many of them go out and do whatever comes naturally without thinking twice about it? You have a statue of a guy in that museum who cursed himself to stone. Say his name and wham-o, there you go up in smoke for it. You have this dame, Vrischika, who goes bouncing against the walls whenever Thaelyn goes in to say hello."

"Well, yes," Aelwyn mutters softly. "She is something of an exception..."

"An exception? Buggers to that, I say! And who's to say what's right or wrong around here, if this story of Ecco is how things work. Is it for me to say, maybe you, or this guy at the other table?" she thumbs over her shoulder. "I just noticed most of these peeps out here simply picked up and walked on like nothing happened, and you hide under the table for it? Stiffen up, girl, this is the life around here," she smiles tenderly.

Aelwyn glared at the young elf for a long moment, spreading her gaze further to Marelle, and then to Kaliya, who simply smiled and nodded as she leaned forward.

"We had a little talk back there in the, um..." she coughs softly as she glances at the brothel, "...professional establishment..."

"Ay," Relissa yips. "Are you taking up the easy side now?"

"Well..." she smiles gingerly. "We were learning a few things from, of all people, a succubus."

"Grace?" Aelwyn muses. "Yes, she is a very sociable individual."

"She was telling us about the polarities and how things become completely neutral in here. Otherwise, in her words, you'd all be tearing each other's throats out. So, I think that tells us anything goes."

"I suppose, but..."

"But? But what? You're a Celestial. What other types of beings do you have either living in, or visiting this place, and what are THEY capable of that they don't hold back on. And YOU are worried for letting out your emotions?"

"But it is embarrassing."

"All right, so it's embarrassing. What side of the polarities are you on again?" she raises her brow inquisitively.

"Huh?"

"Oh buggers, Kaliya," Relissa moans. "Are you pulling rank on her now?"

"I may as well, Relissa, because she's not pulling her own here. Besides, if I'm qualified to call myself half-god, I need to pull my own weight now," she giggles.

"Jiggers, here we go. Now her head will blow up so big, we'll need to haul it around in a cart."

"I am lost…" Aelwyn frowns. "Wait, pull rank…on my polarity?"

"You're Positive, and what does a Positive do?"

Aelwyn gazes at Kaliya for a moment as she realizes her error.

"Powers help us," she wheezes. "I am taking lessons from a Prime now. You mean the Measure of Balance, right?"

"There you go. Vrischika would have a field day with you if you let this out."

As Aelwyn began to piece it together, the logic was so simple, but her inhibitions clearly stood out to spoil the connection. She held a weakness, and she wasn't pressing herself to overcome it, as would be the duty of the Positive side of the Measure of Balance.

"Powers be blessed, Thaelyn, is this part of your work?"

"I am not responsible for this one," he shrugs. "Some part of it may be intuition, and these three are special gems. But I gave them license to seek wisdom here, and Powers help us, what they might do with it afterwards."

"Don't listen to him," Marelle grins. "I've been learning more from him this past year or so than I got in a lifetime back home. He really rubs off on you."

Thaelyn smiled warmly, and Aelwyn felt confident enough to sit upright again. The friendly pep talk gave her a new perspective to think about.

"All my life, Thaelyn…you know how it has been for me."

"Yes, and I suffered through portions of it with you."

"But if this is the result of your teachings on Tae'Eladar, and even if these people are from elsewhere, they are clearly learning from you now. This is astonishing, and I might even say surprising to find on a Prime world."

"I think Tae'Eladar is a special case. But clearly, with the right education, they can be very adaptable."

"Perhaps so, but this is still remarkable to see a society so developed in ways that would otherwise go beyond their current maturity stage. I suppose I must admit, these three are right, and this does reflect on life in this city. But to think of anyone from outside holding such perspectives… Kaliya, I must thank you greatly for exposing my own failure. And Relissa and Marelle, your encouragement is also very enlightening. My introverted nature, and that…shell…I so often enclosed around me, is truly showing it's worth. I must also admit Nemelle is in this same position, and she could do well with this same lesson."

"Is she another empath like you?" Kaliya asks.

"Yes, she is. She is a bit younger than I, but no less for her handicap. I will teach her this, and grant you the credit for the lesson…all of you."

She smiles warmly, and once again, the sensation washes across the table as her emotions seep out to touch the other members.

They divert the topic to other interests to soothe their nerves, hoping to find temporary relief from their troubles, until a collective outpouring of cries and shouts erupts from the street outside the walled space of the Ward. People start dashing through the gates of the plaza, seeking shelter under tables and behind buildings. Calls go out to the citizens in the Ward to take cover and clear the open areas.

"What in all the bleedin' hells is going on out there?" Relissa shouts.

"I think she is here," Thaelyn declares.

The group of women turns their heads at Thaelyn as he leans to peer out through the gates into the street. They attempted to follow his motion, but the vantage point from their angle was insufficient.

"Aelwyn, I will bid you to take charge of my students while I am engaged. Although I am of a fair opinion this interaction should result in a satisfactory outcome, I am no less ill at ease for the prospects."

"Thaelyn!" she starts with a shock of anguish leaping out. "Are you serious? Is there no other way? She is not one to approach for any reason."

"Well, unless you know of any private mailboxes belonging to her, this is the only choice. And she is the ONLY one to approach in this matter. No one else in this city holds this level of authority, and naturally she would need to be involved on some level for such as this."

He places his bag from Vrischika's shop on the table.

"Would one of you ladies mind tending to this for me?"

Marelle reaches over and picks it up.

"My Lord," she assures. "You WILL be coming back to us. Just remember that."

"Aye he will," Relissa moans. "But in how many pieces."

Marelle swings her hand around and whaps Relissa on the shoulder, but keeps her eyes firmly on Thaelyn.

They get up from the table and walk away from the café. Thaelyn directs Aelwyn to usher the girls behind a local building to take cover in the face of the unpredictable. She brings them around the side of the brothel, as it affords the best view. He then straightens himself up, forcing himself into a determined state of mind, and coolly marches out the gate.

Many eyes watch incredulously as the people observe from their hiding places the tall nobleman moving towards the gate. Several whispers pass around as to the mentality and the incomprehensible reasons someone would willingly go out there.

He comes to the gate and passes through. From their hiding place, Aelwyn and her new charges can see him proceeding out onto the street in front of the Ward. They can also see the Lady.

She was wearing an ornately flowing robe and displayed a prominent mask over her face. No part of her actual body was visible. The mask was surrounded by a ring of blades set into the display as a form of ornamentation. She hovered well above the ground, and her attire seemed to weave as if from an imperceptible breeze.

"A question," Marelle whispers. "Is she an Estelar?"

"It is believed by some she might stand among them," Aelwyn responds softly. "But her origins tend to hold some mystery."

"All right, but if she actually is one, is that how they usually appear?"

"Not precisely. In her case, she wears what we might describe as a costume to represent her manifested image. The Estelar are not corporeal beings. They do not have bodies like us. When they manifest themselves before us, they most often take a form within our minds that conforms to our senses, perhaps representing an image similar to one of us. Their true form, however, is quite unique, and beautiful in its own way. In her case, I think it is best to describe it as an overlay for the local environment."

Thaelyn continued into the street, taking a position a respectable distance in front of the deity. The streets were empty except for the two of them facing off.

"Pleasant greetings, Dear Lady," he begins. "I am here with a vital message concerning the safety of the city, the realms, and much more."

"Commencement..." she announces flatly in a reverberating tone. "Supposition..."

"I have discovered the presence of a Primordial in the Prime realms. I have further discovered that he is directing himself on a return path to these realms. I have found evidence to prove this, following the steps taken by minion races he has directed during the course of his actions. It is my belief his minions could be very close to discovering the city if they have not already done so. Of the many issues on my mind, there is one preliminary concern, and this is if you or your servants may have seen any of these within the city thus far."

"Definition..."

"Um..."

He pauses as he considers how to describe the Suuden-Aryku.

Then a quick thought comes up. He turns and signals for Kaliya to stand up and come forward. The tall Daanen'kai female timidly rises to her feet and takes several steps in his direction.

"If you will observe this young lady," he ushers. "She and her kind are refugees that have been trying to escape from the Primordial after he arrived on their native birth world, and are currently in my care. Kaliya, would you be so kind to assist?"

Kaliya steps forward a bit more to present herself.

"My people look generally like this," she glances down at herself. "But the Suuden-Aryku have some differences by now. First is they applied some sort of artificial device on the right side of their cranium, part of an artificial implant inside their neural tissues. Next is they embedded a type of artificial, maybe to say a parasitic lifeform as an augmentation on their back, and it covers a large portion of their bodies by now, disfiguring them, and also causing some discoloration in their skin tone, with a slight reddish blotching. Our males are taller than I am, by maybe half a meter," she reaches a hand up to demonstrate. "They have a larger bone and muscle structure, and much broader torsos. Also, the Suuden-Aryku do not have the glowing eyes. My people received this as we were escaping, and we regard this as a type of blessing from a race of Positive Primes that assisted us."

"Fascination... Acceptance..." the deity muses.

"And another thing, they often wear a form of battle armor, which is based on our technology, and they carry some nasty energy weapons."

"Acknowledgment..."

Kaliya turns to Thaelyn as he nods and directs her to return to the others. As she rejoins the group, Relissa glares at her tall blue friend.

"Jiggers, girl, to think of you going up to someone like that."

"Yeah, when do you get a chance to speak to a god face-to-face?"

Thaelyn now returns to his meeting.

"Have you seen any of these within the city?" he asks.

"Negation..." the Lady responds thoughtfully.

"Very well, perhaps we are ahead of them."

"Insinuation…"

"I am currently engaged in a wartime action as the result of an incursion he made on the Prime world, Tae'Eladar. This incursion arrived through an arcanic portal from another world found in a separate fold, where they were under siege by forces serving this Primordial. The Primordial has a servant who conducts much of this work on his behalf. During the course of my advance, this servant, who is described as Marshal Darumon, began a retreat. But before he was able to depart completely, I was able to make one final conversation with him, and managed to cause him to reveal a clue as to his purpose. He stated that he and others would become a Power once more. But my interpretation, based on what we observed, is that he and his master would not hold this capacity by themselves."

"Affirmation…"

"However, we also discovered a number of additional activities. One of these relates to a portion of his minions who were accumulating large quantities of the enchanted metal adamantium. We discovered this on that new world where we found mining activities and an effort to retrieve a current shipment."

"Motivation…"

"At first, the motivation was a mystery to us, as none of the obvious players carried any innate knowledge on how to use it. But then a suggestion was given that it could be for the production of a weapon. And not any common sort of weapon, but a very unconventional one. For this, we must assume he has a very proprietary operation occurring somewhere. But the suggestion, in itself, is indeed a frightful one. If we consider his current location, which is believed to be in a barren fold, he will not have access to the higher-grade materials likely to be found in such a place as this, therefore the need for this metal as a substitute, and also the need for greater quantities. He is seeking those arcanic energies."

"Agreement…"

"But as for his motivation, you will not like what I have to say, as it reflects on the old Celestial War, specifically that final engagement.

The suggestion given to us is he may hope to create another Agent of Unmaking."

The visage of the woman becomes notably agitated, and a long wailing moan resounds through the streets. The blades surrounding her mask jump out and begin spinning around her head.

The people inside the plaza duck for cover once more, after warily poking their heads out to observe the interaction. Aelwyn and the others pulled back at the infuriated display.

"Take care your words, spirit-brother," she whispers.

The female deity settles back somewhat into the conversation again, but her blades continued to hover in place.

"Continuation!" she directs, her voice now more intense.

"Clearly, if you understand this potential, then you know of the harm it can bring to the realms around us, to the city, and to the Great Powers, clearing the way for him to return unimpeded. But we must also remind ourselves of his statement of becoming a Power again. He proposed this as WE will become a Power once more. But again, if this only includes the two of them, it does not represent much of a statement."

"Agreement... Interpretation..."

"This primary minion race I mentioned holds the technological capacity to create devices capable of establishing trans-dimensional conduits. If they should be successful at infiltrating the city, they could import these materials through the prison gate, which I have come to understand is located here, and build one such device to permit an exit to those inside. This would satisfy the statement of becoming a Power again, within reason, as it would now include the remainder of them. But naturally, as I am sure you are aware, such Doors of this nature require a Key. And in this case, the Key is apparently the essence of a Primordial. This makes the premise entirely viable to pursue."

This statement causes the woman to erupt in a violent display of rage, sending out a tumultuous cry that rattles the nearby buildings. Her blades dart in all directions around the region, chipping off plaster and splinters from nearby buildings, and coming within a hair's breadth of Thaelyn's body. The people watching from their hiding places shrieked in terror. Many take off and run in the opposite direction. Aelwyn and the others winced at the sight, barely able to hold their eyes on the calamitous ordeal unfolding in front of them.

"I'm glad I wasn't standing out there at this time," Kaliya emits softly.

Thaelyn holds his posture stoically, forcing himself to remain still as blades swirl all around him. He blinks slowly as he watches from all sides the flashing of razor-sharp metal. He realizes he must continue his interaction, if only to redirect the Lady from her uncontrolled outbreak.

"If I may have another word," he begs firmly.

The Lady brings her focus back to attention, and the blades slow their motion.

He continues, "Naturally, we all hold similar feelings to this outrage...although most of us do not typically send such dangerous implements flying about recklessly..." he glances conspicuously at the blades hovering in space around him.

The deity pauses to glance at her array of blades, realizing her outburst, as well as his careful suggestion for restraint. She then takes the hint and retracts them back to her side.

"Admission..." she responds softly.

Marelle and Relissa both glared at him for his obvious retort.

"Brazen!" Marelle whispers.

"Aye," Relissa mumbles. "But then, what else can you do before you find yourself sliced to ribbons."

Thaelyn observes as the blades gather back around the Lady.

"Thank you," Thaelyn nods. "Now, it becomes evident for us to safeguard ourselves from this event by securing the gate from unauthorized access. If we can assure ourselves of this, we can block one of his more ambitious attempts to return the Primordials to power."

The Lady seems to calm herself as she considers this.

"Concurrence!" she declares strongly.

"I must also admit that this Primordial seems to treat these minion societies as slaves, either unwilling or unwitting. Although I would not desire to see them, as a society, brought to harm, and instead try to liberate them, the security of this situation must dictate its own demands."

"Agreement…"

"Therefore, I will offer that you attend to this need on your side while I continue on my own. With good fortune and careful planning, perhaps we can find an equitable solution that can also save lives."

"Agreement… Consideration… Infiltration… Disposition…"

"I cannot necessarily suggest how you proceed on this, but the greater need to protect the prison portal must surely take precedence. I am attempting a covert maneuver to approach and dispose of him. Until we can find this opportunity, he cannot know of our efforts directly. Therefore, those who make this attempt may need to be disposed of until we can find a way to prevent it outright."

"Acceptance…"

"In the meantime, I will coordinate my efforts with other members of the Powers as necessary to see that he is brought down."

"Acknowledgement…"

The woman retracts her blades back into their arrangement within her mask. She then turns and floats away through the city, retreating back to her point of origin to consider these unpleasant revelations, and her part to keep the city safe.

Thaelyn stands motionless for a moment longer, drawing a deep sigh of relief and closing his eyes to settle himself.

The other people in the plaza timidly exited from the shadows, cautiously surveying the street to ensure the coast was clear before returning to their previous duties.

Relissa and Marelle had collapsed into a heap leaning against the wall. Kaliya was in no better condition as she hovered over them, mostly due to her larger size. Aelwyn was kneeling on the ground with her face buried in her hands, trying to hide her emotions from the outside world.

Thaelyn turned and made a slow stroll back into the Ward. He attempted to pull his posture upright, but he clearly showed a great amount of fatigue. Relissa and her friends noticed him returning and dragged themselves to their feet. Their motion caught the attention of Aelwyn, who followed behind sluggishly. They moved collectively to meet him halfway.

"Can we go home now?" Marelle pleads.

"Yes, my Children, I think our work here is done."

Chapter 7

CONNECTING
THE DOTS

"Captain, we have something you're going to want to hear," announces a scout coming into the gathering room in the mine. "You're not going to believe this!"

"All right, Cadet, I'm listening."

"We were making rounds in the area of Camp One, trying to find a better vantage point so we could spy on the orcs and see what those odd containers were in their camp. Unfortunately, it seems they've built a number of structures surrounding them, most of which obscure our view. It may be impossible to learn more about them unless you're right on top of them inside the camp."

"Fine, but so far that doesn't sound so promising."

"Yes Sir, I know. We were thinking we could try sending a spy into the camp, maybe at night when most of them are asleep, to see if we can get close enough for a better look."

"The idea may be valid, but not without some careful planning. I want to know about patrols, and which way might prove to be the best approach. Also, we need someone well-practiced in camouflage.

If we're going inside, I want them to look like nothing more than a piece of the local shrubbery."

"A piece of local shrubbery on legs?" Sulíma wonders. "Sounds like a certain girl I know."

"Yes, I suppose it does, also for her use of body paint."

"So far," the scout continues. "It's just something to think about, but considering the placement of the surrounding buildings, this may be the only way to see what it is. Anyway, aside from this, we found something else, which only adds to the mystery, and this will surely cause your horns to fall off."

"I'm still listening, Cadet, what is it?"

"As we were moving around the camp, one of us very literally tripped on something hidden in the underbrush. Sir, we found a pipeline with a power conduit tied to it. It was leading in from the hills southeast of the camp."

"A what?" the Captain shouts.

"We followed it up to the source in the lower foothills. Here is where we found a water pump in a small lake and an array of solar panels on the hillside."

"What in all the nether-space is going on here?! Storage tanks! Water pumps! Solar arrays! Those damnable orcs are doing better than we are, and we're supposed to be the ones with all the best toys!"

"Captain," Sulíma suggests. "Where do you suppose they got all this? There's no way they could've assembled all this by themselves, and I can't imagine any of our people would do it, so who else is there? This has to be the Suuden-Aryku!"

"I'm afraid you're right, Suli. Even though we may have held our suspicions, there's no two ways about it now, the orcs are working with the Suuden-Aryku. Although, how any of this might fit in, I don't know. Maybe if we can ever get inside that camp to see what's going on, we can find our answer."

"That storage tank," she considers. "I wonder if it's receiving the water. But then what's the boxlike thing, and then what else is hidden behind there?"

"If we assume these solar panels are supplying power to something, then that box we saw might be receiving it. And the water pump would surely be using it. So, what do they need water for? Have they finally learned how to take a bath?" he chuckles.

The assembly in the room lets out a boisterous round of laughter.

"I wonder how long it's been out there, Captain. Unless we missed something really important, I can't possibly imagine they're smart enough to run all this, or to maintain it."

"Good question. Someone needs to be watching over this to keep it in working order. Even the best equipment still needs occasional maintenance. And if it's not the orcs, it must be the Suuden-Aryku, so we'll need to inform our patrols to be on the lookout for them, on top of everything else. Dammit, this is getting annoying. They chase us off this world and we still don't get any freedom from them."

"But Captain, why would they be using orcs? Of all creatures, to use something so…well, you know, not, um, as highly sophisticated."

"The Suuden-Aryku have always acted without any perceivable reason. Maybe they're using them as a ground force, like they did with us in the city. I don't recall any reports during the attack of Suuden-Aryku being sighted, but if the orcs were able to cause so much damage, they clearly had help. Whether we're talking about special instruction, or maybe a covert operation by the Suuden-Aryku, I don't know, but it had to be something."

"But this still doesn't answer the one about these solar arrays and the tank."

"I agree, so we may have no choice but to find a way to get inside that camp and see what else is in there. Cadet, we need Tana to give a few lessons on how to be a bush."

"Does this include the behavioral manners?" Sulíma smirks. "Or simply the seasonal fashion appeal?"

"Cute, Suli… She has the best and the longest-term practice, so let's use it. We'll share it with a few others, just so we have a team of people able to move around out there."

"Yes Sir," the scout affirms. "We'll start putting together some disguises right away."

"Also, keep a close eye on their movements. I want to know if they make any regular sweeps through the camp on night watch. If there's a hole of any kind, I want to know about it."

"Yes Sir!"

"Captain?" Sulíma asks. "Whatever the orcs are doing with power, I wonder what they might do if it suddenly turns off."

"I'm not going to take that step until we have more information. And if the Suuden-Aryku are involved, it might not be such a good idea to simply pull the plug, as someone's going to notice, and then they'll come looking for the reason."

"Too bad about that… I would so love to take those for our own use here."

✦✦✦✦✦

"My Lord, it's so good to see you up and about again," the General declares.

Thaelyn had just entered the tactical office for his traditional morning review, having returned home and spent the last few days resting after his ordeal in Sigil.

"…And I see you must've finally paid a visit to your barber," he continues.

"Yes, General, I needed to tidy up a bit after that impromptu trimming I received in the city. I must admit, if my hair could turn any whiter, it would be a few shades above by now."

"We are all very thankful that you returned safely to us. The Lady called some of us into the guild courtyard for a meeting after you left, and I could see in her eyes a very deep sense of worry. But to witness your divine pillar descending upon us again was a glorious sight."

Thaelyn looks at the array of papers and reports on the table, trying to sort through to the most recent selection.

"What do we have occurring out there today, General?" he asks.

"Once again, very little of exceptional interest. The lines are converging steadily, and I had the thought to test a new tactic now that the orcs are condensing in the middle. Also, as we progress, I see a potential opportunity for us to retire a few of our people early."

"And what might that be?"

"First, the new tactic is to fly gryphons overhead between the two opposing lines dropping whatever they can conjure on the heads of our opponents; magical fire, toxic clouds, anything to disturb the orcs and keep them from finding peace. This will make them easier for our ground forces as we move forward. Secondly, as we close in from the north and south, our westward and eastward lines, which are currently being held static, could see an overlapping effect with the others. As such, we could possibly remove some of the outward camps as the main lines cross over."

"Very good, General, and this would give at least some of our troops time to rest."

"I would redirect some of them to the garrison at Portal One, however, and I am examining the configuration of that outpost to see if we could make it more resilient to a large-scale surge by the orcs on the other side."

"Has the situation changed in any way with any of those portals?"

"No change since the last time we spoke. Portal One shows a steady flow while Portal Two seems to be drying up. Portal Three is still inactive."

"This leads me to wonder something, General," Thaelyn reminisces.

"What is that, my Lord?"

"We once discussed the possibility that these portals are being generated by some manner of device, and whether the orcs may have been given instruction to build something, or if it was simply delivered by Darumon."

"Yes, and whether this device might somehow resemble our own Gateways."

"But here we have our quandary. It seems clear to us that Darumon taught them how to use portal magic in order to gain access to our world and return back again. But would he have made such an effort as to teach them how to use any form of technology.

They are described to us by the Daanen-Aryku as incapable even of forging metal. How could they possibly create any manner of technological device?"

"Then the question seems to lead us to conclude it was a gift by him and the Suuden-Aryku."

"And herein lays our next question. If it was a gift, did he build it himself, or instruct the Suuden-Aryku to do so. And if it involves the Suuden-Aryku, it could not be magical in nature, but we do know they can build conveyors."

"For this point, perhaps we should reflect on the Governor's home and his basement. They can clearly build something on a small scale, but that example also seemed to require a rather potent power source."

"Indeed, it did. And surely this would require someone to check on it from time to time for maintenance. But if the proportions are similar in scale to our Gateways, and aimed at an open space..."

Thaelyn turns to address Lieutenant Lapäli, who was once again reviewing the reports but remaining quiet during the conversation.

"Lieutenant, what are your thoughts on this matter? Can a conveyor be configured to point to an open space, as our runes often do, or is it limited only to point to a sister unit to establish a link?"

"From what I studied once," he considers. "The most common form of our old technology is to use two mated endpoint stabilizers in order to establish a permanent conduit. In order for us to assign an open-ended exit point, we would need to carefully calculate the dimensional indexing based on a number of variables, including the movements of both the source and destination celestial bodies, to find and maintain a valid location."

"So far, this is reasonable."

"Our explorations back home provided us with most of this, and further astronomical observations provided even more. This is how we were able to develop the technology within our naval navigation systems."

"But this relates to your ships. What about a conveyor? If we are observing an exit point fixed in three-dimensional space coming out of a source point that could be a device, can we be looking at such as this?"

"It would have to be using either an indexing anchor on the receiving end, repeating a continuous locator beacon for the conveyor's rift generator to lock onto, or else it would need to use a complex set of dynamic virtual indexing algorithms to maintain a destination lock."

"Interesting. In our example, how might this appear if we were to search for it?"

"I think in any situation, you are going to need a system of addressing to identify both the source and endpoints. This might involve the use of a satellite network offering a coordinate addressing matrix to precisely identify any given locational index. Therefore, if we are speaking of an anchor, it would tie into this network and submit a handshaking signal which we might describe as a ping. This ping would locate the anchor within a three-dimensional space, such as on a landform, and relay this information to be packetized as an index array."

"Very good, and again this is reasonable."

"Reasonable on paper, perhaps, but the problem here would be the timing of the calculations, the transmission of this data through a routing network, and finally to unpack the data for the rift generator to create the link, as all these bodies are in motion, and any delay could result in the rift opening in the wrong place, perhaps offset by a catastrophic margin."

"Of course, so you would need an especially rapid form of processing, perhaps also augmented by time indexes that follow a predictable sequencing which can then be accommodated during the transition. But you apparently have this with your existing conveyors, correct?"

"Yes, but these also use large supercomputing networks, which take up space. The question we're asking here is can it be miniaturized enough to fit into a form factor approximating your Gateway device. I don't know if I could answer that directly. But then again, I have no idea how your Gateway works, either," he chuckles.

"Our runes tend to create such anchors, but in our case, it is incorporated into the stone itself as a point of perception imposed upon it by the casting mage. We sometimes refer to this as the rune's perspective. It can be analogized with a person recalling a memory of the location, such as what Kaliya did during her visit to her home, and thus creating a link for her return."

"Yeah, and that simply confuses me even more on how your magic works, as if it wasn't already bad enough," he grins. "I'm still trying to learn some of these details, but it's going slow for me as I need to alternate with my duties here and between the Naarg uy'Sodrad and the Bahlaie Research Center."

"Simply look at it this way. Your mind can perceive your surroundings. This becomes your perspective. If you were to recall this image, you might also recall the various conditions associated with it, which could actually include landmarks, climate conditions, relationships with other bodies that might be present within view, and so on. If you then held such capacity, you could use this to bring yourself back to that precise location simply by thinking of it, recalling the image of that location and all it held for you the last time you were there, then to overlay the aspect of movement from where you are presently to that location."

"Very well, I believe I can understand your meaning, but it just seems like fantasy to me that you can simply think of a place and suddenly you find yourself standing there."

"You are too carefully conditioned to think in such empirical terms as your science dictates. You will need to relieve yourself from some of that if you wish to learn any of these concepts. The mind is a potent force, and under the right conditions, it can overcome many of the limitations your physical science imposes upon you."

"All right, I'll consider this as a way to reimagine these principles."

"Excellent. But now, if we are suggesting the use of these anchors, perhaps we could disrupt them somehow. Such a device as this would need to be powered in some way, correct?"

"Yes, it would, although I couldn't say what method is being used. I don't recall any of these reports mentioning any obvious Suuden-Aryku technology in the area."

"Perhaps it is buried. General, send word to the garrison at Portal Three. Since it is apparently inactive, let us try an experiment with that one. Have the troops begin digging around the portal exit. See if there are any unusual objects or devices buried underground to support this theory of an anchor stabilizing the portal. But next, Lieutenant, about this other idea of yours. If not an anchor, what else can we suggest?"

"The dynamic addressing... This would be more complex, and since we're not using an anchor, we need a way to identify a virtual endpoint. This will surely require some custom technology to make it happen. But if they did, it would follow many of the same principles for the calculations, just that the calculations are conducted elsewhere, like between that satellite network and some sort of processor to manage the endpoint positioning. The method would actually reflect upon how our ships calculate a dynamic endpoint to make a nether-space jump."

"Yes, I suppose this would follow nicely enough, and again, it should be within your capacity."

"Right, so while I suppose it can be done, maybe with geostationary satellites to zero the endpoints on the ground, my next question would be how ambitious the Marshal is to authorize this level of development just to deliver orcs into our backyard."

"He was doing it for three and a half centuries, so perhaps the duration afforded its own value into the equation."

"Maybe so. But if this is the case, it's unlikely we could so easily disable it, if any of these components are outside our immediate reach, like in orbit over our heads."

"Indeed, then we shall consider this if we should ever find a way to reach that high, or depending on how quickly Kaliya can be trained, we might find our solution at the source. And therefore, this means these portals could possibly be the result of conveyors on Ruuki uy'Daan. This does not make life any easier for us, but it does give us something new to think about, and more objectives to look for once we arrive."

"My Lord," the General considers. "If I may offer an idea,

though I think the answer may be obvious at this point... The source to Portal Three is still operational, if only abandoned. If the orcs are unfamiliar with the operation of this technology, they may have simply picked up and moved on without further concern for it. But one must ask how long this portal could remain open without supervision?"

"An interesting proposal, General. This equipment must require maintenance of some kind, and I doubt the orcs are capable of that. Even during the full length of this war, someone would need to tend to it."

"And personally, I would think, if the orcs knew how to operate this equipment, they would turn it off as they left the area. Do you think?"

"This is actually a very good point, General. Similarly, if the Suuden-Aryku have been performing any service, but have now abandoned the orcs, could this equipment also be abandoned, and might simply fail at some moment. Then the portals would close on their own."

"It would be a most convenient solution for us, but I would not feel entirely comfortable making this assumption if one should actually do this. I would much rather find it and confirm the scenario personally."

"Agreed. So, we will continue as planned until then."

◆◆◆◆◆

Sulíma was returning to her shared sleeping quarters after the morning meal. It was a new day, and she was looking forward to helping Túfula with her work in the lab. Túfula was already on her way down there to begin work on making up a new supply of paper. It was a slow process, due to her primitive working conditions, but she was determined to push forward as she knew it was necessary.

Petrith was still in the process of getting himself ready for his daily patrol in the city. Even though the orcs didn't seem to be showing much interest there, he was still tasked with this duty in case the situation changed.

"Petrith, are you still getting dressed for your patrol?" Sulíma asks.

"Yeah, I'm just going a bit slow this morning. What about you?"

"Once I have my horns turned the right way, I'll be joining Túfu down in the lab to help with her work."

"She's still making up a new batch of paper?"

"I think she'll be working on this more than anything else for now, with all the new scouting patrols we're organizing."

"I don't mind her help, and I'm sure it's useful, but it just seems so strange. Us using paper, who would've thought we would see the day."

"A good data-pad would be nicer," she admits. "Just type in your notes and store it in a data chip. But you need the industry to build it, a power source to operate it, and then a communications network to share the information."

"And we don't have any of that," he relents. "So, like the Captain once said, we're reduced to a lower rung on the technological tree... paper."

"Well, hey, let's not knock it too harshly. At least it works. And it's not that easy to make this stuff."

"How does she do it again? Wood pulp spread out on a mat?"

"Basically. She made up a special screen with very fine holes in it, and the wood pulp is soaked in a bath of solvents to make it mushy. Then she spreads this out as a sheet and lets it dry. The result is kind of fragile, but if you're gentle with it, it works."

"What about that other one, the leather strips... Personally, I think I like that one because it's reusable."

"Right, slice them real thin and preserve them to make leather. You can then write on it, wipe it clean...well, sort of...and use it again. The trouble with that one is finding the materials, as it needs animal hides to start."

"Well, good luck with it."

Sulíma eyed him as he finished getting dressed. Although he carried his usual demeanor during their conversation, she noticed him glancing at his cabinet drawer several times as he was assembling himself. His eyes betrayed a hidden distraction to something.

"Petrith, what's wrong today?" she asks. "You seem like you're only half here."

"Oh, nothing, Suli," he sighs as he tidies up his shirt. "And I'm not even sure I would want to tell you anyway. This one is kind of weird and personal."

"Aw, come on, Petrith. How bad can it be?"

"Well, it involves another one of those dreams. But this one… um…well, you'll probably think I've spent too much time hiding behind that row of bushes overlooking the pond."

"Really!" she yips excitedly. "Then you just have to tell me about this one! I've been wondering about you lately. You haven't shown any interest in me or anyone else, so what are you thinking about in those long hours by yourself out there?"

"Suli!" he retorts jokingly. "Like I said before, it's not that I'm not interested, I just have too many other things going around my head right now. For instance, I'm thinking about those orcs more than anything else lately, especially trying to figure out what's going on in that camp over there. If it were just me, I'd probably barge into that camp and take a look personally, but I know the Captain is right to follow these steps."

"Well, fine, but if you're at least having dreams, that's a start. So, what kind of dream was it, and was I in it this time?"

"I, uh…" he chuckles softly. "Well, technically no…"

"Oh!" she pouts. "Well, if not me, then who…Túfu, maybe? She's certainly cute enough."

"Actually, no, not her either."

"In all the nether-space, Petrith! All right, who's the lucky girl tormenting you in your dreams? It's not…her again, is it?" she asks tenderly while glancing at his cabinet drawer.

Petrith catches her action and sighs.

"Actually, it was," he relents.

"Oh…" she turns away and feigns a prominent frown.

"Suli…" he intones.

"You think of her more than me…" she mocks.

"I know you're faking it."

She then returned to the conversation with a supportive smile.

"All right, so tell me what this new one was about. And be sure not to leave out any of the juicy parts."

"You really want to know…" he rolls his eyes. "It's not actually anything dirty, just weird, and I'm sitting here trying to figure out certain parts of it."

"Figuring out certain parts? She's a girl, so what parts do you need to figure out? You know, I'm a real girl, so if you have any questions about anything…"

"Yeah, and I know exactly where this is leading," he laughs.

"So, when you say weird," Sulíma continues. "Is it anything weirder than seeing her in a militia uniform or in something you think was a training academy?"

"Well, yes, in a way. This time she was taking a shower."

"Wow, Petrith! So, maybe all those hoof prints we see behind those bushes really are from you after all!" she giggles. "And, um, was she naked?"

"Suli, this is the part I think I should keep quiet about."

Sulíma slaps him on the arm and exhibits a teasing scowl.

"All right, but you asked for it," he concedes. "Yes, she was, completely, and I watched the whole thing."

"And, um, how does she look?" she inquires innocently. "Not that I'm interested, you know…but as a girl who might be in competition with another, I should probably understand what I'm up against that it attracts your attention so much."

"Right. Suli, I don't think you need to worry about the competition issue. You more than qualify to drive any man crazy…and you very often do," he chuckles. "And this has nothing to do with the pond scene outside."

"All right, thanks," she smiles. "But it still doesn't answer the one about why you always go back to her in these dreams."

"I know, and I don't really have an answer to that."

"I think it's simple. You still think about her, and you can't get over it."

"Maybe you're right, Suli, and I'm sorry. You try so hard, and

I know this. I don't know how to control these dreams. It just happens."

"Well, all right. So, what was so special this time that it leaves you sitting here with your horns drooping trying to figure something out?"

"Um, well..." he coughs subtly. "My issue isn't actually that she was naked and taking a shower, it was more about where she was, what she was doing, and maybe a few things I think I saw along the way."

"Uh huh..." she moans. "Cu'Nar's grace, you're standing there watching a beautiful naked girl taking a shower, and you're more interested in the local scenery? Wow, there go my hopes for any kind of relationship," she smirks.

They share an impulsive laugh together, and then she continues.

"Fine, what was it about all this that got to you?" she asks. "A shower, the local scenery..."

"All right, but don't tease me about this. Sure, it was nice to see her, and yes, I did pay attention to all those little details. But this also reminds me of our previous conversation. She was an adult, so how is it I'm seeing a girl I haven't known since the days we were kids, but here as a fully developed woman."

"Well, yes, I suppose that's a fair question to ask. Let me ask you this. What sort of lessons did you receive about men and women... you know, the adult lessons."

"I got the same as the rest when the instructors started teaching us at around our first centennial about the nature of sex and intimate relations."

"Yes, but...well, maybe what I mean to say is this. Have you ever actually stood out there by the pond to see a real naked girl in the flesh? That is, other than for diagrams and medical charts, do you know what the body looks like to actually have these dreams of naked girls to begin with?"

He sighs deeply as he formulates his response.

"I will admit, just like with a lot of young boys, I suppose, I recall a few times when some of us would take a peek...you know, out of curiosity about the other side of things."

"All right, this is fine, and I think we can all admit to this at some moment. So then, these dreams are simply fantasizing about Kali, trying to pull together some…oh, what can we call it, speculation? About how she might look if she was naked."

"Maybe. But then, what about the rest of it?"

"The rest of it… Then, what was the rest of it?"

"Well, I was there studying her for a while, I think. It continued up until she apparently finished and left, and then I think I woke up from the dream."

"Interesting. So, you pay a visit to see her taking a shower, and go sightseeing instead."

"But this wasn't your typical shower, Suli. This is one of the strange parts."

"And what's so strange about it?"

"Remember when I told you the surrounding environment seems blurred for some reason, so it's hard to tell what's around her."

"Right, I remember this."

"When I first came in, I saw her standing under something that looked like a waterfall, maybe like what we have outside here."

"Hmm, so are we saying you're picturing her out in the pond, like the rest of us?"

"No, I don't think so. This seemed like it was indoors, a room of some kind, and I could see and hear other bodies moving around, so she wasn't alone. It seemed busy."

"An indoor waterfall," she muses. "That's a strange one. Busy… Are we saying busy like a group of us going out to the pond together, like Túfu and I sometimes do?"

"Maybe, but the impression I got was this seemed more like a wave of people getting off work or out of some activity, and then running off to the showers, like what we might see after an outdoor activity session."

"Oh, wait, I think I get it. Ankhia would tell me about this sometimes. This is when she was attending her old university. She and others would finish up their Phys. Ed. class and then run off to the showers to spruce up before going to their next lesson. Something like this?"

"Yeah, I think that's more like it. The trouble here is none of them were like us."

"Oh great, more aliens? But Petrith, this is already confusing. We never had this. With or without the aliens in the picture, we didn't even finish our junior school, to say nothing of a university, so we don't have any experience to give us any images or memories like this. Where did you get this idea?"

"I don't know," he shakes his head morosely.

"All right, but anyway, it sounds like she's still in something like an academy, or at least a learning institution, if I'm interpreting this right. What else?"

"Next, I saw her move out from the waterfall and grab something. It must've been on a shelf or something in the background. She began rubbing this around her body, and it seemed like she was lathering up, like from soap."

"Hang on a second," she snaps. "Soap? This is an object in her hand, and it behaved like soap…a solid form of soap? Petrith, we don't use that…we've never used that. In fact, I can't remember if anyone used that. I recall now where Túfu once mentioned something about this, wishing she knew how to make it, but no one even remembers the formula anymore. Where, in all the nether-space, did you get such an idea as this, then to see it in action in a dream with a girl you never saw naked before, washing up in an indoor waterfall after a Phys. Ed. session in some weird academy with a bunch of aliens?!" she screeches.

"Like I said, this is what I'm trying to figure out, and why I'm so distracted right now."

"I'm going to lose my horns after this one. Is there anything else you can say about it?"

"I recall she washed up thoroughly, stepped under the waterfall again to rinse off, and then I followed her when she apparently walked over to a rack with a white towel, then started drying herself off."

"An indoor waterfall shower, a solid bar of soap, and a white towel hanging on a rack… What next? Did you watch her get dressed in that uniform of hers again?"

"Actually, yes. She walked somewhere. It seemed to lead out of the shower area into another room. I saw her reach into what I think might be a cabinet…or maybe a locker, then pull out some new clothes and get dressed."

"A locker…just like what we might find in a university, or maybe this academy setting, and probably relating to a Phys. Ed. class. This still seems to correlate with what you said about her in some kind of training. All right, so you still see her in a school, and this time following one of those sessions. Petrith, forget what I said about you seeing naked girls, you're starting to worry me for these crazy dreams of yours."

"Me too…"

✦✦✦✦✦

It was approaching midday in Bya'an Tamoranth. The sun was shining, and the air was perfumed by the sweet fragrances of a mid-spring day. The students in the guildhall were just coming out of their morning classes and getting ready for the lunch break. Relissa, Marelle, Haran, and Kaliya all joined together in the cafeteria. It was becoming a habit for them to share this time together to talk about their classes and general gossip from around the compound. The activity of the guildhall was relaxed and well-rehearsed.

The guards who stood watch just outside the front gate held their patient ceremonial stance as a proud reminder of the fortitude of the Order. Then, some distance away, in the center of a large circular driveway in front of the gate, a brilliant column of light descends from high above.

The guards draw their attention to the sudden event, bringing an instant mention of disquiet to their minds on this otherwise peaceful day. The shaft sparkled with wispy streaks, and within this spectacle was the form of a woman being whisked to the ground from places unknown, settling gently as the column faded and disappeared.

She wore a dark blue robe and carried what looked like a travel bag. She paused to glance around the local surroundings, taking in the alien sights, peering up into the clear blue sky, and then over at the midday sun.

"Stellar radiance," she mumbles privately. "So warm and welcoming. We do not have this back home, not for the mirrored landscape of Bitopia."

She returns around to examine the gates and steps forward.

The guards were informed days before of the potential arrival of Aelwyn. They stood at attention and watched this newcomer as she made her way up to the front gate. She stopped just in front, looking at each guard and offering a pleasant smile. She hesitates a moment before speaking, fighting with herself for what approach she might use here.

"Such a curious sensation this is," she mutters distantly.

The nearest guard speaks up to address her.

"Good day to you, fair lady. Might you be the fair Cardinal Aelwyn from the guild up in Sigil?"

"You are already aware of me?"

"Our Lord informed us that you would be making a visit. And your divine column tends to stand out a bit."

"Indeed," she smiles. "But allow me to ask you this. When you see such a thing, how does it affect you to realize such a being as I may be arriving? You are a mortal, and I have very little experience with those from the Primes."

"Maybe so, but we see our Lord Thaelyn use this from time to time, and though it may not be every day, it is common enough to realize what it represents by now. It simply means we have a special visitor coming to us, and we are most honored for the occasion. Indeed, it would be a fine treat to see this more often."

"Really!" she pauses to glance around the city. "This represents my first time visiting this world. Thaelyn has told me much about it, but I would never have imagined people who are still as young as you might hold such comfort with one such as I."

"Perhaps, but the Lord and Lady are both Celestials, let us not forget that. And we might even go so far as to say the city of Sigil could be just as easily described as a dear neighbor, even if we do not make such close association."

"Very well, so be it. It would seem your society has made some important cultural advances, and this might mark you as an exception to the more common rules we tend to follow. But now to my intended purpose. Would Thaelyn be available, or perhaps Aerlie?"

"His Lordship isn't in the city at the moment, but the Lady should be found over yon in the temple," he directs down the hill and along the road. "I could fetch someone to assist you, if you like."

"Yes, please."

The guard turns around and calls through the gate for a page to step forward. A moment later, and a young man rushes outside to meet with the visitor.

"Aye, ma'am," he announces. "What can I do for you?"

Aelwyn studies the pert appearance and eager posture of the young man standing in front of her.

"I am originally seeking my spirit-brother, Thaelyn. But if he is currently too busy, then perhaps Aerlie would be available. Can we investigate?"

"Aye, ma'am, not a problem. The Lady would be in the temple down the road if you'll follow me briefly."

Aelwyn nods, and they stroll down the avenue towards the temple. As they arrive at the door, he opens it to let her through, and then follows after. Once inside, she studies the opulent architecture.

"This is a very lovely building," she muses.

"Aye, it's one of the city's cultural marvels."

"The two of them must have been very busy in this time."

The temple was again mostly empty during this hour of the day. Many of the priests were busy with other duties, or taking their lunch. Aerlie was just finishing up some chores in her office when she sensed a familiar presence approaching. She comes out of her office to meet her caller.

"Aelwyn! It's been so long."

"Aerlie, I have missed you. Why do you not come to visit?"

"I'm sorry Aelwyn, but my duties keep me very busy here. Just as with Thaelyn and all he has on his mind."

"Still, perhaps you could take a brief moment for the sake of old memories."

"I know, and you're right, I should. But some of those old memories still seem a little strange to me, as if I shouldn't be trying to recall them. But for you, I will try. Or perhaps we might finally convince you to stay with us?" she grins optimistically.

"I cannot be sure who is the more imposing between the two of you. However, since I am here and may be staying for a time, I will examine the potential of it."

"Eh, excuse me," the page interrupts gently. "But will the Lady or the good woman here require me for anything further?"

"Oh, we should be fine, thank you," Aerlie responds. "I will take it from here."

The page offers a bow and leaves the two women to recall old memories and discuss the current situation of the war and Kaliya's gift.

They travel back to the guildhall, and the stairs leading up to the palace above, where Aerlie offers Aelwyn the use of one of the guest rooms. They then go back down to the guildhall for a quick tour before she takes them outside to the portal gate. There, they pass through to Firstfall and proceed to the tactical office.

Thaelyn was in a meeting with Tristeen at the time they arrived, discussing a few details about the reconstruction effort in Rolsklinde. As the two women entered, Tristeen made her usual bow to Aerlie, and then turned to see Aelwyn. The most prominent features she noticed were the golden eyes. She turned to examine Thaelyn for comparison, and then back to their newest visitor.

"Spirit-brother," Aelwyn begins. "You have accomplished much in your time here in the Primes. And further, it would seem you have expanded your realm to this world, as well. I think even the Powers would be impressed."

"I would ask them to reserve their judgment until after I have finished this war. If we are successful, they will have a great deal more to impress them. Welcome, Aelwyn, though I wish the circumstances were more pleasant."

"Even with such circumstances, I think my visit here will be an enlightening one."

"Allow me to introduce a few of my officers and political dignitaries," he proposes as he directs his attention to the others in the room. "This would be General Gabarleine, chief in command of our armies currently fighting the war in this world."

The General bows politely as the introduction is made.

"It is my greatest pleasure to make this special occasion, dear Cardinal," he offers. "I trust your stay with us will be an enjoyable one."

"I thank you, General," she replies. "Such a noble gentleman, I wish we had a few like you up in Sigil."

"Aelwyn!" Aerlie chides teasingly. "I thought you had a beau already."

"I do, but he spends so much of his time in the study halls and libraries of his Father, and I in the Sensorium, that we tend to lose ourselves to our work. However, he does promise to make his occasional visits, and during those times we do enjoy our special moments."

"Has he made any proposals yet?"

"He has proposed to make a proposal, in his quaint manner of speech. I am simply waiting for him to find the right moment."

"You need to tell him to hurry up. Neither of you are getting any younger."

"This is true, but then neither are we getting any older," she grins.

"Now there's a statement, if ever I heard one," Tristeen chuckles quietly.

Thaelyn moves to the next in line for his introductions.

"Over here, we have Lieutenant Lapäli, our Daanen'kai intermediary who helps us coordinate our affairs with his people."

"A pleasant greeting to you, Lieutenant," she offers. "Powers behold, and I thought Kaliya was tall."

"Yes, we tend to develop this way," he smiles.

"And finally," Thaelyn continues. "We have a very gifted young lady who has recently joined my advisory council, Tristeen Macaid."

Aelwyn looks into the eyes of the young woman, and took notice of her intent stare. She offers a peaceful smile as she prepares her greeting.

"I am very pleased to meet you, and especially if you have so impressed my dear spirit-brother."

Tristeen feels a gush of warmth roll over her. The sensation was mildly surprising, and she felt almost as if she could fall over backwards. She teeters before catching herself, bringing her eyes back up to meet with Aelwyn.

"Indeed, I am also very pleased to meet you. And I think I am equally impressed that you seem to have abilities in some ways similar to our Lord here. If I may, by looking at your eyes, and then his, are you another of the same people?"

"That I am. I am Aasimar, the same as he, though my gifts may vary from his somewhat as we have different specialties."

"Perhaps a time may come when I can learn a little bit more about this."

Aerlie watched and examined Aelwyn for her unusual manners. She knew of the woman's introverted nature, but this occasion seemed different.

"Aelwyn, you seem rather perky today," she mentions. "Is there something special going on?"

"Not precisely. Perhaps I still feel a somewhat uplifted sensation from Thaelyn's last visit and those students he had with him. If this is indicative of the cultural manner to be found here, I would wish to explore it. Maybe it could help me find a new perspective for myself."

"I heard about that, and from that group especially," she giggles. "Well, you are certainly welcome to stay, if it makes you feel so refreshed."

"Perhaps, but for now I feel I must inquire of my new student. I have been spending some time in deep thought on how I might proceed on this. It is a rather curious circumstance."

"Oh?" Thaelyn wonders. "And how do you think you would proceed, in this case?"

"I would first like to recreate the situation that caused her to discover this talent, and then continue from there to refine it. If this was accidental, we must first learn to control it in a predictable manner. Once we have this, we can move forward and test her limits, there to discover any new elements not previously understood."

"This seems like a fair beginning." Thaelyn admits as he pulls out his timepiece. "At this moment in time, they would be finishing the midday meal, and she will be entering her afternoon classes. We should allow her to finish her schedule for the day and catch her afterwards. Although on this day, we have a special meeting scheduled with Archivist Windsong. Perhaps you would wish to join us, as the subject matter might prove interesting."

"Archivist Windsong…her again," she reflects on the name once mentioned in Sigil.

"Aelwyn," Aerlie begins. "You might recall her from our wedding. She and some others were reciting Adalon's lines when Tyr showed up."

"Yes, this was mentioned during our earlier review. She was young then. And now she works as a historian, how nice."

"She came to us recently," Thaelyn adds. "And she requested a special conference to review some of her latest findings."

"Findings? Is this to say she may have actually deciphered some part of those impossible scribblings by now?" she smiles tenderly.

"Well, this is certainly a curious moment to investigate," he grins.

"Naturally. Well, I would be just as curious to listen, if you do not mind."

"I think it might be a good idea, especially if you are to participate in our studies. She seemed particularly agitated the last time we met, which was just before my journey to Sigil. Apparently, Adalon knew of the prison portal up there."

"What?!" she retorts sharply.

Aelwyn's sudden reaction sent out a jolt of disbelief slamming against those in the room, causing each of them to wince and recoil reflexively.

"Wow," Tristeen giggles. "Yeah, she's one of them, all right. A strong one, too!"

Aelwyn realized almost immediately what she had done, and quickly tried to cover for herself.

"My apologies, please," she ducks her head. "My passions tend to be very potent, and as an empath, they can sometimes escape from me and affect those around me."

"It's quite all right. You're a Celestial, so I'm sure you have all sorts of curious little quirks."

"Little quirks..." she muses intriguingly. "Such an interesting way to describe it. You must know of Relissa and Marelle."

"Actually, I do, we're good friends."

"All right, so be it," she shrugs. "I guess they were right after all. I simply need to stiffen up and accept who I am, as it would seem the rest of you are already there," she shakes her head mildly. "What have you created here?" she glances at Thaelyn and Aerlie. "But anyway, how could Adalon know of this if it is such a closely guarded secret even to the Great Powers?"

"This is a very good question, Aelwyn," Thaelyn admits. "But unless we simply say she peeked in on something using her Sight, I doubt she would let us in on it."

+·+·◆·+·+

"Cadet Nazég," calls the training sergeant. "His Lordship has summoned you to the office in the war camp. Go hit the showers and meet with him promptly."

"Yes Sergeant," she replies, standing at attention as the class is dismissed.

The end of Kaliya's school day has come, and she has just been released from her combat training session. A message came in earlier from Thaelyn that she is to meet with him as part of the conference with the Archivist and other officers.

She gives a salute to the Sergeant and leaves the training hall, then hurries to her dorm room to pick up a change of clothes and a small bag with her bathing kit. She next runs to the guildhall baths to take a quick shower.

The baths were housed in a large building in the rear quarter of the guildhall complex. On entry, one turns down a corridor leading into a changing room with lockers lining the wall. They choose a free locker to store their change of clothes, and any other personal effects. Then they remove their old clothes and drop them into a hamper.

Each member's uniform is required to have a tag stitched inside with the member's name and dorm room number on it. An attendant comes by periodically to pick up the hamper and bring the soiled garments to the laundry room, where they are cleaned and delivered back to the dorm room.

Kaliya takes a locker and stuffs her new clothes inside, then disrobes and drops her training uniform into the bin. She takes her bathing kit from the bag, which acts like a carrying purse, grabs a towel from a handler in the room and heads out into the large bathing lounge.

The lounge was decorated as a pleasant social gathering area, with several small pools, planter boxes with a variety of leafy plants, and benches. The primary feature was an enclosed shower facility with a granite tiled waterfall shower. Underneath the waterfall was an alcove with shelving where bathers could set their soap and shampoo from their bathing kits while they wash. There was also an arrangement of racks set into a closet space behind a curtain where they could leave their towel.

Kaliya stores her towel and sets her bathing kit on a shelf, then goes and soaks herself under the waterfall. The water was maintained at a comfortably warm temperature as it welled up from a downstairs furnace room. She then retrieves her soap to lather up, rinses in the waterfall again, grabs her shampoo to wash her hair, followed by yet another rinse, and finally packs up her bathing kit.

She was rushing through the process today, as she was in a

hurry to meet with her summons. She grabs her towel to dry off, picks up her kit and returns to the locker room for her change of clothing. Once she has herself reassembled, she slings her bag over her shoulder and rushes out to the local gateway to make her meeting with Thaelyn.

On her arrival in the tactical office in Firstfall, she notices the usual officers, but this time with the inclusion of her brother, Kailen, and Ankhia, the Daanen'kai chief medical technician.

Thaelyn and Aerlie sat on one side of the table, along with Aelwyn and the General, while the Daanen'kai members, including Padriyl, all sat on the other side. Vonafel was sitting at the end to give her presentation.

"Kaliya," Thaelyn ushers. "Good to see you. Take a seat with us."

She slides into a chair next to Kailen as the meeting is brought to order.

"Very good," Vonafel announces. "Now that we're all here, I would wish to bring us up to date on a few details I've been collecting over these past several months."

"Of course, Archivist," Thaelyn affirms. "Commander, it is my understanding that you and the Med-tech have become familiar with our language in recent times, correct?"

"Yes, we have," Kailen admits. "Ever since that moment when you informed the Lieutenant that you will need to work more closely with us for the coming military affairs, and also as a result of Lady Aerlie and Ankhia working on those people from the city up north, we realized together how important it was for us to try to find space in your language classes. Fortunately, we finished those just recently, so we are ready for whatever you have in mind."

"Most excellent, this should make our future interactions much easier."

"My Lord," Vonafel begins. "As you know, I've spent most of my life studying Adalon's prophecies. I know I'm not the first, as others have come before me and didn't make any more progress as I could possibly claim, but in more recent times, I am coming to a few very curious and serious conclusions."

"How so on this occasion?"

"As we close in on the end of Book Two, which represents the last work she ever produced, at least to my knowledge, we have deciphered enough of her writings by now to begin making a few associations within the coming quatrains. Not that this really helps us to understand what she's saying, as most of it still involves metaphors and other obscure references, but for those pieces we are sure of, it's starting to paint a very strange picture."

"I recall this from so many long years ago. I believe it was actually during our wedding, Aerlie and I," he glances briskly at his wife, "when you suggested many of these references used clues representing personal knowledge that likely belongs to someone, perhaps a select few, where Adalon is one example, but the others may be unknowable until some specific moment in time when we are destined to discover them."

"Right, I remember that moment, and wow, what a moment," she chuckles. "Adalon has traditionally hidden her meaning behind a veil of these mysterious phrases and metaphors, and our scholars have always been mystified as a result. But I'm coming to the opinion of why, and it's not that she is simply trying to interpret some strange and unfathomable visions into words she can't quite realize. Rather, she's hiding something intentionally."

"That is a rather bold suggestion, Vonafel. What brings you to this conclusion?"

"During these last few months, I've been asking questions, and I also had a few of my assistants acting as, um, spies," she grins bashfully. "I also went out myself, on a few occasions, like that meeting I had with Kaliya in the guildhall cafeteria. We are in the last chapter of Book Two, and this is what I sometimes call the end times. I can't be sure why, but it just feels like an end time, when I reflect on everything else leading us up to this point."

"May I ask a question," Kailen submits. "What is it about this book that is creating so much anxiety in the first place? I'm not as familiar with this so far."

"Right, of course, with you being new here. She is known as

Adalon the Silver, and she holds a long-standing history of prophetic visions. But, unlike others we've seen come and go in our history, this one is different. Her visions seem very specifically oriented towards the life and times of the Lord and Lady, and no one else. It is like she is writing a chronical of their lives before those lives actually occur. This includes who they are, where they come from, things they do during the course of their lifetimes, special events they might be involved in, and so on. It's not as much a series of prophecies as it is a story being told."

"This is very interesting, but why would she be so carefully focused on them?"

"This is one of the mysteries we were never really able to fully understand, except to say our world was engineered by one of the Estelar we call Maker Kuroku. We think she has played a role on at least a few occasions to direct some of these events."

"Engineered?" he winces.

"Tae'Eladar was revitalized from a dead world in an ancient ice age to where it is now, then seeded with life, including all the flora and fauna, plus the human population. The ones who did this are a mysterious race known only as the Sarrukh. We found evidence of their passing in a large time capsule that contained some of their technology and documentation explaining what they did. Then we have a few statements from Adalon herself at one time confirming that Thaelyn and Aerlie are no accident to be among us. We think the Maker put them there intentionally."

"Great cu'Nar! That's enough to twist a few horns, right there."

"Yeah, and it certainly does open a few eyes for what might be coming ahead. And I think it's becoming clear to me now, at least within reason. There have been many references to occasions in our history where one or the other was fated to perform this or that, but I think it is not a simple element of Fate. We are all being directed, in one form or another. Maybe it's intentional or maybe it's incidental, but it's still there."

The gathering all exchanged glances as she prepared to continue.

"For instance, Thaelyn tells us that before he even decided to come to Tae'Eladar, he was confronted by Adalon up in Mount Celestia, and she apparently dropped the suggestion in his lap to come down here to see if he could essentially straighten us out for all the trouble we were causing."

"Trouble?" Ankhia wonders. "What kind of trouble would you be involved with?" she smiles cautiously.

"Our world, at that time, was composed of many nations, some friendly, others not. He came to us and began preaching his philosophies and doctrines as a means of describing a better way of life. Many people saw him as a saint, a messiah, a holy leader with a revolutionary new way of life that could lift us up from our darkness and into a new Age. And they were right. They flocked to his side, forming up a kind of following of disciples. But in his case, him being as much a soldier as a teacher, these disciples became a new order of knights, and from there they spread out to cover our world, uniting all our people together."

"Sounds wonderful, actually. It reminds me of something I learned once in an old history lecture back in my university days."

"However, by his statements over the years, he came to us NOT to be our king, simply to give us a few pointers and let us go from there. He did not even choose to employ his Celestial powers as much, but instead tried to appeal to the people through logic and wisdom, not brute force. Adalon, on the other hand, apparently had other ideas."

"What ideas?"

"After some period of time, she entered the picture. Our history tells us she made contact with Thaelyn and enticed him to join forces together. She revealed to him that he held a larger purpose than to simply teach a few curious lessons about proper manners and conduct. He was…in fact…supposed to lead us."

"In fact?" she winces. "So, if she was the one who suggested this in the first place, up there in Mount Celestia, is this to say she had ulterior motives of some kind?"

"Likely so, as this reflects on Maker Kuroku again, and Adalon is probably an agent of some kind. Our interpretation, after all is said and done, was to entice him voluntarily, where his enthusiasm would carry him, rather than as a work assignment, where it's just one day after another of doing…something."

"Uh huh, the drudgery of work, as opposed to the thrill of achievement. Yes, I can certainly see this much."

"Adalon then provided a considerable amount of wealth into this to get things started. She also contributed her wisdom and guidance along the way, offering her part to suggest new ways to develop us as a society. And then she has these prophecies that seem to suggest there is more waiting ahead of us. Finally, I recall once a mention where she admitted to us, or maybe to him," she points at Thaelyn, "which was later recorded by one of our scribes, that her kind tends to go where they are either needed or maybe assigned by their Maker."

"THEIR Maker? Is this to say this Maker is some sort of governor over their kind?"

"She would be a goddess, a member of the Estelar, and it is said she created their kind."

"Oh dear."

"But like Adalon and her kind, this Maker is also said to be extremely elusive. So, most of what they do is a mystery to people like us."

"That certainly sounds like it could be frustrating."

"Now, as for Adalon, I'm developing the opinion that these prophecies are not simply visions, but statements. She knows what's going on, but she's not revealing it to us in a manner that we can easily follow. My opinion is that like with the Estelar, and for this point, Maker Kuroku, and who knows what else, we're not intended to know everything, but instead need to figure it out for ourselves as part of a learning and discovery process."

Thaelyn listened and began to reflect on some of his old experiences, and then a memory resurfaced.

"To follow our path as it is presented to us. This is what he meant."

"My Lord?"

"Once upon a time, Vonafel… Recall Aerlie and her people,

and those dragons that were bothering them. One was a Blue, and I took him myself. Just before the final blow was dealt, he and I shared a few last words. He asked me what I had accomplished in our world during my progression to take over. He was surprised to see a Celestial parading about, and he hinted that 'she', where I suppose he was referring to the Maker, does not always reveal her ways. Then, he said I have a purpose, and I must follow my course as it is presented to me."

"Spoken just like the Powers themselves," Aerlie muses. "At least they follow the Measure of Balance. And by the sound of it, rather strictly."

"Indeed! Although in his case, this is where he regretted his mistake where your people were concerned."

"Then, my Lord," Vonafel continues. "I think your Fate, if we are to use that word, is being directed, and SHE is the one directing it, using Adalon as an agent of some kind. And this follows nicely with these other suggestions. But now, we are entering into a new phase."

"Very interesting, please continue."

"Throughout our history, Adalon has unveiled one after another curious event in our world that only came into view when that precise moment called for it. For instance, Aerlie and her gift of the Elixir of Visions. She didn't even know she had it until AFTER she was asking about her course schedule at the academy, and Adalon came out to suggest where to find her answer."

"Right, I remember this," Aerlie recalls. "My grandfather was an alchemist, and he had some strange old book he barely ever looked at hidden away in his library, calling for ingredients that were previously unfamiliar to us until that day actually came around."

"That sounds creepy," Ankhia winces.

"Worse, Ankhia," Kaliya adds. "One of those is an alien plant that shouldn't even be there."

"Now, here we are in these end times," Vonafel continues. "And I think everything has been leading up to this last chapter…where neither of them is mentioned at all. Well, mostly…there is one mention, but that's it."

"Vonafel," Thaelyn wonders. "What do you mean? Adalon is no longer writing about us? What does she write about now?"

"People we never knew of, until now," she glances at Kaliya, Kailen, Ankhia, and Padriyl. "As well as references to what I can only describe to be this Primordial and his servant."

"Dear Powers, what is it she actually knows about this? Can you give us some examples?"

"I'll bring us up to date on what we have so far. The chapter begins like this..."

Vonafel pulls out her personal copy of the prophecy book, along with a notebook for reference. She opens it to the chapter page and clears her throat to begin reciting the verses.

"Alone in the dark, they lie in wait, Forgotten and Ignored; two Ancient Ones, from times unmeasured, and a life they once adored."

"The Primordials, it must be. I know the seraphim, among others, might use that term, Ancient Ones, to refer to the Primordials."

"Good. And when recalling my discussion with Kaliya, we might say two individuals, one who is simply forgotten and the other ignored, maybe to say he wasn't much to speak of to begin with."

"Do we know which is which, in this case?"

"Kaliya and I managed to decipher this part, we think, at least within reason. The Forgotten One is mentioned multiple times here, and we already know Darumon is the most active member. So, if he is the Forgotten One, it could be he wasn't worth remembering to begin with. After all, he's a servant, not the main character, and he seems to like to play his role in the background."

"Absolutely, therefore, we would not normally know of him, and thus he might be forgotten."

"We could also say we didn't remember him at all during our journey," Kaliya states. "Only Father even recalled the name, and just barely."

"This is true, and thus another potential for the reference."

"As for Sargeras," Vonafel adds. "We decided if he is in a barren fold, he is without his power source."

"Of course," Aerlie considers. "Therefore, he might be of no concern in that place."

"Yes, this makes sense," Thaelyn nods.

Vonafel continues, "Next is this: The Master sleeps, his servant toils, a plan he does unfold; resurge of hate, avenge of spite, a terror vaguely told."

"Darumon, yes, this would be our answer. And this would then reflect on his work to make a return."

"A terror vaguely told?" Aerlie muses. "This sounds like it is done mostly in secret."

"And this would follow nicely for his observed manners."

"So far," Vonafel resumes. "These make sense, as they appear to have already come true for us. We now know of Sargeras and Darumon, and we've seen them make this return, or at least partially. Now, the following quatrains lead us along a progression of some sort, which I believe is a story of what they're doing, but some references still seem obscure. Listen to this one."

She brings her attention to another line in her book.

"From virgin soil, a nascent breed, the Forgotten One will spur; a spark of whim, a sudden rise, where emergent minds occur. I'm not quite sure how to interpret this one. Does anyone have any suggestions?"

"I do," Aelwyn answers. "This sounds as if that cretin is creating a new form of life to serve him. The Primordials were known for this, and it would not surprise me to see him do it again."

"All right, then this might lead us to the next one. The Forgotten One, long in slumber, seeks to take his prize; a race of Children, slowly grown, shall lead to his demise."

"Really!" she giggles, and spreads her glee across the table. "How very unfortunate, his creations turn on him this time, but I wonder who they were and where they are now."

"This would make for a rather interesting discovery," Thaelyn admits. "If we should have such an occasion to meet them, they might provide us with some curious input."

"I wonder if this relates to that ship of theirs in any way. Perhaps they were the ones who built it? This might then explain who is watching."

"Maybe," he nods.

"Well, so far so good, I suppose," Vonafel affirms. "Like I said, it reads like a book telling a story of someone's lives. It's just not ours anymore."

"But this does bring to mind how and why she is so focused on this new subject matter."

"Oh, it gets better. Listen to this."

She moves to the next page and begins again.

"Higher minds are quick to fall, to intrigue and delight; the lesser-sung shall keep his aim, and others call to flight. Anyone?" she looks around.

"That one is not as easily apparent, thus far," Aelwyn considers. "It would likely require some of this precise input you mentioned earlier."

"But it sounds as though a higher body made an error of some sort," Thaelyn muses. "And then a younger, or lesser privileged member, held a stronger sense of purpose, but it involved leading others into a retreat."

"Cu'Nar's Eyes," Kailen shudders. "Velen…"

Thaelyn and the others all perked up at the mention.

"Commander," he asks urgently. "Do you have something?"

"These lines are indeed very confusing, but this reflects a little on my father. His scientific faction within our old Elder Council on Azgarén was an under-sung division. Many regarded it as an illegitimate form of study, as compared to the more established empirical devotions. But he held firm that it carried a positive merit and pushed for representation within the Council."

"A governing Council based on representative scientific factions?" Aelwyn mentions.

"Yes, Aelwyn," Thaelyn interjects. "I suspect theirs was a curious form of technocracy."

"How interesting, this is not something you see every day. What was his devotion?"

"His faction," Kailen responds, "focused largely on metaphysics and parapsychology, among others."

"Metaphysics?" she gazes at Kaliya. "Are you two related, perhaps?"

"Yeah," she admits. "He's my brother."

"Ah, very nice. And I recall from our discussion in Sigil that your people regard anything outside of the classic empirical studies as a form of..." she grins impishly, "...mysticism. Commander, I can understand your perspective, but let us also consider you come from a barren fold where this is not generally available for you to study. And so, your father is the one who was contacted by these Positive Primes. Therefore, whoever controls them, and also gave you that ship, must be involved with these Primordials from an earlier moment, I suspect."

"But Aelwyn," Aerlie wonders openly. "What are we actually saying here? How does this relate to those previous statements?"

Thaelyn, Aelwyn, and the others all glared at her for the suggestion, then slowly to turn their attention towards the Daanen'kai members.

"Powers help us," Aelwyn wheezes. "Are THESE the people?"

"Huh?" Kaliya retorts brashly. "You can't possibly mean us?!"

"He is on your world right now," Thaelyn ushers. "Is he not?"

"Dammit!" she shouts.

"Can this also explain the discrepancy of their strange evolution?" Aelwyn asks. "An alien influence, perhaps?"

"Perhaps, but then we must ask how and why," Thaelyn notes. "Extreme longevity, the Prodigy Gift... Why would he do this?"

"An anomaly, perhaps. He would certainly not desire this intentionally, would he?"

"Wait, I recall a mention. It was a recording Leesa made one time of the Governor in his office. Overseers, not underlings, this is what he said. The Primordials loved their position of power over other things. So, no, they would not likely desire to engineer something like this intentionally."

"Then he must have used a peculiar method, and this simply came as a result," she pauses to consider this. "They claim this anomalous event in their history… Perhaps…if he is in a barren fold, he would not have access to the dynamistic flows to assist him. But then, how else might he do this…unless…oh dear Powers, he would not do that, would he?"

"What?" Kaliya urges nervously.

"Yeah, what are you people talking about?" Kailen adds.

"And further…yes, I see it now," Aelwyn shudders, and feelings of revulsion wash across the table to splash across the other members. "And here it is in this prophecy, which at this point is much more like a statement. This would explain why you hold Celestial qualities in you now, Kaliya. This is your half-god side. I am so sorry."

"Oh no," she moans. "If you're saying what I think you're saying."

"Kaliya, or someone…" Kailen urges. "What do you mean?"

Kaliya holds up a hand to pause the conversation as she takes a deep breath to collect herself.

"Kailen, Ankhia, Padriyl, you're not going to like this, but if she's right, we have our answer for a number of things all at once. And it won't be nice, so grab your horns now while you still have them."

"Such quaint expressions," Aelwyn muses softly.

"Kailen, we had this long debate up there in Sigil about how our story of life doesn't play out logically. Our extreme longevity simply doesn't give us enough time to develop like we apparently did. Not enough generations passing under the bridge, especially for the Prodigy Gift, which according to her, unless we had some really nether-wild form of evolution, shouldn't exist in us for maybe a billion years or more than what we have now. And our history, at least what I think I know of it, doesn't even seem to show how we made any kind of evolution to earn our longevity."

"And furthermore, Commander," Thaelyn offers. "Let us also consider what Aerlie once said. You still possess too much of your herbivorous physiology to qualify as a species that might try taking over your world by natural means."

"But just a moment," Ankhia argues. "As someone who is studied in biology, at least what we have on our world, I can tell you that our history tells us of fossil records involving the use of tools. This is how our early ancestors first rose up from that herbivore to become a dominant species."

"Very well, Ankhia," Aerlie replies. "But let us ask ourselves, who were you fighting with these tools? If your only concern was the grass under your feet, or the leaves of trees, why do you need tools for that?"

"Well, it was to, um…hunt other animals?" she retorts cautiously.

"Ankhia, if your ancestors were herbivores, those other animals were more likely hunting you. What purpose does it serve to hunt meat if you do not eat meat?"

"Oh wonderful. But our ancestors…" she hesitates. "Well, they supposedly turned to eat meat. Couldn't that afford us an excuse?"

"It could, but then we need to consider the timing. How long does it take for a species to convert from an herbivore to a carnivore, or at least an omnivore? You said it was only half a million years before the first vestiges of civilization, but evolution doesn't work that fast. First you need to make the physiological conversion, which might need to go through a scavenger stage simply to develop a taste for meat."

"A scavenger stage…all right."

"But even this does not give our answer immediately, as you still need to develop the means and the ambition to hunt, and this has to begin with natural tools, not artificial ones. We are speaking of tooth and nail…and only later to develop hunting parties in a coordinated social environment where you might find opportunity to develop thinking minds capable of inventing tools."

"There's also the motivation to actually CHASE things," Kaliya offers. "Which we certainly do NOT have, even now. Not even if our lives depend on it."

"Wonderful," Ankhia moans. "Thank you, Kaliya."

Aerlie continues, "And the period you mention simply does not give us adequate time for all this, especially if we factor in your longevity and how long you might have held this quality, to say nothing of the fact that even in your modern day, just as Kaliya said, you do not represent a vicious predator species. Not physically or mentally."

"I would also wish to add something," Aelwyn offers. "If your history suggests such a short period of development, there must be an error in this. What is the actual cause of this alleged rapid evolution?"

"It was described as a radical environmental event," Ankhia responds. "It was said to have forced our ancestors, which we call Eracyodines, to make this sudden shift, a kind of do-or-die push to survive. The story is delightful, and it often gives us a sense of prestige that our species holds such a strong motivation. But now I'm feeling very weak."

"Let us not despair, as this transition, whatever the means, has clearly given you a few well-pronounced gifts already. But in actuality, any sudden shift would more likely cause you to go extinct rather than push to survive. As I was explaining to Kaliya, many species, both plant and animal, may specialize after a while for certain specific environments. Change this by any, as you say, radical degree, and suddenly you create a calamity where species die off due to the lack of favorable conditions to survive in. As one species dies, those that are dependent on it also fail. And as we travel up the ladder, yours ought not to exist at all by now if this is the case. For this point, I would wish to examine how you came to this conclusion that you had any sort of event at all, or if the entire notion was perhaps fabricated."

"Fabricated?"

"Yes, as I believe you were altered. We generally agreed, up in Sigil, there must have been an external factor involved to mutate you into a new form. Your longevity, your painfully slow growth rate, and the extreme margins of time that you can reproduce…did your species ever modify itself to achieve these numbers, or is this natural for you?"

"Um…longevity, maturing to adulthood, reproduction…I don't recall anything in my medical history about us modifying ourselves to gain these numbers. So, as far as I know, it's always been like this, at least for the recorded history I'm aware of."

"All right, but these numbers are well outside anything I have ever seen with a classic mammaloid-class mortal society. We might not see this until we enter into the Celestial societies, and whatever they achieved. But if you are taking so long with your lifespans, like Kaliya said, you would need several orders of magnitude of time to reach this, especially if we consider this projection gift of yours. That one is truly…godlike…and you would need help for it, at this point."

"Help…?" she wheezes.

"An external factor… And here we have it. Vonafel, what was that line again? From virgin soil, a nascent breed…"

"Um, yeah," she perks up. "A nascent breed…the Forgotten One will spur; a spark of whim, a sudden rise, where emergent minds occur."

"This is the creation of a species by artificial means, whatever the method. And I hesitate to think what he might have done in this case if he did not have the dynamistic flows to assist him. However, one thought, as unpleasant as it may seem, CAN provide us with an answer on multiple counts."

"I don't know if I want to hear this," Ankhia moans. "But what is it?"

"His own seed…"

"Ew! All right, so how do you figure this?"

"Look no further than the three of us sitting here," she directs to herself, Thaelyn, and Aerlie. "We are hybrids between mortals and the Estelar, and we carry a number of qualities you will not find elsewhere, at least not outside the Celestial races. If he is such a potent creature, godlike by comparison with such as you, and if he contributed any part of his essence into modifying your species, these Eracyodines would make a virtually instantaneous alteration to a species capable of many things. This could account for your remarkable longevity, your ability to breed well into your late years, and perhaps also this gift, to say nothing of whatever else you might be capable of."

"Including telepathy?" Kaliya asks briskly.

"Easily, and perhaps more. This could also be exaggerated by your inbreeding as half-siblings since that time. But then, let us review that next one. Vonafel?"

"Yeah," she responds. "The Forgotten One, long in slumber, seeks to take his prize; a race of Children, slowly grown, shall lead to his demise."

"This surely relates to our unfortunate timing of events," Thaelyn muses distantly. "This is where he becomes active."

"Indeed," Aelwyn nods. "And slowly grown...with lifespans reaching a score of millennia. No wonder they are ONLY where they are now. He probably used this gift of longevity to manage them very carefully."

"Managing..." Thaelyn groans. "Oh yes, Aelwyn, we have seen that word pass under our noses a few times, just in this world."

"So, he arrives on Azgarén," Kaliya submits. "At least officially, at this point. Father gets the warning from the cu'Nar, and SOMEONE who is watching all this drops a massive, and probably very expensive colony ship in our laps. But who, at this point, if Adalon is talking about it?"

The group goes silent a moment in consideration, until the General pipes up.

"My money is with Maker Kuroku, if we say Adalon could be an agent here, perhaps also these cu'Nar...beings that should not otherwise be involved at all, but they are. A member of the Estelar could certainly do all this."

"And so," Aerlie offers tenderly. "Our Fate isn't the ONLY Fate in play here."

"But according to this statement," Aelwyn accedes. "These people will turn on him and he will lose control."

"You know," Kaliya relents. "Suddenly, I don't know what to think about all this. I expected to carry this fight back home, but now...this is a completely different picture."

"Vonafel," Thaelyn resumes. "What else can you offer us?"

"Wow, sure," she flusters. "Moving on, we have this next set, but I have no real idea who we're talking about here. I think Adalon is using some new metaphors that might involve private knowledge again."

"Oh great," Aerlie shakes her head. "Another of those? Well, what is it?"

"An imposter waits, with hatred glowing, and a visage weaving boldly…"

"Wait a minute," Kaliya mutters softly. "This sounds a little like that one you mentioned in the cafeteria. An imposter of some kind."

"Yeah, I think I did mention it briefly, but the references here are very obscure. I don't know who this imposter is, or who these others are that come after. Here, listen to the rest. He travels with the Exiled Ones, with eyes upon them coldly."

Kaliya and the other Daanen'kai members collectively draw in droning gasps and wheezes.

"Grace of the cu'Nar!" Kaliya whimpers.

"In all the nether-space!" Ankhia moans.

"That's impossible!" Kailen rants. "How could she know this?"

Vonafel pulled back from the table at the sudden display, while Thaelyn and Aerlie both glanced at each other. Aelwyn withdrew into her seat at the outburst of emotion, trying to contain her reflex reaction.

"Um," Vonafel mutters gently. "Then I guess we have our private knowledge somewhere?"

"Vonafel…" Kaliya blasts. "That's us! The name Daanen-Aryku, in our language, translates as the Exiled Ones."

"Dear gods above, then all this section must relate to your people."

"Can you go over that one again for me?" Kailen urges.

"Yeah. An imposter waits, with hatred glowing, and a visage weaving boldly; he travels with the Exiled Ones, with eyes upon them coldly."

"That sounds like a spy," Kaliya considers.

"Yes, Child," Aelwyn affirms solidly. "And this might offer us a few intriguing answers. For instance, from our earlier conversation of how he was following you, or perhaps pursuing you during this time."

"More like driving, by the sound of it, especially to Ruuki uy'Daan."

"We generally think he was accompanying us," Padriyl interjects. "We had a conversation on this once, that he must've been impersonating someone on at least a few occasions, like that wild jump, to say the least, and also in order to direct their military at us each time."

"Very well," Aelwyn nods. "This might offer us a form of confirmation to the fact. He was participating in order to follow you."

"So, he actually WAS sitting at the nav console," Kaliya huffs. "And since we know he's a shapeshifter, he could be almost anyone at this point."

"Yeah..." Padriyl moans. "And the whole chase was simply a game to him."

"I want to know who he was impersonating," Kailen scorns. "This simply twists my horns now. So many people killed along the way..."

"It would likely be someone familiar and respected," Thaelyn offers. "I doubt he would pose as a janitor or a kitchen cook. He would need access to the critical areas if he were driving you somewhere."

"Of course... That wild jump, for example, is an obvious one."

"And here we come again to an innate ability to fold space naturally, to accompany you, and then return home to direct the others, travelling to-and-fro as needed."

"Right, and this means, at the very least, he had to be present during our jumps."

"Correct, and if he knew about you departing Azgarén at all, he would surely hold contempt for your audacity to disobey his desires, unlike the rest of them. Your father was the only one who apparently held his focus of thought to take the warning of the cu'Nar and leave, while the rest of your Council fell to whatever offer he and Sargeras made."

"All right, I get it so far."

"From what I understand of it," Padriyl offers. "The arrival of that ship didn't go unnoticed in the least."

"And finally," Thaelyn resumes. "To arrive on Ruuki uy'Daan with your wild jump. Here we begin to come full circle."

Thaelyn now reaches behind him to a table where he locates an odd book with a silvery metallic binding tucked between some stacks of supplies and other books. He telekinetically draws it into his hand, much to the amusement of the Daanen-Aryku members, and returns to the table.

Aelwyn also followed his motions, pondering quietly how casually he used his Celestial power in front of the others with little or no reaction from those in attendance.

"Do you see this?" Thaelyn asserts as he brings it into view. "This was found in the Dean's possession in the academy up in Rolsklinde. It represents a detailed study of the flora and fauna of the Outer Planes. He once admitted to us it belongs to the Governor…meaning to say Darumon. Between this and that strange portal we discovered, the one used to draw away the local societies on their migration, and which also took us to the plane of Cynosure, we can say he must have visited our world as part of a study of his old enemies."

"And the delivery of that first batch of orcs to bother you," Kaliya adds.

"Indeed! A priming effort, no doubt. This also reminds me of something, however, and I have no viable explanation of the association here."

"What's that?"

"The portal we found had a number of markings on it in a strange language."

He reaches to the table behind him again, this time to retrieve his trans-com. He pulls up the folder for the image library to display the photos taken during their visit with the giants. He passes it around for review.

"These were taken as we examined the carvings," he explains. "The cave, at the time, was in the possession of a nomadic group of giants, but this was not theirs. Instead, this resembles the language we found in the ruins of the old Creator Race we call the Sarrukh."

"Huh?" Kaliya blurts. "How can that be possible? If we say they helped restore Tae'Eladar from that ice age, and then seed it with all of you…well, some of you…" she chuckles.

"I know. We generally believe it must be the Maker again if she is the one engineering Tae'Eladar. But this now represents a crossover of knowledge between factions I would not otherwise expect to be crossing over."

"Uh huh, and here's a cute new paradox for Aelwyn to chew on," she grins.

"Why thank you, Kaliya," Aelwyn emits satirically. "And would you like for me to give you a taste of how much I truly appreciate the gift?"

"Um, not today, thanks," she blushes.

They all share a quick laugh at the thought.

"Aelwyn," Aerlie reflects humorously. "Such an interesting play. I have never known you to actually ply your gift in a jest of any sort."

"I know! But then, I did not have people like these encouraging me in this way before."

"Perhaps you should reserve one or more of those sensory stones of yours before you finish here. You may have some additional sensations to record."

Thaelyn smiled at his longtime friend as she was clearly settling in with the local ambiance.

"My Lord," the General considers. "Could we be observing a relationship, at least superficially, if she also holds this ancestral knowledge of their kind all the way back to the beginning? This is to say, if she dates back that far, might there be some link to another society, also as old as this, which shared some part of this ancient wisdom, like maybe a predecessor society of beings?"

"This is a very curious mention, General," Thaelyn notes. "If the Sarrukh are so old that they might hold the knowledge and capacity to refurbish an entire world, this could potentially date back that far. Say, for instance, in the modern day, they could be on the scale of a Celestial race. They do apparently speak this language, so they must be a part of it. Then the Maker, like so many other Estelar, might also date back, and perhaps she came to know of them. This ancient race might also relate in some way to the Primordials, and perhaps, just like the Celestials have their common language, here we have another example. This could also explain the bilingual text we found in that time capsule. They left it behind as a kind of ancestral legacy."

"Yes! Very good, and this might now give us an explanation."

"But Thaelyn," Aerlie muses. "This would now suggest the Sarrukh came into contact with the Primordials somehow to learn of this. I wonder what relationship they held. Could they be a survivor race from that period?"

"It is certainly possible," he nods. "And so very fascinating to think of. I wonder what sort of stories they might have to offer by now."

"Grand ones, to be sure."

"Well, back to our subject matter. We have Darumon following along, likely playing a spy, and tracking their motions. This tends to reflect on my initial fears of him peering into our affairs during this time to pry our secrets away,"

"Yes, it does," Kailen nods. "It would also explain how they found us so many times, and without logical reasoning for all of our jumps."

"Yes. And then he drops you on Ruuki uy'Daan, perhaps leaving you for an extended period while he goes in search of his materials, and finally, at some moment, he brings you here to this world, which was serving as a type of collection point before he jumps off to his final goal."

"This is becoming stressful," Kaliya whispers to herself. "So many lives, no wonder Father is so beside himself. Nothing we ever did was our own. He was following us all the way, probably directing us, and the Suuden-Aryku right behind us. But why the long delays in between? It took eight millennia to reach Ruuki uy'Daan, and we had centuries of freedom to rebuild on each new world we passed, only to have them come in and lay waste to everything we created."

"I think I cannot give you a precise answer to that unless there is some external reason for it. Maybe he was distracted by something

outside your view. Or, perhaps, it is simply this game he was playing…
to give you time to grow before he comes along and hits you again."

"Great gods," the General murmurs. "He grants them the luxury
to build a society, then blasts it to oblivion."

"That would surely fit the profile of a Primordial," Aelwyn relents.

"Um, perhaps, but…" Aerlie pauses the topic. "Could he have
been busy with something in between all this. Distracted with
something? Well, building up a potent military would be one thing."

"Yes, it would!" Thaelyn nods. "Furthermore, to train and
condition them, or at the very least to refine the methods, perhaps
also these control devices he uses."

"This could take some time," the General affirms. "Perhaps then
to test the product as it progresses forward."

"Not a nice thing to think of…" Aerlie considers. "But it could
offer a direction to it."

"But then…" Kailen resumes. "Who is he? Or was he… I think
we need to try to understand this, at the very least, to see if he might
still be among us to continue his spying."

"This is true," Thaelyn admits. "Let us consider a few possibilities.
He would need to be someone who was travelling with you, and likely
a familiar face, as my understanding of your society is one that is
very closely knit by now, for all of your suffering."

"Right, we became very familiar with each other after a while."

"So, we must narrow our focus to one who might have travelled
with you for the full journey, at least as far as Ruuki uy'Daan. If we
suggest he has lost interest in you by now, largely because we know
Darumon has abandoned this world and everything on it, then he
may not be with you at present. Although I think I would wish to
take this very cautiously."

"I agree, but how do we protect ourselves against something
like this?"

"If you are marooned here, he should no longer care to follow you,
or maybe to say pursue you, as you can no longer move around. This
might offer an answer, perhaps if we also consider Ruuki uy'Daan and

the sabotage. Something occurred there that changed his manner of conduct. He was discarding you after that."

"I'm not sure if I like that term, but at this moment, I think I like it more than him still holding an interest in us."

"We seem to have a few curious pieces yet to uncover, but for now I think we should keep this very closely to ourselves. He could be anyone. Let us not reveal our knowledge in case he is still listening."

"Agreed."

"Vonafel?" Thaelyn directs. "Anything else?"

"Well," she sighs deeply. "If you don't mind indulging me a bit more…" she returns to her book. "Through chaos and dismay they flee, their vagrancy entails; across the shores of many lands, the harsh pursuit unveils."

"Dear cu'Nar," Kaliya whines. "She was following our movements. This must relate to that bit about the message."

"A message?" Kailen wonders.

"Kailen, wait, please. Let her continue. I'm sure it's coming somewhere."

Vonafel continues, "Upon a shore, they come to rest, the Forgotten One's entice; until a tender moment lends, a Child and its device."

"That's a curious one," Aerlie muses. "Are we now speaking of Ruuki uy'Daan, and that long time they spent there?"

"A tender moment…" Aelwyn puzzles. "A delicate occasion…a sensitive event of some sort. This is surely to involve something we are missing from some input yet to be discovered."

"And now I must ask myself," Thaelyn suggests. "Could this relate to that mention of Darumon's sudden shift of behavior on that world?"

"Maybe," Vonafel accedes. "This next one could hold a clue for us. Here I think we're getting close to our present moment. A final desperate scourge at play, the Forgotten One conspires; the Exiled Ones shall fall to earth, on shores of early mires."

"Here, Therinë," Thaelyn concludes. "Fall to earth, to crash… the sabotage. And he conspired with the Flame Elves, and also the orcs, to do the deed on Ruuki uy'Daan. And early mires, the siege here, or perhaps the migration he invoked, being these people here."

"His collection point," Kaliya muses. "Wonderful. I swear, this Adalon…"

"Sounds good to me so far," Vonafel admits. "Here's that set I mentioned to you, Kaliya. A tide of vulgar manners flow, from a place of unknown shores; the Son and Daughter travel fast, when the sound of battle roars."

"That must be the one that mentions us," Aerlie muses. "And this is the only one?"

"As far as I can tell, based on her strange wording. We've generally decided this has to do with the orcs and the war on our side. But now we have something strange. We're getting into a section that leaves gaps in the writings, like something is missing. I've long asked myself if this was a misprint, or if something was intentionally removed, or simply excluded, but still leaving a gap where it ought to be."

"That would not make much sense to me," Thaelyn wonders. "If it were intentional to be removed, one would think the publisher would simply close the gap. If it was a misprint, someone should have noticed and corrected it, again likely by closing the gap."

"Then something is wrong here, because I see several of these in the coming pages, and if there was supposed to be something there, it's gone now."

"Vonafel," Aerlie asks. "Is this only in the copies, or is it in the original book as well?"

"It's in all of them, the original plus all her authorized copies."

"Then this must be intentional. I doubt she would allow such an error to go uncorrected. This now makes me wonder something. Knowing her manners of hiding details, could it be some sort of hidden text we need to decode?"

"Dear gods, Aerlie, and how am I supposed to know how to decrypt something written by one such as her using whatever glyph or other sort of cloaking cypher she might use?"

"I honestly don't know, so maybe like everything else, it'll be revealed only at that special moment."

"This might make more sense to me," Thaelyn affirms. "Although it would be strange, even for her manners, to encrypt something like this, unless it holds details she did not want revealed under any circumstances until some specific moment."

"Well then, we need to know what that moment is. But I seriously doubt she'll actually tell us."

"Very well, continue with what you have for now."

"Yeah," Vonafel affirms. "Then we have this... A battered home of forlorn souls, in desperation fight; from foreign shores, a haggard chase, is a message borne in flight."

"That's the one!" Kaliya points at Vonafel's book. "That's us, our arrival on this world, already under siege by Darumon and his cronies, and carrying the message of Sargeras arriving on our doorstep back home...to THEM!" she points assertively at Thaelyn and Aerlie. "Perhaps the only two people we could ever possibly meet who would actually know who he is."

"Cu'Nar's eyes...again," Kailen moans feebly. "Then what is this actually saying about our entire journey?"

"And who gave us that ship to do it in?"

"I'll tell you what I think," Vonafel offers. "I think I was right. Adalon knows who you are, probably knows who Sargeras is, knew he was out there, and was waiting for you...and him, for that matter. And then we come back to how WE got here. Thaelyn and Aerlie, two Celestials who might not otherwise take up residence on a world like this, and this war that brought us all together."

"If I thought this was creepy before," Ankhia whimpers. "I think I didn't give it enough credit."

"But Vonafel," Aelwyn considers. "Are we to suggest Adalon is the center of this, or simply using her skills? Even she should answer up to the Maker, correct?"

"Then she's an agent, like I said before."

"But this still brings us back to her role," Thaelyn muses. "If Tae'Eladar was engineered...and then Aerlie and I brought into it..."

"And each of us with our Fate," Aerlie adds. "This sounds like a culmination, if like Vonafel says, this is an end times moment for the writings."

"Great Powers, Aerlie, are we saying this is the ultimate reason of why?"

"Thaelyn, the cu'Nar used a word on them," she points at Kaliya and the others. "It was a specific word, but meaningless to them. Yet, it would hold special meaning to such like the cu'Nar and to us. This was intentional. She clearly knew the orcs would invade our home, and this let us out of the Shell. Intentional or incidental, we would now discover Darumon and Sargeras, the Daanen-Aryku with their special keyword hint at their identity, and this would now drive us to pursue. She's the one following them, and the cu'Nar are spies working for her."

"But wait," Kaliya interjects. "If we're saying she knew, maybe all the way back to the beginning, why didn't she do something about this from a long time ago?"

"I could possibly answer that with a few suggestions," Thaelyn admits. "First, by the sound of it, they were inactive for a long time…Forgotten and Ignored, and therefore of little or no immediate concern. Therefore, they did not represent a viable target. Secondly, we might consider our own perspectives of how they could be a flight risk if anyone should go in search of them that might otherwise stand out."

"Uh huh…" she relents ironically. "And so she goes through this elaborate play of refurbishing a dead world, seeding it with life, putting not one but TWO Celestials on it, recruiting a race of beings that simply do NOT go outside for any reason, then to use them as spies and messengers to deliver the universe's most expensive lifeboat, and telling us to run for our lives while carrying Creation's Most Obscure distress message," she flutters her fingers for emphasis, "to those same two people, so they could chase BACK across Creation using portals and Industrial Age technology to hunt a god. Yeah, if Haran ever said the gods work in strange ways, this one takes the prize," she drops her head into her hands to cover her face.

"And this, coming from beings that are said to be so elusive," Aerlie muses. "Now I think I know why," she giggles.

"I think I am going to have a headache before this day is out," Thaelyn moans and rubs his brow.

Aelwyn simply shook her head at the pure audacity of the statement.

"Mortals…" she reflects. "Did someone mention sensory stones? They will need to open a whole new department for this one."

"Kaliya," Padriyl mumbles as he covers his eyes. "Do you have any spare horns? Mine just disintegrated."

"Don't look at me," she whimpers. "I'm backlogged a couple of years by now."

"I'm asking myself if I want to bring this up to the Council," Kailen ponders distantly. "A part of me is saying…NO! We might not have an asylum, but this doesn't stop them from building one!"

"Well, Kailen, my dear," Ankhia sighs and pats his shoulder. "If it helps any, I can be your personal therapist. I'll be in the room right next to you."

Vonafel grins brightly at each of them as they try to recover from their collective shock.

"Welcome to the Kingdom of Tae'Eladar, everyone," she smiles. "Land of people who don't belong here, and gods that don't explain why. This does make me wonder something, though."

"What might that be?" Ankhia asks.

"Well, back to that ship. An Estelar might hold the resources to do it, but would an Estelar actually build a ship, or instead commission it from someone still in corporeal form?"

"Um, you're losing me, but aside from that, who are you thinking of?"

"Well, if we say the Sarrukh were called in once for Tae'Eladar, could she have called on them for this as well?"

"This is a fine suggestion, Vonafel," Thaelyn offers. "If they are such an advanced race, and given what I saw of that ship out there, this could surely qualify."

"I might also suggest this," the General adds. "If the Maker has been studying these people for so long," he glances at the Daanen'kai members. "She might be well familiar with their manners by now, and this could offer the technical details to accommodate the design work."

"Absolutely, so this might then provide us an answer to this, as well. But this also suggests a long-term premeditation. There must have been a lot of planning involved. I might also ask if she has any other plans ahead of us."

"Your Lordship," Ankhia wonders briskly. "Can you explain these Sarrukh to me briefly, and how they relate to this world?"

"Certainly," he leans forward. "For a long period of Tae'Eladar's geologic history, it was encased in a deep ice age. Then, suddenly, approximately thirty to thirty-five thousand years ago, something happened, and we have new life arriving. And not simply the evolutionary beginnings of life, but already developed life appearing in our fossil record."

"That sounds as bad or worse as what you're saying about Darumon and us."

"Indeed it does. In our case, we found a time capsule by this society calling itself the Sarrukh, along with evidence detailing how they were responsible for this, as well as technology pointing us in the general direction of where it came from."

"Huh? What sort of technology?"

"We call it the Sarrukhan Gate, a technological Gateway device leading to a world where we found the origin point of the flora and fauna, and human forms of life we see today."

"Interesting. Did you ever go there? And how do those humans compare to yours?"

"We did for a time, but just enough to investigate. When last we visited them, which was a few centuries ago, they appeared physically very similar. In fact, if you were to put one of them and one of ours on a street corner, you might not notice any real difference in appearance. Technologically, however, they were well behind us, likely due to following a more natural course of development, as opposed to ours which were first influenced by the elves and such, and then by us," he directs to himself and Aerlie.

"And this accelerated your examples considerably, I suppose."

"Oh, indeed, and then if to include our use of magic, as theirs is apparently also in a barren fold."

"Uh oh," Kaliya moans. "That doesn't sound good for them. You'll outpace them by huge leaps for everything you're doing over here."

"Yes, and until we can feel ourselves ready for a more official step forward, we chose to leave them be. But one day, we may wish to return. Our trouble here becomes what course of action we might take, or to take any at all. We will likely be so far ahead of them by that time that any hope of returning to our ancestral roots would be impossible unless we somehow decide to try augmenting them to evolve a little faster."

"Well, good luck with it. But evolving them faster probably still wouldn't keep up with you here."

"True. Anyway, Vonafel, do we have anything else?"

"At this time, we're arriving at the present moment, I think," she responds. "When Kaliya and I were talking in the cafeteria, we began to suspect these cu'Nar are some sort of spies. But after all this, it seems we have a new Fate for ourselves, with Kaliya's people and the cu'Nar on one side, our people on the other, and apparently this message telling us to do something about it."

"To do something about it..." Kaliya closes her eyes and shakes her head. "You know, when Relissa said you people were wacky, I don't think she knew even half of it," she chuckles.

"Well, Kaliya, I guess if you're chasing a Primordial, you don't fool around."

"But what about that ship? The thing is huge! It would take the gross national product of a full planet to build that thing, and then some. And I'm not even an engineer to try guessing at this."

"She's right," Padriyl adds. "And they apparently just handed it over to us."

"Then whoever it is they serve," the General suggests, "must hold a considerable volume of influence as well as resources. Again, I might point my finger at Maker Kuroku if she holds influence over such bodies as these Sarrukh. And surely, if this is as serious an issue as we all believe, I think money and resources are the least of her concern."

"Well," Kaliya retorts. "If you're going to put it that way, but wow, does she give out grants too?" she smirks.

"Kaliya," Thaelyn wonders. "A brief question… Considering those engineering skills and the overall size, how does it handle, as far as ships are concerned?"

"Um, Kailen, you could answer that better than me."

"I've been inside of it twice now as we had to move around," he recalls. "First, from the world I was born on, called Ghabeel, which came just before Ruuki uy'Daan, and then again on that one. The engines are extremely powerful. The helm was quite responsive, able to take off and land on a planetary surface. The jump drive is unbelievable to take us into a nether-space slipstream smoothly once we power up. It's a dream to fly it, such that you almost don't even realize the thing is the size of a small city."

"Powers behold," Aelwyn mutters. "And where is it now?"

"Buried under a hillside…"

"It's mostly the hill itself," Kaliya winces. "Just take away the layer of dirt that piled up."

"But now," Thaelyn continues. "What kind of power source does it use? I would imagine something of that size would need a massive supply."

"It does," Kailen admits. "We are aware of three compact fusion reactors serving in tandem. They are apparently rigged as mutual backups to each other, so if one goes down, we have others to keep us going. There is a large antimatter chamber for the drive system, and storage cells for emergencies."

"Where does the fuel come from in all of this? You have antimatter and fusion reactors, but you still need fuel, correct?"

"Yes, but this is a mystery to us. There is one section towards the rear that is apparently sealed off. There is no physical access to it, not internal or external. We assume there is something in the compartment, because our studies on the dimensions of the vessel say there is a large area hidden inside, but we can't get to it."

"How curious, they are hiding some critical piece of technology from you, I suspect."

"Thaelyn," Aelwyn submits. "I may not be studied in this, but maybe I could offer an idea. As you said before, these Sarrukh should be on the scale of a Celestial society by now. And something of this size could not be from anything less than a society on this scale. And by this time, I would expect any race worthy of that name would have a rich assortment of arcanic hybrid technology. So, perhaps this is what they are hiding, and especially if these people do not have a clue what this is about."

"Very nicely proposed, Aelwyn. Maybe so, and this could offer the fuel resources."

"Um…" Kaliya mumbles. "If I don't ask this, I might have my horns hanging down to my ankles soon…"

"Oh?" Aelwyn grins. "Have you already grown a new set?"

"Oh! Now SHE'S doing it!" she blurts and points accusingly. "Unbelievable! I swear, that little pep talk up there is bouncing back at me. Yes, but they're still a bit tender. Anyway, how do we describe this technology, because I'm thinking of the stuff you've been using in your…ahem…Early Industrial Age technology, which already blows my horns off."

"Ah, but Kaliya," Thaelyn smiles warmly. "I think I should not burden you with such details as the dynamic generation of hydrogen for your fusion reactors, and the negative matter for the other one. But if they have an arcanic harvester unit in there, this could supply you even in your barren fold."

"A harvester?"

"Think of your own private supply of arcanids providing for you wherever you go."

"Yeah, wow, that does it. Free and unlimited energy…anytime, anywhere."

"Grace of the cu'Nar," Ankhia moans and hides her face. "And it was right under our hooves."

"I'm just barely keeping up with this conversation," Kailen murmurs. "And I'm with Kaliya right now. Padriyl, how about you?"

"Sir, my mother is out there pulling her horns out trying to understand these principles. Assuming she has anything left by the time this is done, I think we're going to see a few revolutions in our technology."

"You know, my Lord," the General muses. "A thought occurs to me as I consider all these prospects, and relate them to those lingering questions we so often find hanging over us."

"Which ones are those, General?" Thaelyn asks.

"How to find our way to Azgarén, for one thing... We have speculated on several things, like portals in the hands of orcs, searching for Morndindor, and so on. But I am of the mind that if our path is being forged by someone who knows the outcome already, just like you said about finding your way as it is presented to you, I think we should not worry as much about the issue of luck. I think, if our purpose is to fulfill our objective, the clues WILL be presented to us, but only at the appointed time when we are ready for them."

"I swear!" Aerlie urges. "When all this is over, I'm going down there to have a good long talk with that old lizard."

"This would further suggest we are indeed intended as a sort of counterforce. Regardless of our level of technology, we are a clever and resourceful people. And with the gifts we received in this time, not the least of which might be the Elixir of Visions, and all that it gives us, we are in a class by ourselves, it would seem. This might qualify us to achieve some rather profound objectives that would not normally be available to us."

"And so, here we have the rationale behind our Fate. Maybe also our outward image to Darumon. We did not have as much time on our side to evolve as they did; therefore, we had to cheat a little to reach at least that point where we could be competitive."

"Cu'Nar's Pity!" Kaliya yips. "Competitive? Early Industrial versus Advanced Space Age? Padriyl, tell your mother she's going to need to invent an automatic horn replenisher before we're done."

"Yeah," he relents. "I'm sure that Professor Cogswoggle over there will be a happy little guy to help out on that one."

"Furthermore," the General continues. "With respect, of course, I might also have to say your father, Kaliya, was apparently chosen for this explicitly. He was an underdog, so maybe we could say he was expendable by your Council. This is to say they would reject him to begin with as he tried giving the warning."

"Maybe so…" she nods solemnly. "And I think we should also consider our faction, metaphysics, the perfect ones who might actually understand any of this magic of yours that we could participate in anything."

"Indeed, this would be like icing on the cake. He was therefore used to lead Darumon into a kind of trap, with us waiting on our side."

"All right, so Darumon had to invade Tae'Eladar, and those orcs made noise along the way, as orcs might normally do. We could say this is incidental to lead you over here to find us. Yeah, Fate at work, one thing cascading into another…and with Thaelyn and Aerlie acting as a, uh…Kailen, what's the word for it? A kind of trigger?"

"You mean for a trap?" he considers. "In this case, maybe a tripwire…"

"Yeah, and Darumon stumbled right over it."

"Great cu'Nar!" Ankhia wheezes. "And THAT would make sense for everything else said here today."

"Then, we were expected to arrive here," Kailen grumbles. "After almost ten millennia of pursuit…with so many losses, so much suffering…"

"Not simply expected, Kailen," Kaliya notes. "It was engineered, at least partially. More of that incidental aspect. He was returning home anyway. But without our message, they might not have the one critical detail to know who he is."

"Commander," Thaelyn soothes. "I am sure we all share great sympathy for your burdens, but under the circumstances, we might find ourselves in a situation where nothing else could be done UNTIL you arrived here. If you came from a barren fold, you might have otherwise been outside our reach. Some folds, to my understanding, are declared off limits by the Estelar for one reason or another. Yours may be one of those."

"Possibly also the reason he is hiding there," Aelwyn mumbles softly. "They would not expect him to be there."

"Yes...and so convenient, too. And therefore, if we are speaking of Maker Kuroku, she may have had to wait for you to come to us before we could help you. Those same restrictions might not apply to a Prime society."

"Wonderful..." Kailen sighs deeply. "All right, so here we are. Now, what do we do about it?"

Kaliya was leaning forward with her elbows on the table and resting her head in her hands. She felt very weary from this long debate. Kailen and Ankhia both shared her misery. Kailen patted her on the shoulder, squeezing gently to reassure his younger sister to hold herself together.

"My Lord," Vonafel continues meekly. "We're approaching that part that got me so upset when you went on your little excursion. May we?"

He nodded silently, as he was also feeling worn.

"First, we have this, and I think this is your victory here against Darumon. A turn of tales, a pursuit engaged, the encroachment in retreat... I'm only guessing here, but based on the placement within these pages, this sounds like you are turning things around on him with all the little games you played up in that new city."

"This seems fair."

"Then... In the shade of the Forgotten One, an unwanted mind will meet. I'm a little at a loss for this one. Can you help?"

"That sounds somewhat like our last conversation," Thaelyn ponders. "In the shade of the Forgotten One, perhaps to mean just outside that command base of his, where I used a trans-com we found in the Governor's Manor...formerly his, I presume...to make my farewells. And I would surely be an unwanted mind at that moment."

"He knew who you were at that time," the General admits. "He was running from you, after your plays in the city, the threats of the Estelar coming in to discover his plans personally, and you being a Celestial would be the last person he would wish to talk to, I should think."

"Indeed," he nods.

"All right, good…" Vonafel resumes. "But now this one… A city of circular marvel spins, a cage as much as a zoo; a secret kept behind a door, shall raise old fears anew."

"Right, the one about Sigil…"

"Unbelievable!" Aelwyn yelps and blasts the table with a shocking jolt of astonishment, causing the rest of them to reel back at the sudden hit. "I recall what you once said, Thaelyn, but to actually hear it…" she shakes her head. "How could one such as she…EVEN one such as she, know about this when no one except perhaps the Lady and Lord Ao himself would hold this knowledge? Who in all Creation is she, or even the Maker, that they knew about this?"

"There are some very deep layers of intrigue at play here," Thaelyn muses gravely. "This Maker must have a long history behind her. It is no wonder she is so elusive."

"Not simply a history, Thaelyn," Aerlie suggests. "She must also have some special privilege."

Vonafel reviews the next few pages of her book to assess their placement with current events.

"All right, I think this is where we stand. The next one talks about these vulgar manners again, but located elsewhere, I think. And given what has been said about it, we must be talking about the orcs' home world."

"What does it say?" Thaelyn asks.

"The vulgar manners home is made, where a Child whose gift can reach; the answer to a question found, and a swirling eye to teach."

"Yes, this would offer us an answer. Kaliya, you and Aelwyn need to get to work on this skill of yours."

"What is that part about a swirling eye?" Ankhia wonders.

"Likely something yet to be discovered," Vonafel offers. "And by the sound of it, only after we arrive…"

"One moment!" Kaliya shouts. "How does that read again?"

Vonafel stares at the girl briefly for the sudden outburst, and then goes back to the verse to reread it.

"It says, the vulgar manners home is made, where a Child whose gift can reach…"

"A child with a gift?" she blurts.

Kailen, Ankhia, and Padriyl all turned to her at the obvious assertion. Vonafel took notice of their reactions and began to wonder what it was about.

"Um, all right, so what does this say to you?"

"My father receives these messages from the cu'Nar, so I guess it already follows that if they're spies working for someone, some of this information is probably being recirculated. But we also take them as prophecies, and the last one, which came to us shortly after we arrived here, mentioned a Child finding its gift…and that Child is apparently me."

"Interesting, so I need to assign a new spy to watch you now," she grins.

"Oh great, put a little more pressure on me."

"Vonafel," Thaelyn begins. "Do we have any other references to this Child?"

"There was that previous one using the same word, but I can't be sure if it's the same child, or simply A child. Beyond that, I don't see any more with what I have here. There's not much more following this. I see mentions of other people, maybe other places, but I think we should find our way through a few steps first. I'll keep you informed as we go along so we can watch for things."

"This is reasonable."

"And then… Oh yeah, she employs one more cute metaphor for someone, and I'm going to guess it somehow relates to their people."

"Indeed," he smiles. "And how do you describe this one."

"She talks about something called the Hooves of Storm rising up. I have absolutely no idea what these Hooves of Storm are about, but it sounds like a fighting force."

"How quaint… Perhaps we will learn more about this somewhere."

"I wonder…" Aelwyn considers. "Could this relate to the earlier mention of Children turning on their Creator?"

"Possibly."

"But in all this," Vonafel relents. "We also have this continued issue of blank spots. And we further have a full page back here that seems empty."

"Then it must be another sequence she wants to hide until some fated moment. It might contain privileged information we are not ready for. Given the pattern we are seeing here, it might involve the final moments, and perhaps she is not taking chances of corruption along the way."

"That makes good sense," Aerlie agrees. "And all the more reason I want to have my long chat with her when this is done. She's apparently driving us nearly as much as Darumon was driving them," she points at the Daanen'kai members.

"For this point, if we consider the General's depiction of us being a counterforce, perhaps this is a very accurate assessment."

"This reminds me of something," Padriyl adds. "Maybe it's like Priestess Sehnisavain once said. She, like Darumon, doesn't reveal anything until the individual needs to know."

"This would certainly follow with her writings," Vonafel offers. "But unfortunately, these writings don't tell us anything until after it occurs."

"And therefore these last few are hidden," Thaelyn conjectures. "They must contain information that is much more apparent, and without as much need to decipher, as by this time we have already understood so much."

"Gracious, so not only is she providing us with a chronical of what's coming up, but she's also realizing by this time how we've been trying so hard to figure it out that we already know what's happening."

"Well," Aerlie sighs. "At least now we know what she does down there all day."

"Yeah, and if you get that chance for a talk, I hope you'll share the highlights with me. Now, after all is said and done, we have one final page with one final quatrain on it, and it seems completely out of place in relation to the rest, with or without the blank spots."

"Very curious…" Thaelyn submits. "And how does that one read?"

"My Lord," she sighs deeply. "I kind of hesitate to mention this without first knowing what leads up to it. It talks about someone new, I think, and uses more metaphors, describing them as crusaders. Then we have an Era in demise, which sounds a little creepy, especially as it's the last item. So, I think our best course would be to see how these other pieces appear, and what's on this last page, as it might actually hold something vital."

"Perhaps so, then we will wait on that, as it is surely ahead of us, and as with so many other things she writes, it likely involves a detail that we will only discover at the right moment."

"As for these blank spots, I'll keep watch on them. I don't know what sort of trigger she has in mind, but if it's a privileged detail we're not supposed to know about until a fated moment, I'll need to pay close attention to it."

"May I ask one thing here," Kailen ushers. "Just for the sake of keeping my horns loosely attached, how would this hidden text somehow magically appear by some trigger mechanism?"

"Adalon and her kind are an ancient race believed to share some knowledge perhaps with the Estelar and other Celestial races. Given this, they can invoke an alteration of some small element of Reality simply by using a trigger event. This could be an action or a word, or some other demonstration that serves like a key."

"Wait…" Kaliya interjects. "Would this be anything like a key for a portal door, like in Sigil?"

"Actually, yes, in some ways. But in this case, you don't need to be physically present for it. She could do this from where she is right now, and it could affect all her books simultaneously."

"Yeah," Kailen sighs and drops his head. "There go my horns, just like I was afraid of."

Kaliya pats her brother on the back to comfort him as she rolls her eyes and sighs.

"Well, if Father ever had a burr up his tail to ask that riddle of metaphysics…"

"Oh please, Kaliya. He's simply too old to bring this up to him."

"Very well, then," Thaelyn asserts. "This is a remarkable series of statements, and it would seem we have some work ahead of us. We will keep you informed as we can, or else you and your, ahem, spies…" he grins, "…if you can at least keep them to one side, can keep you abreast of things, and then come forward again if you discover anything."

"Perfect…" Vonafel smiles. "And thank you all for your time."

She now packs up her books and offers a polite bow before departing.

"And Aelwyn," he concludes. "You should begin your work with Kaliya at your earliest moment. I would imagine, after today's review, we could all use a rest, so perhaps on the morrow."

"I believe this is reasonable, for each of us," she affirms.

Chapter 8

DEVELOPING INTERESTS

It was the start of a weekend, the day after their meeting with Vonafel, which worked out very conveniently for Aelwyn and Kaliya to get an early start on their training. They met in the courtyard and Aelwyn led them through the doors to the administration office and testing rooms. There, they met with Master Sagrid and his assistant, and together they continued further to the meditation room where Kaliya once spent time in preparation for her redemption ritual.

"Now, Kaliya," Aelwyn begins. "Tell me how you first proceeded so we can follow this process again. I wish to repeat your previous steps in an effort to recreate the same conditions you experienced before, as best we can."

"Sure, um, I came into this room, and they had me undress and put on a robe, then they sat me down in this circle facing these candles and incense sticks."

"Master Sagrid, can we have one such robe, please?"

"Right away, Cardinal…"

Master Sagrid sends his assistant to fetch a robe from a closet in another room. While they wait, Aelwyn examines the candles and incense.

"Master Sagrid, what sort of incense is this?"

"It's a special blend His Lordship apparently borrowed from his time in Sigil."

"Really? Hmm, I wonder."

She reaches down and picks up a stick, then sniffs it.

"Yes, of course, I probably should have guessed. I now recall his mention once, as he was asking for a recipe we use in our own guild, that allows one's mind to run free to experience a state of euphoria. This permits them to reach within their innermost thoughts to pull out hidden or repressed feelings."

"Is it some kind of drug?" Kaliya asks.

"It is best to describe it as an herbal therapeutic drug, but not a potent one. In this form, it does not saturate the body. It only helps to release the mind. We sometimes use it as a form of medicinal to ease one's discomfort."

Aelwyn looks up at Kaliya to study her.

"Did you have any repressed feelings at the time you were undertaking this process?"

"Yes, I did. I had a lot of troubles during my earlier life after we were attacked. I was angry, hurt, and frustrated, in part because of our situation with the Suuden-Aryku. And I also didn't like orcs, largely due to a prejudice I held back then. I can't say I like them much even now, but it's not the same as before. And then there was my mother. That was the biggest thing."

"What happened?"

"We were running down the street, trying to get to the ship, when she was hit by one of the orcs. They were using some kind of magic to attack us. It hit her and she went down, twisting into some kind of mutation. I was standing right next to her when it happened, and it horrified me."

"I recall you said once you were a child…how old were you again?"

"Half a century, still early childhood for us."

"Young and impressionable, an unfortunate combination to be involved in a war."

The Adept returns with a robe and a bag to hold Kaliya's existing garments, and she repeats the old routine of undressing and donning the robe. The Mage Master lights the candles and the incense in preparation for the ritual.

Aelwyn supervises the process, taking notice of Kaliya's unusual physical design.

"Curious," she conjectures. "I was expecting different."

"Excuse me?" Kaliya asks as she continues the undressing process.

"Please forgive me for speaking out loud, I do not mean to intrude, but from my experience with the various races we have in Sigil who possess hoofed feet, I was expecting fur-covered legs to match."

"Oh. No, we don't have much in the way of body hair. Only what you see on top."

"This leads me to wonder about your evolutionary design. Did your ancestors have any kind of fur covering, or was it simply bare skin?"

"I have no idea," she chuckles. "What about those up in Sigil?"

"Those we have in Sigil are often a combination of elements from the different source races, many of which possess very different physical features."

"I recall we passed by quite a few as we were walking around. I saw a lot of different kinds, and we even spoke to one which I think you might be referring to. She was inside the brothel. That one named Kimasxi."

"Ah yes, a perfect example. She is a tiefling…part mortal blood, like that of a human, and part fiendish blood like what you would find of the creatures in the Lower Planes. They are often known for their vivid tempers, but are not always of Negative alignment."

"This one sure had a temper, as well as a mouth."

"That is simply her way. She specializes in abusive behavior as a sensation to afford in her trade."

"Well, she's good, I'll say that much. I don't have nearly that level of experience. My family was much too refined to use that sort of language."

Kaliya finishes changing into her robe and prepares to take her seat.

"Now, listen carefully," Aelwyn instructs. "I predict we may have difficulty in the beginning to recreate, and then control this exercise. Particularly if you were under emotional distress the first time, as I suspect you were acting out of desperation before."

"Yeah, you may be right. I was a wreck. In all these years since the attack, after we landed on Therinë, my brother tried to get me involved with counseling to overcome my psychological difficulties, but all I really wanted was revenge."

"Against whom, the Suuden-Aryku?"

"Partly, we had been hunted by them ever since leaving Azgarén, and this always bothered me. But then to have the orcs attack, basically stabbing us in the back and causing so much death and destruction…well, I just wanted to pay them back for it. We never did anything to hurt them, and we even tried carrying on a little cultural interaction. And I learned a few words of orcish along the way, just because it was the thing to do. But after the attack, I felt violated and betrayed. Can you actually blame a person for such feelings?"

"Under those precise conditions, I suppose I cannot, but you also mentioned a form of prejudice, so I feel I must ask what it was about the orcs that disturbed you the most to create so much antipathy."

"Right…and then there's that," she sighs. "I think it centered on our situation, more than anything else. This was after that wild jump when we found their home world. We called it Ruuki uy'Daan, which in our language means Land of Exile. That, in itself, isn't a very nice suggestion, to think of oneself living in a place of exile, also to be described as exiles by our name. And further, living in someone else's backyard. I didn't like living on borrowed space, nothing about it felt like home to me. And then, to borrow it from such as them, where we couldn't interact on a predictable level, and nothing about them made any sense to us. The whole setting just seemed so primitive."

"Did you feel yourselves to be so much superior that you should not interact with such a low species to begin with?"

"That's not really a fair question, but I suppose I did to some degree. We were so much more advanced, and the stories I heard of our old home made it seem so glamorous in comparison to what we were reduced to.”

“So, your prejudice may be better described as disappointment for having lost so much of your former prestige, and now having to take up residence with that which represented such an inferior example by compare, and further to become dependent on it for your living space.”

Kaliya sat down within the circle and sighed deeply. She glanced around at the racks of candles and incense before returning to Aelwyn.

“Yes, I suppose that’s probably the best way to put it, a bit like a slap in the face insult. My people tried to teach me to be thankful for their hospitality, granting us the space to begin with. That ship of ours takes up a lot of space when it sets down on the ground, and then we built a new city around it.”

“I am trying to imagine such a thing of that size being capable of landing on a planetary surface.”

“Yeah, it can do it, if just barely, but you don’t want to be under it at the time,” she chuckles. “One thing that bothered me about the orcs was this strange tribal mysticism they had. Their…magic…” she flutters her fingers for emphasis. “This was pure nonsense to us and our empirical science.”

“Ah, and here we come back to that again.”

“Yeah, and after a while, we simply attributed it to mindless rambling, which further demeaned them in my eyes.”

“So, this opinion might actually have been spread much wider for this point, and you simply picked up on it as a young and impressionable child born of a society longing for better times.”

“My father was also involved in a project to create a kind of compendium of our surviving knowledge into a single memorial work, to be left behind in case we should finally cease to exist. And that didn’t help matters much at all.”

“It would seem you were being hit from multiple directions.”

“Right, and then came the day of the attack. It was so efficient, how they cut our power and communication links, crippling us so easily, that I think I blew a fuse. They likely had help from the

Suuden-Aryku, but to think they could do anything at all was simply humiliating."

"Humiliating in what manner? In such a manner that they could so efficiently disable your higher technology, or in such manner that they might actually have minds with which to think of the answer. We should be careful of our reasoning here."

"You're right, and I understand this now. Maybe it was a little of both. They didn't understand our technology well enough to work it, and even though we later came to the conclusion they must be in league with the Suuden-Aryku, it didn't help matters to think that orcs, of all things, could apparently do all this by themselves, because I don't recall any sightings of Suuden-Aryku on our streets."

"Under these conditions, we must ask ourselves if these Suuden-Aryku gave such careful instructions to the orcs, or if they made some hidden movement to assist."

"Most of us think they probably had a covert operation going on behind our backs. I think some of this went down before the orcs could've reached the associated facilities, to say nothing of gaining access to the critical systems."

"And so we have the varied psychological factors that brought you into this chamber to reconcile yourself."

"I went through some therapy before this. Thaelyn, Aerlie, and others, all started teaching me about these philosophies and morals, some of which were strangely familiar from what my father would teach in his science faction. Suddenly, I started to realize it's not what my people think, or what they were trying to make me think. Instead, it was bigger than that. Here we have a completely new society speaking about things I didn't fully understand from any of my own studies, but to hear someone else speaking of it told me it's not just us."

"He has always carried the light of his Father in him, and I am pleased to see he still shares it with others."

"He even taught me how to use magic."

"Oh? And how did he do this?"

"He gave me a stick of wood and carefully explained how the

flows work. Then, after several failed attempts, I got it to work for me…although I blew the end of the stick apart in the process," she laughs.

"Really!" Aelwyn grins. "For a first-time application, that is an impressive result."

"And here is where I finally began to realize, it's not fantasy."

"The Seas of Creation are vast, Kaliya. You and yours cannot hold such opinions that you understand everything. Even the Great Powers can sometimes find something new to study."

"So, the gods aren't actually as All-Knowing as they say?"

"I think no one can truly attest to that," she smiles.

Kaliya now turns to the incense and begins relaxing into the vapors.

"We shall proceed in this way," Aelwyn advises. "You will perform your meditation in the manner you followed once before, to the best of your ability. I will wait for you in the other room. When your time comes, we will continue to the next step together."

Kaliya nods and begins her ritual while the others leave the room, gently closing the door behind them. The meditation cycle lasts for approximately an hour, although the passage of time becomes lost on Kaliya after a while as the effects of the incense settle in.

Soon, the mage adept returns to call her out. She follows him through the corridors, trying to steady herself against the walls for support, until they reach the antechamber of the ritual room.

"Greetings, Kaliya," Aelwyn announces. "How do you feel?"

"Dizzy…" she mumbles distantly. "And also sleepy…"

"This is normal. Master Sagrid, which room were you using before?"

"Technically speaking," he responds. "It's all one big room with many doors leading inside…we just don't tell the students that," he snickers. "It adds to the intrigue, and we only test one at a time, anyway. But she took the door just left of the center."

"What is inside?"

"The room is empty, but strongly enchanted. His Lordship and a group of his finest mages built it once. He says it resembles a demi-planar construct that simulates the natural permeability of the Outer Planar realms to a person's mental influence."

"Indeed!" she intones eagerly. "That would explain much in this regard."

Aelwyn brings Kaliya over to the door used once before during her original ritual. She opens it to examine the interior. The room is pitch black, and appears empty. They step inside and close the door. Initially, they are unable to see anything, so Aelwyn uses her own skills to reshape space and invokes a beam of light to appear from overhead. This allows them to see each other and make conversation.

Kaliya reflexively angles her head to look up at the light, trying to find the actual source, but nothing seems apparent.

"I did that once...I don't know how, but I did."

"As a Celestial, I hold a number of abilities, but these are often naturally occurring to those like us. If you did this before, it may have been accidental, but it would be nice to see if we can develop this as well. But now, we are here, just as you were before. What were your first thoughts?"

"I was feeling sleepy, and I remember thinking about a chair, like the kind we have back at the Naarg uy'Sodrad. I recall Thaelyn telling me things can appear in here, like with my thoughts bringing them out. I think my mind was drifting. I thought I was dreaming when I saw something appear to the side."

"Most interesting. This, in addition to the light? This could represent another permutation of your gift. Let us see about recreating this now. Can you do it again?"

"I remember later associating this with my Father's metaphysics faction and a riddle we keep pulling our horns out over."

"Oh? What is this riddle? This should be interesting."

"Like I was saying to Grace once, up there in Sigil, it comes in two parts, a theorem and an axiom. The theorem goes like this: Perception enables recognition, existence demands definition, and from this, substance becomes our reality."

"Indeed, how intriguing," she smiles.

"And the axiom goes like this: In a metaphysical reality, nothing unknown exists. It only exists after it is known."

"Truly fascinating," she croons. "And to think, you come from a barren fold. Your father must be very progressive for his time."

"Yeah, but also very unappreciated by all the rest."

"Perhaps so, but if he were able to demonstrate any of this, I think that would have changed."

"I was able to prove this theory in front of him once by playing the fire trick for him. My mind altered the Reality of space by applying my own definition of fire on a stick I was holding."

"What was his reaction to that?"

"Needless to say, he was impressed, especially as I didn't get the full education in a university," she chuckles feebly.

"Well, let us see what else you are capable of. If you made a chair before, we should recreate this scenario."

"I'm not completely sure how I did it the first time. In theory, I think I know, but I was a little lost in my thoughts before, thinking I was going to explore a dream world, not a physical one."

"All right, let us approach it this way. My first lesson to you will be thus... We are in a space that can be affected by the will of the occupant. With a well-directed mind and focus of thoughts, the occupant can alter the space around them, reshaping it to create new objects, even to fold space so one could travel to other locations. From your description, it seems you did some part of this during your first visit, if only unknowingly."

Kaliya mulls the idea over in her mind, recalling her first visit inside the room and the events that occurred at that time. Then a recurring memory surges forward as she reflects on Aelwyn's statement.

"In this space I have will, and my will can alter this space," she mumbles.

"How interesting," Aelwyn muses. "That sounds like a quotation you once heard."

"Yeah... And cu'Nar's grace, if only she could've known how close she was to it. This is from my mother, probably when I was a child."

"Probably? You do not remember?"

"I was young then. My mother discovered this talent probably not long before the attack, and was trying to study it. But she didn't actually tell me what I was doing, apparently to protect me from something, like maybe traumas or psychological abnormalities."

"Possibly, if your society is so fearful of it, and with it being so strange to you."

"Then we had the attack, and I was traumatized from that, so I forgot a lot of things. Then later, Thaelyn did a mind meld on me to share our language, and it must've knocked a few things loose upstairs."

"A melding can certainly invoke a form of shock if you hold any repressed feelings or memories. And since then, this trauma of yours began to break apart, I suppose."

"Yeah, it did. I used to have nightmares and disturbing dreams of a young girl running through ruined streets. It was me from those early days."

"You poor young Child," Aelwyn mourns. "But this is also a fine realization. And now it is time to take it to the next step. Recall that chair again, and do so with great detail, as if you were standing in front of the actual item and studying its every line, contour, texture, and manner of substance. You must create the understanding within your mind that this can be real, a physical presence manifested in the space near you. This is a principle we refer to as Knowing. It is the intellectual recognition of existence by means of our perceptions invoking the manifestation of an object within our space."

"Wow…that sounds so much like my father's faction talking."

"Indeed, there are beings within the Outer Planes who use this not simply for small objects, but they can create much more elaborate settings, even whole cities. And if you already understand this principle, even to partially demonstrate it by now, I feel you should be able to do it again, and not necessarily just inside this chamber."

"But you're speaking of Celestials for this point, right?"

"Yes, but recall what I said before. You clearly hold some small piece of this inside you. Now you must come to terms with it."

"In other words, in this space I have will, and my will can alter this space."

"Precisely!" she asserts energetically. "Now, make it happen!"

Kaliya felt a sense of confidence come into her, although she was still a little hesitant on how to proceed. So, she pulled together whatever pieces of her old studies, as well as the new, to convince her of how this can be done.

She first recalls Thaelyn and his early lesson in magic. She was able to invoke fire on the stick out of absolutely nothing but her desire to do so. The dynamistic flows, this is how they're described by the people of Sigil, an energy cloud that surrounds all things in this space. And apparently, they are highly influential in this place. But it all comes down to the mind. This is the most powerful tool of all.

"Perception enables recognition..." she mumbles. "Existence demands definition..."

She turns to an open area and tries to recall the chair from before. She reflects on her memories of the ship's lounge area, and her favorite chair she so often enjoyed relaxing in after her scouting runs.

"...That chair...in the Naarg uy'Sodrad...in the lounge area... So soft and cushiony...with smooth fabric, you just sink down into it."

She still felt a little dizzy, but rather than struggling against it, she chooses to relax into it, thereby allowing it to release her thoughts. If she tried analyzing it too deeply, she might fail. Science wasn't the application here. There were no empirical numbers involved. It was something else entirely at work, the power of the mind.

She continues recalling her favorite lounge chair from the ship. She envisions it clearly in her mind, isolated from the other items in the room. She imagines how it feels to touch it...to sit in it.

"...And from this, substance becomes our reality."

She recalled Thaelyn's words: Do not be distracted, you want this, you need this, you will stop at nothing to have it. She felt almost as if she could touch the chair in her memory, feeling the cool luxury of it, like it was real and standing before her. And now, she must pull this into the space in front of her.

"...And my will can alter this space..." she mutters determinedly.

As her sensations began to surge, she felt a flow of authority settle in. Deep down, she knew this must be real, she had already demonstrated it, at least in part, and this would take it to the next step, even above her father. She formulated her perception of the chair, and now she would push this into reality…and she could feel space itself beginning to change.

A haze began to form in front of her, indistinct and blurry. She studies this, realizing it needs more substance. She realigns her mind to drag the body further into reality. It was only partially created, but she wanted more.

"Focus, Kaliya," Aelwyn encourages. "Make it real. You must believe in your deepest thoughts that it exists, not just a memory. Convince yourself of this and it will turn for you. The space around you becomes an extension of your mind…of your essence. You work it as you might work your native body."

"To work it. And so, substance becomes our reality. I must feel it with my mind. It must exist!"

Kaliya glares at the image and drives herself harder. She raises a hand to it for better direction of focus.

"I must feel you," she whispers to herself. "I know what you are. You must therefore exist. I've seen you before. You are real, come to me."

Her thoughts seemed to drag the body into better focus. She applies her reasoning that it must have substance, and recalls what that substance is. As she watched the image wavering, her sensations became better defined. She could feel it now, as a subtle sensation of the mind reaching out to the space around her. It was no longer just a point of focus, but all of it. All Reality must turn for this. And with this realization, she would reinterpret the nature of existence.

"Come on, you little tail-puller, I see you hiding there."

Her thoughts began to coalesce to remake existence to her own will. She turns her hand around and coils her fingers in, as if to grip the image and yank it into Reality.

"In this space…"

She draws her hand back in a symbolic gesture to pull the image into stability.

"...I have will..."

Now, she makes a final tug, imposing her will onto the fabric of space to create the substance of her target. She forced herself to feel the item, a physical object created by her sheer desire for it to exist.

The chair snaps into Reality with a soft hiss and crackling, taking on a solid form as the physical matter consolidates. Kaliya relaxes with a contented grin.

"You little tyrant," she muses playfully. "You were fighting me."

"Very nicely done, Child," Aelwyn smiles. "We will clearly need to work on this, but what we have is a good step forward. Within a fold where you have the dynamistic flows, you may find it possible to apply yourself to alter that space. Higher beings can possibly do this even without the flows, but for those of us who belong to a younger race, we may need them to get us started."

Kaliya places a hand on the chair, touching the cushioned arm and sliding it onto the seat.

"I made this. Father, if only you could see me now," she chuckles. "I believed it to exist, I wanted it to exist, and I brought it here through my own will to alter this space. Of course, it defies every law of physics we have on record, but that's beside the point. This is a completely different study," she grins.

"Indeed it is."

"I will also admit this is not the usual way we make chairs back home."

"Yes, I suppose I must admit to that for many of us," she smiles. "But as I said, there are some who apply this on an even greater scale. Now, what was the next thing you did in here?"

"I sat down and apparently fell asleep. Then I think I woke up, stood up out of the chair, walked around, but then weird things started to happen."

"Can you explain? What weird things?"

"Well, aside from the fact I could see myself sleeping in the chair, which in itself was a bit strange, and yet it also felt familiar somehow, but I couldn't place my finger on it."

"Likely an old sensation from your childhood. Perhaps the experience was not completely forgotten."

"Maybe. I was asking myself where I was supposed to go, and what I was supposed to do now that I'm in this dreamlike condition. I believed I had a purpose ahead of me, like some unfinished business I really wanted to tidy up."

"What sort of unfinished business was this?"

"Well, in the end, I believe it was to tell my mother I loved her. That attack left a bad taste in my mouth. I didn't get the chance on Ruuki uy'Daan because I was angry, we were running, and then the orcs hit her with that magic, and I simply lost control. Thaelyn said I should allow this room to fabricate some kind of image for me out of my imagination, but I didn't see anything at first... Except, um...hmm."

"Yes?"

"Well, I thought I could see a few sparkly things moving around... not sure what they were...but it gave me an idea. If my issues were on Ruuki uy'Daan, maybe I needed to visit that place, or at least the memory of it. But for a lack of any other ideas, I might have to imagine going there first."

"Ah, and here we have your translocation effort."

"I guess I let my imagination take over for this point. Without a ship of any kind, I just put the thought of a location in my head and imagined a sensation of movement to carry me from here to there. Next thing I know...bam! That's when things went wild on me. I wanted to go there, and it almost felt like I was flying. Suddenly, I saw clouds of rainbow colors...and then I think I punched through a wall of some kind..."

Aelwyn listened to the depiction with a growing sense of awe. She gazed at Kaliya as she continued her recollection.

"I saw a lot of really strange shapes and images, and it seemed like I was travelling through a tunnel. But ahead of me was a dot, or a hole, or something, and I was aiming to pull myself through to it."

"Powers pay witness," Aelwyn gasps.

"Then I saw another wall, and dear cu'Nar, the thing was huge. I couldn't even see the edges of it."

"A planar membrane… You passed through what I suspect was the Fourth Fold out of our local planar domain and into a new one. This is an incredible experience. Would you care to offer this into a sensory stone one day for us up in Sigil? I think this would make for a truly fascinating addition."

"If you say so, but let's nail this down so I can control it better. The next thing I saw was a lot of glowing things, but I think we might be talking about stars, galaxies, and other celestial bodies, all whizzing past me so fast, all I could see were streaks. And still, this dot in front of me seemed distant, so I was pushing myself harder, until I finally caught a brief glimpse of what I assume was the local galaxy, and cu'Nar's pity, was that a frightening sight."

"You were folding space, and in your case able to perceive of the transitions along the way."

"Then I arrived on Ruuki uy'Daan. And here is where things went from weird to simply wacky. I was a young girl again, and the city was a wreck."

"A young girl? How old?"

"Right about that same age when we left. I was even dressed in my old school clothes."

"Your last viable memory of your time there…so you altered your manifested image to match your recollections. And the city?"

"Destroyed and overgrown with vegetation…at least a few centuries worth of decay."

"How interesting. So, let us try to interpret this now. You fell asleep, but you likely made your projection at that moment, feeling as if you needed to go somewhere and accomplish something. During this course, your desire to achieve your goal pulled you to a perceived destination where you felt this obligation calling you. Your projection then travelled a truly unfathomable distance to a completely different fold. Child, I cannot even begin to predict what level of authority you may carry within you, but this would transcend even the average Celestial."

"Wow, I don't know what to think about that, or if I even want to."

"One thing I think we can already expect is that it may be difficult for us to recreate this, and yet we must. And for this we may find it necessary to imbue you with a similar sense of need. Perhaps if we begin with something simple…I will have you recline in the chair, but rather than sleep, we will see about immersing you into a form of meditation where you may have better control of your thoughts and actions. You should desire an important need again, but not to such tension that you cannot relax into this meditative trance. If I must, I will assist you, but we will allow you to go first."

Kaliya nods and sits down, relaxing in the comfortable seating. She allows herself to enjoy the soothing release of the dizzying flurry of her mind, while closing her eyes and attempting to meditate. She places the thought of an imperative desire to seek a purpose outside her body, but it cannot be while in a wakeful state.

The memories of her previous experience circulated in her mind. On her first visit to this room, she was expecting to experience a dreamlike state, a hallucination generated by her old memories and brought forth by the effects of the incense. The unexpected turn of events that followed shook her when she finally returned from her travels and related them to the people outside. Now, just like she had caused this chair to appear out of nowhere by the desire of her own will, this time she had to make herself appear.

Time passes as she submerges herself into a deep relaxation. Her mind wanders across many thoughts, only to be pulled back as she recalls her purpose. She has many false starts, opening her eyes hoping to find herself standing upright with her body still in the chair, but only to discover she was still physical.

"Attempt it this way, Kaliya," Aelwyn suggests softly. "Normally, your mind and body are one, but at this moment, you wish your mind and your body to be as two disconnected entities. As you relax into meditation, allow yourself to dream that you are floating. Your body drifts away behind you, allowing your spirit to separate and move outward. Do not be afraid of this separation, as you are always linked to your body, and can pull back if need be."

Kaliya tries again, imagining herself as floating, with her body moving one way and her mind another. She feels free and unburdened, a drifting sensation. She struggles to disarm her instinctive fear of loss, and instead to envision a release, an uncoupling of her thoughts. She desires a sentiment of confidence that she can move beyond her body, to lift herself outward.

She attempts to visualize her body falling away, piece-by-piece, as it seemed easier to conceptualize than discarding the whole thing at one time. She pushes her mind into the space around her, sensing a kind of movement, but not the feeling of physical contact with other objects. She first tries turning her head, keeping her eyes closed and only sensing the rotation of her action. She is uncertain of the result, so she gradually opens her eyes.

She is sitting up in the chair, but her form is indistinct. She notices something immediately behind her and slowly turns to look at it, reminding herself to remain calm and focused on her efforts. She sees herself apparently sleeping.

Rather than question the spectacle, she brings herself forward to stand up, then takes a few steps away and turns to look at herself. She sees Aelwyn standing next to the chair, staring in her direction, and beaming a bright smile. Kaliya briefly looks down at herself. Her form looks somewhat transparent. She surmises she is out, but needs further refinement. And so, just as with the chair, she must now bring her body into reality. She recalls her previous lesson and knows she must recognize her own existence, that she must also have substance and form. This exercise seemed to go a little easier, as it was more personal, causing her projected image to solidify.

"This is strange," she muses. "I don't have the same sensation of touch or anything in this form. Are you able to see and hear me?"

"Yes, you are perfectly perceptible to me," Aelwyn nods. "Such a fascinating sight. And so, this is how it is done. Do you believe yourself to be true, Kaliya?"

"I must," she responds mildly. "Just like with the chair, I must perceive myself to exist, although this is a little easier than with a chair. And from this, MY substance will become a form of Reality, at least within the context of whatever it is I'm doing here."

"Very good!" Aelwyn applauds. "We shall practice this many times, until you are able to produce it without the need of the incense. In the meantime, since we are here, let us practice a few simple actions together."

+·+◆+·+

"Captain, we have an update on our report."

"Yes, Cadet, what is it?"

A young male scout returns to the mine where Captain Lapäli has been collecting details from this and other scouting ventures around the region.

The Captain had been embellishing his table in the corner of the large gathering hall in recent times, where he and his officers now made reviews of the reports and plans on how to proceed. Some of the officers were working to train the junior cadets, while the Captain oversaw the greater scale of the operation.

The recent activities outside, with the new, more vigorous scouting efforts, and the strange revelations of the orcs and their bizarre behavior, represented a welcome dose of inspiration for everyone in the group. Where previously, the Captain and so many others were often found in deep depression, now they had something new to think about and look forward to. Nevertheless, the Captain was a cautious one, as he held the highest responsibility to keep everyone safe.

"Camp One is still showing stable behavior," reports the Cadet. "There continue to be new arrivals through the river canyon, but as before, the camp doesn't seem to be growing by the same numbers."

"Fine, but this still doesn't answer our primary concern of where they're going. I'm starting to pull a few suspicions out of this, however, and they're not good. What about the camp patrols?"

"It would seem the orcs are very confident in their own security. They've long since chased all the dangerous animal species out of the area, and nothing else approaches close enough to be a bother to them. And since they feel like they own the place, they don't care much about patrolling it."

"Well, I suppose that makes perfect sense, as they do own the place, and they don't know about us. And further, if they're involved with the Suuden-Aryku, they probably feel an even greater sense of confidence in themselves. So let's use it. How are our spies coming along?"

"Tana's been helping us perfect a few disguises using pieces of local shrubs and ferns. As for the idea of body paint, since we're planning on trying to infiltrate their camp, simply applying a bit of natural color isn't enough, as our skin color still tends to stand out. So, we're basically covering ourselves in a thick layer of mud."

"Sounds glamorous," he chuckles. "Anything else?"

"Another is our size and general weight, complicated by our hoof design leaving very distinctive marks in the soil. So to compensate, we're wrapping our hooves with thick layers of leaves and bark to hide their contours."

"Perfect. They won't know the difference between you and a tree. Now, what about the approach, which way has the least distance and the fewest orcs?"

"Due to the size of the camp, and the number of orcs that have accumulated there, they apparently broke it into two sections, let's call them 'East' and 'West'. Each of these has its own camp center with a large central campfire and rows of huts lining up along a series of lanes. However, there seems to be a kind of dividing line between the two halves. This is where that equipment is found, by the way. You have a row of buildings on either side running along an alleyway, and it looks like it leads right up to the equipment. The buildings face outwards into the camp settings, so a person could sneak in between them and not be seen."

"Which way are we coming in, at this point?"

"The best direction is from the north. From what we can see, this alleyway opens up very close to the edge of their camp on that side."

"And what about this equipment, they need to access it from time to time, so where is that?"

"As best we can tell, it's deeper inside, probably the other end of that alley. We can see a row of buildings on the east side running behind the equipment, so that probably obscures it from that side. This means the equipment is most likely accessed from the west."

"All right then, I guess there's nothing more we can do but to send someone in there. Who are we looking at for our best result, Tana herself, maybe?"

"Yeah, she's got the longest-term practice in moving around out there. She would be my best suggestion. She's trim and slender, so she won't stand out too much, and she's very quiet moving through the underbrush."

"Then let's do it. I'll admit, I'm a bit nervous about sending any of you kids in there, but we need this information. If you think Tana is our best hope, then tell her to keep her tail in line. We'll wait until nightfall and watch the orcs as they close up for the evening. Just remember to move silently and watch all directions at once. Time may be on our side if they don't wander around too much, but let's not get greedy."

"Yes Sir! I'll deliver the word and get them ready."

"And may the cu'Nar watch over us."

✦

Nighttime falls over the orcish camp. The business of the day had mostly been in bringing home food and water from nearby sources, much of it to the east, as that's where the local hunting grounds were located. Wood from local trees had been cut and was being added to the campfires while groups of orcs sat around picking their teeth and scratching their backs. Some conversation was occurring, but mostly about some prized catch made weeks or months before, during a time when they were living in their former habitats elsewhere on the land.

As the sun went down, each of them returned to the hut where they made their bed. Slowly, the camp settles for the night, with only a few still sitting up around the campfires for some late-night chatter.

In the jungle just north of the midpoint of the settlement, there was a modest rustling of leaves and the movement of odd shapes, slow but silent. A collection of strange leafy bodies crept along the ground towards the camp.

"This is it, Tana, it's your game now..." whispers one scout to another.

She nods her head silently and turns to make her approach. She was completely covered from horn to hoof in leafy shrubbery and slathered in mud to hide her natural color. She had also rubbed plant oils on her skin prior to this to help conceal her odors, as orcs were known to hold a keen sense of smell.

She kept herself hidden behind the other local plants and trees, only to move around them after a careful study of the activity around her. She moved slowly to the edge of the camp, paying close attention to watch for any roaming orcs, but they all seemed content to sit around their campfires. In the area immediately near her, it was empty.

There were two large orcish buildings just in front of her, turned in opposite directions with their back walls together. A narrow space between them led along a type of alleyway down the middle between rows of these on either side. She checked both directions before leaving the edge of the jungle landscape, still creeping low to the ground, and crossing the open space from the nearby trees to the edge of the buildings.

She reaches the corners of the large huts and ducks between them, peering out to see if there is any movement approaching from either side. The coast seems clear. She turns to move carefully down the middle, taking care to keep low and trying not to brush the sides of the buildings, as it could make noise and draw attention.

She reaches the end of the first set of buildings and peeks around into the east and west camps to see what sort of movement is occurring out there. There were no orcs in her line of sight to notice her, so she moved forward to the next set.

She continued forward between another set of buildings, now within sight of the first white structure she was sent to examine. It was the tall white cylinder standing upright. She crawled on the ground on her hands and knees, gradually coming up to the next corner. As she approached, she once again peeked around the building on her left, into the east camp. She could just barely see a pair of orcs sitting around the campfire, but with their backs to her. She considered as long as they stayed that way, she should be safe, but the other side was the most troublesome. She could see the assembly of apparatus by now, and it was fully open to the west side.

She laid herself down on the ground and crept forward on her belly. The tall white storage tank would serve as cover, at least until she could pass around it to see the other side. To the right was the large box-like object, and she could hear a humming sound from it.

She first wriggled up to the box, laying a hand against it. It was vibrating slightly. She looked out into the west camp to judge the activity, but it was mostly quiet. There were orcs, but generally facing away from her. She wedged herself between the two units and lifted herself up to reach a hand over the top of the box, testing a theory of what she thought she heard up there. She could feel a flow of warm air blowing upwards from it.

She returned back to the ground to observe the other units in the cluster. She made a series of mental notes as she passed from one to another, recording their position, connections to each other with conduits and piping, and any other significant features.

She was nervous, being in the middle of this array, as well as the middle of the camp. She kept herself wedged between some of the larger units to help conceal her. When she was satisfied with her observations, she worked her way out, taking as much care with her exit as she did her entry, until she rejoined with her fellow scouts out in the bush.

"All right, got it," she whispers. "That's a weird setup they have in there. We should report this in quickly."

The Captain stayed up late waiting for the report. Sulíma, Túfula, and Petrith stayed up with him, also nervous and anxious to hear the report. In fact, a large number of them were sitting around the gathering room waiting, and trying to pass the time with some simple conversation. It was a nervous occasion, and they all wanted to hear the outcome. Many were worried about the spies and hoping all went well.

It was well past midnight, and the group was becoming more anxious as time went by. Then a shout comes in from down the tunnel leading into the mine.

"Captain, they're back!" calls the watchman at the front entrance.

"Thank the cu'Nar!" the Captain exclaims.

Tana and the others dash into the room, panting from their heated run. She was still mostly covered in her plant disguise, and filthy from horn to hoof.

"Looks like someone needs a bath," Sulíma quips.

"You're just jealous because you don't get out as much," she teases.

"At least, when I go out, I don't bring half of it back with me," she giggles.

"I'm just trying to imagine the pond out there," Túfula winces. "You'll leave it so cloudy from all that mud, none of us will get a decent bath for a week."

"Would you prefer I go out to the shoreline for it?" Tana asks. "A nice moonlit dip in the sea might be fun."

"Alone?"

"Oh, of course not! I'll just borrow a few guys to watch my tail," she smirks.

"Hey!" Sulíma protests. "That's supposed to be my line!"

"Easy does it, girls..." the Captain smiles. "Let's keep to the business at hand for the moment. Tana, what do you have for us?"

"Captain, I have a number of things to report, although what it all means is simply beyond me. I've never seen equipment like this before."

"I see. So, we'll take it piece by piece. What do we have going on in there?"

The Captain pulls up a crude piece of paper and a stylus Túfula once made for him to write with, along with a bowl of primitive ink.

"First, there's more to see than just those two pieces," Tana explains. "But then, I guess it goes without saying by now. I can't be sure what I'm looking at, but I'll try to describe it to you. The tall cylinder appears to have a pipe coming in from outside, I think the same one we found coming down from the hills, so it must be holding water. The pipe angles up and enters at the top."

"A fill tube, then. Is there another one coming out?"

"Yes Sir, into the box sitting next to it, which is humming, and I believe there's a fan on top blowing air out. I put my hand up there and it feels warm."

"An exhaust fan to a cooling system... What else?"

"Wow, Captain," Sulíma yips. "We should crash that party! They're serving up cold drinks!"

The room shares a brief round of laughter.

"Not a bad idea, Suli, but somehow, I don't think we'd get past the bouncers. Tana, what's next?"

"There's a smaller pipe coming out the bottom into another tank. It looks like a high-pressure tank, like for a compressed gas."

"What in the name of..." he mumbles. "Fine then, and next?"

"From there, I saw another pipe coming out and leading into the bottom of something... I'm not sure how to describe it. It's a low box on the bottom with a framework on top enclosing a spherical thing with a lot of projections stuck around it. And the projections each had something like a pipe or conduit leading off into the box below. And then there was another conduit, thicker, leading off from the box to something I've never seen before. It was mounted on a platform, and looked like some kind of circular ring standing upright with a swirling vortex in the center of it."

"Is that so..." he considers, sitting back in his chair.

The Captain ponders the situation, piecing it together in his mind and comparing his thoughts to his years of experience and previous service in the Sentinels.

"Were there any distinctive features to any of this? Control panels, display readouts, anything of that sort? Not that I would really expect anything if it's in the possession of orcs. If the Suuden-Aryku are making visits to maintain it, they would probably keep the guts of it locked inside so the orcs couldn't foul it up on them."

"From what I saw, it was all painted white and very plain on the outside."

"All right. So here it is, boys and girls, listen up," he begins. "What we have here is anything but what I would expect to see in the possession of orcs. However, considering we have the Suuden-Aryku involved, it makes sense, though this configuration is new to me."

"Do you know what it is, Captain?" Sulíma asks.

"Let's take this apart one by one. The tank is for water, this much I think is obvious. The box is a cooling system, but I think it's more than that, given the other items on the list. The high-pressure tank is probably holding compressed gas, and I think they're drawing it from the water, an electrolysis reaction to break out the hydrogen."

"Hydrogen? Why in the world do they need that?"

"For the reactor… It seems our friends the Suuden-Aryku have been busy these past few millennia. That sphere sounds like a micro-mini fusion reactor. Although I've never heard of one this small before…impossibly small, if you ask me."

"A fusion reactor!" Sulíma shouts. "Captain, you once asked why in all the nether-space they might want a solar array, but why in all the nether-space would they want a reactor? That's a hundred time's worse, or more!"

"You're right, and by the sound of it, this looks mostly self-contained, a neat little package that wouldn't need more than occasional monitoring. You have the solar panels supplying power to the water pump and the condenser, which breaks out the fuel for the reactor, and keeps everything running nicely, so long as you have sunshine and a water source. And for the amount of precipitation we get off the ocean up here, that little lake of theirs should keep things supplied for a long time."

Sulíma lets out a long moan, and sighs as the description settles in.

"Captain," Petrith wonders. "Why would they need a reactor? And we're still waiting to hear what you think about that last item."

"Yes, the reactor seems to be powering the final item, and this is what I've been worrying about these past few days. The orcs have themselves a conveyor."

Shouts and moans spread around the room as the people started whispering amongst themselves about this startling discovery.

"Captain," Sulíma asserts. "I'm just about ready to lose my mind here, to say nothing of my horns. What are orcs, of all the living creatures in the universe, doing with a conveyor?"

"I think we can answer that with a little bit of analysis. This equipment must belong to the Suuden-Aryku. We've been suspecting the orcs to be working with them for a long time now, and this simply proves it. Although I have to admit, I have no idea why the Suuden-Aryku would want to give them a conveyor. But if to guess, I can only come up with maybe one or two ideas for it."

"All right, so what are they?"

"I suppose we need to apply a few considerations here, mainly how intimately the orcs are working alongside them. But this falls mostly to a relocation effort. We're seeing this migration, which means they must have instructions to move to this location and use it to deport themselves off-world. And if we are suggesting this is to relocate them for some reason, it would surely make sense to provide a conveyor, rather than make so many trips to pick them up and drop them off somewhere."

"But Captain," Petrith interjects. "What would be the purpose of this? Are we still suggesting the Suuden-Aryku are using them as a ground force?"

"You know, I'm asking myself that same question, and also why they would need this. Let's face it, kids, orcs wouldn't compare very favorably to the Suuden-Aryku in a wartime scenario. One good pulse rifle would serve much more effectively than twenty orcs and their spears. And this doesn't even mention their bombardment weapons. So, unless the Suuden-Aryku are using them as an…expendable… ground force, I don't see why they would want them at all…to say nothing of calling so many of them into it. And then, we have to ask where they are going."

"Then the Suuden-Aryku must be at war with someone, that's all I can figure. It wouldn't make sense for them to simply call for, well, how do we describe it…an evacuation…relocation to another world?"

"That's a good point, actually. This is their home world, and they're apparently leaving it to go somewhere else. And the need for them to go there is apparently greater than their motivation to call this world home anymore."

"But who, Petrith?" Sulíma asks. "They attacked us enough times. Who are they attacking this time?"

"What if they found our people again?" he considers. "And now they're calling in orcs to assist."

"Oh great, so what are we saying here? They're attacking our people from the Naarg uy'Sodrad already? That was quick! Captain, how quickly did they find us on previous occasions?"

"Actually," he ponders. "I think it averaged only a few centuries, maybe a bit less. So this might fall into that same range. But if you also count that wild jump we made, well... We were here almost a millennium and a half before we got kicked out."

"And worse, Captain," Petrith adds. "We're apparently in a completely different universe. How do you follow something like that, tracking device or otherwise. It breaks our science just to think of it."

"Yes, you're right. But with this in mind, I'm now forced to wonder something else."

"What's that?"

"How long has this equipment been sitting there, and by association, how long have they been laying siege to our people, or whoever it is on the next world?"

"If we assume the Suuden-Aryku found us sometime before we were attacked, long enough to study us and teach the orcs the best ways to cripple our power and comm networks, then we have to wonder what they were planning. If they wanted to kill us immediately, they could've done so, couldn't they?"

"Yes, indeed they could. Bombardment from space, an invasion of ground troops... They hit us with the orcs nicely enough by surprise; they could've done almost anything."

"But no one ever saw any Suuden'kai troops attack us on the ground."

The Captain pauses to consider the notion. The room goes quiet as he thinks this idea through.

"They wanted us to move again," he concludes. "Each time they found us, they only pushed us off one world and into another. If they wanted us dead, I think we would be dead. They're simply playing with us. According to our history, they've hit us with ground troops, bombardment, but never anything so severe as to completely wipe us out. The Naarg uy'Sodrad, for example, that's a big target. If you want your enemy dead, you don't leave them an escape, but it never took a direct hit."

"Which means," Túfula offers. "Either they're extremely lousy shots that they can't hit the broad side of a massive colony ark, or they only wanted us to pick up and go somewhere. But it doesn't answer why. I mean, in the name of the cu'Nar, what did we ever do to them? Nothing, as far as I know."

"That may be just the point, Túfu. The cu'Nar came and warned us about Sargeras, that he was trouble and would corrupt our people with his lies. They told us he was a remnant of an ancient society which was supposed to be dead. So, if they're supposed to be dead, where did he come from?"

"A sole survivor, perhaps? Whatever killed the rest, he got away?"

"Maybe. And then, I recall it said he came asking for help of some kind in exchange for some advanced knowledge. Whatever the reason he's alive, and whatever the reason he came to us, of all people, and then whatever the reason he wanted our help, it seems clear he did something to the people back home. However, WE ran off. This might be your answer, Túfu. We disobeyed whatever he really wanted out of us."

"All right," Sulíma retorts. "So WE ran off. Then why are THEY chasing us, hitting us only enough to kick us in the tails from one world to another, but never fully removing us for our so-called disobedience? If he wants us to behave like trained animals, he should throw chains around our necks and haul us back home. Either that, or just put us down once and for all."

"That's a good point, and all the more reason we don't understand their methods, unless we just say they're playing with us for some reason, which in itself doesn't really make sense."

"There must be an ulterior motive we're just not aware of," Petrith surmises. "That reason he came to us in the first place. But we ran off too soon to learn what it was."

"Possibly," Túfula nods. "And what…since then, they're playing with us? But why? And how does this fit with the orcs and their new toys?"

"Not nicely," the Captain considers. "I can tell you that much. Is it a war, or a relocation? Is this part of his original plan, or is it incidental? And if we're saying the Suuden-Aryku are at war with someone, maybe our people, maybe someone else, they must be calling in a lot of orcs to do the dirty work. So, the next thing I suppose we COULD ask is what kind of results they're having. Are they using the orcs as expendable labor? What does it look like on the other side?"

"If it's our people from the Naarg uy'Sodrad," Petrith offers. "All things considered; I think we would clean up easily. They hit us by surprise here in the city, but if it came down to a proper fight where you could see them coming, I think we could easily defeat them."

"Assuming we would ever pick up our tails and actually FIGHT for a change…" Tana blasts.

"Yes, Tana," the Captain admits. "I'm sure we all know your feelings on the matter, and I can't blame you. But it was never our way to pick fights with people. And unfortunately, it became MORE of a habit to simply run away."

"Sorry, Captain, but after everything that happened out there, THIS time, I think we should learn a lesson from it…finally!"

"Not just this time. There were plenty of others that had come before. But this was a decision that fell to the Elder Council. And with respect, we all know how Master Velen felt on the subject."

"Yeah. Look, I don't like saying bad things about people, but ONE time of losing people should be enough to teach you to fight for it."

"True. All right, so if we say they're launching an endless stream at someone, the battlefield out there must be tail-deep in bodies by now. But then, what about the Suuden-Aryku in this? What are they doing, just sitting back and watching the show?"

"It must be a madhouse over there," Sulíma adds. "This much seems certain."

"Wait a moment," Túfula interjects. "What about an alternate idea. How long ago did we first notice this change in their behavior? Naturally, the Captain is right to ask how long they had that hole in space siphoning them off, but it wasn't until fairly recently when we first noticed them redirecting away from town and going off somewhere else. So, if it's a madhouse over there, it might be a madhouse turning the other direction. This is why we have this new migration to Camp One. They're calling for reinforcements, and if they're being treated as expendable, it could be simply to throw at something."

"While that's a valid point, Túfu," the Captain offers. "We still have to ask, who are they fighting, and what are the Suuden-Aryku doing about it."

"Maybe they ran off and left the orcs to finish up?" Sulíma muses.

"Finish up what?" Petrith notes. "The other guys or their own race... If Túfu is right, and they're being slaughtered over there, they could go extinct soon."

"You know," Túfula accedes. "Much like with Tana, I don't want this to sound the wrong way, but personally, I wouldn't cry much for that point. Not when you consider where we are right now."

"So," Sulíma concludes. "They send a never-ending stream of orcs at someone, possibly using the last of their species, and for what... simply to remove them from existence, another plaything to watch being killed? What kind of people would do this?"

"I don't know if I could accept the Suuden-Aryku are just sitting back," the Captain resumes. "Let's think back on Sargeras and whatever he actually wanted from our people. He came asking for help. What kind of help. We'll put aside our miseries for now if we simply say he hates us for having minds of our own. These orcs, however, seem willing enough to run to his side, and if we're right in saying they're expendable, it would seem he treats them like dirt, even WITH their dedication to his cause."

"He might treat everything like dirt, if that's the case," Petrith adds. "If his kind is dead, what does he have left to keep him occupied?"

The Captain sits quietly and stares at Petrith for a moment.

"That's an interesting point. I have to wonder what the cu'Nar meant by saying his race is supposed to be dead. Why are they dead…and again, why is he still alive?"

"Captain," Túfula wonders. "If his kind is dead, maybe they crossed paths with someone who didn't like them treating others like dirt."

"There you go," Petrith perks up. "And so, Sargeras runs off to escape, goes into hiding until the dust settles, and now he's back to his old games."

"And the help he wanted from us?"

"Military support. He's alone, his people are dead, what else could he want, but a strong-arm to pick up where he and the others left off. And of course, our people, being the dull-horns they are who don't know any better, fell for it. So he uses us for military power. That's what keeps hitting us. We didn't have this before. He takes our people, builds up a strong military, and now he goes out making trouble for other people, or maybe to get back at those who once made trouble for him and his kind."

"So, the help he was asking for was revenge," the Captain suggests. "But are the orcs a part of this, or are they being used for something else. Anything powerful enough to wipe his kind out of existence, assuming he's actually more advanced than we are, would wipe the orcs a hundred times easier."

"Maybe they were serving a smaller part of the plan," Petrith relents. "Something intermediate or preparatory. We didn't encounter them until we arrived here, so maybe they were a convenient option to serve a role. Whatever the answer, we may never know of it sitting on this side of the universe."

"If you're thinking of jumping through that conveyor, you'd better think again. You still have a lot of orcs on this side, and whatever is on the other side."

"But Captain," Sulíma asserts. "We should try to do something. We can't just sit here and do nothing. If they're actually attacking our people again…or even if not, maybe we could offer some relief by pulling the plug on that thing."

"Should I remind you that someone would take notice of that?"

"All right, we go up there in those hills and…um… Oh! Start a rockslide on those solar cells. You can't blame that on a bunch of refugees hiding in an old mining shaft."

"I'll admit that's an interesting prospect, but before I take any action, I think I'd like to know more about these orcs. For instance, where are they coming from and how many more can we expect to see up here. If we suggest this equipment has been there a while, and I think someone would likely have seen a Suuden-Aryku dropship coming in to check on things, or even to equip them in the first place…"

"Is that with or without us hiding inside this hole," Petrith muses. "And barely peeking outside for anything at all."

"Well, all right. But before this time, when we were still in the city. I think people walking on the streets might see something coming down."

"Unless they came down somewhere outside our immediate view," Túfula suggests. "We might have people walking on the streets, but ONLY in the city. We never travelled anywhere else. We're not a nation. We only cover one tiny corner of this continent. That leaves a lot of space out there they could use for this."

"Yes, Túfu, you're right," he sighs. "So, I guess the lesson here is to pay closer attention. Maybe to put up scanning arrays to watch the skies, even if we don't fly around up there ourselves."

"Scanning arrays," Tana considers. "Early warning beacons, maybe also some defenses. Again, how many times do you have to watch people die in the streets until you finally take the hint to build your own military, along with fortifications and big guns."

"Once again, Tana," the Captain shrugs. "I can't argue with you.

But this again has to fall on the Council, along with our escapist tendencies. No matter how you look at it, it's not a nice scenario."

"Then I might suggest, with respect of course, that we need a different form of government, one that doesn't run away from things. Furthermore, that WE, as a species, learns not to run away from things. After all, some of us don't like dying," she huffs.

"But anyway," Petrith tries to redirect the topic. "After that, we hid in this mine, and this could open up a lot of possibilities for them."

"It can," the Captain nods. "And then we have our recent observations, which were much more vigorous, but without any sightings. So, the last time they made a visit might have been some time ago."

"Before this change in behavior? Which might also suggest a change in THEIR behavior."

"Maybe. And like Túfu said, they only started making this migration as a result of things changing on the other side. Whether to spend them that much faster, or…well, maybe to fill a newly vacant space. In either case, there's not much we can do about it as we are."

"A newly vacant space…" Túfula frowns. "I'm not so sure I like the sound of that."

"Neither do I, but I have to work with what we can be sure of. We're not in a good position to fight as we are. Wherever those orcs are going and whatever they're doing on the other side, if our people are holding their own or not… Well, with so many having gone through already, I don't think it'll make that big a difference if we first try to understand it better on our side. Our position here isn't a very favorable one, and until we can change that, I think we should put some distance between us and that camp. If they're all moving to this one location, let's find out where they're moving from and see if there's any empty space out there."

"We've already got several long-range patrols scouting the areas on the other side of these mountains," Petrith recalls. "What do you have in mind?"

"We'll check further to the south and make a sweep westward from there. From what I remember of our early geographic scans of this world, the orcs were all found on just this one continent. They don't seem to be very good swimmers, and apparently, they're not good at building boats."

"We could build some boats," Sulíma suggests.

"Yes, we could, but under the circumstances, we probably couldn't build anything sturdy enough to cross the ocean, so we're stuck here on this landmass the same as the others. But we also know this continent extends some distance to the south, and the orcs don't apparently go the full distance. They don't seem to like the colder regions. So, if we can find some free space down there, maybe we could relocate. Then it wouldn't be as much a problem for us to start building some industry again, as there wouldn't be any orcs in the area to see our smoke."

"All right, Captain, that sounds good enough. This place is rather dull anyway, and the humidity sometimes causes my clothes to stick to me."

"What clothes?" Petrith smirks as he examines her rags and leather waistcloth.

"Hey, you should speak! You're not much better on most occasions."

"And I'm sure you're looking," he teases.

"All right kids…" the Captain announces cheerily. "I knew this moment would be approaching one of these days, but let's try to keep it…well, at least a little under control. As for looking for a new home, time is on our side so far, so let's send out scouts and see what comes back. In the meantime, we need to keep watch on those orcs."

Chapter 9

THE LOCAL COLORS

"Marelle!" Relissa shouts as she enters the guildhall courtyard. It was after school hours, and Marelle had been in conversation with Tristeen and Haran on one of the benches in the courtyard. Tristeen was once again sharing some of her lessons from the old mage academy in Rolsklinde to help bolster Marelle in her own studies in the guild's classes. Haran was free from his classes and sitting in on the conversation when Relissa arrived outside to join them.

"Hey, Relissa, what took you so long? I lost you after we finished in the showers."

"Aye, I had to run to the requisitions office real quick to pick up a new journal book. My old one is getting a mite full by now."

"Yeah, I was in there last week. They go quick when you have so much to study."

"Are you out here with the other finger-wigglers again?" she smirks. "Just how much do you round-ears need to compare notes, anyway?"

"My dear Relissa," Haran remarks proudly. "We round-ears are very studious learners."

"More like it just takes you longer to wrap your ears around it," she beams.

"And what about you?" Marelle asks. "Are your ears getting the…point…of it," she giggles.

"Oh, that's a good one, Marelle!" she concedes. "You know, the way I see it, it's a bit ironic. All these years I've known Haran and calling him names, and now I'm the one waggling my fingers."

"I'm actually excited about it. I never thought I would learn anything like this. Haran was the only one in our family with the magical inclinations."

"Not in my family. My Mum's a priestess, and she often tried to turn me into one. But in those early years, I had a lot of problems following the old ways and all our ancient traditions. Between her and my Dah, I felt a little buried in all that. Then there were the orcs. They were still hitting us back then, and that just brought home the idea that we're not going to be around long enough to remember it."

"Well, this is the future, and here we are, so get used to it."

"Aye, and I'm fine and happy for it, too!"

"Would you like to sit in with us and hear what's new?"

"I'd love to, but you know, I had something else come bouncing around in my head."

"That sounds painful," Tristeen notes. "How does it feel to have something bouncing around inside your head?"

A bout of laughter goes around the group as Relissa sneers playfully at Tristeen.

"Right then," she grins. "Maybe someday I'll open yours up and show you. But seriously, I remembered something we're supposed to be doing one of these days. I had a little run-by with Kaliya as she was going in for her session with Aelwyn, and this got me to thinking. You know, it's one of those things where this leads to that and then to another."

"How many of these bounces did you have to go through to get to the final idea?"

"Oh, a good three or four, to be sure… Now, if you'll let me finish…" she glares teasingly at the group. "This got me to thinking of Aelwyn, then Sigil and that brothel up there, and then to Thaelyn and that girlfriend of his.”

“He had a girlfriend in a brothel?” Tristeen blushes. “Oh dear, this sounds like something I should keep out of.”

“It’s not that kind of brothel,” Relissa chuckles. “It’s that place we told you about where they do all that head-scratching and name-calling.”

“Oh, that one... Yeah, I liked that part the most. Kimasxi, wasn’t it? I remember when Haran and I visited the lower district in the city back home and saw how some of the people interacted. I heard a few choice words echo across the room on occasion, and I didn’t know what they meant until Haran explained them to me. It was a little embarrassing. But to think someone goes into a sort of therapy session just to experience this, it’s very strange.”

“Apparently, this is their trade,” Marelle interjects. “It’s all part of the guild up there where they study sensations of all kinds.”

“I suppose I would have to live there to fully understand it. Maybe I can learn more about it someday.”

“Anyway,” Relissa continues. “This reminded me of that book Thaelyn was talking about, and I was thinking of going over to the library to check on it. Anyone want to come along?”

“A book...” Marelle wonders. “Which one was that?”

“That prophecy by Adalon the Silver... Remember his story in that demi-plane of his? Well, if we’re ever to figure this one out, we need to go check on it.”

“Adalon...” Tristeen muses. “I’ve been hearing that name a few times lately. She apparently said something once relating to His Lordship’s recent travel up to Sigil, and then a conversation with Cardinal Aelwyn when she visited not long ago in Firstfall.”

“I hear her name on occasion,” Haran mentions. “She’s quite a figure in certain circles.”

“But a prophecy?” Tristeen inquires. “What kind of prophecy? This sounds interesting. I’ve never had a chance to read anything like that before.”

"Would you like to come?" Relissa asks. "It's supposed to be over at the city library."

"Well, if you don't mind… Is this part of a study project for your class?"

"Nah, Thaelyn was giving us this tale while we were waiting for those elves to wake up during that interrogation we were doing once. He told us of this girl he knew, and then how she did something funny once that played him the chump. But apparently this was a good thing. I just don't know what he means by it. He has this way of getting under your skin with a good story, and keeping the juicy bits out for later."

"I've heard about that. It sounds as though he enjoys testing people to encourage their development. He reminds me of my father."

"Aye, so come on. Let's go find ourselves a good book."

They get up and start walking out through the gate onto the avenue leading into the city.

"You see that big building down there and across the way?"

Relissa points to a large ornate building, generally rectangular in shape, with spires coming up at the corners, and a golden dome rising over the roof. The library was only a few blocks away to the right along the cross street from where they were, and would make a healthy stroll down the avenue.

They continue walking away from the guildhall, turning a corner, and passing by several shops and a tavern. On the opposite side of the street were a row of civic buildings where some of the city merchant guilds held their offices, as well as the revenue office. As they passed the nearby tavern, they could hear the typical sounds of music and revelry of the afternoon crowd just getting off their daytime shifts and stopping in for a quick bit of relaxation. The avenue was neatly decorated with potted plants and trees, giving the impression of a city devoted as much to its fondness for nature as it was to the needs of a bustling population.

They finally arrived at the tall and opulently gilded front doors of the library. A sign in the window next to them indicated the operating hours with a smaller attachment hanging below offering to step inside. They enter through the doors into a small foyer.

The main hall of the library extended all the way to the back, with bookshelves both large and small interspaced along the way. To the sides, rows of shelving extended from the walls delineating nooks and alcoves from floor to ceiling. Part way through the hall was a set of wide stairs leading up to the second floor where even more bookcases could be found. Seating areas dotted the floor where people had settled to read their selections during the normal business hours, while a desk situated near the front allowed them to check out books to take home. Tables and chairs also offered space for patrons to copy notes for research and study. The atmosphere was quiet, with only a few mumbling sounds and the shuffling of feet.

"This place is huge!" Relissa whispers cautiously. "Bigger than the one back home by twice or more, and that's just the first floor."

"I don't even dare to mention how small our old library at the academy looked in comparison to this," Tristeen declares.

"Yes, Tristeen," Haran adds. "But keep in mind, ours was also a school, and the books we kept were much more to the needs of our education, what little they actually gave us, while this is a full library with everything. I don't think we had anything quite like this in the whole city."

"Is that before or after the Governor and his cronies threw most of it out?" she chuckles weakly.

"So, where do we start?" Marelle asks.

"I'd say with that desk over there," Relissa suggests. "They should be able to direct us better."

They move over to the front desk to speak to one of the librarians sitting behind it.

"Excuse me," Relissa begs politely.

The librarian on the other side of the desk turns to Relissa's attention. He frowns briefly at seeing her before catching himself for his manners as he takes notice of her uniform. He then passes his glance at the others behind the desk as he quickly tries to compose himself.

"Eh…yes, young lady. May I help you?"

"Aye, and I also caught that look in your eye. I'll bet I know what it was, but I'm no Drow, if that's what you're thinking."

"Oh, please…yes, my apologies. We received a series of notes and public announcements about your people, but sometimes old habits tend to protrude at the least desirable moments. Would you be part of that new group we found recently? Um…what was it… Night Elves?"

"Aye, that's me, I'm a Night Elf," she smiles.

"Well, I hope you will excuse me for my initial reaction. This is the first time for us to see one of your people. Our history tends to leave a lasting impression, so to see one of the Morierea here on the surface would likely turn a few heads no matter the cause."

"On the surface?" she wonders. "Where do they live, underground?"

"Yes, the Drow elves live in a region called the Underdark, which is a series of deep underground caverns. There's a history to this, if you're interested in reading up on it, over in the section of elven lore."

"That sounds like the sort of thing my Dah would like. He's a historian, and might find it interesting to read up on. But as for the rest of us, this is who we are, right and proper. Although a lot of us are a wee bit different from me. I'm a mite rough around the edges."

"Oh, well," he chuckles softly. "I'm sure that's not a problem. We have people from all walks of life among us. We simply attribute this to the fine color of our society. What is it I can help you with today?"

"We're looking for a book telling of some prophecies by someone named Adalon the Silver."

"Someone named Adalon the Silver…" he raises his brow. "So, does this mean you do not actually know who she is?"

"Well, not really. Since we're new here, we're still catching up on a few things."

"Ah, well then this is a good opportunity for you. We have a special section where we place books of this sort, over near Section D, Aisle Six."

"Um, right… This is actually our first time in here, where is that exactly?"

"Oh… You pass through here to that corner off to the right. That is Section D. The shelves are marked, so look for Aisle Six. As you walk along the aisle, you'll come upon the far wall where you'll find a section of shelving with her books on it. You can't miss it."

"That's what they all say," Marelle smirks.

"Aye, maybe so," Relissa grins. "But I think we can manage. Thanks."

Relissa gives a smile and a polite wave before heading off to the section where the librarian indicated she would find her books.

They walk through the main hall to the rear and turn down an aisle marked with a large section heading for the letter D, then along a row of bookshelves until they find one labeled as number six. The multitude of books stacked on the shelves was staggering. The shelving itself was marked with numbers indicating subsections, and the books were grouped in numerical order with small labels that appeared to serve as their location address within the shelf.

Tristeen was taking note of the filing system and comparing it to what they used back home in her old academy.

"This is a very advanced method of categorization. It certainly puts anything I ever learned to shame."

"Keep in mind, Tristeen," Haran advises. "First, you have a society that has been growing for a long time under the guidance of someone like Thaelyn; and second, with so many books to file, simple alphabetical methods might not be adequate."

"Look there," Relissa directs as she spies a likely display on the wall. "The framework around that piece looks a bit fancier than the rest, and the way that guy out there was crossing his eyes at me for not knowing this Adalon girl, I'll bet that's it."

She steps over to a uniquely designed display frame mounted on the wall at the end of the row. The framework was composed of rosewood with a silver trim and supported two hefty books. The books were hardbound and seemed to be silver plated. The titles read Prophecies of Adalon the Silver, Book One and Book Two.

"That looks like it might take a while, Relissa," Marelle suggests. "Do we have time for this today?"

Relissa tries lifting one of the books. Its size is matched only by its weight, and she struggles to pick it up. Haran steps in to assist, and along the way, he takes a close look at the binding and pages inside.

"Everything about this thing seems heavy," he notes. "It's not just the cover, but these pages too. They're not your usual parchment."

"I don't think I want to try walking this all the way out to a table," Relissa concedes. "Maybe we can just sit down right here for a quick peek."

They settle down on the floor in a cozy circle as she opens the cover and proceeds to the first page. She starts to read.

"In the Time of Flowers, a Child of the Wheel,
Will shine through a column upright;
The Son of the Mountain, a millennium proud,
Where justice has been His delight.

Across the Land, they shall herald His name,
And many will follow His course;
Woe be to Evil, wherever it lay,
To be smitten beneath His endorse.

The Pillars of Three shall He bring into cause,
A mighty power beheld;
The fortune of Man, the strength of the Beast,
And the Spirit of nature to meld."

"Oh, I love this!" Tristeen exclaims. "It's like a riddle. You have to solve each verse to understand its meaning."

"Some of this we've already heard about, I think," Relissa denotes. "I'm no bookworm like you, Tristeen, but I'll bet I can already figure a few of these out."

"All right, what do you think so far?"

"Well, this bit up here on being a millennium proud and the next one about justice sounds a bit like someone we all know. I don't know what the Time of Flowers is about, or why he's called the Son of the Mountain."

"Wait a minute, Relissa," Haran interjects. "Thaelyn's home, it's called Mount Celestia, right? We seem to be using metaphors in these verses, so this seems reasonable if we are indeed talking about Thaelyn in this case."

"And the Time of Flowers? That's an odd one if ever I heard."

"That sounds like a reference to a calendar date. I recall from a few of my early apprentice studies where they used to have those in older times. Let me see...the old Tae'Eladaran calendar, the Time of Flowers... Kythorn. It's the sixth month of the year."

"So, we have the sixth month," Tristeen concludes. "But do we know what year? Or does it matter in this case? He's already here, so this looks like old history by now."

"These books do look a mite on the older side of things," Relissa observes. "But I'm wondering now...you mentioned history, so do you think they'll have this on a test someday?" she chuckles. "What's next here...to shine through a column upright, any ideas on that one?"

"Not a clue," Haran offers. "Tristeen, anything out of you?"
She shakes her head.

"Marelle? You're being rather quiet over there."

"Yeah, I'm thinking of our trip to Sigil, and how he took us up there."

"Jiggers!" Relissa yips. "Now there's an entrance!"

"Just remember, the man is halfway to godhood. How do you think he'd make his first appearance in this world?"

"This next set looks fairly straightforward," Tristeen suggests. "Based on what we've learned of him so far...well, he's a King now, so I think the world has already made its statement in his favor. How about we skip that one and move to the next?"

"Aye, easy for you to say," Relissa groans. "I don't know about this. The Pillars of Three? Fortune of Man, strength of the Beast... Hey, wait... Spirit of nature, that's got to be the dryad, Shescellaie. Haran, he said he founded the Order with two others, one of them being her. So, who is the second one, I wonder?"

"For that matter, how do we interpret the first one?" he adds.

"Well, if he's the first one, he's a man…or generally so," she giggles.

"He said he combines the best of each person into his guild," Marelle recalls. "So, the Fortune of Man must be relating to that."

"Then that just leaves the strength of the beast," Tristeen asserts. "So who, or maybe I should ask, what is this beast?"

"He's been mighty secretive about a lot of things so far in this war," Relissa admits. "So, we might not know that one just yet."

She turns the page to see more verses referring to the same individual at what seems like different moments in history. The stories tell of his deeds and journey to fame.

"Are we looking for something special in all this?" Tristeen asks.

"Aye, we're looking for something on his old girlfriend from Sigil. This book here looks like it's mostly just him. Maybe the next one will show it up. Haran, I don't think I can lift this thing off my lap. Will you help swap it over?"

Haran lets out a minor giggle as he steps around to lift the heavy tome back onto the shelf, exchanging it for the second one, then handing it back down to Relissa who was still sitting on the floor. As before, she opens it to the first page and starts reading.

> *"The Daughter of Sky, from realms far beyond,*
> *And hardships many to number;*
> *A quest She did make to seek a lost love,*
> *As a trade for Her ultimate slumber.*
>
> *Through dire plights and turmoil quelled,*
> *She strove to meet with Her choice;*
> *Where rebirth brings Her back again,*
> *To the One who gave Her a voice.*

Twice around, She will come to Him,
The Daughter of Sky at last;
To the Son of the Mountain, for in His mind,
She is an Echo from His past.

The circle complete, the tidings revealed,
Together they will aspire;
The wholeness of Man, the oneness of World,
And the birth of a Proud Empire."

"I'm starting to not like this Adalon girl," Relissa chuckles. "It's like she's intentionally trying to make this hard."

"Maybe she was," Haran suggests.

"How do you mean, Haran?" Tristeen asks.

"Just a thought, really. But now that you ask, didn't Thaelyn once say he didn't like chasing after prophecies?"

"Aye, on that first day he came in!" Relissa recalls. "Other people's dreams, he called it. It was when he was talking about his own power of Sight…when Kaliya was asking those questions."

"So, are we to interpret this as Adalon making it hard on him, personally?" Tristeen asks.

"Well, many of these verses do seem to be specifically directed at him," Haran deduces. "Maybe she didn't want him learning something prematurely?"

"Now I'm wondering just how old these books really are, if he's more than a thousand years himself."

"All right, peeps," Relissa announces. "Right off the top, this looks like what we're after. The Daughter of Sky, from realms far beyond… This sounds like we're talking about a girl, and realms far beyond would certainly include Sigil in my book. The part about seeking a lost love would fit what Thaelyn was saying about the two of them way back in the early days."

"But, good gracious, Relissa," Tristeen muses. "That part talking about hardships, and then the final one in that verse. What did she do, for pity's sake?"

"Thaelyn mentioned some sort of trick she pulled on him. He knew her up in Sigil during her mortal life, up until the day she died, or at least that's how I got it as he was telling the tale."

"All right then, let's continue to the next one. Dire plights, turmoil, striving to meet something… Sounds like she worked hard for it, whatever it was…"

"She couldn't be dead then," Haran notes. "Not completely. So, maybe just before this, especially if she made a trade for it."

"Yes, good one. But now, what is this about rebirth?"

"The One who gave Her a voice…" Relissa mutters. "Marelle! Are you thinking what I'm thinking?"

"Part of it, maybe… Thaelyn said he helped that girl up there get her voice back after some nasty deed by a mage."

"Aye, and then she did this bit to give them a second chance. Marelle, she came back for him! Are we talking about reincarnation? By all the Gods!"

"Gracious!" Haran mumbles. "That's determination for you."

"This could pass as a romance for the Ages," Tristeen concedes.

"Next," Relissa continues, newly inspired by the mystery. "Twice around she comes. What… Once wasn't good enough?" she chuckles. "The Daughter of Sky… Right, so whoever this girl is after being reborn, she's now called the Daughter of Sky. Anyone know what that might mean?"

"More metaphors, as far as I can tell," Haran remarks. "Then we have the one for Thaelyn again, Son of the Mountain, and the next one talking about some kind of echo from his past? Sounds like we're referring to a reflection of an old memory here, especially when you said he was talking about this as a past love."

Relissa suddenly jerks her head up with a revealing insight.

"Buggers, you witch! Echo…Ecco. It's the girl's name! She's playing the words on us. And I'll bet that's why these things are so hard to read. She wanted it to be a surprise. But that means Adalon also knew about it. Who is this dame, anyway, that wrote all this?"

"We still don't have a clue on that part that speaks of coming twice around," Haran reflects. "Did something happen on the first occasion that it didn't complete, or is there another reason?"

"Maybe we can ask on that later. He's got to tell us something after all this. If we're talking about something historical, then it's got to be common knowledge by now."

"So, now we come to this last part," Tristeen directs. "Circle complete, tidings revealed…sounds like they finally came together."

"For all that's Holy," Marelle gasps. "People, has anyone here actually had the thought to look at this from the standpoint of the modern day? I'm looking at those last few lines and just had a shiver run through me. Could this Daughter of Sky be running around the streets right now with a pair of large feathery white wings on her back?"

"Jiggers, Marelle!" Relissa yelps. "But then that means…"

"She came all the way back," Haran concludes. "She married him and became his Queen. But how did she manage this?"

"Wait just a moment," Tristeen interrupts briefly. "Let's summarize. This girl, you say her name was Ecco? And you also say she…well, maybe to say at the end of her life, if not actually dead. If she was somehow reborn, she must've made a deal with someone to enable this."

"Tyr," Marelle whispers. "Aerlie carries his essence in her. She's as much half-god as Thaelyn is."

"Aye," Relissa adds. "She was mortal and came back as a Celestial."

"Wow," Tristeen winces. "That would take something special. But this still doesn't give us the full answer. All right, let's say this god Tyr helped her. If she was living in Sigil, I suppose she might have a way to reach him. What about these lines at the top? She endures a lot of hardship before apparently being reborn."

"And she traded something big for it, too," Haran notes. "…Her ultimate slumber, which I'm going to assume to be the eternal rest of the afterlife. And through all this, she was working for something…hard."

"Criminy!" Relissa yips. "But wait, how might that work…"

"What is it, Relissa?" Haran asks.

"Twice around…could that be a part of it? Or are we talking about something else?"

"Relissa?"

"Just a moment… Let's look at her. She's telepathic, like him; can also apparently project her thoughts to other places, like him. Um, telekinetic…"

"Yes, just recall that orcish patrol on the first day."

"Jiggers, you're right."

"So, where are you going with this?"

"Thaelyn got all his bleedin' powers as gifts from Tyr during his thousand-year contract of service. But what I'm trying to figure now is the timing of it. He said he knew her just a few centuries into his life up in Sigil. So, let's say something like three centuries to make it round."

"How old is he now?" Tristeen asks. "Do you know?"

"Um, Haran, help me on this. I remember something on that first day, but with everything buzzing around me, I was a bit light in the head after a while."

"He said…a millennium and…three-quarters."

"And Aerlie?" Tristeen resumes.

"Four centuries."

"So, if we do some simple arithmetic, we have an offset of about one thousand three hundred and fifty."

"I would even round off that fifty, Tristeen," Haran suggests. "Since we don't really know how old Ecco was when she died, and we don't have a precise age on Aerlie, that half century can serve as a margin."

"Sounds good, and if this was three centuries into Thaelyn's life, that leaves us with just one thousand years."

"Enough for a contract with Tyr," Marelle proposes. "Just like him. And I'll bet part of her payment, if we can use that term here, was the reincarnation. I think I get it now. She knew he was under this contract and couldn't join her in an intimate relationship. So, she finished her mortal life, went to Tyr, made her own contract for a thousand years so she could meet with him after he finished his, and…um, wait a minute, I lost a piece."

"Which one?" Relissa counters. "Sounds like a good enough plan so far."

"Yeah, up until the time her contract ends. How does she know where to find him? We can't be sure if he had plans already made to go to Tae'Eladar after he was done, so she might not know where to go after hers came due."

"I think that's easily answered if you just ask Tyr," Haran surmises. "Surely the father would know where his son has run off to," he smirks.

"Right, that could work. Just one little thing I'm not sure of now."

"And what's that, Sis?"

"Well, other than that part about going twice around, which we might not be able to figure from what we have here… Why Avariel? Do we know what race she was before this? She was mortal, but do elves exist up there? I recall that mention of Aelwyn's friend, an Eladrin, but that's another Celestial, and probably an exception to the rule. And why choose to be reincarnated as a winged elf here on Tae'Eladar? Or maybe it was potluck; she got the next spot that opened up. Wow, that sounds weird…"

"Maybe we should just ask her?" Relissa suggests.

"I'm not even sure if I have the courage to walk up to her with all this, much less ask her. And would she even know the reason? Does a person remember something like this after rebirth?"

"Honestly, Sis," Haran considers. "I don't know of anyone who could answer that, except possibly Aerlie."

✦✦✦✦✦

"Now, Kaliya, we will see about your mobility and physical interactions outside the chamber. Follow me."

Aelwyn and Kaliya were well involved with their session. It had been over a month, with Kaliya taking her lessons a few times a week, keeping it interspaced with her other training practice. Most of it so far had been to refine her ability to project herself out-of-body at will, and to slowly wean her from the need for the incense. By this time, she had learned methods of meditation that allowed her to release herself and move around in free space consistently.

Until now, they had been keeping their practice inside the ritual chamber, as it provided a fertile environment for her mind to manipulate her local space. They practiced picking up objects, moving from location to location using only her thoughts, and further refining her talent to create objects within the unusual space of the chamber. Today, however, was adventure time. They were ready to begin testing her interaction with the outside world.

Aelwyn opened the door and led the two of them into the antechamber. Master Sagrid waited at the table he used to supervise the ritual process. He noticed the two women exit and stood up to greet them.

"Are we finishing already? You just went in there not long ago."

"No, Master Sagrid, we are simply going for a little walk to test some of her abilities."

"Abilities…such as what she did once before?" he asks while watching Kaliya as she approaches the table.

"Were you present at the time?"

"I was monitoring her testing when she came back outside with a most amazing result."

"Indeed, well, we are trying to refine it now. But it is important to keep our work a careful secret to prevent any disturbance that could interfere with her concentration."

"I see."

"Meanwhile, do you have any items we could examine while we are here? Something small, like a pen, or a small book."

The Mage Master looks down at the table and picks up a pen, offering it to Aelwyn. She redirects him to give it to Kaliya, who steps over to pick it up.

Kaliya reaches out for the pen in the man's hand and lifts it without any difficulty. She turns it over in her grip to examine it, then swapping it to the other hand before returning it back to his.

Master Sagrid studied the action carefully, reflecting on Kaliya's earlier ritual event where she came out of the chamber carrying a physical object.

"Cardinal Aelwyn, is this to say she is currently, um…"

"Yes, but we are still very early into the study here, so we must test a variety of examples."

"Incredible. This will surely be an amazing skill, once she raises it up."

"No doubt," Aelwyn smiles. "But for now, if you will excuse us, we would like to take a brief stroll and return shortly."

"Absolutely."

The Mage Master nods, as the two women leave the room. They walk through the corridors and out into the courtyard.

It was late afternoon, and the students were relaxing around the courtyard, some in conversation and others studying their books. Relissa and her friends had finished up in the library and were making their way back up to the guildhall. As they passed through the gates, they saw Aelwyn and Kaliya making rounds and speaking to a few of the other students.

"Kaliya," Relissa shouts. "How are your lessons going?"

Kaliya turns to meet Relissa and her group as they approach.

"Hi, Relissa," she responds placidly. "We're doing very well."

Kaliya reaches out to pat the young elf on the shoulder as she speaks.

"Are you on that dream smoke again? You're acting a little funny."

"No, we finished with that. But I need to keep my calm, so I can remain focused on my lesson."

"Aye, but you're out here, not in that room."

"So I am! Isn't that amazing!" she grins mischievously.

"I think you've had too much of that stuff already, girl," Relissa teases.

"Kaliya," Aelwyn instructs. "Take a moment and walk over to that door for me, and then back across to this wall on the other side."

Kaliya walks across to the administration entrance, then turns and walks back to the wall on the opposite side of the courtyard.

Relissa and the others watch, perplexed as to the meaning of the action. Aelwyn prepares herself for the next instruction.

"Now, recall what we practiced in the chamber. Fold yourself to the point in front of the door."

"Fold?" Relissa ponders out loud. "What do you mean by fold?"

Kaliya places her focus on the point in front of the door. She concentrates, imagining the space between her and the door folding, where space collapses into a point, and thus allowing her spirit projection to simply cross over. She pushes her mind to pass across the gap and into the new location.

Relissa and the others observe as Kaliya's image blurs and streaks across the courtyard to the other side, halting just in front of the door.

"Jiggers!" she shouts. "Kaliya, are you for real on us?"

She turns to look at the shocked expressions, with a wide grin spreading across her face. She walks back over to the group.

"It that really you?" Marelle asks meekly.

"Yes and no, Marelle," Kaliya responds. "I'm projected at the moment. My body is resting inside the chamber."

"That just sounds too weird!"

"Hold out your hand."

Marelle tentatively holds out a hand for Kaliya. The tall Daanen'kai girl reaches out and gently touches Marelle's hand, placing her fingers lightly on the upper surface. To Marelle, it felt solid, just like she might expect of someone touching her, but it also felt like it wasn't quite real. The texture didn't feel like actual skin.

"Do any of you have a book or something I could try holding?" Kaliya inquires.

Relissa pulls out the journal book she picked up earlier, and hands it over to Kaliya. Kaliya takes it and opens it to the first page.

"Hmm, you don't take a lot of notes, Relissa," she remarks as she browses the pages.

"It's a new book. I just got it."

"Ah, sorry... Did you just come from a shop then?"

"No, actually, we just came from the library in town."

"The library?" she asks, returning the book.

"Aye, we were looking up that story Thaelyn gave us on that girlfriend of his."

"Oh, did you learn anything about it?"

"Sure did, and it's a whopper. She apparently started out working for something, probably going into a contract with Tyr, much like Thaelyn did one time. She traded going to the afterlife for a second chance at him. She then got reincarnated so she could join up down here. How do you like that for determination?"

"In all the nether-space, now there's a trick to play! But wait, are we speaking of...Aerlie?" she offers uncertainly.

"Aye, the same, it has to be."

"Cu'Nar help us, and here I am just barely recovering from my last set of horns. No wonder this place is engineered. That woman installed both of them to run everything."

"Woman?" Haran wonders.

"Well, perhaps I'm using the term figuratively, as she's also a goddess. Maker Kuroku. She's the one responsible for refurbishing this world, remember?"

"Oh, her. Wow, but does this mean SHE holds a role?"

"She must be behind some part of it, maybe in collaboration with the others. What did you learn about this?"

"It goes a wee bit like this..." Relissa begins.

Aelwyn listens to the conversation, grinning brightly as it unfolds. Marelle and the others wait as Relissa reviews what they learned in the library, but Marelle also took note of the unusual display on Aelwyn's face.

"Excuse me, Aelwyn," she interjects. "But you look like the cat that ate the mouse here. Do you know anything about this?"

"Perhaps... Recall that I am slightly older than Thaelyn, and we knew each other in those early days, as I also knew Ecco. I followed her life the same as he. We were close friends once. But as her life came to a close, I had to say my own goodbyes, and it left me feeling empty, just like it did him. But she also left a curious note with me. She did not reveal everything, as it was apparently a secret she had to keep. I did not know the full story until later, however, during their wedding, when we had a few details revealed to us."

"So, we're right on this then?" Relissa asks.

"For those portions you have deduced thus far, you are indeed. Very nicely done, Relissa. As for you, Kaliya, yes, I believe I can also say the Maker has played a role in engineering a few things."

"But now," Relissa continues. "What is this twice around bit? We're thinking we might need to go ask her, but it's a mite scary to think about."

"Twice around?" Kaliya muses.

"Aye, it says she came around twice for some reason before they join up officially."

"Interesting. And now as Aerlie... You know, this sounds a little like the story she gave me when I was going through that exam she did."

"Oh? Well maybe you can help us with this part."

"She described a moment in her life when she suffered a really bad experience in her youth, and apparently Thaelyn came to her rescue."

Now Kaliya retells the story Aerlie once gave of her young life in a circus cage, her rescue, and the return home, then the part of her older life and the dragons, with Thaelyn coming to help again, along with the mention of Adalon who joined in.

"That must be weird..." Tristeen winces. "You meet your future wife as a young girl, and then later marry her once she's old enough to become eligible," she giggles.

"That Adalon must get around a bit," Kaliya reflects. "We were speaking of her at length a while back in a meeting with that Archivist Windsong on several of her more recent prophecies...or rather those that mention more recent times."

"I recall her name mentioned once," Marelle reflects. "It was back in Firstfall when we were in a meeting about Darumon trying to sneak around behind us to Tae'Eladar. She would head up a local defense while we pushed forward."

"By the sound of it," Tristeen relents. "She must hold some high authority around here."

"Yeah, it seems so," Kaliya affirms. "Aerlie said she was one of the founders of the guild."

"A founder? But does that mean…"

"Oh great…" Marelle moans. "…The strength of the beast. So Thaelyn, or perhaps the people of this Order, are the fortune of man, the dryad spirit is the nature part, and Adalon represents the strength of the beast?"

"This further implies she knew what was happening," Haran suggests. "So, is this a prophecy, or something planned?"

"Planned, we think," Kaliya admits. "There's surely some prophecy involved, but it reads more like a story fated to happen. We came to a few conclusions about her in that meeting. We think she's an agent, probably working for that Maker Kuroku, who seems directly responsible for Tae'Eladar and everything here, and then Thaelyn and Aerlie, all coming together for a reason. And this reason might just relate to where we are now with Sargeras."

"Buggers girl!" Relissa yips. "So, what are we saying, she made all this just to go after that guy?"

"It sure looks that way, and the cu'Nar are spies."

"Spies?" Tristeen wonders.

"Yeah," Kaliya nods. "These new prophecies we're studying tell the story of my people…all the way back to the beginning when we think we were artificially created to serve Sargeras. But the Maker laid a trap for him. The cu'Nar gave us a message with a special keyword attached, which only certain people would know about, like a Celestial, and then we brought it here so they can take the chase forward."

"Criminy!" Relissa groans. "So, that bit of him taking up this new war isn't really HIM taking up this new war?"

"It's probably incidental at this point, this thing they call Fate around here. Do you recall how he blasted us with that voice of his? Well, that's just his reaction to hearing the word, and naturally it would cascade to him giving chase."

"Jiggers, and to think, I actually signed up here."

"We're starting to think everything around us is a plan to take out Sargeras. Someone was watching him from the beginning, using the cu'Nar as spies, up until the moment when he came to our world. Then they informed my father to pick up and leave. We were expected to be driven…and this is where I think the word comes into best play…driven by Darumon right up to your front door, where we would eventually come into contact with two people who should not otherwise be here, but who know the story of the Primordials."

"That's scary!" Tristeen shudders. "So, where does this leave us?"

"Training for war…and me in study for this crazy gift of mine," she chuckles.

"But who or what is Adalon?" Tristeen asks.

They all suddenly turn to look at Aelwyn for the answer.

"Do not look at me, Children," she refutes. "I am simply an educator. It is not my place to reveal such mysteries."

"Isn't that a contradiction?" Marelle muses.

"Oh bloody wonderful, another one," Relissa complains. "Measure of Balance, my shiny bum."

"Personally, I think they're all like that," Haran considers.

"Right then, so we'll figure it out later, I guess. We got a big part of it, and I think that's good enough for now."

✦ ✦ ✦ ✦ ✦

"Captain, one of our long-range scouts just got back. She says she's got something important to tell."

"Let's hope we finally found the outer limit of the orcs and their territory."

A female scout has returned to the mine to meet with Captain Lapäli. Her assignment was a long-range patrol to the south, hoping to find evidence of orcish camps being abandoned during their migration into the local camp to pass through the conveyor. In the meantime, the Captain had been in conference with Sulíma and Túfula, among others, about the plans to move their hideout to another location.

"Captain," she reports. "I didn't find the outer reach, but I did find something else which I felt was important. There's a small orcish camp to our south, I estimate two weeks run from here, considering the pace we're keeping. It's hard, but at least we're getting used to it."

"Two weeks? And what's so special about this camp?"

"First of all, I'd like to say, it looks bleak out there on the population count. A lot of empty camps along the way. At least until we get to this one. But Sir, here is where we found another of those conveyor units inside."

"What?!" he screeches. "Another one? Just how many do they have out there, for cu'Nar's sake?"

"Captain," Sulíma interrupts. "Perhaps we should try making a study of this situation before we go any further with our plans. If they have more than one, we need to know how many and where."

"And why!" Túfula adds urgently. "It's bad enough to have one, but two?"

"You're absolutely right," the Captain affirms. "Cadet, tell me more about this camp. You said it was small. How small?"

"Yes Sir, tiny, not the same as Camp One. As I said, we saw a lot of empty camps out there in the general area. If we say they're condensing on a point, this might be the local point, and with nothing else to condense into it by now. And we could clearly see the conveyor at a distance. It didn't have as many orcs or their buildings around it."

"Condensing to a point," he muses. "But mostly cleaned out by now. I'm not sure if I like the sound of that, simply for the issue of cleaning things out. What's the terrain like out there?"

"Grasslands, mostly flat, and the camp is situated near a hillside."

"So, we're out of the jungle at this point?"

"Yes Sir, it's mostly meadows and a few small groves of trees. There are hills some distance away, so this might be better described as a valley floor."

The Captain considers the situation for a moment, trying to reconcile the idea of another conveyor, but inside such a small camp.

"There's something wrong about this unless I'm simply missing some important detail. Camp One is bustling like a madhouse. Why isn't this one? If it has a conveyor, it should be just as busy as the first. And if this only began when we saw this change in tactic... Unless...”

“Unless our impression of a consolidation effort is correct,” Sulíma offers. “We were suggesting a migration into Camp One. We also suggested it could be new orders to focus on only this one, maybe because the other side is experiencing trouble or something, and it’s calling everyone to one point.”

“All right, this might make sense. So, at one time, they were making multiple incursions, but something changed, and it’s all being redirected to Camp One.”

“This can also explain the local region,” Túfula suggests. “If this camp has a conveyor, it should be an important center. But if it’s so small, and with so few orcs by now, maybe they’ve already cleaned out the local area, migration or no migration.”

“Possibly. And it also reflects on them being told either to relocate completely, and this area is done now, or else, if like Suli said, they are all redirecting elsewhere for some reason, and this one is no longer viable. We should continue to scout the local region to see if we can confirm this.”

“Sir,” the scout considers. “If we’re saying both of these go to the same general place, like the same world, but the focus is more on the one, this tells me the other one couldn’t be located very conveniently to the first.”

“Maybe, so we might be looking at two incursion points, probably at distance to each other.”

“But Captain,” Sulíma offers. “If this is an invasion to hit our people from the ship, that only represents a single location. I mean, dear cu’Nar, it’s not THAT big.”

“That’s a good point, Suli. So, are we saying this really is our people, or are the Suuden-Aryku making trouble for someone else on this occasion?”

“Using orcs to hit from multiple sides?” Túfula muses. “But then, something must’ve happened on the other side. Could it be only for the reason the other front is no longer valid, or did they simply run out of orcs in the local area to send there.”

"That's also an interesting thought, but it might not answer the one about Camp One. No, I would be more inclined to say this conveyor is no longer needed, or maybe no longer desired. They could be running out of their expendable workforce regardless. But maybe the second front failed, and the exit point is no longer under their control."

"If that's the case, whose control is it under, and could they be friendly to us?"

"While that's certainly something to think about, Túfu, I'm not very anxious to simply jump through and start asking questions about it. For all we know, they cut this one out because they only need the first one now. Maybe they've taken over the place, and like we said before, this is filling in a vacancy."

"Well, as much as I hate to say it, you may be right, but we definitely need to study this more."

"I agree. We'll first wait to see what happens down there, and if this new camp continues to dwindle, then we'll think about what to do with it."

"You know," Sulíma suggests. "If the other side is struggling somehow, this is all the more reason for us to try and do something about Camp One."

"Maybe, but it is also all the more reason for us to put some distance between us. If all their focus is over there, they'll be paying very close attention to it."

"So, we continue our scouting," Túfula admits. "But you know, this makes me wonder if there are any more out there. This new one isn't doing so well, but maybe there's another one out there doing better."

"Fine. Let's designate this new one as Camp Two, and if we find any more, we'll add them to the list. Cadet, keep up the good work. See how far to the south they go and let's consider sweeping to the sides to see what else is out there. Also, assign someone to keep an eye on Camp Two to watch the flow of orcs passing through. Let's organize one of Petrith's relay operations leading back to us here."

Chapter 10

IMPARTING WISDOM

"G eneral," Thaelyn inquires as he makes his morning visit to the tactical office. "Have we closed the lines yet?"

"My Lord, yes!" he announces proudly. "I am pleased to say we got word last night that north has met south and there are no more orcs in-between. Our war, at least in this world, can be officially declared complete. The only concern remaining is the one we can do little about for the present until Kaliya is ready for her service."

"Excellent work, General. Pass my thanks to all of our troops and let us begin sending them home. But now, what is the situation with the portals?"

"The situation seems largely stable and unchanged. Once again, Portal Three is inactive. We continue to see the occasional passage of wildlife in the area through the window, which would indicate a recovery of the natural fauna. This brings me to wonder what the local region looks like there. Perhaps the entire area has been emptied out."

"If they are all consolidating into Portal One, this may very well be. Or perhaps each portal had its own territory to serve, and this one has been fully exploited."

"Perhaps. Portal Two is still showing minor activity, but fewer and farther between. I think that area may be near to depleting. Portal One is still quite active, but we are keeping it under control as they pass through."

"As to the portals themselves," Thaelyn surmises. "Once we arrive in that world, if these portals are still operational, we will need to locate them and bring in some Daanen'kai technicians to shut them down. We do not know what manner of technology is keeping them running, but for it to go this long without Suuden-Aryku support suggests it is either low maintenance or self-maintaining. We are approaching our first year since arriving here. Devices of this sort must require some form of servicing by then, if not sooner, unless the Suuden-Aryku have developed a technology that does not wear so quickly."

"What amazes me about this technology is that it can make such precise calculations to pinpoint the exit portals over time without the need for this anchor we were looking for once. The Suuden-Aryku must have made a very careful study of this world during those early days to discover all the variables involved in this."

"Yes, but the trouble that comes to my mind is not what these conveyors are capable of that points them in our direction, but rather how we may find our way to the next one. If these orcs are simply jumping through due to some command to join the war effort here, not knowing what truly waits for them on this side, we could lose a valuable resource if they possess the knowledge to find Morndindor."

"Do you think they would actually know this secret, or could it be found elsewhere?"

"Adalon's prophecy seems to suggest we will find a way, and if our course is being engineered, I suppose one way or another, we will have our answers. But as I have said so many times in the past, I am not one who enjoys chasing other people's dreams, not even hers," he smiles.

"Under the circumstances, I doubt anyone would enjoy that, the way she presents them. That poor Archivist Windsong sure seems on the edge so much of the time."

"And hers is a good example."

"Then, do you think we should change our strategy on how we deal with the orcs as they come through?"

"We may consider this with Portal One, as this seems to be their focus, and I would imagine their more important members are likely consolidating there, along with everyone else. But the state of affairs seems to suggest Portal One will be with us for a while. It is only their warriors coming through, along with a few supplies, and they are less likely to possess this knowledge than, say, their shamans. We will evaluate the situation as it progresses."

"Yes, my Lord."

"I must also wonder if this information may be recorded in some fashion. From generation to generation, even orcs will pass on knowledge in written form, and we are speaking of something that was once taught many centuries ago. From the time of the orcish invasion, to the time of the elven one, it would need to be preserved in order to teach a new generation of shamans, as the older ones would clearly be dead by then."

"Then perhaps if it's in a written form, it might survive even if all the orcs are sacrificed, and we might still find our way. But this is taking a bit of a gamble."

"Yes, and I do not like to gamble."

⁕⁕⬥⁕⁕

Captain Lapäli had been receiving a series of reports from his spy network extending down towards the orcs in Camp Two in the plains to the south. They were working their way through a chain of outposts trailing back to their hideout in the mine. The final outpost in this chain held a position in a set of hills just opposite of the orcs, and supported a troupe of scouts who were covering the local area. Some had been sent to the western coastal region to investigate any orcish camps on that side, while others continued to the east.

The scouts would often make runs at a jogging pace, coming to a rest periodically and picking up again. This level of activity allowed them to move over large distances while not wearing themselves out entirely. Their sustained efforts had toughened them for the vigorous activity, and with an average speed being more than that of a human, they were able to cover greater distance within the same time.

The relay network had proven itself useful not only to pass messages, but also to serve as outpost markers for scouts to check in for food and drink, and rest from their long runs. The scouts would take turns on patrol, giving each other time to recover before the next duty shift.

Using the relays allowed them to send a message chaining from one outpost to another much more efficiently than for a single scout to run the full distance, which could take weeks and involve a lot of strenuous activity. A runner from one outpost would make a quick dash to the next, hand off the note to another one, and they would continue the movement, keeping the message in motion until it arrived at the home base.

The Captain was in conversation with one of his officers as they reviewed a rough map of the terrain.

"Lieutenant," he begins. "Camp Two, as far as we know, seems to be receiving from this one here to the west," he points at the map, "which is then being fed by the next one to the south. Our last report was they didn't see any more below that, only a few abandoned camps. As far as this region is concerned, it looks like they've mostly cleared it out, leaving only these few leftovers, none of which is anything near as big as Camp One."

"This makes it appear as though Camp Two was being used to clean out the local region. And Camp One has a larger influx because it is pulling in from more settlements. But Sir, I have to wonder how large an area Camp One is actually covering. Camp Two covers the region to the south, but the plains in the southeast would be too far to walk. We might be looking at a hole in the southeast where there should be something."

"I may have to agree. Based on the distance and running times, and then the frequency of our deliveries, I'm hoping to receive something soon…maybe tonight. We sent out a few patrols into that area a couple months ago, chaining our outposts along for support.

The only thing we need to be careful of is crossing any migration lines. We don't want the orcs noticing us."

"Granted, but if there are any more of them out there, it should be in that region."

"Right, our scouts have reported they can't find any more orcs below this line here," he points to the map again. "Not even abandoned camps. Which makes sense to me from our old geographic studies of their territories."

"So, if our eastward patrols are moving into this area," the Lieutenant directs to another point on the map, "we should have a fairly good understanding of their occupation, as we'll be running up against another coastline soon. This should complete our study of where they are. The only thing after that is to decide what to do about it."

"Captain," Sulíma interjects as she listens to the review. "All this talk brings me back to asking why they would want to leave this world. It's their home. Surely even they would hold more interest in it than that to simply walk away, wouldn't they?"

"That's a good question, Suli," he affirms. "I wish I had an appropriate answer for you. The orcs seem to like to fight, so maybe the call to battle is enough to make them jump. But even the most bloodthirsty orc should want to keep something like a home. I've had some time to think this over, and a thought came to me once. We've been saying the orcs were following the Suuden-Aryku, but I think it's more reasonable to say they're following Sargeras. He's the one who goes around apparently corrupting everything he sees, and such a primitive race like orcs would probably see him as a god figure. So, Suli, if your 'god' told you to leave home, would you?"

"Not being one who believes in a god of any kind, I suppose if I were an orc, I might. But this actually brings me to another thought. Camp Two is almost empty, with only what's left in these other camps to spill into it. What do you think will happen to that conveyor afterwards? If there are no more orcs using it, will the Suuden-Aryku come pick it up, or simply leave it to rot. And do you think we could move in and grab it before then."

"That's an interesting idea, but if the Suuden-Aryku do come back to retrieve it, and it's gone, they'll start asking questions. Let's wait till our next few reports come in from the southeast and see what else is out there. Then we'll decide how to go about things."

✦

Relissa, Marelle, and Haran were making progress through their courses. They had just finished the third season schedule and were preparing for the fourth. They had come near to their goal of fulfilling some of the prerequisites for their application, and now their schedule was changing to accommodate some new classes.

The studies they were receiving this first year would place them in-line to finish such courses as the second circle of mage study, as well as to fill out their knowledge on math, science, and a large portion of history and cultural study.

Kaliya continued her practice with Aelwyn these past few months, mostly repeating the same routines until she was competent, and keeping her travels only to the local area. She was no longer using the incense, and could now conduct her meditation outside the ritual chamber to project her image.

Her practice involved retrieving items of different sizes and mass and relocating them elsewhere, as well as interacting with fixed objects like doors and windows, opening and closing boxes, and using small implements. She was also practicing movement using thought rather than simple walking, in which she would focus on her destination and fold her spirit form to zip across to her intended target. So far, she only practiced on destinations within line-of-sight, but today she was going to try something new.

"Kaliya," Aelwyn advises. "It is time to test your ability to travel to places based on the previous experience of your visitations. You will not see them directly, but instead you must envision them within your mind and direct your spirit to phase from the local space into the desired one."

"This sounds like what I did when I travelled to Ruuki uy'Daan."

"It is, and we will develop this skill incrementally until you are proficient, first in the local space, then to other places where we can monitor your progress. Only after that, will I have you attempt to travel outside our observed range."

"How should I proceed?"

"You must recall the place you wish to visit. It will manifest as a memory of somewhere you have been before. The practice of moving your spirit from place to place can still apply here, but rather than seeing your destination with your eyes, you must now reflect upon it in your mind."

"Any suggestions for my first attempt?" she asks.

"I have spoken with your friends Relissa, Marelle, and Haran on this matter, and recruited their help. Relissa is waiting for you in the courtyard while Haran is conducting a little exercise on the lower mage training field. Marelle is waiting near the track field outside the training hall. Visit with each and offer a simple hello, so they can see and interact with you, then return here."

Kaliya nods and sits in the chair she has been using lately for her practice. They were given the use of a quiet study room in the guild, where they could close the doors for privacy and conduct their practice undisturbed by other students. Unlike her first attempts, where she had to disrobe to free herself of any physical burdens, her skills had improved to the point where she could do this fully clothed in any quiet space. In addition, she had learned by now how to manipulate her image to provide an appropriate cover.

As she relaxes in the chair, she begins her meditation, following the familiar practice of releasing her tensions and imagining a floating sensation. Her body feels as though it is drifting, a feeling she has become accustomed to during her training. She draws her spirit away as a separate entity, detaching it from her physical self, then emerging into the room and condensing it as a solid form.

"Good," Aelwyn affirms. "Now, your first assignment is to find Relissa, then go to Haran, and lastly Marelle. After which, you will return here."

Kaliya nods and closes her eyes, recalling the memory of the courtyard. She applies the same technique she had used before to push her spirit through space to a new location, but this time replacing the physical sight with the recalled image. She visualizes the destination, followed by the familiar sensation of folding space, and her image vanishes in a puff of ethereal mist.

Relissa sat on a bench in the courtyard, as requested by Aelwyn, reading one of her study books and waiting. It was a cool autumn day, there was a gentle breeze, and the skies were mostly clear. Several other students passed through the area, some in discussion of their class studies while others were more deeply involved in the local gossip.

In the center of the courtyard, near the benched seating, an image flashed into sight. The shape coalesced into a tall, blue-skinned female standing a short distance away from Relissa. The young elf jumped at the sudden arrival.

"Jiggers, girl," she complains. "I'm not sure if I'll ever get used to that. So, she's got you popping all over the guild today?"

"Yeah, it's my first time trying this out. Looks like I got it right."

"Aye, let me lay a hand on you just to make sure I haven't been sniffing that same smoke you were using before."

"I'm not using it anymore. I got off of that a couple months ago."

Relissa stands up and pats Kaliya's arm to make sure she's real. She makes a quick check around her body to ensure all the pieces are intact before returning to the bench.

"Looks like you made it through. Criminy, girl, just think of when you get all this figured out. We won't know if you're real or a ghost on us!"

"Aelwyn tells me that some of our future lessons will involve me changing form, too. I only take this form because it's natural for me. But just imagine me changing into an animal, or a tree!"

"A tree?" she chuckles. "Aye, but just make sure you don't do it around any woodpeckers!"

"I'll keep that in mind. Well, it's time to go find Haran. I'll see you later."

Kaliya closes her eyes again and this time imagines the mage training field. She had spent a considerable amount of time there during her studies, so it was a well-known location. She brings in her focus and once again disappears in a puff of mist.

Relissa examines the now vacant space and simply shakes her head as she goes back to her book.

Haran was out on the field practicing some of his most recent lessons when Kaliya popped in next to him. He notices the sudden appearance out of the corner of his eye and flinches at the sight of the tall apparition. He had been trying to prepare himself for this occasion, but it didn't help once it actually occurred.

"Kaliya," he calls to her, reaching out to take her hand. "I find it absolutely amazing that you are able to do this."

"Thanks, Haran. I'm still in the early stages, but I'm getting better."

"Are you excited about the prospects of someday returning home again?"

"Yes, I am, but I still have a long way to go before that, and I want to understand everything I can before I do it."

"That's a very good idea," he considers. "I'm just thinking of the old days we had together. You know, on our old scouting runs into the Badlands and such. Seems like an Age ago by now."

"Maybe, and we still have a long way to go together."

"At the very least until Sargeras is brought down. But for now, you still have more work to do. Don't let my reminiscing on the past hold you back."

"All right, bye for now…" she offers, and then closes her eyes for another phasing run.

Marelle was sitting on the bleachers overlooking the track. There were several people out on the field today practicing their exercises and preparing to make runs around the track as part of their scout training. From out of nowhere, Kaliya pops into view on the bottom walkway of the bleachers. Marelle jerks around quickly to study the unexpected sight, then relaxes when she sees it's only her friend.

"I wish I could pop in and out like that," she declares. "Just think of the trouble I could've gotten myself into during my service with the Guard."

"I think Captain Kholgard would've had a heart attack after a while," Kaliya replies as she sits down next to her.

Marelle pats her on the arm, as instructed by Aelwyn to check her form. She studies Kaliya's image, front and back, to make sure all her features are well-defined.

"I'm trying to imagine you as a spy, Kaliya," she states. "You pop in, look around, and pop out, and no one can do anything about it."

"Now there's an interesting thought. And just imagine if I'm able to change my form. You know that cute little saying about a fly on the wall?"

"Now that's scary," she winces.

"Only if we're on the wrong sides…"

"Well, talking about sides, I think you've done your deed on this one, so you'd better get back to report in."

"Right, and thanks for helping, Marelle."

◆◆◆

"Captain, this just came in from our relay network."

It was evening, and a messenger arrived at the mine to deliver a note. The messenger was from the nearest relay post. He turns it in, and then moves off to rest in the gathering room while a replacement runs out to fill his space at the outpost. The message is delivered to the Captain at his strategy table. He opens it up to read it.

"In the cu'Nar's name," he mumbles.

"What is it, Captain?" Sulíma asks.

"Well everybody, we found what we were talking about earlier. We'll call it Camp Three. Another conveyor, but this one looks abandoned. The report tells us there are no orcs in the camp, just some local wildlife running through the region, and nothing else."

"If there's wildlife running around, then that must mean the orcs have been gone long enough for some of it to return, right?"

"It would sure seem that way."

"Captain," Túfula interjects. "If Camp Two still has a few orcs in it, but this one is empty, and for long enough that the local wildlife is coming back, then how do we explain this? Could this be part of the migration moving to Camp One?"

"I suppose that might explain the continued flow we're seeing, if it's pulling in from so far away."

"So this means, whatever happened on the other side of this one, happened a long time ago, but Camp Two is still gathering up a few stragglers. Should we expect to see the remainder of those moving to Camp One also?"

"That's also a good point, and we'll need to keep watch for it."

"But if all this happened some time ago," Sulíma wonders. "How does this relate to when we first saw this change in behavior within the city? Did we miss something that began earlier? And once again, how long has all this been going on if there are no more orcs out there?"

"If there's nothing left out there, I think it must have been occurring for a good long while. And yes, I think this would qualify for us missing something, like not going out any earlier to take a look," he chuckles. "But then, how could we possibly know if they were being called away somewhere. We never saw this anywhere else, and realistically speaking, it wouldn't make sense to involve them if the Suuden-Aryku hold so much capacity that orcs could never meet up to that same challenge."

"True."

"As for the change in behavior, I can't be sure, but whatever it was, it had to be big."

"Big… Big enough to clean out the area to the southeast, big enough to nearly clean out the south, and now it's cleaning out whatever is left to the east. And yet…" she forms a bright grin. "We seem to have an abandoned camp with a shiny new conveyor sitting all alone," she perks up excitedly. "Well…is it my centennial yet?"

"Suli," he chuckles cautiously. "I'll admit, I don't know about your centennial, but this does offer a possibility. I'd like to watch it for a little while to see if anything changes. But if we have wildlife roaming the region and no orcs hunting it, it sure does give the impression of pure abandonment.”

“And with no Suuden-Aryku arriving to pick it up,” Túfula adds. “If they’re aware of this on the other side, and if this equipment is actually so important to them, I think they would’ve come for it by now.”

“She’s right,” Petrith affirms. “If the Suuden-Aryku are actually watching anything at all, they ought to know if the orcs are still using this. So, are we saying they don’t care, or aren’t watching anymore?”

“I may actually have to agree with both of you,” the Captain admits. “But it’s hard to say why they wouldn’t come pick it up unless it simply isn’t important to them. This should represent some valuable equipment. Do they actually throw stuff like this away? And then, if we say they aren’t watching, then we have to ask why they aren’t watching. Could it be like Suli once mentioned that they left the area to the remaining orcs? But then, if they hold no further interest in the area, why do we still see orcs moving in? This represents a kind of paradox.”

“Could it be they were at war with someone, then finished and told the orcs to fill in the space, maybe to regather themselves in a new location for some future campaign?”

“Filling in a vacancy, but selecting one specific location as a gathering spot. Maybe. But I might counter, if they’re using conveyors to move them around, moving out from here would be no different from moving out from anywhere else.”

“Yes, they could just as easily reconfigure the conveyors to a new endpoint.”

“A paradox,” Túfula wonders. “Then how about this. Maybe they lost the battle. Maybe the Suuden-Aryku pulled out, but the orcs, being expendable, are simply being sent in because, like we said once before, Sargeras treats them like dirt, and now he wants them all dead.”

“Wants them all dead?” the Captain frowns. “Why, because they lost the battle? Isn’t that being a little masochistic?”

“Masochistic…like attacking us simply because we didn’t behave as the trained animals he wanted us to be? Maybe they failed somehow, and this is their punishment."

"Well, all right, if you're going to put it that way. But then why to this one location…because of the geographic convenience to this enemy that pushed them out?"

"Maybe. Less distance to walk to your final demise."

"Túfu!" Petrith winces. "You're the one sounding a little masochistic now."

"But it's a reasonable suggestion if you consider how he might treat people…how he's been treating us. If the orcs were expendable from the start, or if they became this way because of a failure, he might simply be angry at them like he is at us. So, he gives them instructions to jump through that hole in space. But they can't see what's on the other side until they land, and then boom…dead orc."

"It doesn't paint a pretty picture," the Captain relents. "But it is a picture. And yet, we can't really be sure of anything from where we are."

"So, what do we do about the conveyor?" Petrith asks. "You're right, and so is Suli; it's a valuable piece of hardware. We shouldn't just let it sit out there."

"I know. We'll watch it for a little while, and if it seems static, we'll see what we can do. But the real question is do we want to bring it back here, or build a new base somewhere else."

"Either way, it sounds like it'll be a long trek, and some of that stuff will be heavy."

"And something else," Sulíma adds. "We should ask, how do we transport it. I'd hate to think of someone trying to carry it, and we don't have any transport vehicles."

"Trying to do this manually would take months," the Captain considers. "Even if to build something like a sled would take forever since we might need to make multiple trips."

"Personally, I think it might be better to bring it here. This is where all our machines are, and all the salvage. There's no sense in taking it halfway across the continent only to transport everything else halfway across the continent to go with it."

"You're right, but what about Camp One in this case?"

"If we had a fusion reactor, couldn't we recharge some of our old weapons and use them to protect ourselves?"

"Suli, most of that equipment has been dead for so long, it's unlikely it could hold a charge anymore. We might have power, but we'll be spending a lot of our time just trying to repair the tools we need to repair the bigger tools that repair the machines that make the tools."

"Wow, so we need to get started thinking of ways to bring all this up here."

"Technically speaking," Petrith notes. "If the only orcs remaining in this world are over there in Camp One, that changes the equation for us significantly. It was one thing to think we might be fighting a full world of orcs. But that camp, regardless of their numbers, puts us in a much better position to rebuild ourselves right where we are. Like Tana said, build some fortifications, some big guns, and then, if they dare try to attack us again, boom, dead orc right here."

"And even more," Túfula asserts. "If they continue jumping through that hole in space, we might not even have to do that much. We might simply inherit this world. And since they don't even know we're here, time is on our side to wait for it."

"All right, kids," the Captain nods. "I'll credit each of you for your arguments. So, our first goal must be to find a way to transport that equipment, and do so reasonably efficiently. You know, I recall there used to be some large vehicles in the city, over at the old Civil Utilities building. A few of those could probably pack up the whole assembly if we're careful."

"But Captain, um..." Sulíma flusters. "How do we transport the transports?"

"Well, Suli," he chuckles. "You once mentioned reinventing the wheel. So, here's your chance."

✦ ✦ ◆ ✦ ✦

The week was soon coming to a close and Aelwyn was meeting with

Aerlie in the guildhall courtyard for a review of Kaliya's progress before another session.

"Aerlie, I have an idea for an exercise for Kaliya, but I may need some assistance from you to see it through."

"Oh, what sort of exercise?" she replies.

"There will be two parts to it. The first is to travel to a place she is not as well familiar with, certainly not like she is with the guild here. The next part is to return an item back."

"If she can only go places that she can recall from a previous visit, where would you have her go?"

"This is where I need your help. I am thinking of sending her to another city, something prominent. What other cities are there nearby where we could send her for study?"

"A large city? We have one just west of us on the coast called Amberdain. Of course, there are others, but this one should do nicely. What is it you want her to pick up?"

"We will first need to send her to examine the city, and in particular to some location that she will return to later, perhaps a local shop. Afterward, we will send her projected form to retrieve a package for us. If you could send word ahead to have something ready for her, she could be our courier in this regard."

"This should be fun," Aerlie smiles. "When do you want to do this?"

"I would imagine it will take some time for her to travel to this place and investigate the location, and I would not wish to interrupt her classes. So, perhaps we could conduct the first part during one of her rest days. Then we can perform the second part during a subsequent session."

"That sounds fair enough, and we have the weekend coming up. So, let me see, where should we send her?"

As the two women conspired, Relissa, Marelle, and Haran were reconvening in the courtyard, as was their habit after class. They saw the women relaxing on one of the benches in conversation and strolled over to pay their respects.

"Hello, everyone," Aerlie announces. "Have you seen Kaliya? We were just talking about her."

"Dreaming up more of those little ghost outings for her?" Relissa asks.

"Oh, of course, and some good ones, too. She'll be the talk of the town soon, and not just this one."

"Oh buggers, that poor girl."

"It won't be that bad, but she does need to practice and test herself on different levels."

"Aye, I'm with you. I just hope you give the rest of us a chance to catch up once you're ready to send her to Ruuki uy'Daan."

"We'll see how it goes. Thaelyn needs her to study up on her mage skills as one part of it, and that'll take time, even if we rush things."

"How high do you need her for this?" Haran wonders.

"To mark a rune with the standard method would typically require a Circle Seven mage. But we think she might need to use something special in this case, since she will be in her projected form, and we're concerned about the results of marking a rune while in that incorporeal phased state."

"I see. Do you think she would be able to channel her energies in this condition? And how would the exit portal appear, maybe to manifest itself in the same state? Do you have any other ideas on how we could do this?"

"These are questions we'll need to answer. We may have to use a special spell scroll to work this solution, or perhaps an effigy. We could have her set the rune on a solid surface, allowing it to phase-sync with the local environment, and then cast the spell on it from there."

"And would she still need a Seventh Circle degree for that?"

"It wouldn't hurt. Thaelyn and I think we may have bought ourselves enough time to play with, at least for the short term, with that visit to Sigil. If the Suuden-Aryku try entering the city, they'll have a really hard time accessing the portal to deliver any equipment into it, and this could stall Darumon long enough for us to make our move."

"What if anyone else enters the city?" Marelle considers. "After all, Darumon seems to like corrupting different kinds of races for different purposes. Couldn't he try another?"

"He could, but it might take time to bring them up to the right level of competence to use them as an alternative to the Suuden-Aryku. And that still buys us time."

"Good, assuming he doesn't already have something. And that means we might be able to move in behind him, but this also asks the question of whether we can find him."

"That is a question we are all asking, but until we can make the step to Ruuki uy'Daan, the answer will have to wait."

The conversation turned to other subjects, including class scheduling and course study until Kaliya arrived in the courtyard to meet with Aelwyn. The two of them excused themselves to go attend their session in the quiet study room while the rest finished their conversation outside.

"So, you also teach classes in the mage academy?" Marelle asks.

"On occasion," Aerlie admits. "I spend a lot of my time teaching in the temple, but since I'm practiced in both, I tend to do as Thaelyn does and share my own experiences in the classrooms."

"What classes do you teach?" Haran inquires.

"I give an introductory lecture to the Third Circle and occasional lessons in the advanced classes. You'll be starting the Third Circle course at the beginning of the year, right?"

"It looks that way. They were pushing us through the first and second circles hard enough."

"Those aren't too hard to study if you're an adult. We spread them out for the children, so they have more time to study and learn the disciplines of the craft. But from the Third Circle on, you need to pay closer attention to the responsibility that comes with your skill level. I remember when I was there. I had a lot to learn in those years."

"What is it that made you choose to be both a mage and a priestess?"

"My mother was a priestess, and my father was a scholar, but he also dabbled in a little magic, and this fascinated me."

"Ay, that sounds a bit like me," Relissa yips.

"Indeed, your mother is also a priestess, and your father a historian. But because of my family, I was uncertain which way to go for my own studies since I was intrigued by both. When I first came here, after Thaelyn helped my people with those dragons, I wanted to try developing my skills in both professions, since his academy was so rich in study potential."

"Those dragons again…" Marelle mentions. "Kaliya was telling us about that story you shared with her during her physical exam. It's amazing how he handled that."

"Aye, and while we're at it," Relissa recalls. "Is this the second time you came around to him? We were reading up on that prophecy of Adalon's. We got most of it, I think, but there were still a few pieces missing."

"Which ones?" Aerlie wonders.

"Well, we got the part about Ecco, and we figure she went to Tyr for one of those thousand-year contracts, like what Thaelyn did, and this is probably how you came about. But jiggers, reincarnation?"

"Yes, this was surprising even to me. I was not aware I had any kind of contract from Tyr before this."

"So, you don't remember anything from it?"

"My current life began as a child believing I was orphaned and found in the woods by my mother."

"Uh, wait," Haran hesitates. "Isn't that a little bit of a contradiction…found by your mother?"

"It is," she smiles. "She had to keep it secret, as she was not pregnant at the time."

"Um, all right…but this kind of spoils some of my lessons on where babies come from."

The group shares a laugh at the notion.

"I can explain this better if you like. We use such a term as cloning for this point. A clone is basically a copy of another entity, in this case my mother. Tyr produced this directly within her body, creating a child that was a copy of the mother, but in this case ascended as a Celestial to create me."

"Right. I think I'll stay with the idea of finding you in the woods, maybe within one of those mushroom rings with little pixies dancing around it."

They let out another boisterous round of laughter.

"All right, fine, but here I am," she smirks. "I didn't know about this until much later, as my mother was under strict instruction by our goddess and a seraph that assisted in my delivery to keep it secret."

"A seraph? Wait a moment, I'm trying to recall a few of my lessons. Aren't those supposed to be some kind of servants to the gods?"

"Yes, they are from one of the more advanced Celestial races. The seraphim are the female component, and have large white feathery wings. Later, when Thaelyn and I met the first time, it was because I was captured and put into a cage in a circus."

"Yes, Kaliya told us about that little adventure of yours as a girl."

"Good, so he brought me back here and helped with my injuries and illness, as I was badly malnourished and feverish. Then he took me home. But he and our Patriarch got into a little argument, mostly because our Patriarch didn't like humans much."

"Humans...so I guess he didn't know Thaelyn isn't actually human?"

"No, he didn't. Our isolation up there in those mountains cut us off from knowing about anything happening elsewhere in the world. And it was partially the result of this argument when I learned my first few pieces. Thaelyn had already left by then, and my mother began scolding the Patriarch for his poor manners, saying it was my purpose to bring Thaelyn up there to help us."

"Oh grand, and now he's gone."

"But apparently it was fated this way, as Thaelyn had previous information from Aerdrie Faenya that there would be TWO occasions to help my people before she gave him her special favor. This is to say, before our people would be free and join up."

"Wait..." Haran interjects. "Fated? How do you mean that?"

"Someone was guiding our way, Haran. And after a while, we began to realize it had to be Maker Kuroku. For instance, recently,

Thaelyn and I, along with Aelwyn and Vonafel…you remember her from that time Thaelyn was going up to Sigil, right?"

"Aye," Relissa affirms. "She came running up to us with that wacky bit about a circular city full of doors."

"Right. Between us, we have been concluding that there may be more at play than previously thought, especially if you consider Adalon and her prophecies about this war. Adalon apparently knows more than she ought to know…about Ecco, and therefore me, about the Daanen-Aryku and their full history, including Sargeras, and a message they were carrying back here to warn us about him. And then, about us, meaning me and Thaelyn, being here to receive it."

"Aye, I remember a few bits of this when I was talking to Kaliya not long ago. She apparently came out of a meeting with you about this."

"Correct. Thaelyn was once directed to come here by Adalon, and later they joined forces to create the Order. So, his involvement seems very direct, and hers alongside it. Now, how do I play into it? Am I to say Ecco just got up one day and decided to do something no one has ever done before by going up to Tyr and propositioning him for a contract? Then, coincidentally to have Aerdrie Faenya get involved to help my people as a secondary objective, and then third that I would discover the Elixir of Visions in my family's library at just the right moment when it was called for."

"That sounds like a lot of coincidences to me," Haran notes.

"Indeed! So, clearly, the Maker made a few backroom deals with both Tyr and Aerdrie Faenya. I was to be a Chosen One to help my people, then to marry Thaelyn, and further to assist in developing our people. It would seem I was chosen by her to be, um, well, I dare to say recycled, but better to say given another chance to join with him."

"That's incredible."

"Just how old is Adalon?" Marelle asks. "By the sound of it, she's been around a while."

"She is presumably as old as Thaelyn. Some have even suggested she may have been born at the same time and for some mysterious reason, perhaps less by coincidence and more by intention."

"Jiggers," Relissa moans. "And put that on top of the rest of it."

"Yes, I suppose we should, at that."

"I don't suppose you'd like to tell us who, and for that matter, what she is? Because we're figuring if the people of the Order are the fortune of man, and Shescellaie is the spirit of nature, then she's got to be the strength of the beast. It sounds a wee bit scary."

"Perhaps, but she is a very kind soul and loves the people, and the people also love her. She doesn't get out much these days...or ever for that matter," she shrugs. "Usually only on special occasions. Instead, she spends most of her time pondering the great mysteries of...well, I'm not even sure if I want to think about it right now, for everything else we're talking about."

"But excuse me, my Lady," Marelle interjects. "I seem to remember something of Kaliya's story where she took on a white dragon by herself. This couldn't be some kind old lady in a rocking chair."

"No, I suppose not," Aerlie giggles. "But it's important for you to meet her someday, especially since you're all students in the guild and need to become familiar with her."

"Well, all right then. I suppose that follows naturally. Where does she live, somewhere nearby?"

"Yes, actually, behind us inside the mountain..."

"Inside...the mountain?" Marelle intones suspiciously.

"Yes, our dwarven engineers once carved out a lovely lair for her during the initial construction phase of the guildhall."

"A lair?" Relissa whines.

"Well, that might explain the beast part," Haran whimpers.

"And now she lives there with her son," Aerlie concludes.

"Oh, how cute," Relissa winces. "And she lives with her son."

"In a lair, inside the mountain," Marelle summarizes. "And how do we get in to see her?"

"I'll probably have to take you, as the passageway leading down to it is sealed by a set of magical doors. Students don't usually go down there, so it's mostly just Thaelyn and me these days."

"Um…and why is it sealed?"

"It's a leftover from the old days when Thaelyn first built the guildhall. Although it's probably not really necessary, we did it to offer a little privacy. In those days, the world was a bit different. He first met her in an underground cavern where she served as a guardian between the surface world and the Underdark, mostly keeping the Drow at bay."

"Oh, but of course, keeping the Drow at bay, how silly of me to ask."

"After they joined forces, she relocated and made her new home here. But to give her some security, we built these magical doors. It's actually not so unusual to have such doors leading into a private chamber like this, and it also reflects a little on our old history…a bit of nostalgia…so we haven't put much thought into changing it."

"I've noticed you do seem to enjoy your history around here," Haran mentions.

"A guardian before the Underdark…" Marelle considers. "…Who's capable of taking on a white dragon by herself, and now lives in a lair inside the mountain behind us. Right, I think I need to make a quick visit back home and bury myself in the mound that used to be the barracks."

"Oh, you kids these days," Aerlie giggles.

✦✦✦✦✦✦

Kaliya was spending her weekend carrying out an assignment to travel to Amberdain, a large metropolitan city on the western coast of Sein'amar. She was using the gateway portal hub located in downtown Bya'an Tamoranth, which sits inside a large transfer station along with a node for the local city network.

The hub operated on a rotating schedule, switching between destinations on a regular timing interval. It was monitored by a conductor who called out the destinations as the rune indexer wheel turned. A clerk stood behind a counter selling tokens to use the facility as a means of collecting revenue for the network maintenance and travel tax. When the wheel turned to their destination, each group would step forward, hand over their tokens and step through.

Kaliya had never used the facility before. She was fascinated by the organized complexity of the service. It reminded her of the old history lessons she studied once in school about Azgarén and the transportation networks they used there. Only in her case it was a public transportation network of hover coaches rather than portal devices.

As she passed though, she arrived in Amberdain in a similar transfer station. From there, she had to find her way to a place known locally as the Promenade District. Not knowing where to go, she had to ask directions, and for this she decided to speak to a local watchman.

"Excuse me," she asks as she walks up to him.

The watchman had noticed the tall, blue-skinned female enter through the portal, as did virtually everyone else in the station. Gasps and whispers were echoing around the floor space as she walked away from the hub facility.

The watchman eyed her carefully as she approached.

"Yes? May I help you?" he replies cautiously.

"I guess you've never seen one of us this far out from B.T., right?"

"B.T.?" he repeats softly, studying her cadet uniform. "Gracious, are you one of those new people His Lordship recruited into the Order?"

"Yes, I am. My people are called Daanen-Aryku, and my name is Kaliya Nazég."

"Ah, I see now. Yes, this is the first time we've seen any of your folk out this way. And my goodness, look at you!" he glances briefly up and down her form. "Such a proud example! Well, welcome to Amberdain, the City of Merchants!"

"Thanks, you people are all so nice. Maybe you could help me find my way around. I'm on assignment and need to find the Promenade District."

"Of course! The quickest way would be to use the local portal gate, located just over there in the next section of the station. If you should feel like going for a stroll through our fine city, I could direct you along the path you would need, but if you are on an assignment for the Order, I guess you aren't here for the sightseeing aspect of it."

"Not this time, but maybe later."

"That's well and good. Please follow me and I'll show you to the local gate."

The watchman brings her into the next section of the station where the city's district portal is found, and begins explaining the various settings she can use to find her way around town.

"We are currently in the Civic District. Here, on the rune wheel, you will find the Promenade District. And when you are ready to return, you should use the gate in that area to return here, then you can find your way home again."

"Good to know. Thanks for the help," she offers.

Kaliya waits for the wheel to turn until it cycles to the setting for the Promenade District, and then jumps through. She arrives in a plaza with a large marketplace set into an oval-shaped bowl-like depression with stepped sides, a bit like an arena. She moves out into the open, once again drawing the attention of nearly every passerby in the area, and recalls her instruction for her assignment. She had been told to descend into the marketplace and look for a confectionary shop on the second step from the bottom.

As she works her way down the stairs, she passes by shops selling a variety of wares, including food, clothing, household items, and other accessories. She spies a couple of taverns, an inn, and a variety of outdoor market stands. In the field on the bottom of the bowl, she saw a stage platform and a small carnival.

Once on the second step, she wanders around the side of the marketplace until she finds her mark. It was a moderately-sized shop with decorative swirls on the front window, and a deliciously sweet aroma wafting out the open door. She steps inside to investigate.

The shopkeeper, along with the other customers inside, all turned to gaze at the tall visitor, cranking their heads up to see her face, then back down again to study her other features. They all stepped aside as she entered the building.

"May I help you?" the shopkeeper asks mildly, uncertain if he wished to speak at all.

Kaliya looked at the man and glanced at the others in the shop, trying to judge their expressions at her appearance.

"I seem to be the center of attention around here today," she states politely.

The shopkeeper passes his gaze at the others in the room, and then turns back to her with a careful smile.

"I suppose it is simply that we haven't seen any like you in this city before. I see you are wearing a uniform, and the colors look like you're from the Order, is this correct?"

"Yes, I am. We're new around here, and so far, we've been busy fighting the war, so we haven't gotten out much."

"Oh, yes, I understand," he declares, feeling more relaxed by now. "I've heard about your race, it's a new one to us here. Hopefully, we'll have more opportunities to meet in the future."

"Yeah, Lady Aerlie and my instructor are setting me up for an assignment soon, and they had me make a run out here to get familiar with the place before that happens."

"Oh? What sort of assignment would bring you here?"

"As I understand it, I'll be picking something up in the next few days. It's a simple thing, just to get me used to travelling around."

"Ah, how interesting! Such a strange assignment for a student of the Order, but I guess if you're new to our world, you need to start somewhere."

"That's right, like learning to use the gateway network, finding my way through cities like this…" she glances outside.

"Ah, but of course, and this might be new to you."

"And this is sure a nice place to start," she looks around the shop. "I'm tempted to spend my last month's wages in here, but I need to stick to my duty," she grins.

"Well, my dear, we're open every day, so if you ever get time away from that, you know where to come," he beams.

"Thanks a lot. But now I need to be on my way…now that I found the place. I have to return to report in," she glances around at the various treats. "And before I lose control of myself. Cu'Nar give me strength!" she giggles.

Kaliya gives a pleasant wave as she leaves the shop.

She returns back the way she came, taking special note of the surroundings and the local atmosphere, the positioning of the shop, the stepped design of the Promenade, and the plaza in general. All these details were important for her to clearly recall this place for her future visit.

✦✦✦✦✦

The week begins with Kaliya returning to her studies. Her schedule progresses until the end of the day when she joins Aelwyn for her latest session.

"Kaliya," Aelwyn advises. "I think you have progressed well enough by now that we can relax your study sessions to give you more time for your other practice. We will take every third day, between your mage practice and combat practice. Aerlie feels that we should allow you to develop those skills strongly in order for you to be ready for your full duty, and I must agree."

"How much more of this training do I need?"

"I would still recommend we carry you in incremental steps, but you have progressed nicely thus far. We have yet to try a variety of applications, and I wish to see you through it gradually to study the results, as some of it may require special attention. As for today, I will have you perform a test to see how well you are able to fold your spirit between different places, and not only in our local environment."

"This has to do with that trip to Amberdain, right?"

"Yes, based on what you learned during your recent expedition to the city, I will have you perform a deed for me to apply a new skill. Aerlie has arranged for a package to be prepared at that same shop you visited before. You will go there, retrieve the package, and then return to me here for a brief review. I will give you further instruction afterwards."

Kaliya nods and takes up her seat. As she has learned to do so many times by now, she relaxes into meditation and projects her spirit form into the open space in front of her. She turns to look at Aelwyn, who simply nods, and then Kaliya closes her eyes and recalls the confectionary shop she visited a few days before, disappearing in her traditional puff of mist.

She arrives just outside the shop. The activity in the Promenade was brisk, with people visiting other shops around the district. The immediate area on the step where she arrived was currently empty, so no one was in view to notice her strange appearance. She walks through the open door of the shop and meets with the shopkeeper again.

"Ah, I see you're back," he greets her. "Would you be interested in something special, or are you on another assignment?"

"On this occasion, I'm on assignment again. Sorry. I'm here to pick up a package for Lady Aerlie. I'm told it should be waiting for me."

"Ah, yes. A courier came in earlier requesting some of her favorite treats to be made ready. I will need a signature on this receipt if you please."

The shopkeeper presents a small paper for Kaliya to sign, and offers her a pen. She takes the pen and signs her name on the paper, neatly printing it on the indicated line. She then sets the pen down and hands the paper back to him.

"Very nice, and here you go, young lady," he hands over the box.

"You might be surprised at just how young I am as compared to my overall lifespan," she smirks.

"Oh really! Do your people have an especially long term to your favor?"

"Quite! And we tend to measure it in centuries," she grins.

"Good gracious!" he chuckles. "Well, I'm sure there are many curious examples across the Seas of Creation."

"More than we can both imagine!"

Kaliya picks up the box from the counter and prepares to leave.

"Try not to eat it along the way, will you?" he jests.

"Yeah, if I had my body with me, it would be buckling over from the temptation. Still, I need to hurry and bring this back to B.T."

"Your…body?" he hesitates.

Kaliya offers a quick wave as she steps back from the counter. She grips the box firmly, closes her eyes, and vanishes in a puff.

"Dear gods above!" the shopkeeper yelps. "What are they training over there?"

Kaliya reappears in the study room, having successfully transported the item with her from the city. Aelwyn had been waiting for her return. She stepped over to study the results of her student's effort, looking inside the box to examine the contents.

"Good," she declares. "You were able to carry the item through the fold along with its contents. This is an important step, as it may occur that you will be called upon to carry other items inside containers. But now we will try something new."

"What do you want next?"

"This item is to be delivered to another location, and this location is outside our dimensional realm, from what I understand. This is an important task, and I want you to be especially focused on your folding practice."

"Outside? Are you sending me to another world?"

"I will have you deliver this with a special blessing from Aerlie to Thaelyn at his command post in the town of Firstfall. You should know the way well enough to find it easily."

"Yes, I do. And what do you want me to do after that?"

"Perhaps engage in a friendly hello, interact with a few objects, and finally return to me."

"I think I can do that," Kaliya grins.

Once again, Kaliya closes her eyes and now places careful concentration in her focus, as this time it was not to any simple location nearby. She would be folding across space and dimensional bounds to another universe.

She envisions the town of Firstfall, the village square, the tactical office, the druid tree, and other sights she had seen on other occasions of her visits. Recalling a location just offset from the tactical office, she concentrates on her objective as a distant point in her perceived imagination, empowering her thoughts to carry her as she fades from sight.

She realizes she must keep her focus on her goal through the full journey, as this is not a simple folding of local space. She finds herself first passing through a haze of rainbow clouds, representing the local Ethereal Maelstrom, then a barrier, followed by a morass of indescribable sights with shapes and dimensions that tested her senses to make any sense out of them. Ahead was another planar wall, and she plunged through it as she continued pressing forward to her perceived goal.

Around her, she now witnessed the myriad streaks of stars and galaxies moving past like rivers of light. Directly in front of her is a point, her final destination. She strains herself to draw closer, using the power of thought as her driving force. The image of her objective grows larger, as she imagines a sensation of reeling herself in. Finally, the flashing images subside, to be replaced by a blur that comes into focus as the village of Firstfall.

Captain Hagmaert was sitting in a chair just outside the door to the tactical office, with his relaxed state being the gift of the end of the local war effort. Kaliya appeared just to the side of the building, causing him to jump out of his chair and instinctively reach a hand to his sword. But when he made the identity of the unexpected arrival, he relaxed back.

"You shouldn't be sneaking up on people like that around here, Cadet."

"Sorry, Captain, I just popped around the corner and didn't realize you were sitting there."

"Where did you just come from, anyway? I didn't even see you walk up."

"Captain!" she grins naughtily. "Don't tell me you're falling asleep out here with no wars to fight."

"Aye," he chuckles reflexively. "It's nice to have the time to relax, but I'd feel better knowing when we could finish this bout."

"I'm working as fast as I can, but these things take time, and it's a little outside my control."

"Granted, that… I recall my own days in the academy. You'll get through it."

"Is His Lordship inside?"

"Aye he is. Do you need him for something?"

"I have a delivery to make."

"Are they making you run their errands now? I thought we had couriers for that."

"Today is special, and I pulled the lucky card for it, I guess."

"Right, then, go ahead."

Kaliya passes around to the door and enters the building. She sees Thaelyn and his officers, along with Tristeen, standing around the table discussing the reconstruction efforts in Rolsklinde.

"Greetings, Kaliya," Thaelyn calls to her. "Taking time away from your practice again?"

"Oh, they gave me a little side errand to run today. Aerlie wanted me to deliver this box to you, and pass along her special wishes at the same time."

Kaliya sets the box on the table as she looks around the room.

"A delivery?" he considers. "I wonder what sort of mischief she is up to today."

"Don't ask me, I'm just the messenger on this occasion. Since I'm here, do we have anything really interesting happening out there? I haven't heard much since we closed the lines and declared the war finished, at least for what we have here."

"We have been keeping a close watch on those portals. The first one seems to be holding steady, but I wonder how much longer it will remain that way. The second one is slowing down on us. We still see some activity on the other side, but they do not seem as anxious to jump through as before."

"Could they be having second thoughts over there?"

"While that might be a possibility, I am going to interpret this as a reduction of the local population. We may see the flow come to a stop entirely before long."

"Then it's just Portal One after that. If they keep this up, they might use their full population. What do we do after that?"

"We might consider a few changes to our plans where Portal One is concerned, but our recent reports of the images from the other side seem to indicate a large mass of family units accumulating in the area."

"Family units…like, with children?"

"Yes, which would actually make sense if you consider they are consolidating on Portal One by drawing in from other locations in the region. Those other camps, which might include local families, would now all form around this one. The next question, at this moment, would be if they are thinking of bringing the entire society across, or to simply use it as a feed to send their younger warriors through as they mature."

"That's just crazy to think they would do this. If they had any idea what's waiting for them on this side… It seems like such a waste."

"Indeed, but they cannot know what is waiting. Since Darumon and the Suuden-Aryku are no longer supporting them, they are most likely acting on their last orders."

"Sacrifices, like all the others," she huffs. "And for so many already sent through… You might think someone would ask a few questions about the end result. If only they knew…" she shakes her head as her thoughts drift away.

Kaliya reaches casually for one of the papers on the table, examining it and turning it over to look at the other side.

"General, can I borrow a pen for a moment?" she asks.

"Certainly," he replies as he passes one over to her.

She takes the pen and writes her name on the paper, then sets the pen down and studies her result before placing the paper back on the stack.

"Um, Kaliya," the General asks curiously. "Is there some meaning to this?"

"Oh, I was curious as to how that pen writes on this style of paper. It looked a little different from my journal back home."

"That is rather curious, but if you say so."

"We don't normally use paper back home; did you know that?"

"Ah, yes, that might offer a twist."

"By the way, Tristeen, how are things coming in the city?"

"A lot of the new housing has been completed," she replies. "And some of the civic buildings are almost done. We'll be working on a new academy soon, as well as facilities for training local watchmen, and a new barracks for civil defense."

"Great cu'Nar, that's a lot of work. You know, you're a real trooper for all this effort," Kaliya smiles assuredly as she gently pats the girl on the shoulder. "Well, folks, I think I should return to my work. It was great talking to you."

"You are doing well in your training, Kaliya," Thaelyn asserts. "Keep it up."

Kaliya steps back from the table, and closes her eyes. She brings to mind a vision of the study room where Aelwyn was waiting patiently for her. As she did before, she places her focus on her goal and vanishes in a puff.

"My Lord!" the General shouts as her image fades.

"Powers be blessed," Thaelyn wheezes and draws back. "And I did not even realize it!"

"What just happened?" Tristeen whimpers.

"Was this her projected form we just saw?" the General wonders. "Great gods, just imagine if she were working for the enemy."

"Indeed!" Thaelyn nods. "One such as those would be potentially devastating. She comes in, carries an innocent conversation, interacts with whatever she pleases, and I dare say, she played a rather polite role for it, as well. That young lady is developing a dangerous talent. If her projection can be made so perfectly, and further to involve the acting skill to go along with it, this represents a rather serious potential, for whomever she might serve."

❖❖❖

Vonafel was making an impromptu visit to the temple in Bya'an Tamoranth. She hurried her way along the sidewalk up to the front doors, and then along the aisle to the dais in front. One of the priests conducting a session with a group of younger clerics saw her approach and stepped forward to receive her.

"Welcome, good Miss," he begins as he examines her obvious professional dress. "Is there something I can help you with?"

"I'm here to see Aerlie, is she in her office?"

"I believe she is. Do you wish me to announce you? You seem to be in a bit of a hurry."

"We're old friends. My name is Vonafel Windsong from the Royal Archives down the road. I have a need to speak with her about a few important matters."

"Ah, very well, her office is just over there," he directs to a rear door.

"Thank you," she offers and continues on.

She strolls over to the office door and knocks gently, then peeks inside.

"Aerlie? It's me, Vonafel."

"Vonafel!" she croons. "Come in…please! What sort of mischief are you into today? Are your spies taking a day off, so you need to come out personally?"

"Well, no, a few are still working," she chuckles. "But you people are making it hard on me! I came to ask you about something, and I think this relates to the next quatrain on my list."

"Oh wonderful," she giggles. "Well, come sit a moment and we'll talk. Is this something you would like to bring to Thaelyn?"

"Eventually, but first I need to understand something."

The two of them sit down and Vonafel sets her traditional stack of books on the desk.

"Vonafel," Aerlie wonders as she examines the pile-up. "Have you ever considered leaving some of this at home?"

"Oh, Aerlie, I have too many notes here, and it seems I need all of them in order to understand these prophecies. You never know whether this or that clue or hint will be the next major breakthrough."

"All right, so what is this you need to ask?"

"It's about Kaliya. During our last meeting, you were talking about a gift she has and how Cardinal Aelwyn was brought down here to teach something. But so far, all I'm getting out of it is a big hush-hush military secret."

"Oh, that…yes. I'm sorry, Vonafel, but until we can be sure she is able to perform, we've been keeping this bottled up in order to give her some freedom from a lot of prying eyes and hallway gossip that could otherwise distract her."

"All right, this is fine. I can still remember back in the day when we were in the academy, and you had that horrid schedule you were trying to put together to study both the priesthood and mage craft together."

"Right, and it was hard enough trying to do this even without everyone studying me for all these crazy prophecies you were whispering about behind my back."

"I'm sorry, but you were such an anomaly back then. Now, it seems poor Kaliya is the anomaly. I managed to get a few clues as to what she's doing, but it's strange and doesn't make a lot of sense so far."

"Oh?" Aerlie grins impishly. "What sort of clues? This is from your spies, I take it."

"Right, there were a couple of recent sightings when she was outside performing some maneuver where she seemed to be vanishing from one location and reappearing in another, almost like she was using some kind of magical hidden door spell to displace herself."

"Really! Well, I suppose if it was out in the open, we can't very well avoid that."

"Yeah, and then you apparently have her performing some really mundane acts that simply don't make sense. Opening and closing doors, using small tools…um, why do we need to teach her how to use this when I think it should go along implicitly that she's smart enough to know this from the beginning?"

"In short, we're testing her limits. She's not actually in corporeal form during these moments."

"What?" she shouts. "Not corporeal! But what does that actually mean? Isn't she a real person? I thought she was."

"She is, but she once demonstrated to us, although accidentally, that she can apparently project her mind outside her body into physical space."

"Do you mean something like astral travelling?"

"Yes, but here in the same physical plane as we are, and her projected image can become tangible, so she can interact with other people and objects. She's in training to perfect this now."

"Incredible! How is she able to do this? Usually, as far as I understand it, a person would go into a form of meditation before travelling outside their body, right?"

"Yes, and she has been in training for this, at first using the incense we use during the Ritual of Redemption, as this is where she first demonstrated this odd skill. Then, we slowly weaned her from that until she can do it on command, and now to explore what she's capable of in this form, all with the ultimate hope to put it to use for us somehow."

"That's simply amazing..." she muses distantly.

Vonafel now reaches for her books and pulls out her journal. She opens it to a marked page where she finds her most recent quandary.

"Aerlie, I want to read a few words to you, and then you give me your opinion on their meaning...whatever comes to mind, all right?"

"Sure, what is it?"

Vonafel brings her attention to a series of lines in the book and begins to read the first part.

"Children of Breed, who walk in their sleep... What does that say to you right off the top?"

"Are we referring to Kaliya, perhaps? Children of Breed would suggest a mortal race, as the Estelar often use the word 'breed' when referring to any of the Child Races. If this is Adalon, and she's working as an agent to Maker Kuroku, she might borrow some of these terms. Then to say they walk in their sleep...well, this could surely apply if we are speaking of this gift. Kaliya must first descend into a kind of torpor condition while meditating. Aelwyn tells us her body behaves like it's sleeping when she projects outside, and reawakens when she returns home to it."

"That sounds a little creepy, if to think of it. I've never actually seen someone project outward, like for astral travelling, but this sounds even worse, because if it occurs right in front of you..." she shivers.

"Yeah, I think I might have to agree," she smiles. "So, what do you think this one could mean?"

"Right off the top, I see it uses the word 'children', which is a plural form. Are there any others that we know of?"

"Her people tell us this is a very rare anomaly that was once discovered on their home world among a few children who just happened to possess it. Her father once said he was part of a research study, but they were never able to learn anything due to something interrupting the studies. And then, of course, we have the arrival of Sargeras that got in the way."

"Yeah, I'll bet that put a kink in a lot of things. But this next line..." her voice trails off.

"Vonafel, what is it?"

"Aerlie, I'm a little unsure how to put this, but there may be a possibility to find more, if we look hard enough. First, because it says they have this slumbering gift."

"A slumbering gift!" she pulls forward in her chair. "That would suggest something dormant."

"And later, we have this mention of those Hooves of Storm rising up, whatever that is."

"Does it say anything else about them?"

"Yeah, they bless something about the battle we're fighting."

✦✦✦

"All right, people, listen up. Here's the plan."

It was morning, and Sulíma had assembled a survey group in the work yard outside the mine. She had been tasked with scouting the city for any utility vehicles they could salvage in preparation to collect the components of the conveyor from Camp Three, assuming there were no complications. The work to make the vehicles useable would take time, and should be attended to while they continued to monitor the situation in the abandoned orcish camp.

"We need to keep a close watch for orcs, mutants, and anything else that walks on two legs that isn't friendly."

"Only two legs?" Petrith jibes.

"Well, maybe more, but I don't think there are too many animals still in the area that could pose a threat. Anyway, the Civil Utilities building is on the other side of town. Let's hope this isn't a wasted trip. With all the damage and decay, we have no idea what condition the vehicles are in, or if we can access them to bring them outside. Beyond that, they probably won't work, so we'll need a way to haul them out and back here for repair and to put wheels under them."

"Those things will be big and heavy," asks a member of the group. "How do we haul them out?"

"Depending on how much debris might be laying around, if we can clear a path, the Captain suggested cutting logs to use as rollers. The problem is lifting them off the ground high enough to stick the rollers underneath. For this, we'll need something to lever them up."

"All right, so we lever them up, put rollers underneath, and roll them out into the street. Then it's just a lot of heavy labor to bring them home."

"We'll have to swap the rollers around as we move along. Heavy labor or not, it has to be done. We've got a fusion reactor just sitting out there collecting dust, and I want it. If we can put enough manpower behind this problem, we can do it. For now, let's just go in and check things out, but be on the lookout for trouble."

Sulíma makes a final check of her group before leading them out of the work yard in the direction of the city. They travelled along the base of the foothills; the standard route most often used when venturing in this direction. They crossed fields and rocky mounds, trying to keep a quick pace, with the full journey taking almost an hour from their home in the mine to the outer edge of the city.

They pass by the low masonry wall of the first residential block, then move into the streets to make their travels more efficient. Unlike her solo trips to the city, where she had to keep low and hide in the shadows, this time she was leading a large group composed of male and female cadets who had been in training by Captain Lapäli and his lieutenants, and all of them carrying weapons. This would represent a respectable force in the eyes of the native mutant inhabitants of the city. They should think twice before trying anything.

They marched through the city streets, working their way across town. As they wended their way through weeds and over broken pavement, an occasional pair of eyes would peek through a window of a nearby structure, attracted by the sound of their hoofed feet. Suli could almost feel their stares on her back as she walked by.

"People, keep your eyes open through here. I feel like we're being watched."

"So long as they keep inside their hidey-holes," Petrith remarks as he walks alongside. "I don't usually see them outside unless they're hunting for food. The poor saps, the best they seem capable of is to catch whatever is crawling by."

"Ew! That sounds awful. Don't they at least try to cook it?"

"I don't even know if they're capable of making fire. It's a sad occasion. These people were once friends and family, but now look at them."

"How do you suppose the orcs did this? We all know they're using this magic stuff, whatever it is, but just how could they make something like this?"

"No idea, Suli, but when you look at one, it hurts a little inside."

They continued along through the streets until they finally arrived at their destination.

The Civil Utilities building was a large structure, even in its collapsed state. The roof had fallen inside one of the larger rooms, and smaller sections had crumbled away in other areas. Some of the walls had peeled away, toppling outwards against neighboring buildings, and a few were broken into fragments with pieces lying inside the office and garage spaces.

A large, segmented door marked the entrance of the garage.

One side was smashed and dented, as if someone was trying to break into the building. The door was set into a track with a motorized gear on top to crank it open. Clearly, this was not in an operable condition by now.

"We need to get inside here," Sulíma notes. "Let's first peek through some of these holes to see if there's an easy way."

They split up and checked the open spaces within the walls. The native vegetation hinders their progress as they need to pull branches and vines out of the way to gain access to the building. Inside, they see remnants of furniture, cabinets, old computer terminals and other office supplies.

"Petrith, do you want to bring home any of these computers while we're here?"

"There's no place to plug it in, and I don't even know what I'd do with it at this point."

"Yeah, but think about it for later. Someone's going to need to shut down that reactor, and I think I know someone who was once very good at cracking computer systems."

"That was a long time ago, Suli. I haven't had one to play with since the attack. And I think the control panel of a reactor would be a lot different from one of these, anyway."

"Suli! Over here," calls a voice from around the corner.

Sulíma and Petrith both follow the sound to find one of the others peeking through an opening they made in the side of the garage.

"What do we have?" she inquires.

"There are several vehicles inside here. It looks like a few of them are intact, and others are buried under a collapsed section of the roof. It might be possible to unbury them, but the big problem is getting them out. That door looks like it's jammed."

Sulíma peers through the hole to examine the interior. She studies the inside of the door. The gear at the top was securely attached to the wall on one side, but the other one, where the door appeared to be smashed in, was hanging loosely.

"I think we have the necessary tools lying around the work yard to pull that door off. Maybe we could also salvage the metal part as lining for our new wheels. We can start chopping trees and cutting pieces to make the wheels, and line them with the metal as treading and reinforcement, but then we need a way to lift those beasts off the ground high enough to set them on the axles."

"We'll need to fashion some kind of crane," Petrith suggests.

"Right, and then we need a way to move them. That means some of you strong men are going to be put to work as beasts of burden," she giggles.

"It won't be easy, but it's all we've got for now. Once we get that reactor up and running, maybe things will pick up for us."

"We need to be gentle with those solar panels, though. I'm sure they'll be delicate."

"And we'll need to carry a sack full of tools with us to disassemble everything properly."

"Not to mention to make repairs on the vehicles along the way in case we have trouble. I'll want to go along to watch over things. And Petrith, like it or not, I want you with me to help figure out how to shut it down."

"Then I'd better get the Captain to start teaching me what he knows about fusion reactors, and anything else I need so I'll know what I'm looking at with those control panels."

"We may need to improvise a lot if they've changed the tech so much since we left."

⋅⋅◆⋅⋅

Once again, Vonafel had called for a meeting in Firstfall, and as before, Kailen, Ankhia, and Kaliya all joined with Thaelyn, Aerlie, and Aelwyn in the tactical office.

"I want to thank all of you for attending," she begins. "Especially on such short notice. But this seemed important. Aerlie and I have come to the conclusion that this next part we are examining might hold an important role for us, and therefore needs to be investigated. But it will require each of us to participate, and likely help cover it up, in case anyone comes around asking questions."

"Cover it up?" Thaelyn wonders. "How do you mean?"

"Thaelyn," Aerlie interjects. "If Darumon has been following them as a spy, and all our previous suggestions of him possibly STILL spying on us, whether real or imagined, the threat speaks for itself."

"Granted," he nods.

"Therefore," Vonafel continues. "If we are to follow this next quatrain for what we believe it holds for us, it must be done very carefully and very quietly."

"Very well, but what sort of suggestion does this one give?"

"Our interpretation is that Kaliya may be a vanguard of a sort."

"Oh no!" Kaliya blasts nervously. "Not me!" she waves it off. "It's bad enough my father once mentioned this. But for all my history, I think I'm not cut out for something like this."

"Kaliya, if I understand this correctly, you are already a vanguard, even now. You are discovering and learning this strange gift of yours, and from what I've heard, you would probably count as the first example ever to do this."

"One moment," Ankhia asserts. "Are you suggesting something about this Prodigy Child gift now? With respect to Kaliya, how can she be regarded as a vanguard when this is such a rare item, only to be seen very infrequently, and from what I've heard, not since Azgarén?"

"Adalon apparently knows about this, which means she must have seen it before and understands what it is. This next quatrain describes something called Children of Breed. Aerlie and I had a discussion recently, trying to understand some of these terms. The term 'breed' is a common form used by members of the Estelar to refer to one or another of the Child Races, and then the word 'children', which is a plural form, to refer to members of that society. Kaliya is only one example, which means there might be others out there."

"Others with this gift? I've never heard of any others…not in recent history. And as the chief med-tech, if there were any new discoveries, I think I'd be the first to know."

"Unless they haven't been discovered yet…"

"Well, all right, if they haven't been discovered. But Vonafel, we already have a problem with this. All those previous discoveries were children, to my knowledge. Even Kaliya first discovered this as a child, though I'll admit she lost it for a while, only to rediscover it recently. But it began as a child. And we haven't had any new children since arriving here."

"But Ankhia, what if you don't actually NEED to be a child for it? She's an adult now, and she's only now discovering how it works. Listen to this…"

Vonafel opens her notebook to her latest focus of attention and begins to read.

"Children of Breed, who walk in their sleep, a slumbering gift possessed… This already tells us it could be a dormant, perhaps latent ability that only SOME of you have so far discovered accidentally, but could be found in many more."

"Dear cu'Nar…" Ankhia wheezes.

"Walk in their sleep?" Kaliya mumbles. "Sleep… To dream… and to walk…"

"Kaliya?" Thaelyn inquires. "Do these words hold meaning to you?"

"Yes, my mother, when I was there that one time and I didn't realize what I was doing, but SHE began to realize it after a while that I was projected and standing in the room. She tried to tell me it wasn't a dream, but that I was sleeping and walking. Her mutation didn't allow her to articulate it clearly enough for me to understand completely, but these words are echoing back to me now."

"Fascinating…" Ankhia whispers. "I'm beginning to wish I could've known more about her research project now. I remember that time when you were little and visited us in the medical lab."

"The medical lab? When was I in there?"

"Apparently, during one of these sessions. She claimed you were in bed asleep, but I had you pulling on my tail and asking questions about my work," she giggles.

"Oh! I did?" she huffs playfully.

The group offers up a quick laugh at the scene.

"Children…" Thaelyn muses thoughtfully. "Even in your example, they are still so delightful."

Vonafel continues, "Let's return a moment to what we were talking about before. We talked about your evolution, your history, and why you might have it in the first place...whether to say that one odd person, or any of you at all. This can't be a natural part of your evolution, but instead a remnant of Darumon's artificial influence. He gave you something you should not otherwise have, and at this moment in your history, you are just now discovering it. You mentioned a few others in the past on Azgarén. They might have been other forerunners. Do we know what happened to them?"

"Um..." Ankhia drifts off.

"Father said something about this," Kailen reflects. "But I don't recall what. Your Lordship, even though we just now mentioned this issue of security, would you mind if I made a quick call to him to ask about this?"

"Does he carry a trans-com?"

"No, but I can send this through my Captain in the control room. I think I can trust him well enough, and I'll simply ask him to forward me for a personal issue. That shouldn't raise any questions."

"Very well, proceed."

Kailen pulls out his trans-com and dials a number. He waits a moment for the line to pick up.

"Captain, it's me..." he issues into the unit. "I need to speak with my Father a moment about some...family business. Can you walk me over there...? Good, thanks."

They wait while the resident officer makes his way through the Naarg uy'Sodrad to meet with Velen in his favorite study. After several long moments, Velen answers the line.

"Father? This is Kailen. I, uh... Um, no, I'm actually over here in Firstfall right now in a meeting... Yes, it is some nice weather we're having out here today..."

Kailen rolls his eyes around at Ankhia and she further rolls them away to meet with Padriyl. Kaliya covers her mouth as she feels a compulsive giggle coming on. Thaelyn folds his arms and leans his head in his hand as he senses another moment of nostalgic rambling fast approaching. Aerlie forms a broad grin as she feels Thaelyn's expectations welling up.

"But anyway, Father," Kailen continues. "This is actually important. First, are you alone in the room...? He's still there...? Then I need you to ask him to return to his desk. This is a private thing... Yes, good...now, as for what I needed to ask you. It's about those early Prodigy Children...you know, back there on Azgarén. Do you remember them...? Ah, good, so I wanted to ask... Uh huh...yeah, it was an extraordinary discovery... Right, I remember how you were once part of the early research, but... Oh, I'm sure it was a big sensation... Wait a minute, it was on the news broadcast? Who was it that released it to the public...? Ah, it was a leak by one of the other factions..."

Kaliya's giggle was turning to an uncontrollable laugh as she still tried to hold it back. Ankhia was covering her eyes and shaking her head. Padriyl simply set an elbow on the table and laid his head in his hand. Aelwyn could sense the variety of emotions and studied each one for its curious interaction. Kailen continued his conversation, now hoping to bring it under control.

"But Father, wait...this actually has to do with what happened after... How many were there...? Really! And for how long...? But when did Sargeras actually arrive during all this? Oh, he did...? And that's when you heard from the cu'Nar for the first time... Yeah, and here we have the Naarg uy'Sodrad arriving...um, Father, can you stop a moment?" he sighs and passes a weary glance around the group. "I know how you love to recall old times, but like I said, I'm in a meeting and we have a question to answer. Good! So, what we're wondering about right now is the history of those early children. I recall you said something about your studies being interrupted, but could you give me a more precise reason as to why this happened?"

The group waited as Kailen listened to the explanation, and watched as his face turned sour for it.

"Really..." he ushers morbidly. "Do we know the cause...? Nothing recognized...but how can that be? What were the symptoms, do we know...? But Father, I'm no medical expert, but that just doesn't sound natural… Right, I'll bet they were… But wait a minute. How do we explain Kaliya for this point…? I see…so THAT'S the reason… All right, I'll consider this and bring it into our conversation. Oh, and Father, we have an issue of security here, so please keep this confidential for now. Good…and thank you."

He ends the link and turns back to the group.

Thaelyn and Aerlie both studied his expression, as did Aelwyn, who could also feel his emotions vividly.

"Commander," Thaelyn ushers gently. "I sense something bad. What is it?"

Kailen first glanced longingly at Kaliya, and then turned to look at Ankhia before returning to the table.

"They died," he responds curtly.

Both Thaelyn and Aerlie frowned at the mention and leaned forward, then turned to study Kaliya for her reaction. Kaliya was clearly stunned, and suddenly began to show worry. Ankhia and Padriyl both gazed at Kailen incredulously.

"Kailen," Ankhia emits softly. "Are you saying they died as children?"

"Yeah, each one, and not long after they were first discovered. This is why we don't know anything about it, because we didn't have enough time to learn something."

"But what about her, is she in danger? How did they die?"

"Mysteriously… There were no recognizable symptoms, no obvious injuries, no signs of illness, nothing. He said this is the reason for the security, and also apparently why Mother didn't tell her as a child. She was trying to protect Kaliya, as if such a thing might be possible, since we don't know how the others died."

He pauses to gaze at Kaliya, who still appeared in shock.

"He says there was an initial statement in the news media describing this as a fantastic medical sensation, but then it turned into a medical anomaly, invoking panic of a new kind of disease, possibly of alien origin. The children showed a strange physical deterioration at the time of death. They were fine one moment, and the next time anyone saw them, they appeared to have had the life literally sucked out of them. They even appeared as partially desiccated, maybe even mummified, as if their bodies had shriveled up."

"That's ridiculous!" she shrieks. "How can a body simply do that overnight, because…"

"It wasn't overnight, Ankhia. It was, 'turn your back and poof'…"

"Turn your back and poof?!" she screeches. "That's even worse! It's not physically possible for a body to do this in a matter of seconds. This sounds as if…"

"…It was not natural," Aelwyn interjects.

Ankhia turns to Aelwyn's address, then passing her gaze among the others.

"The symptoms you are describing sound familiar to me," Aelwyn continues. "Including the time factor. But this is not something I would commonly hear about, not even in Sigil. Your mention of having the life sucked out may be closer than you realize, as it probably was. The body contains a life force, what we may often describe as its living essence. This essence can exist in all corporeal bodies, but it becomes much better defined in higher lifeforms, especially those with complex neurological processes to shape and refine it into what many Child Races would call a spirit."

"I'm not religious, so can you put this into terms a scientist can understand?"

"Your conscious mind, and the energy that drives your living body. Religious or otherwise, it is all the same. The Powers would understand this on a much more intimate level, as they might interact with such things in ways similar to how you would interact with your medical practice. For you, we might describe this in such terms as the inherent bioelectrochemical interactions of living matter, but it tends to run deeper than that, at least in part, as I said, due to the complex neurological refinement. However, if you should hold such capacity as to be able to drain this away, especially in a forceful manner, the result might be something like the Commander's depiction of these children."

"All right, I think I'm with you…at least in theory. But now, how might this actually happen, and in each of these children consistently? Is this some kind of harmful side effect of the Prodigy Gift?"

"I have never heard of a person who held any such gift as this somehow losing control of it and dying, to say nothing of dying in such a fashion as this. This sounds much more like a form of attack than a consequence of this gift."

"An attack?!" she screams.

"Yes, of course," Thaelyn muses silently. "And it would surely make sense to me."

"Would one of you please speak in complete sentences? I'm about to pull my horns out now."

"Darumon…again. Med-tech, Kaliya has not shown any unpleasant symptoms of any kind during her training, and in fact, it is just the opposite. She is showing herself to be very strong, and growing more so as her skills improve. Even if we were to suggest these early children, one or all, should have an accident, I cannot imagine the result appearing as anything like this. However, as Aelwyn suggested, a forceful method, perhaps suggesting a vampiric interaction, could surely do the job. And who might conduct such as this, but the one who did not want you to learn of this fantastic new medical sensation…as it represents a power you should not otherwise have. Darumon…"

"Damn him!" Kailen roars and pounds his fist on the table. "Isn't it bad enough he created us to be his pet species to do all his dirty work, and for those of us who didn't want to follow his blessed idea of utopia, he has to hunt us halfway to extinction, only to grant us these brief respites before hunting us again. Now he kills our children just to deny us one more aspect of what he did to us."

Ankhia reaches over and wraps her arms around Kailen to calm his outrage.

"Thankfully for us," she soothes. "Kaliya managed to escape from this. Maybe he didn't notice her there on Ruuki uy'Daan."

"Mother was conducting that research project. If he was spying on us, could he have heard of it?"

"If he knew anything about it, I think we would know the result."

"Maybe. All right, so where does this leave us? We might still have a spy watching us, so we can't say or do anything…cu'Nar's pity, we already have. The Elder Council, to say the least, and virtually everyone else has heard of at least a few words of it by now."

"Commander," Thaelyn considers. "Perhaps we might be able to suggest he is no longer watching, because if this offends him so, he might have taken action already. Either that, or perhaps he knows she is out of his reach."

"Would he even know who she is, precisely?" Aerlie wonders. "If your mother was performing this research, did she actually mention a name? You mentioned something about security..."

"Yes..." Ankhia nods. "Technically, it wouldn't be very professional to do so, if for no other reason than to keep the patient anonymous. I knew about it mostly through my personal relationship with their family, but most others would not."

"So then, even if he was spying on you, perhaps he wasn't spying in those particular circles where she was performing this research."

"Or perhaps he was absent during this time," Thaelyn adds. "Maybe to go in search of the materials for his weapon."

"Fine..." Kailen relents. "So, we'll need to try to keep the rest of it under our control."

"Vonafel," Aerlie redirects. "There was more to that quatrain, as I recall. May we continue, please?"

"Right..." she sighs as she glances around the group. "Um, so we have this slumbering gift, which could mean we have something latent we need to look for. But all things considered, it'll need to be quiet, I'm sure."

"Thaelyn," Aerlie asserts. "If we do this, I want to be placed in charge of this project, at least until we can gain control of this aspect of the spy. If the Commander could check around, maybe ask for a few volunteers, but quietly, we could conduct some testing to see who and how many might be available to us."

"This is reasonable," he accedes. "How would you wish to proceed?"

"I would first conduct interviews in my office, just to be sure. I can use my telepathic skills to conduct a passive scan to ensure we have real people, not this imposter Vonafel speaks of, and I might also suggest we select from those in diminutive positions of labor, rather than ranking members. If Darumon is present, I doubt he would want to work as a janitor, but rather a position where he had access to the critical information."

"This makes good sense to me. Commander?"

"Yes, I think I would agree," he nods. "But if we start pulling people out of their positions, someone might start taking notice after a while."

"Then we will need an excuse," Aerlie suggests. "Perhaps a new study relating to something innocent… You are building a lot of new industry, and I already know many of your people are expressing an interest in studying our magic. We use this in many areas, so perhaps some of them are exploring such avenues as arts and crafts, or other cultural affairs. This would surely offer us a fair enough explanation for their temporary absence."

"All right, I think we can do this easily enough. But now, how many are we talking about, and where are we eventually going with it?"

"I might say we take a dozen or so to start, and maybe cycle through a few batches, just to get an idea at first. As for where it goes…Vonafel, could you please finish for us?"

"But of course!" she smiles playfully. "Here is where we have that mention of those Hooves of Storm, by the way. I still don't know what it is, but knowing Adalon as I do, if she's giving it a name, even as a metaphor, it must hold a special meaning."

She again refers to her book, now to finish her recital.

"Children of Breed, who walk in their sleep, a slumbering gift possessed; their Hooves of Storm will rise anew, and the turn of battle blessed."

"Dear Powers, Vonafel," Thaelyn mutters. "That sounds like an army."

"Not simply an army, Thaelyn," Aerlie mentions. "…'Will rise anew' means it's been there before."

TO BE CONTINUED